Robert Crais

THREE GREAT NOVELS

ALSO BY ROBERT CRAIS

Hostage
Demolition Angel
L.A. Requiem
Indigo Slam
Sunset Express
Voodoo River
Free Fall

Robert Crais

THREE GREAT NOVELS

....

The Monkey's Raincoat

Stalking the Angel

Lullaby Town

ORION

First published in Great Britain in 2001 by
Orion Books
an imprint of The Orion Publishing Group
Orion House, 5 Upper St Martin's Lane, London WC2H 9EA

A CIP catalogue record for this book is available
from the British Library

(cased) ISBN 0 75283 865 2
(Trade paperback) ISBN 0 75283 866 0

Typeset by Deltatype Ltd, Birkenhead, Merseyside
Printed and bound in Great Britain by
Clays Ltd, St Ives plc

Contents

How it Began

BY ROBERT CRAIS

Truth be told, all I was trying to do was write a book that wouldn't embarrass me too badly. An author should never admit this; instead one should describe the compulsion of uncontrolled muses or the mystical bliss of channeling creative energies from the deepest wells of the human heart. These latter excuses for a novel are more endearing to the literary intelligentsia than admitting an aversion to shame. But I had been a writer for a long time, I had already completed a couple of manuscripts, and they were damned poor. To this day, they remain hidden in the bottom of my drawer; sealed, strapped, and secured in the strongest box I could find, forever safe from human view. Now, from the vantage point of a career twenty years in the making and ten published novels, I realize that those earlier works failed because I had no story to tell. You can have all the elegant language you wish, fill umpteen pages with emotional anguish and snappy dialogue, type until your fingers are bloody and the world is hidden by towering stacks of pages, but it all comes to naught without a story. I had none.

Then, in 1985, my father died.

It's like this: My parents had been married well over forty years, and were of an age and from a place where, by tradition, the woman made the meals and tended the children, and the man earned the living and paid the bills. They lived their lives that way for the almost fifty years that they shared. Never once during those years had my mother written a check or paid a bill or tended to the financial business of life. She did not have to; that was his job.

Then he was gone.

In the ensuing months, as I struggled to teach my mother those skills which she would need in order to maintain herself – how to write a check and balance a checkbook, the ins and outs of bank deposits and withdrawals, the magic reality of credit cards – I often

I

doubted that I was up to the task at hand. As I often do when troubled or confused, I used my fiction to help myself divine order from the chaos of the real world. Where I was unsure that I could, indeed, help my mother grow into the person she needed to become, I created a fictional world wherein I would have more control. My mother's plight was transformed into that of the character Ellen Lang, a much younger woman with small children and a missing husband. To save Ellen (or, at least, aid in her transformation), I created the hero of my tale, Elvis Coke, a smarter, stronger, more capable and competent savior than ever I might be.

My father's death and my mother's plight provided the story that became *The Monkey's Raincoat*, and Elvis Cole became the mirror through which I reflect the world as I see it. When I wrote that first book, I never dreamed that *Stalking the Angel* or *Lullaby Town* would follow, or that the series – now numbering eight published novels with many more on the way – would become bestsellers around the world. I simply wanted the story to make sense; I only wanted to save my mother.

The Monkey's Raincoat

AN ELVIS COLE NOVEL

For Pat, who met Joe Pike and
decided to hang around.

That ain't tactics, baby. That's
just the beast in me.
– Elvis Presley,
Jailhouse Rock
(the movie)

Winter downpour –
even the monkey
needs a raincoat.
– Basho

CHAPTER I

'I'm sorry, Mr. Cole, this has nothing to do with you. Please excuse me.' Ellen Lang stood up out of the director's chair across from my desk. I'd had it and its mate fitted in a nice pastel burgundy a year ago. The leather was broken in and soft and did not crack when she stood. 'We shouldn't have come here, Janet,' she said. 'I feel awkward.'

Janet Simon said, 'For Christ's sake, Ellen, sit down.'

Ellen sat.

Janet Simon said, 'Talk to him, Ellen. Eric says he's very good at this sort of thing. He can help.'

Speak, Ellen. Arf. I rearranged two of the Jiminy Cricket figurines on my desk and wondered who the hell Eric was.

Ellen Lang adjusted her glasses, clutched her hands, and faded back into the director's chair. She looked small, even though she wasn't. Some people are like that. Janet Simon looked like a dancer who'd spent a lot of time at it. Lean and strong. Good bones. She wore tight beige cotton pants and a loose cotton shirt striped with shades of blue and pink and red. No panty line. I hoped she didn't think I was *déclassé* in my white Levi's and Hawaiian shirt. Maybe the shoulder holster made up for it.

Ellen Lang smiled at me, trying to feign comfort in an uncomfortable situation. She said, 'Well, perhaps if you told me about yourself.'

Janet Simon sighed, giving it the weight of the world. 'Mr. Cole is a private detective. He detects for money. You give him some money and he'll find Mort. Then you can get Perry back and kiss off Mort and get your life together.' She said it like she was talking to someone with brain damage. Great legs, though.

'Thanks, Mom,' I said.

Janet Simon gave me a look, then turned away and stared at the

Pinocchio clock. It's on the wall beside the door that leads to my partner's office, just above the little sign that says *The Elvis Cole Detective Agency*. As the second hand sweeps around, Pinocchio's eyes move from side to side. Janet Simon had been glancing at it since they walked in. Probably thought it was peculiar.

Ellen fidgeted. 'I was just curious, that's all. I'm sorry.'

'You don't have to be sorry, Mrs. Lang,' I said. 'I'm thirty-five years old and I've been licensed as a private investigator for seven years. The state of California requires three thousand hours of experience before they'll give you the license. I spent that time with a man named George Feider. Mr. Feider was an investigator here in Los Angeles for almost forty years. Before that I was a security guard, and before that I spent some time in the Army. I'm five feet eleven and one-half inches tall, I weigh one hundred seventy-six pounds, and I'm licensed to carry a firearm. How's that?'

She blinked.

'Yeah, it impresses me, too,' I said. 'I don't take custody work. I might find your husband and your son but after that it's up to you. I don't steal children unless there's reason to believe the child is in danger.'

Ellen Lang looked as if I'd kicked her. 'Oh, no. No, no. Mort's a good man, Mr. Cole, please don't think he isn't.' Janet Simon said something like *shumphf*. 'You have to understand. He's been under enormous strain. He left ICM last year to start his own talent agency and things just haven't gone the way they should. He's had to worry about the house payments and the cars and schools. It's been terrible for him.'

Janet Simon said, 'Mort's an asshole.' She was standing by the sliding glass doors that lead out to the little balcony. On a clear day I could go out there and see all the way down Santa Monica Boulevard to the water. The view had been the selling point. Janet Simon fit nicely with the view.

'I just want Perry home, that's all.' Ellen Lang's eyes went from Janet Simon to me, sort of like the Pinocchio clock. 'Mort will settle for McDonald's. He'll let Perry stay up all hours –'

I cleared my throat. 'Mrs. Lang, I don't bill by the day. I charge a flat fee exclusive of expenses and I get it in advance. You're looking at about two grand here. Why don't you wait? Mort might call.' McDonald's. Christ.

'Yes,' Ellen Lang said. She looked relieved. 'I'm sure you're right.'

'Bullshit,' Janet Simon said. She turned away from the balcony to sit in the other director's chair. 'That's not right and she knows it. Mort's been threatening to leave for almost a year. Mort treats her like a sop. He runs around.' Ellen Lang made a little gurgling noise. 'He's even hit her twice that I know of. Now he's taken their son and disappeared. She wants her son back. That's all she wants. It's very important to her.'

Ellen Lang's eyes widened but didn't seem to be looking at anything. 'Ms. Simon,' I said evenly, 'as much as I'd like to lick chocolate syrup off your body, I want you to shut up.'

Ellen Lang said, 'Oh, my.' Janet Simon stood up and then Ellen Lang stood up. Janet Simon put a hand on Ellen Lang's shoulder and shoved her back down. 'Who do you think you're talking to?' she said.

'A woman who's very concerned with her friend's problem. But a woman who, right now, is acting like a royal pain in the ass. If the sexual nature of my comment surprised you it's only because I needed to be shocking to get your attention.'

She chewed at the inside of her cheek, trying to decide about me, then nodded and took her seat.

'Also,' I said, 'I find you devastatingly attractive and it's been on my mind.'

She leaned forward and said, 'Eric told us you had a partner. Maybe we should speak with him.'

Eric again. The Mystery Man. 'Fine by me.'

Janet Simon looked at the door beneath the Pinocchio clock. If she looked close enough she'd see the little ridge in the jamb from the time someone had forced the lock. Three coats of paint, and you could still see the crack. She didn't notice. 'Is that his office?' she said.

'Unh-hunh.'

'Well?'

'Well, what?'

'Aren't you going to introduce us?'

'Nope.'

Janet Simon stood up, steamed over to the door, and went through. I smiled at Ellen Lang. Ellen Lang looked nervous but smiled back. After a while Janet Simon rejoined us.

'That's no office,' she said. 'There's no desk, no furniture, nothing. What kind of office is that?'

'Italian moderne?'

She cocked her head a little to the side. 'Eric said you'd be like this.'

Eric. 'How do you know Eric?' I smiled. Mr. Sly. I have quite a charming smile. Like Peter Pan. Innocent, but with a touch of the rake.

'We worked together when I was in the legal department at Universal.'

That brought it back. Eric Filer. Three years ago.

'He said you found some film negatives for him. He said it wasn't easy. He recommends you highly.'

'M'man Eric.'

'He also said you were like this.'

'Were you ever a dancer?' I said.

If she wanted to smile, she fought it. She took out a pack of Salem Lights, lit up in the office but stood in the balcony door, blowing smoke out over West Hollywood. I liked the way her neck looked when she lifted her chin to send out a plume of smoke. Some woman. I bet her mouth tasted like an ashtray.

'Listen, Mrs. Lang,' I said, turning back to Ellen, 'I don't know if Mort is going to call or not, or what you want, or what Mort wants. A couple hundred women have sat where you're sitting, and usually their husbands call. But not always. You're going to have to decide which way you want to jump.'

Ellen Lang nodded. Pinocchio's eyes shifted back and forth a few times. Janet Simon smoked. After a while Ellen Lang took two photographs out of her purse and put them carefully on the desk. 'On Friday Mort always picks up Perry from school. Perry goes to Oakhurst and the girls go to Westridge. That's Cindy and Carrie. Fridays, Perry gets out two hours earlier. Only this past Friday they never came home. I tried all weekend to find Mort. I phoned Oakhurst Monday but Perry wasn't there, and I phoned again this morning and he still wasn't there. They've been gone for four days.'

I looked at the pictures. Mort was four or five years older than me, balding on top with a round face, thin lifeless hair, and skinny arms. He was wearing a tee shirt that said *U.S.S. Bluegill, Maui, Hawaii*. He had the sort of eyes that had just been looking somewhere else. On the back of the picture someone had written *Morton Lang, age 39, 5' 10", 145 lbs, brown hair and brown eyes, no visible scars or tattoos, mole on right forearm*. The writing was even and firm, all of the letters identical in size.

'I wrote that,' Ellen said. God bless television.

The other picture was a wallet-size school photo of a little boy who looked like a smaller, less-worn version of Mort. Perry Lang, age 9, 4' 8", 64 pounds, brown hair and brown eyes, no visible scars or tattoos or moles.

I put the pictures on the desk, then opened my right top desk drawer and took out a Bic pen and a blank yellow legal pad. I had to move my gun to get the pad. The gun was a Dan Wesson .38 Special with the 4-inch barrel, a gift from George Feider the day I got my license. It was a good gun. I closed the drawer, put the pad beside the pictures and the Bic on the pad.

'Okay,' I said. 'Did Mort leave a note?'

'No.'

'Why would Mort take your son but not your two girls?'

'I don't know.'

'Was Perry Mort's favorite?'

'That would be Carrie, our youngest daughter. I asked her if Mort said anything about this to her, thinking he might have, but she said no.'

I nodded and wrote *Carrie* on the pad.

'Your husband make any large withdrawals recently?'

Ellen Lang said, 'I'm not very good with figures. Mort handles all our business affairs.' She said it apologetically.

'How about work? Someone there who might know what was on your husband's mind?'

Ellen Lang looked at the floor. 'Well, he's not part of an office anymore, like I said. He worked out of the house, and he didn't really talk ...' She trailed off and turned red, her lips a tight purple knot.

I tapped the Bic against the pad, which wasn't exactly brimming with information.

I looked at Janet Simon. She had a tight, sexy grin on her face. Or maybe it was a sneer. 'I wouldn't think of interfering,' she said.

'Maybe if I said please.'

Janet Simon took a final pull on her cigarette, tossed it out over the railing, and came back inside. 'Tell him about the girlfriend, Ellen.'

Ellen Lang's voice was so soft I could barely hear her. 'He has a girlfriend. She lives at the Piedmont Arms off Barrington in Brentwood.'

'Her name is Kimberly Marsh,' Janet Simon said. 'She's one of his clients. 412 Gorham, just above San Vicente. Apartment 4, on the ground, in the back. An actress.' She took two rolodex cards from her purse and flipped them down on the desk next to the photographs. The top one had KIMBERLY MARSH typed on it along with the address and a phone number.

'We followed him.' Ellen Lang said it the way you say something that embarrasses you.

I looked at Janet Simon. 'And I'll bet you drove.'

She looked back. 'And I got out of the car and I checked the apartment number and I matched it to a name on the mailbox.' Some woman, all right.

'Okay,' I said. 'What about friends?'

Neither of us bothered to look at Ellen Lang. 'Mort was trying to get a film project off the ground with a producer named Garrett Rice. That's his name and number on the second card. It was one of those deals where you do a lot of talking about firming up Redford with a commitment from Coppola so you can get the money from Arab investors. That kind of thing. They call it "blue-sky."'

I nodded. 'How come you know more about her life than she does?'

Ellen Lang leaned forward out of the director's chair. It was the first time she'd shown any animation since they'd walked into my office twenty minutes ago. 'Garrett is an old friend. We used to play bridge with Garrett and his wife Lila until they were divorced, oh, I guess it was five years ago. We used to play every week for almost a year. Mort was so happy to be back in contact with him. Garrett was Mort's best friend. I guess that's why he told me.'

Janet Simon sighed the way you sigh when you've been holding your breath at a horror movie, and said, 'Mort didn't believe in sharing his life. At least, not with his wife.'

'Well, that was his way,' Ellen Lang said. Her eyes were still wide. 'Mort would just die if he knew about this, Mr. Cole. That's why I wouldn't go to the police, even though Janet said that's what I should do. I couldn't get my own husband in trouble with the police. He'd never forgive me. You can see that, can't you?'

Maybe it was my expression. Ellen Lang's face got dark, her chin trembled, and she said, 'What's wrong with a woman caring how her husband feels?' I got the feeling she'd been saying it a lot lately.

'You'll take the job?' Janet Simon said.

'There's the matter of the fee.'

Ellen looked away from me again. 'I'm afraid I forgot my checkbook.'

Janet said, 'She's not used to this. Mort always paid for everything, so she didn't think to bring it.'

I tapped the Bic against the pad.

'You can understand that, can't you?' Janet said.

I stood up. 'Yep, I can understand that. Why don't I come by your house this afternoon, Mrs. Lang? You can give me the check and we can go through your husband's things.'

'Why do you have to do that?'

'Clues, Mrs. Lang.'

Janet Simon said, 'You look like John Cassavetes twenty years ago.'

'Who do I look like now?'

Janet Simon smiled grimly and stood up. Ellen Lang stood up, too, and this time Janet Simon didn't push her back down. They left.

I wrote *old friends* on the pad, drew a box around it, then tore off the sheet and threw it away.

Some notes.

CHAPTER 2

I went out on the balcony and watched the street. After a few minutes they pulled out from beneath the building in a sky-blue Mustang convertible. Janet Simon was driving. It was the GT handling package. Great maneuverability. Tight in the curves. Without sacrificing a smooth ride.

I went back into my office, called the deli on the ground floor to order a pastrami on rye with Chinese hot mustard, and then I called Joe Pike.

A man's voice said, 'Gun shop.'

'Give me Joe.'

The phone got put down on something hard. There were noises and words I couldn't understand, and then the phone got picked up again. 'Pike.'

'We just had another complaint about your office. Woman goes in there, comes out, says what kind of office is that, empty, no phone, no desk? What could I tell her?'

'Tell her she likes the office so much she can live there.'

'It's a good thing we don't depend on you to sweet-talk the customers.'

'I don't do this for the customers.' Pike's voice was flat. No smile. No humor. Normal, for Pike.

'That's why I like to call,' I said. 'Always the pleasant word. Always the cheery hello.'

Nothing came back over the line. After a while I said, 'We added a new client today. Thought you'd like to know.'

'Any heat?' Pike's only interest.

'We got through the interview with a minimum of gunshots.'

'You need me, you know where to find me.'

He hung up. I shook my head. Some partner.

An entire afternoon ahead of me and nary a thing to do except drive out to Ellen Lang's and dig through six or seven months of phone bills, bank statements, and credit card receipts. Yuck. I decided to go see Kimberly Marsh. The Other Woman.

I slipped the Dan Wesson into my holster, put on the white cotton jacket, and picked up the sandwich on my way to the parking garage. I ate in the car driving up Fairfax, turning left at Sunset toward Brentwood. I've got a Jamaica-yellow 1966 Corvette convertible. It would have been easier to take Santa Monica, but with the top down Sunset was a nicer drive.

It was shaping up as another brutal Los Angeles winter, low seventies, scattered clouds, clearing. The sky was that deep blue we get just before or just after a rain. The white stucco houses along the ridges were sharp and brilliant in the sun. I passed the coed-specked running paths of UCLA, then wound my way past a house that may have been the one William Holden used to slip the repossessors in *Sunset Boulevard*. Old Spanish. Same cornices and pilasters. The ghosts of old Hollywood haunting the eaves. I've wondered about that house since I discovered it, just two days after I mustered out of the Army in 1972. I've wondered, but I've never wanted to know for sure. After the Army, magic was in short supply and when you found some, you held on tight. It wouldn't be the same if I knew the house belonged to some guy who made his millions inventing Fruit Loops.

A half mile past the San Diego Freeway I turned left on Barrington and dropped south toward San Vicente, then hung another left on Gorham. The Piedmont Arms is on the south side of the street in a stretch of apartment houses and condominiums. I drove past, turned around at a cross street, and parked. It looked like a nice place to live. An older woman with wispy white hair eased a Hughes Market cart off a curb and across a street. She smiled at a man and a woman in their twenties, the man with his shirt off, the woman in an airy Navajo top. L.A. winter. They smiled back. Two women in jogging suits were walking back toward Barrington, probably off to lunch at one of the little nouveaux restaurants on San Vicente. Hot duck salad with raspberry sauce. A sturdily built Chicano woman with a purse the size of a mobile home waited at a bus stop, squinting into the sun. Somewhere a screw gun started up, then cut short. There were gulls and a scent of the sea. Nice. Four cars in front of me, north side of the street, two guys sat in a dark blue '69 Nova with a bad rust spot on the left rear fender. Chicanos. The driver tried to scowl like

Charles Bronson as I cruised past. Maybe they were from the government.

The Piedmont is a clean, two-story, U-shaped stucco building with a garden entry at the front braced by stairs that go up to the second floor. Around each stair is a stand of bamboo and a couple of banana trees for that always-popular rain forest look. There are two rows of brass-burnished mailboxes in front of the bamboo, with a big open bin beneath them for magazines and packages and Pygmies with blowguns. Kimberly Marsh's drop was the fourth from the left on the top row. I could see eight or nine envelopes through the slot. In the bin there were three catalogs and a couple of those giveaway flyers that everyone gets. Lot of mail. Maybe four days' worth.

I walked through the little courtyard past some more banana trees. Apartment 4 was all the way back on the left. That Janet. I knocked, but there was no answer. I walked back up to apartment 1, where a little sign on the door said MANAGER. A fat man built like a pear came around the mailboxes, started up the stairs, and saw me. 'Jo-Jo isn't here,' he said. 'He's got the aerobics class on Tuesday.'

'Jo-Jo the manager?'

He nodded. 'He'll be back around five or six. But I can tell you, there aren't any vacancies.'

'Maybe I could pitch a tent.'

He thought about that. 'Oh, that was a joke.'

'You know Kimberly Marsh?' I said. 'In number four.'

He said, 'Number four,' and thought about it. 'That the pretty blonde girl?'

'Yes.'

He shrugged. 'You see her around, that's all. I said hi once and she said hi back, that's all.'

I took out the photograph of Mort. 'You see this guy around with her?'

He squinted at me. 'Mr. Suspicious I don't know who you are,' he said.

'Johnny Staccato, Confidential Investigations.'

He nodded and stared at the picture and rubbed his arm. 'Well, I dunno,' he said. 'Gee.' Gee.

I thanked him and walked around until I heard a door upstairs open and close. Then I walked back to number 4. I knocked again in case she had been in the shower, then took out two little tools I

18

keep in my wallet and popped Kimberly Marsh's deadbolt lock. 'Ms. Marsh?' Maybe she was taking a nap. Maybe she just hadn't wanted to answer the door. Maybe she was waiting behind it with an ice pick she had dipped in rat poison.

No answer.

I pushed open the door and went in.

There was a davenport against one wall with a wicker and glass coffee table in front of it and a matching Morris chair at the far end. From the doorway, I could see across the living room to the dining area and the kitchen. To the left was a short hall. Above the couch was a slickly framed poster of James Dean walking in the rain. He looked lonely.

A dozen brown daisies sat in a glass bowl on the coffee table. Propped against the bowl was a little lavender card. *For the girl who gives me life, all my love, Mort.* Papery petals had rained around the card.

On the end table there was a Panasonic phone-answering machine. I passed it, walked back to the kitchen, then glanced down the little hall to the bedroom before I went into the bath. No bodies. No messages scrawled in blood. No stopped-up toilet with red-tinted water. There were two towels on the bathroom floor as if someone had stepped out of the shower, toweled off, then dropped the towels. They were dry, at least two days old. There was a little chrome toothbrush holder with the stains those things get when you park a toothbrush in them, only there was no toothbrush. The medicine cabinet held all the stuff medicine cabinets hold, though maybe there were a couple of spaces where things had been but now weren't. I went back out into the living room and checked the message machine. The message counter said zero – no messages. I played it back anyway. The counter was right.

I went into the bedroom. The bed was made and neat. There was a little desk in the corner beneath the window, cluttered and messy with old copies of the *L.A. Times*, *Vogue*, I. Magnin shopping bags, and other junk. Halfway down a stack of trade papers and *Casting Calls* I found the kind of 8×10 black-and-white stills actors bring to readings. Most were head shots of a pretty blonde with clean healthy features. At the bottom of the 8×10 it said *Kimberly Marsh* in an elegant flowing script. On the back was stapled a Xeroxed copy of her acting credits, her training, and her physical description. She was 5' 6", 120 pounds, had honey hair and green eyes. She was 26 years old and wore a size 8. She could play tennis, enjoyed water sports, could ski, and ride both Western and English. Her credits as an actress didn't amount to much. Mostly regional theater from Arizona. She claimed to have studied with Nina Foch. Farther down the stack I found some full body shots, one with Kimberly in a fur bikini doing her best to look like a Pictish warrior. She looked pretty good in that fur bikini. I thought of Ellen Lang invisible in my director's chair. Sit, Ellen. Speak. I put one of the head shots in my pocket.

I finished with the desk and moved to the closet. There were twelve shoe boxes stacked against the wall. I found a snapshot of a sleeping dog in one of them. There was a large empty space about the size of a suitcase on the right side of the closet shelf. Maybe Morton Lang had called and said, *I've finally had my fill of this invisible sexless drudge I'm married to so how's about you and me and Perry hit the beach in Hawaii?* And maybe Kimberly Marsh had said, *You bet, but I havta get back for this role I got on 'One Life to Live,'* so she'd pulled down the suitcase and packed her toothbrush and enough clothes for a week and they had split. Sounded good to me. Ellen Lang wouldn't like it, but there you are.

I shut the closet and went through the dresser, starting with the top drawer and working down. In the third drawer from the top I found a small wooden box containing a plastic bag of marijuana, three joints, two well-used pipes, a small bong, a broken mirror, four empty glass vials, and a short candle. Well, well, well. There was a 9 × 12 envelope under the stash box, folded in half and held tight by a rubber band. There was a pack of photographs in it. The first picture featured a nude Kimberly seated on her davenport, stark white triangles offsetting a rich tan. Not all of the shots were raw. A couple showed her posing on the back of a Triumph motorcycle, a couple more had her at the beach with a big, well-muscled, sandy-haired kid who had probably played end for the University of Mars. Near the bottom of the pack I found Morton Lang. He was naked on the bed, grinning, propped up on one elbow. A well-tanned female leg reached in from the bottom of the picture to play toesies with his privates. Mort. You jerk. I tore the picture of Morton in two and put it in my pocket. I put the rest of the stuff back, closed the drawers, and made sure the apartment was the way I'd found it. Then I let myself out.

The pear-shaped man was standing by the mailboxes on a little plot of grass they have there, waiting for a rat-sized dog on a silver leash. The dog was straining so hard its back was bent double. It edged sideways as it strained. Awful, the things you see in my line of work. The pear-shaped man said, 'You're not Johnny Staccato. That was an old TV series with John Cassavetes.'

'Caught me,' I said. 'That's the trouble with trying to be smart, there's always someone smarter.' The pear-shaped man nodded and looked superior. I gave him a card. 'You see Ms. Marsh around, I'd appreciate a call.'

The Mexicans in the Nova were still there, only now they were arguing. Charlie Bronson gestured angrily, then fired up their car and swung off down the street. Hot-blooded. The pear-shaped man put the card in his pants. 'You aren't the only one looking for that woman,' he said.

I looked at him. 'No?'

'There was another man. I didn't speak to him, but I saw him knocking on number 4. A big man.'

I gave him my All-Knowing Operative look. 'Good-looking kid. Six-three. Sandy-haired. Could be a football player.'

He looked at the dog. 'No, this man was dark. Black hair. Bigger than that.'

So much for the All-Knowing Operative. 'When was this?'

'Last week. Thursday or Friday.' He belched softly, said 'That's a sweetie' to the dog, then eyed me again. 'I think she had quite a few men friends.'

I nodded.

The pear-shaped man *tsked* at the little dog and gently jerked the leash, as if that would be coaxing. The dog looked up with sad, protruding eyes. The pear-shaped man said, 'I'd feed him dog meal, but he whines so much for chicken necks. That's all he'll eat. He loves the skin so.'

I nodded again. 'Same with people,' I said. 'You never like what's good for you.'

CHAPTER 3

I walked back along Gorham and down to San Vicente where I phoned Ellen Lang from a Shell station, and got no answer. I took out the rolodex cards Janet Simon had given me. There were two phone numbers typed on Garrett Rice's card, one with a Beverly Hills prefix, one from The Burbank Studios in beautiful downtown Burbank. It was almost four and traffic was starting to build, the sky already a pallid exhaust orange. Ugly. Bumper to bumper. Fifty-five delightful minutes later I was on another pay phone across from the Warner Brothers gate asking a secretary I knew for a walk-on pass. I would have phoned Garrett Rice directly, but people tend not to be in for private cops. Even when they brave the rush hour.

I jaywalked across Olive Street and gave the guard my name. He flipped through a little file where they keep the passes after the teletype prints them out and said, 'Yes, sir.'

I said, 'I'm going to see Garrett Rice. Can you tell me where that is?'

'What's that name again?'

Usually, you tell these guys a name, they're spitting out directions before you finish saying it. This guy had to look in a little book. Maybe nobody ever asked for Garrett Rice. Maybe I was the first ever and would win some kind of prize. 'Here we go,' he said, and told me.

A lot of production companies share space at The Burbank Studios. Warner Brothers and Columbia are the big two. Aaron Spelling Productions rents space there. So do a couple zillion lesser companies. All tucked away in warm sand-colored buildings with red tile roofs and pseudo-adobe walls. Mature oaks fill the spaces between the buildings, making a nice shade. The quality of the space reflects your position within the industry.

Garrett Rice was beneath the water tower at the back of the lot. I missed the building twice until a cross-eyed kid on a bicycle pointed it out. It was a squat two-story brick box, six single offices on the bottom and six more on top, with a metal stair at either end. There were palm trees at either end, too, and more palms in a little plot right out front. The palms didn't look like they were doing too well. A backhoe and a bulldozer were parked beside the building, taking up most of a tiny parking lot. This probably wasn't where they put Paul Newman or David Lean. I looked at the names stenciled on the parking curbs. Second from the right was Garrett Rice. Room 217. The backhoe was in his spot.

I went up the stairs and found his office without having anybody point it out. The door was open. There was a little secretary's cubicle, but no secretary. A spine-rolled copy of *Black Belt* magazine was on the secretary's desk, open to an article about hand-to-hand combat in low-visibility situations. Some secretary.

Behind the secretary's space was another door. I opened it and there was Garrett Rice. He stood behind his desk with the phone pressed to his ear, bouncing from foot to foot like he had to go to the bathroom. There was a dying plant on the desk and another on the end table by a worn green couch. There was a can of Lysol air freshener on a file cabinet. The cap was off.

When he saw me, he pressed his hip against the desk, closing a drawer that had been open. He did this in what some might call an understated fashion, then murmured into the phone and hung up.

Rice was about six-one with thin bones and the crepey skin you get from too much sun lamp. There was a mouse under his left eye and another on the left side of his forehead. He had tried to cover them with Indian earth. He had beer wings and shouldn't have been wearing a form-fit shirt.

I handed him one of my cards. 'Nice office,' I said. 'I'm trying to find Morton Lang. I'm told you and he were close and that maybe you can help me out.'

He glanced at the card, then looked at me with wet, shining eyes. Nervous. 'How'd you get in here?'

'My uncle owns the studio.'

'Bullshit.'

I gave him a shrug. 'Mort's been missing since Friday. He took his boy with him and didn't leave word. His wife's worried. Since you and he were associates, it makes sense that he might've said something to you.'

He licked his lips and I thought of Bambi's mother, the way her

23

head jerked up at the first sound of the hunters. Only she was pleasant to look at. The longer I looked at Garrett Rice, the more I wanted to cover my face with a handkerchief and fog the air with the Lysol.

He read the card again and flexed it back and forth, thinking. Then he said. 'Fuckin' asshole, Mort.'

I nodded. 'That's the one. When did you see him last?'

He glanced at the doorway behind me and spread his hands. 'You shoulda called. I'm busy. I got calls.'

'Consider it a favor to the Forces of Good.'

'I got calls.'

'So make'm. I've got time.' I sat down on the couch between his briefcase and a large brown stain. The stain looked like Mickey Mouse run over by a Kenworth. It went well with the decor.

Garrett Rice hustled over and closed the case. Maybe he had the new Hot Property in there. Maybe Steven Spielberg had been calling him, begging to get a peek. Maybe I could sap Garrett Rice, make my getaway with the Hot Property, and sell it to George Lucas for a million bucks. I put my arm up on the back of the couch so the jacket would open and he could see the Dan Wesson. I waited.

He was breathing harder now, the way a fat man does after a flight of stairs. He looked at the door again. Maybe he was waiting for a pizza delivery. 'I got calls,' he said. 'I dunno where Mort is. I haven't seen him for a week, maybe longer. What do I look like, his keeper?' He went back to his desk with the case.

I stared at him.

He fidgeted. 'What?'

'Who beat you up, Garrett?'

He held the briefcase to his chest like a shield. 'You'd better not fuck with me. I'm warning you.'

'I don't want to fuck with you, Mr. Rice. I just want to ask you about Morton Lang.'

He looked past me at the door again, only this time he said, 'Well, thank Christ! Where the hell you been?'

The man in the doorway was a little taller than me and a lot wider, with the sort of squared-off shoulders boxers get. He wore a heavy Fu moustache, a little business under his lower lip, and a two-inch Afro that was thicker on top than on the sides. Not quite the Carl Lewis look. He was very, very black. He looked at me. He looked at Garrett Rice. 'Nature call. You didn't want me to mess the floor, right?'

Rice said, 'Throw this asshole outta here. C'mon.'

The black guy looked back at me and sucked a tooth. 'How 'bout that, Elvis? Think I oughta throw your ass outta here?'

I sucked a tooth back at him. 'She-it,' I said. 'How's it goin,' Cleon?'

Garrett Rice looked from Cleon Tyner to me and back to Cleon. 'What the hell is this?' "Cleon. Elvis. Howzitgoin?" Throw the sonofabitch out, goddamnit!'

Cleon said, 'Unh-unh,' and let himself down in the chair opposite Rice's desk. He wrapped one arm over the back of the chair so I could see his Smith. It was in a pretty, gray brushed-leather rig. Cleon was wearing dark blue designer jeans, a ruffled white tuxedo shirt, and a gray sharkskin jacket. The jacket was tight across his shoulders and biceps. 'You're looking good,' I said.

He tried to give me modest. 'Cut down on the grits. Dropped a few pounds. Workin' out again. How's Joe?'

Garrett Rice said, 'Hey, hey, this guy walks in here, he's got a gun. Look right there, under his goddamned arm. He starts pumpin' me, he won't leave when I ask, he could be anybody, goddamnit, and you're shootin' the shit with him. What in hell I hire you for?' His forehead was damp.

Cleon let out a long, deep breath and shifted forward in the chair. Rice jerked back an inch. Probably didn't even know he'd done it. Cleon's voice was polite. 'I know this man, Mr. Rice. He won't take muscle work. If he *does* decide to move on you now, why, then I'll step in. That's what I take the money for. But if all he wants to do is ask you about something or other, then you talk to him. That's the smart thing.' Cleon gave me the sleepy eyes. 'That's all you wanna do, blood, is talk, am I right?'

'Sure.'

Cleon looked back at Rice. 'There. You see. Why make somethin' out of nothing?'

Garrett Rice chewed his lip. He said, 'I don't know where Mort is, all right. I told you.'

'You told me you saw him about a week ago. He say anything about leaving his wife?'

'Look, it was a party, see? A social situation. We were meeting with a potential backer about this project of mine. Mort had some bimbo with him. An actress. It was good times, that's all. Mort wouldn't've brought up any shit about his wife.'

'Kimberly Marsh?'

'Yeah, I guess that was her name. The bitch was all over me. That's the way it is, see? These bimbos find out you're a producer, they're all over you.' Talking about that brought him to life.

'Sounds rewarding.'

He leered and made a pistol with his fingers and shot me. I considered returning the gesture with my .38. Cleon picked his thumb, ignoring us. I said, 'Can you think of anyone else Mort might've talked to?'

'How the hell should I know?'

'You were friends.'

'We had business.'

'You played cards with them. Every week for almost a year.'

'Hey, I'm everybody's friend. You want me to be your friend? I'll be your friend, too. I'll even play cards with you. I'll even *lose*, you want me to.'

I looked at Cleon. He shrugged. 'It's a gig, man.'

'Not what you call your quality employment.'

'Is it ever?'

I stood up. Cleon shifted, rolling the big shoulders. 'Leaving,' I said. Cleon nodded but stayed forward. Cleon knew the moves. I looked back at Garrett. 'I like the bruises. They go with the liver spots.'

'Some asshole thought I stole his script. That happens, this business.'

'Must be some asshole, you hiring on Cleon.'

'Man just dig quality, bro, that's all.'

I nodded. Garrett Rice gnawed at his lip.

I said, 'This has been disappointing, Garrett. I bucked rush hour for this.'

'Tough.'

I said, 'I see Ellen Lang, I'll give her your best.'

'Tell her Mort's an asshole.'

'She might agree.'

'She's an asshole, too. So are you.'

I looked at Cleon. There was a little smile to his eye, but you'd never know it unless you knew him well.

I went out along the cement walk and down the metal stairs and took the long walk back to my car. I drove to Studio City to pick up

26

eggplant parmesan and an antipasto from a place called Sonny's and a six-pack of Wheat beer from the liquor store next door. By the time I got out of Sonny's, the sky was a deep purple, coal red in the west behind black palm-tree cutouts. I drove south on Laurel Canyon, up the hill toward home.

I had very much wanted to turn up some good news for Ellen Lang. But good news, like magic, is sometimes in short supply.

CHAPTER 4

It was eight o'clock when I pulled into the carport. I put the eggplant in the microwave to reheat and ate the antipasto while I waited. Oily. Sonny's had gone downhill. The little metal hatch I'd built into the door off the kitchen clattered and the cat walked in. He's black and he walks with his head sort of cocked to the side because someone once shot him with a .22. I poured a little of the Wheat beer in a saucer and put out some cat food. He drank the beer first then ate the cat food then looked at me for more beer. He was purring. 'Forget it,' I said. The purring stopped and he walked away.

When the eggplant was ready I carried it and the beer and the cordless phone out onto the deck. The rich black of the canyon was dotted with jack-o'-lantern lit houses, orange and white and yellow and red in the night. Where the canyon flattened out into Hollywood and the basin beyond, the lights concentrated into thousands of blue-white diamonds spilled over the earth. I liked that.

I'm in a rustic A-frame on a little road off Woodrow Wilson Drive above Hollywood. The only other house is a cantilevered job to my east. A stuntman I know lives there with his girlfriend and their two little boys. Sometimes during the day they come out on their deck and we'll see each other and wave. The boys call my place the teepee house. I like that, too.

When I bought the house four years ago I tore off the deck railing and rebuilt it so the center section was detachable. I detached it now, and sat on the edge of the deck with my feet hanging down, eggplant in my lap, and nothing between me and Out There. The chill air felt good. After a while the cat came out and stared at me. 'Okay,' I said. I poured some more of the Wheat beer on the deck. He blinked, then lapped at it.

When the eggplant was gone I called the answering machine at my office. There were three messages from Ellen Lang and one from Janet Simon. Ellen Lang sounded scared in the first two and teary in the third. Janet Simon sounded like Janet Simon. I called Ellen Lang. Janet Simon answered. It works like that sometimes.

'Mort came back and tore up the house. Could you come over here?'

'Is she okay?'

'He was gone when she got here. I made her call the police but now she's saying she won't let them in the house.'

'Want me to pistol-whip her?'

'Don't you ever let up?'

Apparently not. It took me eighteen minutes to push the Corvette down the valley side of Laurel, up onto the freeway, and over to Encino. Ellen Lang lived in the flat part above Ventura Boulevard in what's called a sprawling California Tudor by realtors and Encino Baroque by people with taste. Janet Simon's pale blue Mustang was on the street in front of the house. I pulled into the drive behind a Subaru wagon, cut the engine, and went up to the door. It opened before I could knock. Ellen Lang was pinched and thin behind her glasses, more so than this morning. She said, 'I called you. I called and called and you weren't there. I came to you so the police wouldn't get involved and now they are.'

Janet said, 'Oh, for God's sake, Ellen.'

I had one of those dull aches you get behind the eyes when your beer drinking is interrupted.

Ellen Lang said, 'Well, it's Mort's house, isn't it? He can do what he wants here, can't he? Can't we call the police back and tell them it was a mistake?'

I followed them like that into the living room.

Every large piece of furniture had been turned over and the bottom cloth ripped away. Books had been pulled off the shelves and cabinets thrown open. The back was off the television. A palm had been worked out of its heavy brass pot, scattering dirt over the beige carpet. The Zenith console stereo was turned on its face and about two hundred record albums spilled out on the floor. One of those large ceramic greyhounds you see in department stores was cracked open on the hearth, its head intact but lying on the carpet upside down. It looked asleep.

Some mistake.

'How long ago did you call?' I said to Ellen Lang.

Janet Simon answered. 'About forty-five minutes. She told them it wasn't an emergency.'

'If you had they'd have been here forty minutes ago. As it is, they've called it out to a radio car. They'll be here any time.'

Ellen Lang crossed her arms in the keep-me-warm posture and began nibbling the side of her mouth. Every light in the house was on, as if Janet or Ellen had gone through, making a point of driving out as much darkness as possible. There was a little night-light behind a wingback chair beside the fireplace. Even it glowed.

'He leave a note?' I said.

She shook her head.

'Take any clothes for the boy?'

Shook her head again.

'Take anything else?'

She squinted and did something funny with her mouth, blowing air out the corners while keeping the lips together. 'I checked my things. I checked the silver. The Neil Diamond records are still here. Mort loves Neil Diamond.'

'This is A-plus help you're giving me, Mrs. Lang.'

She looked at me like I was fading out and tough to see. 'Mort isn't a thief. If he took anything of his, that isn't thievery, is it? He paid for it, didn't he? He paid for all this and that gives him some rights, doesn't it?' She said that to Janet Simon.

Janet Simon reached a cigarette out of a little blue purse, tamped it, fired up, and pulled enough smoke into her chest to fill the Goodyear blimp. 'When are you going to wake up?' she said.

I left them to it and went down the hall. There was a door on the left, closed, with the sounds of running water. 'That's the bathroom,' Janet Simon called. 'The girls are in there.' The girls' bedroom was just past the bath but on the right. It was pink and white and had twin canopy beds and probably used to be quite nice. Now, the mattresses were half on and half off and one of the box springs had been turned upside down. There was a dresser and a chest, but all the drawers were out and the clothes were scattered on the floor. Bruce Springsteen was on the closet door, which spoke highly for at least one of the girls. Clothes hung neatly on the crossbar even though the closet floor had been trashed. Just outside the closet, there were two three-ring binders and two stacks of schoolbooks. The binders and the dust covers on the books were covered with doodles and designs and words. *Cindy loves Frank. B.T. + C.L. Robby Robby Robby, I want you for my hobby. BOOK*

YOU. I found a folded piece of three-hole paper in Cindy Lang's geography book with a message written on it in pencil. The message was ELAM FREID BITES THE BIG ONE!!!!! I wondered if Elam Freid knew that. I wondered how much he'd pay to find out.

I went to the boy's room next. It was smaller than the girls', with a single bed and a dresser and a big oak chest. The chest was turned over and the dresser was on its side and the mattress and box springs leaned drunkenly against the wall. I had wanted to go over the boy's room. I had wanted to read his diary and sift through his comics and peek under his mattress. I had wanted to go through the wads of paper in his trash and page through his notebooks and study the drawings that he made and pinned to the wall. A week before they left, maybe Mort had said something to the boy and the boy had left a clue. All of that was gone. There was only a big mess here that made me hope the boy wouldn't suddenly come through the front door, run back here, and see it.

The master bedroom was at the back of the house looking out on the pool through some nice French doors. It smelled of Anaïs Anaïs. I pulled the bolts at the top of each French door and ran my fingers along the stiles. They hadn't been jimmied. There was a kingsize platform bed, a dresser, a chest, and a desk, and all of it was torn up pretty much like the others. They had one of those sliding wall closets with the mirrored hanging doors. The left half was Ellen and the right Mort. Boxes and shoe bags and a Minolta camera case and a larger box that said Bekins had been tossed out to the center of the room. Mort had some nice pants and some nice shirts and half a dozen pair of Bally shoes. There was a tan Nino Cerruti shirt I liked a lot hanging beside three dark gray Sy Devore suit bags and two from Carroll's in Westwood. A lot of clothes to leave behind, but maybe Mort traveled light.

A collection of family pictures hung over the bed. The kids. Mort and the kids. Ellen. Mort and Ellen. Mort didn't seem to be playing favorites. The nicest had Mort in the pool with the younger girl on his shoulders and Perry and the older girl in his arms. Nothing looked wrong in those pictures. Mort didn't look crazy. Ellen didn't look small. Nothing ever looks wrong in the pictures. Everything always goes wrong when the camera's turned away.

The bathroom door was still closed, the water was still running, Janet Simon was still smoking, Ellen Lang was still standing with her arms crossed, cold. I went into the kitchen. Every cupboard had been emptied, every bag of sugar and rice and flour and box of cereal

31

spilled. The grill had been pulled off the bottom of the refrigerator and the stove had been dragged away from the wall, scarring the vinyl with ragged furrows. I found a bottle of Extra Strength Bayer aspirin in a mound of Corn Chex, ate three, then went back out into the living room.

Janet Simon gave me frozen eyes. Ellen Lang watched the floor. I cleared my throat. 'Someone was looking for something and someone knew where someone else might want to hide it,' I said. 'This was professional. Mort didn't do this. You're going to need the police.' Stating the obvious is something I do well.

Ellen Lang said, 'No.' Softly.

Janet Simon crushed out her cigarette and said, '*Yes*.' Firmly.

I took a deep breath and smiled sweetly. 'I'm going to check around outside,' I said.

It was either that, or hit them with a chair.

CHAPTER 5

I went out to the Corvette and got the big five-cell I keep in the trunk. I looked for jimmy marks on the front door lock stile and the doorjamb, but didn't find any. Three bay windows at the front of the house overlooked a flower bed with azaleas and snapdragons. The windows weren't jimmied and the flowers weren't trampled. I walked around the north side of the house and there were four more windows, two and a space and then two more, each still locked on the inside. I let myself through a wooden gate and walked the back of the house past a little beaded bathroom window to the pool. No openings punched in the wall, no sliding door off its track, no circular holes cut into glass. No one slugged me with a ball peen hammer and disappeared into the night.

I stopped by the pool and listened. Motor sounds from the freeway to the south. Water gurgling through pipes to the little bathroom. Somewhere a radio going, Tina Turner coughing out *What's Love Got to Do With It?*. Through the glass doors, I could see Ellen and Janet in the living room, Ellen with her arms squeezed across her chest, Janet making an explanatory gesture with her cigarette, Ellen shaking her head, Janet looking disgusted. I thought of great teams from the past: Burns and Allen, Bergen and McCarthy, Heckle and Jeckle. I took a deep breath, smelled jasmine, and kept going.

On the south side of the house it was the same thing. No footprints beneath the windows. No jimmy marks. No sign of forced entry. That meant a key or a lock pick. Maybe Mort had hired somebody to go in there and given them his key. But if so, what could he have wanted? Stock certificates? Negotiable bonds? Nudie shots he was scared Ellen would show their friends?

I went back out to the front just as a black and white pulled up. They pegged me with their spotlight and told me not to move.

33

'Should I grab sky?' I said.

The same voice came back, 'Just stand there, shithead.' Service with a smile.

One of the cops came forward with his hand on his gun. The other stayed behind the light. You can never see what they're doing behind those lights, which is why they stay there. The cop who came out was about my height but thicker in the butt and legs. It didn't detract from his presence. His name tag read SIMMS.

I spread my arms, careful not to point the five-cell in their direction. 'White pants and jacket. The latest in cat burglar apparel.'

Simms said, 'Little man, I've cuffed'm that went out in red tights. Let's see some ID.'

'I'm Cole. I work for the owner. Private investigator. There's a Dan Wesson .38 under my left arm.'

He said okay, told me he was going to reach under and take the gun, then did it. 'Now the paper,' he said.

I produced the PI license and the license to carry, and watched him read them. 'Elvis. This some kind of bullshit or what?'

'After my mother.'

He looked at me the way cops look at you when they're thinking about trying you out, then gave me the benefit of the doubt. 'Guess you take some riding about that.'

'My brother Edna had it worse.'

He thought about it again, figured I wasn't worth the paperwork and handed back the gun. 'Okay. We got a B&E call.' The other cop came around and joined us but left the spotlight on. I clicked off the five-cell.

'They're inside,' I said. 'The client's name is Ellen Lang. She owns the place. She came home and found it busted up. Another woman is with her. I checked the windows and the doors but it looks okay.'

The new cop said, 'You don't mind if we see for ourselves, do you?'

I said, 'This guy is good, Simms. He's a comer.'

Simms put his hand on my arm and pointed me toward the house. 'Come on, let's you and me go see the ladies. Eddie, take a walk around.'

When we got into the living room I said, 'Look what the cat dragged in.' Ellen Lang said, 'Oh, Lord,' and sat down as the two girls walked in. The oldest was fourteen, the youngest maybe

34

eleven. The older one was tall and gawky and had a couple of major league pimples forming up on her forehead. The younger one was slender and dark and looked a little bit like Ellen. They were carrying pink-and-white overnighters. The oldest had a pissed-off look on her face. 'We're packed,' she said. She ignored me and the cop.

'Oh, honey, that's not warm enough. Get a sweater.'

The younger one stared at Simms, then at me. 'Is he the detective?'

'Wanna see my sap?' I said.

Ellen Lang took off her glasses, rubbed at her eyes, put her glasses back on, and said, 'Please, Mr. Cole.'

The younger one said, 'What's a sap?'

Simms ignored all that. 'This place looks like hell.'

The older one said, 'It's not the arctic, Mother. We're only going to Janet's.' Her face reeked of disapproval. Teenage girls reek of disapproval better than anyone I know.

'Oh, honey, please,' Ellen Lang said. It wasn't nice to hear. It's never nice to hear an adult whine to a child. The older one closed her eyes, sighed dramatically, and said, 'Come on.' They went back down the hall and disappeared.

Simms said, 'I'm Officer Simms. There's another officer outside checking the yard. What we're going to do is look around, then sit down with you and talk about it, okay?' He had a good style. Relaxed and easy.

Ellen Lang's 'Yes' was very soft.

Eddie tapped at the glass doors that led off the dining room out to the pool and Simms went over. They mumbled together, then Simms said, 'Poolhouse is inside out. I'll be right back,' and went out to see. The jasmine floated in the open door.

I said, 'You want the cops in on this or not? They're in now and it's smarter if they stay in.'

She shook her head without looking at me.

Janet Simon said, 'Oh, for God's sake, Ellen,' for maybe the 400th time, and took a seat on the hearth.

I said, 'It is my professional opinion that you allow the police to investigate. I checked Kimberly Marsh's apartment this afternoon. It looks like she went away for a few days. If she did, there's a good chance she went somewhere with Mort. If Mort's out of town, then he couldn't have done this. That means you had a stranger in your house. Even if Mort hired somebody, that's over the line and the cops should know.'

Janet Simon said, 'Wow. You work fast.'

Ellen Lang went white when I mentioned Kimberly Marsh. She tried to swallow, looked like she had a little trouble, then stood up and said, 'I won't have the police after my husband. I won't do that to him. I don't want the police here. I don't want ABPs. I don't want Mort in any trouble.'

'APB,' I said. 'All Points Bulletin. That went out with Al Capone.'

'I don't want that, either.'

My head throbbed. The muscles along my neck were tight. Pretty soon I'd have knots in the trapezius muscles and sour stomach. 'Listen,' I said. 'It wasn't Mort.'

Ellen Lang started to cry. No whimpering, no trembling chin. Just water spilling out her eyes. 'Please do something,' she said. She made no move to hide her face.

The cops came back and glanced into the kitchen. Eddie mumbled some more to Simms and headed out to the radio car. Simms stayed with us. 'We're gonna get the detectives in on this,' he said.

Ellen Lang folded up and sat down like she'd just been told the biopsy was positive. 'Oh, God, I can't do anything right.'

I watched her a moment, then took a long breath in through the nose, let it out, and said, 'Simms?'

Simms' eyes flicked my way. Flat, bored eyes. Street-cop eyes.

I brought him aside. 'She thinks it was her husband,' I said. 'It's a domestic beef. They're separated.'

Simms said 'Shit' under his breath and called out the front door for Eddie to wait. He stood in the living room, one thick hand on his gun butt and one on his nightstick, looking around the place like he was standing hip deep in dog shit. The older girl came back in, saw her mother crying, and looked disgusted. 'Oh, for Christ's sake, Mother.' She went back down the hall. Maybe she wanted to grow up to be Janet Simon.

Ellen Lang cried harder. I went over to her, put my hand on her shoulder, and said, 'Stop that' into her ear. She nodded and tried to stop. She did a pretty good job.

Simms said, 'All right. Do you want to report anything missing?'

She shook her head without looking at him, either.

'A lot of this stuff is ruined,' he said. 'You could maybe file a vandalism claim with the insurance, but only if we file a report, and only if we can't prove it's your husband. Okay, even if we forget your husband, the detectives still gotta come out here and file a vandalism report. That's the insurance company, see?'

'You're okay, Simms,' I said.

He ignored me. Ellen blew her nose on a little bit of Kleenex and shook her head again. 'I'm very sorry for the bother,' she said.

Simms frowned around the room. 'Husband, huh?'

Janet Simon said, 'Ellen, you should have this for court.' I felt Ellen Lang tighten like a flexed muscle.

'Forget that,' I said.

Simms stood there a second longer, breathing heavily, then nodded and walked out.

Nobody moved for a long time. Then Janet Simon pulled out another cigarette. 'You're a dope.'

Ellen Lang began to tremble. I felt it deep in my chest and up through my arm, a high-strung from-the-lonely-place resonance that left the tips of her collar shaking like leaves in a chill breeze. 'You want me to stay?' I asked. 'I can bunk on the couch.'

Ellen lifted off her glasses, wiped at the wet around her eyes, and sniffled. 'Thank you, no. We're going to stay the night with Janet.'

I gave Janet a look. 'Gosh, I was hoping I could. I'm into pain.' Janet ignored me, but Ellen Lang smiled. It wasn't much of a smile, but it was real.

I told her I'd be back tomorrow to look over the bills and bank statements and that she should gather them. I let myself out. The chill had a bite to it now and I could smell a eucalyptus from a neighbor's yard along with the jasmine. There were times when I thought it might be nice to have a jasmine and a eucalyptus to smell. But not always.

CHAPTER 6

I woke up just before nine the next morning and caught the tail end of *Sesame Street*. Today's episode was brought to us by the letter D. For Depressed Detective. I pulled on a pair of tennis shoes and went out onto the deck for the traditional twelve sun salutes of the hatha-yoga, then segued smoothly to the tai chi, third and eighth cycles, Tiger and Crane work. I started slow the way you're supposed to, then increased the pace the way you're not until the tai chi became a wing chun *kata* and sweat trickled down the sides of my face and my muscles burned and I was feeling pretty good again. I finished in *vrischikasan*, the second-stage scorpion pose, and held it for almost six minutes.

The cat was waiting in the kitchen. I gave him the big smile and a cheery hello. 'Held the scorpion for six minutes,' I said. Proudly.

The cat thought about that, then licked his scrotum. Some people you can never please.

I made us eggs. His with tuna, mine with a couple of shots of Tabasco. We ate in silence. After the meal I phoned General Entertainment Studios.

A young woman's voice said, 'Casting.'

'Patricia Kyle, please.'

'Who's calling?'

'Elvis Cole.'

'Pardon me?'

'Don't be cruel,' I said.

'I'm not. I – oh.' A giggle. '*That* Elvis. Hold on.'

Patricia Kyle came on the phone, voice loud enough to be heard in Swaziland. 'You got me pregnant, you bastard!' That Patricia. What a kidder.

I said, 'I need to pump you.'

'Oh, ho!'

'For information.'

'That's what they all say.' She told me that she would be there until lunch, that there would be a drive-on pass at the main gate, and that I should come by anytime.

'That's what they all say,' I said. And hung up.

Forty minutes later, showered, dusted, deodorized, and dressed, I was on the GE lot walking toward the casting offices.

GE has one of the few remaining old-time studio lots. Huge gray sound stages packed belly-to-butt with bunkerlike offices, navigable only by a grid of narrow streets usually fouled with the big semis production companies employ to carry cameras and lights and costumes to location. On any given day you could see almost anyone walking those slim tarmac streets. As a tour bus passed I waved and the people waved back. Ah, the land of make-believe.

I went in a door that said Emergency Exit Only and took the first flight of stairs I came to, turned down a short hall and passed seven of the most beautiful women on Earth, strolled past the casting office receptionist like I owned the place, went through a glass door and down another short hall past a man and a woman who were arguing softly, and stopped outside Patricia Kyle's door. She was on the phone.

I said loudly, 'Have the abortion. It's the only way.' I looked at the man and the woman. 'Herpes.' Then a hand yanked me into Patricia Kyle's office and the door slammed amid a gale of red-faced laughter.

'You nut, that's my boss!'

'Not for long.'

She picked up the phone and cupped the receiver. 'Business. I'll just be a second.'

I took a seat in a chair beneath a wall-sized poster of Raquel Welch from the movie *1,000,000 Years B.C.* Someone had taken a Magic Marker and drawn a voice balloon over her head so that Raquel was saying, 'Mess with me, buster, I'll gut you like a fish!!!'

Patricia Kyle is forty-four years old, five-four and slim the way a female gymnast is slim, all long, lithe muscle and defined curves, with a pretty Irish face framed by curly auburn hair. When we met four years ago she weighed in at one seventy-three and had just gotten out of the world's worst marriage. Only her ex didn't see it that way. He'd show up all hours, drunk and stumbling around, knocking over the garbage cans, doing Stanley Kowalski. To prove how much he loved her, he put a brick through the rear window of her BMW and used an ice pick on the tires and that's when she called me. I took care of it. She dumped the weight and quit smoking and took up Nautilus and started running. She got the job at General Entertainment. Things were looking up.

She apologized into the phone, told whoever it was that GE and the producers really wanted their actor but couldn't pay more than Top of the Show, that she knew the actor's wife had just had a baby and so he'd probably want the work and the money, and that he'd be just so *right* for the part she really wished he'd do it. She listened, then smiled, said fine, and hung up.

'He's going to take the role?'

She nodded. 'It's twenty-five hundred dollars for two days' work.'

'Yeah, but those guys earn it.'

She laughed. I've never heard Patricia giggle. It's either a smile or a full blown laugh, but nothing in between. I gave her the once-over. 'Nice,' I said.

She put a thousand watts out through her teeth. 'One-twelve,' she said. 'I ran in my first Ten-K last week, *AND* I've got a new boyfriend.'

'He's just after your mind.'

'God, I hope not.'

'Tell me everything you know about an agent named Morton Lang.'

She pushed back in her chair. 'He used to work for ICM, I think, then he left about a year ago to start his own agency. He calls maybe once a month, sometimes more, to push a client or ask about upcoming roles.'

'Talk to him anytime in the past week or so?'

'Unh-unh.' She leaned forward, gave me dimples and an eager look. 'What's the dirt?'

I tried to give her the sort of look I'd always imagined Mike Hammer giving to dames and broads who got out of line. 'It's the game, doll. You know that.'

Her left eyebrow arched. 'Doll?'

I spread my hands. 'Let's pretend you didn't commit this major gaff by asking about a client, and continue. Mort had business with a producer named Garrett Rice.'

'Garrett Rice. Yuck.'

'Crepey skin, lecherous demeanor, sour body odor. What's not to like?'

She looked at me as if she were trying to think of a concise way to say it. 'When you're in high school, and you first start thinking you'd like to work in this business and you tell your parents and they freak out, they're freaking out because they're thinking of men like Garrett Rice.'

'Can you think of any reason why he might need a bodyguard?'

'You're kidding me.'

'Nope. Guy named Cleon Tyner. He's pretty good. Not world class, but okay in a bar. Somebody put a couple of marks on Mr. Rice and scared him. Ergo, Cleon.'

Patricia thought about it, then laid a finger alongside her nose. 'I've heard there's some of this.'

'Cocaine.'

'Just talk. I don't know for sure. Garrett has this reputation. He came on to one of the girls here by offering her a toot, that kind of thing.'

I saw him closing the drawer, closing the briefcase. 'Mort, too?'

She looked surprised. 'I wouldn't think so.'

'Okay, that's Garrett's problem. Mort ever mention any friends, anyone he might've been close to?'

'Not that I remember. I can ask the other people here. I'll call a friend at Universal Casting and he can ask around over there.'

I unfolded the 8 × 10 of Kimberly Marsh. Patricia looked at it, turned it over and read the résumé, then shook her head. 'Sorry.'

'If Mort calls, will you try to get a number and let me know?'

'You going to tell me what this is about?'

'Mort's peddling government secrets to the Arabs.'

She stuck her tongue at me.

'Tell me the truth,' I said. 'Do I look like John Cassavetes twenty years ago?'

'I didn't know you twenty years ago.'

Everyone's a comedian. I stood up and went to the door.

'It's too bad about Mort,' she said. 'I remember when he was with ICM. He was well-placed. He had a fair clients list.' She leaned back, putting her feet on her desk. She was wearing dark blue Espadrilles and tight Jag jeans. 'You only start dealing with a Garrett Rice when you're scared. It's the kiss of death. A guy like Garrett Rice, he rents space over at TBS but he couldn't get a deal with Warners or Columbia. Nobody wants him around.' She frowned. 'I met Mort twice maybe a year and a half ago when he was with ICM. He seemed like a nice man.'

'Yeah, they're all nice men. This business is rife with nice men.'

'You're a cynic, Elvis.'

'No, I've just never met anyone in this business who believed in anything worthwhile and was willing to go the distance for it.'

'Oh, foo,' she said. That's one of the reasons I like her, she said things like 'oh, foo.' She slapped her desk, then got up and came around and punched my arm. 'Hey, when are you going to come to the house for dinner?'

'Then I'll have to meet your boyfriend.'

'That's the idea.'

'What if I don't approve?'

'You'll lie and tell me he's the greatest thing in the world.'

I squeezed her butt and walked out. 'It works like that, doesn't it.'

CHAPTER 7

I pulled up at Ellen Lang's house at ten minutes before noon. She came to the door in cutoffs, bare feet, and a man's white-with-blue-stripes shirt tied at the waist. Her hair was done up in a knot. 'Oh, God,' she said. 'Oh, God.'

I smiled serenely. 'To some, yes.'

'I wasn't expecting you. I'm not dressed.'

I went past her into the living room. The books and records were back on their shelves and most of the furniture was righted and in some semblance of order. There was a staple gun and packaging tape by the big couch, which was still upside down. Too heavy for her. I whistled. 'You do all this by yourself?'

'Of course.'

'Without Janet?'

She flushed and touched her hair where it was wispy out from the knot. 'I must look horrible.'

'You look better than yesterday. You look like someone who's been working hard and had her mind off her troubles. You look okay.'

She flushed some more and turned back toward the dining room. Half a sandwich was laid out on a paper towel on the table. It looked like a single slice of processed chicken loaf on whole wheat, cut diagonally. There was half a Fred Flintstone glass of skim milk beside it.

She said, 'I want to apologize to you for last night. And to thank you for what you did.'

'Forget it.'

She looked away, picking at the knot that held the shirttails together. 'Well, you came all the way out here and I was so silly.'

'No, you weren't. You were upset. You had a right to be. It would have been smart to keep the cops but you didn't and now it's past, so forget it.'

She nodded, again without looking at me. Habit. As if she had never been quite strong enough to carry on a conversation in person. 'Why did you let the police leave?'

'You wanted them to.'

'But you and Janet didn't.'

'I don't work for Janet.' Ellen Lang went very red. 'When you hire me I work for you. That means I'm on your side. I act on your behalf. I respect your confidences. My job doesn't mean cribbing off what the cops dig up. So if you don't want the cops then I'll try to live by that.'

She looked at me, then remembered herself and glanced away. 'You're the first private investigator I've ever met.'

'The others aren't as good looking.'

A little bit of a smile came to one side of her face, then left. Progress. She turned and handed me a small stack of white and green envelopes from the table. 'I found these by Mort's desk.' There were phone bills, some charge receipts from Bullocks and the Broadway and Visa, and some gas receipts from Mobil. All neatly sorted.

'There's only two phone bills here,' I said.

'That's all I found.'

'I want everything for the last six months, and the checkbook and the passbooks and anything from your broker if you have one, including ILA accounts and things like that.'

'Well, like I said –' The awkward look was back.

'Mort handled all the money.'

'I'm so bad with figures. I'm sorry.'

'Unh-huh.' I pointed at the sandwich. 'Why don't you fix me one of those, only put some food on mine, and when I come back we can talk.'

I went back through the living room and down the hall to the master. The mattress had been pulled back onto the box spring. The clothes and personal items had been picked up and folded into neat piles on the bed, his and hers, outer garments and underwear, all waiting to go back into the drawers. The drawers were back in the chest and dresser, and the room, like the rest of the house, looked in order. She must have started at 3 A.M.

Two shoe boxes and the Bekins box were on Mort's desk, filled with envelopes and file folders and actors' résumés and more of those glossy 8 × 10s. On the back of each 8 × 10 someone had stamped 'The Morton Lang Agency' in red ink. I went through his rolodex, pulled cards for the clients I recognized, and put them in my pocket. In the second shoe box I found registration papers for a Walther .32-caliber automatic pistol purchased in 1980. Well, well. I stood up and looked at the room but didn't see the gun sticking out of any place conspicuous. Halfway down the Bekins box, under a three-year-old copy of *Playboy*, I found an unframed diploma from Kansas State University in Morton Keith Lang's name. It was water-stained. The bills and receipts and bank stuff were near the bottom of the box. Grand total search time: eight minutes. Maybe the box had hidden from Ellen when she came into the room. I have socks that do that.

When I got back to the dining room, a full-grown sandwich sat on a black china plate atop a blue and gray pastel place mat. The sandwich was cut into two triangles, each sporting a toothpick with an electric blue tassel. Four orange slices and four raspberries and a sprig of parsley offset the tassels. A water goblet sat to the right of the plate. To the left was a matching saucer with sweet pickles and pitted olives and Tuscan peppers, and a little gold fork to spear them with. A blue and gray linen napkin was rolled and peaked and sitting above the plate.

Ellen Lang sat at her place, staring out through the glass doors into her backyard. When she heard me she turned. 'I put out water because I didn't know what else you might want. We have Diet Coke or milk or Pabst beer. I could make coffee if you'd like.'

The table was perfect. 'No, this is fine,' I said. 'Thank you.'

She shifted in the chair. I sat and ate a Tuscan pepper. I prefer chili peppers or serranos, but Tuscans are fun, too.

'Did you find what you were looking for?' she said.

'In the box on the desk.' I showed her the stack of paper.

She closed her eyes. 'Oh, God. I'm sorry. I put those things in there this morning. I don't know why I didn't see them.'

'Stress. You give a person enough stress and they begin to fog out. People start having little fender benders in parking lots. People forget their keys. People can't see things right under their noses. It happens to everybody. Even Janet Simon.'

She took a nibble of her sandwich, then rearranged it on the plate. 'You don't like her very much, do you?'

I didn't say anything.

'She's my friend. She's a very strong lady. She understands.' Sit, Ellen. Speak.

'She's your anchor,' I said. 'She is that because she's abusive and insulting and she reinforces your lousy self-image, which is what you want. If she's right about you, then Mort's right about you. If Mort's right about you then you deserve to be treated the way he treats you and you shouldn't rock the boat which is something you do not want to do.' Mr. Sensitive. 'Other than that, I like her fine.'

'You made a joke.'

I had said a very hard thing and she wasn't angry. She should've been, but she wasn't. Maybe enough years of Janet Simon will do that to you. Or maybe she hadn't heard.

I shrugged. 'Being funny, that's one way to deal with stress. Investigators, cops, paramedics. Paramedics are the funniest people I know. Have you in stitches.'

She looked at me. Blank.

'Paramedics are the funniest people I know. *Have you in stitches.*'

'Oh.'

'Another little joke.'

We smiled at each other. Just your basic lunchtime conversation. 'Did you mean that, what you said about Janet?'

Maybe she had heard. Maybe, deep down, she was even angry. 'Yes.'

'You're wrong.'

'Okay.'

She took another microscopic bite of her sandwich, then pushed it away. Maybe she absorbed nutrients from her surroundings. 'You must like being a private investigator,' she said.

'Yes. Very much.' I took the top off one of the sandwich halves, pulled the stems off two of the peppers, put the peppers on the sandwich, sealed it up again.

'Did you go to college for that?'

'University of Southeast Asia. Two-year program.'

'Vietnam?'

'Unh-huh.' I finished the first half of the sandwich, put three peppers on the remaining half, and started on that one.

'That must have been awful,' she said.

'There were some very real disadvantages to being there, yes.' I swallowed, took a sip of water, patted my lips with the napkin. 'But adversity has a way of strengthening. If it doesn't kill you, you

46

learn things. For instance, that's when I learned I wanted to be Peter Pan.'

She didn't quite frown. She quizzled. 'You're quizzling.'

'Pardon me?' Confused.

'Me being funny again. I learned to be funny in Vietnam. Funny is a survival mechanism. I started yoga. Pranayamic breathing is a great way to keep your mind right. We'd be in a bunker, six of us, breathing in one nostril, out the other, *om*ing to beat hell as the rockets came in. You see how this gets funny?'

'Of course.'

'Yoga led to tai chi, tai chi led to tae kwan do, which is Korean karate, and wing chun, which is an offshoot of Chinese kung fu. All very centering, stabilizing activities.' I spread my hands. 'I am a bastion of calm in a chaotic world.'

Blank eyes.

'I learned that I could survive. I learned what I would do to keep breathing, and what I wouldn't do, and what was important to me, and what wasn't. Just like you're going to learn that you can survive what's happening to you.'

She pursed her lips, looking away to pick at a bread crumb on her milk glass.

'If I can survive Vietnam, you can survive Encino,' I said. 'Try yoga. Be good for you.'

'Yoga.'

Apparently she didn't consider yoga an appropriate substitute for a husband. 'Mrs. Lang, do you know where Mort kept his gun?'

She looked surprised. 'Mort didn't have a gun.'

I showed her the receipt. 'Well, this is years ago,' she said.

'Guns tend to hang around. Keep an eye out for it.'

She nodded. 'All right. I'm sorry.'

'You say that a lot. You don't have to be sorry. You look away a lot, too, and that's something else you don't have to do.'

'I'm sorry.'

'Quite all right.'

She took a sip of her milk. It left a moustache on her upper lip. 'You are funny,' she said.

'It's either that or be smart.' I killed the rest of the sandwich and sorted the paperwork: bank stuff together, credit card billings together, phone stuff by itself. Without Janet Simon around, she was much more relaxed. You could look past the frightened eyes and mottled face and slumped shoulders and get glimpses of her

47

from better days. I said, 'I'll bet you were the third prettiest girl in eleventh grade.'

Happy-lines came to the corners of her eyes. She touched at her hair again. '*Second* prettiest,' she said.

It was good when she smiled. She probably hadn't done a lot of that lately. 'You meet Mort in college?'

'High school. Clarence Darrow Senior High in Elverton. That's where we grew up. In Kansas.'

'High school sweethearts.'

She smiled. 'Yes. Isn't that awful?'

'Not at all. You go to college together?'

Her eyes turned a little wistful. 'Mort was in theater arts and business. His parents had quite a large paint store there, in Elverton. They wanted him to take it over but Mort wanted to act. No one can understand that in Elverton. You say you want to act and they just look at you.'

I shrugged. 'Mort didn't have it so bad.'

She looked at me.

'He had the second prettiest girl at Clarence Darrow Senior High, didn't he?'

She looked at me some more until she realized what I was doing, then she grinned, and nodded, and finally gave a short uncertain laugh. She told me I was terrible.

I pushed the paperwork across the table to her. 'Be that as it may, I want you to go through and notate all the phone numbers that you can identify. Go through the credit card billings and see if the purchases make sense to you. Same with the bank statements and the check stubs.'

She looked at the stacks of paper. The smile disappeared. No happy-lines around the eyes. 'Isn't that what I'm paying you for?' she said softly.

'We're going to have to take care of that, too. So far, you're not paying me anything.'

'Yes, of course.' Awkward and uncomfortable.

I sighed. 'Look, I could do this, sure, but it's faster if you do it. I won't know any of these phone numbers, but you will, and that will save time. I don't know what you people bought from the Broadway or on Visa. I see a Visa charge from The Ivy for a hundred dollars a week every week, I don't know you and Janet make a regular thing of it there every Thursday.'

'There's nothing like that.'

48

'There might be something else.'

She was looking at the paper like it was going to jump at her. 'It's not that I don't want to,' she said, 'it's just that I'm not very good at these things.'

'You'll surprise youself.'

'I'm so bad with figures.'

'Try.'

'I'll mess it up.' I leaned back in the chair and put my hands on the table. At the Grand Canyon, I'd seen a man with acrophobia force himself toward the guardrail because his daughter wanted to look down. He almost made it; both hands on the rail, leaning forward in a lunge with his feet as far back as possible, before the cold sweats cut his knees out from under him and he collapsed to the pavement. Ellen Lang's eyes looked like his eyes.

She tried to smile again, but it came out broken this time. 'It really will be better if you do it, don't you see?'

I saw. 'Mort really did it to you, didn't he.'

She stood quickly and scooped up what was left of her sandwich and the Fred Flintstone glass. 'You stop that right now. You sound just like Janet.'

'Nope. With me it was just an observation.'

She stood breathing hard for a second and then she went into the kitchen. I waited. When she came back out she said, 'All right. Tell me what to do again.'

I told her. 'Now, about my fee.'

'Yes, of course.'

'Two thousand, exclusive of expenses.'

'I remember.'

I looked at her. She looked at me. Nobody moved. After twenty or thirty years I said, 'Well?'

'I'll get it to you.'

I took the checkbook out of the stack of bank paper and pushed it across the table to her. 'What's wrong with now?'

A tic started on her right eye. 'Do you ... take Visa?'

It was very still in the house. I could hear a single-engine light plane climbing out of Van Nuys Airport to the north. Somewhere down the street a dog with a deep, barrel-chested voice barked. There was a little breeze, but the jasmine was soured by the smog. I slid the checkbook back and looked at it. Most of the couples I know have the husband's name printed out, with the wife's name printed beneath it, two individuals. Theirs read: *Mr. and Mrs.*

49

Morton K. Lang. There was a balance of $3426.15. All of the stubs were written in the same masculine hand. I said quietly, 'Go get a pen and I'll show you how.'

She went back into the kitchen. When she didn't come out for a while I went to see. She was standing with one hand on the counter and one hand atop her head. Her glasses were off and her chest was heaving and there was a puddle of tears on the tile counter by the glasses. Streamers of mucus ran down from her nose. All of that, but you couldn't hear her. 'It's okay,' I said.

She broke and turned into my chest, sucking great gasping sobs. I held her tight, feeling the wet soak through my shirt. 'I'm thirty-nine years old and I can't do anything. What did I do to myself? What did I do? I've got to have him back. Oh, God, I need him.'

I knew she wasn't talking about Perry.

I held her until the heaving stopped and then I wrapped some ice in a dish towel and wet it and told her to put it on her face.

After a while we went back out to the dining room and I showed her how to fill in the check and how to maintain the balance on the stub. She was fine with the figures once she knew where to put them.

When the check was written she tried to smile but all the life had gone out of her. 'I guess I'll need to do this to pay the bills.'

'Yes.'

'Excuse me.'

She went down the hall toward her bedroom. I sat at the table for a while, then brought the dishes into the kitchen. I washed both glasses and the plate and the saucer, and dried them with paper towels, then I went back out, gathered together the bank records, and went into the living room by the overturned couch. She'd done a fair job of stapling the bottom cloth back on, but she would have a helluva time righting it. I listened, but couldn't hear her moving around. I turned the couch over and put it where I thought it should go and left.

CHAPTER 8

Forty minutes later I was back at my office. It was nicer there. I liked the view. I liked the Pinocchio clock. I liked my director's chairs. I arranged the rolodex cards I'd taken from Morton Lang's desk neatly on top of his bank statements. I took out my bankbook and the two thousand dollar check Ellen Lang had written. Her first check. I filled out a deposit slip, endorsed the check, stamped *FOR DEPOSIT ONLY* over my signature, put it all in the bankbook, put everything back in my desk, closed the drawer, and put my brain in neutral, a relatively easy task.

The outer door opened and Clarence Wu stuck his grapefruit head and thin shoulders into the little waiting room. 'Is now a bad time?'

Pinocchio's eyes went side to side, side to side.

Clarence came in with his briefcase. Clarence owned Wu's Quality Engraving on the second floor, above the bank. I had stopped in a week ago to see about the business cards and stationery, telling him I wanted a more businesslike image. 'I made up the samples,' he said. 'You had some wonderful ideas.'

I didn't remember having any wonderful ideas, but there you go. He put the briefcase on the desk, took some cards out of his shirt pocket, and laid them out on the case like a blackjack dealer. I looked at Pinocchio. Clarence frowned. 'You seem preoccupied,' he said.

'A small loss of faith in the human condition. It'll pass. Continue.'

He turned the case around. '*Voilà.*'

There were four cards, two white, one sort of light blue, and one cream. One of the white ones had a human eye rendered in charcoal in the center with *The Elvis Cole Detective Agency* arced above it and the legend *on your case* beneath. 'Businesslike,' I said. He beamed. The other white card had my name spelled out in bullet holes with a smoking machine gun underneath. Had I thought of that? The sort-of-blue card had a magnifying glass laid over a deerstalker hat in the upper left corner and the agency's name in script. 'Victorian,' I said.

'A certain elegance,' he nodded.

The cream card had my name centered in modern block letters with the word *detective* beneath it and a .45 Colt Automatic in the upper right quad. I looked at that one the longest. I said, 'Get rid of the gun and you've got something.'

He looked confused. 'No art?'

'No art.'

He looked confused some more and then he beamed. 'Inspired.'

'Yeah. Gimme five hundred with my name and the *detective* and another five hundred that say The Elvis Cole Detective Agency. Put the phone number in the lower right corner and the address in the lower left.'

'You want cards for Mr. Pike?'

'Mr. Pike won't use cards.'

'Of course.' Of course. He nodded and beamed again, and said, 'Next Thursday,' and left.

Maybe I could find Mort by next Thursday. Maybe I could find him this afternoon. There would be advantages. No more trips to Encino. No more Ellen Lang. No more depression. I would be The Happy Detective. I could call Wu and have him change the card. *Elvis Cole, The Happy Detective, specializing in Happy Cases.* Inspired.

I went down to the deli, bought an Evian water, drank it on the way back up, then went through Mort's finances. As of two weeks ago Monday, Morton Lang had $4265.18 in a passbook savings account. There was one three-year CD in his name worth $5000 that matured in August. I could find no evidence of any stocks or other income-producing investment in either his name, Ellen's name, or in the names of the children. Irregular deposits totaling $5200 had been made into savings over the past six months. During the same period, $2200 was transferred to checking every two weeks. Figure $1600 note and taxes, $800 food, $500 cars, another $200 gardener and pool service, another $500 or $600 because you got three kids and you live in Encino. Forty-five hundred a month to live, next to nothing coming in. *You only start dealing with a Garrett Rice when you're scared.*

I dialed ICM. They gave me to someone in the television department who had known Morton Lang when he worked there fourteen months ago. He had known Mort, but not very well, and if I was looking for representation perhaps he could help me out, ICM being a full-service agency representing artists in all media. I dialed Morton's Lang's clients. Edmund Harris wasn't home. Kaitlin Rosenberg hadn't spoken to Mort in three weeks, and I should tell him the play was going fine. Cynthia Alport hadn't heard from him in over a month and why the hell hadn't he returned her calls? Ric-with-no-K Lloyd hadn't returned Mort's call of six weeks ago because he'd changed agents and would I please pass that along to Mort? Darren Fips had spoken with Mort about two weeks ago because the contracts had never arrived but Mort hadn't gotten back to him and Darren was getting damned pissed. Tracey Cormer's line was busy. Fourteen minutes after I started, the rolodex cards were back in their stack and I still had no useful information. I dialed Kimberly Marsh, thinking maybe she hadn't run off with Mort after all, and got her answering machine. I called Ellen Lang, thinking maybe she'd found something in the phone bills, or, if not, maybe she just needed a kind word. No answer. I called Janet Simon, thinking maybe Ellen Lang had gone over there, or, if not, Janet might know where she had gone. No answer. I got up, opened the glass doors, and went out onto the balcony to stand in the smog.

All dressed up and no place to go.

The phone rang. 'Elvis Cole Detective Agency. Top rates paid for top clues.'

It was Lou Poitras, this cop I know who works out of North Hollywood Division. 'Howzitgoin, Hound Dog?'

'Your wife's here. We're having a Wesson oil party.'

There was a grunt. 'You workin' for a guy named Morton Lang?'

'His wife. Ellen Lang. How'd you know?'

It got very still in the office. I watched Pinocchio's eyes. Side to side, side to side. 'What's going on, Lou?'

'Bout an hour ago some Chippies found Morton Lang sittin' in his Caddie up near Lancaster. Shot to death.'

There was a loud shushing noise and my fingers began to tingle and I had to go to the bathroom. My voice didn't want to work. 'The boy?'

Lou didn't say anything.

'Lou?'

'What boy?' he said.

After a while I hung up and took out the photo of Morton Lang. I turned it over and reread the description his wife had written. I looked at the picture of the boy. Maybe he was with Kimberly Marsh. Maybe he was fine and safe and away from whoever had shot his father to death. Maybe not. I opened the drawer and took out my passbook and the check and the deposit slip. I put the passbook back and closed the drawer. I tore the deposit slip in quarters and threw it away. I wrote VOID across the face of the check. Her first check. I folded it in two and put it in my wallet and then I went to see Lou Poitras.

CHAPTER 9

I parked in the little lot they have next to the North Hollywood Police Department headquarters and went around front to this big linoleum-floored room. There were hardwood benches on two of the walls, a couple of Coke and candy machines, and a bulletin board. A poster on the bulletin board said POLICE FUND RAISER – A NIGHT OF BOXING ENTERTAINMENT – COPS VERSUS FIREMEN! SPECIAL EXHIBITION BOUT: BULLDOG PARKER AND MUSTAFA HAMSHO. Beside the poster a skinny white kid with stringy hair spoke softly into a pay phone. He leaned against the wall with one foot back on a toe, his heel nervously rocking.

I went around two Chicano men in Caterpillar hats with green jackets and dirty broken work shoes and through a reinforced door, up one flight of stairs, and down a short hall into the detectives' squad room. Also known as Xanadu.

The detectives live in a long gray room with all the desks against the north wall and three little offices at the far end. Across from the desks are a shower, a locker room, and a holding cell. *Days of Our Lives* was going on the locker room TV. Two brown hands were sticking out through the holding cell bars. They looked tired. Poitras' office was the first of the three at the far end.

Lou Poitras has a face like a frying pan and a back as wide as a Coupe de Ville. His arms are so swollen from the weights he pumps they look like fourteen pound hams squeezed into his sleeves. He has a scar breaking the hairline above his left eye where a guy who should've known better got silly and laid a jack handle. It lent character. Poitras was leaning back behind his desk as I walked in, kielbasa fingers laced over his belly. Even reclined, he took up most of the room.

He said, 'You didn't bring that sonofabitch Pike, did you?'

'I'm fine, Lou. And you?'

Simms was sitting in a hard chair in front of Lou's desk. There was another chair against the wall, but it was stacked high with files and folders. First come, first served. Simms wore street clothes: blue jeans and a faded khaki safari shirt with an ink stain on the pocket and tread-worn Converse All Stars. 'You get promoted?' I said.

'Day off.'

Lou said, 'Forget that. Gimme the kid's picture.'

I handed him the little school picture of gap-toothed Perry Lang. He yelled, 'Penny!' and flipped the photo over to read the back, jaw working.

Penny came in. There was a lot of dusty red hair and tanned skin. She had to be six feet tall. 'Sheena, right?' I said. She ignored me. Lou gave her the little picture. 'Color-copy this, front and back, and have a set phoned up to McGill in Lancaster right away.' When she left, Simms looked after her. So did I.

'She's new,' I said.

Simms smiled. 'Uh-huh.'

Poitras looked sour. 'You two try to control your glands.'

'You get anything new on the cause of death?' I said.

'I called the States up by Lancaster after we talked. They say four shots, close range. ME's out there now.'

'What about the boy?'

'McGill up there, he's okay. McGill said there was nothing in the Caddie to indicate the boy was in the car when his old man got it. They put some people out to search the roadside, but it's gonna be a while before we hear.'

'Okay.'

Poitras leaned forward and looked at me, his forehead wrinkling up like a street map of Bangkok. 'Simms says you're in on this.'

I started from the beginning, telling them how Ellen Lang had hired me and why. I told them about Kimberly Marsh and said her address twice so Lou could write it down, and then about Garrett Rice and what Patricia Kyle had given me as background information. I told them what I knew about Mort from Kansas and his failing business and his heavy monthly note and his midlife crisis. It didn't take long. Somewhere in there Simms went out and came back with three coffees. Mine was cold. When I finished, Lou said, 'All right. You come up with any angles on Lang?'

'No.'

'Enemies?'

56

'No.'

'How about connections?'

'Unh-uh.'

Simms liked that. 'Sounds like you been busting your ass.'

Lou drummed his fingers on the desk. It sounded like firecrackers going off. I'd once seen Lou Poitras dead-lift the front end of a '69 Volkswagen Bug. 'Simms said somebody went through their house last night.'

'Simms knows what I know. The wife figures the husband did it. I don't figure it that way, but it's possible. I think somebody went in there looking for something.'

Simms cracked a knuckle. 'You think the wife's holding out?'

'No.'

Lou said, 'What would somebody want?'

'I got no idea.'

A tall thin man in a dark gray three-piece suit walked in and gave me the checkout. He had a tight puckered face that made me think of Raid Ant & Roach Killer. He said, 'This asshole works with Joe Pike?'

I smiled at Poitras. 'You two rehearse this?'

Lou said, 'Wait outside, Hound Dog.'

Simms got up so the new guy could sit down, and Poitras shut the door behind me. It made me feel left out. The squad room was empty. Tail end of the lunch hour, all the dicks were still out scoring half-price meals. The big redhead came back with a sheaf of color copies and stopped when she saw the closed door. I was sitting behind one of the desks with my feet up, reading a *Daily Variety*. Half the desks on the floor sported show business trade papers. One of the desks even had *American Cinematographer*. These cops. She looked at me. I said, 'Conference with Washington. Very hush-hush.' Then I wiggled my eyebrows. She stared at me a half a heartbeat longer and walked away.

I got up and wandered into the locker room for more coffee. An older cop with a bad toup and lots of gold around his neck was watching *Wheel of Fortune*. The place smelled like a ripe jock but he didn't seem to mind. I poured two cups and brought one out to the holding cell but it was empty.

I was standing by myself in the middle of the squad room with a cup of coffee in each hand when Poitras' door opened and Simms looked out. 'I always take two,' I said. 'One for me. One for my ego.'

'Inside. Bring a chair.'

I put the coffees down, took a chair from beside one of the squad desks, and went in. Lou said, 'Elvis, this is Lieutenant Baishe. He took over from Gianelli a couple months ago.'

Baishe said, 'He doesn't need my pedigree.'

I looked at him.

Baishe was leaning into the corner behind Poitras' desk, looking at me like he'd had to scrape me off the bottom of his shoe. Without waiting he went on, 'I know about you. Big deal in the Army, security guard at a couple of studios, sucking around town with that bastard Joe Pike. They say you think you're tough. They say you think you're cute. They also say you're pretty good. Okay. Here's what we've got. The highway patrol up by Lancaster finds Morton Lang shot to death behind the wheel of his car, an '82 Cadillac Seville. He's got three in the chest and one in the temple, close range.' Baishe touched his forehead. Wasn't much hair there to get in the way. 'No shell casings in the car, but the people up there say it looks like a 9mm. There's blood, but not a whole lot, and some peculiar lividity patterns so maybe he wasn't popped there in his car. Maybe he got it somewhere else and he was put there. No sign of the kid. Car's been wiped clean. Robbery's out. He's still got his wallet and the credit cards and forty-six bucks and his watch. Keys are in the ignition. You got all that?'

'I'm watching your lips, yes, sir.'

Baishe looked at me, then at Lou. Lou said, 'Cole has a brain imbalance, Lieutenant.'

Baishe unwrapped his arms, came out of the corner, leaned on Poitras' desk and looked at me. He looked like a Daddy Longlegs. 'Don't fuck with me, boy.'

I pretended to be intimidated. After a bit he said, 'How do you fit into this?'

I went through it again. Baishe said, 'How long have you known the wife?'

'Since yesterday.'

'You sure it hasn't been longer?'

I looked from Baishe to Poitras to Simms and back to Baishe. Poitras and Simms were looking at Baishe, too. I said, 'Come off it, Baishe. You got nothing.'

'Maybe we dig into this we see a bigger connection. Maybe you two are pretty good friends, so good you decide to get rid of her old man. Maybe you rig the whole act and you pull the trigger. Setup City.'

'Setup City?' I looked at Poitras. His mouth was open. Simms was staring at a spot somewhere out around the orbit of Pluto. I looked back at Baishe with what we in the trade call 'disbelief.' He was looking at me with what we in the trade call 'distaste.'

I said, '*The Postman Always Rings Twice*, right? 1938?'

'Keep it up,' Baishe said.

'That's a real good thought, Lieutenant,' Lou said, 'only Cole here is known to me personally. He's a good dick.' I expected Baishe to laugh maniacally. *Only the Shadow knooowwzz*. I was getting tired and just a little bit cranky. I said, 'Is that it?'

Baishe said, 'We'll tell you when that's it.'

I stood up. 'Screw that. I didn't come down here so you guys could work out. You got any other questions, book me or call my lawyer.'

Baishe went purple and started around the desk. Lou stood up, just happening to block his way. 'Lieutenant, could I talk to you a sec? Outside.'

Baishe glared at me. 'Have your ass in that chair when I get back, peep.'

'Peep. You're really up on the patois, aren't you?'

Baishe's jaw knotted but they went out. I glared at Simms. He looked bored. I glared at Lou's desk. Behind the desk on a gray metal file cabinet were pictures of a pretty brunette and three children and a three bedroom ranch-style home in Chatsworth. One shot showed a couple of comfortable lawn chairs in the backyard beneath a poplar tree, just right for drinking a beer and listening to a ball game while kids played in the backyard. There was a picture of Lou doing just that. I had taken the picture.

Lou came back in alone. 'He expects your continued cooperation.'

Simms laughed softly.

I said, 'You notify the wife yet?'

'Not home. We got a car there waiting for her.' I could see a couple of street monsters parked in her drive, scratching their balls and waiting for a fadeaway woman in a light green Subaru wagon with two little girls in the back. Sensitive guys. Guys like Baishe. *Sorry, lady, your old man caught four and he's history*. I said, 'Maybe I'd better do it.'

Lou shrugged. 'You sure you want to?'

'You bet, Lou. Nothing I want more than to sit down with this woman and give her the news her husband's dead and her nine-year-old son is missing. Maybe I'll even break the word to the two little girls, too, for the capper.'

'Take it easy.'

'I'm taking it easy,' I said. Simms had stopped smiling.

The redhead came back in with the color copies and the little picture. She put the copies on Lou's desk and the little picture on top of the copies. She looked at me. 'What, no cracks?'

'They broke my spirit.'

She smiled nicely. 'Penny Brotman. Studio City.' And swayed away. Simms said, 'Sonofabitch.'

I took the little picture and put it in my pocket. I sneered at Simms, then gave Lou a flat look. 'If we're finished, I want to get out of here.'

He looked at his hands. 'I didn't know he was gonna pull that, Hound Dog. I'm sorry.'

'Yeah.'

I went back along the short hall, down the flight of stairs and out through the reinforced door. Nothing had changed. The Chicano guys still stood by the front desk, the white kid still murmured into the phone. People came in and went out. A fat woman bought a Coke; it wasn't a diet drink. A black cop with heavy arms led a man past the desk and through swinging doors. The man's fragile wrists were cuffed. There were knots in my trapezius muscles and in my latissimus dorsi and my head throbbed. I went up behind the kid on the phone and stood very close. He looked at me. Then he murmured something into the phone, hung up, and sat on one of the wooden benches with his head in his hands. I dialed Janet Simon and let it ring. On the thirty-second buzz she answered, breathless. I said, 'Does Ellen Lang have any close relatives nearby? Sister or mother or something like that?'

'No. No, Ellen doesn't have any relatives that I know of. She's an only child. I think there could be an aunt back in Kansas, but her parents are dead. Why?'

'Can you meet me at her house in twenty minutes?'

There was a long pause. 'What is it?'

I told her. I had to stop once because she was crying. When I was through I said, 'I'm on my way,' then I hung up. I stood with my hand on the phone for several seconds, breathing deeply, in through the nose, out through the mouth, making my body relax. After a while, I went over to the kid on the bench, said I was sorry, and put a quarter on the bench beside him. It was shaping up as a helluva day.

CHAPTER 10

At twenty minutes before three I pulled into Ellen Lang's drive and parked behind Janet Simon's Mustang. Ellen's Subaru wasn't there. I went to the front door and knocked. Out on the street, cars driven by moms went past, each carrying kids home from school or off to soccer practice. It was that time of the day. Pretty soon Ellen Lang would turn in with her two girls. She'd see the Corvette and the Mustang and her eyes would get nervous.

I knocked again, and Janet Simon opened the door. Her hair was pulled back and large purple sunglasses sat on top of her head. Every woman in Encino wears large purple sunglasses. It's *de rigueur*. She held a tall glass filled with amber liquid and ice. More ice than liquid. She said, 'Well, well. The private dick.' It wasn't her first drink.

Ellen Lang had made the house spotless for Mort's return. Everything was back in its place, everything was clean. The effort had been enormous. Janet Simon brought her drink to the couch and sat. The ashtray beside her had four butts in it. I said, 'You know when she'll get home?'

Janet Simon fished in her pack for a fresh cigarette, lit it, and blew out a heavy volume of smoke. Maybe she hadn't heard me. Maybe I'd spoken Russian without realizing it and had confused her.

'In a while. Does it matter?' She took some of the drink.

'How many of those have you had?'

'Don't get snippy. This is only my second. Do you want one?'

'I'll stay straight. Ellen might appreciate coherence from the person telling her that her husband is dead.'

She looked at me over the top of the glass, then took some of the cigarette. She said, 'I'm upset. This is very hard for me.'

'Yeah. Because you loved Mort so much.'

'You bastard.'

The leaders on either side of my neck were as tight as bowstrings. My head throbbed. I went out to the kitchen, cracked ice into a glass, and filled it with water. I drank it, then went back into the living room. Her eyes were red. 'I'm sorry I said that,' I said. 'I've done this before, and I know what it's going to be like, so my guts are in knots. Part of me wants to be up in Lancaster trying to get something on the boy, but I've got to do this first. The rest of me is pissed because the cops had me in so an asshole named Baishe could give me a hard time and feel tough. He did, it wasn't fun, and I feel lousy. I shouldn't have taken it out on you.'

She listened to all that, then quietly said, 'She always runs a couple of errands after she picks up the girls. They might go to Baskin-Robbins.'

'Okay.' I sat down in the big chair opposite the couch. She kept looking at me. She brought the cigarette to her mouth, inhaled, paused, exhaled. I got up and opened the front door to air the place out.

She said, 'You don't like me, do you?'

'I think you're swell.'

'You think I ride Ellen too hard.'

I didn't say anything. From where I was sitting I could see the street and the drive through the big front window. And Janet Simon.

She said, 'What the hell do you know,' then finished off her drink and went into the dining room. I heard glass against glass, then she came back in and stood at the hearth, staring out the window.

I said, 'She's your friend, but you don't show her any respect. You treat her like she's backward and you're ashamed of it, like you've got some sort of paradigm for modern womanhood and it burns your ass that she doesn't fit it. So you put her down. Maybe if you put her down enough, what she wants will change and she'll begin to fit the paradigm.'

'My. Don't we have me figured out.'

'I read *Cosmo* when I'm on stakeout.'

She took a long sip of the drink, set it down on the mantel, crossed her arms, and leaned against the wall to stare at me. 'What shit.'

I shrugged.

'Ellen and I have been friends since our kids were in nursery. I'm the one she cries to. I'm the one who holds her when she breaks down in the middle of the morning. I'm the only goddamned friend she has.' More cigarette, more drink. 'You haven't seen the bags under her eyes from the sleepless nights or heard the horror stories.'

'And you have. I respect that.'

'All right.'

'The problem is that you're shoving too hard. Ellen has to move at her own rate, not yours. I'm not talking about where you want to go. I agree with that. I'm talking about how you get there. Your method. I think it weakens the one you're hoping to strengthen.'

She raised an eyebrow. 'My. Aren't we sensitive. Aren't we caring.'

'Don't forget brave and handsome.'

She cupped her hands around her upper arms the way you do when you're standing in a draft, the way Ellen Lang often did.

'Maybe you're too close,' I said. 'Maybe you're so close and hurting so much you can only know how you'd react and that isn't necessarily the way Ellen should react. You're not Ellen.'

'Perhaps I used to be.'

I shook my head. 'You were never Ellen Lang.'

She stared at me a little longer, then shrugged. 'I was alone, and it was rough. I was taken advantage of. Even my women friends deserted me. Their husbands were business friends of Stan's. They went with the money.'

'But you'll stick with Ellen.'

'I'll help any way I can.'

'It must've been worse than rough.'

She nodded, barely moving.

'You should've called me,' I said. 'I'm in the book.'

She put her eyes on mine and left them there. 'Yes. Maybe I should have.' She bent down to stub out her cigarette in a little ceramic ashtray one of the kids made in school. She was wearing tight jeans and a clinging brown top that was cut just above the beltline and open-toed strap sandals with a medium heel. When she bent over, the top pulled up to show tanned skin and the ridge of her spine. A good looking woman. She picked up the drink, drained half the glass, and took a deep breath. It was a lot of booze. 'What was all that crap you gave Ellen about yoga and karate and Vietnam?'

'You guys tell each other everything?'

'Friends havta stick together.' You could hear the booze in her voice. 'You look too young for Vietnam.'

63

'I looked old when I got back.'

She smiled. You could see the booze in her smile, too. 'Peter Pan. You told Ellen you wanted to be Peter Pan.'

'Unh-hunh.'

'That's crap. Stay a little boy forever.'

'It's not age. Childhood, maybe. All the good things are in childhood. Innocence. Loyalty. Truth. You're eighteen years old. You're sitting in a rice paddy. Most guys give it up. I decided eighteen was too young to be old. I work at maintaining myself.'

'So at thirty-five, you're still eighteen.'

'Fourteen. Fourteen's my ideal age.'

The left corner of her mouth ticked. 'Stan,' she said, face soft. 'Stan gave it up. But he doesn't have Vietnam to blame it on.'

'There are different kinds of war.'

'Of course.'

I didn't say anything. She was thinking. When she finished, she said, 'How'd you get a name like Elvis? You were born before anyone knew who Elvis Presley was.'

'My name was Phillip James Cole until I was six years old. Then my mother saw The King in concert. She changed my name to Elvis the next afternoon.'

'Legally?'

'Legally.'

'Oh, God. And you've never changed it back?'

'It's what she named me.'

Janet Simon shook her head, putting her eyes back on mine. With her face relaxed and the booze taking the edge off, she seemed stronger. Sexier. She crossed her ankles and rocked. She took more of the drink. 'Have you ever been shot?'

'I caught some frag in the war.'

'Did it hurt?'

'At first it feels like you've been slapped, then it starts to burn and the muscle tightens up. With me, it wasn't too bad so I could take it. Other guys who had it worse, it was worse.'

'So it probably hurt Mort.'

'If the head shot was first, he didn't feel a thing. If not, he hurt a lot.'

She nodded, then put the glass back on the mantel. It was empty except for the ice. 'If Ellen asks, please don't tell her that.'

'I wouldn't.'

'I forgot. Sensitive and caring.'

'"Prove yourself brave, truthful, and unselfish, and someday you will be a real boy." The Blue Fairy said that. In *Pinocchio*.'

She looked at me a very long time, then her eyes got red and she turned toward the window. Past her, I could see three little girls walking north down the middle of the street, one of them skipping. They were laughing, but we were too far away to hear them. The house was quiet. 'Ellen's never home before four,' she whispered.

It was five minutes until three.

'Did you hear me?' Still facing the window.

'Yes.'

Janet Simon began to shiver, then tremble, then cry. I went over to her and let her sob into me like Ellen Lang had done. This time I got an erection. I tried to ease away but she pressed against me. Then her head came up and her mouth found me and that was that.

She squeezed hard and bruised my lips with her teeth and bit me. She was as lithe and strong as she looked. I lifted her away from the hearth and the big window and put her on the floor. She pulled off her clothes while I closed and locked the door. Her body was lean and firm and tan with smallish breasts and definition to her abdominals with nice ribs.

She came twice before I did. She bit my shoulders and scratched me and said 'Yes' a lot. When it ended we lay on our backs, wet and breathing hard, staring at the ceiling. She got up without a word, picked up her clothes, and disappeared down the hall. After a moment I heard water running.

I dressed and went into the kitchen for a glass of water. When I went back out to the living room, Janet Simon was there. 'Well,' she said.

'Well,' I said.

The phone rang. While Janet answered it, I took a peek out the big window. No light green Subaru. No Ellen Lang. No boys on bicycles or little girls in the middle of the street. Everything was on this side of the door.

Janet hung up and said, 'That was the girls. They're still at school. Ellen never picked them up.'

My watch showed three twenty-two.

'What time does school let out?'

'Two forty-five.' She looked uneasy. 'The girls want me to go get them.'

'Can you drive?'

She gave me a small tight smile without a lot of humor in it. 'I've been sobered.'

I nodded. 'I'll stay here for Ellen.'

'What do I say to them about Mort?'

'Don't say anything. We wait for their mother for that.'

'But she didn't pick them up.'

'She's got a lot on her mind.'

We stood there for a while, neither moving toward the other. Then Janet nodded and left. I went back to the chair and drank my water. Then I got up and went back to the big window and watched the drive. Ellen Lang didn't turn in.

CHAPTER 11

Janet Simon was back with the two girls in less than forty minutes. The older one came in first, sullen and red-eyed, and went straight back to her room, slamming her door. Janet and the younger one came in together. Janet gave a little shake of her head, meaning that she hadn't told them anything. She said, 'Did Ellen call?'

'Nope.'

The younger one dropped her books on the long table they have in the entry, then ran past me to the TV, turned it on, and sat on the floor about two feet from the screen. *3–2–1 Contact* was starting. It was the episode about directions and map-making. I'd seen it before. 'My name's Elvis. What's yours?'

'Carrie.'

She inched closer to the set. I guess I was making too much noise.

Janet Simon sat on the hearth, as far from me as she could get and still be in the room. I went over and sat by her. She didn't look up. I went back to the couch. Here were these two children and their father was dead and here were we, faking it, holding back The Big News.

We watched *3–2–1 Contact* until five, then switched channels for *Masters of the Universe* until five-thirty, then switched again for *Leave It to Beaver*. It was the one where Eddie Haskell talks Wally into buying a watch so Wally can make like he stole it to get in solid with some tough kids. I'd seen that one before, too. Halfway through *Leave It to Beaver*, Janet went back to see the older girl, Cindy. I heard a door close, then muffled screaming, Cindy shrieking that they were both crazy and she hated them. She hated him and she hated her mother and she wished she lived in Africa. Carrie inched closer to the television. I said, 'Hey, you hungry?'

She shook her head. Even with the lousy angle I had I could see her eyes swelling.

'Listen, you think you could help me find something? It's your kitchen, right? You know where things are.' She turned up the volume. I said, 'I could really go for a donkeyburger. Or the hairball soup. Or the breast of puppy.' She looked at me. 'Or the stuffed toad au gratin with duck fuzz.' She giggled and said, 'I can make soup.'

In the kitchen, we couldn't hear Cindy. The kid got a three-quart pot from beneath the sink, a large spoon from the drawer beside the refrigerator, a glass measuring bowl, and a packet of Lipton chicken noodle soup mix. She put the pot on the stove, filled the measuring bowl with three cups of water, then put the water in the pot. She covered it and put the heat on high. She put the packet of soup mix on the counter with the spoon beside it and the measuring bowl in the sink. 'We have to wait for the water to boil,' she said.

'Okay.'

We stood there a while, sneaking glances at each other. Finally she couldn't stand it anymore. 'You got a gun?'

'Yeah.'

'Can I see it?'

'It's in the car. I don't carry it when I don't have to. It weighs a lot.'

'What if you get jumped?'

I looked over my shoulder. 'Here in the house?'

She said, 'You see *Bateman and Evans*?'

'What's that?'

'This TV show. You know, *Bateman and Evans*. It used to be on Wednesday nights.'

'No.'

'Why not?'

'I don't watch much nighttime TV.'

'Why not?'

'I think it promotes cancer.'

'You're silly.'

'I guess.'

She said, 'My daddy used to represent Evans. I met him once. He was a detective and he always carried a gun.'

'You see, if I carried my gun I'd probably be on television.'

'Well, you have to be an actor, too.' Wouldn't know it from watching most of those guys.

'I got to meet Lee Majors that time, too, and this other time my

68

daddy got this actor a job on *Knightrider* and brought me over to Universal and David Hasselhoff was standing there and I got to meet him, too.'

'Unh-huh.'

'Are you going to find my daddy?'

Something long and thin and cold went in just below my stomach and up into my chest. 'Soup smells good,' I said.

She said, 'I bet I know where he is.'

I nodded. 'You want a bowl or a cup?' Some big-time private cop, you want a bowl or a cup?

She said, 'We've got soup cups in that cabinet there. Blue ones. If I tell you, you can't say I told you, okay? Cause nobody knows this but me and Daddy and he wouldn't like it if I said, okay?'

'Okay.' My voice was hoarse.

'Wait here.'

She ran out of the kitchen, then ran back thirty seconds later with a thick green photo album. It was the older kind, with heavy cardboard covers and black felt paper and the pictures held to the pages by little corner tabs. On the front of the album it said, *'Home.'*

On the first page there were faded sepia pictures dated June 1947 of a man and a woman and a baby. Mort. Adult faces changed or disappeared, but the child's face grew. Mort as a toddler. Mort riding his bike. Mort and a skinny, long-tongued dog emerging from an infinite field of Kansas wheat.

'My momma made this book up and gave it to my daddy when they moved out here. You see, these are all of my daddy back in Elverton, that's where Daddy and Momma are from in Kansas. It's got pictures of Gramma and Grampa and their house and Daddy in school and this dog my daddy had named Teddy and this girl named Joline Price that Momma used to tease Daddy about and all this stuff.'

She flipped the pages for me, taking me on a guided tour of Morton Lang's life. She would point. I would nod. Isn't that nice? Mort in grade school. Mort at the paint store in a clerk's apron. Mort and three buddies sitting around a bedroom, laughing. Crew cuts one year, duck's ass pompadours the next. Mort in a '58 Dodge. Mort looking good and strong and proud. Mort in a play. Mort and Ellen. Their prom. She was pretty. Very pretty. Isn't that nice?

Carrie was saying, 'I got up real late to go to the bathroom one night and Daddy was sitting in the living room. He was looking at this book and he was crying, looking at the pictures and crying and I started crying, too, so we looked at the book together and he said, 'I don't know what any of this is.' I said, 'That's Gramma and Grampa, that's Teddy, that's Joline Price.' He always says how much he hated Kansas and how he doesn't even want to go back there to visit, but I'll bet that's where he went. I bet if you went back to Elverton, Kansas, and looked you could find him and make him come home.'

I said, 'I think the soup's ready.'

I ladled out the soup into two blue mugs while she got two spoons and two napkins. Out in the dining room you couldn't hear Cindy anymore. We sat down and ate, Carrie with the book beside her on the table. Her last meal believing her daddy was alive, could walk in the door and make it better. I got up and found the dark stuff Janet Simon had been drinking and brought it back to the table. Carrie's nose wrinkled. 'Yuck.'

Yeah, kid. After a while Janet came out of the back of the house and asked to see me in the kitchen.

When we were in there she stood well away from me. 'It's after six, Elvis. Ellen wouldn't stay out like this.' Her face was white.

'Okay,' I said, feeling cold. I picked up the phone and called Lou Poitras.

CHAPTER 12

I told Poitras that I had been at Ellen Lang's since I'd left him earlier that day and that she hadn't come home. I told him that Ellen had failed to pick up her children from school and that there had been no messages. I told him I was worried. There was a long pause on his end, then some noise I couldn't make out, and then he asked questions. I gave him Ellen Lang's description and the make and model of her car. Janet Simon knew the license number, KLX774. He told me to stay put and hung up. I think I caught him going home to dinner.

Janet said, 'What do we do?'

'Cops are on the way. Is there someplace we can put the kids so they don't have to hear it?'

There was. Mrs. Martinson's, across the street. While Janet walked the girls over – Carrie scared and Cindy sullen – I found directions for a Toshiba automatic coffee maker and fresh Vienna cinnamon beans in the freezer and put on a pot. Then I went out to the Corvette, took the Dan Wesson out of the glove box, put it on, and got out a pale blue cotton jacket I keep in the trunk to wear over it. Made me feel like I was doing something. Maybe I should go across to Mrs. Martinson's and show the Dan Wesson to Carrie. Maybe it would make her feel like I was doing something, too.

I stood out on the drive until Janet came back across and the western sky began to pinken and the first chill of the night settled through Encino.

'Are you just going to stand here?' Janet said.

'For a while. I made coffee.'

She looked like she wanted to say something, then turned and went into the house.

Poitras pulled up at twenty minutes to eight. It was dark enough for the first wave of jasmine to be filtering into the air and for drivers to begin using their headlamps. Poitras had brought an older dick with him, gray-haired and crew cut with a face he'd left out of doors a couple centuries too long, named Griggs. When he saw me, Griggs feigned surprise and said, 'You still got a license?'

Griggs is a scream.

We managed to get Poitras through the door and into the living room without tearing out a wall. After we were settled with coffee and some little biscuits Janet found, I went through it all again, from when I left Poitras earlier in the afternoon until now. There wasn't much to tell. Poitras took out a little pad and a gold Cross pen and gave them to Janet and asked her to list all the places Ellen frequented: where she got her hair done, where she did the marketing, where she bought clothes, that kind of thing. Janet took the pad and pen into the dining room. After she was gone Lou said, 'This guy, Lang, he was into something.'

I nodded. 'Unh-huh.'

Poitras gave me empty cop eyes. 'And you got no idea what.'

'Mere unfounded speculations.'

Griggs grunted. 'Our favorite kind.'

'What?' Poitras said.

'Lang was going broke. He needed five grand a month to keep this place going but in the last eleven months he's only made fifty-two hundred. His savings were depleted. He might've tried going to a bank, but a bank wouldn't let him refinance the house because he was effectively unemployed. He could've gone to someone less reputable for some carry-over cash and been unable to pay the vig.'

Poitras thought about it. 'You welch on ten, fifteen grand, they maybe only break you up. They don't put four in you.'

I shrugged. 'I told you. Speculation.'

Poitras was still thinking. 'Not anyone sane, at any rate.' He looked at Griggs and Griggs got up and went into the kitchen to use the phone.

I said, 'Did you guys follow up on Kimberly Marsh?'

'We rolled by and had the manager let us in. Looks like she took off. But it looks like she's coming back, too. Talked to some fat guy there with a little dog. He said you told him you were Johnny Staccato. Shit.'

Griggs came back in and sat down.

'How about Rice?'

'Couldn't reach him. Left word at his studio and a card on his front stoop.'

Griggs spread his mouth in a strictured smile. 'Yeah. We're hell with those calling cards.'

Lou shrugged. 'You do what you can.'

Griggs said, 'Hey, you happen to find out where Lang bought his gas?'

'Missed that, somehow.'

'Yeah, be a hot shot. That's how the feds busted Carlo "The Hammer" Peritini, mouthing off to the guy at the Exxon station pumped his gas. Peritini, shit, all his millions, head of a whole goddamned family, he had to be a big shot to the guy who pumped his gas, told him everything.'

Poitras and I were staring at him. Griggs spread his hands. 'That's how they got The Hammer.'

'You'll do well with Baishe,' I said.

'Up yours.'

Janet Simon came back and handed Poitras the note pad. 'This is all I can think of.'

There were nine places listed, some under headings. *Hair: Lolly's* on Ventura at Balboa. *Food: Gelson's* at Ventura & Hayvenhurst, *Ralph's* on Ventura (Encino). *Fashion Square*, Sherman Oaks. *Saks*, Woodland Hills. *Books: Scene of the Crime* in Sherman Oaks. Like that.

I would've thought her writing would be strong and measured and connected, only it wasn't. She wrote in a small, uneven hand in lines that curved up. She wrote the way I thought Ellen Lang would write, only Ellen Lang didn't write that way. Ellen wrote the way I had thought Janet Simon would write.

Griggs took the pad into the kitchen to make another phone call. When he came out again he had a fresh cup of coffee and another plate of the biscuits.

Poitras asked Janet to run through it from her point of view, from the last time she'd seen Ellen Lang. He watched her as she did, with that flat, impassive face of his that says maybe the sun comes up tomorrow, maybe not, maybe he'll hit the Pick Six at Santa Anita for two mil, maybe not. Janet's hand was resting on the arm of the sofa by me. I patted it. She pulled away. Ah, romance.

Poitras said, 'You and Mrs. Lang seem to be pretty close.'

Janet nodded. 'She's my best friend.'

'So if she's gonna tell anybody anything, it's going to be you.'

'I guess. Yes. It would be me.'

'A guy doesn't get it in the chest for no reason.'

73

I sat forward. 'Hey.'

Poitras' eyes shifted to me. There was a little bit of a smile there, but maybe not. 'I'm just asking her to think back and think hard.'

'I know what you're asking her and I don't like the way you were asking it.'

Janet Simon snapped, 'I don't need you to defend me,' then went eye-to-eye with Poitras. 'What is it you mean, Sergeant?'

Poitras said, 'It doesn't have to be right now, but I'd just like you to see if you can remember anything Mrs. Lang or Mr. Lang might've said, that's all. Okay?'

Janet said, 'Of course,' but she was a little stiff when she said it.

The phone rang. Janet got up and went into the kitchen to answer it. Griggs grinned at me. 'She's a fine looking woman,' he said.

'There's something between your teeth.'

He tried to laugh it off but when he looked away I could tell he was sucking at his teeth.

Janet came out a moment later and looked at Poitras. 'It's for you.'

He went into the kitchen, stayed about a minute, then came out. Same frying-pan blank face. 'They found her car,' he said to me. 'You wanna come?'

I nodded.

Janet stood very still, then said, 'I'd better pack for the girls. They can sleep at my place until she's back.' She went out of the living room and down the hall without looking at us. Griggs stayed at the house while I rode over with Poitras.

Ellen Lang's light green Subaru wagon KLX774 was under a streetlamp at Ralph's supermarket on Ventura in Encino, the third place on Janet Simon's list. Ralph's had closed at eight-thirty, so the lot was empty except for the Subaru, a radio car, and a sunfaded Galaxy 500 belonging to the night watchman an old geez who stood out on the tarmac talking cop-shop with the uniforms. We pulled up to them and got out, Poitras flashing his shield, making sure the watchman saw it.

Poitras said, 'You got any idea how long it's been here?'

The old man jerked his head once, to the side. His white hair looked purple in the streetlight. So did my jacket and so did Poitras' white Hathaway shirt. Twenty feet above us the lamp buzzed like an angry firefly. 'It's been here since before I come on,' he said.

'Okay. You got the manager's number?'

The old guy jerked his head toward the store. 'It's inside.'

'Get it. Call him and have him come out here. I wanna talk to his bag boys and stock clerks and anyone else who might've been out here.'

The old guy looked scared he was getting cut out of the action. 'What's up, Sarge?'

'Go call.'

The old man frowned but nodded his head and gimped away. Walter Brennan. Out on Ventura, traffic had slowed to a crawl, drivers looking our way to see what was going on. I walked over to the car. Four bags of groceries were lined up on the back deck behind the rear seat. She'd done her shopping, then come back, and was probably approached while she loaded the bags. 'Okay to try the door?'

Poitras said yeah. One of the uniforms drifted over and stood behind me. Young guy, muscled arms, Tom Selleck moustache. I pulled on the rear door handle and it lifted. The tailgate swung out and me and the uniform stepped back.

'Bad milk,' Poitras said. He walked over, dug through the bags. Wilted lettuce. Wrinkled strawberries. A burst tomato. It gets hot in a sealed car on a sunny afternoon in Los Angeles. Hot enough to kill someone. Poitras finally came out with an opened pint of skim milk, like she'd had a little, just a sip while she was shopping, then sealed it up again to bring it home. I said, 'Probably been here since early afternoon. Could've been here since I was with you.'

Poitras grunted. He opened the driver's side door and stuck his head in. When he leaned against the little car, it settled on its springs. Then he dropped down into a push-up position on the ground. He got up, went to the tail end of the car, and dropped down again. This time he reached under the car and came out with a pair of white and lavender glasses. The left temple was broken.

'Ellen Lang's,' I said.

Poitras nodded and watched the cars go by on Ventura. He set the glasses on the Subaru's hood, leaned against the fender, and stared at me, eyes empty. The streetlamp was suddenly much louder. 'Old Mort,' Poitras said slowly, 'he was into something all right.'

CHAPTER 13

Later, Poitras had one of the uniforms drive me back to Ellen Lang's for my car. Janet Simon was sitting on the ottoman when I walked in, the little blue ashtray beside her full and the living room cloudy with smoke. I didn't make any cracks. She said, 'Well?'

'Looks like someone grabbed her.'

She nodded as if it were unimportant and stood up. There were two small suitcases by the entry, one light blue, the other tan. She said, 'I'd better get the girls.'

'Are you sorry it happened between us?'

She went ashen around her lips as if she were very angry. Maybe she was. As if in opening herself she had violated a promise she held very dear. Maybe she had. 'No,' she said. 'Of course not.'

I nodded. 'Want some help with the girls?'

'No.'

'Maybe some company, when you tell them?'

'No. I'm sorry, but no. Do you see?' She was a pale, creamy coffee color beneath her tan, her lips and nostrils and temples touched with blue. She wasn't making eye contact. She was at a place like Ellen Lang, where putting your eyes to someone else's cost too much, only Janet Simon wasn't used to it.

'Sure,' I said. 'You've got my number.'

She nodded, once, looking down at her cigarette.

I left.

I stopped at a Westward Ho market to pick up two six-packs of Falstaff, the best cheap beer around, and went home and put George Thorogood on loud and drank beer with the cat and thought about things. Ellen Lang and Janet Simon. They weren't so very different. Maybe Janet Simon *had* been Ellen Lang. Maybe Ellen Lang would one day be Janet Simon. *If* she were still alive. I drank more beer, and cranked the speakers up to distortion when George got to *Bad to the Bone*. I listen to that song, I always feel tough. I drank more beer. At some point very late that night I became a flying monkey, one of thousands chasing Morton Lang toward the Emerald City.

The next morning I hurt, but it was manageable. The cat was on the floor beside me, belly up. 'Have something ready when I get back, okay?' He ignored me. I stripped down to my shorts, went out onto the deck, and went from the twelve sun salutes to the tae kwan do. I took air in deep, using my stomach muscles, saturating my blood with oxygen until my ears rang. I pushed hard, spinning through low space to mid space to high space, using the big muscles in my back and chest and legs the way I'd been taught, working to burn out the Bad Things and finding a proof of it in the pain singing in my muscles.

After I shaved and showered and dressed I made soft-boiled eggs and raisin muffins and sliced bananas. While I ate them I made four sandwiches, brewed a pot of coffee, and poured it into the big thermos. I took out a six-pack of RC 100, two Budweisers, and a jar of jalapeño-stuffed olives. I put all that in a double-strength paper bag on top of a couple of books by Elmore Leonard, *Hombre* and *Valdez Is Coming*. I took my clip-on holster out of the closet, put the Dan Wesson in it, and selected a jacket to go with my khaki Meronas. By eight-twenty I was staking out Kimberly Marsh's apartment. I was cranky. If the fat guy brought his dog out today, maybe I'd shoot it. They'd probably arrest John Cassavetes, and wouldn't Gena Rowlands be surprised.

There were still letters in Kimberly Marsh's mail drop and still bulk-rate flyers in the big open bin. I walked back past the banana trees to number 4 and let myself in. The rest of the petals had fallen from the dead daisies. A guy named Sid had left a message on the machine saying they'd met at Marion's and how much he'd like to get together with her because his planets were rising in the lower quadrant and if she was a happening babe she'd give him a buzz. I let myself out, closed the door, and locked it. The walkway continued past number 4, turning right to pass a laundry room, then down one flight of stairs to the underground parking. I went down and found one other stair at the opposite side of the garage that opened out into the complex. That was it. Anybody wanted to get to number 4 they'd have to go past me through the entry, or down the parking drive, also past me. All I had to do was stay awake and I had the place covered.

I walked back to the Corvette, pulled the top up, and climbed into the passenger side. I was armed, supplied, and ready for siege. I could hang in as long as it took. Even until lunch.

Seven minutes later the dark blue Nova with the bad rust spot on its left rear fender rolled past and pulled to the curb about six cars ahead of me. Same two Chicano guys. Curiouser and curiouser. The driver got out and trotted across the street to disappear behind the banana trees. He was back there a long time. Maybe Pygmies got him. Just when I got my hopes up he came back, still scowling, still trying to look like Charles Bronson, still not making it. It's tough to look like Charles Bronson when you got no chin. He walked into the street in front of an elderly lady driving a big bronze Mercury. She had to stop. He scowled at her. Tough, all right. I heard his car door slam, then a minute later faint Mexican music. These guys were good.

A couple minutes before nine, two cars eased up out of the garage, a little metallic-brown Toyota Celica and a green LTD. About nine-fifteen a beige Volvo sedan turned in. Kimberly Marsh wasn't driving and probably wasn't hiding in the trunk. At ten-fourteen the fat guy came out with his little dog. I held my fire so as not to tip the guys in the Nova. The little dog didn't have any better luck than last time. At ten fifty-five the mail was delivered. Kimberly Marsh got a couple more letters. At six minutes before noon the Nova cracked open again and a different guy walked back past me on the sidewalk, heading toward Barrington. This one was taller, with a relaxed face and prominent Adam's apple. This one, maybe you could talk to. I scrunched down onto the floor, no easy feat in a '66 Corvette, and counted to forty before I looked up. Thirty-five minutes later he came back, whistling and carrying a white paper bag with grease stains at the bottom. Tacos or burritos, one. I ate a salami sandwich, followed it with a turkey, and drank a warm Budweiser. Bud holds up better warm than any other beer. Great for that tailgate party when you're on stakeout.

At ten minutes after three, a dirty red Porsche 914 double-parked in front of the Piedmont Arms and a good-looking kid the size of a tree got out and went to the mailboxes. Kimberly Marsh's mailbox, in particular. Then I had him. The beach picture in Kimberly Marsh's dresser drawer. Six-three. Two-fifteen. Brown-almost-blond hair and toothpaste-commercial features. I lifted myself up in the seat and tried to see the guys in the Nova. They didn't seem to be paying any attention, the driver talking and gesturing and the passenger nodding his head and the Mexican music going with a lot of trumpet. The big kid cleaned out the box, dug through the bin, then went back to his car. Sonofabitch, stay with the Nova or follow the kid? The Mexican driver was still explaining something with his hands. The passenger fired the wadded-up white paper bag into the shrubs around the apartments. They turned up the music. Marimbas. I went with the kid.

He cruised back toward Barrington, then left on San Vicente to Wilshire and the San Diego Freeway, north. I stayed three or four cars back up through the Sepulveda Pass into the valley and onto the Ventura Freeway, east. He took the Woodman exit and headed to Burbank Boulevard where he pulled into an auto parts store, running in like he was in a hurry. I swung the Corvette into the Shell station across the street and stopped by the pay phone. I kept one eye on the parts store, fed money into the phone, and called Joe Pike.

A man's voice said, 'Gun shop.'

'Joe Pike, please.'

Five seconds. Ten, tops. 'Pike.'

'It's warming up. You feel like work?'

I could tell Pike covered the mouthpiece. When he took his hand away the background at his shop was quiet. 'What do you want me to do?'

'There're two Mexicans sitting in a dark blue Chevy Nova at 412 Gorham, just above San Vicente in Brentwood. Bad rust spot on the left rear fender behind the wheel well. I want to know where they go.'

'You want me to clean and dress them after?'

'Just the address.' With Pike you had to be careful. You never knew when he meant it.

I followed my man back down Woodman to the freeway again, up and east until the Universal City exit, then down to the boulevard and climbed almost at once into the hills above Universal Studios. The streets there are old and narrow, built back when hill streets were poured cement and curbed for cars with high, skinny wheels. The houses are pink and yellow and gray and white, stucco and wood, old Spanish and new Ultramodern, little places jammed together on tiny lots, some bare, some shaded with old, gnarled trees and knotted vines. The 914 pulled into a small wood and stone contemporary on the mountain side of the street. I continued past around the curve, then reversed in someone's drive and parked at the curb.

I took the .38 out of the glove box and clipped it onto my waistband over my wallet. I got out and pulled on the jacket, then dug around under the seat until I found a roll of nickels. I slipped the nickel roll in my right pocket and walked back to the house.

The 914 was ticking in a little carport dug into the side of the mountain. The flat-roofed house sat on top of the garage and spilled to the right, nestling in an ivy bed as did so many houses in Los Angeles. There was a big plate glass window to the right of the door and a dormer window a little beyond that. The landscaping was uneven and shabby. Dead vines twined with live; lonely Saint Augustine runners purchased in bare spots along the unmaintained slope, outlining just as lonely sprigs of ice plant and cactus. Everything looked dusty: the 914, the carport, the brick steps leading up to the house, the house, the plants, the bugs crawling on the plants. Classy.

I crept up the steps to the door and listened. Murmurs, maybe, but impossible to tell if it was people or TV. I left the stoop and went to the right, creeping along on all fours under the big window and hoping the local rent-a-cops didn't pick now to cruise by. I raised my head and looked. Living room. Big and empty and open all the way through to the back of the house. There was a kitchen in the back on the left and a freestanding fireplace just to the right of the big window. A shabby couch covered with something that looked like a bedspread stood next to the kind of bookshelves college kids make out of boards and cinder blocks. No books; just a stereo and some records and a big aquarium with green sides and too many plants and green around the water line. In the back, off the kitchen, there was a round dining table with spindly legs and two chairs. Newspaper sections were spread across the table, pinned there by a glass, a quarter filled with something I couldn't identify. I was staring at the glass when Kimberly Marsh walked out of the kitchen and into the living room without a stitch of clothes. When she saw me she said, 'Hey!' so loud I could hear her through the glass.

I waved at her and smiled. Then the front door opened and the Son of Kong appeared.

CHAPTER 14

Up close, he was shorter than I had guessed, but his thighs and calves were thicker than in the picture and there was maybe a little more muscle across his chest. He'd changed clothes. His shirt was off, and he was wearing a pair of red gym shorts, so old and faded I couldn't make out the name of the school. He was barefoot. There was a four-inch crescent-shaped scar on the front of his left shoulder and two long ugly zipper scars bracketing his left knee. The girl appeared in the doorway behind him, holding a sheet around herself. There were stains on the sheet. I said, 'Hi, Kimberly. My name's Elvis Cole. I want to talk to you about Morton Lang.'

She said, 'Larry.'

Larry flicked his fingers back toward the house without taking his eyes off me. 'Go pack. I'll take care of this.' Larry's voice had a whiny quality, as if he were a rich kid from a small town who'd been Mister Everything in school and was spoiled by it.

I ignored him. 'I'm a private investigator, Kimberly. Morton Lang is dead.'

'Dead,' she said.

I nodded. If she was ready to collapse with grief, it didn't show. 'Yeah. We need to talk about it.'

Larry gestured to the house again. 'Go on, Kimmie.' Kimmie. Okay, Jody. Let's go, Buffy. He sort of nodded to himself, making a big deal out of sizing me up. 'I got this guy by forty pounds. He's mine.'

I said, 'Larry, you wanna be dominant male, that's okay by me. But it's important that Kimberly and I talk about this.'

He shook his head. 'Beat it, asshole.'

I pushed my jacket back so he could see the gun. 'This ain't like playing football, boy.'

81

He blinked, and the hard lines around his eyes softened, making him look even younger, then he yelled and came at me, leading with his face like a lot of ballplayers do. It only took him two hard strides to get to me, but moving so fast on the crumbly slope, his footing was weak and he was off-balance. I took one step uphill, planted, then hit him as hard as I could with the roll of nickels, getting some umph into it from my hips and carrying it up through my shoulder. His nose burst in a red and pink spray and he folded, stumbling and sliding downhill before the ivy and ice plants snagged him. He flopped around for a while, then grabbed his face and moaned. 'Come on, Kimmie,' I said, 'help me get him inside.'

We put him on the couch with his head back over the arm and gave him ice wrapped in a wet towel to hold on his face, then she went into the back to dress. While she was gone I filled a small pot with water, cracked in some ice cubes, and brought it to the dining room table to soak my hand. Larry stirred and looked at me out the corners of his eyes, trying not to bend his head much. 'You hit me with something.' Sort of accusatory, like, *You cheated.*

Kimberly came back wearing a faded pair of cut-off jeans and a black POLTERGEIST tee shirt cut just below her breasts so her belly was exposed. Her body was lean and firm but she didn't look as good as the 8 × 10. Take away the lights and the makeup and the pose, her nose had an uncomplimentary bend to it and her eyes said nothing. Even with the tan and the dimple in her chin, she looked puffy and worn. Life in the fast lane.

I said, 'Why are two Mexicans sitting on your apartment and what does that have to do with Morton Lang?'

She glanced sort of vaguely at Larry, who stirred on the couch, then struggled up and gave me the eye. I took out the Dan Wesson. 'If you come off that couch,' I said, 'I'll shoot you in the chest.'

He stayed where he was, both hands holding the red-splotched towel to his face. Kimberly positioned herself between me and the kitchen door, thumbs hooked down in the top of her shorts. Posing. She said, 'Are you the police?'

I put the gun on the table, took out the photostat of my license with my dry hand and held it up. I said, 'Think back five minutes, when we were outside, what I said.' Beneath the smell of kitchen grease and fishbowl was the burned tar scent of marijuana and sandalwood. And maybe the metallic after-smell that ether leaves from freebasing.

She didn't look at the license. 'Oh, yeah, private investigator.'

'Right. That means I don't have to be nice. I don't have to read rights. I don't have to wait for your lawyer. I can kick the shit out of people and nobody can say dick.' Mr. Threat.

She shook her head and used her right foot to scratch her left. 'I don't know who they are.'

'Mort dropped out of sight last Friday. You with me, Kimmie?'

'Unh-hunh.'

'He took his son with him. Perry. You ever meet Perry?'

'Unh-unh.'

'Yesterday, the cops found Mort dead up by Lancaster. He was shot to death. The boy's missing. Now Mort's wife is missing. Maybe kidnapped. Those two Mexicans, maybe they want to make you missing, too.'

Larry grunted. 'Spics.'

'What was the trouble about?' I said.

'I don't *know*,' she said, picking at her fingernail polish.

I looked past her to Larry. 'Bullshit, Kimberly. Mort loved you. He would've said something to you.'

She followed my eyes to Larry and tried to remember how to look offended. 'Mort was my mentor and my friend,' she said. I think she *moued*.

I looked back at Larry. 'You her mentor, too?'

'Fuck off.'

I could see Mort's card hanging by the thin wire from the wilted flower: *For the girl who gives me life, all my love.* Right, Mort. Asshole.

She paced in a small circle with her thumbs back in her shorts, then stood in the middle of the room. Show-and-tell time. 'I'm scared.'

'With good ol' Larry here?'

Larry gave me his tough look. She said, 'Mort took me to this party to meet some guy. A guy from Mexico. A Financier.' She said financier like it was Duke or Earl or Governor. 'Mort's friend Garrett found him. Garrett's a producer. When you're starting out you have to meet producers and directors and the power people.'

'When was this?'

'Early last week. Tuesday.' Tuesday, Mort was still living at home, Ellen wasn't yet being badgered into seeking a private investigator, the Lang children's lives were shaky but still intact.

'Okay.'

'Mort said that Dom was thinking about backing one of Garrett's movies, so it'd be good if they knew me for parts.'

'Yours or theirs?'

'Hunh?'

'Is Dom the Mexican?'

She nodded. 'All they said was Dom. I don't know his last name.' She giggled. I hate women who giggle. 'He's an older man. Really neat. Sort of old-fashioned, you know. He called me Miss Marsh.' She giggled again. 'He used to be a bullfighter, only now he's got oil and stuff.'

'Good connection,' Larry agreed.

I frowned at him.

'It was a big deal,' Kimberly said. 'Mort told me to dress sexy and be real nice, you know, laugh at their jokes and smile a lot and follow his lead. Mort knew just what to do, you know. He's great at getting with the right people and making the right connections.'

I thought of Mort sitting in his chair, looking at his photo album, crying. I thought of his steadily shrinking bank balance, all out and no in. I thought of Mort with four bullets in him. 'Yeah, his strong point. Where was the party?'

She looked confused and gestured somewhere off into outer space. 'Somewhere over the hill. I dunno. It was dark.'

'All right. What happened?'

'It was rad. We were hanging out, talking, doing lines. Everyone was very sophisticated. The dope was first-rate.'

'Mort, too?'

'What?'

'Doing coke.'

'Sure.'

I could see it: palatial living room, marble coffee table, crystal bowl with the white powder, everybody playing Pass the Mirror. Old Mort right in there with them direct from Elverton, Kansas, by way of Oz, laughing when they laugh, nodding when they nod, eyes nervous, darting, wondering if they accept him or if they're just faking it. I couldn't make the pictures fit. I couldn't clip Mort out of the snapshot in his pool with the three kids, color in Versace threads, and drop him around that marble table with this woman and Garrett Rice and that life. Maybe Mort couldn't make the picture fit, either. Maybe that had been his problem.

Kimberly giggled. 'Dom really liked me, you know.'

I was getting tired of 'you know'. Larry took the towel away and grinned, but there was no humor in it. 'It's the business, man.' His nose was a mess.

'You're going to need a doctor,' I said. 'It's broken.'

He stood up, wobbled, then went to the shelves by the slimy fishbowl. He took a slender blue cigarette from a little painted box and lit up, pulling deep. 'For the pain.'

'Was anyone else there?'

'These people from Italy. They said they might want to get into movies, too. You know –'

'Yeah. Financiers. How much did Dom like you, Kimberly?'

She tried to look embarrassed but they probably hadn't covered that in acting school. 'Dom, you know, wanted to get to know me.' Giggle. That made four.

'How'd Mort feel about that?'

A shrug. 'You know.'

'No, I don't know,' I said carefully. 'If I knew I wouldn't be here with you and him listening to this.'

Larry giggled.

Kimberly focused on me like she wasn't quite sure what I had said and gave me a pout. 'Mort had to act like such an asshole. Dom is *rich*. Dom said he might make a three-picture deal and I could be in *all* of them.'

Larry giggled again. 'The old spic fucked her brains out.'

I looked at him. 'Shut up.'

Larry frowned and stared at the slime in the fish tank.

'When Dom and I came back, Mort got all upset and Dom started yelling in Spanish and Garrett was yelling and this Italian woman just kept laughing. Then Garrett got everybody calmed down and they went off and talked for a while and then Mort came back and we left. It just went all wrong. Mort had to act like such an asshole.'

Her story could explain Garrett Rice. A guy like Rice, he'd get pissed if his friend blew a deal just because he didn't want his girlfriend humping for dollars. Guy like Garrett Rice, that'd be a pisser, and Rice certainly had been pissed.

'Mort tell you what they talked about when they went out?'

'We didn't talk on the way home. I was so mad.'

'Sure,' I said. 'Who could blame you.'

She cocked her head and gave me that sort-of-confused look again. 'The next day he calls me and says we're in trouble. He says he can't talk because his wife is in the next room, but if anybody comes around the apartment I wasn't to answer the door and that he'd call when it was okay again. I got so scared I called Larry and came up here.'

Larry sat up straighter and nodded. Defender of damsels.

'Did Mort say anything about the boy?'

'Unh-unh.' Kimberly started to sniffle. 'I kept checking my answer machine but Mort never called back. Now you say he's dead and there's guys watching my apartment and I'm scared.'

Larry smirked. It didn't look like much, considering his nose had evolved into a rutabaga. 'Coupla spics. Let'm come and see what happens.'

'Yeah. Like with me.'

He frowned. 'You hit me with something.'

'Mort got hit with four 9mm Parabellums, stupid.' I was at my limit. 'A cop named Poitras is going to come around. Talk to him. He won't hassle you about things that don't matter. Just don't try to act tough. He's not as nice as me.'

I walked out through the living room past the fishbowl. It smelled like a toilet. Algae were thick and furry around the sides and on top and over the big rocks at the bottom, and there was a dense mat of seaweed that looked like colonic polyps. A white fish of indeterminate genus lay bloated and belly-up at the surface. I stopped at the front door and looked back at them. Larry took a toke on his joint and the tip glowed.

'Kimberly?'

She turned toward me, putting her hands in her back pockets and letting me see her body. It was nice. A long time ago she could've been a cheerleader or even the homecoming queen in Elverton, Kansas. Every boy's desire. 'Hunh?' she said.

'Mort was an asshole because he loved you.'

She put her right hand up under her Poltergeist tee shirt and scratched her right breast.

I went out and slammed the door.

CHAPTER 15

The next morning I woke with brilliant white sunlight in my face, smelling coffee. The sliding glass doors were open and Joe Pike was out on the deck. He was wearing faded jeans and a gray sweat shirt with the sleeves cut off and blue Nikes and government issue pilot's sunglasses. He rarely takes the glasses off. He never smiles. He never laughs. I'd known Joe Pike since 1973 and he has never violated those statements. He's six feet one with short brown hair and muscled the way a fast cornerback is muscled, weighing in somewhere between one eighty-five and one-ninety. He had a red arrow tattooed on the outside of each shoulder when he was in The Nam. They pointed forward.

Pike had the rail section out and was sitting on the edge of the deck. The cat was in his lap. I pulled on a pair of sweat pants and went out. I said, 'Goddamnit. If you broke the alarm again, you pay for it.'

'Slipped the latch on the sliding doors with a hacksaw blade. You didn't arm the system. You don't arm the system, it won't keep out the bad guys.' Pike stroked the cat along the top of the shoulders, using slow, careful passes the way the cat likes.

I said, 'I don't like to keep out the bad guys. I like to let'm in and work out on them.'

'You should get a dog. A good dog, properly trained, you don't need to arm him. He's always armed.'

'What? You don't think I'm tough enough?'

Pike sat silently.

'I got the cat.'

Pike nodded. 'That is a problem.' He put the cat down. The cat flattened his ears, hissed, grabbed Pike's hand and bit him, then darted away to the other side of the deck to crouch under my grill. He growled deep in his throat. Helluva cat. Pike stood up. 'Come on,' he said, 'I've got breakfast, then we can take a ride.'

Pike had put out plates and napkins and flatware. There was a bowl of pancake batter beside the stove and four eggs and a small pot of water simmering on a back burner. The big skillet was greased and waiting for the batter. I said, 'How long you been here?'

'About an hour. You want eggs?'

'Yeah.' About an hour, doing all this. I might just as well have been on the moon.

Pike poured the coffee, then spooned the eggs into the simmering water and looked at his watch. It was a big steel Rolex. He said, 'Tell me about it.'

By the time we sat down, each with two soft-boiled eggs smushed atop six pancakes and syrup and butter, I had told him. Pike nodded, forked in some pancake and egg, swallowed. 'We're not overburdened with useful intelligence.'

'One might say that, yes.'

'She say this guy Dom's a matador?'

'Yes.' The pancakes were good. I wondered if he'd put cottage cheese in them.

'I put cottage cheese in these,' he said, reading my mind. 'What do you think?'

I shrugged. 'Okay.'

He ate. 'You know what matador means?'

'Bullfighter.'

He shook his head. I could see little images of me in his glasses. 'Bullfight is an American concept. It has no relevance to the actual event. Not only is the term irrelevant, it's insulting. If a matador fights a bull, then they're adversaries. That's not what it's about. The matador has to dominate the bull, not be equal to it. The bull's death is preordained. The matador's job is to bring him to it.'

What a thing to wake up to. I said, 'So what does it mean?'

The corner of Pike's mouth twitched. That's the closest he comes to a smile. 'Means "bringer of death." Nifty, huh?'

I sipped the coffee. Bush coffee, bitter and black, made by putting grounds in a pot, adding water, and boiling it down. Amazing, what you can grow to like. 'How do you know so much about it?'

The twitch again. 'I'm into ritualized death. You know that.'

I ate more pancake. 'Is this your contribution to the case?'

'What'd you have in mind?'

'A small clue, perhaps. A small note, a small eye-witness. Anything, really. I'm easy to please.'

'We'll see.'

I got up, found two bananas in the living room, and brought them back to the table. I put one by Pike and sliced the other over my pancakes. Pike didn't touch his. He said, 'I don't see how you stand dealing with these screwups.'

'People didn't screw up, we'd be out of a job. Screwups are our business.' I liked the sound of that. Maybe I should call Wu, have him put it on the cards.

Joe said, 'Guy like Mort, laughing when they laugh, nodding when they nod, sucking up the slimeballs.' The cat came in off the deck, hopped up onto the table, and stared at Pike. He held out a bit of egg. The cat ate it with delicate bites. 'I know this Mort. I've known men like him. I don't like people with no will and no commitment and no pride.'

'Your problem is your lack of a clear-cut opinion.'

Joe stopped feeding the cat, so the cat walked across the table and sat beside me. I ignored him.

'It's never that simple,' I said. I told him about Carrie, about the photo album, about the pictures of Mort and Ellen and the kids around the pool.

Joe said, 'Everybody's got pictures. People *pose* for pictures. I've got pictures of me and my old man with our arms around each other, smiling, and I haven't spoken to the sonofabitch in twelve years.'

I didn't say anything. I had pictures, too. I finished off the pancakes and the eggs and speared the last slice of banana. 'Mort gave himself up,' I said.

Joe Pike sat erect at the table, chewing, mirrored lenses immobile, lean jaws flexing, one veined, muscled arm in his lap, the other against the table, elbow not touching. He swallowed, finished his coffee, wiped his mouth. Impeccable. He said, 'No. He gave nothing. He lost himself. The distinction is important.'

After a while I gathered the dishes, brought them into the kitchen and rinsed them. When I finished, Pike was back out on the deck, holding the cat, staring off toward Hollywood. I went out to the rail. He didn't turn around. 'Somebody screws up, I clean up after them. That's why people come to the agency. That's what I'm good at. You're good at it, too.'

'Hell of a way to make a living,' he said.

'Yeah,' I turned and went back inside. 'Come on, Yukio. Let's take that ride.'

CHAPTER 16

Pike had parked his red Jeep Cherokee off the road by the carport. It was one of the older, full-size models, blocky and tall and resting on immense knobbed tires. It dwarfed the Corvette. Three years ago we'd taken it north into the mountains, fishing. I'd used the fender for a shaving mirror. You still could. I shook my head. 'Hate a man lets his car go to hell.'

Joe nodded, looking grim. 'Me, too.' He wiped a finger along the Corvette. It came away dark.

'The wind,' I said. 'Blows the dirt right through the carport. Hell on the rolling stock.'

Joe stared at his finger like it was something from Jupiter, then grunted and said, 'You amaze me.'

We dropped down Laurel Canyon and swung east on Hollywood Boulevard. It was warm and sunny and Hollywood was in full flower: a wino sat on a bench eating mayonnaise from a jar with his finger; four girls with hair like sea anemone smoked in front of a record store while boys in berets and red-splattered fatigue shirts buzzed around them like flies; young men with thick necks, broad backs, and crew cuts drifted in twos and threes past the shops and porno parlors – marines on leave, come up from Pendleton looking for action.

Ah, Hollywood. *Down these mean streets, a man must walk who is himself not mean. How mean ARE they!!!! So mean . . . well, just ask Morton Lang . . .*

We turned north at Western and climbed past Franklin toward Griffith Park, then right on Los Feliz Boulevard, winding our way past the park into the cool green of the Los Feliz hills. On a clear day, when the sun is bright and a breeze is in from the sea and the eucalyptus are throwing off their scent, Los Feliz is one of the finest places on earth. The hills are lush with plants and the right houses have a view all the way to the ocean. Hollywood legends lived and died here in homes built by Frank Lloyd Wright and Richard Neutra and Rudolf Schindler. People who made fortunes in oil or off the railroad built mansions that are now bought by gay couples, renovated, and resold for fortunes themselves. But with poor Hispanic areas to the south and east and the Hollywood slimepit to the west, New Money now buys above the Sunset Strip and points west. Los Feliz has seen its day.

Pike left Los Feliz Boulevard for a narrow, overgrown street that wound its way higher in tight curves, climbing steeply in some spots, leveling or dropping in others. Traffic thinned to nothing, just us and a woman in a champagne-colored Jaguar. Then she turned off. Three quarters of a mile from where we'd left the boulevard we cruised past the sort of stone gateposts I had always imagined guarding Fort Knox. Pike pulled to the curb and killed the engine.

It was so quiet the engine's ticking sounded like finger snaps. Pike got out and walked to the gate. It was black and ornate and iron. It probably weighed as much as the Corvette. There were crossed swords over some kind of coat of arms centered on the gate. The tips of the swords were bent. Sometimes I felt bent, too. Maybe it was phallic.

I got out, opening the door easy, like when I was a kid sneaking out to do something bad and not wanting anyone to hear. This place did that to you.

An eight-foot-high mortared stone wall grew off the gateposts. It was overgrown with ivy and followed the street both uphill and down to disappear around the curves. There were eucalyptus and scrub oak and olive trees inside the wall and out. Old trees. Gnarled and gray and established and quiet. I walked over to the gate and stood by Pike. The drive rose rapidly and disappeared behind a knoll. You couldn't see the house. You couldn't see anything. The trees were so thick it was dark. Ten o'clock in the morning and it was dark. 'That does it. From now on I carry a crucifix and a sharpened stake.'

Pike said, 'The Nova came here. Other side of that knoll there's a motor court and the main house. Garage for eight cars. There's a pool in the back with a poolhouse, a tennis court to the northeast of it, and a guesthouse. Main house has two levels. These walls follow the topography. This gate is the only way in or out, unless you go over.'

I looked at him. Pike shrugged. 'I took a look.'

'I suspect you went over.'

'Unh-hunh.'

'You get the Nova's tag number?'

'Unh-hunh.' He handed me a slip of paper with a license number written on it.

'I suspect the guys driving the Nova, they don't own that place.'

'Unh-unh. Had a few other guys walking around in there. Big necks.'

We walked back to the Jeep. I leaned against the fender. Pike didn't mind. 'Dom,' I said.

'Unh-hunh. On the gate, that sword with the bent tip. It's called an *estoque*. It's what the matador uses to kill the bull.'

I looked at him.

'I checked the address. Domingo Garcia Duran.'

I looked at him some more.

Pike's mouth twitched. 'You said you wanted a clue.'

CHAPTER 17

Joe dropped me back at the house to pick up the Corvette, then I drove in to the office. I parked in the basement and rode up alone, listening to an instrumental rendering of *Hey, Jude* that John probably would not have liked. I unlocked the outer door and went in. Nobody sapped me. Nobody stuck a gun in my face. I went to my desk, put the Dan Wesson in the top right drawer, sat, and stared out the glass doors.

Other detectives have partners with whom they could discuss the case. Me, I get dropped off in my driveway, grunted at, and left to fend for myself. Did Percival drop off Galahad? Did Archer drop off Spade?

Garrett Rice had mentioned a party. Kimberly Marsh said Morton Lang had taken her to a party. The party had been at the home of a Mexican gentleman named Dom. Dom had grown angry with Morton, probably about Kimberly Marsh, so Mort and Kimberly had left. The next day Morton Lang phoned Kimberly Marsh and told her he was in trouble and not to answer the door. A large dark man, possibly Mexican, was reported asking for Kimberly Marsh. Later, two men of Hispanic descent in a blue Nova spent hours outside Kimberly Marsh's apartment. Joe Pike followed them to a home belonging to Domingo Garcia Duran. Men with thick necks were observed.

I tapped the desk. I shifted from my right side to my left. My stomach growled and produced a vision of myself riding down to the deli for a lean corned beef with hot Chinese mustard on rye. Maybe I would sit at a little table for one they have down there. Maybe the slim blonde behind the register liked John Cassavetes. Maybe a lot of things.

It did not seem credible that Morton Lang had been murdered

because he objected to Kimberly Marsh sleeping with Domingo Duran.

Men with thick necks.

I picked up the phone and called Eddie Ditko at the *Examiner*. He said, 'What? I'm busy. What?'

'That's why I like talking to you, Eddie. Always anxious to share a human moment.'

'You want a human moment? I got bowel trouble. I'm worried I gotta get cut and wear a bag the rest of my life.'

That Eddie. Class all the way. I said, 'You got any clippings on a guy named Domingo Garcia Duran?'

'Shit, know him from when I used to work sports. Bullfighter. A Mexican. Right up there with El Cordobes and Belmonde, those guys, when he was young. Made millions. Got himself into oil, Acapulco beachfront, hotels. Liked the high life. Always something on the wire about him hanging with the guys from Phoenix, Jersey, Bolivia, like that. I think he retired around '68, '69, something.'

'He step over the line himself?'

'He's supposed to be worth, what?, a couple hundred million? You flip up the rock, he's in bed with the wrong people somewhere. His name came up in a laundering scheme once, then again with some assholes who were transporting dope up from South America. No indictments. No convictions. Shit, he's always on Rudy Gambino's yacht, that kind of thing. What, Rudy's gonna have him around because he likes tacos?'

We shot the breeze a little longer, me trying to cadge some freebie Dodgers tickets for the upcoming season and him pretending not to hear, then we hung up. I tapped the desk some more. Cocaine. Organized crime. Rudy Gambino. Murder was beginning to seem more credible.

I picked up the phone and punched the numbers for the North Hollywood P.D. A voice said, 'Detectives.'

'Lou Poitras, please.'

'He's out. Take a message?'

'Ask him to call Elvis Cole. He's got the number.'

I hung up.

Outside, a brown gull floated on the breeze. He looked at me. I made my left hand into a gun and pointed it at him. He banked away from the building and disappeared. I called Janet Simon. She answered on the sixth ring. 'How are you doing?'

'Okay.' Her voice was flat.

'Was it rough?'

A hesitation. 'I couldn't tell them.'

I nodded, but she probably didn't see it. 'What'd you tell them about Ellen?'

'I really can't talk now.'

'Why don't I pick up some sandwiches or some chicken and come over?'

'No.'

'I guess I'm calling at a bad time.'

'Yes.'

'Well, you have my number.'

'Yes, that I do.'

We hung up. It's always gratifying to be appreciated.

I called the deli, ordered a lean corned beef with Chinese hot mustard, told them I'd be down in ten minutes, and went out onto the balcony. There was a slight haze to the south and west and a thin band of cirrus clouds up high over the Santa Monica mountains to the north. The air felt glassy and damp. It hadn't turned hot yet, but it would soon. That was L.A.

I thought about Mort, wearing his *U.S.S. Bluegill* tee shirt in the little snapshot. Mort from Kansas. Mort of the paint store. Mort with his traditional wife and his traditional kids and his not-so-traditional life. *Don't look now, Toto, but this ain't Kansas. . . .* Would Mort be stupid enough to try to move some dope? *Laugh when they laugh, nod when they nod.* Partners with Rice, not on a movie deal, but on a dope deal that had gone bad? Had Mort picked up the boy from school, then been kidnapped on the way home? That would explain why Mort's clothes were still at the house and why he'd left no note. But with Mort dead, why grab Ellen and tear up the house? Because somebody thought Mort had something and thought Ellen Lang knew about it. Maybe that somebody was Domingo Garcia Duran. Maybe Ellen and the boy were up at his place now.

I was thinking about the big walls and the big gate and the big swords with the big bent tips when the outer door opened and the biggest human being I'd ever seen off a playing field walked in. If anything, I am consistent. First I thought Mexican, then Indian, then Samoan. Lots of Samoans come over to play middle guard for USC. He was six-eight easy and slim the way I'm slim, but on him that meant two-forty. When he moved I thought shark, sliding through the water. He had large, thick-fingered hands and big

95

bones. His cheeks were high and flat. So was his forehead. So was his nose. His eyes were black and empty and made me think shark again. A shorter man came in after him, this one Mexican for sure. Shorter than me, but wider and heavier. About one-ninety. Beer barrel body on little pin legs. You could tell he thought he was a hitter because he carried himself sort of hunched over with his arms away from his body. His hair was short and combed straight back the way Chicano kids do when they're in a gang. His right eyebrow was broken into three pieces by vertical scars. A long time ago someone had hit him very hard on the left side of his mouth and it hadn't healed right. I said, 'Wrong door. Beauty supply is down the hall.'

The big guy stopped just inside the inner door, but the Mexican came in all the way. He opened Joe Pike's door, glanced in, then closed it again. He turned in a full circle, looking at the cartoon characters on the wall and the clock and the stuff I keep around. His mouth was open. He said something in Spanish I didn't get, then shook his head and put his left foot on my desk and looked at me. I didn't like the foot on my desk. I also didn't like the lump in his windbreaker beneath his left arm.

The big one said, 'Are you Elvis Cole?' Perfect diction with a slight accent I couldn't place. I was back to thinking American Indian.

'Sometimes. Sometimes I'm the Blue Beetle.'

He said, 'Domingo Duran wants to see you. You're to come with us.' Talk about hard evidence.

I didn't move. 'Navajo?' I'd just read Tony Hillerman.

'Eskimo.'

'Some heat down here, huh?'

The Eskimo reached behind his back and came out with a black automatic. Looked to be a .380 but it could have been a 9mm. He held it loosely down at his side. 'Come on,' he said.

I stared at the Eskimo for a very long time. He let me. He was probably the guy who asked around at Kimberly Marsh's place. He may have been the guy who pulled the trigger on Mort. We started. I didn't like him and I didn't like what was happening.

The Mexican was handling one of the figures of Jiminy Cricket on the desk. I walked over, took it from him, put it back in its place. He said something in Spanish. 'I don't speak it,' I said.

'It's just as well,' the Eskimo said. 'Manolo doesn't like you.'

'Tell Manolo to get his goddamned foot off my desk.'

The Eskimo studied me for a while longer, then made a sighing sound and took a step back, taking himself out of it. He rested his gun arm on top of the file cabinet. He said something in Spanish. The Mexican's eyes narrowed and he smiled. One of his front teeth had a design etched into it. He said something back.

The Eskimo said, 'He wants you to take it off for him.'

'Tell him it'll hurt.'

He did. The Mexican gave one barking laugh, then put his right hand under his windbreaker. I stepped in, swept his support leg out from under him, kicked him in the groin when he hit the floor, and followed it down hard, driving my knee in his chest. Something gave with a loud snap. I hit him twice on the jaw with my right hand. His eyes rolled back, shiny and black as marbles, he stopped trying to cover up, and that was it.

The Eskimo hadn't moved.

'He'll need a doctor,' I said. 'Maybe for the groin shot, but more likely for the chest. A couple of ribs went. Could be some liver damage.'

Manolo rolled onto his side and coughed. The Eskimo looked at him with bottomless eyes. Maybe your eyes get that way from looking down through thin ice to see killer whales looking back at you. I read somewhere that in the Deep Ice Tribes young kids still have to kill polar bears to pass into manhood. By themselves. With sticks.

The Eskimo turned the eyes to me, nodded at whatever he saw, and made the .380 disappear. 'Let's go.'

'I didn't want you guys to think I was too easy.'

'No problem.'

He picked up Manolo like I'd lift an overnight bag. Manolo moaned. I said, 'Those ribs are probably grating together.'

'No problem.'

We went out my office, along the hall, down the elevator, across the lobby, and out the side of the building.

CHAPTER 18

A black Cadillac limo waited in the service alley. The Eskimo put me against the car, patted me down, then said, 'Okay.' He shoved Manolo into the front, then he and I got into the back. There was an Asian guy at the wheel. I said, 'Hey, just like the Green Hornet.'

The Asian guy glanced at me in the mirror. The Eskimo said, 'Shut up,' then settled back and closed his eyes. I nodded and did what I was told.

We went east on Santa Monica, then north on Highland to pick up the Hollywood Freeway north, passing Universal Studios with its ominous black tower and skyscraper hotels and array of sound stages so numerous it looked like a breeding ground for airplane hangars. In the San Fernando valley we looped onto the Ventura Freeway and rolled west for a long time. The big Cadillac was whisper quiet. The Eskimo was to my left, slouched down on his spine, eyes still closed. Maybe sleeping, maybe faking it and waiting for me to make my move. A lot like seal hunting, I guessed. The driver never looked back, never moved, just drove. Manolo shifted every once in a while, a lump in the front seat ahead of me. Quiet. I whistled the opening bars to *The Bridge on the River Kwai*.

The Eskimo said, 'Shut up.'

Yassuh.

We passed Woodland Hills and Reseda and Thousand Oaks. Pretty soon we left the west valley and were moving toward Camarillo. Manolo coughed twice, groaned, then sat up. He rubbed at his face, then shrugged his shoulders and rolled his head from side to side. He twisted around and looked at me. There wasn't any threat in his look; it was more like he'd discovered a new species of rhododendron.

The sprawl and clutter of the valley gave way to hilly pasture land, green from the winter rains. There was the occasional scrub oak and the occasional dirt road and Jersey and Hereford cattle spotted on the steeper slopes. In summer, the same hills would be brown and dead and would look like desert. A few minutes past Camarillo we left the freeway. There was nothing around but a Union 76 station and an old two-lane state road running to the northwest and what was maybe a grain elevator from the forties. I said, 'If you guys are lost we should ask.'

The Eskimo said nothing. Maybe I was wearing him down.

We went northwest. Ten minutes later we turned through an arched metal gate that said *Cachon Ranches* and followed a well-maintained composition road about a mile up into the hills until we came to what I guessed was the ranch. A maze of steel pipe corrals, one wooden main office, and three corrugated metal buildings. A heavy-duty livestock truck was backing up to the corrals as sweaty men in worn jeans and work shirts and broken fiber cowboy hats waited to receive it. Another limo was parked by the wooden office and there were three or four dusty pickups by the largest metal building. We pulled up beside the pickups and got out. The Eskimo said, 'Come on.' Manolo fell out of the front seat. No one rushed to help him.

Domingo Garcia Duran stood at one of the smaller corrals, his back to us. He was standing next to a fat man. Duran was about five-ten, slim and strong-looking with narrow hips and wide shoulders and black hair shot through with silver. He was wearing tan Gucci loafers and dark slacks and a cream-colored pullover shirt that showed his build. He stood erect, much like Ricardo Montalban. He looked wealthy, also like Ricardo Montalban. Maybe if I said, 'Boss! Boss! De plane! De plane!' he'd think I was funny. He and the fat man were watching a black cow walk in slow circles about the corral. Every once in a while the fat man said something and pointed at the cow and Duran would nod. Duran was holding a slender sword in his left hand. About three feet long, with a bent tip. Ixnay on the Villechaise.

The Eskimo said something to them and the fat guy went away. The black cow was short and squat and nervous. She saw us, lowered her head, then twitched and jumped away to resume her walk. No resemblance to Elsie. Duran looked at me and said, 'We will talk. I will ask you questions, you will answer. I will give you instructions, you will act on them. First, do you know who I am?'

'Karl Malden.'

99

Something hit me hard in the left shoulder blade. I grunted and bent over but didn't fall. The Eskimo stared at me.

Duran said, 'He will hit you as many times as I wish. There are others who will hit you, also. After they are done, still others will put your body there,' he pointed the sword into the hills 'so that it will never be found. Do you understand these things?'

'Do I get penalized for questions?'

The hard thing hit me again and this time I went over, my left arm dead from my shoulder blade out. He should have hit me in the head. In the head, he would've broken his hand and knocked some sense into me. Somebody lifted me and held me up before Duran. Life as a puppetoon. I said, 'Do you have Ellen Lang or Perry Lang or know of their whereabouts?'

I tensed for the next shot but it didn't come. Duran looked at me like he was looking at a retard. He said, 'A man named Morton Lang came to my home. I did not know this man, yet I welcomed him and allowed him in as a guest. He repays my hospitality by stealing from my home two kilograms of cocaine. Very special cocaine. Not easy to get. Medical quality, you see, the cocaine they study in laboratories and hospitals. Now I'm told you have it.'

I looked at Duran. I looked at the Eskimo. I looked back at Duran. He looked at the cow. 'She's beautiful, no?'

'Somebody told you I had your cocaine?'

'Come. I show you something.'

The Eskimo shoved me after Duran toward the bigger corral. The truck had backed to the loading ramp and killed its engine. The ranch hands were swarming around the rear gate, pulling chains and metal latchbars. Duran said, 'Do you know *toreo?*'

'No.' *Toreo.* Next it would be Thai cuisine or decorative macramé. A guy like Duran, you've got to let him run his course. Especially if you don't want to get hit a lot.

'To the shame of the United States. It's an art of great passion and beauty.'

'Yeah, all that red.'

He shouted something to one of the men working at the truck, then turned back to me. 'Much of what happens between the man and the *toro* grows out of *jurisdicción*. To cite the *toro*, to make him charge, you must place yourself in his *jurisdicción*. You invade his place. You offer yourself to his horn.' He looked at the sword, then touched it to my chest. The point curved down. If he shoved it in, the blade would follow the curve to my heart. 'The most courageous matador, he offers his balls.'

I looked at the Eskimo, who was staring off across the yard, probably watching for narwhals. My back hurt, but feeling had returned to my arm. Maybe I could take him. Maybe I could do something to his eyes, then put him down on the ground to neutralize his size and go to work on his throat and groin. Sure. I looked back at Duran. 'You mean the whole idea is that the bull is coming for your balls.'

'Yes.'

I shook my head. 'Dumb.' I think the Eskimo smiled, but I wouldn't swear to it.

The ranch hands slammed open the truck's gate. A brown and gray steer looked out, then trotted slowly down the ramp and into the pen. He didn't look like much. Then, almost as if in slow motion, a heavy black bull not quite the size of Godzilla came down the ramp to stand beside the steer. He stood very still, feet squarely placed, head up, looking first at the ranch hands, then at us. A Russell sculpture. It was impossible to imagine a chest and shoulders more powerfully formed. His horns came up and out then curved back in. They were very sharp. Duran nodded. 'See how he carries his head, see the way he looks about. This is *pundonor*. Great pride, a very great jealousy of his *jurisdicción*. He accepts the duty of protecting what is his.'

Maybe Duran was thinking about adopting him. I said, 'Why the steer?'

'*Cabestros*. To calm the bull for the journey. The herd instinct, you see? They are friends.' He looked at me again. 'Would you offer yourself to such an animal?'

'Maybe with a rocket launcher.'

'Imagine standing before his charge, watching him come, waiting for him.' Duran smiled, maybe remembering. 'We will breed them, the bull and the cow. The young one will inherit the looks of the father, the courage of the mother. She is very brave. She killed a man in the Pampas.'

I said, 'I don't have your cocaine. I don't know anything about your cocaine.'

'I am told you do.'

'You were told wrong. I was hired to find Morton Lang. He's been found. I don't guess you guys know anything about that. Now I'm looking for his wife and his little boy. I think you've got them.'

He touched me with the sword again. I wondered if I could take it away from him before the Eskimo nailed me. I said, 'Maybe Morton Lang didn't steal your cocaine. Maybe somebody else did.'

'No.'

'Maybe Nanuk here took it.'

'No.'

'Look, if Mort had taken the dope and now I had it, wouldn't I be trying to sell it back to you?'

Duran touched a button on my shirt with the point of the sword. He pressed. The button split. 'Return my property. Perhaps then you'll find the woman and the boy.'

The ranch hands began to chatter. When I looked, the bull had lifted his snout and begun to trot around the pen. The hands scurried to open a gate on the far side, but Duran snapped an order and they stopped. The bull made a coughing sound and lowered his head. There was drool streaming out of his mouth. The steer, eyes wide and rolling, edged away.

Duran said, 'He smells the female.'

The bull charged the steer. When they hit, it sounded like a mortar round, *whump*. The bull caught him in the gut by the hindquarters, then lifted and twisted, ripping forward into the ribs. You could hear them pop like green wood. The steer brayed and went down. The bull stayed with him, lowering the thick neck and hooking his horns two lefts and a right like a boxer throwing combinations, once almost lifting the steer off the ground. Then Duran nodded and the hands threw open the far gate, shouting and waving their hats. The bull backed away from the steer. His horns glistened red. He pawed the ground then ran through the gate. The steer flopped around for a while, then managed to gain its feet. When it did, most of its intestine fell out onto the ground. It wobbled and staggered but stayed up. Some friend.

Duran looked at me, then vaulted the fence. I was dismissed. The Eskimo led me back to the limo and opened the door. A full-service thug. Kato was still behind the wheel. The Eskimo said, 'He'll take you where you tell him.'

'What if I tell him the police?'

'He'll take you there.'

'That easy.'

The Eskimo shrugged. 'Play it the way you want. Mr. Duran was lunching at the Marina today. He can prove that. If you consider what has happened and what could, he won't have to. You will do as he tells you.'

'I don't have the dope.'

He looked at me.

I said, 'The woman and the boy, they'd better be all right.'

Something like a grin touched the Eskimo's lips. He said, 'Nanuk,' then turned and walked back toward the corrals.

I got into the car. The last thing I saw was Domingo Garcia Duran approach the steer and drive the sword to its hilt down through the steer's shoulders at the base of its neck. The steer dropped, the ranch hands cheered, and I shut the door.

CHAPTER 19

When I got back to my building I went to the deli to pick up the corned beef sandwich. They'd saved it and weren't happy about it. I wasn't so happy about it myself. I snapped at the blonde behind the register to prove I was still tough, then brought the sandwich and three bottles of Heineken up to my office. I was so tough I forgot I didn't have an opener and had to ride all the way back down to the deli to buy one of theirs. Buck sixty-five for a piece of tin.

I let myself into the office and locked the outer door. There were two messages on my machine: the first from an auto parts store letting me know that the genuine 1966 Chevrolet Corvette shifter skirt I'd ordered four months ago was finally in, the second from Lou Poitras, returning my call. I reset the machine, opened the balcony doors for air, sat down behind the desk, opened the first Heineken, and drank most of it.

The smart move would be to call the cops. That's what I'd advised Ellen Lang. More often than not, the cops crack the case, the cops get their man, the kidnapped come back alive when the cops are involved. The Feds will supply you with statistics that bear this out. Lots of neat black lettering on clean white sheets that don't have much at all to do with some dead-eyed psychopathic sonofabitch saying that if the police come in a little kid and a woman get dead. *Well, no, Your Honor, he didn't actually* say *it, but he* strongly hinted *that that would be the case. . . .*

I finished the rest of the Heineken, dropped the bottle into the trash, opened another, and unwrapped the sandwich. It was cold and the bread was stale. My back hurt where the Eskimo had hit me and my hand hurt from hitting Kimberly Marsh's boyfriend and the thick-necked Mexican. I ate some of the sandwich and drank more of the beer and thought about all this.

I couldn't see Morton Lang ripping two keys of cocaine off

Domingo Garcia Duran. Trying to set up a deal and blowing it, that's one thing. But to shove two plastic packs of dope in your jockeys right in the man's house and walk out, unh-unh. That took *cojones*. There was Garrett Rice, but he didn't strike me as being particularly well-endowed either. Maybe someone else. Anyone else. The Eskimo, the guys in the Nova, Manolo, the fat guy at the ranch. Maybe the rich Italian Kimberly Marsh had mentioned. I drank more beer and ate more sandwich. What did I know? Maybe Mort had swiped it and Ellen knew about it and that's why she hadn't wanted the cops involved. Maybe she'd known all along and right now the dope was buried in a coffee can under the swing set in her back yard. I killed the second Heiny and opened the last one.

No chance. Maybe Mort had ripped off the dope but there was no way Ellen had known about it. Mort, I hadn't met, hadn't touched, hadn't sat with. Ellen, we'd breathed the same air. If Mort had ripped off the Crown jewels of London, Ellen hadn't known it. She'd been enduring, going through the necessary chore of shopping for groceries to feed her kids, probably wondering why life had turned so unfair since leaving Kansas when a man or men approached to show her just how unfair life could get. They would take her somewhere and ask her about the dope and maybe hurt her. And she would cry and maybe be angry but mostly be scared. After a while, when the fear wasn't so new and her head began to work, she'd think of me. Mr. White Knight. Dragons slain. Maidens rescued. She'd say, 'Mr. Cole has it,' because that would take the heat off her and maybe bring me into it and I could help. Maybe.

I finished the sandwich and the third Heineken and put the wax paper in the waste basket and the empty bottle beside the other two. Okay, Ellen, I'm your guy. Shield shined and charger shod. I got up and fished around in the little cooler by the file cabinet and found a Miller High Life. The Champagne of Bottled Beers. Domingo Garcia Duran has a couple of thugs deliver me and lays it out like he's talking to a dog who can't repeat it or report it or use the information in any way. Not that I had anything to repeat or report. I could tie Mort to Duran's little party through Kimberly Marsh and Garrett Rice, but Duran had admitted that much and would probably be willing to admit it again. He hadn't admitted offing Mort or holding Ellen and the boy. All I had for evidence was a phone call from Mort to Kimberly where Mort said he was in trouble with someone named Dom. Big deal. Still, I could run to the cops and let them worry about digging up the evidence. Maybe

Duran didn't care. Maybe he was so connected he could take the heat and shut off or divert an investigation. Maybe if he couldn't, his friend Rudy Gambino could. Rudy Gambino. Christ. I had seen Rudy Gambino once in Houston before I became an op. He was being led through the lobby of the Whitworth Hotel, surrounded by a swarm of attorneys and state marshals, on his way to face charges of statutory rape, rape, mayhem, assault, and sodomy against a twelve-year-old girl. Quite a guy, that Rudy. The charges were later dropped.

I finished the Miller and put it with the other empties. Saturday during a Dodgers game the pile would look respectable. Midweek during a case made me look like a drunkard. I dialed Lou Poitras. 'You ever hear of a guy, Domingo Garcia Duran?'

'Runs a bodywork shop on Alvarado.'

'Different Duran. This guy used to fight bulls. Now he's rich, has investments, friends, like that.'

'This got anything to do with Lang?'

I ignored him. 'This guy, he's seen around with Rudy Gambino and those guys. Think you could ask around, see what kind of weight he could handle?'

'You mean like, can he get a ticket fixed? Like that?'

'Like that.'

'You didn't answer me, Hound Dog.'

'No, it doesn't have anything to do with Lang.'

There was a pause. 'Okay,' he said, and hung up. I frowned at the phone. Galahad lying to Percival. It made me feel small.

I brought my typewriter from its little stand in the corner over to the desk and typed up a complete report from the time Ellen Lang hired me three days ago until Kato brought me back to the building. When I finished, it was four single-spaced pages long. I corrected the typos, numbered, dated, and signed each page, then brought them to the insurance office across the hall. The secretary there lets me use their copy machine whenever the boss' door is closed. It was closed. I made two copies and tried not to breathe in the secretary's face. I took the copies back to my office, signed and dated each sheet again and wrote in longhand that there should be no erasures or deletions from any page. The original and one copy went into my office file. The other I sealed in an envelope, stamped, and addressed it to my home. Then I went down, put the letter in the drop outside the bank, and went back into the deli. I bought a bottle of aspirin and a large black coffee to go. I chewed four of the aspirin while the blonde watched, then took the steps, two at a time, all the way up. For every sin, there must be penance.

Back in the office I ate two more aspirin, sipped the coffee, and thought about what I might do. Ellen and the boy would be safe as long as Duran thought he could trade them for the dope, only I had no dope to trade. Maybe I could break into his manse at three in the morning, ram a gun in his mouth, and demand their release. Unh-huh. Maybe I could kite some bad checks, score a hundred grand worth of dope, and pull the trade that way. Unh-huh. The problem was that once Duran had the dope, Ellen and Perry had to disappear. Wouldn't matter how connected he was, he couldn't buck eyewitness testimony. And that meant Elvis had to disappear, too. I watched Pinocchio's eyes move back and forth. Portrait of the investigator: young man in search of a plan.

Maybe I could poke around and trip over some heretofore unknown bit of evidence. I dug out the rolodex card with Garrett Rice's phone numbers and dialed his office. A woman answered, 'Mr. Rice's office,' and told me he'd gone for the day. I asked if Mr. Tyner was about. She said he had gone with Mr. Rice. I dialed Rice's home number and waited while it rang. Maybe Garrett Rice knew something he wasn't telling. Maybe I could use some form of nonlethal persuasion to find out. On the fifteenth ring I hung up. Not home. Some plan, all right.

I took out my wallet and looked at the license number that Joe Pike had copied off the Nova, then called a lady at the Department of Motor Vehicles. I identified myself, gave her the number of my PI license, and asked for the Nova's registration. She told me to wait, then came back with a name and an address. I thanked her, hung up, then finished the coffee. The beer and the aspirin had helped my back. I pulled on the shoulder rig without too much pain, got the Dan Wesson out of my desk, put on the cotton jacket, and went out. It was eight minutes after four.

I still didn't have a plan. Maybe the guys in the Nova, maybe they had a plan. Maybe I could borrow it.

CHAPTER 20

Forty minutes later I turned down a small residential street in an older part of Los Angeles between Echo Park and Dodger Stadium. The houses were flat-topped stucco bungalows, mostly off-white or sand or yellow in color. Most had porches and most of the porches had tricycles and big potted geraniums and old Chicano women sitting in lawn chairs. You could smell chili sauce and *machaca* simmering and the doughy scent of fresh, hand-thrown flour tortillas. It was a good, clean smell.

The DMV had said that the dark blue Nova belonged to a man named Arturo Sanchez who lived in the fourth house from the corner on the north side of the street. It was a light brown bungalow with a two-strip drive, a porch, and four ratty rose bushes. The Nova wasn't in the drive, nor was it parked on the street. I cruised past the house to the end of the block and turned into a little street-corner shopping center. There was a laundromat and a 7-Eleven and a taco stand and a billboard advertising Virginia Slims. *¡Hiciste mucho progreso, chiquita!*

I parked under the Virginia Slims sign, bought a taco and an iced tea, and sat with them at one of the little picnic benches in a place where I could watch Arturo Sanchez's house. It was a real taco, with chunk beef and chilis, fried in oil and doused with the sort of sauce that would bring a Taco Bell taco to its knees. Heaven. I had finished the first and started on a second when the blue Nova turned down the street and into Sanchez's drive. The poor man's Charles Bronson got out, looking sullen, kicked at something on the ground, kicked at it again, then entered the front door. Still tough, all right.

I waited.

The sun settled and the cars that passed began to burn their headlamps. It grew chill. Two teenage girls in tight pants and too much makeup walked past the taco stand and into the 7-Eleven. Cars pulled into the lot. Guys who looked like they worked hard for a living got out, went into the 7-Eleven and came out with six-packs or cartons of milk. It got dark. A beat-up station wagon discharged a short, thick-boned woman with two large baskets of clothes. The two baskets were almost as big as the woman. She edged sideways through the laundromat doors, set the baskets onto the floor near the closest machine, and sorted through her wash. She saw me watching her. I smiled. She smiled. She went on with her wash. Another close brush with dangerous inner-city life.

The guy in the taco stand was beginning to look at me, too, only he wasn't smiling. I threw the rest of my iced tea into a steel trash bin and went over to the 7-Eleven and pretended to make a call from the pay phone. The guy in the taco stand watched me. Four make-believe calls later I gave up, went back to the taco stand, and smiled in the little window. 'Ever thought about licensing a franchise?' I said.

The guy never took his eyes off me. He had his right hand where I couldn't see it behind the Orange Crush machine. Probably embarrassed by a hangnail.

At ten minutes before eight Arturo Sanchez kicked open the screen door to his house and stormed out to his Nova. The porch light came on and a heavy woman appeared in the door, screaming something in Spanish. Arturo gunned the Nova, screeched backward out of the drive, and roared down the street away from me.

I caught up to him a block and a half down Elysian Park heading toward Dodger Stadium. With the baseball season still a couple of months off, traffic was light; two months from now with the Dodgers in a home game I might have had problems. We went up Stadium Way through Chavez Ravine and north on Riverside paralleling the Golden State Freeway. About a mile and a half up he swung right onto a crowded side street without signaling. Some guys are assholes all the way through.

The Nova pulled into a small apartment building. A man passed through his headlights and climbed in. It wasn't the same guy who'd been with Sanchez in front of Kimberly Marsh's place. This guy was shorter and built like an in-shape welterweight, compact and hard and mean. The kind of guy who just naturally wanted to make something of it. The Nova came back onto Riverside and continued north.

When we got to Los Feliz Boulevard they surprised me, turning west toward Hollywood instead of east toward Domingo Duran's. On Franklin they parked in front of a liquor store and the welterweight got out. He went into the store, came out with a bagged pint, and made a call on the pay phone. Probably to his broker. They continued down Franklin to Beachwood, then hung a right up into the Hollywood hills. Halfway up they turned off Beachwood and climbed into a little nest of cramped, winding streets beneath the Hollywood sign. I killed my lights and backed off, guessing turns by watching their lights bounce off the houses and trees above me. We went higher, Hollywood and Los Angeles spreading out below in a hypnotic panorama so wide and deep that you could lose yourself in the lights.

When I saw their car again it was parked at the curb of a little white clapboard bungalow. I eased to a stop, then let the Corvette roll backward and swing into an empty drive. I took my gun out from under the seat and held it at my side as I walked up to the house. My heart was pounding. That really happens when you're scared.

There were three men standing in the living room, Sanchez and the welterweight and a third guy. The third guy was holding a can of Budweiser beer in his teeth and pulling on a white shirt. He had spiderwebs tattooed on each shoulder along with assorted daggers and skulls and female breasts. He also had a shoulder holster. Behind them was a short hall running back to what looked like the kitchen. The welterweight peeled the bag off his pint, set it on the coffee table, and laughed at something. Probably not the other guy's tattoos.

I went around the side of the house and peeked in a window. It was a little bedroom off the hall, decorated in early poverty. Ellen Lang sat in a chair. Her hands were tied behind her back and there was a Mayfair Market grocery bag over her head. I went back to the front and around the other side, looking in each window for the boy. I didn't see him. At the back of the house, there was a wooden door off the kitchen, opened to catch the breeze. I stood just outside the wedge of light, trying to hear into the front room. The men were still laughing. Maybe if I yelled *Fire!* they'd run. I eased back the hammer on my gun and stepped into the house.

Alarms didn't go off. The Eskimo didn't swoop out of the sky. The kitchen was dingy and yellow and hadn't been cleaned in a long time. There was a roach trap on the floor under the dinette, Taco Bell and Burrito King wrappers on the counter, and the stink of old hot sauce. Someone had built a pyramid of Coors cans on the dinette. From where I was standing I could look down the hall and see the back of Sanchez's head. I took one step out into the hall, then turned right into the bedroom with Ellen Lang. I could hear her breath hissing softly against the paper bag. She shifted once, then sat motionless. Out in the living room, the men talked and laughed and I heard a bottle clunk the table. I went to Ellen Lang and said quietly, 'Don't speak and don't move. It's me.'

I thought it would end then. I thought she would gasp or moan or stumble out of the chair but she didn't. Her body tensed and she drew up very, very straight. I slipped the bag off her head and untied her wrists. Her eyes were puffy and she had one small red mark in the left corner of her mouth but that was all. She stared at me without blinking.

'Can you walk?'

She nodded once.

'Is Perry here?'

She shook her head.

'I'm going to slip your shoes off. We're going to go out that door, turn left, and go out through the kitchen. On the deck, we'll turn right and out to the street. You'll go first so I can cover our backs.'

She nodded. I slipped her shoes off and handed them to her. Just as she stood up, a toilet flushed and a door across the hall opened and a fourth man came out of the bathroom. He was shorter than me and fat, carrying a *Times* sports section. He said something in Spanish to the living room and then he saw me. I shot him twice in the chest and he fell sideways. There were shouts and a thump like a chair hitting the floor. I yanked Ellen Lang toward the hall.

The welterweight came around the corner, firing as fast as he could pull the trigger. One of his slugs caught the doorjamb and kicked some splinters into my cheek. I shot him in the face, then shoved Ellen through the kitchen and half carried her around the house and out onto the street. The Tattooed Man popped out of the front door and fired five shots – *bapbapbapbapbap* – then dove back into the house.

Porch lights were coming on and someone was yelling and Wang Chung was coming out over somebody's radio. I shoved Ellen into the Corvette, fired up, and ran over two garbage cans pulling away. I was shaking and my shirt was wet with sweat and I wasn't having a great deal of luck seeing past the little silver flashes that bobbed around in front of my eyes. I drove. Slow. Steady. Just trying to get away from there. I think I ran over a dog.

At the bottom of Beachwood, I pulled into an Exxon station and waited for the shakes to pass. When they did I looked at Ellen Lang. She was drawn and pale in the fluorescent Exxon light, and sitting absolutely still. She didn't whimper and she didn't tremble but I'm not quite sure she felt anything, either. I touched her hand. It was cold. 'Do you need a doctor?'

She shook her head once like back at the house, and looked at me with dulled eyes. I peeled off my jacket, put it around her shoulders, then leaned my head back on the seat. My heart was hammering. Outside on Franklin, night-time Hollywood traffic edged past. A tall skinny kid wearing an old Stetson and a threadbare Levi jacket thumbed for a ride. The Exxon attendant leaned against the gas pump, staring at us, probably wondering what the hell we were doing over in the shadows, probably thinking maybe he should walk over and see, probably deciding nope, this is Hollywood. The attendant went into a service bay.

I closed my eyes. I'd killed one man for sure and probably another. The cops would have to come in, and they wouldn't like it. I didn't much like it myself.

I heard her say, 'Mort's dead, isn't he?'

I turned my head to see her. 'Yes.'

'Did he steal those drugs like they said?'

'I don't know.'

She nodded once more, and that was it. We stayed in the shadows on the side of the Exxon station for a long time. Then I restarted the Corvette, pulled into traffic, and drove slowly toward Laurel Canyon.

CHAPTER 21

The Corvette moved easily up the mountain. When cars came up behind us, I steered into turnouts to let them pass. At the far edge of the passenger seat, Ellen Lang sat huddled in the jacket, eyes forward, as I told her what I knew. She only spoke twice. Once to ask me about the girls, and once to answer 'no' when I told her the girls were with Janet and asked if she wanted me to bring her there.

We pulled into the carport, killed the engine, and went into the kitchen through the carport door. When we were inside she asked me to please be sure to lock the door, so I had her watch me throw the bolt. I went out to the living room for a bottle of Glenlivet and a couple of glasses that looked like they were made for something besides jam. When I got back she was holding one of my R.H. Forschner steak knives. I put ice into each glass, filled them with the scotch, then pried the steak knife out of her hand and replaced it with a glass. 'Drink this, then I'll show you what we have.'

I dumped mine back, threw out the ice, then refilled the glass and downed that, too. You can't beat Glenlivet for the smooth mellow glow it gives you, especially after you kill some people. I felt my nose and eyes fill and something large in my throat and I thought I was going to burst. But I bit down on it and managed some more of the scotch and it passed. When she had taken half of hers I led her through the house, first the dining area and living room and powder room on the main floor, then the loft bed above and the master bath. The bottle of scotch went with us. I turned on every light in each room and left it on. We looked in closets and in the storage space under the platform bed. I showed her that the windows and the front door and the sliding glass doors were all locked and I showed her the red light that meant the burglar alarm was armed. When we finished the tour upstairs by the master bath I refilled her drink and said, 'You can bathe in here. I've got an oversized hot-water heater, so use all you want. There's buttermilk soap and shampoo in the cabinet and extra towels under the sink.' I went out to the closet and brought back the big white terry robe. 'You can wear this. If you'd rather have some clothes, I've got a sweat shirt and some jogging shorts that a friend left over. They should fit.'

'Where will you be?'

'In the kitchen. I have to make a call, and then I'll make us something to eat.'

She thanked me and shut the door. I waited until I heard the water running, then the scotch and I went back to the kitchen. I took off my pistol, put it on the counter, then went into the bathroom and plucked my face. It was like playing buried treasure with a needle and a bright light. I dug out six little pieces of wood, washed, dabbed on alcohol, then looked at myself in the mirror. No permanent damage. At least nothing that you could see.

Back out in the kitchen, I refilled my glass, then dialed Lou Poitras at home. He said, 'Do you know what time it is? I got kids in bed.'

'Ellen Lang's over here. To get her I had to kill a couple of guys up in Beachwood Canyon, in a house just under the Hollywood sign.'

Lou said, 'Hold on.' There was a knocking sound, like the receiver had been put down on a table, then nothing, then some scuffing sounds as the phone was picked up, then a little girl's voice, giggling. 'Judy bit my heiny.'

An extension was lifted and Poitras yelled he had it. A hang-up, and it was just me and Lou again. He said, 'You get the boy, too?'

'No.'

'You home?'

'Yeah.'

'Does this have anything to do with you asking about Domingo Duran?'

'Yes.'

Another pause, this one the kind when the background static becomes real noise. Then he said, 'You're an asshole, Elvis. I'm on my way.'

He hung up. I hung up. I sipped the scotch. Asshole. That Lou. What a kidder.

I called Joe Pike. He answered on the first ring, a little breathless, as if he were finishing a long run or a couple hundred push-ups. 'Pike.'

I could hear his stereo system in the background. Oldies but goodies. The Doors. 'It's gotten hot,' I said. I gave him the short version.

Pike asked no questions, made no comment. 'Button up,' he said. 'I'm coming in.'

Pike thinks Clint Eastwood talks too much.

I took eight eggs, cream, butter, and mushrooms out of the refrigerator. I got out the big pan, put it on the stove, and was opening three raisin muffins when Ellen Lang came down and stood in the little passageway between the counter and the wall.

She was wearing the terry robe and a pair of my socks. Her hair was damp and combed out and looked clean. So did her face. She looked good. She looked younger and maybe willing to laugh if you gave her something worth laughing at. 'How are you doing?' I asked.

'You must be terribly tired,' she said. 'Let me do that.' She moved to the stove.

'It's okay.' I put the muffins face up in the toaster oven.

'Don't be silly,' she said. 'You've had a hard day. If you want to do something, you can make the coffee.' Her eyes had turned to poached eggs. Her smile was weak but somehow pleasant, the sort of smile you get when you practice smiling because you think you have to. Like with Mort. Only now the poached-egg eyes were rimmed with something that could have been desperation.

I smiled as if everything was fine, and stepped back out of her way. 'Okay.'

She opened each cabinet, saw what was inside, then closed it and moved on. She looked over the food I had out, then put the cream back into the fridge and took peanut oil out of the cupboard. The oil and a little bit of the butter she put into the big pan. While they heated she beat the eggs with a little water, then placed the spoon neatly beside the bowl when the eggs were frothy. I could see Carrie in her. I said, 'I always put in cream.'

She chopped the mushrooms. 'You men. Cream makes the eggs stick. Never put cream. Would you like to shower before we eat?'

'Later, thank you.'

She moved around the kitchen as if I weren't there, or if I was, I was somebody else. We talked, but I didn't think she was talking to me. She was Barbara Billingsley and I was Hugh Beaumont. But not. I drank more of the scotch.

She got out two plates, forks, knives, and spoons, and brought them to the counter. She had to move the Dan Wesson to set out the plates, and stared at it before she did.

I went into the dining area to get placemats out of the buffet. When I looked at Ellen again she had picked up the gun. She held it like that, then brought it close and smelled it. I stood up. 'There're placemats and napkins,' I said.

She set the places even though I offered.

She put the eggs in the pan and turned on the toaster oven and put out butter and strawberry jam and salt and pepper, and then she told me to sit. She nursed the omelette, then eased it onto a serving plate, added a sprig of mint leaf as garnish, and brought it to the counter. A lovely presentation. She brought out cups and poured the coffee and asked me if I took cream and sugar. I said no. She said she hoped I would like it. I said it smelled wonderful. She asked if there was anything else I might want. I said no, this would be fine. She said it would be no trouble if there were. I said if I thought of something, I'd ask for it. I wanted to cry.

We didn't speak as we ate. She took one spoon of eggs and one side of a muffin. She ate that, then took some more. She ended up eating more eggs than me and half of the muffins. That was okay. I was happy with the scotch.

When she was finished she took a breath and let out a sigh like her body was trying to rid itself of ten years' accumulated poison.

I said, 'A couple of friends of mine are on their way over. Joe Pike, who owns the agency with me, and a guy named Lou Poitras. Poitras is a sergeant with the LAPD. He's also a friend. We're going to have to talk to him and tell him what we know. Do you have any objection to that?'

She sipped some of the coffee and put down the cup. Her voice came out softly. 'If I had let the police search the house when you wanted, would Mort still be alive?' Steam from the coffee crept around her hand like delicate vines. I watched the way the overhead light worked the planes of her face. She had a nice face when she didn't slump.

'No,' I said. 'Mort was already dead. There wasn't anything in the house that could've told us where he was.'

She nodded. I drank more of the scotch. She drank more of the coffee. That's what we did until Poitras arrived.

CHAPTER 22

Poitras said, 'Okay, let's have it.'

I told him everything from following the beach boy to Kimberly Marsh all the way up to what had just happened in Beachwood. He didn't laugh when I told him about Duran and the bull. He just chewed his lower lip and listened. Ellen Lang listened closely, too, as if she were taking notes on her own life. I kept my version of what Kimberly had said about Mort and the party at Duran's as brief as possible without leaving anything out. When I finished, Poitras went into the kitchen and used the phone.

I patted Ellen's arm. 'You okay?'

She gave a little shrug. I drained the rest of the scotch, went to the cabinet for some more. Out of Glenlivet. Damn. I cracked a bottle of Chivas that a cheap client had given me as a present and brought it back to the couch. I drank some. Hell, it wasn't much different from the Glenlivet after all.

Ellen went into the dining area and came back with a coaster and a napkin. She put the coaster on the coffee table in front of me and the napkin on the arm of the couch by my hand. 'There,' she said.

Poitras came back and asked for her side of it. When he saw the Chivas bottle he gave me a look. I gave him a look back.

Ellen spoke slowly, in short, declarative sentences, describing how two men had approached her in the Ralph's parking lot, forced her into the backseat of their car, and taped a sack over her head. One of them was the tattooed man. They drove around for a while, Mexican music playing and one of them occasionally patting her rump, until they arrived at the Beachwood house. They told her that Mort had stolen cocaine from them and that they had killed him and would kill her, too, if she didn't tell them where Mort had hidden the dope. They wouldn't believe her when she told them she didn't know what they were talking about. They put a gun to

117

her head and snapped the trigger and touched her breasts and between her legs and threatened to rape her, though they hadn't. One of them, the fat one, brought in Perry and slapped the boy repeatedly while the other asked her about the drugs. She screamed for them to leave Perry alone, but they wouldn't, and that was when she told them that Mort had hidden the cocaine but that now I had it. After that, another man came and they took the boy away and hadn't brought him back.

I watched her tell it and sipped at the Chivas and felt bad. Once when she mentioned Perry her voice broke. Other than that, she was fine. I decided she'd started out a pretty tough lady, back there in Kansas. So tough she took life-with-Mort on the chin for so long that it finally changed her into what Janet Simon had dragged into my office three days ago. I wondered if she could heal back to the person she had been. Could anyone, ever?

When she finished, Poitras ticked his fingers on his belt buckle and frowned at me. 'Can you talk or are you incoherent?'

I sampled more of the scotch. Chivas ain't so bad no matter what they say. Probably just elitists, anyway.

Poitras excused himself to Ellen, then got up, and we went over to the kitchen. I brought my drink. He poured himself a cup of coffee and stared at me for a while. 'You think Lang took the dope?'

I said, 'I think Mort's lousy for it. I see him for the patsy. It's either inside or it's Garrett Rice or it's both. I'm thinking Duran's guys would be smarter than to try to screw the old man, so that puts it on Rice.'

Poitras nodded. 'We been trying to find him.'

'Aha.' My voice was loud.

Poitras looked at me. He didn't like what he saw a whole lot. 'We talked with your friend Kimberly Marsh. Her boyfriend looked like he'd had a little trouble.'

'Clumsy, that guy.' It was getting tough to stand up straight, but I was doing okay.

Poitras said, 'You think she had anything to do with it?'

'She'd go for it,' I said. 'Only she had no way to get away with it. Party like that, she'd be dressed sexy, showing as much skin as she could, no big pockets, no big purse, no way to hide four and a half pounds of dust.'

He tapped his belt some more. 'So now Duran has the boy.'

I took more of the scotch and looked across the dining area out the glass doors. A police helicopter was pulling a tight orbit somewhere over Hollywood, its big spot tracking something on the ground.

Poitras said, 'You asked me how much weight Duran could carry, remember? That was when I asked you if this had anything to do with Morton Lang, and you lied?'

I looked at him. He was angry. He was also out of focus.

'We've got files since 1964 connecting Duran to the Rudy Gambino family, operating out of Phoenix and Los Angeles,' he said. 'He's what the feds call a clean associate. Duran won't set up a dope deal or muscle into a business, but he invests through a guy like Gambino. The feds have been trying to bust Duran for years, only they can't because he keeps himself clean. They've got him placed as an investor with dope up from Colombia, with hotel kickbacks in Phoenix and Tucson. He owns a couple of banks in Mexico City and he's on the board of a bank in New Orleans. Gambino launders his Gulf Coast pornography take through Duran's New Orleans bank and gives Duran a cut. It goes on like that. This give you some idea what kind of weight he can handle?'

'Yeah.'

'Yeah.' Poitras walked away from me, back into the living room. 'Mrs. Lang, who was the man who came and took your son?'

She said, 'I don't think they called him by name. He spoke to the other men in Spanish, then he told Perry they were leaving. He said that in English with a different accent. It wasn't Spanish.'

'That would be the Eskimo,' I said.

Poitras said to her, 'Did you see anyone who might've been Domingo Duran, or did any of the men in the house refer to him?'

She looked at me with a little bit of the fear back in her eyes. 'What's wrong?' she said.

'He isn't liking it. He's coming in late in the game and we've got bad cards.'

'You got no cards at all.' Poitras looked big and grim and ominous, like the Michelin Man with a bad headache. He said, 'You should've put me in on this as soon as you suspected, Elvis.'

Ellen Lang said, 'What're you talking about? What's wrong?' The first bright tinge of panic.

I said, 'What's wrong is that Duran can beat what we have. He's kept himself away from it except for me and he can beat my story easy enough if people in the right place are willing to say the wrong thing. They will be. My statement gives the cops probable cause to go in to Duran's, but Duran won't have Perry in his home. He'll deny everything, and all we've done is jeopardize Perry with nothing but a guy named Sanchez to show for it.' It came out harder than I liked, but I was angry with Poitras and too drunk to handle it.

Lou said, 'That's about it.'

Ellen Lang got white and the corner of her mouth with the red mark began to tremble. I put my hand over hers and squeezed. Her jaw clenched and the trembling stopped. 'I'm all right,' she said.

The phone rang and Poitras went back into the kitchen for it. I poured some of the Chivas into Ellen's coffee cup and put it in her hand. 'It's going to be fine,' I said. 'Trust me. It'll work out.' I gave her my everything-under-control smile. She didn't look convinced. Maybe it's tough for a drunk to look convincing. I saw the Eskimo put a size 18 hand on the boy's shoulder. I saw them walk out to the long black limo. I saw the limo disappearing into the high desert hills. I saw Domingo Duran, jabbing his sword toward the hills, saying *Then other men will come, and put your body there, where you will not be found.*

I spilled another inch of Chivas into my glass, then went into the kitchen so Ellen Lang couldn't see me drink it. Poitras was talking in that low mumble cops use that only other cops can hear and understand. After a while he hung up and said, 'Okay. You left two in the house, like you thought. Fat guy in the hall and another one in the living room. The house is listed to a man named Louis Foley. The neighbors up there say Foley moved to Seattle two months ago and that the house has been up for sale. Your guys probably just pulled up the sign and cracked the lock box.'

'That's great. They'll promote you to Lieutenant along with Baishe for this kinda work.'

He looked at me. 'You're pushing it, Hound Dog.'

'And you're acting like an asshole with that woman in there. She's been through hell and all you got to say is a lot of bullshit about how I didn't call you in and how we got nothing. Negative bullshit that she doesn't need to deal with. She's missing a child, Poitras. She's lost her husband.'

I was very close to him. His big face was calm. He said, 'Take a step back, Elvis.'

It was quiet in the kitchen with just his breathing and my breathing and the hum of the electric clock over the sink. The cat door clacked and the cat walked in. Staring at Poitras, I couldn't see him but I heard him growl, low and deep in his chest at finding a stranger in the kitchen. I heard the *snick-snick* of claws on the floor, then the crunch of hard food.

Poitras said softly, 'You're drunk, man.'

I nodded.

He said, 'You found the lady and you went in and the boy wasn't there. You pulled the trigger. I know you, I know it's because you had to. You wouldn't have played it that way if you'd had a choice. But there weren't any choices. It was lousy that the kid wasn't there. You didn't lose the kid. He just wasn't there to be had.'

I felt my eyes grow hot. I took more of the Chivas.

He made his voice quieter. 'You always get in too deep, don't you? Always get too close to the client. Fall a little bit in love.'

'Go to hell.'

Poitras took the glass out of my hands and emptied it in the sink. He went out into the living room, bent over Ellen Lang, and spoke in that cop mumble. After a while she nodded and gave him a tiny smile. The cat walked over and sat by my feet. *Snick-snick-snick.* He stared up at me and purred. Sometimes a little love can be important.

Poitras came back and leaned against the counter with his arms crossed.

'Thanks,' I said.

He nodded. 'Even drunk you make a point.'

I put on a fresh pot of coffee while Poitras made more phone calls, most local but at least one up to Sacramento. Between the calls we went through it again, and this time Poitras took notes. When the coffee was ready I poured fresh cups and brought one out to Ellen Lang. She had fallen asleep with the old cup in her hand. I went up to the loft, turned down the bed, then went back down. Ellen woke when I touched her arm, then followed me up and climbed into the bed still wearing the robe and the socks. She curled into a ball on her side, knees up, hands together under her chin. Fetal position, only with her eyes open. Large, liquid Bambi eyes. Something stirred in the empty part of my stomach, the part the scotch didn't fill.

'I'm scared,' she said.

'Don't be,' I said. 'I never fail.'

She looked at me and then she fell back to sleep.

I went downstairs and found Pike standing in the entry. Poitras was in the dining area, the coiled phone cord stretched taut from his coming out of the kitchen to see who had walked in. Poitras' gun was in his right hand hanging loose at his side. He stared at Pike a couple seconds, then went back into the kitchen to get off the phone.

Pike said, 'You okay?' He was wearing a cammie Marine Corps field jacket.

'Good. You want something to eat or drink?'

Pike shook his head as Poitras came back out of the kitchen. The cat stuck his head out, saw Pike, made a wide are around Poitras, and padded over to rub against Pike's legs. 'Well, well. The big time cop,' Pike said.

Poitras' face was empty the way a traffic cop's face is empty when he's listening to you try to talk your way out of a ticket. 'You ever wanna work out, bo. You know where the gym is.'

Pike's mouth twitched.

Poitras' shoulders flexed, filling most of the dining area with his bulk.

'Here's to good friends,' I said. 'Lemme see if I've got some Löwenbräu.' Mr. Levity.

Pike's mouth twitched again, his dark glasses never moving away from Poitras. 'You got the woman here?'

I said yes.

'You going to stay in all night?'

I said yes again. Poitras kept his eyes on Pike. Motionless. Two tomcats squaring off across a property line.

'You need me, I'll be around.' Pike reached back to the door, looked at Poitras before he opened it. 'We don't see each other enough anymore, Lou.'

'Drop dead, Pike.'

Pike's mouth twitched and he left, holding the door long enough for the cat to follow. The tension level dropped around three hundred points.

'I'll have to have you two guys over for lunch sometime,' I said. 'Or maybe a dinner party.'

Poitras flexed his jaw, put .50-caliber eyes on me. 'You tell me the next time that sonofabitch is going to be around.'

'Sure, Lou.'

Poitras went into the kitchen, made another phone call, then came back into the living room carrying a cup of coffee. His face was smooth and calm, as if Pike had never been. 'There might be a way to work this Duran thing.'

'Unh-huh.'

'You willing to stay in it?'

I said, 'Duran's expecting me to produce the dope. Maybe I can. Maybe I can put the dope and Duran and the boy together. If I can do that, we own him. If I can do that without tipping him to what's going on, we can get the boy back.'

Poitras sipped more of the coffee. 'Sometimes you think like a pretty good cop.'

'We all have our weak moments.'

Poitras nodded. 'You think Duran wants the dope that bad?'

'I don't think he cares about the dope at all. He's pissed that someone would steal from him in his own home. He's got a highly developed sense of territory.'

Poitras smiled crookedly. 'Macho.'

I nodded.

Poitras said, 'Yeah, me and you are thinking along the same lines. Maybe I can help you with the dope. I'll see. I'll have to run it up the line and get it okayed.'

'Up the line through Baishe?'

'You don't make it to lieutenant without something on the ball, Hound Dog. Even Baishe.'

'My confidence is bolstered.'

'That's all we care about down at the PD, keepin' you confident.' He folded up his note pad, slipped it in his back pocket, and headed toward the door. 'Come around first thing tomorrow and we'll work this thing out. If anything happens between now and then, let me know. When things start to break it'll be tricky. You'll have to play it our way.'

'Can't we do it professionally instead?'

Poitras grinned hard and without humor. He said, 'You know something, Hound Dog? It sounded to me like Duran maybe thought you and he had an understanding. Now you break out the woman and kill a couple of his soldiers. He's probably gonna be pissed. He might even come after you.'

'There's Pike.'

Poitras' face went dead. He opened the door and stepped out. 'You got lousy taste in partners.'

'Who else would put up with me?'

I stood in the door until Poitras drove away. Off to the left I heard the cat growl, and Joe Pike answer, 'Good cat.'

CHAPTER 23

I showered and shaved, then went through the house dousing the extra lights that I had turned on for Ellen Lang. The house was quiet, warm in the gold light from the lamp beside the couch, and comfortable. There were books on the shelves that I liked to read and reread, and prints and originals on the walls that I liked to look at. Like the office, I was proud of it. Like the office, it was the result of a process and the process was ongoing. The house lived, as did the person within it. Upstairs, Ellen Lang shifted under the covers.

I got six aspirin from the powder room, ate them, then got my sleeping bag from the entry closet, spread it on the couch, and stretched out. My head rocked from side to side, floating on the scotch, and started to spin. I sat up.

It was too late for the final sports recap. Too late for Ted Koppel. Maybe I could luck into a rerun of Howard Hawks' The Thing with Ken Tobey. When I was a boy, Ken Tobey kept the monsters away. He battled things from other worlds and creatures from the bottom of the sea and prehistoric beasts and he always won. Ken Tobey fought the monsters and kept us safe. He always won. That was the trick. Any jerk can get his ass creamed.

The cat came in a little while later, jumped onto the couch next to me, stepped into my lap, and began to purr. His fur was chill from having been out. I petted him. And petting him, fell asleep.

I dreamed I was in a hot dusty arena and Domingo Duran, replete with Suit of Lights, was advancing toward me, little sword before him and cape extended. The crowd was cheering, and beautiful women threw roses. I figured I was supposed to be the bull, but when I looked down I saw my regular arms and my regular feet. Where the hell was the bull? Just then, Duran's cape flew up and a dark, satanic bull charged me. Not just any bull. This one wore mukluks and sealskin boots. When I dream, you don't have to hop the Concorde to Vienna to figure it out. Just as the bull was about to horn me with something looking suspiciously like a harpoon, I felt myself spinning out of the arena, spinning up and up until I was awake in my still-dark house.

Ellen Lang stood at the glass doors, her back to me, arms at her sides, staring down into Hollywood. Beside me the cat shifted, out of it. Some watchcat.

I listened to the house, listened to my breath. She never moved. After a while I said, quietly so as not to startle her, 'We'll find him.'

She turned. Her face was shadowed. 'I didn't want to wake you.'

'You didn't.'

She made a little sound in her throat and came over to the big chair by the couch. She didn't sit. I had fallen asleep on top of the sleeping bag and was cold but didn't want to move. I could see her face now, blue in the moonlight.

She looked out at Hollywood, then down at me. She said, 'They wouldn't believe me. I told them I didn't know what they were talking about but they just kept asking. Then they brought in Perry. They kept saying I knew and I had to tell them, and they kept slapping him and feeling me and saying that they would rape me in front of Perry, and that I had better tell them. I thought of you. I told them I thought you had it.'

'It's okay.'

'I'm sorry.'

'You don't have to be sorry.'

'I'm ashamed of myself. It wasn't right.'

I lifted the cat, sat up, then put the cat back down beside me. She said, 'Would you like coffee?'

'No, thanks.'

'If you're hungry, I could make something.'

I shook my head. 'If I want anything, I'll get it. But thank you.'

She nodded and curled up in the big chair across from me, her feet tucked under her.

I said, 'Would you like me to turn on a light?'

'If it's what you want.'

I left the light off.

After a while the cat stood up, stretched, turned in a circle, and lay back down. He said, *roawmph*. Ellen said, 'I didn't know you had a cat.'

'I don't. He lives here because I'm easy to sucker for beer and food. Don't try to pet him. He's mean and he bites.'

She smiled, her teeth blue in the reflected moonlight.

'Besides that, he's dirty and he carries germs.'

Her smile widened for an instant, then faded.

We sat some more. Outside, another police helicopter flew very low up the canyon and over the house. When I was little we lived near an air base and I was terrified that the airplanes and helicopters would scare away Santa Claus. Years later, in Vietnam, I grew to like the sound. It meant someone was coming to save me.

Ellen Lang said quietly, 'I don't know if there's any money. I don't know if I can feed the children. I don't know if I can pay for the house or the school or any of those things.'

'I'll check the insurance for you. If worse comes to worst, you can sell the house. You would sell Mort's car, anyway. The kids can go to public schools. You'll adapt. You'll do all right and so will the kids.'

She sat very still. 'I've never been alone before.'

'I know.' The helicopter looped back and disappeared toward the reservoir. I wondered if Joe Pike was watching it. 'You've got the children. There's me. When it's over doesn't mean you never see me again.'

She nodded.

'I'm a full-service op. I provide follow-up service and yearly maintenance just like Mr. Goodwrench.'

She nodded again.

'Just like the Shell Answer Man.'

She didn't respond. This stuff would kill'm in the Comedy Store. Maybe she only laughed at cat jokes. I looked at the cat. He offered little inspiration.

'There's even Janet.'

'Who reinforces my lousy self-image?'

'Keep you humble.'

She said, 'You're sweet, trying to cheer me up like this. Thank you.'

We sat. Ellen stared out the window. I stared at Ellen. Her hair was dry and brushed out and offset her small narrow face nicely. The pale light softened her features and I could see the girl back in Kansas, a nice girl who'd be great to bring to a football game on a cold night, who'd sit close to you and jump up when the home team scored and who'd feel good to hug. After a very long time, she said softly, 'It must be beautiful, living up here.'

'It is.'

'Are there coyotes?'

'Yes. They like the hills above the reservoir.'

She looked at the cat. 'I heard they take cats. I had a friend in Nichols Canyon who lost two that way.'

I touched the cats head between his ears. It was broad and flat and lumpy with scars. A good cat head.

She shifted in the chair. She was sitting on her feet, and when she moved she was careful to keep the robe over her knees. She said, 'Tell me, how can you live with someone for so long and know so little about them?'

'You can know only what someone shows you.'

'But I lived with Mort for fourteen years. I knew Garrett Rice for five years. I was married to Mort for eight years before I even knew there were other women. Now I find out about drugs. I never knew there were drugs.' Her lips barely moved, matching the stillness of the rest of her. 'He said it was me. He said I was killing him. He said he would lie in bed some nights, hoping I would die and thinking of ways to hurt me.'

'It wasn't you.'

'Then how could Mort be that person, and how could I not know? His wife. What does that say about me?' A whisper.

'It says you trusted a man who didn't deserve your trust. It says you gave of yourself completely because you loved him. It comments on Mort's quality, not yours.'

'I've been so wrong about things. Everything's been such a lie. I'm thirty-nine years old and I feel like I've thrown my life away.'

'Look at me,' I said.

She looked.

'When you marry someone, and put your trust in them, you have a right to expect that they will be there for you. The marriage doesn't have to be perfect. *You* don't have to be perfect. By virtue of the commitment, your partner is supposed to be there. Without having to look around, you have to know they're there. When you looked, Mort wasn't there. Mort hadn't been there for a long time. It doesn't matter about his problems. He failed to live up to you. Mort lived the lie. Not you. Mort threw it away. Not you.'

Her head moved. 'That sounds so harsh.'

'I'm feeling a little harsh toward Mort right now.' I took short breaths, feeling the booze still there. The big room had grown warmer.

We sat like that for several minutes. I was slouched on the sofa

127

with my abdominal muscles forming neat rows leading up to my ribs. My legs were extended, my feet on the coffee table. I looked blue.

'I don't mean to whine,' she said.

'You hurt. It's okay.'

She brought her feet out from under her with a soft rustle, and sat forward. I heard her draw a deep breath and sigh it out. She said, 'You're a very nice man.'

'Unh-hunh.'

She said, 'What happened' – she leaned forward out of the chair and touched my stomach – 'here?'

When she touched me the muscles in my stomach and pelvic girdle and thighs bunched. Her finger was very warm, almost hot. I said, 'I got into a fight with a man in Texas City, Texas. He cut me with a piece of glass.'

She moved her finger about an inch along the scar. I stood up, pulling her to me. She held on tight and whispered something into my chest that I did not hear.

I carried her upstairs and made love to her. She called me Mort. Afterward I held her, but it was a long time before she slept. And when she slept it was fitful and without rest.

CHAPTER 24

The morning sky was a rich orange when I left the bed. Ellen was up, wearing the socks and the big terry robe. She had the washing machine going, doing two towels and the clothes she had been in since Ralph's, and had started breakfast by the time I was showered and dressed.

'I called Janet,' she said.

'What a way to start your day.'

'I asked her to tell the girls that I was in San Francisco and that I'd have to be there a few days. Do you think that's all right?'

'It's smart if you don't go home.'

She nodded.

'You could stay here.'

She nodded again.

'That okay with Janet?'

The young pretty part of her momentarily surfaced. 'I'll call her and ask.' Definite progress.

The cat door clacked and the cat came in, his fur misted with dew. He saw Ellen, went to her ankle, sniffed, and started to growl.

I said, 'Get away from there.'

The cat sprinted back through his door. *Clack-clack*.

There was a knock, then Joe Pike walked in. He was misted with dew, also. 'Couple of black-and-whites cruised you just before sunup. Other than that, nada.'

I introduced him to Ellen.

She said, 'You're the one in the pictures.' There were pictures up in the bedroom of me and Pike after billfish off Cabo San Lucas at the tip of Baha.

'I'm the only one in the pictures,' he said. Enigmatically. Then he left.

'He's like that,' I said.

'Mr. Pike is your partner?'

'Unh-hunh.'

'He was out there all night?'

'All night.'

'Why?'

'To watch over us, why else?'

Joe came back with an Eastern Airlines flight bag and a brown leather rifle case and without the field jacket. He put the rifle case in the entry closet, took a Colt .357 Python in a clip-on holster from the flight bag, and put it on his hip. He took two boxes of .357 Softnose out of the bag, then rezipped it and put it in the closet next to the rifle. The boxes of extra ammo he brought to the coffee table by Ellen Lang. She watched every move the way a canary watches a cat, her eyes going from his tattoos to the gun at his waist – it was the big Python, with the 6-inch combat barrel – to the polished sunglasses. Pike was in uniform: faded Levis', blue Nikes, white sweat socks, steel Rolex, sleeveless sweat shirt. When he had everything where he wanted it, he looked at her again. 'I'm sorry to hear of your trouble,' he said.

She tried out a small, faltering smile. 'Would you like something to eat?'

'It's nice of you to offer. No. Not right now.'

He stood close, dwarfing her with his size and his energy and his capacity for violence. He did it without thinking about it. He could do it to almost anyone I knew, even men much taller and much heavier. Anyone except Lou Poitras.

Pike went into the kitchen. Ellen watched him, large-eyed and uneasy. 'You'll be fine,' I said. 'The Amal militia couldn't touch you with him here.'

She kept her eyes on Pike. Joe was standing in the kitchen, staring at a closed cabinet, unmoving. It was easy to imagine him standing all night like that.

'I'm going to swing by your house before I go to the cops,' I said. 'Can I bring back some clothes for you?'

'Yes. If you would. And my toothbrush. It's the green one.'

'Would you like to come with me?'

She glanced at the floor. 'I don't want to go back there right now.'

The drive to Encino was easy. This early, traffic down the valley side of Laurel Canyon was light and the freeway west seemed empty. I parked in Ellen's drive and let myself in the front door. There is no quiet the way a house is quiet when its family is gone.

I found an empty Ralph's bag in the kitchen and brought it back to the master bath. I packed her green toothbrush in it, along with a bottle of Almay roll-on that was probably hers, and a Personal Touch shaver. I opened the counter drawers and stared into them a while, wondering what she might want. I took out three little white Georgette Klinger face cream jars, two lip gloss tubes, a marbled plastic box of Clinique blush, a Clinique eye liner pencil, and two silver tins of Clinique eye shadow, and put them in the bag. You never can tell. Out in the bedroom, I selected panties, bras, a pair of white New Balance running shoes, three light tops, two pairs of cotton pants, and one pair of Jordache jeans. Mort's insurance policy was in the same box where I had found his banking papers. He had purchased a $200,000 policy three years before but had borrowed against past premiums. Its current value was written down to $40,000. Not a lot, but she wasn't broke. She'd have to plan. I put the policy back in the box and went through the room for Mort's .32. Nothing. I went through the living room, the dining room, the kitchen. Nothing. I went through the kids' rooms. Zip.

At twenty minutes after eight I parked beside the North Hollywood station house and went up to the detectives' squad room. Poitras was standing by a desk, talking to Griggs in a low voice. Griggs was sipping coffee from a mug that said #1 DADDY and nodding. When Poitras saw me he said something else to Griggs, then jerked his head back toward his office. He didn't look happy. 'Come on,' he said.

'Top of the morning to you, too, Louis.'

A thin blond man sat in the hard chair in Poitras' office. He wore brown slacks and brand-new tan Bally loafers with little tassels and a brown coarse-knit jacket with patches on the elbows. He had a dark beige shirt and a yellow tie with little white camels. Silk. He glowed the way skinny guys glow when they get up early and play three sets at the club. I made him for Stanford Law. Poitras dropped into his chair behind the desk and said, 'This is O'Bannon.' When Poitras looked at O'Bannon his flat face hardened and his eyes ticked. 'From Special Operations.'

O'Bannon didn't offer to shake my hand. He said, 'From the California Attorney General's office, attached to Spec Op.'

Spec Op. Stanford Law, all right. 'You say that to girls when you try to pick'm up?' I said.

O'Bannon smiled the way a fish smiles when it's been on ice all day. 'No, only to smart guys who've been tagged for two bodies up in Beachwood Canyon. You want to push it?'

They make'm tough up at Stanford.

'I thought not. Tell me about your encounter with Duran.'

I started at the beginning, when Ellen Lang and Janet Simon came to my office. O'Bannon stopped me. 'Poitras filled me in on the background. Just tell me about your contact with Domingo Duran.'

I started again. I told him how the Eskimo and Manolo picked me up in my office and brought me out to the bull ranch, and I told him what happened out there. Listening to myself describe Duran and reconstruct the dialogue and sequence of events, I came out sounding pretty good. It's easy to sound good. All you do is leave in the parts where you act tough and forget the parts where you get shoved around. At one point we got up and went out into the squad room where they have a big map of L.A. and the surrounding counties so I could ballpark the ranch. O'Bannon wrote down everything I said. He reminded me of Jimmy Olsen, only nastier.

When I finished, O'Bannon stared at me like I was the biggest disappointment of his life. 'That it?'

'I could make up more if you want.'

'Did the Lang woman have any direct contact with Duran?'

'The Lang woman's name is Ellen, or Ms. Lang.'

O'Bannon gave me you're-wasting-my-time eyes. I get those a lot.

'No, no direct contact.'

He folded his note pad and put it in his inside jacket pocket, unconcerned that it might ruin the line. Daring, he was. Gotta be daring for Spec Op. He said, 'All right. We may need to talk to her later.'

I looked at Lou. 'Later?'

O'Bannon nodded. 'There a problem with that?'

'I figured maybe we could do a little better than later. You know, with her son missing and all.'

O'Bannon pulled a brown briefcase from beside the hard chair. 'There's no "we." This is a Spec Op case now. You're out. We're handling the investigation.'

Poitras' jaw worked and he picked at something invisible on his desk. He said, carefully, 'Somebody downtown decided Special Operations was better suited to cover Duran.'

'What the hell does that mean?'

His voice came out ugly. 'What the hell does it sound like, Elvis? You took an IQ reducer since last night? We're out. You're out. That's the end of it.'

I said, 'O'Bannon, there's a nine-year-old kid out there. You don't need a goddamned investigation. I'm handing you the scam and the setup and the bust.'

O'Bannon took a manila file folder off the end of Poitras' desk, put it in his briefcase, snapped the brass latches. It was a Gucci case. He hefted it, then turned and looked at me the way prosecutors look at jurors when they're showing off. 'Spec Op will handle it, Cole. You're out. You're not to approach Duran, nor to proceed with this in any way. He's off limits. You go near him, I'll yank your license for violating the Private Investigators Act of California. You got that?'

'I'll bet you can't get it up, can you, O'Bannon?'

He tried to give me the sort of glare he'd seen fighters give on TV. Then he walked out.

The big redheaded secretary was talking to Griggs down by the rec room door. She watched O'Bannon pass and shook her head. I didn't move for a very long time and neither did Poitras. Then I got up, carefully shut Poitras' door, and went back to my chair. 'Who shut it off, Lou?' I said, softly.

'It ain't been shut off. Other people are handling it, that's all.'

'Bullshit.'

Poitras' eyes were small and hard. Kielbasa fingers worked against each other with no purpose. Someone knocked at the door. Poitras went red. He yelled, 'Beat it!'

The door opened anyway and Griggs came in. He closed the door behind him and leaned against it, arms crossed. Only a couple of hours into the morning and he already looked rumpled and tired.

I said, 'It's still kidnapping, Lou. You can pass it to the feds.'

Griggs said quietly, 'You know the rules, bo. You pass it up the line, up the line has to refer it.'

'Did Baishe bring them in?'

'Goddamn it, it wasn't Baishe,' Lou said. 'You got Baishe on the brain. Forget him. He was for it.'

'What do I tell Ellen Lang?'

'Tell her it's a Special Operations bust. Tell her someone from Special Operations might come talk to her.'

'Later.'

'Yeah. Later.'

'Is that what I tell Duran when he calls?'

'You're off Duran. That's the word. You go around Duran, O'Bannon will use those two bodies up Beachwood to grind you up.'

'They grow'm hard up at Stanford Law,' Griggs said. 'Only a hard guy could wear a tie with little white camels like that, right, Lou?'

Lou didn't say anything.

I said, 'This smells like buy-off, Lou. Like Duran picked up the phone.'

Poitras leaned back in his chair and swiveled to look at the file cabinet. Or maybe he was looking at the pictures of his kids. 'Get the hell out of here, Elvis.'

I got up and went to the door. Griggs gave me sleepy eyes, then peeled himself away from the door and opened it.

I looked back at Lou. 'The cops up in Lancaster happen to find a Walther .32 automatic in Lang's car?'

'How the hell do I know?'

'He had one.'

'Good-bye.'

I walked out. The door closed behind me, and I heard something heavy hit something hard. I kept walking.

The redhead was gone. I walked out past the rec room and the holding cell and into the stairwell. I met Baishe coming up. His face looked softer and older. He stopped me on the stairs. 'I got a prowlcar making extra passes at Duran's place. That's the best I can do.'

We nodded at each other, then he went up to the squad room and I went down and out to my car.

CHAPTER 25

It was already hot out in the parking lot. I pushed down the top on the Corvette, climbed in, and sat thinking about Perry Lang and his mother and how O'Bannon might want to talk to her. Later. That was probably okay with Perry. He was probably having a good time. The Eskimo was probably showing him how to eat seal fat and Manolo was probably giving him piggyback rides and Duran was probably teaching him the correct technique for a *verónica*, with *temple*. Of course, when Duran called and I told him he was now a Spec Op, he'd probably get pissed and stop the lessons. Then it wouldn't be very much fun at all. I took out my wallet, looked at my license for a long time, then folded the wallet again and put it back in my pocket. Screw you, O'Bannon.

I peeled out of the parking lot and laid a strip of Goodyear rubber halfway down the street.

Ten minutes later I was parked across from the Burbank Studios and walking back toward Garrett Rice's office. The backhoe and the bulldozer were tearing up the little parking lot and kicking up a lot of dust that I had to walk through to get to the stairs. Rice's door was closed and locked. I knocked and looked through the glass panel next to the door. The outer office was dark, Rice's inner office darker still. I went to the next office.

The door was propped open, and an almost-pretty blonde in a green LaCoste shirt was fanning herself with a *Daily Variety* behind the desk. She raised her eyebrows at me, something my mother had done quite a bit. I said, 'Has Mr. Rice been in?'

'I don't think so, today. Sheila left about a half hour ago.'

'Sheila the secretary?'

'Unh-huh. You an actor?'

'Look sorta like John Cassavetes, right?'

She stuck her lips out and shook her head. 'No, you just have the look, that's all. I know the look. Hungry.'

'A man is defined by his appetites.'

Her eyes smiled. 'Unh-huh.'

I gave her one of my better smiles and walked loudly back to the stairs, waited a few seconds to see if she'd stir, then eased back to Rice's door, picked the lock, and let myself in.

Nothing much had changed since the last time I was there. The furnishings were still cheap, the dead mouse stain still marked the couch, the plants still clung to life. There were crumbs beneath the couch cushions, along with three pennies, a nickel, two dimes, and a Winston cigarette. The top three drawers of the file cabinet held yellowing scripts and news clippings, and articles and short stories that had been snipped from magazines. The bottom drawer was actors' résumés and correspondence and interoffice memos. More than one of the memos warned Rice against any further evidence of copyright infringement.

Behind the memos there was a mason jar of marijuana, two packs of Zig Zag papers, and three porno magazines. One titled *Lesbian Delight*, another *Women in Pain*, and the last *Little Lovers*. *Little Lovers* was kids.

I took a deep breath and stood up and felt tired. You feel tired a lot in this business.

I shredded *Little Lovers* into a metal waste can and brought the can over to the window looking out at the water tower. There was a book of matches in the top drawer of the desk. I put the can beneath the window and burned away the images of the children and what some animal had made those children do. If Rice walked in, maybe I'd burn him, too.

When I finished with that I went through the rest of the desk. There was no cocaine. No clues to Garrett Rice's whereabouts. No unexpected or surprising evidence. In the middle drawer on the right side of his desk there was a small yellowed envelope postmarked June 1958. It was a handwritten note from Jane Fonda, saying how much she had enjoyed working with Garrett during a recent summer stock production and that Garrett was one of the most professional stage managers it had been her pleasure to meet. It was signed, *Love, Jane*. The edges of the note and the envelope were smudged and gray, as if Rice took it out and read it often.

I went out to the secretary's office and checked her calendar. There weren't any special notes or appointments scheduled for Mr.

136

Rice. There weren't even any unspecial ones. I looked up Garrett Rice in her rolodex and pulled the card. It had his home phone, which I already had, but it also had his home address, which I didn't. I gave him a call, let it ring twenty-two times, then hung up. Maybe he was taking an early lunch.

I called my office and had the answer machine play back the messages. There weren't any. I didn't like that. After last night, the Eskimo should've called. I punched another line and dialed my house.

One ring. 'Pike.'

'There's an address book upstairs on the left side of the phone. I need Cleon Tyner's home number.'

'Wait.'

In a few moments the upstairs extension lifted and Pike gave me the number.

'Ellen okay?' I said.

'She likes to wait on people.'

'It's all she knows how to do.'

'She's cleaning the house. If you came back now, she'd probably wash your car.'

'Have her check the Cherokee. It looked a little dirty on my way out this morning.'

Pike gave me Hard Silence. Then: 'How'd it go with the cops?'

I told him.

'Special Operations,' he said. 'That's shit.'

'Close enough to smell bad.'

'Poitras is good. Poitras won't shit you.'

'Poitras doesn't like it any more than me. Someone up the line yanks the deal from Poitras, this asshole O'Bannon tells me to back away. Nobody knows anything. If it's a buy-out then they're selling the kid to let Duran handle us himself.'

'What's Cleon got to do with this?'

'He was working for Garrett Rice. Only I can't see Cleon on the other side. I can't see him selling muscle to take down a dope deal. You know Cleon.'

'People change.'

'You haven't changed since 1975.'

'Other people.'

I hung up, then dialed Cleon Tyner. A woman with a hoarse bar singer's voice answered.

I said, 'I was trying to get Eartha Kitt for the Sands, but everybody says Betty Tyner is sexier.'

She laughed. 'Oh? And how would everybody know?'

'Her walk, her talk –'

'The way she crawls on her belly like a reptile?'

I said, 'Now you're embarrassing me.'

She laughed louder, the strong healthy laugh of a woman at ease with herself. We spent a few minutes bringing each other up to date and trading friendly insults before she said, 'Well, since you ain't asked me to marry you yet, I'll bet you're calling for that shiftless brother of mine.'

'Amazing. The woman not only is fantastic in bed, but she mind-reads, too.'

'How you think I got to be so fantastic?'

'Practice?'

She suggested an anatomical impossibility. 'Cleon's working. He ain't been here for a couple of days.'

'He go out of town?'

'I don't know, babe. He just said something about staying with the client. Said the man was walking sideways he was so scared.'

We shot the breeze another few minutes, with me promising to give a call soon, and her saying I'd better, then we hung up. The door in the next office closed, and the blonde secretary walked by, carrying a large blue purse. She didn't glance in and she didn't see me sitting in the dark at Sheila's desk, staring at Garrett Rice's address.

I opened the door enough to see that no one was on the walk, then let myself out and drove to Garrett Rice's house in the hills above the Sunset Strip.

Rice lived in a low-slung white stucco modern on a little cul-de-sac off Sunset Plaza Drive. It was the sort of place that went for half a million plus today, but if you were lucky enough to be working in the sixties it didn't cost you more than eighty or ninety thou. I drove into the cul-de-sac, circled, then parked at the curb in front of Rice's house. Each house was set back enough to have some sort of gate and some sort of motor court and some sort of lush greenery, mostly ivy and banana trees and giant ferns. There were walls between each house and tall skinny cyprus so you wouldn't have to see the next guy's roofline, and none of the houses had very much in the way of windows looking out toward the street. Easier to forget the world if you didn't have to see it. They probably gave great block parties, though.

I walked up through the little motor court to Garrett Rice's door. There was a little white form envelope from the LAPD thumb-tacked to the jamb. Inside there would be a little white form note informing (*Mr. Garrett Rice*) that (*officer's name written in*) wished to speak with him and requesting that (*Mr. Garrett Rice*) call (*officer's phone number*) at his earliest opportunity. I had seen these notes before. I wondered if Elliot Ness ever saw them. Probably what killed him.

I rang the bell. No answer. I knocked. Still no answer. Across the street a woman in pink frou frou slippers and a pretentious silver housecoat watched me from her drive as a Yorkie sniffed at the thick ivy in front of their house. I nodded at the woman and smiled. She nodded back but didn't smile. Probably too early to smile. Can't smile when you're still in the housecoat.

There was no car in the motor court, no way to see into the garage, and nothing parked on the street but my Vette. Cleon drove a black '83 Trans Am. I didn't know what Garrett Rice drove. I went back to my car, climbed in, and thought about it.

Poitras said the cops had tried to see Rice two days ago. That meant the little call-back note had been posted for two days and Rice hadn't seen it. Or maybe he had, but wanted the cops to think he hadn't, and left it there.

Or maybe Garrett Rice, who was so scared he asked Cleon Tyner, not the most social of people, to move in with him, had blown town. That made sense if he had had the dope, and then moved it. Cashed in and ran from Duran. He'd still be scared enough to want a muscle like Cleon along so he could sleep at night. He'd sport for the plane fare and head for parts unknown. Sure. That made sense. But Cleon being part of it, that didn't. Betty had once chased the dragon with a lounge owner from Riverside. Cleon found out when she ended the chase in the Riverside ER. The lounge mysteriously burned. The lounge owner's Caddie mysteriously blew up. The lounge owner himself mysteriously disappeared. Cleon Tyner suffered neither dope nor dopers. So. Dilemma, dilemma.

The woman in the silver lamé housecoat came out into the street and stared at me with her hands on her hips, then pointed at a little sign planted in the ivy by her drive. Every house on the street had one, a little red sign that said *Bel Air Patrol – Armed Response*. I stuck my tongue out at her and crossed my eyes. She gave me the finger and went back into her compound. Another close brush with dangerous, affluent-class life-forms.

I took a deep breath, let it out, and started my car. I was tired of sitting and thinking and getting nowhere. I also didn't want to lose time hassling with a Rent-a-Cop with the kid still out there. I blew the horn as I swung around the cul-de-sac – twice – then drove away.

Scared hell out that Yorkie.

CHAPTER 26

At the bottom of Sunset Plaza I parked behind a gelato place and used the pay phone to call Pat Kyle at General Entertainment and ask her if she'd heard anything more about Mort or Garrett. She asked if she could call me right back. I gave her the number on the pay phone, then hung up, bought a cup of double chocolate banana, and enjoyed the extra butterfat.

The minutes ticked by, slow and heavy. I took small bites of the gelato and thought about the girl behind the counter to keep from thinking about Perry Lang and Ellen Lang and Domingo Duran and a guy named O'Bannon. She caught me staring and stared back. She couldn't have been more than sixteen, pretty despite yellow and black eyeshadow, yellow lip gloss, and yellow and black paint in her hair. The hair was spiked and stood out straight from her head like thick fuzz. The bumblebee look. She had a nice even tan and large breasts and probably two parents who wouldn't think kindly of a thirty-five-year-old man wondering what their baby looked like without clothes.

I said, 'I'm John Cassavetes.'

'Who?'

I said, 'Tell me the truth, do I look more like John Cassavetes or Tony Dow?'

She cocked her head. 'I think you look like Andy Summers, only bigger and more athletic-looking.'

'Nah, I don't look like Andy Summers.'

'I bet you don't even know who Andy Summers is.'

'Useta play lead for The Police.'

She grinned. Her teeth were even and white. 'Yeah,' she said, 'You look like him. Thoughtful and smart and sensitive.'

Maybe if everyone wore yellow and black makeup the world would be a better place. I sat up straighter and was considering marriage when the phone rang. Pat said. 'Sorry. I had someone in the office.'

'It's okay. I fell in love during the wait.'

She made her voice cool. 'Perhaps I should call back later. Give you time to consummate the relationship.'

'It's as consummated as it's going to get. What's the word?'

'I didn't hear anything new about Mort, but I did confirm those rumors about Garrett Rice. He's a glad-hander with the weasel dust. He gets invited to parties because he always brings along a little something and he's willing to share it.'

'Gosh, you mean what I hear about those Hollywood parties is true?'

'No. I mean what you hear about *some* of those Hollywood parties is true.'

'How'd you confirm it?'

'Friend of a friend at another studio. Someone who is very much involved in that world and who knew firsthand.'

I said, 'Patricia, if I had two kilograms of pure cocaine that I wanted to sell and I was around the studios like Garrett Rice who would I call?'

She laughed. 'You're talking to the wrong person, Elvis. I'm into health and the perfect body.'

'Would your friend of a friend know?'

'I can't tell you her name.'

'Would you ask for me?'

She sighed. 'I don't know. She might be scared.'

'It's important, kid.'

She said okay, then hung up. I went back to my seat at the table and looked at the counter girl some more. She said, 'What's going on?'

I said, 'Can you keep a secret?'

'Sure.'

'A mobster from Mexico is holding a little kid ransom for two keys of cocaine. I'm trying to get the cocaine back so I can trade it for the kid and maybe nail the mobster at the same time.'

She laughed. 'What bullshit,' she said.

'No bullshit. I'm a private detective.'

'Yeah.'

'Wanna see my gun?'

She put her hands behind her and gave me a look. 'I know what you want to show me.'

Such cynicism. Two women who were probably Persian walked in and the counter girl went over to them. The phone rang and I picked it up. Pat said, 'My reputation may be ruined. I was just invited to a freebasing party.'

'You get a name?'

'Barry Fein. He's probably the guy Garrett dealt with.'

I thanked her, hung up, and called the North Hollywood PD. The same tired voice said, 'Detectives.'

'Lou Poitras, please.'

'He ain't here.'

'How about Griggs?'

There was a pause, then Griggs came on. 'Griggs.'

'It's Cole. You guys got anything on a guy named Barry Fein?'

'You got some nut, you know that. We don't run a goddamned library service here.'

'Considering what I saw this morning, it ain't much of a cop house, either.'

He hung up. I took a deep breath, let it out, called back. A different bored voice answered this time, 'North Hollywood Detectives.'

'Let me have Griggs, please.'

'Hold on.'

A minute, then Griggs picked up. 'Griggs.'

'I'm sorry,' I said. 'I shouldn't have said that. It was dumb, and I apologize. I know you guys don't like it any more than I did, and I know it's tougher for you than it is for me.'

'You're fuckin'-A right it is, bubba. Lou's downtown raising hell right now, goddamnit. Even Baishe is down there, that sonofabitch. So we don't need any bullshit from you.'

'Can you give me an address on Fein?'

'Hold on.'

While I waited, the counter girl gave one cup of something light-colored to one of the women and a cup of something so brown it was almost black to the other. They took their gelato to a little table at the front of the shop and spoke to each other in Farsi. Two men entered, one wearing a conservative gray Brooks Brothers, the other something resembling a pale orange pressure suit. The spaceman looked intense, and snapped his fingers at the girl. I didn't like that.

Griggs came back on the line. 'Fein's a goddamned dope dealer.'

'Yeah.'

'You're supposed to stay the hell away from this Duran thing.'
'I know.'

I could hear him breathing into the phone. In the background, I could hear other cops talking and phones ringing and typewriters tapping and a deep, coarse laugh. Cop sounds. The sort of sounds Griggs would miss if he had to stop hearing them. Griggs said, 'Try 11001 Wilshire, Suite 601. That's in Westwood.'

'Thanks.'

'Cole, the wrong people find out I gave you this, it's my badge.'

'Gave me what?'

Griggs said, 'Yeah' and hung up.

The counter girl was holding a cup in one hand and a scoop in the other, waiting for the guy in the pressure suit to make up his mind. He kept asking to taste the different flavors, then making a big deal about a place in Santa Monica that made this place look like shit. The two Persian women glanced at him.

The counter girl put down her scoop, looked my way, and chewed her fingernail. I hung up, walked over, smiled at the counter girl, and said, 'The double chocolate banana was excellent, thank you.' Then I turned to Captain New Wave. I was very close to him. 'Do you dance?' Smiling.

He had a healthy tan and coarse black hair and a gold Patek Philippe watch. There'd be the health club and handball and somewhere along the way he would've taken judo and been pretty good at it. His eyes flicked to the guy he'd come in with, wondering, what the hell is this?

'Not with boys,' he said. Tough, but uncertain. In over his head and just beginning to realize it. He had walked through a door and now he was in something and it could go in any direction, and in any direction he'd lose.

I put my hand in the small of his back and pulled him close. He should've stepped back sooner, but he hadn't because he was tough. Now he couldn't. One of the Persian women stood up.

'Try the double chocolate banana,' I said softly.

He wet his lips, again glancing at the man he'd entered with. The man hadn't moved. I pulled him tighter, letting him feel the gun.

'The double chocolate banana,' I said.

'The double chocolate banana.'

'To her.'

'Chocolate banana.' To her.

'Please.'

'Please.' To her.

'Good. You'll like it.'

I let him go. He started to say something, wet his lips again, then stepped back.

The counter girl was frozen with wide bumblebee eyes. More scared now than when it started. Some days, you can't win.

'I'm sorry,' I said. 'It's been hell the past few days.'

She nodded and gave me a shy, quiet smile, more young girl than grown-up woman, which is the way it should be when you're sixteen. Everything's gonna be okay, the smile said.

I leaned over the counter and put one of my cards by the cash register.

'If anyone ever bothers you,' I said, shooting a glance at the guy in the spacesuit, 'let me know.'

I walked out the door, went to my car, and drove west along Sunset toward Westwood and Barry Fein.

CHAPTER 27

11001 Wilshire is a nine-story high-rise done up quite nicely in gray and white and glass, what the big ads in the real-estate section of the *Times* call 'a luxury address.' There is a circular drive of gray cobblestone running up beneath a tremendous white and gray awning to the large glass lobby and two waiting doormen. A Rolls and a Jaguar were parked by the glass doors. In the lobby was a security officer behind an elaborately paneled security station who probably took great pride in collecting the mail and calling the elevator and giving the arm to peepers and process servers and similar social debris. It was not a place where you could go to a call box, press a lot of buttons, and count on someone buzzing you in.

I turned up one of the little side streets that ran north through a pleasant residential section, parked by a sign that said Permit Parking Only, and walked back to the high-rise. On the east side of 11001 there was a parking garage with a card key gate leading down, elegantly landscaped with poplar saplings and California poppies. I sat on the ground by the poplars. It was getting hotter, but the smog was manageable. After about ten minutes, the gate groaned to life, folded up into the roof of the building, and a long forest green Cadillac nosed out onto the street. By the time the gate closed, I was in the garage.

There were two cars parked in the slot for 601, a powder blue Porsche 928 and a steel DeLorean. Barry Fein was home. I looked for the elevator and found it on the other side of the garage, but it was one of those security jobs that didn't have buttons down in the garage, just another card key slot. There would be stairs, but the stairs would go up to the lobby and the guards and I wasn't ready for them yet. I went back to the gate, pressed the service switch, and let myself out.

It was a six-block walk to Westwood Village along elm-shaded sidewalks.

If you ignore the surroundings, Westwood Village could be the center of a college town in Iowa or Massachusetts or Alabama. Lots of fast food vendors, restaurants, collegiate clothing stores, bookshops, art galleries, record stores. Lots of pretty girls. Lots of young guys with muscles who thought playing high school football and being able to lift 200 pounds made them memorable. Lots of bicycles. In a drugstore next to a falafel stand I bought a box of envelopes, a roll of fiber wrapping tape, a stamper that said PRIORITY, an ink pad, and a Bic pen. On the way out I spotted a little sheet of stick-on labels that said things like HANDLE WITH CARE. I bought that, too.

Back at the car I tore an old McDonald's Happy Meal box into strips, put it in an envelope, sealed it, and wrote *Mr. Barry Fein* on the front. I put the wrapping tape along all four edges, then across the flap on the back, making sure to keep the fiber bands even. Even in crime, neatness counts. I stamped PRIORITY twice on the front and twice more on the back, then put a sticker that said DO NOT BEND where you normally put the stamp. I looked at it. Not bad. I bent it twice, then put it on the ground and stepped on it hard. Better.

I walked back to 11001 Wilshire and went in to the guard at the reception desk. 'Got something here for Mr. Barry Fein,' I said.

The guard looked at me like I was somebody else's bad breath and held out a hand. 'I'll take it.' He'd crossed the line into his fifties a couple years back. He had a broad face and a thick nose that had been broken more than once, and eyes that stayed with you. Ex-cop.

I shook my head. 'Unh-unh. Hand delivery.'

'Hand deliveries are made to me.'

'Not this one.' I waved the envelope under his nose. 'My ass is in the grinder as it is. Guy tells me, get this to Mr. Fein and be careful with it, right? Like a dope I drop it and some asshole kicks it and the wind picks it up and I gotta chase it half across Westwood against the traffic.'

He was impressed. 'This is as far as you go.'

I put the letter in my pocket. 'Okay, you're a hard ass and you don't give a shit if I get chewed. Call Fein. Tell him it's from Mr. Garrett Rice. Tell him that even though he wants this you've decided that he shouldn't have it.'

The guard's eyes never moved.

I said, 'Look, Sarge, either you call Mr. Fein now or Mr. Rice is gonna call him when I bring this thing back, and then my ass won't be the only one in the grinder.'

We stared at each other. After a while his mouth tightened and he picked up the phone and pressed three buttons. One of the doormen had come inside and was looking at us. The guard put down the phone and scowled at me, not liking it that I'd showed him up.

He said, 'You think I'm letting you upstairs with the piece, forget it.'

He was good. The way I'm built, most people never see the gun under the light jacket I wear. I grinned and spread the jacket. He reached across, fingered it out, and put it under his desk. 'It'll be here when you come down,' he said.

'Sure.'

'When you get out of the elevator, turn right, then right again.'

I took the elevator up to six, got out into the H-shaped hall, turned right, then right again by a little gold sign that said 601 & 603». Blue-gray carpet, white walls, cream light fixtures, Italian moderne artwork. It was so hushed and so clean and so sterile, I wondered if people really lived there. Maybe just androids, or people so old they stayed in bed all day and fed from tubes. I thought of Keir Dullea as an old man in *2001*.

At the end of the hall a blond man stood in the door to 601 waiting for me. He was blond the way straw blonds are blond, so light it was almost white. He wore a white LaCoste shirt and white slacks and white deck shoes, all of which made his dark tan look even darker. On the young side, maybe 24, with a boyish face, and built the way you're built when you lift for strength rather than bulk. Like Pike. Unlike Pike, he was short, not over five-eight.

'Mr. Fein?' I said.

'I'm Charles. Are you from Mr. Rice?' His voice was higher pitched than you would've guessed, and soft, like a sensitive fourteen-year-old's. Five-eight was short for this kind of work.

'Yeah. I'm supposed to give this to Mr. Fein.'

Charles took the envelope, opened the door, and stepped to the side to let me in. The first two knuckles of each hand were large and swollen, the way they get doing push-ups on them and pounding sacks of rice and breaking boards. Maybe five-eight wasn't so much of a problem for him.

148

We went through a blue-tiled entry, down two steps, and into a room not quite the size of Pauley Pavillion. It was very bright, the outer wall all glass and opening out on a balcony lush with greenery. The glass was open and, very faintly, you could hear the cars below like a whisper. The place was done in pastels: gray and blue and raspberry and white. The tile gave way to carpets, and ultramodern Italian furniture sprouted up out of the carpet. Barry Fein was sipping cognac at a hammered-copper bar. The copper clashed horribly with the pastels. So did Barry. He was short and skinny and dark, with close-to-the-skull hair and furry arms and furry, bandy legs. He was wearing red plaid Bermuda shorts and a dark blue tee shirt that said *RKO Pictures*. There was a hole in the shirt on his left shoulder. He was barefoot.

He said, 'You the guy from Gary?' Charles gave him the envelope.

'Indiana?'

He looked at me, cocking his head. 'Garrett Rice, stupid. Gary. Jesus fuckin' Christ.'

'Well, not really.'

'Whattaya mean, not really?' He finished the cognac, then refilled the snifter from a bottle of Courvoisier. There was a hard pack of Marlboros and a heavy Zippo lighter beside the bottle and a large marble ashtray filled with butts. Maybe I could introduce him to Janet Simon and they could have a smoke-off.

Barry Fein opened the envelope and looked in and saw Ronald McDonald. 'What the fuck is this?'

I said, 'Can I get my wallet out and show you something?'

Charles put his fists on his hips and stared at me thoughtlessly. Barry said, 'Aw, shit, you ain't a cop, are you?'

'Unh-unh.' I got out my wallet, went over to the bar, and showed him my license. 'It's very important that I find out if Garrett Rice has tried to sell you two kilograms of cocaine.'

Barry grinned at me and looked at Charles. 'Is this guy serious or what?'

Charles smiled benignly. Perhaps repartée was beyond him.

I said, 'Listen to me. I'm sorry I used a ruse to get up here, but I didn't think you'd see me if I played it straight. I'm not here to bring you trouble. Garrett Rice may have stolen two kilograms of lab-quality cocaine from a very bad man. Now that man wants it back and he's holding a little boy hostage. I think if Garrett stole the dope he'll try to move it. You're a guy he might move it through.'

Barry Fein shrugged and jerked his head at Charles. 'Get rid of'm.'

I looked at Charles. 'I'm in a rush here, Barry. He won't be able to do it.'

Barry shrugged again. Charles whistled sharply between his teeth, and a moment later another Charles walked in from the balcony with a watering can. Five-eight, blond, muscled, white shirt and pants and shoes. Twins all the way down to the big knuckles.

Barry said, 'Jonathan, we got some trouble here.'

Jonathan set the watering can down and came over to stand a little in front of me, Charles a little behind. They stood with their feet spread for balance and their hands loose at their sides. Jonathan had the same perfect skin and vacant eyes as Charles. Idiot angels. The two of them reminded me of the kids down in Westwood who thought they were tough. Only these guys weren't down in Westwood. And they probably were tough.

'Attractive, Barry,' I said. 'Bet they're great in bed, too.'

Charles said, 'It's time to leave,' and stepped in to take my arm. I threw Barry's snifter of Courvoisier on Charles. Jonathan hit me hard twice, not as hard as he should've because I was moving, but hard enough to hurt. I shoved Barry off his stool, making Jonathan hop back to keep from getting bowled over. Charles was coming at me sideways and planting for a spin kick when I grabbed the big Zippo and set him on fire. The Courvoisier went off with a blue alcohol whoosh. Charles screamed and slapped at his face and dropped to the carpet. Jonathan yelled, 'Hey!' and forgot about me. He tried to turn Charles onto his belly to smother the flames. I broke one of the barstools across Jonathan's back. He was tough. He tried to get up, tears leaking down along his nose, then fell over and moaned.

Barry was down on his hands and knees where he'd fallen, staring at me, saying, 'Jesus fuckin' Christ' over and over. I grabbed his hair and pulled him up. He said, 'Jesus fuckin' Christ.'

I shook him. 'You think I'm playing with you, Barry? Tell me about Rice.'

Barry looked at me with eyes like pissholes in fresh snow and tried to scramble away. I slapped him. 'Stand still!'

'Jesus fuckin' Christ, you set the sonofabitch on fire.'

'What about Rice?'

'No, no. I ain't heard from Rice in a couple of weeks.'

'He hasn't tried to sell any dope to you?'

'I swear to Christ.'

'He ask you where he could?'

'No. No.' He looked over my shoulder at Charles, then at me, then back to Charles again. 'Jesus fuckin' Christ.'

I shook him again. 'Your card key.'

'What?'

'Your card key. What you use to open the gate downstairs. Give it to me.'

We went to the near end of the bar and took the card key out of a brass tray where it sat with keys and change and a black alligator wallet.

I said, 'Rice had two keys of lab-quality cocaine. Not all that common, so if he tried to shop it around, people would remember. Ask around. I'm going to come back here tomorrow, and you're going to have something for me. Right, Barry?'

'Jesus fuckin' Christ.'

I bent down and checked Charles. His shirtfront was browned and his hair was singed and he was starting to blister in a couple of spots, but that was about it. Cognac burns off fast. His eye flickered open and he looked at me. His lashes were gone.

'You've got to be a lot better than you are to get away with a spin kick, Charles. They look great on the mat, but in real life they take too long.'

I stood up.

'Remember this, Barry,' I said. 'Don't fuck with the Human Torch.'

Barry said, 'Jesus fuckin' Christ.'

I went back along the hall, down the elevator, and collected my gun from the guard, who nodded and told me to have a nice day.

CHAPTER 28

Until I heard from Barry Fein, there weren't a whole lot of options left for me to pursue. I could go back to my house and brood about things there. I could cover ground I had already been over and brood. Or I could go to my office and brood, and maybe be there when the Eskimo or Duran called. I drove to my office.

The fourth-floor hall was empty. Office doors were closed the way they always were; none was cracked open, no one peeked out of the broom closet. I went down the hall as quietly as I could, not even making the little shushing sound shoes will make on carpet. I took my gun out, held it down along my thigh, and keyed the office lock with my left hand. Wouldn't this be a sight for the insurance secretaries across the hall. *Oh, look, Elvis is scared someone's going to shoot him again!* When the knob turned I pushed open the door and went in low. No one shot me. No one was pressed along the ceiling, waiting to drop down. The Eskimo wasn't crouching under the desk. Safe again.

There was one call on the answering machine. The auto parts clerk, telling me that if I didn't want the shifter skirt he knew plenty of guys who did. I turned off the machine, opened the balcony doors, and sat at my desk to wait. Sooner or later Duran would call or send the Eskimo. He'd have to. He lost two men last night and the woman and he wouldn't like it. Maybe Poitras was right and he'd like it so little he'd just say *aw fuck it* and send somebody to blow me away. Or maybe he'd just say, *Give me the dope* now *or I'll kill the kid.* Then what would I do?

The air was warm and moist and a small breeze was blowing in from the south. Down the coastline, toward San Pedro and Newport Beach, there were a couple of dark cumulus out over the water. Looking at them, I smiled. Where I grew up, there was much rain of the beating, pounding, falling-in-sheets variety that Southern California almost never enjoys. I missed it. Rain was a Good Thing. If there were more rain, there would be less smog.

I took out the Dan Wesson, checked the load, then laid it on the desk. If the Eskimo came in, maybe he'd think it was one of those fancy office lighters and ignore it.

I settled in and I waited.

Three hours later the phone rang. 'Elvis Cole Detective Agency, we find more for less. Check our prices.'

The Eskimo said, 'You made a very bad mistake, Mr. Cole.'

'Would it help to say I'm sorry?'

He said, 'We know the woman is at your home and we know a man wearing a sidearm is staying with her. Mr. Duran trusted that you would do as you were told, but you didn't.'

'That couldn't be helped.'

'We still have what we have.'

'I know that.'

'Mr. Duran still wants his property. Go home now.'

He hung up. No mention of a trade, no demand for an explanation. I called the house. Pike answered on the second ring.

I said, 'I just heard from the Eskimo. They know Ellen's at the house and they know you're with her.'

There was a pause. 'Spotter. They could have found out your address, then put someone up the hill or in an empty house across the canyon.'

'Better keep her away from the windows and the deck.'

'No reason. Guy with the right weapon could have taken us any time he wanted. I get into that with her, we'll have to pull all the drapes and lock her in the bathroom. Be worse for her.'

'The Eskimo told me to go home. He's got to have a reason for wanting me there.'

Pike grunted. 'Maybe pulling the drapes isn't so bad an idea after all.'

'Do it without alarming her.'

'Unh-huh.'

'We need anything?'

'Unh-unh.'

'I'm coming in.'

When I got to the house, the drapes were pulled across the sliding glass doors and Pike was making dinner. Ellen was wearing her cleaned Ralph's clothes and was standing by the counter, watching him cook. She looked uncomfortable, probably because he was in the kitchen and she wasn't. I put the bag of her fresh clothes and makeup on the stairs.

'What's for dinner, girls?' Mr. Nonchalance.

Pike said, 'Red beans and rice, ham hocks, cornbread.' He was still wearing the sunglasses and the gun.

'He wouldn't let me help.' Ellen took a sip of iced scotch from a short glass. The glass was sitting in a puddle of condensation. She'd probably been taking little sips all day. Just enough to keep things manageable.

I nodded. 'He's very territorial about his kitchen.'

I pushed under the drapes, opened the glass doors, then reclosed the drapes. I opened the little jalousie window off the powder room, then the kitchen window.

'Good idea,' Pike said. 'It was getting stuffy.' It would be easier to hear with the glass open.

Ellen said, 'Janet called.'

'Delightful.'

'She was worried.'

I leaned against the powder room doorjamb. The powder room window opened on the front of the house. If anyone came, they'd have to come from the front. The downslope off the back of the house is too steep for any sort of assault.

Ellen sipped the scotch. 'She wanted to put the girls on. I said no. I didn't know what to say. I don't think I could talk to them without crying.'

I nodded, listening but not listening, straining to hear outside. Ellen didn't notice.

'Janet said they need me to be strong now, and I don't know if I can. I'm thirty-nine years old. I don't want to be weak. I don't want to be scared.'

'Then don't be,' Pike said.

Ellen and I both looked at him. He used the flat of a heavy knife to push diced onion into a small bowl. He covered the bowl with Saran Wrap.

'Don't be,' she repeated.

'This Janet your friend?' Pike said.

'Of course.'

Pike shook his head and put the bowl in the ice box.

The phone rang. I picked it up.

154

A thick voice with a heavy Mexican accent said, 'The boy wants to speak with his mother.'

'Who is this?'

'Put on the mother.'

I motioned Ellen over, raising a finger to make her pause as I ran to pick up the living-room extension. She looked confused. When I had the phone I mouthed, 'Perry.'

She blurted, 'Perry?' into the phone as Pike moved to stand by her, watching me.

The harsh voice said, 'Listen.'

There was a thump on the line, then a scuffling, whimpering sound, then a long, piercing little-boy shriek that made a clammy sweat leak out over my face and chest and back. Ellen Lang screamed. Pike jerked the phone away from her. She screamed '*No!*' and slapped at him, clawing to get the receiver back. He pulled her close, holding her tight against him. She hit and clawed and made a deep-in-the-throat gargling sound and got the edge of his hand in her mouth and bit until blood spouted down along her chin and wrist and onto Pike's shirt. He didn't pull away.

I shouted something into the phone.

The shrieking didn't stop, but the voice came back on. It said, 'You won't fuck up again.'

I said, 'No.'

'The boy is alive. You can hear him.'

'Yes.' I felt like I was going to choke.

'We call you again.'

I looked at Pike over the dead connection.

CHAPTER 29

Ellen thrashed and cried and finally grew still, but even then her pain was a physical presence in the room.

Pike went into the little bathroom, stayed a few minutes, then came out with gauze taped to his hand and his skin orange from Merthiolate. Ellen squeezed her eyes shut when she saw his hand.

Pike said, 'Do you have any Valium or Darvon for her?'

I told him no. He slipped out the kitchen door. I poured more scotch and brought it to her. She shook her head. 'I've been drinking all day.'

'Sure?'

She nodded.

'Want a hug?'

She nodded again, and sighed deeply as I held her. After a while she said, 'I want to wash.'

She took the bag of clothes upstairs, and in a few minutes the water began to run. I turned on the evening news with Jess Marlowe and Sandy Hill, Sandy talked about Navy spies in San Diego. Not particularly relevant to Perry Lang unless Duran was smuggling state secrets to the Russkies. But in L.A., anything is possible. The water ran for a long time.

When Ellen came back downstairs she was wearing some of the clothes I'd brought and the white New Balance. Her face looked clean and blank, less vulnerable than at any time since I'd met her. She said something that surprised me. She said, 'God, I could use a cigarette.'

I couldn't see her having ever smoked. 'When Joe gets back, I'll get you some.'

She nodded slightly, then shook her head. 'No.' She stood next to the TV and crossed her arms. I couldn't tell if she was looking at me or past me. 'I quit almost six years ago. I just stopped. Janet says she goes crazy after about a day, but when I wanted to stop, I just stopped.'

'Tough to do.'

She said, 'What did the police say?'

I thought about lying, but couldn't think of anything good enough to explain why the cops weren't here or we weren't there, so I said, 'It's a Special Operations case now.'

'What does that mean?'

'It means the case was taken away from Poitras to be handled by some hotshots downtown.'

'What are they doing?'

'I don't know. They shut Poitras and me out. They said they might come out to talk to you.'

'When?'

'Later.'

She looked at me calmly. She said, 'But what are they doing about . . . all of this?' She gestured around her.

'I spoke with Joe this morning. Did he tell you anything that happened when I went to the cops?'

She shook her head, so I told her. When I was done she asked if she could have a glass of water. When I came back with it she looked just as she'd looked when I left. As if the idea that somebody on the police force could cave in to political pressure was an everyday and undisturbing event.

She said, 'Sergeant Poitras goes along with this?'

'He has to. But he doesn't like it, and he's fighting it. He and his lieutenant were downtown this afternoon, trying to find out who's damming the works.'

She said, 'Unh-huh,' and drank the water. When the glass was empty she said, 'My older daughter, Cindy, she hates me. She screams that if I were a better wife, her father would be happier.' She said it as if she were telling me she preferred tan shoes to cordovan.

'She's wrong.'

'I tried being the best wife I could.'

'I know.'

'I tried.'

'There's some insurance,' I said. 'Not a lot. But some.'

She didn't ask how much.

I sipped some of the scotch I'd poured for her. I said, 'Look, I'll find the dope or where the dope went and who has it and we'll work something out with Duran. Then we'll bring Poitras in and put it in his lap, and this will end.'

'But that man, O'Bannon, he said you were supposed to stay away.'

I shrugged.

She nodded and turned away and looked at the books and the figurines and the photos and the dark steel knight's heraldry that line my shelves. A girlfriend who was a pretty good carpenter built the shelves for me from unfinished redwood. A place for me to keep my junk, she said. The TV sat at about eye level, the stereo beneath it, my books and mementos and treasures on either side. The latex Frankenstein mask was on a Styrofoam head. My junk. Out from the canyon, we could hear the first faint yelps of the coyotes, gearing up for a sing.

I drank more of the scotch but found it sour. I took the glass into the kitchen, threw out the booze, and went back into the living room with a can of pineapple juice.

'Mr. Pike says you read these same books over and over,' Ellen said.

'That's true.'

She touched different volumes. 'I know some of these. I read the histories of King Arthur when I was in college. I worked as a teacher's aide. I read them to the children when the teachers went on break.'

'I'll bet you enjoyed that.'

'Yes.' Ellen turned to me from the books. 'Was Mr. Pike really a policeman?'

I was impressed. 'He must like you. I've never known him to tell that to anyone.'

'Then he was.'

'For a while. Pike will never lie to you. You don't have to doubt anything he says.'

'He says he's a professional soldier.'

'He has a gun shop in Culver City. He owns the agency with me. But sometimes he goes to places like El Salvador or Botswana or the Sudan. So I guess that makes him a part-time professional soldier.'

'Was he in Vietnam with you?'

'Not with me. He was in the Marines. We didn't meet until after we'd mustered out and were back here in L.A. Pike was riding in a black-and-white. I was working with George Feider. We met on the job. When Pike and the cops parted company, I made the offer.'

'He told me he wasn't a successful policeman.'

'He wasn't successful, but he was outstanding. Pike and some of the cops he worked with had what we might call a grave philosophical difference. Guy like Pike, philosophy is all. He rode a black-and-white for three years and for three years he was outstanding. Even splendid. He just wasn't successful.'

'He likes you quite a bit.'

'That's the Marine. Marines are all fairies at heart.'

'Did he get those tattoos in Vietnam?'

'Yeah.'

'What for?'

'Ask him.'

'I did. He said I wouldn't understand.'

'Joe's got a little credo he lives by. Never back up. That's what the arrows on his shoulders are for. They point forward. They keep him from backing up.'

She stared at the end of the sofa. 'I understand that.'

I finished the pineapple juice and crushed the can. 'Don't let Joe get to you. Life is very simple to him, but it isn't always the way he'd like it to be. Part of his problem with the cops.'

She nodded but didn't look any less empty.

'Think of a samurai,' I said. 'A warrior who requires order. That's Pike.'

'The arrows.'

'Yeah. The arrows allow him to impose order on chaos. A professional soldier needs that.'

She thought about it. 'And that's what you are?'

'Not me. I'm just a private cop. I am also the antithesis of order.'

'He said you were a better soldier than he. He said you won a lot of decorations in the war.'

'Ha ha, that Pike. You see what a card that guy is? A million laughs.'

'He said you'd deny it.'

'A scream, that guy.'

'He said that everything of any real value that he's learned, he's learned from you.'

'Flip it to channel 11, wouldja?' I said. 'I think *Wheel of Fortune*'s on.'

She stared at me for a very long time. She didn't change the channel. 'I can't be the person I was anymore, can I?'

I gave her gentle eyes. 'No.'

She nodded, but probably not to me. 'All right,' she said. 'I can understand that, too.'

CHAPTER 30

When Joe got back he had a bottle of Dalmane and six Valiums. We put out the red beans and rice and cornbread, and ate. Ellen stared at her plate and said, 'I've never eaten a ham hock before,' so I slit the skin and showed her how to get out the meat.

She ate quietly and completely, finishing what Pike put on her plate. Joe and I drank beer, Ellen had milk. I pointed out a few of the more uproarious ironies of life, but neither Ellen nor Joe showed much in the way of appreciation. I was used to it from Pike.

We finished the meal, did the dishes, then went into the living room. No one said more than five words at a time. I put on a Credence Clearwater album, then went into the entry closet and came back wearing my Groucho Marx nose.

'Appropriate, as always,' Pike said, then went out onto the deck. Ellen smiled once, then looked away. After a while I took off the nose and picked up *Valdez Is Coming*.

I was almost through it when Ellen made a hoarse sighing sound from her end of the couch. When I looked up, her eyes were red and tears dripped down her cheeks. I reached across and touched her leg. She took my fingers and said, 'What did they do to make him scream like that?'

Pike stepped in off the deck. I slid across the couch and held Ellen for a while, until she asked for two of the Dalmane and said she would go up to bed. I went up with her and stood at the foot until the Dalmane had done its work, then I shut the light and went down.

Pike said, 'I like her.'

'You told her you were on the cops.'

'I like her a lot.'

I got two Falstaff from the box. We offed all the lights in the house, turned the stereo low, then went out onto the deck. A couple of cars moved through the canyon roads to the south and east, appearing then disappearing behind the houses that dotted the hillside. The coyotes were quiet.

Pike hung his feet off the deck. I joined him. Just like Tom and Huck.

I said, 'Duran's spotter had a good deer rifle, we'd be history.'

'Maybe.'

We sat. Heavy clouds blocked out the moon and most of the stars. You could smell the coming rain in the air. Springsteen sang about tough kids and broken hearts on KLSX.

I said, 'Remember the other day, when I said Mort had given himself up?'

'Yes.'

'He didn't. She did.'

'I know.'

'She's over the edge right now. Mort, the kid, who she is. She doesn't have as much self-esteem as a piece of bread.' Pike's beer can raised, tilted, lowered. 'I want her to make it back,' I said.

'Unh-huh.'

I took a pull on my Falstaff. 'Does it strike you odd that Duran's giving me so much time to turn over his dope?'

'It does.'

'Like maybe he knows I don't have it, but he's using me to find it for him.'

'Unh-huh.'

'Joe, how the hell can you see at night with the sunglasses?'

'I am one with the night.' Raise, tilt, lower. You never know whether he's serious. 'Duran wants you to find the dope because he doesn't know how. If he tells his people to find something, all they know how to do is rack ass. That doesn't get you very far, and maybe eliminates someone with some important information.'

'It would've been easier to hire me.'

'Maybe.'

'Only maybe I won't hire, and I turn it over to the cops.'

'He probably shit himself, thinking about that one.'

I nodded and sipped the beer and listened to Springsteen's courage flow into Mellencamp's raucous honesty. 'Joseph, what have you learned from me?'

'Good things.'

'Like what?'

He didn't answer. I finished the Falstaff, then crimped the can square and crushed it. 'A guy like Duran, worth a couple hundred million, a hundred K can't be worth the hassle.'

'He's not doing it for the money.'

'That's what I don't like. Maybe we're all just running out of time. Maybe Duran says to hell with it and smokes the kid and the rest of us.'

Pike finished his beer, set the can on the deck. Pike never crushes cans. I guess he's man enough without that. 'Maybe you should find the dope before that happens.'

A big *splat* sounded behind me, then again to my left, then something wet hit my forehead. Joe stood up. 'Good time for a walk.'

He went in through the living room and let himself out the kitchen door, locking it behind. I picked up our cans and went in out of the rain. My father, rest him, would've been proud.

The rain slapped at the deck and ran down along the glass. When I was little, I would sit in my window and watch the rain and feel easy and at peace. I didn't feel that way often anymore, though I kept trying out windows and rainstorms and probably always would.

I turned the stereo off, put on the lamp at the head of the couch, stretched out, and finished *Valdez*. Much later, Pike let himself into the kitchen, moving like a dark shadow across the edges of the lamplight. He put muddy Nikes in the sink, peeled out of his wet shirt and wet pants and went into the little bathroom. 'You up?' A voice in the dark.

'Yeah.'

He came out of the bathroom in jockey shorts with a towel over his shoulders. 'I found the spotters. Two guys in the yellow house ten o'clock east, just up from Nichols Canyon. Asshole in a lawn chair on the back deck, squinting through a pair of field glasses.'

'What about the other guy?'

'Sacked out on a waterbed.'

There was more. 'You took them?'

'Yes.'

Pike sat down on the floor beside the glass doors, his back to the wall. He sat *sukhasen*. Yoga. A sitting pose that allows relaxation. Did Pike do yoga before he met me? I couldn't remember.

I said, 'Your knife?'

'A house contains all sorts of useful appliances, Elvis. You know that.'

'Duran won't like it, Joe. He'll take it out on the kid.'

Joe's eyes were pinpoints of light in the dark. They did not move. 'He won't know what happened, Elvis. No one will. Ever. They're gone. It's like they never were.'

I nodded, and felt cold.

The rain beat down, hammering noisily on the glass and the roof and Pike's Jeep parked out past the front door. I thought about the cat, holed up under a car somewhere. After a while I slept and dreamed about the Eskimo and Perry Lang and my friend Joe Pike. But what I dreamed I did not remember.

CHAPTER 31

The sky was still gray the next morning when I drove back to Garrett Rice's house. All down the mountain, little rivulets of debris and mud veined the roads. Traffic moved quickly, as it always did during the rains, with the Angelenos' innate belief that driving in rain is the same as driving in dry, only wetter.

Maybe Barry Fein would be able to turn a lead on Garrett Rice, but maybe he wouldn't. Maybe Garrett and the dope and Cleon Tyner were long gone. If they were, I had to know. If the dope was gone, I'd have to come up with another way to deal with Domingo Duran. Maybe severe public reprimands.

I left my car on Sunset Plaza and walked up the little cul-de-sac, gun loose in the holster and ready for the housecoated woman and her killer Yorkie.

Everything looked just as it had yesterday, only damp. No sign of Cleon's Trans Am or any other car. No one had moved the letter tacked up by the cops. No lights or sounds came from the house. I walked straight up the drive, across the little motor court, and into the narrow alley alongside Rice's garage as if I knew exactly where I was going and as if the gentleman of the house expected me.

There were three large plastic garbage cans, wet from the rain, with a heavy musty smell, and a chest-high chain-link gate knotted with ivy and bougainvillea. A little Master combo lock secured the latch. I looked back toward the street. Still free from dogs and neighbors and armed response patrols. I hopped the fence, walked the length of the garage, turned right past a pool pump and filter, then out a redwood gate to Garrett Rice's pool deck. The pool was a tasteful oval, small, but still filling most of the backyard. The deck and the patio areas were flagstone. A flagstone retaining wall followed the curve of the pool where Rice's lot had been carved out of the hillside, and the hill angled and rose away up behind the house. Little piles of pebbles and silt were on the back deck where they'd run off the hillside with the rain.

The back of the house was mostly glass, landscaped with ferns and bamboo and something that looked like a mimosa tree. There was a nice, glade-like feel to the place. Secluded. Probably just right for skinny-dipping with starlets and playing grabass.

The musty smell was stronger, the way a dark room in an old house might smell, wet and moldy and slightly sour. I kept trying to put it on the rain. Only it wasn't the rain. Cleon Tyner was face down under a giant fern at the back of Garrett Rice's house.

I slipped out my gun and went up to him, watching the windows and big glass doors. One of the big glass doors was open.

There was no pulse in his neck. His skin was cold and pliable over stiff muscles. He was lying mostly on the right side of his face, the left looking up and back toward the pool. His left eye was open but droopy, and rolled back in his head. I tried to close it but the eyelid wouldn't go down. There were no pools of blood or bullet holes in his back. I tilted him up, saw chest wounds, then lowered him. Cleon had been out here quite a while, out here while I was ringing the front door bell yesterday, out here while the rain came down and churned the ground beneath him to mud. *That Cleon, what a stick-in-the-mud.*

I went into the house. It was damp and cold and wet on the floor where the rain had driven in under the soffit and through the open door. There was a Westec Alarm box just inside the draw drapes. All the lights showed green. It had been turned off.

Garrett Rice was on the kitchen floor beside a cook island. He was naked, and even in death his flesh hung loose and crinkly and pale, his sunlamp tan ending abruptly on his upper chest. There were contusions on his face and dried blood on his mouth and nose, and a single small-caliber bullet hole above his right ear. On the back of his left thigh was an ugly spiral burn the size and shape of the largest burner on the cooktop. There was another burn like it on his stomach. He'd voided himself.

I went back out through the living room to the open glass door, sucked in wet air, then searched what used to be Garrett Rice's house for the dope. It didn't take long, mostly because I knew I wouldn't find anything. If the dope had been here, Garrett Rice would've turned it over long before his clothes were yanked off and he was pressed down onto a red-glowing stovetop.

Perry Lang!

166

I made an anonymous report to the cops, then tore down a shower curtain, took it outside, and covered Cleon Tyner's body. I squatted by him, trying to think of something to say, but all that came to mind were questions. *Sorry, Cleon. I'll check on Betty, time to time.* I went back to my car and drove into Westwood.

By the time I reached 11001, the clouds had broken the way they break when they're going to seal up again. I used Barry Fein's card key to get into his building through the parking garage. The cars were still in his parking slot, only they were reversed, the DeLorean on the inside now, the Porsche behind. I put the Corvette in the No Parking zone in front of the elevators, used the card key again, and rode up to 6.

Jonathan opened the door but didn't step back, playing it tough. He stood a little crooked, as if his back bothered him. I was in the right mood to make it bother him a little more. I said, 'Fuck with me I'll kill you.'

Barry Fein's voice came from inside. 'For Christ's sake, Jonathan. Jesus Christ, in the goddamn hall.'

A little smile broke crookedly on Jonathan's face. He stepped out of the door, lifting his hands to show me they were empty. We went inside, him first.

Barry Fein was fidgeting around the big room. Charles sat on the couch, leaning forward with his forearms on his knees and his hands empty. A large gauze bandage was taped along his left jawline and another smaller gauze patch spotted his left cheek. His neck and the lower half of his face were shiny, as if he were wearing suntan lotion. His eyebrows were gone.

He said, 'One day.'

I ignored him. 'Where'd Rice move the dope, Barry?'

Barry paced. He said, 'Listen, I asked everybody I could think of, right?, where Garrett might try to unload?'

Jonathan moved away from me to sit on the arm of the couch next to Charles. He rubbed Charles's shoulders, then let his hidden hand drift down behind Charles's back. I took out my gun and pointed it at Barry's furry stomach. I said, 'I'll shoot him, Barry. And you, too.'

Barry rubbed at his hair. 'Jesus Christ, Jonathan, would you get outta there. Shit!'

Jonathan went to stand beside the bar. I suggested Charles stand with him, and when he got up you could see the butt of a piece sticking out from behind the cushion. 'Jesus fuckin' Christ, I didn't

167

know!' Barry screamed. He picked up a couch pillow and threw it at them. *'You shits, you shits trying to get me killed!'*

Jonathan and Charles looked sullen and mean, like a couple of fourth-grade psychopaths caught sticking pins into puppies.

I put the gun back on Barry. 'You asked everyone you know,' I reminded him.

He hopped around, rolling his eyes and trying to pick up the thread. Ten in the morning and he was already in another universe. 'Yeah, right. Look, you gotta open your mind, see? I called around. I asked. Everybody I ask, and believe me, I know everybody Garrett Rice would know, they say Garrett ain't called. He ain't been trying to move nothing.'

I shook my head. 'That's not what you're supposed to tell me, Barry. You're supposed to tell me who Rice sold it to and when he made the trade.' I dropped the muzzle down to his crotch, let it circle, raised it back to his eyes.

He squirmed like he had to pee. 'I swear to Christ. I called. I asked. Rice ain't been trying to move *anything.*'

I took short breaths, thinking. Jonathan and Charles glared. Barry hopped up and down. Jesus Christ, what if Garrett Rice hadn't had the dope after all? What if, all along, it had been an inside job, the Eskimo taking down two keys to sock away for his retirement, or one of the Italian guests Kimberly Marsh described. Or a cat burglar, just passing by. I stopped breathing altogether, then took a deep breath using my stomach, held it, then let it out slow. Focus and relax. I put my head on Perry Lang and kept it there; anyplace else and everything starts to fall apart, and maybe Perry and Ellen and the two girls with it.

I said, 'You ask about two kilograms of lab-quality coke, it's going to come up if anyone else has been trying to sell some.'

'Yeah. Sure.'

'Tell me.'

'This guy I know, he says a friend of his wants to sell some. You know, called him up, shopping price.'

'What and when?'

'Key and a half. Said it was 99 percent pure. Said the guy called him three or four days ago, you know, like I said, calling around shopping price.'

'Who's the seller?'

'Guy named Larson Fisk.'

Great. Larson Fisk. 'Who the hell is Larson Fisk?'

Barry looked impatient. 'He's an actor. You probably seen his face a million times. Day player, you know. I sold him some stuff. Come here.'

Barry hopped over to the bar past Jonathan and Charles. He pulled down a thick *Academy Players Directory* from a shelf beside the bar. 'I got lotsa clients in here,' Barry said. 'Shit, I get jokes all the time how I oughta have my own star on Hollywood Boulevard. Maybe one day, eh?'

He showed me Larson Fisk. Sure, I'd seen him before. Larson Fisk was Larry, Kimberly Marsh's boyfriend.

CHAPTER 32

The house above Universal was empty but not abandoned. The little red 914 was gone, but a rumpled shirt lay on the living room floor and a couple of Carl's Junior shake cups sat on the dining room table. Lights burned in a back bathroom. I parked my car out of sight above the house, then came back, picked the front door lock, and let myself in. I walked through the house once, gun out, to see if maybe the cocaine had been left lying out in the open. It hadn't.

I had ripped the rear bedroom apart and was starting on the little bath next to it when I heard car doors slam down below and a woman's laugh, light and lute-like.

Kimberly Marsh and Larson Fisk were climbing the steps. She was in shorts and rumpled cream safari shirt tied off beneath her breasts with the sleeves rolled up, carrying her sandals. Sexy. Fisk was in blue gym trunks, beat-up Adidas running shoes, and a black muscle shirt. He was carrying a bag of groceries in each arm and smiling. She was smiling, too.

I went back to the front of the house, took out my gun, and stepped into the little coat closet behind the front door as their key went into the lock. The front door opened. Kimberly Marsh walked in. Larson Fisk followed her. When they were past me, I shoved open the closet door, took one step, planted my left foot, and kicked Larson Fisk on the outside of his left knee as hard as I could. His left knee was the one with the scars.

There was a wet snap similar to what you hear when you joint a chicken. Larry screamed and fell, dropping the grocery bags to catch himself. Something glass shattered and the near bag turned dark and wet. Oranges and pippin apples rolled out across the floor. One made it all the way into the dining room. Kimberly Marsh gasped sharply, spun around to look at Larry, and saw me. Larry was rocking back and forth on the floor, sometimes gripping his leg, sometimes pounding the floor with his right fist. His face was purple.

He called me a sonofabitch.

I waved my gun at him. 'Come on, Larry. A sonofabitch would've put one behind your ear. Besides, now you can add another scar to your collection.'

He closed his eyes and rocked back, calling me a sonofabitch again, like a mantra, very softly. I shook my head. 'You see,' I said to Kimberly, 'some people are never satisfied.'

She had backed away until the plank shelves were pressing into her back. The big green fish tank with the dead fish was to her right. Why do blondes look good with green?

She didn't appear particularly frightened. She said, 'What are you doing?'

'Removing Larry as an active threat. He may be stupid, but he is strong. And mean.' I smiled at her.

Larry said, 'It *hurts!*'

She was relaxing. Her eyes never went to Larry, but her shoulders dropped just a hair, and her hands went down, and she stopped clenching her teeth. I imagined a window in her forehead, behind it little watchwork wheels and gears, spinning and rocking and making ticking sounds. I smiled wider.

She smiled back. 'Did you find out what happened to Mort?'

'Unh-huh.'

'Thank God. Can I move back to my apartment now?'

'Nah. Not right now. Now, I want you to give me the cocaine.'

Her eyes got a little bigger, and that was it. She just stood there. The gears spun faster. The ticking got louder. I think of the damnedest things.

I wiggled the gun. I stopped smiling. 'Dom wants his dope back, Kimberly.'

Her eyes flicked to Larry, then back. 'I don't know what you're talking about.'

I cocked the gun and I pointed it at Larry. 'She doesn't know, Larry.' Larry was watching the gun and clutching the knee. I said, 'She sees the stuff just sitting around over at Duran's, right? And thinks, boy, wouldn't that be great to have. Only she's got no way to get it out of the house. So she finds a phone and gives you a call and gets you involved. She throws it out the window and tells you where and you sneak over and pick it up. Risky, Larry. That took balls, with all the goons Duran keeps around. You do all that, and here I am pointing a gun at you, and now she doesn't know what I'm talking about.'

She flipped her head to get the blonde hair out of her eyes and smiled at me as if I'd just told her I thought she had sexy toenails. 'That's silly.' She stepped away from the shelves and cocked her head at me, lifting her ribs to pull her abdomen tight and pushing out her hips to the side. Moving on me. Like she'd seen gun molls do in a thousand movies.

I said, 'How about you tell me, Larry? Before I do your other knee.'

Neither of them said anything, but you could hear the breathing.

I said, 'Right now you guys are in a survivable position. If the cops walked in, all they could hang on you is possession with intent to distribute and obstruction of justice. They might push for an accessory to murder charge because of Mort but they wouldn't get it. You give me the dope, then you're no longer possessing. You give me the dope, and even though you're a couple of scumbags, I'll put in a word with the cops.'

Neither of them said anything, but the breathing was louder.

'Okay,' I said, 'let's go back to basics.' I pointed the gun at Larry's good knee. 'It'll be a bone shot, Larry. You'll limp.'

Larry nodded. 'Okay.' His voice cracked.

'Don't tell him.' Kimberly was calm.

'Sure,' I said. 'It's not your knee.'

Kimberly Marsh's eyes got dark. 'This stuff is worth a lot of money,' she said. 'We could share. We could share a lot.'

'What about the boy?'

'What about him?'

Something hot throbbed in my head and I felt my face grow tight. 'No wonder Mort went for you, Kimmie. You're all class.' I toed Larry's bad knee. He went purple again. 'The dope.'

Kimberly yelled, 'No!' then snatched something from the shelves, threw it at me, and plunged her hands into the slimy aquarium. As she did, Larry grabbed my legs. I hit him with the butt of the pistol, but he hung on, digging at my crotch. I hit him again, harder. His forehead split and blood spilled down over his nose and brow. Kimberly pulled what looked like a large brick from the algae and seaweed, and ran back toward the kitchen. Her arms were green from the slime, and the stink of fish was strong. Larry

172

gasped, still trying to pull me down, but his grip was weaker. I hit him twice more, this time over his ear, and he let go.

I stumbled away from him and ran toward the back of the house, around through the dining room, and into the kitchen. Kimberly Marsh was clawing at the back door when I caught her and slapped her as hard as I could. She made an *unh!* sound and dropped the brick. It was about the size of a five-pound sack of Gold Medal flour. Bits of scum and seaweed still clung to it.

She scrambled after it, kicking at me and making grunting noises. There were flecks of saliva on her chin. I lifted her by the arm and hit her again. It was hot in the kitchen. I shook her and hit her once more, hard enough to knock her down. It hadn't been necessary, but then, most things aren't.

On the floor, she started to cry.

I picked up the dope and went back through the house. Larry was where he had fallen, lying on his back, staring at the ceiling. He looked the way pro wrestlers look when they've popped blood capsules all over their faces, only he hurt. He hurt bad.

'She went all the way for you, Lar,' I said slowly. 'Just like she did for Mort.'

Larry's eyes began to leak.

I went out the door and down the steps. He was crying. She was crying. But they weren't crying for the same thing.

CHAPTER 33

I drove to my office, called a woman I know at the phone company, and gave her Domingo Duran's address in Los Feliz. She told me four phone numbers registered to Duran's address. The first one gave me a tentative female voice with a heavy accent. When I asked to speak with Mr. Duran, she didn't seem to understand, then there was a long pause and she hung up. Probably kitchen help.

On the second number a man with a very light accent said, 'Mr. Duran's residence.'

I said, 'This is Elvis Cole, calling for Mr. Duran.'

The voice said pleasantly, 'Mr. Duran is not available at present.'

'He'll talk to me.'

'I'm afraid that's not possible. Mr. Duran is entertaining guests, you see.'

'Tell him it's Cole. Tell him I want to talk about the dope.'

The line went dead. I hung up. Pinocchio's eyes tocked back and forth, the second hand swept his face. I picked up one of the Jiminy Crickets, inspected it, and blew off dust. I should dust more often. What had Jiminy Cricket said? *'Hey, enough's enough!'* The phone rang.

'Cole.'

The Eskimo said, 'You do not help yourself.'

'It's been that kind of day. Let's talk trade. I got the dope.'

'Be at the curb in front of your building in twenty minutes.'

'What if I don't want to?'

He didn't say anything.

'Just a joke,' I said.

Fifteen minutes later the limo pulled up and the rear door opened. I got in, and we pulled into the alley beside the building. Kato wasn't driving. This was another guy, probably a machete killer specially imported from Brazil. The Eskimo said, 'Where is it?'

'Are we going to fool around or are we going to do business?'

He looked at me without moving. I think he was chewing a piece of Dentyne. He nodded. 'All right.'

'We pick a time and a place for the trade. I come alone, so do you. I give you the dope, you give me the boy.'

'All right.'

'Griffith Park,' I said. 'Noon tomorrow, back by the tunnel. You drive up, I drive up. I bring out the dope, you bring out the kid. We swap, go back to our cars, that's it.'

The driver was staring at me through the rearview. Maybe he had a gun in his lap. Maybe the Eskimo would suddenly yell *Kill him!* and the driver would open up through the seat. There are so many maybes in my life that they begin to lose all meaning. Maybe I should retire.

The Eskimo said, 'There could be many people in the park.'

I made my eyes wide. 'Garsh, I never thoughta that.' I do a pretty good Goofy.

He stared at me, nodded. 'Bring the boy's mother.'

'No.'

'I do not want to meet you for the exchange. Send the mother out with the cocaine. I'll send the boy alone. She can leave the dope on the ground and bring her son back to you before I move forward for the dope.'

'No.'

'The boy's hand is injured. He is frightened. Knowing the mother is there will calm him. If the child isn't calm, it will not go well.'

'No.'

The Eskimo spread his hands. 'Then we still have a problem. Perhaps you should keep the cocaine and we should keep the boy. Or perhaps we will simply come take the cocaine.'

'You'll never find it.'

He was pressing hard for the mother. Maybe he wanted a family snapshot for his memory book. He spread his hands again and looked at me.

'All right,' I said. 'Tomorrow noon. I send the mother. You send the kid. Back by the tunnel. You're alone. I'm alone.'

'Yes.'

I got out of the limo, watched them pull away into traffic, then went in and down to my car.

Pike and Ellen were standing on the east side of my house when I pulled up. I got out of the car with the foil brick and walked around the front of the house toward them. Pike was saying, 'You're holding it too hard. Hold it firmly, but don't clutch it. It won't fly away from you.'

They were standing in the grass on the part of the hillside that tabled out and was flat before falling away. Ellen Lang was aiming a blued Ruger .25 automatic at one of the two young gum trees that I'd planted there last year. Pike was standing to her right, adjusting her form with a touch here, a touch there. Her right arm held the gun out straight, her left bent slightly at the elbow so she could use her left hand to cup and brace her right. 'Okay,' Pike said.

She exhaled, steadied, then there was a loud *snap!* Dry firing. Pike looked at me. 'She's pretty good. Her body's quiet.'

'What does that mean?' Ellen said. When she wasn't aiming the gun she cradled it in both hands against her stomach.

'It means your body damps your pulse and your muscles don't quiver when you try to hold still. That's natural. You can't learn it.' Pike nodded his head at the foil brick. 'Who had the dope?'

Ellen's eyes went to the brick as if Pike had just said, *'Who's the Martian?'* She said, 'Mort didn't steal that?'

'No. Kimberly Marsh and her boyfriend stole it.'

'That woman had a boyfriend?'

'Yeah.'

'Someone besides Mort?'

'Yes.'

'Behind Mort's back?'

I nodded.

Ellen pulled back the slide to cock the .25, then aimed at the gum tree again. *Snap!*

Pike said, 'You set it up with Duran?'

'The Eskimo. Noon tomorrow back by the tunnel at Griffith Park. Ellen brings the dope to the tunnel, puts it on the ground, then they send out Perry. She brings Perry back to me, the Eskimo goes out for the dope. End of deal.'

Ellen looked at me. Pike was looking at me, too. His mouth twitched. 'So. They're going to let you and Ellen and the kid walk away and expect everybody to keep their mouths shut.'

Ellen looked at him.

'No,' I said. 'What happens is something like this: they set up some soldiers early, and when we're all together they eliminate us,

176

recover the dope, and an hour later the Eskimo and the soldiers are on Duran's private jet, heading for Acapulco and a long, expenses-paid vacation.'

'Ah,' Joe said, 'reality raises its ugly head.'

Ellen said, 'Shouldn't you call Sergeant Poitras?'

'Not if Duran owns somebody downtown. If all we can get is a couple of soldiers, you've still got a problem.'

'Then what are we going to do?'

'We get there earlier than they do. We watch them set up. we see if I'm right about their intentions. If I am, we figure a way to get Perry away from them. If I'm not, we go through with the trade and worry about Duran after you and the boy and the girls are away from here and safe.'

'What if they don't wait?' Ellen said. 'If they want these drugs and they know you have them, won't they just come here instead?'

Pike's mouth twitched again. For Pike, that's a laughing fit. 'It'll cost too much,' he said. 'Here, we're dug in. Here, a cop car could roll by, there's neighbors, bad access. In Griffith, they're hoping we'll be exposed. They can set up a free fire zone, snipers, ambushes, roadblocks, you name it.' You could tell he was pleased.

I cleared my throat. Loudly. 'They want the dope,' I said, rationally. 'I told the Eskimo it was hidden somewhere and that I'd have to get it. That's why they won't come.' I glared hard at Pike. *'Right?'*

Pike said, 'Gonna get a guitar. Back later.' He disappeared around the front of the house. Purring.

Ellen said, 'Does he play?'

I just looked at her, then went into the house and opened two Evian water. Ellen had come in and had just thanked me for the water when the phone rang. She went as white as a sheet of clean new paper.

I answered. Janet Simon said, 'Elvis? It's Janet Simon.'

I covered the mouthpiece and told Ellen it was Janet. She was relieved, but she wasn't thrilled. She made that funny mouth gesture where she keeps the front of her lips together and blows out the sides.

'I was beginning to think you never wanted to speak to me again,' I said into the phone. Mr. Charm.

'Yes. Well.' Janet's voice was low and measured and sounded like she never wanted to speak to me again, only now she had to. It's a sound I've heard before.

'How is Ellen?' she said.

'Sitting on a rainbow.'

'Is it almost over?'

'Yep.'

'Is she keeping it together?'

'She's doing okay.'

'I could come over.'

'Not a great idea.'

'She might need me to do something.'

I didn't say anything. Ellen looked suspicious and uneasy and not anxious to talk. But that could have been my imagination.

Janet said, 'Maybe there's something I could do. She might have dry cleaning. She might have a prescription. She forgets things.'

I held out the phone to Ellen Lang. 'For you.'

Ellen made the blowing gesture again and took the phone. She cradled the receiver into her neck beneath her jaw and said, 'Hello?' She listened a while, then said, 'Actually, I'm fine. How're the girls?' Not thrilled. Definitely not thrilled.

She said, 'I don't know that yet. I don't know if he's dead or alive or what.'

She did not look faded or uneasy or intimidated.

'I should go now.'

She looked angry and bored.

'No, I'll call you.'

She hung up. She did not do so lightly.

I took the two Evians out onto the deck. After a while, Ellen joined me. She said, 'Janet,' as if she were going to follow it with a lot more, but then she fell silent.

An hour and forty minutes later Pike was back. Ellen and I were sitting on the edge of the deck, listening to a Lakers game and not talking about Janet Simon. The Lakers were out at Washington playing the Bullets. It sounded like a physical game. The Evian water was warm.

Pike unloaded a large green duffel bag and two olive-green guitar cases from his Jeep and carried them toward the house. Ellen went over to the side rail to watch him.

'Do you know Segovia?' she asked.

'Rock 'n roll,' he said.

He brought his things into the living room through the front door. Ellen went in, then came out a few minutes later, looking distant.

'Those aren't guitars.'

'Nope.'

'He has guns.'

I nodded. The Lakers were down by four but Kareem had just scored six straight from inside.

She said, 'You seem so calm.'

'I'm working at it.'

'I know this is what we have to do, but it seems so unreal.'

'Unh-hunh.' Fantasy in fantasyland.

She said, 'It's like a war, right here in Los Angeles.'

I nodded some more.

After a very long time, she said, 'I hope we kick their asses.'

I looked at her. I drank the warm Evian water. Kareem made it eight in a row.

CHAPTER 34

It began to rain again just after four the next morning, a slow leaking drizzle that fell out of silver clouds, lit from beneath by cityglow. Pike sat at the dining table in the dark, sipping at a finger of bourbon in a tall glass. He said, 'It's about time you were up.'

I went into the little bathroom without saying anything and dressed. Levi's, gray Beverly Hills Gun Club tee shirt, CJ Bass desert boots. A client had given me the Gun Club tee shirt, but I'd never worn it. When I went out to the kitchen Pike looked at the shirt and shook his head.

There was coffee in the pot and a plate of dry toast, and Pike's big Coleman thermos, also filled with coffee. I got out a loaf of white and a half loaf of whole wheat and laid out bread for nine sandwiches. There were two packs of pressed ham, most of a pack of processed chicken, and two ham hocks left in the refrigerator. Enough for nine. I wrapped sweet gherkins and jalapeño-stuffed olives in foil, put them in a Gelson's bag with napkins, then put the sandwiches on top. In another sack I put two six-packs of RC 100, a plastic bottle of water, cups, and some Handi Wipes.

When the food was ready, Pike took the bags out through the kitchen door and put them in his Jeep. Cold air came in through the open door. While he was out, Ellen Lang, dressed in her jeans and one of my sweatshirts, came down and sat quietly on the stairs, elbows on knees.

'How ya doing?' I said.

She nodded.

'Want some coffee?' I poured half a cup and brought that and a slice of the dry toast to her. 'It's good to have something in your stomach.'

'I don't think I can.'

'Nibble.'

From the entry closet I took out a slicker for Ellen and a nylon rain shell for me. I put Pike's duffel bag and the two guitar cases by the couch. The duffel bag weighed a ton. I shrugged into my shoulder holster, checked the load in the Dan Wesson, and snapped the catch. I went upstairs, found my clip-on holster, and took a 9mm Beretta automatic from the drawer beside my bed and two extra clips. Each clip held fourteen hollow-point hot loads. Pike had made them for me a long time ago. Illegal. But what's that to a tough guy like me? With the rain shell on, you couldn't see either gun. It wouldn't be easy to get to the Dan Wesson, but I didn't expect to have to quick-draw walking out to the Jeep.

When Pike came back, he was wearing the cammie field jacket. He opened the first guitar case and took out a Weatherby Mark V .30–06 deer buster with an 8-power Bushnell scope and a box of cartridges. He fed four into the gun, locked the bolt, then stood the gun against the arm of the couch. When he opened the second case, Ellen Lang leaned forward. She said, 'What's that?'

'Heckler and Koch .308 assault rifle,' Pike said.

'Pike shows it to people to scare them,' I said. 'It doesn't really shoot.'

Pike's mouth twitched. The HK was entirely black. With its Fiberglas stock, pistol grip, carry handle, and flash suppressor, it was an ugly, mean gun. Pike snapped the bolt, then took a sixty-shot banana clip from the duffel bag and seated it. He sprayed the external metal parts of each rifle with a mist of WD40, then wiped each lightly with a greasy cloth. His hands worked with a precise economy. Finished, he stood up, said, 'Whenever,' and brought the big guns and the duffel out to the Cherokee.

I gave the slicker to Ellen. 'Put this on.'

She put it on.

I put the foil brick into a third shopping bag and gave it to her. 'Are you scared?' I said.

She nodded.

I said, 'Try to be like me. I'm never scared.'

She carried the dope out to the Cherokee. I watched her climb into the backseat from the kitchen, then stood around, wondering if I'd forgotten anything.

The cat walked in and looked at me. I fed him, poured out a saucer of beer, then locked the door. We drove to Griffith Park in a rain so light it was very much like falling dew.

CHAPTER 35

At ten minutes before six, the park was dark and empty and cold, with only light traffic passing the entrance off Los Feliz Boulevard. We turned in and cruised to the back of the park toward the tunnel, past the picnic tables and green lawns and public rest rooms that are habitat for bums, muggers, and homosexual mashers. An old Volkswagen microbus and a Norton motorcycle were parked in the spaces past the rest rooms, but there was no sign of life.

Pike had the radio tuned to the farm reports. To the best of my knowledge, Joe Pike has never been on a farm in his life. Ellen sat in the backseat, the dope on her lap, her eyes luminous in the glow from reflected streetlights.

At the tunnel the road split, one fork disappearing into the tunnel, the other taking a hard right to climb into the mountains up to the observatory. A steel pipe gate blocked the fork that went up. I said, 'There's a fire road about a half mile ahead that's good for us.'

Pike nodded.

I got out, picked the Yale on the pipe gate, let Pike through, then swung the gate back across and relocked it. It was colder here in Griffith than in my own canyon, with clouds pushing down out of the sky to touch the mountains above us, and my breath fogging the air as I worked against the gate.

The sky along the ridgeline to the east was just beginning to turn violet when Pike engaged the four-wheel-drive and turned off onto the fire road. We went out along the ridge between scrub oak and tumbleweed and yucca trees for about a hundred yards until we came to a small grove of scrub oak. Below, the flat of the park spread in an irregular green triangle, from its apex at the tunnel widening all the way out to the park's entrance off Los Feliz. We could see everything we would need to.

Pike nodded approvingly. 'Nice view.'

'Glad you like it.'

He killed the engine but left the radio on.

We waited.

At ten minutes to seven a Park Service Bronco came out of the tunnel and turned up toward the pipe gate. A woman in a brown Park Service uniform unlocked the gate, swung it out of the road, then climbed back into her Bronco and disappeared through the tunnel. I ate a processed chicken on white and drank coffee. Ellen didn't have anything. Neither did Pike.

The world brightened even though the sky remained dark gray. The clouds pushed lower, now sitting halfway down the mountains, slowly bleeding moisture. Traffic grew heavy down on the boulevard, and people began to gather at the bus stop, mostly short, stocky Chicano women carrying large purses. Some of them had umbrellas, but some didn't, and not everybody looked willing to share.

In the back, Ellen pulled her feet up, leaned against the cab wall, and slept. Or pretended to. Pike slouched down behind the wheel, his eyes closed to little slits. That Ellen, that Pike, what a couple of wet blankets. Just when I was going to suggest charades.

At seven-thirty, a white Cadillac turned in off Los Feliz and rolled down past the picnic tables to park across from the rest rooms. Ten minutes later, a cruising police prowl car stopped beside the Volkswagen microbus. Two cops in black slickers got out. One of them rapped on the bus' side door with his nightstick while the other stayed by their black-and-white with his hand on the butt of his Smith. A young guy in jeans and no shirt climbed out of the bus and talked to the cops for a while and did a lot of nodding and a lot of shivering. Then the cops got back in their car and the kid went back into his bus and the cops drove away. I drank more coffee and ate a sweet gherkin and watched. Two lean women in racing tights pedaled fancy bicycles up through the park from out of the Hollywood traffic and zinged back through the tunnel, their bikes throwing up sprays of water, their fine legs churning. An occasional car took the same path but turned up the mountain instead, passing us moments later. Probably people who worked at the observatory. A tall Hispanic man in tight black pants, plaid shirt, and down vest came up from Hollywood under a pale pink umbrella. He stopped under the restroom awning, shook out his umbrella, then went inside. After a minute, the Caddie opened and a middle-aged white man in designer jeans, tweed sport coat, and glasses hustled across, hands over his head against the rain, and also went into the restroom. More cars passed, more cyclists, some runners. The kid came out of his bus, this time wearing a shirt and shoes and rain jacket, wiped off the Norton's seat with a piece of newspaper, fired it up, and took off. The middle-aged guy came out of the restroom, hustled back to his Caddie, and drove away. Then the tall man came out, looked at the sky as if expecting it might have cleared, opened his umbrella, and headed back to Hollywood. I ate four jalapeño olives and drank more coffee. Life is drama.

Just after nine, the clouds let go. Rain banged down in big heavy drops that sounded like hail against the Jeep. Pike took a sandwich from the bag and ate it without saying anything. Ellen stirred and sat up but neither ate nor drank.

Just before ten, a Mercury Montego turned into the park and stopped by the picnic tables. There were three men inside, two in the front, one in the back. I said, 'Joe.'

'Got'm.'

Ellen Lang leaned forward.

Five minutes later two more sedans pulled up next to the Montego, and five minutes after that, two more cars came. The second-to-last car was the blue Nova.

'He's fielding a goddamned army for this,' Pike said.

'Sure. He's heard of us.'

'I don't see Perry,' Ellen said.

'There's still time,' I said.

Pike frowned and looked back out the window.

The Tattooed Man got out of the third car and walked up to the Montego. You couldn't see his tattoos because of the rain jacket he wore, but Ellen said softly, 'He's one of them.' I nodded and finished the jalapeño olives. No one else had had any. Pity.

The Tattooed Man leaned into the Montego, spoke briefly to its driver, then it pulled away, heading toward us. It slowed at the mouth of the tunnel, then swung onto the gated road and came up. The rain had slacked to a dull gray drizzle again. The Montego climbed past us, probably all the way to the observatory, then came back down and pulled up by the other cars. The Tattooed Man got out of his car again, spoke with the Montego, then gestured at the other cars. Men stepped out into the rain. The Tattooed Man pointed to different spots along the parking perimeter, then to different spots along the hills surrounding the tunnel, then at the kid's microbus. A chunky guy with slicked-back hair put his right hand in his coat pocket and went over to the bus. He knocked, then went around to peer in the windshield. He said something to the Tattooed Man and shook his head, then joined the others. Close for the kid on the Norton. Very close. Pike took field glasses out of the glove box and watched them. Some of the men took long guns out of their cars and walked into the woods holding the guns close to their bodies. When everyone was out and armed, the drivers spread their cars, parking two by the restrooms, two more by the picnic tables, another at the mouth of the park by the entrance. The Tattooed Man spoke to Sanchez, who nodded and trotted off to an olive grove in the low hills behind the restrooms. Then the Tattooed Man got back in his own car. After a while you could see him sipping something. Rank hath its privileges.

At twenty-two minutes before noon, a black stretch limo turned in off Los Feliz Boulevard, cruised the length of the park road, and parked under an elm tree by the mouth of the tunnel. Kato was driving. Ellen Lang dug her fingers into my shoulder like pliers' jaws and made a noise in her throat.

Pike sighted down through the Weatherby's scope, then lowered the gun and shook his head. 'Can't see. Back in ten.'

Pike left the Cherokee with the Weatherby, easing the door shut with a soft *click*, then disappeared down the hill. Ellen said, 'Where's he going?'

'To see if Perry's in the limo.'

She edged sideways in the seat. 'Of course he's down there. He has to be, doesn't he? They want to trade for the drugs, don't they?'

I didn't say anything. With the artillery they'd deployed it was clear that Duran's plan was what I thought it would be: let us in, but not out. The only question was whether they would do the boy here, with us, or later, after we were gone. If the boy wasn't here we'd have to find him.

I ate a ham hock sandwich. I ate more sweet gherkins. I drank most of an RC 100. Halfway through the RC, Pike opened the door and climbed in, wet and muddy. He got a Kleenex from the glove box, took off his sunglasses, and cleaned them. It was the first time in weeks that I had seen Pike's eyes, and I'd forgotten how blue they were, so clear and rich and deep that they looked artificial. When the glasses were clean and dry again, he refitted them. 'No kid,' he said. 'Gook behind the wheel, a couple of bruisers in back. One looks like he could be your Eskimo.'

Ellen began to shake. Her face tightened and turned red and her lips came away from her teeth and her eyes filled. Not pain this time. Anger. I squeezed her arm hard and said, 'He's alive. They have to keep him alive in case this fails. If he were dead and they blew this, they'd have nothing. So they'll keep him alive. See?'

She nodded, neck rigid.

Pike said, 'Any ideas?'

I said, 'Yeah. The guy who owns the blue Nova, Sanchez, he's in the trees behind the john.'

Pike nodded. 'I'm better in the bush than you. I'm also better at getting people to talk.'

'Woods, Joe. Here in America it's called the woods, not the bush.'

Pike put the Weatherby back by the HK, then left the car again. I dug up under my rain shell, took out the Dan Wesson, and gave it to Ellen. 'We're not going to be long,' I said. 'If we're not back in twenty minutes or if you see something bad happen, drive out of here, back the way we came. Use the gun if you have to. Go to the North Hollywood P.D. and see Poitras.'

She stared at the gun in her hands.

'Are you all right?'

She nodded, then said, 'Yes. Yes, I'm all right.'

The rain had eroded deep grooves into the hillside and made the earth slick and the footing treacherous. I slipped more than Pike, but the rain splattering on leaves and grass and rocks and road masked our sounds. Dead leaves were wet and spongy and no longer crackled. Whip grass gave way easily, heavy with water. Twigs bent without breaking. We moved down off of our ridge onto a low rise that bottomed out behind the picnic tables and the restrooms, staying low under scrub oak and olive and the occasional elm, Pike moving like something from another age, like part of a medieval mist, slewing down over the ground and between the trees with no apparent effort and without apparent effect. The jabberwock. When we were most of the way down the prowl car came back, driving smoothly back toward the tunnel, oblivious, then turning up the mountain to cruise the observatory.

When we saw Sanchez, sitting on a paper bag beside an olive tree sixty yards down the slope, he was not alone. Pike, out front, held up a hand, pointed at them. I nodded. The man with Sanchez was short and squat with a beaked nose and a pockmarked face. He was picking a Styrofoam cup to pieces and murmuring to Sanchez, who grunted every once in a while. There was a 12-gauge Ithaca pump gun across the squat man's legs.

I caught Pike's eye and made a fist. He nodded. We waited. After a few minutes, the prowl car came back down off the mountain, continued on through the park and back out into the Hollywood traffic. Pike looked at me. I eased out the 9mm, then nodded.

We separated and worked our way through the trees until we were on opposite sides of them. Then I stood up, walked out from behind a tree that was to their left, and showed them the gun.

Sanchez gasped, eyes bulging, but stayed where he was. The other guy rolled sideways, scrambling to come up with the Ithaca and saying '¡Hueta!' quite loud. Pike grabbed his face from behind, twisted it hard to the side, and jammed his Marine Corps knife into the base of his skull, angling up and twisting. It sounded like empty peanut shells when you step on them at the ball park. The man collapsed, his body jerking and trembling, but no longer trying to yell or trying to shoot us. Pike eased the body down, and put a knee on its back to keep the jerking from getting too wild. His bowels and his bladder went at the same time. On TV, a guy gets knifed or shot and he's dead. In the world, dying takes a while and it smells bad. Sanchez stared at his friend. Pike stared at Sanchez, the reflective lenses blank. I touched Sanchez with the pistol, and when he looked at me, put a finger to my lips. His face was the color of wheat. He nodded.

When Pike pulled out the knife it made a wet sound.

I said, 'If you lie to me, he'll do that to you. Do you speak English?'

Sanchez answered without taking his eyes off Pike. '*Sí*. Yes.'

'Is Duran sending the boy here for the trade?'

Sanchez shook his head, watching Pike wipe his knife on the dead man's shirt.

'Where do they have the boy?'

'I don't know.'

I put the barrel of the 9mm under his eye. He jerked, then looked away from Pike to me. 'I don't know. They been keeping him at a place in Silverlake but they moved him this morning. I don't know where.'

Pike gestured at the surrounding area. 'Would any of these guys know?'

'If one of them drove. If one of them heard. I don't know.'

'The Eskimo would know,' I said.

Sanchez nodded. 'Luca,' he said.

'Yeah, Luca.'

Pike said, 'He in the limo?'

Sanchez nodded again. Pike looked at me. 'You want Luca, it's going to be loud and messy. We're going to have to go through a few of these guys.'

'Duran would know,' I said.

Pike's mouth twitched.

I touched Sanchez gently with the gun barrel. 'Is Duran at home?' He nodded.

I looked back at Pike. 'All his soldiers are here.'

Pike squinted out through the misted trees. 'It's ten of, now. Pretty soon these clucks are going to figure out they've been stood up. Then they're going to go back home. Not much time.'

I slid the muzzle of the 9mm down the length of Sanchez's nose and rested it at the tip. 'How many are left at the house?'

Sanchez shook his head. 'The *patrón* has guests. Important people.' Sweat on his forehead mixed with the drizzle.

'If he's got guests,' I said, 'he won't want a bunch of pugs standing around his living room. There's twelve here. How many soldiers can he have?'

Pike's mouth twitched again. 'Didn't somebody say that about the Viet Cong?'

The three of us started back up the hill. By the time we made the Jeep, the drizzle had evolved back into rain – heavy, gravid drops that beat at you, and thudded into your head with a sound I imagined to be like that of the hooves of bulls, pounding damp earth, earth damp with blood.

CHAPTER 36

The Cherokee was thick with the smell of wet clothes and mud and sweat and fear. We eased down off the mountain under the canopy of rain, Ellen under the dash up front, me and Sanchez squeezed onto the rear floorboard, Pike driving. I'd wrapped Sanchez's wrists behind his back with duct tape. I'd once kept a car running for years, held together by duct tape. There's nothing like it. I put the 9mm between Sanchez's legs and told him if he made a sound he could kiss them good-bye.

When the road finally leveled out down by the tunnel, Pike said, 'Uh-oh, the Eskimo just jumped out and is waving at us.' I shoved the gun harder into Sanchez's crotch and felt the drop-stick feeling you get from adrenaline rush. Then Pike said, 'Ha ha. Just kidding.'

That Pike.

The Cherokee moved steadily forward for several minutes, then slowed and Pike said, 'We're out of the park. You can get up.'

'Is this another joke?'

'Trust me.'

We turned left into the heavy lunch-hour traffic on Los Feliz. When we were up in the seats, I stripped the tape from Sanchez's wrists and rebound them, taking time to make sure the job was done right. Ellen watched Sanchez as I did it, her face empty. Maybe she was studying to be like Pike.

She said, 'What did you do to my son to make him scream like that?'

Sanchez looked at me. He'd probably never seen her face. Just a woman with a bag for a head.

'She's the boy's mother,' I said.

Sanchez shook his head.

Ellen continued to stare at him as we eased to a stop at a traffic light. The pounding rain had slacked to a misty drizzle. A black kid in a big yellow Ryder truck pulled up next to us with his radio blasting out Mozart's *Piano Concerto in D Minor*. Probably trying to found a new stereotype. Pike took a sandwich out of the bag under Ellen Lang's seat, ham and white bread, and ate.

Ellen lifted the Dan Wesson and pointed it at Sanchez's face. 'Are you the one who murdered my husband?'

Sanchez straightened. I didn't move. Pike took another bite of sandwich, chewed, swallowed. His lenses were blank in the rearview mirror. Sanchez said, 'I swear to God I know nothing.'

Ellen looked at me. 'I could kill him.' Her voice was calm and steady.

'I know.'

The .38's muzzle didn't waver. Pike was right. She had a quiet body. She said, 'But we might need him to get Perry.'

'Unh-huh.'

She lowered the .38. Something like a smile pinched the corners of her mouth. She turned around and sat forward, resting the gun in her lap. Joe reached across and patted her leg.

I said, 'We should drop these two off somewhere.'

Pike said, 'Where? Your Eskimo's probably tapping his watch right now. Maybe they've already found the body.'

'This isn't going to be easy,' I said. 'It might go wrong.'

Pike shrugged. 'She can handle it. Can't you?'

'Yes,' Ellen said. 'Let's get Perry.'

Five minutes later, we came to the massive mortared wall, followed it up past the gate, turned around at the side street, then drove back down. We parked the Cherokee off the road about a block from the corner of Duran's estate. Pike got out, said, 'C'mere, you,' and pulled Sanchez out into the street. Pike turned him around, then hit him behind the right ear with the flat of his pistol. Sanchez smacked against the Cherokee and collasped. Pike hoisted him into the rear seat again, then dug out the duct tape and put strips over his mouth and eyes, and bound his ankles.

I helped Ellen into the driver's seat, then closed the door and spoke to her through the open window. 'If anyone comes, get out of here and go for the cops. If they stand in front of the car, run over them. If you hear shots, go for the cops. If Sanchez tries to make trouble, shoot him. When you see us coming, start up and be ready to go.'

'All right.'

Pike slammed the rear door, then came around and looked at

Ellen. He looked at her the way you examine something that you don't want to make a mistake about. 'There's going to be killing,' he said.

She nodded. 'I know.'

'You might have to do some.'

Another nod.

'You got a lipstick, something?'

She shook her head.

'Look in the glove box.'

Ellen bent across the seat. Sanchez moaned and shifted in the back of the Jeep. 'Joe,' I said.

Ellen leaned back into the window. She had a brown plastic tube. Estée Lauder Scarlet Haze. Pike ran the color out, then drew a bright red line down his forehead and along the bridge of his nose and two parallel lines across each cheek under his eyes.

'You're getting crazy on me, Joe,' I said.

She watched him without a word, and she held steady when he did the same with her. 'Not crazy,' he said. 'She's going to want to forget, so reality ends now. It's easy to forget the unreal. In a year, in five, she thinks of this, it's all the more absurd.'

'You two look silly,' I said.

Ellen Lang twisted the sideview mirror so she could see herself, first one side, then the other. No smile, now. Just consideration.

Nobody said good-bye or I'll be seeing you or keep a stiff upper lip. When Sanchez was secure and the doors were closed and locked, Pike and I trotted back up the hill toward Duran's, me carrying the 9mm loosely in my hand, Pike the HK.

When we came to the estate, we turned onto the side street and followed the wall until we came to an ancient olive tree, grown gnarled and crooked with huge limbs twisting up and over. Pike said, 'You remember what I said about the layout?'

'You look dumb with that lipstick on.'

'You don't remember, do you?'

'Just past the front knoll is the motor court. Main house with two levels. Guest house in the rear. Pool and poolhouse. Tennis court to the northeast of the pool.'

He nodded. Pike went up first. I handed up the HK, stuck the 9mm in my belt and followed. Water from the rain-heavy leaves showered down on us every time the tree shook. When we dropped down, I thought we were behind the Mexico City Hilton, but Pike said no, it was only the guest house, the main residence was larger.

We followed the perimeter of the guest house toward the rear of the estate and came out by a small stand of newly planted magnolia trees. Three women and four men were standing around a sheltered brick barbeque off the poolhouse, cooking hamburgers. They were wearing sweaters and long pants and one of the men wore a hat. It never rains in Southern California. They looked comfortable and at ease and more than a little drunk. None of the men was Domingo Duran. The man with the hat laughed loudly, then grabbed the breast of the nearest woman. She swatted him away and he laughed louder. He had a flat, round face and a nose with jagged scars from the time someone had tried to bite it off, and he dressed like a hick from back east: black lace-up shoes, Sears pants, and a lime green golfing sweater over a white Arrow shirt, all of which went beautifully with his crushed gray felt hat. I looked at him and smiled and said, 'Well, well.'

'What?' Pike said.

'You see the gentleman in the hat?'

'Yeah.'

'Rudy Gambino.'

'What's a Rudy Gambino?' Pike refused to keep himself current on underworld figures.

'Mobster from Arizona. From Newark originally, until his own people sent him out west because they couldn't control him. Duran's connected with him. Buddies.'

Pike said, 'I like his nose.'

Inside the poolhouse, two young thick-necked Chicano kids in black suits leaned against a pinball machine and smoked. Muscle to keep Uncle Rudy safe.

We went back past the guest house, slipped along a narrow shrub-lined walk, and edged up against the side of a fountain behind pale red oleander. The drizzle had stopped altogether now, but the clouds were still dark. We had a clear view of the front of the guest house, as well as the pool and the poolhouse and the back side of the main house. As big as the guest house was, the main house was larger. An enormous white Spanish Mediterranean, heavy-walled, with quarry-tiled patios and red-tiled roofs and oversized beams. The patios were covered and partially hidden behind lush landscaping. A man in a trench coat sat at a small glass table, well out of the rain. He was holding a paperback copy of Stephen King's *The Dead Zone* but he wasn't reading. A Remington over/under shotgun rested on the table. Arizona muscle.

The guest house had three separate facing doors, like a triplex. The door farthest away from us opened and two thugs came out with Perry Lang between them. The boy was blindfolded and his left hand was heavily bandaged. He walked the way you walk when you haven't slept well in a while. I felt Pike shift next to me. Good luck, and bad. Good luck, that the boy had been brought here. We wouldn't have to force his whereabouts out of anyone. It wasn't smart for them to have him here, but Sanchez said they'd moved the boy this morning. They'd probably been keeping him in a safe house, but decided to bring him closer in case something went wrong with the ambush and they needed a little extra leverage. Maybe I should call Poitras. I could tell him the kid was here and he would act on it. But maybe by the time I got to a phone and called the cops and the cops got here, the Eskimo would've come and gone and taken the boy with him, maybe not quite as alive as last reported.

Bad luck because of Gambino. How many Arizona soldiers did he have hanging around the guest house and the main house and the garage? What would Gambino do when Pike and I made our move? Normal business practice would be noninterference. But he was a guest in Duran's home. They were friends. Besides that, he wouldn't know for sure if we weren't coming for him. Shit.

Gambino left the barbeque and sloshed across to the main house. He carried a Coors and belched so loudly we could hear him sixty yards away. Classy. He didn't bother with the walkways. Guess he didn't give a shit if he tracked messy into his good friend Domingo Duran's home. Maybe he figured Mexicans didn't mind.

The two guys holding Perry stopped outside of the guest-house, talking, then one of them continued on with the kid across to the main house. The second one came our way, toward the garage. We dropped along the row of oleander until we were out of sight of the rear yard, then came out onto the walk.

'If we're going into the main house,' Pike said, 'we're not going to do it through the back. Too many people.'

We were zipping along, backpedaling along the walk toward the garage. 'Did you see a way in through the front?' I said.

'Sure. Windows. Doors.'

Smartass. 'You always carry lipstick in your truck?'

'You wouldn't believe what I got in there.'

The walk ended at a door off the rear of the garage in a nice circular spot strewn with pretty white rocks. There was a heavy adobe wall to the right, as thick as but lower than the main wall, extending from the garage to the main house. To the left the grounds sloped away to an open rolling lawn. It was through the door or across the lawn. On the lawn, we could be seen. The door was locked.

We stepped back off the walk into the shrubs and waited. There were footsteps, then the second thug came along, hissing air through his teeth and digging in his pocket. When he stopped at the door and took out a silver key, I stepped out and hit him once in the ear, hard. He sat down and I hit him again. Pike picked up the key. 'Not bad.'

I waffled my hand from side to side. 'Eh.'

Pike put the key in the lock and opened the door. A short Mexican with a broad face and a gray zoot suit took one step out, pushed a gold Llama automatic into Pike's chest, and pulled the trigger. There was a deep muffled *POP*, then Pike came up and around with his right foot faster than I could see. There was a louder sound, what you might hear if you drop an overripe casaba melon onto a tile floor. The Mexican collapsed, his neck limp. Pike looked down at himself, put one hand over a growing spot high and to the right of his chest, then sat down. 'Keep going,' he said. 'Get the kid.'

I felt like I might scream. I looked at him, nodded, then pushed through the door. Forward. Never back up.

There were three Cadillac limos, two Rolls-Royces, and a bright yellow Ferrari Boxer in the garage, but no more thugs. I went out to the edge of the motor court and looked at the front of the house. Another limo was there. A service drive branched off the motor court and ran around to the side of the house, then looped back around to the garage. That would be the kitchen. I walked out across the motor court to the service and followed it around to the side of the mansion. Maybe the way to get the kid was to walk up to things and shoot them and when I ran out of things to shoot I'd either have the kid or be dead.

The service drive led to a carport attached to the house. There was a single door there, and a little metal buzzer. When I pushed the buzzer a tiny woman, as nicely browned as good leather, opened the door. She looked disgusted. '¡No más comer!' she said.

'Do you speak English?'

'No, no.' She shook her head and tried to push me out of the door. Probably thought I was one of Gambino's goons.

I showed her the gun and jerked my head out toward the front gate. 'Vamoose!' Then I went into the kitchen.

Manolo was eating a sandwich at a chopping block table. His jacket was off and he was wearing a shoulder holster over a blue shirt with white collar and cuffs. When he saw me, he clawed at his gun. I shot him twice. The hollow-points picked him up and kicked him back off the stool. The 9mm high-velocity loads echoed like a cannon in the tile kitchen.

I went out through a serving hall and into a living room that made Barry Fein's place look like a phone booth. Gambino's hood was coming in off the balcony with his shotgun. When he saw me he said, 'What the hell was that?'

I said, 'This,' and clubbed him in the side of the face with the gun. He stumbled and dropped the shotgun but didn't pass out. I pulled him up to his feet and shook him and pressed the muzzle up under his jaw. 'They just brought a kid in here. Where?'

'I swear to God I don't know. I swear.'

I hit him in the mouth with the butt of the gun. His teeth went and blood sprayed out along my arm and he went down to his knees. 'Where?'

'Shwear to Chri I dunno.' Hard to talk with a ruined mouth.

'Where's Duran?'

'Offishe. Upshtairs.'

'Show me.'

I could see out the elegant French doors, across the patio and the lawn to the poolhouse. If they'd heard the shots, no one showed it. Burgers still sizzled, music still played, men and women still laughed. I was vaguely aware that Ellen Lang, sitting out in Pike's Cherokee without benefit of laughter or music or gaiety, might have heard the shots. And having heard them, might be on her way to call the cops.

I pulled him up again and we went out the living room, up a monstrous semicircular stairway to the second floor. Voices and the sound of closing doors came from the back of the house. On the upper landing, I said, 'Where are you taking me?'

'Offishe.' He looked to the left down a curving hall. 'Door, wish a couple guysh. Go shrough into she offishe.'

'Just a couple of guys, huh?'

'Yesh.'

'There another way in or out?'

195

He looked confused, then shook his head. It hurt him to do that. 'I don't live here, man. It'sh tight. Shoundproo.'

Shoundproo. Perfect.

'Why are you people here?'

His eyes flagged and he started to crumple. I hoisted him up, gave him a shake, asked him again.

'Bushnesh,' he said.

'Business. Dope deal?'

He nodded.

The hall was long and paneled with a very rich grade of walnut. Impressive. The St. Francis Hotel in San Francisco has walls like that. I stopped us before we got to the door, held up the Beretta, and touched my lips.

He said, 'I beliee you.'

A slim, well-manicured Mexican sat at a bank president's desk and spoke into a phone. A tall, blocky blond guy had half his ass on the edge of the desk, listening in with his arms crossed. Across the room there was a handsome copper-façaded door that would lead to Duran's sanctum sanctorum. The blond guy was in a pale yellow sport coat. The Mexican wore a charcoal gray Brooks Brothers three-piece and looked better than the blond guy. Executive secretary, no doubt. He was speaking English, asking about the noises he'd just heard. I shoved Mr. Teeth in through the doorway, walked in after him and shot the Mexican and the blond once each. The hollow-points flipped the Mexican over backward out of his chair and knocked the blond guy off the desk.

I looked at the door. It was thick and heavy and I didn't know how I was going to get in there. No knob. *Knock, knock, knock, Chicken Delight!* There would probably be a buzzer somewhere around the secretary's desk that would make little metal gears push little metal rods to swing open the door. They would have to be strong rods. It was a big door.

Mr. Teeth and I were halfway across the outer office when the copper door opened and Rudy Gambino stepped out, saying, 'The fuck's goin' on out –'

He had a Smith Police Special in his left hand. He dropped it when he saw me.

'Back up, fat man,' I said.

He backed. And in we went.

CHAPTER 37

Perry Lang was not in the room.

Domingo Garcia Duran was sitting on a maroon leather couch under a wall of black-and-white photographs. Most of the shots were of bullrings and bulls and Duran, I supposed, in his Suit of Lights. Still others showed Duran with other matadors and Duran with various political personalities and Duran with assorted celebrities. Everyone smiled. Everyone was friends. *Hooray for Holley-wood!* There were trophies and black horns mounted to teak plaques and tattered black ears mounted to still other teak plaques. Gray-black hooves stood hoof up off little wooden pedestals like demented ashtrays. You could smell death in the room like mildewed satin. A cape was hanging off a tall leather pedestal near the window, and crossed swords like the ones on the front gate, only real-size, were fixed on the wall above it. The walls were hung with oil paintings of bulls and an enormous life-size rendering of Duran poised for the kill. Still more statues of bulls and matadors and men on horses with long lances lined the bookcases.

'Really, Dom,' I said. 'A bit much, don't you think?'

Rudy Gambino said, 'Your ass is shit, bubba.'

I said, 'I got the gun, Rudy.'

There was a marble coffee table in front of Duran with an open briefcase on top of it. The briefcase was filled with neat stacks of hundred-dollar bills. Duran's well-worn bent sword was on top of it. Duran leaned forward, picked up the sword, and closed the case. *Estoque*, Pike had said. The sword used for the kill.

I pushed Mr. Teeth down onto the floor and told him to stay there, then pointed the gun at Duran. 'I want the boy *now*, Dom.' I could see Pike bleeding to death out in the yard. I could see Sanchez getting loose, getting Ellen's gun . . .

Rudy said, 'The fuck is this, Dom? He knows who I am.'

I fired a round into the couch next to Duran. The leather dimpled a foot from his shoulder as the bullet yanked through the cushion. The high-velocity load was so loud my ears rang. Rudy jumped but Duran didn't, and he never took his eyes off me. Balls, all right. He said, 'We will trade.'

I shook my head. 'Get me the kid.'

Rudy moved forward, swinging his right arm in a broad gesture and talking to me like we were used to this. Maybe he was. 'How the hell you know who I am?'

'I stayed at the same hotel as you once. In Houston. I saw you walk through the lobby.'

'Bullshit.' He shook his finger at Duran. 'No one's supposed to know I'm here, goddamnit. Carlos and Lenny find out I'm here right now instead of in Colombia I'll have to go through all kindsa shit.'

'Shut up, Rudy,' I said. 'You cutting out your partners is the least of your worries.' I didn't know who the hell Carlos and Lenny were. But there was a briefcase of money on the table. Carlos and Lenny thought Rudy Gambino was in Colombia. There was a known dope connection between Gambino and Duran, as well as a history of investment partnerships. It looked good that Gambino was moving dope through Duran to cut out the middleman.

Gambino screamed, 'I ain't cutting out nobody, goddamnit!'

I fired another round, this one slamming through a picture into the wall beside Duran. Four inches from his ear. He didn't flinch. I wouldn't be that good. 'I take the kid, and I go for the police,' I said. 'If you're good, you can make an airport.'

He didn't say anything.

This wasn't working. I was making a lot of noise and taking a lot of time and not getting any closer to Perry Lang. Sooner or later someone would come. When enough someones came, that would be it.

'Okay, motherfucker,' I said, 'bring me to the kid or eat one.' I aimed the Beretta between Duran's eyes. I meant it.

He shook his head. 'No. I do not have to.'

Something hard pressed against my neck and the Eskimo said, 'That's enough.'

Rudy Gambino hopped over, jerked my gun away, then hit me in the face twice with his right hand. His punches split my lip but didn't put me down. 'Now what you got?' he shouted. 'You got dick is what you got!'

Gambino went over to Mr. Teeth and kicked him. 'Eddie?' Eddie was passed out.

Duran leaned forward again and tapped the marble table with the sword. He said, 'Here is how I will deal with you. I will kill you, and I will kill the boy, and I will kill the mother, and then it will be done.' He looked serenely calm as he said it, almost in repose, and I knew this must be the way he used to look when he faced the bulls. Assured and in absolute control of the pageant. The Bringer of Death.

'But you won't have your property.'

He shrugged. 'The property was never what was important.'

'Sure.' The Eskimo was an enormous presence behind me, something dark and gargantuan and primordial. I could feel the gun there, hovering. I took deep breaths through my nose, filling my lungs with air, trying to will my body to relax, to calm. *Pranayama.* Start with the feet. Prepare yourself. Focus *ki.* If Gambino or Duran moved close enough, if I could move fast enough . . . If I couldn't, it wouldn't make much difference.

Rudy Gambino leveled the 9mm at me and said, 'This kinda shit ain't supposed to happen when I'm here, Dom.' When he said 'Dom' there was a sharp *pow* out in the secretary's office. A red spot grew low on Gambino's abdomen. As he looked down at himself there was another *pow*, this one closer, in the doorway, and his right leg kicked back and he fell.

Ellen Lang stood in the doorway with my .38, right arm out straight, left bent at the elbow and cupping the right, just the way Pike taught her. The lipstick didn't look silly anymore. She was dark and alien and threatening, the way guys in the Nam who wore paint had looked. Duran saw the lipstick and smiled.

When the Eskimo's gun moved I went into him, grabbing his gun hand with both of mine and forcing it in toward the elbow and away from his body. The gun kicked free and the Eskimo hit me on top of my right shoulder with an MX missile. My whole side went numb. I stayed inside, wrapping his hips and lifting and driving him away from the gun. His hands came down on my back, he pushed backward, and I let go. He landed on the floor sideways and went over on his hands and knees. I drove straight in with a power kick to the ribs and followed it with two punches, one to the same spot on the ribs, the other behind his left ear. The head punch broke one of my knuckles. Head punches will do that. I hit him a third time, this one beneath the ear where it was softer. The Eskimo grunted and heaved himself up. He didn't look too much the worse for wear. You couldn't say that about me.

Ellen was still in the door. Duran was on his feet now, saying something to her, but I couldn't hear what. I said, 'Only pussies kill seals and polar bears.'

The Eskimo smiled.

I threw an ashtray at him. It bounced off his arm.

He smiled some more.

I threw a Waterford lamp at him. He batted it aside.

There are any number of innovative ways to best an opponent. I simply had to think of one.

The Eskimo came for me. I faked to the outside, planted my left foot, and roundhouse kicked him in the face. His head snapped back and his nose burst into a red mist. He looked down at himself, then charged again. I dropped, spun, and kicked the outside of his knee. His leg buckled and he went down. I went in close, hitting his smashed nose with the heel of my hand and driving in behind it hard with my knees. His head rocked back and his eyes looked funny. I hit him with my left hand and lost a second knuckle. Bruce Lee could fight a thousand guys and not even split a fingernail. Karma. I saw Duran moving toward Ellen, walking across the room, the little sword in front of him.

'Ellen,' I said.

The Eskimo came up from underneath, locked his arms around my chest, and squeezed. It felt the way they describe a massive coronary: your lungs stop working, an elephant sits on your chest, and you know with absolute certainty that you are going to die.

Ellen stepped toward Duran and there was a loud *BANG*, louder than before because she was in the room now. Duran missed a step, then kept going, holding the sword straight out now and picking up speed.

I hammered down into the Eskimo's face, hitting him on the top of the head and in the temples and in the eyes. He squeezed his eyes tight and hugged me closer. I felt something snap in my lower back. Short rib. What the hell, don't need'm anyhow.

Ellen's gun went off again. *BANG.*

I wanted to yell for her to get out of here, but knew if I gave up what breath I had I wouldn't get any more. I stopped punching and tried to dig my thumbs into the Eskimo's eyes, but he pressed his face into my chest. Everything in my peripheral vision began to grow fuzz. From out of another solar system I heard a gutty *choonk-*

choonk-choonk, choonk-choonk. The HK. Pike. Not lucky for them, finding Pike. Ruin their whole day.

I reached above my head and brought my elbow down on the crown of the Eskimo's head. A sharp pain lanced up my arm and another rib went, this one higher in my back.

Ellen's gun sounded again. *BANG*. Duran stopped and staggered sideways a step. Then he went on.

I brought my elbow down again, and this time the Eskimo sobbed. I did it again and his arms loosened. Whenever I hit him, something hot flashed in my elbow, letting me know the bone was broken. That didn't seem to matter much. Not much mattered at all. Life's priorities tend to shift when you're in the process of dying.

I was seeing mostly gray shadows and squiggly bright things. I heard another *BANG*. That would be six. Ellen wouldn't have any more. I hit the Eskimo again, and this time his arms released. I backed away, sucking air, each breath sending razors through my chest. The Eskimo tried to stand, pushing himself up onto one leg, then the other. He looked at me, swayed, and fell. Some tough sonofabitch.

Domingo Duran was on the floor at Ellen's feet. She lowered the gun. Then she spit on him. She hadn't moved, or flinched, or cowered. She hadn't backed up.

I walked over to her, but it took a while. Not much was working right. I seemed to go sideways when I wanted to go straight, and I very badly wanted to throw up.

'Perry,' I said. 'Perry.'

Then there was a lot of noise in the hall, and I dropped down to the rug, trying to find my pistol. I couldn't and I started to cry. It had to be there somewhere. I had to find it because the game wasn't over. It couldn't be over until we had the boy, only the goons were coming and there didn't seem to be anything I could do to stop them.

Men with blue rain shells that said FBI or POLICE on the back came in with M-16s. O'Bannon was with them. He saw Ellen Lang, and then he saw me, and he said, 'You sonofabitch.'

I remember smiling. Then I passed out.

CHAPTER 38

For one of the few times in my life, I thought wouldn't it be grand if I smoked. I was in the Hollywood Presbyterian Emergency Room watching the nurses, one nurse in particular, and waiting for my elbow cast to dry. They had the cast held away from my body by a little metal and plastic brace. A kid waiting to get his lip stitched asked me how I'd busted it, and I said fighting spies loud enough for my nurse to hear. All I needed now was a London Fog slung casually over my shoulders and a cigarette dangling from my lip, and she'd probably rape me.

Poitras came though a set of swinging doors, with O'Bannon playing shadow. Poitras was big and blank and carrying two Styrofoam cups of coffee. They looked like thimbles in his hands. O'Bannon looked like he'd bitten into a Quarter-pounder and found an ear. Everyone in the waiting room stared at Poitras. Even the doctors. What a specimen.

'My,' I said. 'What a delightful surprise.'

Poitras held out one of the coffees. 'Black, right?'

'Black.'

The doctor had put three layers of tape around my ribs, splinted my hand, and given me an analgesic, but it still hurt to reach for the coffee. Driving would be an adventure.

'How's the kid?' I said.

They'd found him hidden away in a closet on the first floor. He was still blindfolded and didn't know what was happening. 'Okay,' Lou said. 'Cleaned up his hand, gave him some shots. You know. His mom took him down to the cafeteria. He wanted a hamburger.'

One of Duran's thugs had put an ice pick through the boy's hand to make him scream. I didn't know who. With any luck I'd killed him. 'You talk to him yet?'

'Mm-hmm.' Lou said, 'You left a lot of bodies back there, Ace. Sorta like Rambo Goes To Hollywood.'

I nodded.

'Between you and Pike and Mrs. Lang, if we include the one in Griffith park, looks to be eleven stiffs.'

'Me and Pike. Mrs. Lang had nothing to do with it.'

'Yeah.'

O'Bannon leaned toward me. His face was very tight and getting tighter. If it got much tighter his brain would probably pop out. He said, 'Goddamn you, you ruined four months of undercover work, do you know that? We knew Gambino was setting up a move with Duran. We had his phone bugged, his bed bugged, his goddamned jock strap bugged. We ate, slept, and shit with that sonofabitch.'

'I can tell,' I said. 'Try Lavoris.'

Poitras said, 'They had the house across the street. You had two Feds watch you and Pike hop the fence, wondering what the hell was going on. They like to shit, you and Pike jogging down the road like a couple of National Guardsmen, Pike with that howitzer of his, paint all over his face.' Poitras looked at O'Bannon and made a hard, nasty grin. 'Only no one could make a decision until the big boss got there. No one knew jack shit who was doing what since no one had been told anything.' O'Bannon chewed at his lip. Poitras finished, 'They thought you guys might be cops, so they just sat on things until Mrs. Lang went in through the front gate. Then they hoofed it across the street.'

I nodded. Figured it had to be something like that. If Ellen had called the cops, blue suits and prowl cars would've come.

O'Bannon said, 'We ran an efficient, tight, *secure* operation.'

'Swinging,' I said. The coffee felt gritty in my mouth, like it was mostly sediment. Maybe I should ask the nurse to have a look-see.

'Goddamnit,' O'Bannon said, 'do you know how much this has cost the taxpayers?'

Poitras said, 'Shit.'

O'Bannon's Stanford Law/three-sets-before-breakfast tan was a nice mottled color. He said, 'We were finally going to nail Gambino and Duran both. They were making a major cocaine buy together. We *had* them, and you fucked it up, Cole. You were ordered to stay away from this and you didn't. Your goddamned license is *mine*.'

I stared at him. There was a petulance to his face that one does not often see in law-enforcement personnel. I wanted very much to pat his head, tell him everything would be okay, and send him to his room. Instead, I carefully set the cup down on the seat next to me and stood up. It hurt to stand.

'Screw you, O'Bannon,' I said. 'You were ready to trade the kid for that bust.'

He stood, breathing very hard, his hands balled into fists at his sides. 'We would have moved when the time was right to maximize our results.'

The nurse behind the station was looking at us. I wondered if she'd ever seen someone split a brand-new cast over a Spec Op before. 'Right,' I said.

Poitras edged between O'Bannon and me, dwarfing us both. 'Go back to Special Operations, O'Bannon,' he said. 'Tell them the results have been maximized. Tell them that they won't have to waste any more of the taxpayers' dollars on Domingo Duran or Rudy Gambino.'

O'Bannon pointed his finger at me. 'Your ass is mine.'

I said, 'Get out of here before I beat you to death.'

O'Bannon gave Poitras another attempt at a bad look, then walked away. It was sort of a cross between a wince and a squint. I guess it really wilted them in court.

Poitras said, 'The kid doesn't know about his father. We're going to let the mother tell him.'

I was still staring after O'Bannon. Then I looked over at the nurse. She smiled. It was a nice smile.

'We did a little talking,' Lou said. 'Mort and the kid weren't kidnapped on their way home from school. Mort didn't even get to pick the kid up. One of Duran's people snatched him when he was walking out to his father's car.'

I stared at him.

'I talked to Lancaster,' he said. 'They didn't find a .32 in Lang's Caddie.'

'No?'

'So I had the ME run a paraffin. Came back positive.'

I nodded, thinking about Ellen Lang, thinking about Mort and his .32, thinking about a positive paraffin test.

Poitras said, 'Hound Dog?'

'Yeah?'

'When you knew for certain, you shoulda come to me. O'Bannon or no O'Bannon, downtown or not, I woulda moved on it. It's my job. I woulda done it.'

'I know.'

'I don't like any goddamned cowboys thinking they can go off half-cocked, goddamned Pike running down the street with a goddamned HK-91.'

I felt very tired, the sort of deep, bled-to-the-bone tired you feel when you've tried very hard to keep something dear to you only to lose it. I said, 'Are we going to be charged with anything?'

'Baishe has already been with the D.A. O'Bannon got there first, but Baishe thinks we might be able to square it. I don't know about Pike. He gets picked up, they say what's your occupation, he says mercenary, goddamned paint all over his face like he's still in the jungle. Nobody likes that. Nobody on the department likes Pike anyway.'

'If the department kept more guys like Pike, they'd have less guys like O'Bannon.'

Poitras didn't say anything.

'If you charge Joe, you charge me.'

Poitras took a deep breath, sighed. He needed a shave. 'I want you to come in. We gotta get a statement.'

'Can you wait?'

He stared at me for a while, then nodded. 'No later than noon tomorrow.'

We shook hands. 'Tell Baishe thanks,' I said.

Poitras nodded again.

I took off the little brace and started for the door. The nurse had left her station with a tall black orderly who looked like Julius Erving. Good looking. Neat moustache. He'd said something funny and she'd laughed. Screw him.

Poitras said, 'Hound Dog?'

I stopped.

'At least it wasn't a buy-off. That's something.'

'Sure.'

CHAPTER 39

I found Ellen and Perry Lang sitting alone at a big table in the back of the cafeteria. I went up behind them, put my good hand on Ellen's shoulder, and said, 'Come on. It's time to go home.'

She looked back at me silently for a moment, then nodded. She had cleaned the lipstick off, leaving her face pink and fresh from the scrubbing. 'I should get the things I left at your house.'

We picked up Pike's Cherokee from a cop out front and took the drive west to Fairfax, then north up Laurel and into the hills. It was almost six when we got there. The cloud cover had broken, and the air had a fresh, scrubbed smell. Nice. A red-winged hawk rode the wind pushing up the canyon above my house. I could see his head turn, looking for mice.

When Ellen got out, Perry got out with her. He had made her sit in the backseat with him, and he wasn't about to let her get out of reach now.

The cat was sitting in the middle of the floor, waiting, when we walked in. He hissed when he saw Perry and crept under the couch, ears down. Ever the gracious host.

While Ellen and Perry were upstairs, I went into the kitchen, drank two glasses of water, then called the hospital and asked after Pike. A woman with a very direct voice told me he was out of surgery now, in serious but stable condition, with a good prognosis. He would be fine. I thanked her and hung up.

When Ellen and Perry came back, she was carrying the Ralph's bag I'd brought from her house. She had taken off my sweat shirt and the dirty jeans and replaced them with a pretty pink top and cotton pants. Pike was right. A year from now, she would not remember the smell of gun-powder or ferocious red marks on her face. At the bottom of the stairs, Perry Lang asked her about his father.

She went white and looked at me, but I did not help her with the decision. She had to do what she thought she could do. After a while, she took Perry into the living room, sat him on the couch, and told him that his father was dead.

They sat together a very long time. Perry cried, then grew quiet, then cried again until he fell asleep in her lap. At ten minutes before eight, she said, 'We can go now,' and stood up with her nine-year-old son cradled in her arms like a baby.

We put him, groggy and whimpering, into the back of the Cherokee, then took the long drive to Encino. Coming down off the mountain into the valley, the lights were like brilliant crystal jewels in the rain-washed air. Better than that. It was as if the stars had fallen from the sky and lay stewn along the desert.

'I can do this,' she said.

'Yep.'

'I can pull us together, and keep us together, and go back to school maybe, and go forward.'

'Never any doubt.'

She looked at me. 'I won't back up.'

I nodded.

'Not ever,' she said.

I exited the freeway and rolled down the cool silent Encino streets to Janet Simon's house. It was brightly lit, inside and out. The older daughter, Cindy, passed by the front window as we pulled into the drive. 'Would you like me to be there when you tell them?' I said.

She sat silently, chewing her lip, staring at the house. 'No. If I need help there, let it come from Perry.'

I nodded. A car passed, washing her with light and revealing something ageless in her face. A sort of maturity and life that hadn't been there before, and that you never see in most people. The look of someone who has assumed responsibility.

We got out. I liked it that she didn't expect me to open the door for her.

'You didn't throw away your life with Mort,' I said.

She stared up at me.

'Mort wasn't kidnapped and Mort wasn't dealing with these people. Duran's goons took the boy and Mort went after them. That's where the .32 was. Maybe Mort wasn't there for you anymore, but he tried to be there for Perry. He died trying to save his boy.'

Her eyes looked deep in the night. 'How do you know?'

'Poitras ran a paraffin test. The test says Mort fired a gun. He wouldn't have had to do any shooting unless he was trying to get his son back.'

She took a very deep breath, let it out, and stared down the street. Then she nodded, raised up on her toes, and kissed me. 'Thank you.'

The front door opened and Janet Simon appeared in the light. We didn't move toward her and she didn't move out toward us.

'There's more to bring away from this than firing a pistol,' I said.

'I know.'

'You're different now.'

She looked at Janet Simon. 'They'll have to get used to that, won't they?'

I helped her lift Perry out. His face was puffy and pale and he clung to her even in sleep. She said, 'Would you like to come in?'

I shook my head. 'Not if you don't need me. If you need me, I'll stay. If you don't, I'll go sit with Joe.'

She smiled and told me she'd come see Joe tomorrow, then she kissed my cheek once more and walked up to the house. Janet Simon stepped aside to let them in, then shut the door.

Perhaps Janet hadn't seen me.

I stood there, breathing deep, and looked at Pike's Jeep. Even in the dark, I could see it was a mess, muddy and streaked and dusty. I found a self-wash on Ventura Boulevard that was still open, and worked there until the Cherokee sparkled. Then I rolled down the windows and drove slowly in the cool fresh air, drove back to the hospital to wait for Joe Pike.

Stalking The Angel

AN ELVIS COLE NOVEL

For Lauren
whose parents will always love her,
& for Carol and Bill, who have made me larger by
sharing their lives.

I love to hear the story
which angel voices tell.
—*The Little Corporal*
Emily Miller

When the truth is found to be lies,
and all the joy within you dies,
don't you want somebody to love?
—Jefferson Airplane

CHAPTER I

I was standing on my head in the middle of my office when the door opened and the best looking woman I'd seen in three weeks walked in. She stopped in the door to stare, then remembered herself and moved aside for a grim-faced man who frowned when he saw me. A sure sign of disapproval. The woman said, 'Mr. Cole, I'm Jillian Becker. This is Bradley Warren. May we speak with you?'

Jillian Becker was in her early thirties, slender in gray pants and a white ruffled shirt with a fluffy bow at the neck and a gray jacket. She held a cordovan Gucci briefcase that complemented the gray nicely, and had very blond hair and eyes that I would call amber but she would call green. Good eyes. There was an intelligent humour in them that the Serious Businesswoman look didn't diminish.

I said, 'You should try this. Invigorates the scalp. Retards the aging process. Makes for embarrassing moments when prospective clients walk in.' Upside down, my face was the color of beef liver.

Jillian Becker smiled politely. 'Mr. Warren and I don't have very much time,' she said. 'Mr. Warren and I have to catch the noon flight to Kyoto, Japan.' Mr. Warren.

'Of course.'

I dropped down from the headstand, held one of the two director's chairs opposite my desk for Jillian Becker, shook hands with Mr. Warren, then tucked in my shirt and took a seat at my desk. I had taken off the shoulder holster earlier so it wouldn't flop into my face when I was upside down. 'What can I do for you?' I said. Clever opening lines are my forte.

Bradley Warren looked around the office and frowned again. He was ten years older than Jillian, and had the manicured, no-hair-out-of-place look that serious corporate types go for. There was an $8000 gold Rolex watch on his left wrist and a $3000 Wesley Barron pinstripe suit on the rest of him and he didn't seem too worried that I'd slug him and steal the Rolex. Probably had another just like it at home. 'Are you in business by yourself, Mr. Cole?' He'd have been more comfortable if I'd been in a suit and had a couple of wanted posters lying around.

'I have a partner named Joe Pike. Mr. Pike is not a licensed private investigator. He is a former Los Angeles police officer. I hold the license.' I pointed out the framed pink license that the Bureau of Collections of the State of California had issued to me. 'You see. Elvis Cole.' The license hangs beside this animation cel I've got of the Blue Fairy and Pinocchio. Pinocchio is as close as I come to a wanted poster.

Bradley Warren stared at the Blue Fairy and looked doubtful. He said, 'Something very valuable was stolen from my home four days ago. I need someone to find it.'

'Okay.'

'Do you know anything about the Japanese culture?'

'I read *Shōgun*.'

Warren made a quick hand gesture and said, 'Jillian.' His manner was brusque and I didn't like it much. Jillian Becker didn't seem to mind, but she was probably used to it.

Jillian said, 'The Japanese culture was once predicated on a very specific code of behavior and personal conduct developed by the samurai during Japan's feudal period.'

Samurai. Better buckle the old seat belt for this one.

'In the eighteenth century, a man named Jōchō Yamamoto outlined every aspect of proper behavior for the samurai in manuscript form. It was called "Recorded Words of the Hagakure Master," or, simply, the Hagakure, and only a few of the original editions survive. Mr. Warren had arranged the loan of one of these from the Tashiro family in Kyoto, with whom his company has extensive business dealings. The manuscript was in his home safe when it was stolen.'

As Jillian spoke, Bradley Warren looked around the office again and did some more frowning. He frowned at the Mickey Mouse phone. He frowned at the little figurines of Jiminy Cricket. He frowned at the Spider-Man mug. I considered taking out my gun and letting him frown at that, too, but thought it might seem peevish. 'How much is the Hagakure worth?'

Jillian Becker said, 'A little over three million dollars.'

'Insured?'

'Yes. But the policy won't begin to cover the millions our company will lose in business with the Tashiros unless their manuscript is recovered.'

'The police are pretty good. Why not go to them?'

Bradley Warren sighed loudly, letting us know he was bored, then frowned at the gold Rolex. Time equals money.

Jillian said, 'The police are involved, Mr. Cole, but we'd like things to proceed faster than they seem able to manage. That's why we came to you.'

'Oh,' I said. 'I thought you came to me so Bradley could practice frowning.'

Bradley looked at me. Pointedly. 'I'm the president of Warren Investments Corporation. We form real estate partnerships with Japanese investors.' He leaned forward and raised his eyebrows. 'I have a big operation. I'm in Hawaii. I'm in L.A., San Diego, Seattle.' He made an opera out of looking around my office. 'Try to imagine the money involved.'

Jillian Becker said, 'Mr. Warren's newest hotel has just opened downtown in Little Tokyo.'

Bradley said, 'Thirty-two stories. Eight million square feet.'

I nodded. 'Big.'

He nodded back at me.

Jillian said, 'We wanted to have the Hagakure on display there next week when the Pacific Men's Club names Bradley Man of the Month.'

Bradley gave me more of the eyebrows. 'I'm the first Caucasian they've honored this way. You know why? I've pumped three hundred million dollars into the local Asian community in the last thirty-six months. You got any idea how much money that is?'

'Excuse me,' I said. I pushed away from my desk, pitched myself out of my chair onto the floor, then got up, brushed myself off, and sat again. 'There. I'm finished being impressed. We can go on.'

Jillian Becker's face went white. Bradley Warren's face went dark red. His nostrils flared and his lips tightened and he stood up. It was lovely. He said, 'I don't like your attitude.'

'That's okay. I'm not selling it.' I opened the drawer in the center of my desk and tossed a cream-colored card toward him. He looked at it. 'What's this?'

'Pinkerton's. They're large. They're good. They're who you want. But they probably won't like your attitude any more than I do.' I stood up with him.

Jillian Becker stood up, too, and held out her hand the way you do when you want things to settle down. 'Mr. Cole, I think we've started on the wrong foot here.'

I leaned forward. 'One of us did.'

She turned toward Warren. 'It's a small firm, Bradley, but it's a quality firm. Two attorneys in the prosecutor's office recommended him. He's been an investigator for eight years and the police think highly of him. His references are impeccable.' Impeccable. I liked that.

Bradley Warren held the Pink's card and flexed it back and forth, breathing hard. He looked the way a man looks when he doesn't have any other choice and the choice he has is lousy. There's a Pinocchio clock on the wall beside the door that leads to Joe Pike's office. It has eyes that move from side to side. You go to the Pinkerton's, they don't have a clock like that. Jillian Becker said, 'Bradley, he's who you want to hire.'

After a while the heavy breathing passed and Bradley nodded. 'All right, Cole. I'll go along with Jillian on this and hire you.'

'No,' I said. 'You won't.'

Jillian Becker stiffened. Bradley Warren looked at Jillian Becker, then looked back at me. 'What do you mean, I won't?'

'I don't want to work for you.'

'Why not?'

'I don't like you.'

Bradley Warren started to say something, then stopped. His mouth opened, then closed. Jillian Becker looked confused. Maybe no one had ever before said no to Bradley Warren. Maybe it was against the law. Maybe Bradley Warren's personal police were about to crash through the door and arrest me for defying the One True Way. Jillian shook her head. 'They said you could be difficult.'

I shrugged. 'They should've said that when I'm pushed, I push back. They also should've said that when I do things, I do them my way.' I looked at Bradley. 'The check rents. It does not buy.'

Bradley Warren stared at me as if I had just beamed down from the *Enterprise*. He stood very still. So did Jillian Becker. They stood like that until a tic started beneath his left eye and he said, 'Jillian.'

Jillian Becker said, 'Mr. Cole, we need the Hagakure found, and we want you to find it. If we in some way offended you, we apologize.'

We.

'Will you help us?'

Her makeup was understated and appropriate, and there was a tasteful gold chain around her right wrist. She was bright and attractive and I wondered how many times she'd had to apologize for him and how it made her feel.

I gave her the Jack Nicholson smile and made a big deal out of sitting down again. 'For you, babe, anything.' Can you stand it?

Bradley Warren's face was red and purple and splotched, and the tic was a mad flicker. He made the hand gesture as quick as a cracking whip, and said, 'Write him a check and leave it blank. I'll be down in the limo.'

He left without looking at me and without offering his hand and without waiting for Jillian. When he was gone I said, 'My, my. Man of the Month.'

Jillian Becker took a deep breath, let it out, then sat in one of the director's chairs and opened the Gucci briefcase in her lap. She took out a corporate checkbook and spoke while she wrote. 'Mr. Cole, please understand that Bradley's under enormous pressure. We're on our way to Kyoto to tell the Tashiros what has happened. That will be neither pleasant nor easy.'

'Sorry,' I said. 'I should be more sensitive.'

She glanced up from the check with cool eyes. 'Maybe you should.'

So much for humor.

After a while, she put the check and a 3 × 5 index card on my desk. I didn't look at the check. She said, 'The card has Bradley's home and office addresses and phone numbers. It also has mine. You may call me at any time, day or night, for anything that pertains to this case.'

'Okay.'

'Will you need anything else?'

'Access to the house. I want to see where the book was and talk to anyone who knew that the book was there. Also, if there's a photograph or description of the manuscript, I'll need it.'

'Bradley's wife can supply that. At the house.'

'What's her name?'

'Sheila. Their daughter Mimi lives at the house, also, along with two housekeepers. I'll call Sheila and tell her to expect you.'

'Fine.'

'Fine.'

We were getting along just great.

Jillian Becker closed the Gucci briefcase, snapped its latch, stood, and went to the door. Maybe she hadn't always been this serious. Maybe working for Bradley brought it out in her.

'You do that well,' I said.

She looked back. 'What?'

'Walk.'

She gave me the cool eyes again. 'This is a business relationship, Mr. Cole. Let's leave it at that.'

'Sure.'

She opened the door.

'One more thing.'

She turned back to me.

'You always look this good, or is today a special occasion?'

She stood like that for a while, not moving, and then she shook her head. 'You really are something, aren't you?'

I made a gun out of my hand, pointed it at her, and gave her another dose of the Nicholson. 'I hope he pays you well.'

She went out and slammed the door.

CHAPTER 2

When the door closed I looked at the check. Blank. She hadn't dated it 1889 or April 1. It had been signed by Bradley Warren and, as far as I could tell, in ink that wouldn't vanish. Maybe a better detective would have known for sure about the ink, but I'd have to risk it. Son of a gun. My big chance. I could nick him for a hundred thousand dollars, but that was probably playing it small. Maybe I should put a one and write zeros until my arm fell off and endorse it Elvis Cole, Yachtsman.

I folded the check in half, put it in my wallet, and took a Dan Wesson .38 in a shoulder rig out of my top right-hand drawer. I pulled a white cotton jacket on to cover the Dan Wesson, then went down to my car. The car is a Jamaica-yellow 1966 Corvette convertible that looks pretty snazzy. Maybe with the white jacket and the convertible and the blank check in my pocket, someone would think I was Donald Trump.

I put the Corvette out onto Santa Monica and cruised west through Beverly Hills and the upper rim of Century City, then north up Beverly Glen past rows of palm trees and stuccoed apartment houses and Persian-owned construction projects. L.A. in late June is bright. With the smog pressed down by an inversion layer, the sky turns white and the sun glares brilliantly from signs and awnings and reflective building glass and deep-waxed fenders and miles and miles of molten chrome bumpers. There were shirtless kids with skateboards on their way into Westwood and older women with big hats coming back from markets and construction workers tearing up the streets and Hispanic women waiting for buses and everybody wore sunglasses. It looked like a Ray Ban commercial.

I stayed with Beverly Glen up past the Los Angeles Country Club golf course until I got to Sunset Boulevard, then hung a right and a quick left into upper Holmby Hills. Holmby is a smaller, more expensive version of the very best part of Beverly Hills to the east. It is old and elegant, and the streets are wide and neat with proper curbs and large homes hidden behind hedgerows and mortar walls and black wrought iron gates. Many of the houses are near the street, but a few are set back and quite a few you can't see at all.

The Warrens' home was the one with the guard. He was sitting in a light blue Thunderbird with a sticker on its side that said TITAN SECURITIES. He got out when he saw me slow down and stood with his hands on his hips. Late forties, big across the back, in a brown off-the-rack Sears suit. Wrinkled. He'd taken a couple of hard ones on the bridge of his nose, but that had been a long time ago. I turned into the drive, and showed him the license. 'Cole. They're expecting me.'

He nodded at the license and leaned against the door. 'She sent the kid down to tell me you were on the way. I'm Hatcher.' He didn't offer to shake my hand.

I said, 'Anyone try storming the house?'

He looked back at the house, then shook his head. 'Shit. I been out here since they got hit and I ain't seen dick.' He shot me a wink. 'Leastways, not what you're talking about.'

I said, 'Are you tipping me off or is something in your eye?'

He smirked. 'You been out before?'

'Uh-uh.'

He gave me some more of the smirk, then ambled back to the Thunderbird. 'You'll see.'

Bradley Warren lived in a French Normandy mansion just about the size of Kansas. A large Spanish oak in the center of the motor court put filigreed shadows on the Normandy's steep roof, and three or four thousand snapdragons spilled out of the beds that bordered the drive and the perimeter of the house. There was a porchlike overhang at the front of the house with the front door recessed in a wide alcove. It was a single door, but it was a good nine feet high and four feet wide. Maybe Bradley Warren had bought the place from the Munsters.

I parked under the big oak, walked over to the door, and rang the bell. Hatcher was twisted around in his T-bird, watching. I rang the bell two more times before the door opened and a woman wearing a white Love tennis outfit and holding a tall glass with something clear in it looked up at me. She said, 'Are you the detective?'

'Usually I wear a deerstalker cap,' I said, 'but today it's at the cleaners.'

She laughed too loud and put out her hand. 'Sheila Warren,' she said. 'You're a good-looking devil, aren't you.' Twenty minutes before noon and she was drunk.

I looked back at Hatcher. He was grinning.

Sheila Warren was in her forties, with tanned skin and a sharp nose and bright blue eyes and auburn hair. She had the sort of deep lines you get when you play a lot of tennis or golf or otherwise hang out in the sun. The hair was pulled back in a pony tail and she wore a white headband. She looked good in the tennis outfit, but not athletic. Probably did more hanging out than playing.

She opened the door wider and gestured with the glass for me to come in. Ice tinkled. 'I suppose you want to see where he had the damn book.' She said it like we were talking about an eighth-grade history book.

'Sure.'

She gestured with the glass again. 'I always like to have something cool when I come in off the court. All that sweat. Can I get you something?'

'Maybe later.'

We walked back through about six thousand miles of entry and a living room they could rent out as an airplane hangar and a dining room with seating for Congress. She stayed a step in front of me and swayed as she walked. I said, 'Was anyone home the night it was stolen?'

'We were in Canada. Bradley's building a hotel in Edmonton so we flew up. Bradley usually flies alone, but the kid and I wanted to go so we went.' The kid.

'How about the help?'

'They've all got family living down in Little Tokyo. They beat it down there as soon as we're out of the house.' She looked back at me. 'The police asked all this, you know.'

'I like to check up on them.'

She said, 'Oh, you.'

We went down a long hall with a tile floor and into a cavern that turned out to be the master bedroom. At the end of the hall there was an open marble atrium with a lot of green leafy plants in it, and to the left of the atrium there were glass doors looking out to the back lawn and the pool. Where one of the glass doors had been, there was now a 4 × 8 sheet of plywood as if the glass had been broken and the plywood put there until the glass could be replaced. Opposite the atrium, there was a black lacquer platform bed and a lot of black lacquer furniture. We went past the bed and through a doorway into a *his* dressing room. The *hers* had a separate entrance.

The *his* held a full-length three-way dressing mirror and a black granite dressing table and about a mile and a half of coats and slacks and suits and enough shoes to shod a small American city. At the foot of the dressing mirror the carpet had been rolled back and there was a Citabria-Wilcox floor safe large enough for a man to squat in.

Sheila Warren gestured toward it with the glass and made a face. 'The big shot's safe.'

The top was lying open like a manhole cover swung over on a hinge. It was quarter-inch plate steel with two tumblers and three half-inch shear pins. There was black powder on everything from when the crime scene guys dusted for prints. Nothing else seemed disturbed. The ice tinkled behind me. 'Was the safe like this when you found it?'

'It was closed. The police left it open.'

'How about the alarm?'

'The police said they must've known how to turn it off. Or maybe we forgot to turn it on.' She gave a little shrug when she said it, like it didn't matter very much in the first place and she was tired of talking about it. She was leaning against the door-jamb with her arms crossed, watching me. Maybe she thought that when detectives flew into action it was something you didn't want to miss. 'You should've seen the glass,' she said. 'He brings the damn book here and look what happens. I walk barefoot on the carpet and I still pick up slivers. Mr. Big Shot Businessman.' She didn't say the last part to me.

'Has anyone called, or delivered a ransom note?'

'For what?'

'The book. When something rare and easily identifiable is stolen, it's usually stolen to sell it back to the owner or his insurance company.'

She made another face. 'That's silly.'

I guess that meant no. I stood up. 'Your husband said there were pictures of the book.'

She finished the drink and said, 'I wish he'd take care of these things himself.' Then she left. Maybe I could go out and Hatcher could come in and question her for me. Maybe Hatcher already had.

Maybe I should call the airport and catch Bradley's plane and tell him he could keep his check and his job. Nah. What would Donald Trump think?

When Sheila Warren came back, she had gotten rid of the glass and was carrying a color 8 × 10 showing Bradley accepting something that looked like a photo album from a dignified white-haired Japanese gentleman. There were other men around, all Japanese, but not all of them looked dignified. The book was a dark rich brown, probably leather-covered board, and would probably crumble if you sneered at it. Jillian Becker was in the picture.

Sheila Warren said, 'I hope this is what you want.' The top three buttons on her tennis outfit had been undone.

'This will be fine,' I said. I folded the picture and put it in my pocket.

She wet her lips. 'Are you sure I can't get you something to drink?'

'Positive, thanks.'

She looked down at her shoes, said, 'Ooo, these darn laces,' then turned her back and bent over from the hip. The laces hadn't looked untied to me, but I miss a lot. She played with one lace and then she played with the other, and while she was playing with them I walked out. I wandered back through to the kitchen and from there to the rear yard. There was a dichondra lawn that sloped gently away from the house toward a fifty-foot Greek Revival swimming pool and a small pool house with a sunken conversation pit around a circular grill. I stood at the deep end of the pool and looked around and shook my head. Man. First him. Now her. What a pair.

Whoever had gone into the house had probably known the combination or known where to find it. Combinations are easy to get. One day when no one's around, a gardener slips in, finds the scrap of paper on which people like Bradley Warren always write their combinations, then sells it to the right guy for the right price. Or maybe one day Sheila flexed a little too much upper-class muscle with the hundred-buck-a-week housekeeper, and the housekeeper says, Okay, bitch, here's one for you, and feeds the numbers to her out-of-work boyfriend. You could go on.

I walked along the pool deck past the tennis court and along the edge of the property and then back toward the house. There were no guard dogs and no closed-circuit cameras and no fancy surveillance equipment. The wall around the perimeter wasn't electrified, and if there was a guard tower it was disguised as a palm tree. Half the kids on Hollywood Boulevard could loot the place blind. Maybe I'd go down there and question them. Only take me three or four years.

When I got back to the house, a teenage girl was sitting on one of four couches in the den. She was cross-legged, staring down into the oversized pages of a book that could've been titled *Andrew Wyeth's Bleakest Landscapes*.

I said, 'Hi, my name's Elvis. Are you Mimi?'

She looked up at me the way you look at someone when you open your front door and see it's a Jehovah's Witness. She was maybe sixteen and had close-cropped brown hair that framed her face like a small inner tube. It made her face rounder than it was. I would have suggested something upswept or shag-cut to give her face some length, but she hadn't asked me. There was no makeup and no nail polish and some would have been in order. She wasn't pretty. She rubbed at her nose and said, 'Are you the detective?'

'Uh-huh. You got any clues about the big theft?'

She rubbed at her nose again.

'Clues,' I said. 'Did you see a shadow skulk across the lawn? Did you overhear a snatch of mysterious conversation? That kind of thing.'

Maybe she was looking at me. Maybe she wasn't. There was sort of a cockeyed grin on her face that made me wonder if she was high.

'Would you like to get back to your book?'

She didn't nod or blink or run screaming from the room. She just stared.

I went back through the dining room and the entry and out to my Corvette and cranked it up and eased down the drive. When I got to the street, Hatcher grinned over from his T-bird, and said, 'How'd you like it?'

'Up yours,' I said.

He laughed and I drove away.

CHAPTER 3

Three years ago I'd done some work for a man named Berke Feldstein who owns a very nice art gallery in Venice on the beach below Santa Monica. It's one of those converted industrial spaces where they slap on a coat of stark white paint to maintain the industrial look and all the art is white boxes with colored paper inside. For Christmas that year, Berke had given me a large mug with the words MONSTER FIGHTER emblazoned on its side. I like it a lot.

I dropped down out of Holmby Hills into Westwood, parked at a falafel stand, and used their pay phone to call Berke's gallery. A woman's voice answered, 'ArtWerks Gallery.'

I said, 'This is Michael Delacroix's representative calling. Is Mr. Feldman receiving?' A black kid in a UCLA tee shirt was slumped at one of the picnic tables they have out there, reading a sociology text.

Her voice came back hesitant. 'You mean Mr. Feldstein?'

I gave her imperious. 'Is *that* his name?'

She asked me to hold. There were the sounds of something or someone moving around in the background, and then Berke Feldstein said, 'Who is this, please?'

'The King of Rock 'n' Roll.'

A dry, sardonic laugh. Berke Feldstein does sardonic better than anyone else I know. 'Don't tell me. You're trying to decide between the Monet and the Degas and you need my advice.'

I said, 'Something very rare from eighteenth-century Japan has been stolen. Who might have some ideas about that?' The black kid closed the book and looked at me.

Berke Feldstein put me on hold. After a minute, he was on the line again. His voice was flat and serious. 'I won't be connected with this?'

227

'Berke.' I gave him miffed.

He said, 'There's a Gallery on Cañon Drive in Beverly Hills. The Sun Tree Gallery. It's owned by a guy named Malcolm Denning. I can't *swear* by this, but I've heard that Denning's occasionally a conduit for less than honest transactions.'

'"Less than honest." I like that. Do we mean "criminal"?' The black kid got up and walked away.

'Don't be smug,' Berke said.

'How come you hear about these less than honest transactions, Berke? You got something going on the side?'

He hung up.

There were several ways to locate the Sun Tree Gallery. I could call one of the contacts I maintain in the police department and have them search through their secret files. I could drive about aimlessly, stopping at every gallery I passed until I found someone who knew the location, then force the information from him. Or I could look in the Yellow Pages. I looked in the Yellow Pages.

The Sun Tree Gallery of Beverly Hills rested atop a jewelry store two blocks over from Rodeo Drive amidst some of the world's most exclusive shopping. There were plenty of boutiques with Arabic or Italian names, and small plaques that said BY APPOINTMENT ONLY. The shoppers were rich, the cars were German, and the doormen were mostly young and handsome and looking to land a lead in an action-adventure series. You could smell the crime in the air.

I passed the gallery twice without finding a parking spot, continued north up Cañon above Santa Monica Boulevard to the residential part of the Beverly Hills flats, parked there, and walked back. A heavy glass door was next to the jewelry store with a small, tasteful brass sign that said SUN TREE GALLERY, HOURS 10:00 A.M. UNTIL 5:00 P.M., TUESDAY THROUGH SATURDAY; DARK, SUNDAY AND MONDAY. I went through the door and climbed a flight of plush stairs that led up to a landing where there was a much heavier door with another brass sign that said RING BELL. Maybe when you rang the bell, a guy in a beret with a long scar beside his nose slithered out and asked if you wanted to buy some stolen art. I rang the bell.

A very attractive brunette in a claret-colored pants suit appeared in the door, buzzed me in, and said brightly, 'I hope you're having a good day.' These criminals will do anything to gain your confidence.

'I could take it or leave it until you said that. Is Mr. Denning in?'

'Yes, but I'm afraid he's on long distance just now. If you could wait a moment, I'd love to help you.' There was an older, balding man and a silver-haired woman standing at the front of the place by a long glass wall that faced down on the street. The man was looking at a shiny black helmet not unlike that worn by Darth Vader. It was sitting on a sleek red pedestal and was covered by a glass dome.

'Sure,' I said. 'Mind if I browse?'

She handed me a price catalog and another big smile. 'Not at all.' These crooks.

The gallery was one large room that had been sectioned off by three false walls to form little viewing alcoves. There weren't many pieces on display, but what was there seemed authentic. Vases and bowls sat on pedestals beneath elegant watercolors done on thin cloth that had been stretched over a bamboo frame. The cloth was yellow with age. There were quite a few wood-block prints that I liked, including a very nice double print that was two separate prints mounted side by side. Each was of the same man in a bamboo house overlooking a river as a storm raged at the horizon and lightning flashed. Each man held a bit of blue cloth that trailed away out of the picture. The pictures were mounted so that the cloth trailed from one picture to the other, connecting the men. It was a lovely piece and would be a fine addition to my home. I looked up the price. $14,000. Maybe I could find something more appropriate to my decor.

At the rear of the gallery there was a sleek Elliot Ryerson desk, three beige corduroy chairs for sitting down and discussing the financing of your purchase, and a good stand of the indoor palms I am always trying to grow in my office but which are always dying. These were thriving. Behind the palms was a door. It opened, and a man in a pink LaCoste shirt and khaki slacks came out and began looking for something on the desk. Mid-forties. Short hair with a sprinkling of gray. The brunette looked over and said, 'Mr. Denning, this gentleman would like to see you.'

Malcolm Denning gave me a friendly smile and put out his hand. He had sad eyes. 'Can you give me a minute? I'm on the phone with a client in Paris.' Good handshake.

'Sure.'

'Thanks. I won't be any longer than necessary.' He gave me another smile, found what he was looking for, then disappeared back through the door. Malcolm Denning, Considerate Crook.

The brunette resumed talking to the older couple and I resumed browsing and when everything was back the way it had been, I went through the door. There was a short hall with a bathroom on the left, what looked like a storage and packing area at the rear, and a small office on the right. Malcolm Denning was in the office, seated at a cluttered rolltop desk, speaking French into the phone. He looked up when he saw me, cupped the receiver, and said, 'I'm sorry. This will take another minute or so.'

I took out my license and held it for him to see. I could've showed him a card, but the license looked more official. 'Elvis Cole's the name, private detecting's the game.' One of those things you always want to say. 'I've got a few questions about feudal Japanese art and I'm told you're the man to ask.'

Without taking his eyes from me, he spoke more French into the phone, nodded at something I couldn't hear, then hung up. There were four photographs along the top of the desk, one of an overweight woman with a pleasant smile, and another of three teenage boys. One of the pictures was of a Little League team with Malcolm Denning and another man both wearing shirts that said COACH. 'May I ask who referred you to me?'

'You can ask, but I'm afraid I couldn't tell you. Somebody tells me something, I try to protect the source. Especially if what they've told me can be incriminating. You see?'

'Incriminating?'

'*Especially* if it's incriminating.'

He nodded.

'You know what the Hagakure is, Mr. Denning?'

Nervous. 'Well, the Hagakure isn't really a piece of what we might call art. It's a book, you know.' He put one hand on his desk and the other in his lap. There was a red mug on the desk that said DAD.

'But it's fair to say that whoever might have an interest in early Japanese art might also have an interest in the Hagakure, wouldn't it?'

'I guess.'

'One of the original copies of the Hagakure was stolen a few days ago. Would you have heard anything about that?'

'Why on earth would I hear anything about it?'

'Because you've been known to broker a rip-off or two.'

He pushed back his chair and stood up. The two of us in the little office was like being in a phone booth. 'I think you should leave,' he said.

'Come on, Malcolm. Give us both a break. You don't want to be hassled and I can hassle you.'

The outer door opened and the pretty brunette came back into the little hall. She saw us standing there, broke into the smile, said, 'Oh, I wondered where you'd gone.' Then she saw the look on Denning's face. 'Mr. Denning?'

He looked at me and I looked back. Then he glanced at her. 'Yes, Barbara?'

Nervousness is contagious. She looked from Denning to me and back to Denning. She said, 'The Kendals want to purchase the Myori.'

I said, 'Maybe the Kendals can help me.'

Malcolm Denning stared at me for a long time and then he sat down. He said, 'I'll be right out.'

When she was gone, he said, 'I can sue you for this. I can get an injunction to bar you from the premises. I can have you arrested.' His voice was hoarse. An I-always-thought-this-would-happen-and-now-it-has voice.

'Sure,' I said.

He stared at me, breathing hard, thinking it through, wondering how far he'd have to go if he picked up the ball, and how much it would cost him.

I said, 'If someone wanted the Hagakure, who might arrange for its theft? If the Hagakure were for sale, who might buy it?'

His eyes flicked over the pictures on the desk. The wife, the sons. The Little League. I watched the sad eyes. He was a nice man. Maybe even a good man. Sometimes, in this job, you wonder how someone managed to take the wrong turn. You wonder where it happened and when and why. But you don't really want to know. If you knew, it would break your heart.

He said, 'There's a man in Little Tokyo. He has some sort of import business. Nobu Ishida.' He told me where I could find Ishida. He stared at the pictures as he told me.

After a while I went out through the gallery and down the stairs and along Cañon to my car. It was past three and traffic was starting to build, so it took the better part of an hour to move back along Sunset and climb the mountain to the little A-frame I have off Woodrow Wilson Drive above Hollywood. When I got inside, I took two cold Falstaff beers out of the fridge, pulled off my shirt, and went out onto my deck.

There was a black cat crouched under a Weber charcoal grill that

I keep out there. He's big and he's mean and he's black all over except for the white scars that lace his fur like spider webs. He keeps one ear up and one ear sort of cocked to the side because someone once shot him. Head shot. He hasn't been right since.

'You want some beer?'

He growled.

'Forget it, then.'

The growling stopped.

I took out the center section of the railing that runs around the deck, sat on the edge, and opened the first Falstaff. From my deck you can see across a long twisting canyon that widens and spreads into Hollywood. I like to sit there with my feet hanging down and drink and think about things. It's about thirty feet from the deck to the slope below, but that's okay. I like the height. Sometimes the hawks come and float above the canyon and above the smog. They like the height, too.

I drank some of the beer and thought about Bradley and Sheila and Jillian Becker and Malcolm Denning. Bradley would be sitting comfortably in first class, dictating important business notes to Jillian Becker, who would be writing them down and nodding. Sheila would be out on her tennis court, bending over to show Hatcher her rear end, and squealing, *Ooo, these darn laces!* Malcolm Denning would be staring at the pictures of his wife and his boys and his Little League team and wondering when it would all go to hell.

'You ever notice,' I said to the cat, 'that sometimes the bad guys are better people than the good guys?'

The cat crept out from beneath the Weber, walked over, and sniffed at my beer. I poured a little out onto the deck for him and touched his back as he drank. It was soft.

Sometimes he bites, but not always.

CHAPTER 4

The next morning it was warm and bright in my loft, with the summer sun slanting in through the big glass A that is the back of my house. The cat was curled on the bed next to me, bits of leaf and dust in his fur, smelling of eucalyptus.

I rolled out of bed and pulled on some shorts and went downstairs. I opened the glass sliding doors for the breeze, then went back into the living room and turned on the TV. News. I changed channels. Rocky and Bullwinkle. There was a thump upstairs and then the cat came down. Bullwinkle said, 'Nothing up my sleeve!' and ripped off his sleeve to prove it. Rocky said, 'Oh, no, not again!' and flew around in a circle. The cat hopped up on the couch and stared at them. *The Adventures of Rocky and Bullwinkle* is his favorite show.

I went back out onto the deck and did twelve sun salutes to stretch out the kinks. I did neck rolls and shoulder rolls and the spine rock and the cobra and the locust, and I began to sweat. Inside, Mr. Peabody and Sherman were setting the Way Back Machine for the Early Mesopotamian Age. I put myself into the peacock posture with my legs straight out behind me and I held it like that until my back screamed and the sweat left dark splatters on the deck, and then I went into the Dragon *kata* from the tae kwon do, and then the Crane *kata*, driving myself until the sweat ran in my eyes and my muscles failed and my nerves refused to carry another signal and I sat on the deck and felt like a million bucks. Endorphin heaven. So clients weren't perfect. So being a private cop wasn't perfect. So life wasn't perfect. I could always get new cards printed up. They would say: *Elvis Cole, Perfect Detective.*

Forty minutes later I was on the Hollywood Freeway heading southeast toward downtown Los Angeles and Little Tokyo and feeling pretty good about myself. Ah, perfection. It lends comfort in troubled times.

I stayed with the Hollywood past the Pasadena interchange, then took the Broadway exit into downtown L.A. Downtown Los Angeles features dirty inner-city streets, close-packed inner-city skyscrapers, and aromatic inner-city street life. The men who work there wear suits and the women wear heels and you see people carrying umbrellas as if it might rain. Downtown Los Angeles does not feel like Los Angeles. It is Boston or Chicago or Detroit or Manhattan. It feels like someplace else that had come out to visit and decided to stay. Maybe one day they'll put a dome over it and charge admission. They could call it Banal-land.

I took Broadway down to First Street, hung a left, and two blocks later I was in Little Tokyo.

The buildings were old, mostly brick or stone facade, but they had been kept up and the streets were clean. Paper lanterns hung in front of some of the shops, and red and green and yellow and blue wind socks in front of others, and all the signs were in Japanese. The sidewalks were crowded. Summer is tourist season, and most of the white faces and many of the yellow ones had Nikons or Pentaxes slung under them. A knot of sailors in Italian navy uniforms stood at a street corner, grinning at a couple of girls in a Camaro who grinned back at them. One of the sailors carried a Disneyland bag with Mickey Mouse on the side. Souvenirs from distant lands.

Nobu Ishida's import business was exactly where Malcolm Denning said it would be, in an older building on Ki Street between a fish market and a Japanese-language bookstore, with a yakitori grill across the street.

I rolled past Ishida's place, found a parking spot in front of one of the souvenir shops they have for people from Cleveland, and walked back. There was a little bell on the door that rang as I went in and three men sitting around two tables at the rear of the place. It looked more like a warehouse than a retail outlet, with boxes stacked floor to ceiling and lots of freestanding metal shelves. A few things were on display, mostly garish lacquered boxes and miniature pagodas and dragons that looked like Barkley from *Sesame Street*. I smiled at the three men. 'Nice stuff.'

One of them said, 'What do you want?' He was a lot younger than the other two, maybe in his early twenties. No accent. Born and raised in Southern California with a surfer's tan to prove it. He was big for someone of Japanese extraction, just over six feet, with muscular arms and lean jaws and the sort of wildly overdeveloped trapezius muscles you get when you spend a lot of time with the weights. He wore a tight knit shirt with a crew neck and three-quarter sleeves even though it was ninety degrees outside. The other two guys were both in their thirties. One of them had a bad left eye as if he had taken a hard one there and it had never healed, and the other had the pinkie missing from his right hand. I made the young one for Ishida's advertising manager and the other two for buyers from Neiman-Marcus.

'My name's Elvis Cole,' I said. 'Are you Nobu Ishida?' I put one of my cards on the second table.

The one with the missing finger grinned at the big kid and said, 'Hey, Eddie, are you Nobu Ishida?'

Eddie said, 'You have business with Mr. Ishida?'

'Well, it's what we might call personal.'

The one with the bad eye said something in Japanese.

'Sorry,' I said. 'Japanese is one of the four known languages I don't speak.'

Eddie said, 'Maybe you'll understand this, dude. Fuck off.'

They probably weren't from Neiman-Marcus. I said, 'You'd better ask Mr. Ishida. Tell him it's about eighteenth-century Japan.'

Eddie thought about it for a while, then picked up my card, and said, 'Wait here.' He disappeared behind stacks of what looked like sushi trays and bamboo steamers.

The guy with the bad eye and the guy with no finger stared at me. I said, 'I guess Mr. Ishida keeps you guys around to take inventory.'

The guy with no finger smiled, but I don't think he was being friendly.

A little bit later Eddie came back without the card and said, 'Time for you to go.'

I said, 'Ask him again. I won't take much of his time.'

'You're leaving.'

I looked from Eddie to the other two and back to Eddie. 'Nope. I'm going to stay and I'm going to talk to Ishida or I'm going to tip the cops that you guys deal stolen goods.' Mr. Threat.

The guy with the bad eye mumbled something else and they all laughed. Eddie pulled his sleeves up to his elbows and flexed his arms. Big, all right. Elaborate, multicolored tattoos started about an inch below his elbows and continued up beneath the sleeves. They looked like fish scales. His hands were square and blocky and his

235

knuckles were thick. He said something in Japanese and the guy with the missing finger came around the tables like he was going to show me the door. When he reached to take my arm I pushed his hand away. He stopped smiling and threw a pretty fast backfist. I pushed the fist past me and hit him in the neck with my left hand. He made the sound a drunk in a cheap restaurant makes with a piece of meat caught in his throat and went down. The guy with the bad eye was coming around the tables when an older man came out from behind the bamboo steamers and spoke sharply and the guy with the bad eye stopped.

Nobu Ishida was in his early fifties with short gray hair and hard black eyes and a paunch for a belly. Even with the paunch, the other guys seemed to straighten up and pay attention. Those who could stand.

He looked at me the way you look at a disappearing menu, then shook his head. The guy on the floor was making small coughing noises but Nobu Ishida didn't look at him and neither did anyone else. Ishida was carrying my card. 'What are you, crazy? You know I could have you arrested for this?' Nobu Ishida didn't have an accent, either.

I gave him a little shrug. 'Go ahead.'

He said, 'What do you want?'

I told him about the Hagakure.

Nobu Ishida listened without moving and then he tried to give me good-natured confusion. 'I don't get it. Why come to me?'

The guy with the missing finger stopped making noises and pushed himself up to his knees. He was holding his throat. I said, 'You're interested in samurai artifacts. The Hagakure was stolen. You've purchased stolen artworks in the past. You see how this works?'

The good-natured confusion went away. Ishida's mouth tightened and something dark washed his face. Telltale signs of guilt. 'Who says I've bought stolen art?'

'Akira Kurosawa gave me a call.'

Ishida stared at me a very long time. 'Oh, we've got a funny one here, Eddie.'

Eddie said, 'I don't like him.' Eddie.

I said, 'I think you might have the Hagakure. If you don't, I think you might know the people who stole it or who have it.'

Ishida gave me the stare a little more, thinking, and then the tension went out of his face and his shoulders relaxed and he

236

smiled. This time the smile was real, as if in all the thinking he had seen something and what he had seen had been funny as hell. He glanced at Eddie and then at the other two guys and then back at me. 'You got no idea how stupid you are,' he said.

'People hint.'

He laughed and Eddie laughed, too. Eddie crossed his arms and made the huge trapezius muscles swell like a couple of demented air bladders. You could see that the tattoos climbed over his elbows and up his biceps. Pretty soon, everybody was laughing but me and the guy on the floor.

Ishida held up my card and looked at it, then crumpled it up and tossed it toward an open crate of little plastic pagodas. He said, 'Your problem is, you don't look like a private detective.'

'What's a private detective look like?'

'Like Mickey Spillane. You see those Lite beer commercials? Mickey Spillane looks tough.'

I hooked a glance at the guy with the crushed neck. 'Ask him.'

Nobu Ishida nodded, but it didn't seem to matter much. The smile went away and the serious eyes came back. Hard. 'Don't come down here anymore, boy. You don't know what you're messing with down here.'

I said, 'What about the Hagakure?'

Nobu Ishida gave me what I guess was supposed to be an enigmatic look, then he turned and melted away behind the bamboo steamers.

I looked at Eddie. 'Is the interview over?'

Eddie made the tattoos disappear, then sat down behind the tables again and stared at me. The guy with the bad eye sat down beside him, put his feet up, and laced his hands behind his head. The guy with the missing finger pulled one foot beneath himself, then the other, then shoved himself up into sort of a hunched crouch. If I stood around much longer, they'd probably send me out for Chinese.

'Some days are the pits,' I said. 'Drive all the way down here and don't get so much as one clue.'

The guy with the bad eye nodded, agreeing.

Eddie nodded, too. 'Watch those Lite beer commercials,' he said. 'If you looked more like a detective, people might be more cooperative.'

CHAPTER 5

I walked back along Ki to the first cross street, turned north, then turned again into an alley that ran along behind Ishida's shop. There were delivery vans and trash cans and dumpsters and lots of very old, very small people who did not look at me. An ice truck was parked behind the fish market. At the back of Ishida's place there was a metal loading dock for deliveries and another door about six feet to the right for people and a small, dirty window with a steel grid over it between the doors. An anonymous tan delivery van was parked by the people door. Nobu Ishida probably did not use the van as his personal car. He probably drove a Lincoln or a Mercedes into the parking garage down the block, then walked back to the office. It was either that or matter transference.

I continued along the alley to the next street, then went south back to Ki and into the yakitori grill across the street.

I sat at the counter near the front so I could keep an eye on Ishida's and ordered two skewers of chicken and two of giant clam and a pot of green tea. The cook was an x-ray thin guy in his fifties who wore a pristine white apron and a little white cap and had gold worked into his front teeth like Mike Tyson. He said, 'You want spicy?'

I said sure.

He said, 'It hot.'

I said I was tough.

He brought over the tea in a little metal pot with a heavy white teacup and set a fork and a spoon and a paper napkin in front of me. No-frills service. He opened the little metal refrigerator and took out two strips of chicken breast and a fresh geoduck clam that looked like a bull's penis. He forced each strip of chicken lengthways onto a long wooden skewer, then skinned the geoduck and sliced two strips of the long muscle with a cleaver that could take a man's arm. When the geoduck was skewered he looked doubtfully back at me. 'Spicy very hot,' he said. He pronounced the *r* fine.

'Double spicy,' I said.

The gold in his teeth flashed and he took a blue bowl off a shelf and poured a thick powder of crushed chili peppers onto his work surface. He pressed each skewer of meat down into the powder, first one side, then the other, then arranged all four skewers on the grill. Other side of the counter, I could still feel the heat. 'We see,' he said. Then he went into the back.

I sipped tea and watched Ishida's. After a few minutes, Eddie and the guy with no finger came out, got in a dark green Alfa Romeo parked at the curb, and drove away. Eddie didn't look happy. I sipped more tea and did more watching, but nobody else came out. Real going concern, that place.

The cook came back and flipped the skewers. He put a little white saucer of red chili paste in front of me. It was the real stuff, the kind they make in Asia, not the junk you buy at the supermarket. Real chili paste will eat through porcelain. He gave me a big smile. 'In case not hot enough.' Don't you love a wiseass?

When the edges of the chicken and clam were blackened, he took the skewers off the grill. He dipped them in a pan of yakitori sauce, put them in a paperlined plastic basket, put the basket beside the chili paste, then leaned back against his grill and watched me.

I took a mouthful of the chicken, chewed, swallowed. Not bad. I dipped some of the chicken in the chili paste, took another bite. 'Could be hotter,' I said.

He looked disappointed and went into the back.

I sipped more tea, finished the first chicken, then started on the first geoduck. The clam was tough and hard and chewy, but I like that. The tea was good. While I was chewing, a Japanese guy wearing a Grateful Dead tee shirt came in and went up to the counter. He looked at the chalkboard where the daily menu was written, then looked at what was left of the geoduck lying beside the grill and made a face. He turned away and walked back to a pay phone they had in the rear. Some guys you can never please.

Twenty minutes later I was on my second pot of tea when Nobu Ishida came out and started up the street toward the parking garage. I paid, left a nice tip, then went out onto the sidewalk. When Ishida disappeared into the garage, I trotted back down to my car, got in, and waited. Maybe Ishida had a secret vault dug into the core of a mountain where he kept stolen treasure. Maybe he called this secret place The Fortress of Solitude. Maybe he was going there now and I could follow him and find the Hagakure and solve several heretofore unsolved art thefts. Then again, maybe not. I was three cars behind him when he pulled out in a black Cadillac Eldorado and turned right toward downtown.

We left Little Tokyo and went past Union Station and Olvera Street with its gaudy Mexican colors and food booths and souvenir shops. There were about nine million tourists, all desperately snapping pictures of how 'the Mexicans' lived, and buying sombreros and ponchos and stuffed iguanas that would start to ripen about a week after they got home. We swung around the Civic Center and were sitting in traffic at Pershing Square, me now four cars behind and counting the homeless bag ladies around the Square, when I spotted the guy in the Grateful Dead tee shirt from the yakitori grill. He was sitting behind the wheel of a maroon Ford Taurus two cars in back of me and one lane over. There was another Asian guy with him. Hmmmm. When the light changed and Ishida went straight, I hung a left onto Sixth. Two cars later, the Taurus followed. I stayed on Sixth to San Pedro and went south. The Taurus came south, too. I took the Dan Wesson out of the glove box and put it between my legs. Freud would've loved that.

At a spotlight on the corner of Fourteenth Street and Commerce, the Taurus pulled up on my left. I looked over. The guy in the Grateful Dead shirt and the other guy were staring at me and they were not smiling. I gripped the Dan Wesson in my right hand and said, 'Sony makes a fine TV.'

The guy on the passenger side said something to the driver, then turned back to me and flipped open a small black leather case with a silver and gold L.A.P.D. badge in it. 'Put it over to the curb, asshole.'

'*Moi*?'

The Taurus bucked out ahead under the red light and jerked to the right, blocking me. They were out and coming before the Taurus stopped rocking. I put both hands on the top of the steering wheel and left them there.

The guy who had shown me the badge came directly at me. The other guy walked the long way around the car and came up from behind. The car behind us blew its horn. I said, 'I swear to God, Officer. I came to a full stop.'

The one with the badge had the sort of face they hand out to bantamweights, all flat planes and busted nose, and a knotty build to go with it. I made him for forty but he could've been younger. He said, 'Get out of the car.'

I kept my hands on the wheel. 'There's a Dan Wesson .38 sitting here between my legs.'

Grateful Dead had a gun under my ear before I finished the sentence. The other cop brought his gun out, too, and put it in my face and reached through the window and lifted out the Dan Wesson. Grateful Dead pulled me out of the Corvette and shoved me against the fender and frisked me and took my wallet. Other horns were blowing but nobody seemed to give a damn.

I said, 'Why are you guys watching Nobu Ishida?'

The bantamweight saw the license and said, 'PI.'

Grateful Dead said, 'Shit.' He put away his gun.

The boxer tossed my wallet into the Corvette and dropped the Dan Wesson into the roof bay behind the driver's seat. I said, 'How about those search and seizure laws, huh?'

They got back in their Taurus and left, and pretty soon the horns stopped blowing and traffic began to move. Well, well, well.

I drove back to my office and called the cops. A voice said, 'North Hollywood detectives.'

'Lou Poitras, please.'

I got put on hold and had to wait and then somebody said, 'Poitras.'

'There's an importer down on Ki Street in Little Tokyo named Nobu Ishida.' I spelled it for him. 'I was on him today when two Asian cops come out of my trunk and take me off the board.'

Lou Poitras said, 'You got that four bucks you owe me?' These cops.

'Don't be small, Lou. I call up with a matter of great import and you bring up a paltry four dollars.'

'Great import. Shit.'

'They took me out just long enough to lose Ishida. They don't say three words. They flash their guns all over Pershing Square and they don't even rub my nose in it the way you cops like to do. Maybe they're cops. Maybe they're just two guys pretending to be cops.'

He thought about that. I could hear him breathe over the phone. 'You see a badge?'

'Not long enough to get a number.'

'How about a tag?'

'Maroon Ford Taurus. Three-W-W-L-seven-eight-eight.'

Poitras said, 'Stick around. I'll get back to you,' and hung up.

I got up, opened the glass doors that lead out to the little balcony, went back to my desk, and put my feet up. Stick around.

Half an hour later I got up again and went out onto the balcony. Sometimes, when the smog is gone and the weather is clear, you can stand on the balcony and see all the way down Santa Monica Boulevard to the ocean. Now, the heat was up and the smog was in and I felt lucky to see across the street.

I went back in the office, dug around in the little refrigerator I have there, and found a bottle of Negra Modelo beer. Negra Modelo is a dark Mexican beer and may be the best dark beer brewed anywhere in the world. I sipped some and watched the Pinocchio clock. After a while I turned on the radio and tuned to KLSX. Bananarama singing it was a cruel summer. They're not George Thoroughgood, but they're not bad. I went back onto the balcony and looked out over Los Angeles and thought about what it would be like to marry and have children. I would have two or three daughters and we would watch *Sesame Street* and *Mr. Rogers* together and then roll around on the floor like puppies. When they grew up they would like Kenneth Tobey movies. Would they look like me, or their mother? I went back into the office, closed the glass doors, and sat in one of the director's chairs. You think the damnedest things when you're waiting for a call.

Maybe Lou Poitras had lost my phone number and was desperately searching the police computers in his attempts to contact me. Maybe he had obtained forbidden information concerning the two cops who'd fronted me and was now lying dead in a pool of blood behind the wheel of his Oldsmobile. Maybe I was bored stiff.

At five minutes after seven I was flat on my back on the floor, staring at the ceiling and wondering if aliens from space had ever visited the earth. At ten minutes after seven, the phone rang. I got up off the floor as if I had not been waiting most of the day, sauntered over, and casually picked up the receiver. 'Laid-back Detectives, where your problems are no problem.'

It wasn't Lou Poitras. It was Sheila Warren. She was crying. She said, 'Mr. Cole? Are you there? Who is this?' The words spilled out around coughing sobs. It was tough to understand her. She still sounded drunk.

I said, 'Is anyone hurt?'

'They said they would kill me. They said they would kill Bradley and me and that they would burn the house down.'

'Who?'

'The people who stole the book. You've got to come over. Please. I'm terrified.' She said something else but she was sobbing again and I couldn't make it out.

I hung up. One thing about this business, it doesn't stay boring for long.

CHAPTER 6

When I got to the Warren home it was still standing. There was no fire, no hazy smoke blotting out a blood-red sun, no siege tower breaching the front wall. It was dark and cool and pleasant, the way it gets at twilight just as the sun settles beneath the horizon. Hatcher sat in the same light blue Titan Securities Thunderbird and watched me pull into the drive and park. He came over. He didn't look too worried.

I said, 'Everything all right?'

'She phone you about the call?'

'Seemed pretty upset.'

'Yeah. Well.' He hacked up something thick and phlegmy and spit it at the bushes. Sinus.

I said, 'You don't act like anything out of the ordinary has happened.'

He patted his jacket below his left arm. 'Anything out of the ordinary comes around here, I'll give it some of this.'

'Wow,' I said. 'I'm surprised she bothered to call me with you out here.'

Hatcher snorted and went back to the T-bird. 'You'll see. You're around here enough, you'll see.'

The voice of experience.

I walked over to the front door, rang the bell twice, and waited. In a little bit, Sheila Warren's voice came from behind the door. 'Who's there?'

'Elvis Cole.'

The locks were thrown and the door opened. She was wearing a silver satin nightgown that looked like it had been poured over her body and silver high-heeled sandals. Her eyes were pink and puffy and her mascara had run and been wiped away and not fixed. She was holding a handkerchief with dark blue smudges on it. The mascara. She said, 'Thank God it's you. We've been terrified.'

I shrugged toward the front gate. 'Not much is going to get past Wyatt Earp.'

'He could've been clubbed.'

Some things you can't argue. I went in past her, watched her lock the door, then followed her back through the house. She walked with a slight lean to the right as if the floor wasn't quite level, and she cut too short through the doorways, brushing her inside shoulder. 'Who's home?' I said.

'Just myself and Mimi. Mimi's in the back.'

She led me to the den. The bar was in the den.

'Tell me about the call.'

'I thought it was Tammy. Tammy's my girlfriend. We play tennis, we go to movies, like that. But it was a man.' There was a capless bottle of Bombay gin and a short heavy glass with a couple of melting ice cubes in it sitting on the bar. She picked up the glass and finished what was left, and said, 'Would you like something to drink?'

'You got a Falstaff?' I walked over to the big French doors that open out to the rear, and looked behind the drapes. Each door was locked and secure.

'What's that?' she said.

'This beer they brew in Tumwater, Washington.'

'All we have are Japanese beers.' Her voice took on an edge when she said it.

'That'll be fine.'

She went behind the bar, put more ice in her glass, and glugged in some of the gin. That brought the Bombay down about to the halfway point. The bottle cap was sitting in an ashtray at the end of the bar. A strip of bright clean Bonded paper was lying beside it. The Bombay had been full when she'd started. She disappeared down behind the bar for a little bit, then stood up with a bottle of Asahi. There was a tight smile on her face and a smear of mascara on her left cheek like a bruise. 'Did I tell you that I find you quite attractive?'

'It was the first thing you said to me.'

'Well, I do.'

'Everyone says I look like John Cassavetes.'

'Do they?'

'I think I look like Joe Isuzu.'

She cocked her hips and her head and rested her drink along her jawline, posing. She still hadn't given me the beer. 'I think you look like Joe Theismann,' she said. 'Do you know who Joe Theismann is?'

'Sure. Used to quarterback for the Redskins.'

She gave me a giggle. 'No, you silly. Joe Theismann is married to Cathy Lee Crosby.'

'Oh. That Joe Theismann.'

She opened the Asahi, put a paper coaster that said New Asia Hotels on the bar, then set the Asahi on the coaster. She took an icy beer mug from somewhere beneath the bar and put it beside the bottle. I ignored the mug. 'You were telling me about the call.'

The smile went away. She looked down into her drink and swirled it and her eyes began to redden and puff. 'He had an ugly voice. He said he had that goddamned book, and that he knew we had the police involved and that we had hired a private investigator. He said that was a mistake. He said if we didn't stop looking he was going to do things.' Her voice got higher, probably the way it had been ten years ago. It was nice. 'He said they were watching me and could strike at any time. He told me when I left the house this morning and what I was wearing and who I met and when I came back. He knew my perfume. He knew I use Maxipads. He knew Tammy came over at four and that we played tennis and that Tammy was wearing green shorts and a halter top and –' She closed her eyes and took more of the gin and said, 'Damn.'

'Did you call the police?'

She shook her head, keeping her eyes closed. 'Bradley would shit.'

'Calling the cops is the smart thing.'

'We do things Bradley's way, mister, or we never hear the end of it.' She shook her head again and had more gin. 'God damn him.'

I said, 'Did you recognize the voice?'

She took a deep breath, let it out, then came around to my side of the bar and stood next to me. Petulant. The first fright was past and the gin was working. She said, 'I don't want to talk about this anymore. I needed someone here.' I guess she hadn't recognized the voice.

'I know. I'll check the house and make sure it's tight. You'll be all right. A guy calls like this, it's only to scare you. If he was going to do anything, he'd have done it.'

She gave her head a flick to get the hair out of her face. Her hair was lush and rich and if it was dyed it was a helluva good job. She reached out and touched my forearm with her finger. 'I'll walk with you.'

I moved my arm. 'You look cold,' I said. 'Go put something on.'

She looked down at herself. The silver gown made an upside-down V over each breast with a thin silver cord running from the apex of one V up her chest and around behind her neck and back down to the apex of the other V. Her shoulders were smooth and bare and tanned. She said, 'I'm not cold. See?' She picked up my hand in both of hers and brought it to her chest.

I said, 'Your daughter's in the house.'

'I don't give a good goddamn who's in the house.'

'I do. And even if she wasn't, your husband hired me, and he didn't hire me to lay his wife.'

'Do you have to be hired for that?'

'Go put something on.'

She pressed against me and kissed me. The silver gown felt warm and slick. I eased her back. 'Go put something on.'

'Fuck you.' She slid past me and hurried out of the room, bouncing a thigh off the near couch as she left. She hadn't seen her daughter standing in one of the doorways leading from the rear of the house, as motionless as a reed in still air. Neither had I.

I put the Asahi on the bar. 'I'm sorry that happened,' I said. 'She's very scared and she's had too much to drink.'

Mimi Warren said, 'She's very good in bed. Everyone says so.' Sixteen.

I didn't say anything to her and she didn't say anything to me, and then she turned and walked away. I watched little drops of condensation sprout on the Asahi until their weight pulled them down to the bar, then I took a rambling tour of the house, checking each window and door and making sure they were tight and locked and that the alarms were armed. I looked for the girl.

At the back of the house, a little hall branched away from the kitchen with a couple of doors on one side and glass looking out toward the pool on the other. If you looked out the glass you could see down across the lawn to the flat mirrored surface of the pool and the dark silhouette of palm trees behind it. I watched the quarter moon bounce on the pool's still surface, then tried the first door. It was open and the room was dark. I turned on the light.

Mimi was lying on her back across a single bed, legs straight up

247

against the wall, head hanging down over the bedside, eyes wide and unfocused. I said, 'You okay?'

She said nothing.

'You want to talk to your mom, we can do it together. That might be easier.'

She did not move. The room was white on white, as stark and cold as the Wyeth landscapes she had been staring at earlier. There were no posters on the walls or record albums on the floor or clothes spilling out of a hamper or diet soda cans or anything at all that would mark the room as a sixteen-year-old girl's. On a glass-topped white desk at the foot of the bed there were three oversized art books by someone named Kiro Asano and a paperback edition of Yukio Mishima's *The Sailor Who Fell from Grace with the Sea*. The Mishima looked as if it had been read a hundred times. There was a small Hitachi color TV on the desk, and a scent in the room that might have been marijuana, but if it was it was not recent.

I said, 'You gotta be angry.' Mr. Sensitive.

'To be angry is to waste life,' she said, not moving. 'One must have a cruel heart.'

Great.

I finished my circuit of the house and found my way back to the den. Sheila was there, sitting on a bar stool, sipping from the short glass. She was wearing a man's denim work shirt buttoned over the gown and she'd done something about her makeup. She looked good. I wondered how anyone who drank so much could stay that lean. Maybe when she was on the court she played harder than I had thought.

I said, 'The house is tight. All the windows are secure and the doors are locked. The alarm is armed and in order. With Hatcher out front, you're not going to have a problem.'

'If you say so.'

I said, 'Your daughter saw you kiss me. You might want to talk to her.'

'Are you scared Bradley's going to fire you?'

A pulse began behind my right eye. 'No. You might want to talk to her because she saw her mother kiss a strange man and that had to be frightening.'

'She won't tell. She never says anything. All she does is sit in her room and watch TV.'

'Maybe she should tell. Maybe that's the point.'

Sheila drained the glass. 'Bradley's not going to fire you, if that's what you're worried about.'

The pulse began to throb. 'I'm not worried about it. I don't give a damn if Bradley fires me or not.'

Sheila set the glass down hard. Red spots flared on her cheeks. 'You must think I have it pretty good, don't you? Big house, big money. Here's this woman, plays tennis all day, what does she have to gripe about? Well, I've got shit is what I've got. What the hell's a big house if there's nothing in it?' She turned and stalked out the way she'd seen women do a hundred times on *Dallas* and *Falcon Crest*. Drama.

I stood by the bar and breathed hard and waited for something else to happen, but nothing did. Somewhere a door slammed. Somewhere else a TV played. Maybe this was a dream. Maybe I would wake up and find myself in a 7-Eleven parking lot and think, *Oh, Elvis, ha-ha, you really dreamed up some zingo clients this time!*

I let myself out and got in the Corvette and had to stop at the gate to let a yellow Pantera with two teenagers in it pass. Hatcher was in his T-bird, a smug grin on his face.

I leaned toward him. 'If you say anything, Hatcher,' I said, 'I'll shoot you.'

CHAPTER 7

At nine-forty the next morning my phone rang and Jillian Becker said, 'Did I wake you?'

'Impossible. I never sleep.'

'We're back from Kyoto. Bradley wants to see you.'

I had fallen asleep on the couch, watching a two A.M. rerun of *It Came from Beneath the Sea* with Ken Tobey and Faith Domergue. The cat had watched it with me and had fallen asleep on my chest. He was still there. I said, 'I went by Bradley's house last night. Someone called and scared the hell out of Sheila.'

'That's one of the reasons Bradley wants to see you. We're at the Century City office. May we expect you in thirty minutes?'

'Better gimme a little longer. I want to think up something real funny to see if I can make you laugh.'

She hung up.

I lifted off the cat, went into the kitchen, filled a large glass with water, drank it, and filled it once more when the phone rang again. Lou Poitras. He said, 'I made some calls. Those two guys who sixed you yesterday were Asian Task Force cops.'

'Gee, you mean Nobu Ishida isn't a simple businessman?'

'If ATF people are in, Hound Dog, it's gotta be heavy.'

Poitras hung up. Asian Task Force, huh? Maybe I had been right about old Nobu. Maybe he was the mastermind of an international stolen art cartel. Maybe I would crack The Big Case and be hailed as The World's Greatest Detective. Wow.

I fed myself and the cat, then showered, dressed, and was turning down Century Park East Boulevard forty minutes later. It was clear and sunny and cooler than yesterday, with a lot of women on the sidewalks, all of them wearing lightweight summer outfits with no backs and no sleeves. Century City was once the back lot of Twentieth Century-Fox Studios. Now it is an orchard of high-rise office buildings done in designer shades of bronze and black and metallic blue glass, each carefully spaced for that planned-community look and landscaped with small pods of green lawn and California poplar trees. The streets have names like Constellation Boulevard and Avenue of the Stars and Galaxy Way. We are nothing if not grandiose.

The Century Plaza Towers are a matching set of triangular buildings, thirty-five floors each of agents, lawyers, accountants, lawyers, business managers, lawyers, record executives, lawyers, and Porsche owners. Most of whom are lawyers. The Century Plaza Towers are the biggest buildings in Century City. They have to be to squeeze in the egos. Warren Investments occupied half of the seventeenth floor of the north tower. Rent alone had to exceed the Swedish gross national product.

I stepped off the elevator into an enormous glass and chrome waiting room filled with white leather chairs that were occupied by important-looking men and women holding important-looking briefcases. They looked like they had been waiting a long time. A sleek black woman sat in the center of a U-shaped command post. She wore a wire-thin headphone set that curved around to her mouth with a microphone the size of a pencil lead. 'Elvis Cole,' I said. 'For Mr. Warren.'

She touched buttons and murmured into the microphone and told me someone would be right out. The important-looking men and women glared enviously. Moments later, an older woman with gray hair in a tight bun and a nice manner led me back along a mile and a half of corridor, through a heavy glass door, and into what could only have been an executive secretary's office. There was a double door wide enough to drive a street cleaner through at the far end. 'Go right in,' she said. I did.

Bradley Warren was sitting on the edge of a black marble desk not quite as long as a bowling alley with his arms crossed and a J. Jonah Jameson smile on his face. He was smiling at five dour-faced Japanese men. Three of the Japanese men were sitting on a white silk couch and were old the way only Asians can be old, with that sort of weathered papery skin and eternal presence. The other two Japanese men stood at either end of the couch, and were much younger and much larger, maybe two inches shorter than me and twenty pounds heavier. They had broad flat faces and eyes that stared at you and didn't give a damn if you minded or not. The one on the right was wearing a custom-cut Lawrence Marx suit that made him look fat. If you knew what to look for, though, you knew he wasn't fat. He was all wedges and heavy muscle. The one on the left was in a brown herringbone, and had gone to the same tailor. Odd Job and his clone. Jillian Becker sat primly on the edge of a white silk chair, framed neatly in a full wall of glass that looked north. She looked nice. Yuppie, but nice.

'Where's Bush?' I said. 'Couldn't he make it?'

Bradley Warren said, 'You're late. We've had to wait.' Mr. Personality.

'Why don't we cancel this meeting and schedule another to begin in ten minutes? Then I can be early.'

Bradley Warren said, 'I'm not paying you for jokes.'

'I throw those in for free.'

Today Jillian Becker was wearing a burgundy skirt and jacket with a white shirt and very sheer burgundy hose with tiny leaf designs and broken-leather burgundy pumps. With her legs crossed, her top knee gleamed. I gave her a beaming smile, but she didn't smile back. Maybe I'd go easy on the jokes for a while.

Bradley Warren slid off his desk and said something in Japanese to the men on the couch. His speech was fluid and natural, as if he had spoken the language as a child. The older man in the center said something back to him, also in Japanese, and everybody laughed. Especially Jillian Becker. Bradley said, 'These men are members of the Tashiro family, who own the Hagakure. They're here to make sure every best effort is made to recover the manuscript.' The guy in the brown herringbone spoke softly in Japanese, translating.

'All right.'

Bradley Warren said, 'Have you found it yet?' I had expected him to ask about the threat against his wife first, but there you go.

'No.' More mumbling from the guy in the brown herringbone.

'Are you close?'

'Hot on its trail.'

The guy in the brown herringbone frowned, and translated, and the old guys on the couch frowned, too. Bradley saw all the frowning going on and joined in. So that was where he got it. He said, 'I'm disappointed. I expected more.'

'It's been two days, Bradley. In those two days I have begun identifying people who deal in or collect feudal Japanese artwork. I will do more of that. Eventually, one of the people I contact will know something about the Hagakure, or about someone who does.

That's the way it's done. Stealing something like this is like stealing the *Mona Lisa*. There's only a half dozen people on earth who would do it or be involved in it, and once you know who they are it's only a matter of time. Collectors make no secret about what they want, and once they have it they like to brag.'

Bradley gave the Japanese men a superior look and said, '*Harumph*.'

The Japanese man sitting in the center of the couch nodded thoughtfully and said, 'I think that he has made a reasonable beginning.'

Bradley said, 'Huh?'

The Japanese man said, 'Has there been a ransom demand?' He was the oldest of the three seated men, but his eyes were clear and steady and stayed with you. His English was heavily accented.

I shook my head. 'None that I'm aware of.'

Bradley looked from the old man to me and back to the old man. 'What's this about a ransom?'

The old man kept his eyes on me. 'If a ransom is demanded, we will pay it.'

'Okay.'

'If you must pay for information, price is of no concern.'

'Okay.'

The old man looked at Bradley. 'Is this clear?'

Bradley said, 'Yes, sir.'

The old man stood, and the large men quickly moved to his side in case he needed their help. He didn't. He stared at me for a very long time, and then he said, 'You must understand this: the Hagakure is Japan. It is the heart and the spirit of the people. It defines how we act and what we believe and what is right and what is wrong and how we live and how we die. It is who we are. If you feel these things, you would know why this book must be found.'

He meant it. He meant it all the way down deep where it is very important to mean what you say. 'I'll do what I can.'

The old man kept the steady eyes on me, then mumbled something in Japanese and the other two old men stood up. No one said *I'll be seeing you* or *Nice to have met you* or *See you again some time*. Bradley walked the Tashiros to the door, but I don't think they looked at him. Then they were gone.

When Bradley came back, he said, 'I didn't appreciate all the smart talk in front of the Tashiros. They're nervous as hell and breathing down my neck. You'd be a lot farther along without the wit.'

'Yeah, but along to where?'

His jaw knotted but he didn't say anything. He strode over to the glass wall and looked out. Holmby Hills was due north. With a good pair of field glasses he could probably see his house. 'Now,' he said. 'My wife is frightened because of this threat she received. Do you think there's any merit to it?'

'I don't know,' I said. 'It's not professional. You steal something, you're looking at ten years. You kill someone, you're looking at life. Besides that, the cops are already in and these guys know it. If they're hanging around, that means they want something else. What else do you have that they would want?'

'Nothing.' Offended.

'Has there been any communication between you and them that I have not heard about?'

'Of course not.' Pissed.

'Then I'd treat it seriously until we know more.'

Bradley went back to his desk and began to flip through papers as if he couldn't wait to get back to work. Maybe he couldn't. 'In that case, we should expand your services. I want you to oversee the security of my family.'

'You've got Titan.'

Jillian Becker said, 'Sheila was not comfortable with Titan. They've been let go.'

I spread my hands. 'All right. I can put someone in your house.'

Bradley Warren nodded. 'Good. Just be sure that the Hagakure investigation continues to proceed.' First things first.

'Of course.'

'And the Man of the Month banquet is tomorrow,' he said. 'We can't forget that.'

'Maybe you shouldn't go.'

The frown came back and he shook his head. 'Out of the question. The Tashiros will be there.' He tamped some papers together and fingered their edges and looked thoughtful. 'Mr. Tashiro liked you. That's good. That's very, very good.' You could see the business wheels turning.

I said, 'Bradley.'

The frown.

'If someone is genuinely committed to killing you or your family, there isn't much we can do to stop them.'

The skin beneath his left eye began to tic, just like it had in my office.

'You understand that, don't you?'

'Of course.'

His phone buzzed and he picked it up. He listened for a few seconds, still staring at me, then broke into a Cheshire cat smile and asked someone on the other end of the line how the Graintech takeover had gone. He glanced at Jillian Becker and made a dismissal gesture with his free hand. Jillian stood up and showed me to the door. Bradley laughed very loud at something and put his feet up and said he'd like to get some of those profits into a new hotel he was building on Maui.

When we got to the door, Bradley cupped a hand over the receiver's mouthpiece, leaned out of his chair, and called, 'Cole. Keep me posted, will you?'

I said sure.

Bradley Warren uncupped the receiver, laughed like he'd just heard the best joke he'd heard all year, then swiveled back toward the big glass wall.

I left.

With the security of his family now in my trusted hands, apparently it was safe to resume business.

CHAPTER 8

Twenty minutes after Bradley and Jillian resumed business, I drove down to a flat, gray building on Venice Boulevard in Culver City, and parked beside a red Jeep Cherokee with a finish like polished glass. It's industrial down there, so all the buildings are flat and gray, but most of them don't have the Cherokee or an electronically locked steel door or a sign that says BARTON'S PISTOL RANGE. I had to ring a bell and someone inside had to buzz open the steel door before I could enter.

The lobby is big and bright, with high ceilings and Coke machines and posters of Clint Eastwood as Dirty Harry and Sylvester Stallone as Rambo. Someone had put up a poster of Huey, Dewey, and Louie, with a little sign on it that said WE ARE THE NRA. These gun nuts. There was a long counter filled with targets and gun cleaning supplies and pistols you could rent, and a couple of couches you could sit on while you were waiting for a shooting stall to open up. Three men in business suits and a woman in a jogging suit and another woman in a dress were waiting to shoot, but they weren't waiting on the couches. They were at the head of the counter and they didn't look happy. One of the men was tall and forty pounds too fat and had a red face. He was leaning over the counter at Rick Barton, saying, 'I made an appointment, goddamnit. I don't see why I have to stand around and wait.'

Rick Barton said, calmly, 'I'm terribly sorry for the inconvenience, sir, but we've had to momentarily close the range. It will open again in about fifteen minutes.'

'Closed my ass! I hear *somebody* shooting back there!'

Rick Barton nodded, calmly. 'Yes, sir. Another fifteen minutes. Excuse me, please.' Rick came down the long counter and nodded at me. He was short and slight and had put in twelve years in the Marine Corps. Eight of those years he had shot on the Marine Corps

256

pistol team. He said, 'Thank Christ you walked in. I hadda "sir" that fat fuck one more time, I'da lubed his gear box for him.'

'Ah, Rick. You always did have a gift for the public.'

Rick said, 'You want to pop some caps?'

I shook my head. 'The gun shop said Joe was here.'

Rick looked at his watch. 'Go on back. Tell him he's got another ten, then I chuck his ass out.'

He tossed me a set of ear covers, and I went back toward the range. Behind me, the fat guy said, 'Hey, how come *he* gets to go back there?'

You go through the door, then down a long, dim corridor with a lot of signs that say things like EAR AND EYE PROTECTION MUST BE WORN AT ALL TIMES and NO RAPID FIRING, and then you go through another sound-proofed door and you're on the firing range. There are twelve side-by-side stalls from which people can shoot at targets that they send down-range using little electric pulleys. Usually, the range is bright, and well lighted, but now the lights had been turned off so that only the targets were lit. A tape player had been hooked up, and Bob Seger was screaming *I like that old time rock 'n' roll* . . . so loud that you could hear him through the ear covers. Anyone else would find his partner on the golf course or the tennis courts.

Joe Pike was shooting at six targets that he had placed as far down-range as possible. He was firing a Colt Python .357 Magnum with a four-inch barrel, moving left-to-right, right-to-left, shooting at the targets in precise time with the music. *That kind of music just soothes the soul* . . . He was wearing faded Levi's and blue Nike running shoes and a gray sweatshirt with the sleeves cut off and a big steel Rolex and mirrored pilot's glasses. The gun and the glasses and the Rolex gleamed in the darkness as if they had been polished to a high luster. Pike moved without hesitation or doubt, as precise and controlled as a well-made machine. *Bang bang bang.* The Python would move, and flash, and a hole would burst near the center of a target. The dark glasses seemed not to adversely affect his vision. Maybe the sunglasses didn't matter because Pike had his eyes closed. Maybe somehow Pike and the target were one, and we could write a book titled *Zen and the Art of Small Arms Fire* and make a fortune. Wow.

He stopped to reload, still facing down-range, and said, 'Want to shoot a few?' You see? Cosmic.

I went to the stall where he had set up Rick's tape player and clicked off the music. 'How'd you know I was here?'

Shrug.

'We've got a job.'

'Yeah?' Pike loves to talk.

We walked down-range, collected his targets, then examined them. Every shot had been within two inches of center. He was delighted. You could tell because the corner of his mouth twitched. Joe Pike does not smile. Joe Pike never smiles. After a while you get used to it. I said, 'Eh. Not bad.'

We gathered his things and walked back along the dim corridor, me telling him about Bradley and Sheila and the stolen Hagakure and the phone call from person or persons unknown that had scared the hell out of Sheila Warren.

He said, 'Threat like that doesn't make any sense.'

'Nope.'

'Maybe there wasn't a threat. Maybe somebody's having a little fun.'

'Maybe.'

'Maybe the lady made it up.'

'Maybe. But we don't know that. I figure you can stay with the woman and the kid while I look for the book.'

'Uh-huh.'

Pike was pulling off his sweatshirt when we walked out into the lobby. The fat man said, 'Well, it's about goddamned time,' and then he saw Joe Pike and shut up. Pike is an inch taller than me, and more heavily muscled, and when he was in Vietnam he'd had a bright red arrow tattooed on the outside of each deltoid. The arrows pointed forward. There is an ugly pucker scar high on the left side of his chest from the time a Mexican in a zoot suit shot him with a gold Llama automatic, and two more scars low on his back above his right kidney. After the fat guy looked at the tattoos and the muscles, he looked at the scars and then he looked away. Rick Barton was grinning from ear to ear.

Pike said, 'Use your shower, Rick?'

'No problem, bo.'

While Pike was in the shower I used a pay phone to call Sheila Warren. 'I'm on the way over,' I said. 'Bradley hired me to look out for you.'

'Well,' she said, 'I should hope so.'

'I'm bringing my partner, Joe Pike. He'll make sure the house and grounds are secure and be there in case there's a problem.'

There was a pause. 'Who's Joe Pike?'

Maybe I had lapsed into Urdu the first time. 'My partner. He owns the agency with me.'

'You won't be here?'

'Somebody has to look for the book.'

'Maybe this Joe Pike should look for the book.'

'I'm better at finding. He's better at guarding.'

You could hear her breathing into the phone. The breaths were deep and irregular and I thought I could hear ice move in a glass but maybe that was the TV. I said, 'You were pretty gone last night. How's your head?'

'You go to hell.' She hung up.

Five minutes later Pike came back with a blue leather gym bag and we drove across town, me leading and Pike following in the Cherokee. When we got to the Warren house, Pike parked in the drive, then got out with the gym bag, walked back, and climbed into my car. Hatcher and his T-bird were gone. I told Pike about Berke Feldstein in the Sun Tree Gallery and Nobu Ishida and the two Asian Task Force cops.

'Asian Task Force are tough dudes,' Pike said. 'You think Ishida's got the book?'

'I think that a couple of hours after I saw him, someone threatened the Warrens. If Ishida doesn't have it, maybe he'll want to find out who does. Maybe he'll ask around.'

Pike nodded. 'And maybe you'll be there when he gets some answers.'

'Uh-huh.'

The twitch. 'Nice.'

The front door opened and Sheila Warren stepped out. She was in Jordache jeans over a red Danskin top that showed a fine torso. She put her palms on her hips, fingertips down the way women do, and stared at us.

Pike said, 'The lady of the house?'

'Yep.'

Pike opened the gym bag, took out a Walther 9mm automatic in a strap holster, hitched up his right pant, fastened the gun around his ankle, then pulled the pant down over it and got out of the car. Maybe he was saving the .357 for heavy work.

'Be careful,' I said.

Pike nodded without saying anything, then took the gym bag and walked up to the house. He stopped in front of Sheila Warren and put out his hand and she took it. She glanced my way, then back up at Pike and gave him a big smile. Twenty kilowatts. She touched his gym bag and then his forearm and said something and laughed. She slid her hand up his arm to his shoulder and showed him into the house. I think she may have licked her lips. I eased the Corvette into gear and drove away. It's a good thing Pike's tough.

CHAPTER 9

Little Tokyo was jammed with the lunch hour rush. Every restaurant on the block had a line of Caucasian secretaries and their bosses queued up out front, and the smell of hot peanut oil and vinegar sauces made my stomach rumble.

A small CLOSED sign was taped in the door at Nobu Ishida's place. It was one of those cruddy hand-lettered things and not at all what you would expect from a big-time importer and art connoisseur, but there you go. I turned into the alley behind Ishida's just to check, and, sure enough, it looked closed from back there, too. Probably out for lunch.

I turned back to Ki, then went up Broadway past the Hollywood Freeway into Chinatown. Chinatown is much bigger than Little Tokyo and not as clean, but the best honey-dipped duck and spring rolls in America can be had at a place called Yang Chow's on Broadway just past Ord. If bad guys can break for lunch, so can good guys.

I parked in front of a live poultry market and walked back to Yang Chow's and bought half a duck, three spring rolls, fried rice, and two Tsingtao to go. They put extra spice in the spring rolls for me.

Ten minutes later I was back on Ki Street, pulling into a parking lot sandwiched between two restaurants. It was crowded but all of the lots this time of day were crowded. I was a block and a half down from Ishida's, and if anyone went into his shop through the front or came out through the front or turned over the CLOSED sign, I'd be able to see it. If they came or went through the back I was screwed. You learn to live with failure.

The parking attendant said, 'You here to eat?'

'Yeah.'

'Three-fifty.'

261

I gave him three-fifty.

'Park anywhere. Give me the key.'

I took a spot at the front of the lot, blocking in a white Volvo so that I had an easy eyes-forward view of Ishida's shop. I got out of the Corvette, pulled the top up to cut the sun, then climbed back in. I opened a Tsingtao, drank some, then went to work on the rice.

'I thought you here to eat.' The parking attendant was standing by my door.

I showed him the rice.

'In there.' He pointed at one of the restaurants.

I shook my head. 'Out here.'

'You no eat out here. In there for eating.'

'I'm a health inspector. I go in there I'll close the place down.'

'You got to give me key.' Maybe he didn't believe me.

'No key. I keep the key.'

He pointed at the Volvo. 'What if owner come out? I got to move.' He rapped knuckles on the Corvette's door.

'I'm here. I'll move it.'

'You no insured here.'

'Okay. I'll get out and let you move it.'

'What if you leave.'

'If I leave, I'll give you the key.' People like this are put here to test us.

He was going to say more when two Asian women and a black man came out of the restaurant. The black man wore a navy suit and had a small mustache and looked successful. The attendant hustled over to them, got a claim check, then hustled to the back of the lot. One of the Asian women said something to the black man and they all laughed. The attendant drove up in a Mercedes 420 Turbo Diesel. Bronze. He closed the door after each woman, and the black man gave him a tip. Maybe the tip made him feel better about things. He went back to the little attendant's shack and looked at me but left me alone.

The honey-dipped duck was wonderful.

Four hours and twenty minutes later the Volvo was gone and the first of the early evening dinner crowd were starting to show up. The lot had emptied after lunch and another attendant had come on duty, an older man who looked at me once and didn't seem to care if I stayed or left or homesteaded. No one had gone into Ishida's shop or come out or touched the little CLOSED sign. Maybe nobody would, ever again.

At ten minutes after five the cop who had made me in the yakitori grill walked past carrying a large white paper bag and a six-pack of diet Coke. The Grateful Dead tee shirt was gone. Now it was ZZ Top. I got out of the car and watched him saunter down Ki Street and turn into a doorway next to the yakitori grill. I waited to see if he would come out and when he didn't I did a little sauntering myself and took a look. He and a cop I hadn't seen before were across from Ishida's in a State Farm Insurance office above the yakitori grill. Those sneaky devils. *Who watches the watchers?*

I walked back along Ki, crossed over at the little side street, and turned up the alley behind Ishida's shop. It looked the way it looked when I drove past six hours earlier. Empty. I went up to the loading dock doors and didn't like the lock and went over to the people door and took out the wires I keep in my wallet and opened it. If the cops had had the rear of the place staked out there would be trouble, but all the cops were on the street side eating cheeseburgers.

I let myself in, eased the door shut behind me, and waited for my eyes to adjust. I was in a dim, high-ceilinged freight room. Dirty light came through the little window beside the door and a skylight twenty feet up, but that was it. Boxes and crates were stacked ten feet up the wall. Some were wooden but most were cardboard, and most had Styrofoam packaging pellets or shredded Japanese newspapers spilling out. There was a metal stair against one wall that went up to a steel-grate catwalk and loft. There were more boxes and crates up there and a little office. If the Hagakure were here it should only take about six years to find it.

I went through a hall at the head of the freight room and past shelves of bamboo steamers and into the showroom. The two desks were still there but the Hagakure hadn't been left sitting on them. No one had left a note suggesting a safe place to store the manuscript or a photograph of the new owner with his prize collectible. There were memo pads and paper clips and a little purple stapler and assorted pens and pencils and a Panasonic pencil sharpener and an old issue of *Batman* with the back cover gone. I was hoping for a clue but I would have settled for Ishida's home phone and address. *Nada.*

I went into the brighter light near the front of the shop, put my hands in my pockets, and wondered what to do. From the edge of the shadows you could see into the insurance office above the yakitori grill. The cop I didn't know was sitting a few feet back from the window with his feet up, drinking a diet Coke out of a can with a straw.

I went back into the freight room. Ishida had come from the back. Maybe the little office on the catwalk was where he worked. Maybe there would be a little desk with pictures of the kids and a note to bring home some sushi and a Rolodex or some personal correspondence that would tell me where he lived.

I climbed the steel stair and went along the narrow catwalk and opened the white door with the pebbled glass panel in it and smelled the blood and the cold meat and the death. It's the smell that comes only from a great quantity of blood and human waste. It can sting your nose and throat like a bad smog. It's a smell so strong and so alive that it has a taste and the taste is like when you were a kid and found a nickel in the winter and the metal was cold and you put it in your mouth to see what it would be like and your mother screamed that you would die from the germs and so you spit it out but the cold taste and the fear of the germs stayed.

The little office was heavy with shadow. I took out my handkerchief and found the light switch and snapped it on. The guy with the missing finger who'd been out front my first time around was curled atop a gray metal file cabinet. His head and his right arm were hanging over the edge. His neck was limp, the front and side of it purple as if he had been hit there very hard. Someone had cleared Nobu Ishida's desk of papers and ledgers and pencil can and phone. They had put all that on his swivel chair along with his clothes and then pushed the chair out of the way and tied Ishida spread-eagled on his desk, naked, arms and legs bound to the desk legs with brown electrical cord. They had used a knife on him. There were cuts on his arms and his legs and his torso and his face and his genitals. Some of the cuts were very deep. His bladder and his bowels had let go. The blood had crusted into delicate red-brown rivers along his arms and legs and had pooled on the desk and then dripped heavily onto the floor to mix with other things. The pool on the floor had spread almost to the door and looked slick and tacky. A gray stuffed Godzilla had been jammed in his mouth to smother the screams.

I stepped around the blood to the chair and looked through the things that had been on the desk. Ishida's wallet was still in his right back pants pocket. I took it out, opened it, copied down his home address, then put the wallet back the way I'd found it. I used my handkerchief to pick up the phone and called Lou Poitras. He said, 'What now?'

'I'm at Ishida's place of business. He's dead.'

There was a pause. 'Did you kill him?'

'No.' I watched the pool of blood.

'Don't leave the scene. Don't touch anything. Don't let anyone else in. I'm on my way. There'll be other cops but I'll get there first.'

He hung up. I put the phone down and stepped around the blood back onto the catwalk and pulled the door closed. I worked up spit and swallowed and took several deep breaths. I expanded my lungs from the diaphragm and expelled the air in stages from the lower lobes to the mid-lobes to the upper lobes. I tried everything I could think of but I couldn't get rid of the taste or the smell. I never could. Like every encounter with death, it had become a part of me.

CHAPTER 10

I went downstairs and sat at one of the two tables in the deepening darkness until Lou Poitras pulled up out front in a light green Dodge. A black-and-white pulled up behind him and the plain white van the crime scene guys use pulled up behind the van. Cops on parade.

I went to the front door and opened it. Across the street, the ATF cops were on their feet in the big window, ZZ Top screaming into the phone, the other one pulling on a jacket. I gave them a little wave.

Poitras said, 'Knock off that shit and come in here.'

If Lou Poitras wasn't a cop he could rent himself out as Mighty Joe Young. He spends about an hour and a half every morning six days a week pumping iron in a little weight room in his back yard in Northridge, trying to see how big he can get. He's good at it. I'd once seen him punch through a Cadillac's windshield and pull a big man out over the steering wheel.

He shouldered past me. 'Where?'

'In the back. Up the stairs.'

One of the uniforms was a black guy with a bullet head and a thick neck and hands four sizes too big for him. His name tag read LEONARD. His partner was a blond kid with a skimpy Larry Bird mustache and hard eyes. Leonard mumbled something and the blond kid took the crime scene guys into the back after Poitras.

'You don't want to see?' I said.

Leonard said, 'I seen enough.'

I went back to the two tables and sat. Leonard found the lights, turned them on, then went back up front. He leaned against a floor-to-ceiling case of toy robots with his arms crossed, and stared out into the street. You do this job long enough, you know what's going to be back there even without going back there.

The little door chime rang and the two ATF cops from the insurance office came in. They showed their badges to Leonard and then they went into the rear. When they passed me, the one in the ZZ Top tee shirt said, 'You're in deep shit, asshole.'

Lou Poitras came back around the bamboo steamers and said, 'Jesus Christ.' He looked pale.

I nodded.

The blond kid came out like it was nothing. He went back to Leonard and said, 'You should see that, Lenny.' His voice was loud.

In fifteen minutes the place was swarming with cops like flies on a nervous dog. Someone had found a Dunkin' Donuts and brought back two boxes of crullers and about twenty little Styrofoam cups of coffee. Crime scene specialists from the Hollenbeck Division were dusting everything and snapping pictures and asking me every two minutes if I had moved anything before they got there, and every time they asked I said no. Two guys came in from the L.A. County Medical Examiner's Office, but neither of them looked like Jack Klugman. One of them had a twitch. More than one cop came out of the back and sat down with his face in his hands, and everybody pretended not to notice when they did.

I was working on my second cup of coffee when the bell tinkled and the ATF cop with the bantamweight's face came in. He was wearing tan chinos and a pale lavender rugby shirt and a light khaki windbreaker and Topsiders with no socks. Like he'd been at home about to sit down to dinner with his family. Poitras went over and talked with him and then they went into the back. When they came back, ZZ Top was with them. Poitras and the bantamweight came over to me. ZZ Top pushed aside the cruller box, sat on the table, crossed his arms, and glared at me. Cops are tough when they've got you outnumbered.

Poitras said, 'This is Terry Ito. He works out of the Asian Task Force, Japanese sub-unit.'

I put out my hand. Ito didn't take it. He said, 'What were you doing with Nobu Ishida?'

'Taking chopsticks lessons.' The muscles in the tops of my shoulders and down through my mid-back were tight and aching.

Ito looked at Poitras. Poitras shrugged. 'He's like that.'

Ito looked back at me. 'I think maybe you got shit for brains. You think that's possible?'

I looked from Ito to the cop at the cruller table and back to Ito. I could still smell what I'd smelled in Ishida's office. I said, 'I think somebody dropped the ball. I think someone walked in here under ZZ Top's nose and did this and walked out again and nobody said dick.'

The cop on the cruller table uncrossed his arms and stood up and said, 'Fuck you, asshole.'

'Good line,' I said. 'Schwarzenegger, right? *The Terminator.*'

Poitras said, 'Cut the bullshit.'

Ito said, 'Jimmy.'

A tall black uniform came out of the back, took off his hat, and said, 'Who'd do something like that?' Then he went outside. I was breathing hard and Jimmy was breathing hard but everybody else looked bored. Jimmy sat down again but didn't cross his arms.

Ito turned away from Jimmy and looked at me. 'How long were you outside, hotshot?'

'Maybe six hours.'

'You see anybody?'

I sipped some coffee.

Ito nodded. 'Yeah, that's what I thought.' He went over to the cruller table, picked up a cup of the coffee, peeled off its top, and took a long sip. Steam was rising off the cup but the heat didn't seem to bother him. He said, 'Who's your client?'

'A guy named Bradley Warren. The Pacific Men's Club is naming him Man of the Month tomorrow.'

'Man of the Month.'

'Yeah. You should get in on that.'

Jimmy said, 'Shit.'

I told them who Warren was and that he had hired me to find the Hagakure and that I had turned up Nobu Ishida's name as a place to start. Terry Ito listened and sipped the hot coffee and stared at me without blinking. Detectives and crime scene guys and uniforms moved around us. The two guys from the ME's office went out to their van and came back with a gurney. Ito called to them.

'When did it happen?'

The shorter of the two said, 'Maybe eight hours.'

Ito looked at me and nodded. I shrugged. Ito looked at Jimmy, but Jimmy was staring at the floor and flexing his jaws.

I drank coffee and told them about my first visit to Ishida's shop and about the three guys sitting at the tables and about Ishida. I said, 'The stiff upstairs with the missing finger was one of them. There was another guy with a bad left eye, and a big kid, young, named Eddie.'

Ito looked at Jimmy again. Jimmy looked up and said, 'Eddie have tattoos? Here?' He touched his arms just below the elbows.

'Yeah.'

Jimmy looked at Ito and nodded. 'Eddie Tang.'

I said, 'About three hours after I left Ishida's, the client's wife got a phone call saying they'd burn the house down if the Warrens didn't call off the cops. I wanted to work Ishida some more, maybe take a look around his house, that kind of thing, so I came back here today.'

Jimmy said, 'That's horseshit. You don't threaten somebody to make the cops back off.'

I said, 'Yeah. You cops are tough, all right.'

Ito said, 'You're some smart for a guy standing where you're standing.'

'It's not hard in this company.'

Jimmy didn't say anything.

I could feel the pulse in my temples and a sharp pain behind my right eye. It made me blink. Ito stared at me a long time, then gave a little nod. 'Yeah, you're smart. Maybe if you're smart enough you can get what's in that room back there out of your head. Maybe if you're tough enough, what you saw back there won't bother you.' His voice was softer than you would've expected.

I took a deep breath and let it out. I rolled my shoulders to try to work out some of the tension. Poitras was leaning against a shelf of tea trays and little lacquer cups with his arms crossed. Crossed like that, they looked swollen even more than normal. Ito was good, all right.

He said, 'Thing is, what's back there ain't so special around here. This is Little Tokyo, Chinatown. You oughta see what the Mung have going down in Little Saigon.'

Jimmy said, 'How about those pricks in Koreatown?'

Ito nodded at him, then looked back at me. Thinking about those pricks in Koreatown made him smile. 'This ain't America, white boy. This is Little Asia, and it's ten thousand years old. We've got stuff down here like nothing you've ever seen.'

I said, 'Yeah.' Mr. Tough.

He said, 'If Nobu Ishida wanted you out of the picture, he wouldn't do it by calling up some broad and making a threat.' He swiveled around and looked at Jimmy. 'Call Hollenbeck Robbery and see who has this book thing. Find out what they know.'

'Sure, Terry.' Jimmy didn't move.

I said, 'What's the big deal with Nobu Ishida?'

Ito looked back at me and thought about it for a while. Like maybe he would tell me and maybe he wouldn't. 'You know what the yakuza is?'

'Japanese mafia.'

Jimmy smiled, wide and mindless, the way a pit bull smiles before he bites you. He said, 'How about that, Terry. You think we got something as pussy as the mafia down here?'

Ito said, 'Call Hollenbeck.'

I said, 'Ishida was in the yakuza?'

Jimmy smiled some more, then pushed off the cruller table and walked out. Ito turned back to me. 'The yakuza is big in white slavery and dope and loan-sharking like the mafia, but that's where it stops. The stiff in back with the missing finger, he's what you would think of as a mafia soldier. But the mafia doesn't have any soldiers like him. These guys, they've got a little code they live by. Somewhere along the line this guy screwed up and the code required him to chop off his own finger to make up for it. I've seen guys with three, four fingers missing from one hand.'

I drank more coffee.

Ito said, 'The real headcases get their entire body tattooed from just below the elbows to just above the knees. Those guys are yakuza assassins.' He touched his forehead. 'Bug fuck.'

'Eddie,' I said.

Ito nodded. 'Yeah. Eddie's a real up-and-comer. Local kid. Arrest record could fill a book. We got him made for half a dozen killings but we can't prove it. That's the bitch with the yakuza. You can't prove it. People down here, something happens, they don't see it and they don't talk about it. So you've got to put a guy like Ishida's business under surveillance for eight months and pray some hotshot private license doesn't come along and tip him that he's being watched and blow the whole thing. You don't want that to happen because Ishida is overseeing a major operation to import brown heroin from China and Thailand for a guy named Yuki Torobuni who runs the yakuza here in L.A. and if you get Ishida maybe you get Torobuni and shut the whole fucking thing down.' Behind us, the two guys from the coroner's office wheeled out the gurney. There was a dark gray body bag sitting on it. Whatever was in the bag looked rumpled.

I said, 'If they're moving dope in, the guys down in Watts and

East L.A. aren't going to like it. Maybe what happened in back is an effort to eliminate competition.'

Ito looked at Poitras. 'You were right, Poitras. This boy is bright.'

'He has his days.'

'Unless,' I said, 'it has something to do with the Hagakure.'

Terry Ito smiled at me, then walked over to the cruller box and selected one with green icing. He said, 'You're smart, all right, but not smart enough. This isn't your world, white boy. People disappear. Entire families vanish in the most outrageous manner. And there's never a witness, never a clue.' Ito gave me a little more of the smile. 'Have you read a translation of the Hagakure?'

'No.'

The smile went nasty. 'There's a little thing in there called Bushido. Bushido says that the way of the warrior is death.' Ito stopped smiling. 'Whoever took your little book, pray it's not the yakuza.' He stared at me for a little while longer, then he took his cruller and went into the back.

Poitras uncrossed the huge arms and shook his head. 'Sometimes, Hound Dog, you are a real asshole.'

'Et tu, Brute?'

He walked away.

They kept me around until a dick from Hollenbeck got there and took my statement. It was 3:14 in the morning when they finished with me, and Poitras had long since gone. I went out into the cool night air onto streets that were empty of round-eyed faces. I thought about the yakuza and people disappearing and I tried to imagine things like nothing I'd ever seen. I tried, but all I kept seeing was what someone had done to Nobu Ishida.

The walk to the car was long and through dark streets, but only once did I look behind me.

CHAPTER II

The next morning Jillian Becker called me at eight-fifteen and asked me if I had yet recovered the Hagakure. I told her no, that in the fourteen hours that had passed since we last spoke, I had not recovered it, but should I stumble upon it as I walked out to retrieve my morning paper, I would call her at once. She then reminded me that today was the Pacific Men's Club Man of the Month banquet. The banquet was to begin at one, we were expected to arrive at the hotel by noon, and would I please dress appropriate to the occasion? I told her that my formal black suede holster was being cleaned, but that I would do the best I could. She asked me why I always had something flip to say. I said that I didn't know, but having been blessed with the gift, I felt obliged to use it.

At ten minutes after ten I pulled into the Warrens' drive and parked behind a dark gray presidential stretch limousine. The driver was sitting across the front seat, head down, reading the *Times* sports section. There was a chocolate-brown 1988 Rolls-Royce Corniche by the four-car garage with a white BMW 633i beside it. I made the BMW for Jillian Becker. Pike's red Jeep was at the edge of the drive out by the gate. It was as far from the other vehicles as possible. Even Pike's transportation is anti-social.

When I rang the bell, Jillian Becker answered, her face tight. She said, 'They've just gotten another call. This time the caller said they'd hurt Mimi.'

She led me back along the entry and into the big den. Sheila Warren was sitting in one of the overstuffed chairs, feet pulled up beneath her, a glass on the little table beside the chair. She was wrapped in a white terry bathrobe. Joe Pike was leaning against the far wall, thumbs hooked in his Levi's, and Mimi Warren was on the big couch across from the bar. Her eyes were large and glassy, and she looked excited. Bradley Warren came in from his library at the back of the den, immaculate in a charcoal three-piece suit, and said, 'Sheila. You're just sitting there. We don't want to be late.'

I looked back at Jillian Becker. 'Tell me about the call.'

She said, 'A half hour after you and I spoke the phone rang. Whoever it was started talking to Mimi, then must've realized she wasn't an adult and asked for her father.'

'What'd they say, Bradley?'

Bradley looked annoyed. He adjusted each cuff and examined himself in the mirror behind the bar. Sheila Warren watched him, shook her head, and drained her glass. He said, 'They told me that they knew we hadn't stopped searching for the Hagakure and that they were growing angry. They said they would be at the Man of the Month banquet and that if I knew what was good for me and my family, I'd call it off.'

Sheila Warren said, 'Bastards.' Her s's were a little slurred.

Bradley said, 'They told me they knew our every move and we were at their mercy and if I didn't do what they said they'd kill Mimi.'

I looked at Mimi. She was in a shapeless brown silk dress and flat shoes and her hair was pulled back. There still wasn't any makeup. I said, 'Pretty scary.'

She nodded.

I looked back at Bradley Warren. He was picking at something on his right lapel. 'Is that the way they said it, using those words?'

'As near as I can remember. Why?' Not used to being questioned by an employee.

'Because it is so theatrical. "If you know what's good for you." "Know your every move." "At their mercy." Most of the crooks I know have better imaginations. Also, it's pretty clear now that we aren't just talking about robbery. The calls you're getting seem like harassment calls. Someone wants to hurt your business and embarrass you, and that's probably why the Hagakure was stolen.'

I went over to the big couch and sat down next to Mimi. She was watching everything the way a goldfish watches the world from its bowl, all big eyes and vulnerability and with an assumption of invisibility. Maybe that was easy to assume when Bradley and Sheila were your parents. I said, 'What'd they say to you, babe?'

Mimi giggled.

Sheila said, 'For Christ's sake, Mimi.'

Mimi blinked. Serious. 'He told me it wasn't ours. He told me it

273

is the last legacy of Japan's lost heart and that it belongs to the spirit of Japan.'

Sheila Warren said, 'Spirit my ass.' She got up from the chair and brought her glass over to the bar. She wasn't wearing anything under the robe. 'Well, I guess it's time to get ready for the Man of the Month's divine moment.' She said it loudly, then turned away from the bar and leered at Joe Pike. 'Want to stand guard while I'm in the bath, rough guy?'

Jillian Becker coughed. Pike stood solemn and cat-like, mirrored lenses filled with the empty life of a television after a station sign-off. Bradley Warren found a hair out of place and leaned toward the mirror to adjust it. Mimi's face grew dark and blotched. At the bar, Sheila shook her head at no one in particular, mumbled something about there being no takers, then left.

Bradley Warren stepped away from the mirror, temporarily satisfied with his appearance, and looked at his daughter. 'Finish dressing, Mimi. We're going to leave soon.'

'I hate to be the wet blanket,' I said, 'but maybe we should forgo the Man of the Month celebration.'

Bradley frowned. 'I told you before. That's impossible.'

I said, 'The banquet will be in a large ballroom at the hotel. There will be a couple of hundred people plus the hotel and kitchen employees. People will want to speak with you before the presentation and after, and with your wife, and your family will be spread all to hell and back. If we assume that there is merit to the threats you've received, you'll be vulnerable. So will your wife and daughter.'

Mimi's left eye began to twitch in the same way that Bradley's had. What a trait to inherit. Her face was small and pinched and closed, but her eyes were watchful in spite of the tic, and made me think of a small animal hiding at the edge of a forest.

Bradley said, 'Nothing's going to happen to my best girl.' He went over to her with an Ozzie Nelson smile and put his hands on her shoulders.

Mimi jumped when he touched her as if an electrical current had arced between them. He didn't notice. He said, 'My best girl knows I have to attend. She knows that if we're not at the banquet, the Tashiros will see me as weak.'

His best girl nodded. Dutifully.

Bradley turned the Ozzie Nelson smile on me. 'There. You see?'

274

'Okay,' I said. 'Go without your family. Pike will stay with them, here, and I'll go with you.'

Ozzie Nelson grew impatient. 'You don't seem to understand,' he said. 'What you're asking would be bad for business.'

'Silly me,' I said. 'Of course.'

Jillian Becker stared out the front window toward a grove of bamboo. Joe Pike moved to the bar and crossed his arms the way he does when he's disgusted. I took a deep breath and told myself to pretend Bradley Warren was a four-year-old. I spoke slowly and wished Mimi wasn't with us. I said, 'A threat was made to your wife, and now a threat has been made to your daughter. A person who may or may not have been connected with the theft of the Hagakure was murdered. Whether the two are linked or not, I don't know, but the situation is worsening and it would be smart to take these threats seriously.'

Jillian Becker turned from the window. 'Bradley, maybe we should call the police. They could help with extra security.'

Bradley made a face like she'd pissed on his leg. He said, 'Absolutely not.'

Mimi stood, then, and went over to her father. 'I put on this dress especially for the banquet. Isn't it pretty?'

Bradley Warren looked at her and frowned. 'Can't you do something about your hair?'

Mimi's left eye fluttered like a moth in a jar. She rubbed at the eye and opened her mouth and closed it, and then she left.

Joe Pike shook his head and he left, too.

Bradley Warren looked at himself in the mirror again. 'Maybe I should change shoes,' he said. Then he started out, too.

I said, 'Bradley.'

He stopped in the door.

'Your daughter is terrified.'

'Of course she's frightened,' he said. 'Some maniac said he was going to kill her.'

I nodded. Slowly. 'The right thing for you to do is to call this off. Stay home. Take care of your family. They're scared now, and possibly in danger, and they need your help.'

Bradley Warren gave me the famous Bradley Warren frown, then shook his head. 'Don't you see?' he said. 'A lot of cops would ruin the banquet.'

I nodded. Of course. I looked at Jillian Becker, but she was busy with her briefcase.

CHAPTER 12

'Who heads security at Bradley's hotel?'

Jillian Becker said, 'A man named Jack Ellis.'

'May I have his phone number?'

Jillian Becker held my gaze for a moment, then turned away and found Jack Ellis's number in her briefcase. I used the phone behind the bar, called Ellis at the hotel, told him what was going on and that I had been hired by Mr. Warren for Mr. Warren's personal security. Jillian Becker took the phone and confirmed it. Ellis had a thick, coarse voice that put him in his fifties. He said, 'What do the cops think about all this?'

'The cops don't know. Mr. Warren thinks they'd be bad for business.' When I said it Jillian Becker pursed her lips and went back to shuffling papers within the briefcase. Disapproving my tone of voice, no doubt.

Ellis said, 'You like that?'

'I think it's lousy.' More disapproval. The down-turned mouth. The posture. That kind of thing.

Ellis said, 'I'll bring in my night people. That'll be enough to cover the Angeles Room, where they're gonna be, follow him in and out, watch the kitchen and the hallways.' There was a pause. 'He didn't tell the cops, huh?'

'Bad for business. Also, too many unsightly cops might ruin the banquet.' Jillian Becker put the Cross pen down and looked at me with the cool eyes.

'Son of a bitch.'

'That's right.'

I hung up and looked at Jillian Becker looking at me. I smiled. 'Want to hear my Mel Gibson imitation?'

She said, 'If you knew more about Bradley, you wouldn't dislike him the way you do.'

'I don't know. I sort of like disliking him.'

'That's obvious. Either way, as long as you're in his employ, you might be more circumspect in sharing your feelings with fellow employees. It breeds discontent.'

'Discontent. How Upper Management.'

The nostrils tightened.

I said, 'I think he's behaving like a self-absorbed ass, and so do you.'

Her left eyebrow arched. 'However he's behaving, he's still my employer. I will treat him accordingly. So should you.' My country right or wrong.

Pretty soon Joe Pike came back, scrubbed and fresh and bright-eyed. It's never easy to tell if someone is bright-eyed when they're wearing sunglasses, but one makes certain assumptions.

He put his gym bag on the floor, then leaned with his back against the bar and his elbows up on the bar rail and stared out at infinity. 'You really know how to pick'm,' he said.

A little bit after that Bradley Warren came back resplendent in different shoes, and Sheila Warren came back smelling fresh and clean, and Mimi Warren came back looking and smelling pretty much the same, and we were all together. One big happy family. We trooped out to the limo, Bradley and Jillian and Sheila and me and Mimi and Pike, all single file. I broke into 'Whistle While You Work,' but no one got it. Pike might've got it, but he never tells. Bradley and Jillian took the forward-facing seat and Mimi and Sheila and I got the seat facing the rear, Sheila and Mimi on either side of me, Sheila sitting so that her leg was pressed against mine. Sheila said, 'Don't they have a bar in these damn things?' Everyone ignored her. Pike said something to the limo driver, then went over to his Jeep. Sheila Warren said, 'He's not coming with us?'

'Nope.'

'Mother fuck.'

Traffic was light. We went down Beverly Glen to Wilshire, then east. We stayed on Wilshire through Beverly Hills and past the La Brea tar pits with the full-sized models of the mammoths they have there and past MacArthur Park and into downtown L.A. until Wilshire ended at Grand. We went up to Seventh, then over on Broadway, and pulled up under the entrance of the New Nippon Hotel.

One thing you could say about Bradley Warren, he built a helluva hotel. The New Nippon was a thirty-two-story cylindrical column of metallic blue glass and snow-white concrete midway between Little Tokyo, Chinatown, and downtown L.A. There were dozens of limos and taxis and MBs and Jaguars. Suitcases were going in and out and doormen in red uniforms were whistling for the next taxi in line and guys I took to be tourists who looked like they made a lot of money were with tall slender women who looked like they cost a lot of money to keep up. None of them looked like gunsels or thugs or art thief-maniacs, but you can never be sure.

'You got a McDonald's in there?' I said.

Bradley Warren smiled at me.

Sheila Warren murmured, 'Piece of shit.'

We pulled to a stop by a clump of men and women who smiled as they watched the limo drive up. Two doormen trotted over, one with a lot of braid who was probably the boss, and opened the doors. Pike pulled up behind us, gave his keys to a parking attendant, and moved to stand by the lobby entrance twenty feet away.

The group of smiling people gathered around Bradley and congratulated him and said it was long deserved and didn't Sheila look lovely and wasn't Mimi getting pretty. Somebody took a photo. Sheila gave everyone an arc-light smile and draped herself on her husband's arm and looked adoring and proud and was everything he could have wanted her to be. She didn't look like she hated it or hated him or hated the goddamned building. Nancy Reagan would've been proud.

A square-faced guy in gray slacks and a blue blazer and a gold and yellow rep tie moved up to Jillian's elbow, said something, then the two of them moved over to me. He put out his hand. 'Jack Ellis. You Cole?'

'Yeah. Where'd you do your time?' Ellis wore *ex-cop* like a bad coat.

'You can tell, huh?'

'Sure.'

'Detroit.'

'Rough beat.'

Ellis nodded, pleased. 'Murder City, brother. Murder City.' Murder City. These cops.

We moved into the lobby and up an escalator to the mezzanine floor. The lower three floors were boutiques and travel agencies and bookstores and art galleries surrounding a lobby interior big enough to park the Goodyear blimp. There was a sign at the top of the escalator that read PACIFIC MEN'S CLUB LUNCHEON with ANGELES ROOM beneath it and an arrow pointing down a short corridor. People who looked like guests milled around and two overweight guys dressed like Ellis stood off to the side, looking like security. Ellis said, 'I've got eight people in for this. Two up here on the mezzanine, two more in the Angeles Room, two in the lobby, and two in the kitchen entrance behind the podium.'

Bradley and his knot of admirers continued along the corridor, passing the Angeles Room. I thought about saying something, but after all, it was their hotel. They should know where we were going.

I said, 'There any other halls or entrances off the Angeles Room besides the kitchen entrance?'

'The Blue Corridor. I got no people there because that's where we'll be. We wait in there and when they're ready for the show to start we can get into the Angeles Room from a side door.'

I nodded and looked at Jillian Becker. 'What's on the program?'

'It shouldn't take more than an hour and a half. First, lunch is served, then the president of the association makes a few introductory remarks, and then Bradley speaks for about fifteen minutes and we go home.'

We went through an unmarked door and along a sterile tile corridor and through another unmarked door and then we were in the Blue Corridor and then the Blue Room. Both the corridor and the room were blue. Four successful-looking Asian-American men were there, along with a tall black man and an older white guy with glasses and the mayor of Los Angeles. Everybody smiled and kissed Sheila's cheek and shook Bradley's hand. There was back-slapping and more photographs and everybody ignored Mimi. She stood to the side with her head down as if she were looking for lint on her dress.

I leaned close to her and whispered, 'How you doin'?'

She looked up at me the way you look at someone when they've said something that surprises you. I patted her shoulder and said softly, 'Stay close, kid. I'll take care of you.'

She gave me the serious goldfish face, then went back to staring at her dress.

'Hey, Mimi.'

She looked at me again.

'I think the dress looks great.'

Her mouth tightened and bent. A smile.

279

Jillian Becker came up behind me and tapped at her wrist. 'Ten minutes.'

'Maybe we should synchronize watches.'

She frowned.

'I'm going to take a look outside. I'll be back in five.' I told Ellis to stay with Bradley and told both Mimi and Sheila to stay put. Mimi made the crooked mouth again. Sheila told me she was horny, and asked wouldn't I like to do something about it. Nothing like cooperation.

I went along the Blue Corridor and out into what a little sign said was the Angeles Room and thought, nope, maybe the sign was wrong. Maybe this was really the UN. Maybe a king was about to be crowned. Maybe aliens had landed and this was where they were going to make their address. Then I saw Joe Pike. It was the Angeles Room, all right.

Eighty tables, eight people per table. Video cams set up on a little platform at the rear of a place that might be called a grand ballroom if you thought small. Press people. A dais with seating for twenty-four. Pacific Men's Club Man of the Month. Who would've thought it. About sixty percent of the faces were Asian. The rest were black and white and brown and nobody looked too concerned about making the next Mercedes payment. I recognized five city council members and a red-haired television newswoman I'd had a crush on for about three years and the Tashiros. Maybe the Pacific Men's Club was *the* hot ticket in town. Maybe Steven Spielberg had tried to get in and been turned away. Maybe I could get the news-woman's phone number.

Pike drifted up to me. 'This sucks.'

That Joe.

'I could off anybody in this place five times over.'

'Could you off someone and get away with you here?'

Head shake. 'I'm too good even for me.'

I said, 'It starts in ten minutes. Door I came from is off the Blue Corridor. They're in a room down the corridor. We come out that room, along the corridor, through the door, and up to the dais.' I told him where Ellis had put his men. 'You take the right side of the dais. I'll come out with them and take the left.'

Pike nodded and drifted away, head slowly swiveling as he scanned the crowd from behind the sunglasses.

I went back to the Blue Room. Bradley Warren was seated on a nice leather couch, smiling with four or five new arrivals, probably

280

people who would sit on the dais. The little room was getting crowded and smoky and I didn't like it. Jack Ellis looked nervous. Bradley laughed at something somebody said, then got up and went to a little table where someone had put out white wine and San Pellegrino water. I edged up to him and said, 'Do you know all these people?'

'Of course.'

'Any way to clear them out?'

'Don't be absurd, Cole. Does everything look all right?'

'You're asking my opinion, I say blow this off and go home.'

'Don't be absurd.' I guess he liked the sound of it.

'All right.'

'You're being paid to protect us. Do that.'

If he kept it up, he was going to have to pay someone to protect him from me.

More people squeezed into the little room. Jack Ellis went out and then came back. There were maybe twenty-five people in the room now, more coming in and some going out, and then Jillian Becker went over to Bradley and said, 'It's time,' loud enough for me to hear. I looked around, figuring to get Sheila and Mimi and Bradley into a group. Sheila was nodding at a very heavy white guy who smiled a great deal. I said, 'Where's Mimi?'

Sheila looked confused. 'Mimi?'

I went out into the hall. There were more people coming along the corridor and others going into the Angeles Room but there was no Mimi. Jack Ellis came out and then Jillian Becker. Ellis said, 'She asked one of the busboys for the bathroom.'

'Where is it?'

'Just around the corner to the left. I got a man down there.' We were trotting as he said it, picking up speed, Ellis breathing hard after twenty feet. We went around one corner then around another and into a dirty white hall with an exit sign at the far end. There was a men's room door and a women's room door halfway down its length. Jack Ellis's man was lying facedown in front of the women's room door with one leg crossed over the other and his right hand behind his back. Ellis said, 'Christ, Davis,' and puffed forward. Davis groaned and rolled over as he said it.

I pulled my gun and pushed first into the women's room and then into the men's. Empty. I ran down to the exit door and kicked through it and ran down two flights of stairs and through another door into the hotel's laundry. There were huge commercial washers and steam-circulating systems and dryers that could handle a hundred sheets at a crack. But there was no Mimi.

In Vietnam I had learned that the worst parts of life and death are not where you look for them. Like the sniper's bullet that takes off a buddy's head as you stand side by side at a latrine griping about foot sores, the worst parts hover softly in the shadows and happen when you are not looking. The worst of life stays hidden until death.

On a heavy gray security door that led onto a service drive beneath the hotel, someone had written WE WARNED YOU in red spray paint. Beneath it they had drawn a rising sun.

CHAPTER 13

When the first wave of cops and FBI got there, they sealed off the Blue Corridor and herded all the principals into the Blue Room and sealed that off, too. An FBI agent named Reese put the arm on me and Ellis and brought us outside and walked us past the restrooms and down the stairs. Reese was about fifty, with very long arms and pool player's hands. He was about the color of fine French roast coffee, and he looked like he hadn't had a good night's sleep in twenty years.

He said, 'How long this guy Davis been working for you, Ellis?'

'Two years. He's an ex-cop. All my guys are ex-cops. So am I.' He said it nervous.

Reese nodded. 'Davis says he's standing down the hall back up by the bathrooms grabbing a smoke when the girl comes by, goes into the women's room. Says the next thing he knows this gook dude is coming out the women's room and gives him one on the head and that's it.' Reese squinted at us. Maybe doing his impression of a gook dude. 'That sound good to you?'

Jack Ellis chewed the inside of his mouth and said, 'Uh-huh.'

In the laundry there were cops and feds taking pictures of the paint job and talking to Chicano guys in green coveralls with NEW NIPPON HOTEL on the back. Reese ignored them. 'Didn't anybody tell the girl not to go off alone?' He squatted down to look at something on the floor as he said it. Maybe a clue.

Ellis looked at me. I said, 'She was told.'

Reese got up, maybe saw another clue, squatted again in a different place. 'But she went anyway. And when she went, nobody went with her.'

I said, 'That's it.'

He stood up again and looked at us. 'Little girl gotta go potty. That's no big deal. Happens every day. Nothing to worry about, right?' A little smile hit at the corner of his mouth and went away. 'Only when you got serious criminals out there, and they're saying things, maybe going potty, maybe that's something to think about. Maybe calling the police when the threats are made, maybe that's something to think about, too.' He looked from Ellis to me and back to Ellis. 'Maybe the cops are here, maybe the little girl does her diddle and comes back and this never happens.'

Ellis didn't say anything.

Reese looked at me. 'I talked to a dick named Poitras about you. He said you know the moves. What happened, this one get outta hand?'

Ellis said, 'Look, Mr. Warren signs the checks, right? He says jump, I say which side of my ass you want me to land on?'

Reese's eyes went back to Ellis and flagged to half-mast. I think it was his disdainful look. 'How long were you a cop?'

Ellis chewed harder at his mouth.

I said, 'You gonna bust our ass about this all day or we gonna try to get something done?'

Reese put the look on me.

I said, 'We shoulda brought you guys in. We wanted to bring you guys in. But Ellis is right. It's Warren's ticket and he said no. That's half-assed, but there it is. So this is what we're left with. We can stand here and you can work out on us or we can move past it.'

Reese's eyes went to half-mast again, then he turned to look at the door with the paint. He sucked at a tooth while he looked. 'Poitras said you got Joe Pike for a partner. That true?'

'Yeah.'

Reese shook his head. 'Ain't that some shit.' He finished sucking on the tooth and turned back to me. 'Tell me what you got, from the beginning.'

I gave it to him from the beginning. I had told it so many times to so many cops I thought about making mimeographed copies and handing them out. When I told the part about Nobu Ishida, Jack Ellis said, 'Holy shit.'

We went back up the stairs to the Blue Room. There were cops talking to Bradley Warren and Sheila Warren and the hotel manager and the people who organized the Pacific Men's Club luncheon. Reese stopped in the door and said, 'Which one's Pike?'

Pike was standing in a corner, out of the way. 'Him.'

Reese nodded and sucked the tooth again. 'Do tell,' he said softly.

'You want to meet him?'

Reese gave me flat eyes, then went over and stood by two dicks who were talking to Bradley Warren. Sheila was sitting on the couch, leaning forward into the detective who was interviewing her, touching his thigh every once in a while for emphasis. Jillian Becker stood by the bar. Her eyes were puffy and her mascara had run.

When Bradley saw me, he glared, and said, 'What happened to my daughter?' His face was flushed.

Jillian said, 'Brad.'

He snapped his eyes to her. 'I asked him an appropriate question. Should I have you research his answer?'

Jillian went very red.

I said, 'They knew you were going to be here. They had someone come up through the laundry. Maybe he waited in the restroom or maybe he walked around and was in here with us. We won't know that until we find him.'

'I don't like these "maybes." Maybe is a weak word.'

Reese said, 'Maybe somebody shoulda brought the cops in.'

Bradley ignored him. 'I paid for security and I got nothing.' He stabbed a finger at Jack Ellis. 'You're fired.'

Ellis really worked at the inside of his mouth. Bradley Warren looked at me. 'And you? What did you do?' He looked at Jillian Becker again. 'The one you insisted I hire. What did you say about him?'

I said, 'Be careful, Bradley.'

Warren pointed at me. 'You're fired, too.' He looked at Pike. 'You, too. Get out. Get out. All of you.'

Everyone in the small tight room was staring at us. Even the cops had stopped doing cop things. Jack Ellis swallowed hard, started to say something, but finally just nodded and walked out. I looked at Sheila Warren. There was something bright and anxious in her eyes. Her hand was on the arm of the big cop, frozen there. Jillian Becker stared at the floor.

Reese said, 'Take it easy, Mr. Warren. I got a few questions.'

Bradley Warren sucked in some air, let it out, then glanced at his watch. 'I hope it won't take too long,' he said. 'Maybe they can still make the presentation.'

Joe Pike said, 'Fuck you.'

We left.

CHAPTER 14

Pike took me back to the Warren house, dropped me off, and drove away without saying anything. I got into the Corvette, went down Beverly Glen into Westwood, and stopped at a little Vietnamese place I know. Ten tables, most of them doubles, cleanly done in pale pinks and pastel blues and run by a Vietnamese man and his wife and their two daughters. The daughters are in their twenties and quite pretty. At the back of the restaurant, where they have the cash register, there's a little color snapshot of the man wearing a South Vietnamese Regular Army uniform. Major. He looked a lot younger then. I spent eleven months in Vietnam, but I've never told the man. I often eat in his restaurant.

The man smiled when he saw me. 'The usual?'

I gave him one of my best smiles. 'Sure. To go.'

I sat at the little table for two they have in the window of the place and waited and watched the people moving past along Westwood Boulevard and felt hollow. There were college kids and general-issue pedestrians and two cops walking a beat, one of them smiling at a girl in a gauzy cotton halter and white and black tiger-striped aerobic tights. The tights started just above her navel and stopped just below her knees. Her calves were tanned. I wondered if the cop would be smiling as much if he had just gotten fired from a job because a kid he had been hired to protect had gotten snatched anyway. Probably not. I wondered if the girl in the white and black tights would smile back quite so brightly. Probably not.

The oldest daughter brought my food from the kitchen while her father rang up the bill. She put the bag on the table and said, 'Squid with garlic and pepper, and a double order of vegetable rice.' I wondered if she could see it on my forehead: *Elvis Cole, Failed Protector*. She gave me a warm smile and said, 'I put a container of chili sauce in the bag, like always.' Nope. Probably couldn't see it.

286

I went down to Santa Monica and east to my office. At any number of traffic lights and intersections I waited for people to look my way and point and say nasty things, but no one did. Word was still under wraps.

I put the Corvette in its spot in the parking garage and rode up in the elevator and went into my office and closed the door. There was a message on my answering machine from someone looking for Bob, but that was probably a wrong number. Or maybe it wasn't a wrong number. Maybe I was in the wrong office. Maybe I was in the wrong life.

I put the food on my desk and took off my jacket and put it on a wooden coat hanger and hung it on the back of the door. I took the Dan Wesson out of its holster and put it in my top right drawer, then slipped out of the rig and tossed it onto one of the director's chairs across from my desk, then went over to the little refrigerator and got out a bottle of Negra Modelo beer and opened it and went back to my desk and sat and listened to the quiet. It was peaceful in the office. I liked that. No worries. No sense of loss or unfulfilled obligations. No guilt. I thought about a song a little friend of mine sings: *I'm a big brown mouse, I go marching through the house, and I'm not afraid of anything!* I sang it softly to myself and sipped the Modelo. Modelo is ideal for soothing that hollow feeling. I think that's why they make it.

After a while I opened the bag and took out the container of squid and the larger container of rice and the little plastic cup of bright red chili paste and the napkins and the chopsticks. I had to move the little figures of Jiminy Cricket and Mickey Mouse to make room for the food. What was it Jiminy Cricket said? *Little man, you've had a busy night.* I put some of the chili paste on the squid and some on the rice and mixed it and ate and drank the beer. *I'm a big brown mouse, I go marching through the house, and I'm noooot afraid of anything!*

The sun was low above Catalina, pushing bright yellow rectangles up my eastern wall when the door opened and Joe Pike walked in. I tipped what was maybe the second or third Modelo bottle at him. 'Life in the fast lane,' I said. Maybe it was the fourth.

'Uh-huh.'

He came over to the desk, looked in what was left of the carton of squid, then the carton of rice. 'Any meat in this?'

I shook my head. Pike had turned vegetarian about four months ago.

He dumped what was left of the squid into the rice, took a set of chopsticks, sat in one of the director's chairs, and ate. Southeast Asians almost never use chopsticks. If you go to Vietnam or Thailand or Cambodia, you never see a chopstick. Even in the boonies. They use forks and large spoons but when they come here and open a little restaurant they put out chopsticks because that's what Americans expect. Ain't life a bitch?

I said, 'There's chili paste.'

Pike shook what was left of the chili paste into the rice, stirred it, continued to eat.

'There's another Modelo in the box.'

He shook his head.

'How long since you've come to the office?'

Shrug.

'Must be four, five months.' There was a door to an adjoining office that belonged to Pike. He never used it and didn't bother to glance at it now. He shoveled in rice and broccoli and peas, chewed, swallowed.

I sipped the last of the Modelo, then dropped the empty into the waste basket. 'I was just kidding,' I said. 'That's really pork-fried rice.'

Pike said, 'I don't like losing the girl.'

I took a deep breath and leaned back in the chair. The office was quiet and still. Only the eyes in the Pinocchio clock moved. 'Maybe, whatever reason, Warren wanted the Hagakure stolen and wants people to know and also wants them to know that he's had a child kidnapped because of his efforts to recover it. Maybe he's looking for a certain image here, figuring he can make a big deal out of recovering the book and his daughter. That sound like Bradley to you?'

Pike got up, went to the little refrigerator, and took out a can of tomato juice. 'Maybe,' he said. 'Maybe it's the other way. Maybe somebody wants Warren to look bad and they don't give a damn about the book just so they stir up as much publicity as they can. Maybe what they want is to make the big Japanese connections lose interest. Or maybe they just want to hurt him. Maybe he owes money.'

'A lot of maybes,' I said.

Pike nodded. 'Maybe is a weak word.'

I said, 'Maybe it's the yakuza.'

Pike shook the little can of tomato juice and peeled off the foil sealer tab and drank. A tiny drop ran down from the corner of his mouth. It looked like blood. He wiped it away with a napkin. 'We could sit here maybe all night and the girl's still gone.'

I got up and went to the glass doors and opened them. Traffic noise was loud but the evening air was beginning to cool. 'I don't like losing her either. I don't like getting fired and told to forget it. I don't like it that she's out there and in trouble and we're not in it anymore.'

Mirrored lenses caught the setting sun. The sun made the lenses glow.

'I think we should stay in,' I said.

Pike tossed the little can on top of the empty Modelo bottles.

'We stay with the yakuza because they're what we have,' I said. 'Forget the other stuff. We push until someone pushes back and then we see where we are.'

'All we have to do is find the yakuza.'

'Right. All we have to do is find the yakuza.'

Pike's mouth twitched. 'We can do that.'

CHAPTER 15

Nobu Ishida had lived in an older split-level house on a Leave-It-to-Beaver street in Cheviot Hills, a couple of miles south of the Twentieth Century-Fox lot. It was dark, just after nine when we rolled past his home, rounded the block, and parked at the curb fifty yards up the street. Somewhere nearby, a dog barked.

The house was brick and board and painted a light, bright color you couldn't make out at night. Ishida's Eldorado was in the drive, with a tiny, two-tone Merkur behind it. There was an enormous plate glass picture window to the left of the front door, ideal for revealing the house's brightly lit interior. A woman in her fifties passed by the window talking to a young man in his twenties. Both the woman and the man looked sad. Mrs. Ishida and a son. With Dad not yet cold in the grave, there was plenty to be sad about.

Pike said, 'Me or you?'

'Me.'

I got out of the car as if I were out for an evening stroll. A block and a half down, I turned, came back, slipped off the walk into the shadows, and went to the west side of the Ishida house. There were two frame windows off what looked like a bedroom. The bedroom was dark. Past the windows, there was a redwood gate with a neatly painted sign that said BEWARE OF DOG. I whistled softly through my teeth, then broke off a hedge branch and brushed it against the inside of the gate. No dog. I slipped back to the street, then followed a hedgerow to the east side of the house. The garage was on that side, locked tight and windowless, with a narrow chain link gate leading to the back yard. I eased open the gate and walked along the side of the house to a little window about midway down. A young woman in a print dress sat at the dining room table, holding a baby. She touched her nose to the baby's and smiled. The baby smiled back. Not exactly a yakuza stronghold.

I went back to the car. Pike said, 'Just family, right?'

'Or clever impersonators.'

Forty minutes later the front door opened and the young man and the woman with the baby came out. The young man had a pink carry-bag with teddy bears on the side, probably stuffed with Pampers and baby bottles and teething rattles and Bert and Ernie dolls. Mrs. Ishida kissed everyone good-bye and watched them walk out to the little Merkur and waved as they drove away. 'You see that?' I said.

Pike nodded.

'Classic yakuza misdirection.'

Pike said, 'You're a pip on stakeout.'

Just before midnight, an L.A.P.D. prowl car turned the corner and cruised the block, arcing its big spot over the houses to scare away burglars and peepers. At one-twenty, two men jogged down the middle of the street, one white, one black, breathing in unison, matching strides. By three, I was stiff and hungry. Pike had not moved. Maybe he was dead. 'You awake?'

'If you're tired, go to sleep.'

Some partner.

At twenty-five minutes after five, an Alta-Dena milk truck rolled down the street and made four stops. By six-oh-five, the sky in the east was starting to pinken, and lights were on in two houses down the block. At fourteen minutes after eight o'clock, after jobs had been gone to and children had been brought to school and lives had been put under way, Nobu Ishida's widow came out of her house carrying a Saks Fifth Avenue shopping bag and wearing a black suit. She locked the door, walked to the Eldorado, got in, and drove away.

I said, 'Let's do it.'

We climbed out of the Corvette, went through the little chain link gate next to the garage, then around to the back. There was a standard frame door off the kitchen, and French doors opening off the family room to a small, kidney-shaped swimming pool. We went in through the French doors.

Pike said, 'I'll take the back of the house.'

'Okay.'

He disappeared down the hall without making a sound.

The family room was a nice-sized space with Early American furniture and pictures of the kids and a Zenith console color TV and absolutely nothing to indicate that Nobu Ishida had an interest in feudal Japanese artifacts. *People* magazine sat on the hearth and a box of Ritz crackers was on the coffee table and someone was reading the latest Jackie Collins. Imagine that. Portrait of the criminal as a Middle-Class American.

There was a yellow dial phone on a little table beside a Barcalounger chair across from the Zenith. Beneath the phone was an address book with listings for things like paramedics, doctor, fire, police, Ed and Diane Waters, and Bobby's school. Probably code names for yakuza thugs. I put the address book down and went into the kitchen. There were messages held to the refrigerator by little plastic magnets that looked like Snoopy and Charlie Brown and baskets of flowers. A picture of Ishida's wife sat on the counter in a frame that said KISS THE COOK. She looked like a nice woman and a good mom. Did she know what her husband had done for a living? When they were young and courting, had he said, 'Stick with me, babe, I'm gonna be the biggest thug in Little Tokyo,' or had he simply found himself there while she found herself with children and PTA and a loving husband who kept business to himself and made a comfortable life? Maybe I should introduce her to Malcolm Denning's wife. Maybe they would have a lot to talk about.

Pike materialized in the doorway. 'Back here,' he said.

We went back through the family room and down a short hall to what had probably once been a child's bedroom. Now, it wasn't.

'Well, well, well,' I said. 'Welcome to Nippon.'

We were in a small room with a lot of furniture and all the furniture was lacquered rosewood. There was a low table in the center of the room with a pillow for a chair and one of those lacquered boxes with a phone inside. A matching file cabinet stood in the corner, and a low table ran along two walls. On the table were four little stands, each stand holding a pair of horizontal samurai swords, a longer one on the bottom, a shorter one above it. The swords were inlaid with pearls and gems and had silk ribbons wound about the handles. Separating the stands were very old samurai battle helmets shaped like the helmets the Federation Storm Troopers had worn in *Star Wars*. A beautiful silk robe was framed on the wall above the helmets. It looked like a giant butterfly. There were wood-block prints on the opposite walls and a silk-screened watercolor under glass that looked so delicate that a ripple of air might fray it, and two tiny bonsai trees growing in glass globes. On the outside wall, shoji screens softened and filtered the early morning sunlight. It was a beautiful room.

Pike went to the low table and said, 'Look.'

Three books were stacked on the edge of the table. The top book was an excerpted English translation of the Hagakure. The second book was a different translation. The third was titled *Bushido: The Warrior's Soul*. Pike thumbed through the top Hagakure translation. 'They've been read a lot.'

'If Ishida had the real thing, maybe someone found out and wanted it bad enough to try to make him turn it over to them.'

'Uh-huh.' Pike found something he liked and stopped to read.

'Perhaps we can find a clue as to whom.'

Pike kept reading.

'As soon as we finish reading.'

Joe read a moment longer, then put the book back on the table. 'I'll go up front and keep watch.'

When he was gone, I looked around. There was nothing on the low desk but the books and the phone, and nothing on the wall tables but the swords and the helmets. Not even dust. The file cabinet was absolutely clean, too, but at least there were the drawers to look into. The top drawer had neatly labeled files devoted to home and family: the kids' schools, medical payments, insurance policies. The bottom drawer held art catalogs, vacation brochures, and supply catalogs from Ishida's import business. There were no financial records from his business. Those were probably with his accountant. Filed under *C* for Crime.

In the third folder from the back of the drawer I found Ishida's personal credit card records. The charges were substantial.

Nobu Ishida had two Visa cards and two MasterCards and American Express Platinum and Optima and Diners Club. Most of the charges were at restaurants or hotels or various boutiques and department stores. The Ishidas had gone out a lot, and spent a lot more than people living in this house in this neighborhood might spend. I was looking for patterns, but there didn't seem to be any. All the hotels were one-shots and so were most of the restaurants. Go someplace for a bite, maybe not go back for another couple of months, if you went back at all. There were a few repeats, but those mostly to places I recognized. Ma Maison is not a yakuza hangout.

I had gone through the old stuff and was working on the recent when I noticed that two or three times a week, every week for the past three months, Ishida had gone to a place called Mr. Moto's.

There were mostly small charges, as if he had gone by himself to have a couple of drinks, but once every two weeks, usually on a Thursday, there was a single large charge of between four and five hundred dollars. Hmmmm.

I put the credit card receipts back in their file and the file back in its folder and left the cabinet as I had found it and went back to the low table. I used the phone and called information.

A woman's voice said, 'What city?'

'Los Angeles. I need a number and address for a restaurant or bar named Mr. Moto's.'

If all you want is a number, they put on the computer. If you want the address, a person has to tell you. The person gave me the number and the address and told me to have a good day. Something the computer never does. I hung up and wiped the beautiful lacquered box free of unsightly fingerprints, then went out to Joe Pike.

He nodded when he saw me. 'Didn't take long.'

'The best clues never do.'

We let ourselves out, walked back along the side of the house, got into the Corvette, and drove to Mr. Moto's.

CHAPTER 16

Mr. Moto's was a storefront dance club just off Sixth downtown. Hi-tech deco. Whitewashed front with port-hole windows outlined in aqua and peach, and *Mr. Moto's* spelled out in neon triangles. Japanese and Chinese cuisine. Very *nouveau*. There would be buffalo mozzarella spring rolls and black pasta miso and waiters with new wave football player haircuts and more neon triangles on the inside. A sign on the door said CLOSED. Another sign said LUNCH – DINNER – COCKTAILS – OPEN 11:30 A.M. It was twenty minutes after ten.

We drove another three blocks and stopped at a Bob's Big Boy to clean up in their restroom. There was an older guy with a copy of the *Jewish Daily News* standing at one of the lavatories combing his hair when we walked in. Pike went to the lavatory next to him, pulled off his sweatshirt, then unhooked his hip holster and put his gun on top of the soap dispenser. The old man looked at the gun, then at Pike, then left. He forgot his newspaper.

When we were as clean as about a million paper towels and soap that smelled like Pledge could make us, we walked the three blocks down to Mr. Moto's. It was ten minutes before noon when we went in the front door and the slim Japanese maître d' said, 'Two for lunch?' The hair on the right side of his head was shaved down to a quarter-inch buzz cut, the hair on the left was long and frizzed. New wave, all right.

I said, 'We'll sit at the bar for a while.'

It was a nice-looking place, even with the neon. The front was all aqua plastic tables and peach wrought iron chairs and a tile floor the color of steel. There was a sushi bar on the right, with maybe twenty stools and four sushi chefs wearing white and red head-bands and yelling anytime somebody walked into the place. About halfway back, the room cut in half. Tables continued along the wall on the right all the way to the kitchen in the back. On the left, you could step up underlit tile steps to a full bar and a little drinking area they had there with more tables and plants and neon triangles. A modern steel rail ran around the edge of the drinking platform to keep drunks from falling into someone's California roll. There were three women together at one of the little tables up in the bar area, and four couples in the dining room. Business people on their lunch hour. Pike and I went back through the dining area and up the little steps to the bar, one of the three women staring at Pike's tattoos.

The bartender was a Japanese woman in her late twenties. Hard face and too much green eye shadow and a rich ocher tan. She was wearing black, sprayed-on pants and a blue and black *hapi* coat with red trim that had been tied off just below the breasts so her midriff was bare. A tattoo of a butterfly floated two inches to the right of her navel. She said, 'What'll it be, guys?'

I said, 'Not too busy.'

'It picks up about twelve-thirty.'

We ordered a couple of Sapporo in the short bottles, and Pike asked for the men's room. The bartender told him, and Pike went back through the kitchen. I said, 'First time here. A friend of mine raves about the place, though. You might know him. A regular.'

She reached under the bar and music started to play. A Joan Jett rip-off. 'Who's that?'

'Nobu Ishida.'

The bartender shrugged. 'So many faces,' she said.

A man and a woman took two stools at the end of the bar. The bartender went down to them. I leaned over the bar to watch her. Nice legs.

The three women at the table took their drinks and went down to the dining area. I brought my beer and Pike's and took their table. Pike came out of the back a couple of minutes later. He said, 'Restroom in the back with a pay phone. L-shaped kitchen running the width of the building and a cold room. Door out the back. Office off the kitchen. Five men and four women working the place.'

We sipped our beer. Mr. Moto's filled with lots of men in Giorgio Armani suits and women in black biking tights and female lawyers. You could tell the lawyers because they drank too much and looked nervous. There was a smattering of Asians in the place, but most everybody else was white or black. 'You'll notice,' Pike said, 'that the only people in here who look like thugs are me and you.'

'You, maybe. I look like Don Johnson. You look like Fred Flintstone.'

Sixteen hours with nothing to eat and the Sapporo was working wonders. Pike flagged a waitress and we ordered sashimi, sushi, white rice, miso soup, and more Sapporo. Sapporo is great when your back is stiff from an all-night stakeout.

Several young women who looked like models came in. They were tall and thin and wore their hair in flashes and swirls and bobs that looked okay in a magazine but looked silly in real life. They spent a lot of time touching themselves.

Pike said, 'Maybe we should interrogate them.'

The food came. We'd ordered toro and yellowtail and octopus and freshwater eel and sea urchin. The urchin and eel and octopus were prepared as sushi, each slice draped over a molded bullet of rice and held there by a band of seaweed. Sashimi is sliced fish without the rice. The waitress brought two little trays of a dark brown dipping sauce with a sprinkling of chopped green onion in it for the sashimi. In an empty tray I mixed soy sauce and hot green mustard for the sushi. I dipped a piece of the octopus sushi in the sauce, let the rice absorb the sauce, then took a bite. Delicious. Pike was looking in his miso soup. 'There's something in here.'

'Black pasta,' I said. '*Nouveau* cuisine.'

Pike pushed the soup aside.

By one o'clock the place was packed. It was SRO up by the maître d' and the crowd noise was threatening to drown out the music. Just after one a second bartender came on duty. He was younger than the Butterfly Lady, with short spiky hair and very smooth skin and a little-boy face. Someone's grad student nephew, given a part-time job to make a few extra bucks during the summer. The Butterfly Lady said something and the new kid looked our way. Worried. I smiled at Pike. 'Well, well. I think we're making progress.'

I got up and went over to the new kid's end of the bar. 'You guys have Falstaff?'

The grad student shook his head. The Butterfly Lady came over, gave me a look, said something in Japanese to the kid, then went back to her end of the bar. The grad student began building a margarita. I said, 'How about Corona?'

'Just Japanese.'

I nodded. 'Sapporo in a short bottle. Two.'

He poured the margarita mixture into three round glasses. The

297

Butterfly Lady came back, got them, went away. I smiled at the kid. Mr. Friendly. 'Get many thugs in here?'

He said, 'What?'

I winked at him, and took the two Sapporos back to the table. Our dishes had been cleared. Pike said, 'Look.'

Across the room, at a little corner table by some leafy plants, three men were being seated. An older Japanese man, a much younger Japanese man with heavy shoulders, and a tall, thin black man. The black man looked like Lou Gossett except for the scar that started at the crown of his head and ran down across his temple and curved back to lop off the top of his left ear. The two Asian men were smiling broadly and laughing with a slight man in a dark suit whose long hair was pulled back in a punk version of the traditional Japanese topknot. Manager. 'Something tells me we are no longer the only thugs in the place,' I said.

'Know the black guy from when I was a cop,' Pike said. 'Richards Sangoise. Dope dealer from Crenshaw.'

'You see,' I said. 'Gangsters.'

'Could just be coincidence they're here.'

'Could be.'

'But maybe not.'

'Maybe those two Asian gentlemen are yakuza executives in search of an expanding business opportunity.'

Pike nodded.

I went back to the grad student and gave him the same Mr. Friendly. 'Excuse me,' I said. 'Do you see the three gentlemen seated there?'

'Uh-huh.' Uneasy.

'I have reason to believe that those men are criminals, and that they may be engaged in the criminal act of conspiracy, and I felt obligated to tell someone. You might want to call the police.'

The kid gave me Ping-Pong ball eyes. I walked back and sat down with Pike. 'Just a little push,' I said.

We watched the bar. The grad student said something to the Butterfly Lady. She snagged a waiter, said something, and the waiter went down onto the main floor to the manager. The manager came back into the bar and went over to the Butterfly Lady. They looked our way, then the manager left the bar and went back toward the kitchen. A little while later he reappeared and came over to our table. 'Excuse me, gentlemen.' Mr. Cordiality. 'We're terribly busy, as you can see. Since you've finished your meal, would it be too much of an imposition for me to ask that you make room for others?'

'Yes,' Pike said, 'it would.'

I said, 'My friend Nobu told me that if I came here I would be treated better than this.'

The manager looked past me for a moment. 'You're a friend of Mr. Ishida?'

I said, 'Mr. Ishida is dead. Murdered. I want to know who he was with the last time he was in here.'

The manager shook his head and gave me a smile that wobbled. 'You should leave now.'

'We like it here,' Pike said. 'We might stay forever.'

The manager worked his mouth, then went back down to the dining room and into the kitchen. Pike said, 'I think we're becoming a problem.'

I nodded. 'Fun, isn't it?'

Pike went down into the dining area and over to the table with the two Japanese men and the black man. He stood very close to the table, so that the men had to lean back to look up at him. He said something to Richards Sangoise. Sangoise's eyes widened. Pike leaned over, put a hand on Sangoise's shoulder, and said something else. Sangoise looked at me. I made a gun with my hand, pointed it at him, and pulled the trigger. Sangoise shoved his chair back and left. The younger Japanese man jumped to his feet. The older man looked from Pike to me and back to Pike. Angry. They hurried out after Sangoise. The manager came running out of the back in time to see the end of it. He looked angry, too. The grad student looked even more worried and said something to the Butterfly Lady. She said something sharp and walked away from him. Pike came back to the table and sat down.

'Nice,' I said.

Pike nodded.

When the grad student came out from behind the bar and went back toward the kitchen, I followed him.

The kitchen was all steel and white with a high industrial ceiling. It was hot, even with the kitchen's blowers going at top speed. There was a narrow hall at the right rear of the kitchen with a door that said OFFICE. On the left, there was another little hall with a pay phone and a sign that said RESTROOMS. I passed a woman carrying a tray of pot sticker dumplings and went into the men's room.

It was small and white, with one stall for the toilet and one urinal and one sink and one of those blowers that never get your hands dry and a smudged sign above the sink that said that employees MUST wash with soap. The grad student was standing at the urinal. He looked over and saw it was me and you would've thought I'd kicked him in the groin. I gave him the smile, then I threw the little bolt that locked the door. He said, 'You'd better not touch me.'

I said, 'Is this place owned by the yakuza?'

Scared. Very scared. 'Open the door. Come on.'

'I'll open the door after we talk.'

He zipped up and moved away from the urinal. His mouth was working like maybe he'd cry, like he'd spent a lot of time thinking that something like this would happen one day and now it was. Malcolm Denning. I said, 'The shit is about to hit the fan, boy. Do you know what the yakuza is?'

He shook his head.

I said, 'Did you know a man named Nobu Ishida?'

He shook his head again and I slapped him in the center of the chest with an open right hand. It made a deep hollow thump and knocked him back and frightened him more than hurt him. I said, 'Do not bullshit me. Nobu Ishida was in here three times a week for three months. He spent big and he tipped big and you know him.'

Someone tried the door, then knocked. I opened my jacket to show the Dan Wesson to the kid and said, 'Occupied. Out in a minute.' The kid's eyes were big, and his mouth opened and closed like a fish. Koi. He said, 'I didn't know him. He was a customer.'

'But you know the name.'

'Yes, sir.' Yes, sir.

I said, 'Nobu Ishida was a member of the yakuza. Every two weeks he was here with other people and those people were probably in the yakuza, too. A girl named Mimi Warren has been kidnapped, maybe by the yakuza, and maybe by someone who knew Ishida. I want their names.'

The kid looked up from the place under my jacket where the Dan Wesson lived. 'Mimi was kidnapped?'

I looked at him. 'You know Mimi Warren?'

He nodded. 'She comes here sometimes.'

'Here?'

'With her friends.'

'Friends?' Witness interrogation had always been a strong point.

'A girl named Carol. Another girl named Kerri. I really didn't know them. They're around, you see them, you say hi. They'd come and dance and hang out. We get pretty good bands.' He was looking past me at the door. Like maybe somebody was going to kick it in. 'I don't know anything about a kidnapping. I swear I don't. They're going to miss me and come looking. I'll get in trouble.'

'Tell me about Ishida.'

The kid spread his hands. Helpless. 'There were always three other men. The only one I know was Mr. Torobuni. He owns the place, *Please*.' Terry Ito had said that Yuki Torobuni runs the L.A. yakuza.

I opened the door and let the kid out. A pink-faced guy in a nice Ross Hobbs suit gave me a helluva look when I walked out after the kid.

Mimi Warren? *Here?*

When I got back to the bar, three men were waiting at the table with Joe Pike. There was an older guy with a lot of loose skin and a cheap sharkskin coat over an orange shirt, and a very short guy with two fingers off his left hand and the sort of baleful stare you get when life's a mystery. There was also a tall kid with too many muscles in a three-quarter-sleeve pullover. Eddie Tang. He grinned at me. 'What do ya know. It's Mickey Spillane.'

Pike's mouth twitched. 'You missed all the fun,' he said. 'While you were out, somebody phoned for reinforcements.'

CHAPTER 17

The older man in the cheap sharkskin looked at Eddie. 'You know this one?' No accent.

Eddie nodded. 'He came into Ishida's.'

I said, 'Wow, Eddie. Last week you're working for Nobu Ishida, then Ishida gets osterized, and now you're working for Yuki Torobuni. You're really on the rise.'

Yuki Torobuni said, 'How do you know who I am?'

'You're either Torobuni or Fu Manchu.'

Torobuni dipped his chin at Eddie. 'Let's go in the back.'

Torobuni moved past me and went down the steps toward the kitchen. The midget swaggered after him the way midgets will. Pike and I went next, and Eddie trailed behind. The Butterfly Lady watched us go, lean hips moving to The Smiths, little butterfly dancing. Nice moves.

Eddie said, 'You like that, huh?'

Some guys.

When we got into the kitchen, Yuki Torobuni leaned against a steel table and said, 'Eddie.' Everything was Eddie. Maybe the midget was a moron.

Eddie moved to pat Pike down. Pike pushed Eddie's hand away from his body. 'No.'

The midget took out a Browning .45 automatic about eighteen sizes too big for him. The smell of sesame oil and tahini and mint was strong and the kitchen help was careful not to look our way.

Eddie and Pike were just about the same height but Eddie was heavier and his shoulders sloped more because of the insanely developed trapezius muscles. Eddie sneered at Pike's red arrows. 'Those are shit tattoos.'

Torobuni made a little forget-it gesture with his left hand. 'Let's not waste our time.' He looked at me. 'What do you want?'

'I want a sixteen-year-old girl named Mimi Warren.'

Eddie Tang laughed. Torobuni smiled at Eddie, then shook his head and gave me bored. 'So what?'

'Maybe you have her.'

Torobuni said, 'Boy, I never heard of this girl. What is she, a princess, some kind of movie star?' Eddie thought that was a riot.

I said, 'Something called the Hagakure was stolen from her parents, and whoever got it kidnapped the girl to stop the search. It's a good bet that whoever wanted the Hagakure is also in the yakuza. Maybe that's you.'

Torobuni's face darkened. He barked out a couple of words of Japanese and Eddie stopped laughing. 'Whoever stole the Hagakure kidnaps the girl to stop you looking for it?'

'That's the way it looks.'

'Not too bright.'

'Geniuses rarely go into crime.'

Torobuni stared at me a moment, then walked over to a giant U.S. range where a woman was taking a fresh load of tempura shrimp from the deep fat. He mumbled something and she plucked out a shrimp on a little metal skewer and handed it to him. He took a small bite. He said, 'Two years ago I had a man's face put in here.' He gestured at the grease vat. 'You ever see a fried face?'

'No. How'd it taste?'

Torobuni finished the shrimp and wiped his hands on a cloth that was lying on the steel table. He shook his head. 'You're out of your mind to come here like this. You know my name, but do you have any idea who I am?'

'Who killed Nobu Ishida?'

He leaned against the table again and looked at me. Eddie shifted closer, his eyes on Pike. The midget with the .45 beamed. Torobuni folded the towel neatly and put it down. 'Maybe you killed him.'

'Sure.'

Behind us cooking fat bubbled and cleavers bit into hardwood cutting boards and damp heat billowed out of steamers. Torobuni stared at me for another couple of centuries, then spoke again in Japanese. The midget put away the gun. Torobuni came very close to me, so close the cheap sharkskin brushed my chest. He looked first in my right eye, then in my left. He said, 'Yakuza is a terrible monster to arouse. If you come down here again, yakuza will eat you.' His voice was like late-night music.

'I'm going to find the girl.'

303

Torobuni smiled a smile to match the voice. 'Good luck.'

He turned and went out the back of the kitchen, the midget swaggering behind him. Eddie Tang went with them, walking backward and keeping his eyes on Joe Pike. He stopped in the door, gave Pike a nasty grin, then peeled up his sleeves to show the tattoos. He worked his arms to make the tattoos dance, then snarled and flexed the huge traps so they grew out of his back like spiny wings. Then he left.

Pike said, 'Wow.'

We went out through the dining room and past the bar. The kid I'd talked to was gone. The Butterfly Lady was busy with customers. People ate. People drank. Life went on.

When we got back to the Big Boy lot, Pike said, 'He knows something.'

'You got that feeling, huh?'

Nod.

'Somebody else might know something, too. Mimi Warren used to come here.'

The sunglasses moved. 'Mimi?' He was doing it, too.

'She came with friends and she hung out and she probably met a wide variety of sleazy people. Maybe whoever grabbed her was someone she met here and bragged to about what her daddy had sitting in his home safe.'

'And if we can find the friends, they might know who.'

'That's it.'

The sunglasses moved again. 'Uh-huh.'

Forty minutes later I pulled the Corvette into my carport, parked, went in through the kitchen, and phoned Jillian Becker at her office. She said, 'Yes?'

'It's Elvis Cole. I'd like to talk with you about Mimi and her father and all of this.'

'You were fired.'

'That may be, but I'm going to find her. Maybe you can help me do that.'

There was a pause, and sounds in the background. 'I can't talk now.'

'Would you have dinner with me tonight at Musso and Frank?'

Another pause. Thinking about it. 'All right.' She didn't sound particularly enthusiastic. 'What time?'

'Eight o'clock. You can meet me there, or I'll pick you up. Whichever you prefer.'

'I'll meet you there.' It was clear what she preferred.

After we hung up I pulled off my clothes, took a shower, then fell into a deep uneasy sleep.

CHAPTER 18

I woke just after six feeling drained and stiff, as if sleeping had been hard work. I went downstairs and flipped on the TV news, and after a while there was something about Mimi's kidnapping.

A blond woman who looked like she played racquet-ball twice a day gave the update standing in front of the New Nippon Hotel, 'site of the kidnapping'. She said the police and the FBI still had no information as to Mimi's whereabouts or condition, but were working diligently to effect a positive resolution. The screen cut to a close-up of a photograph of Mimi with a phone number beneath her chin. After the blond woman asked anyone who might have information to call the number, the news anchor segued nicely into a story about a recruitment drive the L.A.P.D. was launching. There was a number to call for that, too.

Mimi Warren had been given seventeen seconds.

At seven o'clock I went into the kitchen, drank two glasses of water, then went upstairs to shave and shower. I ran the water hot and rubbed the soap in hard and after the shower I felt a little better. Maybe I was getting used to the pain. Or maybe it was just the thought of dinner with an MBA.

When I was dry and deodorized, I stood in the door to my closet and wondered what I should wear. Hmmm. I could wear my Groucho Marx nose, but Jillian already thought I joked around too much. My Metaluna Mutant mask? Nah. I pulled on a pair of brown outback pants and gray CJ Bass desert boots and a white Indian hiking shirt and a light blue waiter's jacket. I looked like an ad for Banana Republic. Maybe Banana Republic would give me a job. They could put my picture in their little catalog and under it they could say: *Elvis Cole, famous detective, outfitted for his latest adventure in rugged inner-city climes!* Did Banana Republic sell shoulder holsters?

I went downstairs, put out food for the cat, then locked up and drove down into deepest, darkest Hollywood. Yep. Thinking about dinner with Jillian was working wonders.

At two minutes before eight, I parked behind Musso and Frank's Grill on Hollywood Boulevard and went in. Jillian Becker walked in behind me. She was wearing a conservative eggshell pants suit over a light brown shirt and beige pumps. Her nails and her lip gloss were one of those colors between pink and flesh, and went well with the eggshell. Her fingers were slim and manicured and there was a single strand of white pearls around her neck. She looked tired and harassed, but I couldn't tell that until she was closer. She said, 'I'm sorry I'm late.' It was one minute after eight.

'Would you like a drink?'

'At the table.'

A bald man led us into Musso's huge back room to a very nice booth. There's a long bar back there and leather booths and it looks very much the way it looked in 1918, when Musso's opened. A busboy came with sourdough bread and water, then a waiter appeared, giving us menus and asking if we cared for something to drink. I ordered a Dos Equis. Jillian Becker ordered a double Stoly on the rocks. Must have been some kind of day.

'This room,' I said, 'is where Dashiell Hammett first laid eyes on Lillian Hellman. It was a romance that lasted ages.'

Jillian Becker glanced at her watch. 'What did you want to talk about?' So much for romance.

'Have the cops come up with anything?'

'No.'

'Have there been any demands from the kidnappers?'

'No. The police and the FBI talk to us a dozen times a day. They have a tap on Bradley's home phone. They have a tap on the office phone. But there's been nothing.'

The waiter came back with the drinks. Usually it takes about a year to get your drinks, but sometimes they're fast. 'Are you ready to order?' he said, pencil poised.

Jillian said, 'I'll have the crab salad.'

The waiter looked at me.

'Grilled chicken. Home fries. Broccoli.'

He nodded twice and wrote it down and left. Jillian lifted her glass and took a long drink.

'Rough day?'

'Mr. Cole, I'd rather not discuss my day if it's all the same to you. You could have asked me what the police had over the phone.'

'But then I wouldn't have been able to admire your beauty.'

She tapped her glass with a manicured fingernail. Guess we'd proceed directly to business.

I said, 'Have you ever heard the name Yuki Torobuni?'

'No.'

'Yuki Torobuni owns a dance club downtown called Mr. Moto's. It's very new wave, very hip, cocaine in the bathrooms, that kind of place. Yuki Torobuni also heads the yakuza here in L.A. Do you know what the yakuza is?'

'Like the mafia.'

'Yeah. How about a guy named Eddie Tang? Ever heard his name?'

'No.' Impatient. 'Why are you asking if I've heard of these people? Do you think Bradley's involved with them?'

'It crossed my mind.'

She lifted her glass and took a careful sip, thinking about that. She thought about it for a very long time. When she put the glass down, she said, 'All right. It's reasonable for you to consider every possible solution to a problem.' Business school. 'But Bradley is not involved with organized crime. I see where the money comes from, and I see where it goes. If there were something shady going on, I'd know it, or at least suspect it, and I don't.'

'Maybe it's very well hidden.'

She shook her head. 'I'm too good for that.'

I nodded. 'Okay. Let's try this. I talked to a guy at Mr. Moto's who told me that Mimi came there often, and that she came with friends.'

'Mimi?' Everybody does it.

'Uh-huh. A girl named Carol and another girl named Kerri.'

Jillian took another sip of her drink. 'She's never mentioned them to me. Not that she necessarily would.'

'How about other friends?'

Jillian shook her head again. 'I'm sorry. Mimi always seemed very withdrawn. Sheila complains endlessly that she never leaves the house.' Jillian put her glass down and eyed it coolly. 'Sheila is something else.'

The waiter came with a little stand and all of our plates on a large oval tray. He put the stand down by the table, then the tray on the stand. He set out Jillian's crab salad, then my chicken and broccoli and home fries, and then he took the tray and the stand and left. The chicken smelled wonderful. It always did.

Jillian said, 'Bradley's not going to pay you a dime, you know. He intends to sue you, if he has to, to recover the money he's already paid.'

'He won't have to do that.' Bradley Warren's blank check was still in my wallet. I took it out, tore it in quarters, and put it on the table by Jillian Becker's plate.

Jillian Becker looked at the check and then at me. She shook her head. 'And you're still going to look for Mimi?'

'Yes.'

'Why?'

'I told Mimi I would take care of her.'

'And that's enough.'

I shrugged. 'It's an ugly job, but somebody has to do it.'

Jillian frowned and ate some of the crab salad. I had some of the chicken, then a couple of the home fries. Excellent.

I said, 'I need to find out who Mimi hangs out with. Bradley and Sheila might be able to tell me. If they won't talk to me, maybe you could talk to them for me.'

Jillian frowned more deeply and put her fork in the crab but only played with it. 'Bradley had to fly to Kyoto.'

The Dos Equis was cold and bitter. I sipped it. I had a little more of the chicken. I had a little of the broccoli. Two guys at the edge of the bar crowd were looking our way. One of the guys was overweight and balding. The other guy was very tall with dark hair and thick glasses and a heavy jaw. He looked like Stephen King. The shorter guy was drinking what looked like scotch rocks. The taller, Campari and soda. They were staring at Jillian and the taller guy was smiling. 'His daughter is gone,' I said, 'but business continues.'

Jillian Becker's lips tightened and she put down her fork and I thought she was going to stand. She didn't. She said, 'Bradley has been very fair to me. He's treated me just as he's treated everyone else in his organization. He's recognized and rewarded my abilities. It's a good job.'

'And you've got the BMW to prove it.'

'It's so easy for you, isn't it? Tearing up checks. Standing on your head in your office.'

'How about Sheila? You think I could talk with her?'

Silence.

'Sheila went with him.'

Slow nod.

I finished off the Dos Equis. 'Parents of the Year, all right.'

Jillian started to say something, then stopped. She looked angry and embarrassed.

I said, 'You could get me into their house. We could look in Mimi's room.'

'Bradley would fire me.'

'Maybe.'

Her jaw worked and she sipped some water and didn't say anything for a long time. When she did, she said, 'I don't like you.'

I nodded.

Her jaw flexed again, and she stood up. 'God damn you,' she said. 'Let's go. I have a key.'

CHAPTER 19

We took two cars, Jillian pulling out in her white BMW and me following her west along Sunset toward Beverly Hills, then up Beverly Glen to the Warrens'. Jillian parked by the front of the house and I parked next to her. She had the front door open by the time I got out of my car. She said, 'Mimi's room is in the rear. I'll walk back with you.' She walked in ahead without waiting.

The big house was as cold as a mausoleum, and our footsteps echoed on the terrazzo entry. I hadn't heard it when I'd been in the house before, but when I was in the house before there'd been other people and things going on. Now the house seemed abandoned and desolate. Life in an Andrew Wyeth landscape.

Mimi's room was big and white and empty the way I remembered it. The single bed was made and tight and the desk was neat and the walls bare and the high shelf of *Britannica* and Laura Ingalls Wilder just as it had been before. I had hoped that since the last time I had seen the room, posters would have gone up on the walls and someone would have doodled on the desk and a pile of dirty clothes would've grown in the corner. Jillian said, 'Sixteen years old.' She was standing with her arms crossed and her hands cupping her upper arms, feeling the cold.

I nodded. 'Uh-huh.'

She looked at me. 'As long as I'm here, I may as well help you.'

'Take the desk.'

'What are we looking for?'

'Address books, yearbooks, letters, a diary. Anything that might have names and phone numbers. Search one drawer at a time. Empty it item by item, then put it back together. Make yourself go slowly.'

Jillian went over to the desk and opened the large bottom drawer.

Hesitant. She said, 'You do this a lot, don't you? Look through people's things.'

'Yes. People keep secrets. You have to look into personal places to find them.'

'It makes me uncomfortable.'

'It makes me uncomfortable, too, but there's no other way.'

She looked at me some more, then bent to the drawer and started taking out things. I went to the bed, stripped down the covers, threw them into the center of the room, and lifted the mattress off the box springs. No hidden diary. No secret compartments cut into the side of the mattress. I tilted the bed up on its edge. Nothing beneath the box springs. I put the bed back the way it had been, then I looked through the *Britannica* and the matched set of Laura Ingalls Wilder. A pink $50 Monopoly money bill fell out of volume E of the *Britannica*. The Laura Ingalls Wilder books had never been opened.

To the left of the desk there was a walk-in closet. A rail of clothes hung on the right side of the closet with a shoe board and shoes beneath the clothes, each pair neatly together and all the shoes forming a nice neat row. On the left side of the closet there were shelves with more books and game boxes. On the lowest shelf there was a blue hat that said *Disneyland* and a little stuffed monkey and what had once been an ant farm but was now just an empty plastic box. Next to the ant farm there was a very old set of a children's encyclopedia and a book about standard poodles that looked like it had been read a lot and four brochures on the work of a Japanese artist named Kira Asano. The brochures showed reproductions of bleak landscapes and described Asano as a dynamic, charismatic visionary whose gallery showings and lectures were not to be missed. One of the brochures had a picture of Asano made up like a samurai with a white and red headband, no shirt, and a samurai sword. Visionary, all right. Beneath the brochures were two slim volumes of what looked like Japanese poetry. There was something handwritten in Japanese in the front of each volume. I put the volumes of poetry aside and called Jillian.

'Can you read this?'

'Haiku by Bashō and Issa.' She read the inscriptions and smiled. 'They were a gift from someone named Edo. "May there always be warm sun."'

'Can Mimi read Japanese?'

'Maybe a little. I don't really know.' Mimi Warren, the Invisible Child.

I put the poetry back on the shelf. 'Did you finish going through the desk?'

'I didn't find anything.'

I nodded. 'Okay. I'll finish here in a minute.'

'We could carry this stuff out and I could help.'

'If we carried this stuff out, we wouldn't remember where it belongs.'

She cocked her head at me. Curious.

'These aren't our things,' I said. 'We have to respect that.'

She stared at me some more, then stepped back. 'Of course. I'll wait in the front.'

Halfway through the games, I found seven smudged envelopes in a Parcheesi box. They were postmarked Westwood and had been addressed to Ms. Mimi Warren at the Shintazi Hotel in Kyoto, Japan, and were return-addressed to Traci Louise Fishman, 816 Chandelle Road, Beverly Hills. Both the address and return had been neatly printed in bright, violet ink, with plenty of curlicues and swirls and hearts rather than dots over the *i*'s. I took out each letter and read it. Traci Louise Fishman was sixteen years old, and wondered why Mimi's father had to ruin every vacation by dragging her best friend off to Japan. In one letter, she had a crush on a boy named David who went to Birmingham High in Van Nuys, and desperately wanted him to 'make her a woman.' In another, David had become a stuck-up shit who wouldn't look at her, being a typical shallow Valley dude more interested in brainless bimbos with surfer-chick tans than women of intellect and sensitivity. Traci smoked too much, but was going to quit, having read a *Harvard Medical School Health Letter* which said that teenage girls who smoke would almost certainly have deformed children and breast cancer. She really really really liked Bruce Willis, but she'd just die if she could ever meet Judd Nelson, even though he had a funny-looking nose. Her dad had promised her a new car if she took two summer-session classes at the Glenlake School for Girls so maybe she could graduate one semester early. She was gonna do it 'cause what she wanted more than anything else in the world was a snow-white Volkswagen Rabbit convertible even though her old man was such a cheap shit it would probably never happen. She couldn't wait for Mimi to get home, she missed their talks soooooooon much! And – ohmyGod, fur shure! – she had

313

spotted in a pair of white pants through a *Super* Tampax and was so embarrassed she thought she would die!!!! The letters went on. The stuff of life.

When I had read all seven letters, I returned them to the Parcheesi box, then went through the rest of the boxes, but found nothing else. When I left the closet, Jillian Becker was gone. I made sure the closet was as I had found it, fixed the bed, shut the light, then left and went back through the dark house to the front.

Jillian was leaning against a little table in the entry with her arms crossed when I got there. I thought she might have looked sad, but maybe not. She said, 'Did you find anything?' Her voice was quiet.

'No mention of Carol or Kerri, but I found seven letters from someone named Traci Louise Fishman. Traci Louise Fishman told Mimi everything that was going on in her life. Maybe Mimi returned the favor.'

Jillian uncrossed her arms. 'Good. I'm glad this was helpful. Now let me lock up.'

I went out and waited. It was cool in upper Holmby and the earth smelled damp from having been recently watered. When Jillian came out, I said, 'Thanks for getting me in here.'

She walked past without looking at me and went to her BMW. She opened her door, then she closed it and turned back to me. Her eyes were bright. She said, 'I worked my butt off for a job like this.'

'I know.'

'You don't walk away from something you've worked so hard for.'

'I know.'

She opened her car door again, but still didn't get in. Out in the street some rich kid's Firebird with a Glaspak muffler blasted past, wrecking the calm. She said, 'You go to school, you work hard, you play the game. When you're in school, they don't tell you how much it costs. They don't tell you what you've got to give up to get to where you want to be.'

'They never do.'

Jillian looked at me some more, then she said good night and got into her white BMW and drove away. I watched her. Then I drove away, too.

CHAPTER 20

Glenlake School for Girls is on a manicured green campus at the border between Westwood and Bel Air, in the midst of some of the most expensive real estate in the world. It is a fine school for fine girls from fine families, the sort of place that would not take kindly to an unemployed private cop asking to be alone with one of its young ladies. Real cops would probably be called. As would the young lady's parents. When you got to that point, you could just about always count on the kid clamming up. So. Ixnay on the direct approach.

There were other options. I could go to Traci Louise's home, but that, too, would involve parents and an equal possibility of clamming. Or I could stake out the Glenlake campus and abduct Traci Louise Fishman as she arrived. This seemed the most likely option. There was only one problem. I had no idea what Traci Louise Fishman looked like.

The next morning I forwent my usual wardrobe and selected a conservative blue three-piece pinstripe suit and black Bally loafers. I hadn't worn the Ballys for over a year. There was dust on them. When the tie was tied and the vest buttoned and the jacket in place and riding squarely on my shoulders, the cat topped the stairs and looked at me.

'Pretty nice, huh?'

His ears went down and he ran under the bed. Some people are never happy.

At twenty minutes after nine I parked in the Glenlake visitors' lot, found my way to the office, went up to an overweight lady behind the counter, and said, 'My name's Cole. I'm thinking about applying to Glenlake for my daughter. Would it be all right if I looked around?'

The woman said, 'Let me get Mrs. Farley.'

A thin woman in her early fifties came out of an office and over to the counter. She had blond hair going to gray and sharp blue eyes and a smile as toothy as a Pontiac's grill. I tried to look like I made two hundred thou a year. She said, 'Hello, Mr. Cole, I'm Mrs. Farley. Mrs. Engle said you wished to see the school.'

'That's right.'

She looked me over. 'Had you made an appointment?'

'I didn't think one was necessary. Should I have called?'

'I'm afraid so. I have an interview scheduled with another couple in ten minutes.'

I nodded gravely, and tried to look like I would look if I was recalling an overbooked personal calendar, then shook my head. 'Of course. Being a single parent and having just been made a partner in the firm, my schedule tends to get out of hand, but maybe I can get back in a couple of weeks.' I let my eyes drift down the line of her body and linger.

She shifted behind the counter and glanced at her watch. 'It seems a shame not to see the school after you've gone to such trouble,' she said.

'True. But I understand if you can't make the time.' I touched her arm.

The tip of her tongue peeked out and wet the left corner of her mouth. 'Well,' she said, 'maybe if we hurry I can give you a short tour.' She said it deviously.

Some guys can charm the stitches off a baseball.

Mrs. Farley came around the counter, put her hand on my back, and gave me the short tour. The short tour included a lot of laughing at unfunny things, a lot of her feeling my shoulder and arm, and a lot of her breathing in my face. Violets. We saw the new gymnasium and the new science labs and the newly expanded library and the new theater arts building and a lot of coeds with moussed hair and bright plastic hair clips and skin cancer tans. Five girls were standing in a little knot outside the cafeteria when Mrs. Farley and I walked past, Mrs. Farley's hand on my back. One of the girls said something and the others laughed. Maybe Mrs. Farley didn't require as much charming as I thought.

When we got back to the office, a man in a flowered shirt and a woman in sweat pants and a New Balance running shirt were waiting. Mrs. Farley's appointment. She smiled at them and told them she would only be another moment, then thanked me for my interest in Glenlake, holding my hand a very long time as she did, and apologized twice for not having more time. She offered to be available whenever I might have more questions. I asked her if it would be all right to take a short stroll around on my way out. She took my hand again and said of course. I smiled at the man in the flowered shirt and the woman in the sweat pants. They smiled back. To think that I dressed for this.

Two minutes later I was back in the library. There was a birch-and-Formica information table as you walked in, and a girl sitting behind the table chewing bubble gum and reading a Danielle Steel novel. The girl had the same moussed, sun-streaked hair and walnut tan that every other girl at Glenlake had, and the same large plastic hair clip. I said, 'I thought Glenlake didn't require its students to wear uniforms.'

She gave me blank eyes and blew a bubble.

'Where could I find last year's yearbook?'

The bubble popped. 'In reference, over there on the shelf above California history. You see the David Bowie poster? To the left of that.'

Traci Louise Fishman was on page 87 of last year's yearbook, sandwiched between Krystle Fisher and Tiffany Ann Fletcher. She had a heart-shaped face and a flat nose and pale frizzy hair and round, wire-framed glasses. Her lips were thin and tight, and her eyebrows looked like they would have a tendency to grow together. Like her friend Mimi, she wasn't what you would call pretty. From the look on her face, you could tell she knew it. I put the yearbook back on the shelf, left the library, went back to the Corvette, cranked it up, drove off the campus, and parked in the shade of a large elm just outside the school's front gate. Traci's letters to Mimi said she would be taking two morning classes to leave her afternoons free. It was 10:20.

At 11:45, Traci Fishman came around the rear of the administration building, walked into the student parking lot, and unlocked a white Volkswagen Rabbit convertible. Dad wasn't such a cheap shit after all. She was putting the top down when I walked up behind her. 'Traci?'

'Yes?' She pronounced the word clearly.

'My name's Elvis Cole. I'm a private detective. Could I talk with you for a few minutes?' I showed her my license.

She stopped futzing with the top, looked at the little plastic card, then looked at me out of round, expressive eyes. No glasses. Maybe when you started thinking in terms of having some guy 'make you a woman,' you ditched the glasses and got contacts. 'What do you want to talk with me about?'

I put my license away. 'Mimi Warren.'

'Mimi's been kidnapped.'

'I know. I'm trying to find her. I'm hoping you can help me.'

The big eyes blinked. The contacts didn't fit well, but in a world of plastic hair clips and chocolate fudge tans, she was going to wear them or die trying. Also, she was scared. She said, 'I don't know. Are you working for her parents?'

'I was. Now I'm working for me.'

'How come you're not working for Mimi's parents if you're trying to find Mimi?'

'They fired me. I was supposed to be taking care of her when she got snatched.'

She nodded and glanced toward the front of the school. More girls were coming from behind the administration building and from other places and were going to their cars or heading through the gates to the street where parked cars waited. Traci chewed at her upper lip and stared at them through blinking alien eyes. Her frizzy hair was cut short and stuck out from her head. She was heavy and her posture was bad. Some of the girls looked our way. More than a couple traded looks and made faces. Traci said, 'You want to sit in my car?'

'Sure.' I held the door for her, then closed it and went around to the other side.

Three girls with moussed hair and plastic clips and mahogany tans and pearl-white lip gloss walked past the Rabbit to a catch-me red Porsche 944 Turbo. I watched Traci watch them. She tried to do it sneaky, out the corner of her eye so they couldn't tell. The girls at the Porsche leaned against its fenders and looked past each other so they could see the Rabbit and me and Traci, and there was lots of laughter. One of them stared openly. I said, 'You think they share the same lip gloss tube?'

Traci giggled. She looked at me sort of the same way she looked at them, out from under her eyes, as if she really didn't want you to know she was looking, as if she thought that if you knew, you'd say something sharp or do something hurtful. 'Don't you think they look like clones?' she said. 'They have no individuality. They're scared of being unique, and therefore alone, so they mask their fear by sameness and denigrate those who do not share their fear.' She just tossed that off, like saying, *Hey, buddy, how about a bag of nuts!* She said, 'They're talking about us, you know. They're wondering who's that guy and why are you sitting with me.'

'I know that.'

'I knew they would. That's why I wanted us to get into the car.'

'I know that, too.'

She looked at me a long time, then looked away. 'Do you think that's shallow? I hate to be shallow. I try not to be.' Sixteen.

'Traci,' I said, 'I think maybe Mimi was mixed up with some people who might've had something to do with her kidnapping. People she might've thought were her friends and who she might've gone out with.'

Traci pooched out her lips and chewed them and shrugged. 'Friends?'

Even Traci Louise Fishman did it. I said, 'Do you know a couple of Mimi's friends named Carol and Kerri?'

'Uh-uh.'

'You sure?'

Traci chewed the lips some more and shrugged again. Nervous. 'Why would I know them?'

'Because you guys were buddies.'

Shrug.

I said, 'Traci, I've seen seven letters that you wrote to Mimi last year when she was away. I've read them.'

She looked shocked. 'You read other people's mail?'

'Monstrous, isn't it?'

She chewed harder. 'If you find her, what are you going to do?'

'Rescue her.' Sir Elvis.

'You won't tell her that I'm the one who said?'

I said, 'I know you want to protect your friend, babe, but you have to understand that right now she is in a world of trouble. We're not talking about her shoplifting a radio and you telling. Bad people have her and whatever you know might be able to help me find her.'

She chewed harder and then she nodded. 'You really think it was people she thought were her friends that did it?'

'Yes.'

The irritated eyes grew pink and blinked faster. Maybe starting to cry. 'It's just that Mimi liked to make things up, you know. She was always telling me about these stud guys and the parties they would have and how they would ride around in limousines and go to clubs and all these things that you just knew she'd made up.'

'Bigger-than-life stuff.'

'Uh-huh.' She began to sniffle. 'So when she told me about these new people, I didn't believe her at first. She said she had these new friends and that they weren't full of bullshit like everybody else in her life. She said she had a boyfriend and she said he was really buff and they partied every night and had real good cocaine and stuff and that they were the seeds of a revolution and all this crazy stuff, and after a while I said, "Mimi, you're full of crap," just like I always did, and she said it was true and she'd prove it.'

Traci Louise Fishman dug through her purse and took out a battered red leather wallet and dug through that and pulled out a bent color snapshot. 'A couple of days later she gave me this. Kerri's the girl with the white hair. I don't know about Carol. I really don't.'

The photograph had been taken on the street at night and was of half a dozen smiling young men and women. Mimi Warren was standing next to a girl with white hair, but Mimi Warren wasn't Mimi Warren as I had ever seen her. She had blue electroshock hair and heavy emerald eye shadow and she was giving the finger to the camera. She was also standing beside a big, good-looking kid with huge shoulders. The big guy was giving us the bird with his right hand and had his left hand on Mimi's breast. I took a deep breath, then let it out. Carol and Kerri didn't matter anymore. The big kid was Eddie Tang.

I touched his image in the photograph. 'And this is Mimi's boyfriend?'

'Uh-huh. That's what she said.'

CHAPTER 21

One of the moussed girls by the 944 went around to the driver's side, got in, and leaned across to unlock the passenger door. The other girls climbed in, but the Porsche didn't start. One of the girls lit up. The one in the tiny back seat turned crosswise, and kept raking her fingers through her hair. Music blasted out of the Porsche's door-mounted speakers, rolling across the parking lot, and you could see them passing around an Evian bottle. They had gotten in the car, apparently, to better watch us from Black Forest comfort.

I looked at the photograph that Traci had given me and at the people in it. Eddie was the oldest, and the biggest. The other two guys were probably not out of their teens and were slight, one wearing narrow-legged jeans and a white shirt and a couple-of-sizes-too-big cloth jacket with a lot of buckles and studs, the other a uniform that looked like something a Red Chinese National would wear, all gray and plain with a single row of buttons down the front and a Nehru collar and a Red Army cap. The kid in the uniform was Asian. He didn't look like a yakuza thug, but maybe he was executive material. Kerri and the other woman were also Asian. The one Traci didn't know was dressed in Jordache jeans and a plaid shirt with the sleeves rolled up and a Swatch watch. Normal. Kerri was a Clorox blonde with a spike cut and a powdered face and neon-red lips and nails. There was a dog collar around her neck. Billy Idol. I said, 'Traci, this is important. Did Mimi ever say what she talked about with these people?'

'Uh-huh.'

'Was it about something called the Hagakure?'

'Uh-uh.'

'What did she talk about?'

'Stuff I didn't understand. She said they were real. She said they loved her. She said they were the first people she'd ever met who truly had purpose.' I looked out the window. Purpose. When you're sixteen, maybe all life is drama. I looked back at Traci. Her big eyes went from pink to red and she rubbed at them and said, 'I gotta put in drops.'

She took a little plastic bottle from her purse and put two drops of something into each eye and sat with her eyes closed for a couple of minutes. Trying not to cry.

'When was the last time you spoke to her?'

Nervous shrug. 'About three weeks ago.'

'Did you tell you what she would do when she was hanging out with these people?'

Traci stared at the photograph. I handed it back and watched her put it in her wallet like something precious that had to be handled carefully.

'She told me they went to all these clubs. She told me they did all these drugs and had sex and it sounded just like when she would make stuff up only this time I believed her. I said she ought not. I said she was gonna get in trouble or get fucked up or get arrested, and Mimi got real mad so I shut up. This one time she got so mad at me she didn't talk to me for a month. You have to be careful.' Traci said it like she was telling me a secret that only she knew, like it was important and special and I had probably never heard anything like it ever before.

I said, 'Mimi could sneak out, make herself up and change her clothes, and be with these people, then undo it all and go back home and be a different Mimi and her parents never knew.'

Traci nodded, sniffling.

'Man.' I stared out the front of the Rabbit at the Administration Building. It was large and clean and old with thick Spanish walls and a red tile roof. The hedges and the lawn and the trees were neat and well-groomed. Small knots of girls still moved along the walks, some carrying books, some not, but almost all were smiling. I shook my head.

Traci Louise Fishman picked at the steering wheel some more, then gave me the Special Secret look again. Like there was something else I'd never heard before, and something Traci had never been able to tell, and now she wanted to. 'You want me to tell you something really weird?'

I looked at her.

'Last year, we were up in my room, smoking. My room is on the second floor and in the back, so I can open the window and no one knows.'

'Uh-huh.'

'We were smoking and talking and Mimi said, "Watch this," and she pulled up her shirt and put the hot part of the cigarette on her stomach and held it there.' I sat in the Rabbit, listening to sixteen-year-old Traci Louise Fishman, and my back went cold. 'It was so weird I couldn't even say anything. I just watched, and it seemed like she held it there forever, and I yelled, "That's crazy, Mimi, you'll have a scar," and she said she didn't care, and then she pushed down her pants and there were these two dark marks just above her hair down there and she said, "Pain gives us meaning, Traci," and then she took a real deep drag on the cigarette and got the tip glowing bright red and then she did it again.' Traci Louise Fishman's eyes were round and bulging. She was scared, as if telling me these things she had been keeping secret for so long was in some way giving them reality for the first time, and the reality was a shameful, frightful thing.

I ran my tongue across the backs of my teeth and thought about Mimi Warren and couldn't shake the cold feeling. 'Did she do things like that often?'

Traci Louise Fishman began to sob, great heaving sobs that shook her and made her gag. The secret had been held a long time, and it had been scary. Perhaps even incomprehensible. When the sobs died, she said, 'You'll find her? You'll find her and bring her back?'

'Yes.'

'I told her *I* was real. I told her *I* had purpose.'

I nodded.

'She's my friend,' she said. Her voice was hoarse and bubbly.

I nodded. 'I know, babe.'

The sobs erupted once more and took a long time to die. I gave her my handkerchief. With the pale skin and the out-from-under eyes and the heavy little-girl face, there was a quality of loneliness to her that comes when your only friend walks away and you don't know why and there's no one else and never will be. A left-behind look.

We sat like that for another few minutes, Traci rubbing at her flat nose and me breathing deeply and thinking about Mimi and Eddie Tang and what that might mean. Most of the cars had long since gone, but the red 944 still sat in its spot, music playing, girls within pretending not to stare toward Traci Louise Fishman's white Volkswagen Rabbit. After a while I said, 'They're still watching us.'

Traci nodded. The eyes weren't watering anymore and the nose was dry and she gave back my handkerchief. 'They can't believe a good-looking guy like you is sitting here with me.'

'Maybe,' I said, 'they can't believe a good-looking girl like you is letting me.'

She smiled and looked down at her steering wheel again, and again picked at the plastic. She said, 'Please bring her back.'

I looked at the Porsche. The girl in the back seat was staring our way. I said, 'Traci?'

She looked up at me.

I leaned across and kissed her on the lips. She didn't move, and when I pulled back she was a vivid red. I said, 'Thanks for the help.'

Her chin went down into her neck and she swallowed hard and looked mortified. She touched her lips and looked over at the girls in the Porsche. They were gaping at us. Traci Louise Fishman blinked at them, and looked back at me. Then she squared her shoulders, touched her lips again, and folded both hands very neatly in her lap.

I got out of the Rabbit, went back to the Corvette, and drove to my office.

CHAPTER 22

I parked in the bottom of my building, went into the deli, bought a pastrami sandwich with Chinese hot mustard, then used the stairs to go up to the office. Walking the stairs made it easier not to think about Mimi Warren holding a lit cigarette to her skin. Maybe Traci Louise Fishman had made up that part. Maybe she'd made up all of it. Maybe if I didn't think about Mimi Warren or Traci Louise Fishman or Eddie Tang they would all disappear and living would be easy. Elvis Cole, Existential Detective. I liked that. Not thinking, properly done, creates a pleasant numbed sensation in the brain that I like a lot. There are women who will tell you that not thinking is one of my best things.

I let myself into the office, got a Falstaff out of the little fridge, put the sandwich on a paper plate, and called Lou Poitras.

Lou said, 'Don't tell me. You've cracked the case.'

I said, 'The girl knew Eddie Tang.'

He told me to hang on and then he put me on hold. When he put me on hold, the phone started playing music. Michael Jackson singing about how bad he was. Our tax dollars at work.

Lou came back and said, 'Go on.'

'She used to sneak out of the house and go to clubs. She hung out and met people and one of the people she met was Tang. She might've mentioned the book to him. She told people that Eddie Tang was her boyfriend.'

'She know Tang was yakuza?'

'I don't know.'

'Eddie hears about the book, he maybe figures it's a good thing to steal.'

'Uh-huh.'

Lou Poitras didn't say anything for a while. He's got three kids.

325

Two of them are daughters. 'Thanks for the tip, Hound Dog. I'll look into it.'

'Always happy to cooperate with the police.'

'Right.'

We hung up. I watched Pinocchio's eyes slide from side to side and ate the sandwich. Terry Ito had said Eddie Tang was on his way up. Maybe Eddie figured taking advantage of Mimi Warren and stealing the Hagakure were the keys to ascendancy. Hmmm. I finished the sandwich, then called the phone company. I asked if they had a street address for a guy named Eddie or Edward Tang. They did. Forty minutes later, I was there.

Eddie Tang lived in an apartment building in the flat part of L.A. just south of Century City off Pico Boulevard. It's older in there, and used to be middle class, but now there're lots of trendy restaurants and singles places and New Age health clubs. Eddie's complex had been redone about five years ago with mauve stucco and redwood inlays and black slate steps that twisted up from the walk in a slow curve to a glass security door. To the right of the entry a driveway angled down beneath the building and was blocked by a wrought iron gate. To either side of the garage, bougainvillea had been planted but not long enough ago to flourish. It was a good-looking building. Proof positive that crime pays.

I parked fifty yards down the block in the shade from a gum tree and waited. Maybe Eddie was home and maybe he had Mimi bound and gagged and hidden away in a closet, but maybe not. Boxes buried a couple of feet under the desert up in Sun Valley were more along the lines reserved for kidnap victims than upscale apartment houses in West Los Angeles.

At four-ten a brown unmarked copmobile pulled to a stop by the fire hydrant in front of Eddie's building. You know it's a copmobile because nobody in L.A. would buy anything as boring as a stripped-down four-door Dodge sedan except the cops. A bald-headed dick with freckles and a younger dick with a deep tan and heavy lines around his eyes climbed out and went up to the glass security door. The bald-headed guy was in a suit that looked like it hadn't been pressed in two months. The younger guy was in a dark blue Calvin Klein cord jacket and charcoal slacks with creases so sharp they could have been registered as deadly weapons. Poitras had made some phone calls and this was the follow-up.

They stood at the glass door and pretty soon a young woman in jeans and no shoes and a Sports Connection T-shirt came and opened the door. Manager. The younger cop showed her his badge and they all went inside and about fifteen minutes later they all came back out again. Eddie wasn't home, and Mimi hadn't been in a closet. The bald-headed cop went out to the car. The younger cop stood at the security door and talked to the woman for a while, both of them smiling a lot. When the woman went back inside, the younger cop watched her closely. Probably alert for suspicious moves. The cops left.

Just before five, Eddie Tang came down the street in a dark green Alfa Romeo Spider. There might've been blood stains on Eddie's shirt, but if there were, I couldn't see them. The garage gate lifted and Eddie Tang disappeared beneath his building and the gate closed and I waited.

At a quarter after six, the garage gate lifted again and Eddie and the Alfa turned north past me, heading toward Olympic. I followed him. We turned west on Olympic, then south to Washington, and stayed on Washington until we came to a clapboard warehouse in Culver City three blocks from MGM. Eddie pulled into the warehouse, then almost lost me when he pulled out again while I was looking for a place to park. We went west into Marina del Rey. Eddie drove slowly, as if he wasn't sure where he was going, and that made it tough. I had to keep cars between us and I had to drop further and further back to do it. In the Marina, we turned off Washington onto Via Dolce Drive and passed tall, cubist houses on little tiny lots that sold for over a million bucks each. Eddie parked at the curb of a brick and wood monstrosity with a sea horse in the window and got out of the Alfa carrying a red nylon gym bag. A slender man with a beard and thick glasses opened the door, took the gym bag without a word, then closed the door. Criminals rarely observe the social graces. We went back out to Washington and drove east. After a while Eddie stopped at a Texaco station and used the pay phone, then drove south to pick up the I-10 free-way. In Hollywood, a heavily muscled black guy in a tank top climbed into Eddie's car and the two of them talked, the black guy getting agitated and waving his arms. Eddie threw a snapping backfist, and after that the arm-waving stopped. The black guy put a handkerchief to his mouth for the bleeding. There was more driving and more stops and more phone calls and not once did I see anyone dressed like a ninja or carrying a sword.

At eight-twenty that evening, Eddie Tang turned west onto Sunset from Fairfax, drove two blocks, and pulled to the curb at a new wave dance place called the Pago Pago Club. We were right in the heart of the Sunset Strip. There were two men and three women waiting for him. One of the women was Mimi Warren.

Kidnapped, all right.

CHAPTER 23

Mimi Warren wasn't tied up and no one was holding a gun on her. She was wearing tight white pants and a green sequined halter top and spike-heeled silver sandals. Her hair stuck out at odd angles and her nails were bright blue and she wore too much makeup the way teenage girls do when they think it's sexy. She still wasn't very pretty. Eddie pulled to the curb and gave her a big smile.

I drove past the club, turned around at Tower Records, and crept back. The Strip was bright with flashing neon signs and the sidewalks were jammed with overage hipsters trying to look like Phil Collins or Sheena Easton. There were two baby-blue spotlights on the back of a flatbed trailer parked in front of a shoe store. The lights arced in counter-rotating circles, the light shafts crisscrossing again and again like matched sabers.

When I got back, Mimi and the white-haired girl Traci Louise Fishman had identified as Kerri were climbing into the Alfa. Eddie gave Mimi a kiss. There was a lot of laughing and a lot of waving and then they drove away, heading west on Sunset across Beverly Hills. I thought about shooting out the tires, but that would have been showing off.

Eddie turned north, following Rexford as it turned into Coldwater Canyon, and climbed into the Santa Monica mountains. He wasn't bringing her home and he wasn't bringing her back to his place. Maybe he was bringing her to a party. There's always a party in Hollywood.

At the top of the mountain, Eddie turned west on Mulholland Drive. Mulholland runs along the top of the mountains like some great black python. There were no streetlights and no other cars. The only light came from the waxing moon high overhead and from the San Fernando Valley, spreading out on the right like gold

329

and yellow and red glitter. I turned off my headlamps and dropped back and hoped nothing was lying in the road.

Just before Benedict Canyon, the Alfa's brake lights flared and it pulled into a drive cut into the hillside. The drive was private and well lit and there was a modern metal gate growing out of the rock and one of those little voice boxes so you can announce yourself. The gate rolled out of the way and the Alfa went in. Then the gate closed.

I stopped about a hundred yards short of where the Alfa disappeared, backed into another drive, and killed the engine. The air was chill and clean and there was a breeze coming up the canyons. If you listened hard, you could hear the faraway hiss of the Ventura Freeway riding the breeze. I sat for twenty minutes and then the gate opened again and the Alfa came out. Eddie was still driving, but if Mimi and Kerri were with him, they were in the trunk.

Hmmm.

I got out of the Corvette, walked up to the gate, and took a look. The drive followed the curve of the hillside for about sixty yards to where the mountain had been cut away for a large neat lawn and a large, well-lit Bauhaus house. There were garages on the right of the property with what looked like a tennis court peeking out from behind, and a guy and a girl standing just outside the entry to the house. They were both wearing pale gray pants and pale gray Nehru jackets with black leather belts. That good old Red Army look. Mimi and Kerri were framed in a large picture window to the left of the entry, talking with another boy and girl. The boy was Asian, but the girl wasn't. The girl wore the same pale gray uniform. The boy wore baggy white pants and a too-big tee shirt. The four of them stood in the window for a while, then walked out of my line of sight. There came no cries for help, no sharp crack of gunfire, no blood-curdling screams.

I went back to the Corvette, got in, and stared at the gate. Mimi was in the house, and it appeared that she planned to stay there. It also appeared that she was safe. The smart thing would be to find a phone and call the cops. It was also the obvious thing. I sat there and stared, and after a while I started up and drove west.

Just off Beverly Glen at Mulholland I found a Stop & Go convenience store and used their pay phone. I called the phone company again, gave them my name and the number off my license, then told them the Mulholland address, and asked who lived there. The phone company voice said that there were four numbers installed at that address, all unlisted, two being billed to something called Gray Shield Enterprises and two being billed to a Mr. Kira Asano, all billings being sent care of an accountancy firm with a Wilshire address. I said, 'Kira Asano, the artist?'

The voice said, 'Pardon me, sir?'

I hung up.

I went into the Stop & Go, got more change, then called the *Herald Examiner* and asked if Eddie Ditko was on the night desk. He was.

Eddie came on with a phlegmy cough and said, 'Elvis Cole, shit. I heard you got shot to death down in San Diego. What in hell you want?' Eddie loves me like a son.

'Know anything about a guy named Eddie Tang?'

'What, I'm supposed to know about some guy just because we got the same goddamn first name?' You see? Always the kind word.

'Try out Yuki Torobuni.'

Eddie made a gargling sound, then spit.

'How about a guy named Kira Asano?'

'Asano's the gook artist, right?'

'That's what I like about you, Eddie. Sensitive.'

'Shit. You want Asano or you want sensitive?'

'Asano.'

'Okay. Made *Time* back in the sixties. Back then, he was some kinda hot shit artist from Japan, mostly because of a lot of minimalist landscape work showing empty beaches and crap. He stopped painting and came here, saying America was gonna be the new Japan, and he was gonna instill the samurai spirit in American youth. Some shit, huh?'

'The Hagakure,' I said.

'Huh?'

'What else?'

Eddie made the gargling sound again, then said, 'Jesus. You wouldn't believe what I got coming out of me.' That Eddie. 'Asano founded something called the Gray Army and got a couple hundred kids to join. That was a long time ago, though. Old news. I ain't heard about him in years.'

I said, 'Is he dangerous?'

'Hell, *I'm* dangerous. Asano's just crazy.'

I hung up and got back in the Corvette but didn't start it. Sonofagun. Maybe Kira Asano was behind the theft of the

Hagakure. Mimi would have gotten involved with his organization because she didn't have anything else in her life, and Asano would've pointed out what a grand fine place the Hagakure would have in the movement. Only now Eddie knew about the Hagakure, and wanted it, and was playing on Mimi to get to it. *You and me, babe.* My, my.

A fat man in baggy shorts came out of the Stop & Go with a brown paper bag. Inside, the Persian clerk stared at a miniature TV. The fat man looked at me, nodded, then got into a black Jaguar and drove away. When the Jaguar was gone, the little parking lot was quiet except for the insectile buzz of the street lamps. Here in the mountains, the Stop & Go was an island of light.

I had come to rescue Mimi, and that would be easy enough. I could call the cops, and let them do it, or I could return to Asano's, crash through the gate, and drag Mimi back to the safe tranquility of Holmby Hills and her mother and father. Only she probably wouldn't stay. Something had driven her away. Something had turned her into a kid who burned herself with cigarettes and adopted a different personality for everyone in her life and had made her want to get away from home so badly and hurt her parents so much that she had gone to incredible lengths to do it. Something wasn't right.

I sat and I stared into the warm light of the Stop & Go and I thought about all the different Mimis. The Mimi that I'd met and the Mimi that Bradley and Sheila knew and Traci Louise Fishman's Mimi and the Mimi who thought the kids in the gray uniforms had 'purpose.' *I'm with people who love me now.* Maybe there would even be a different Mimi tomorrow. Maybe I needed to know which Mimi was the real Mimi before I'd know what to do.

At eighteen minutes after ten I started my car, pulled out onto Mulholland Drive, and went home.

CHAPTER 24

At nine-forty the next morning I drove back along Mulholland, pulled up at Asano's gate, and pressed a blue metal button on the call box. A female voice said, 'May I help you?'

I said, 'Yes, you may. My name is Elvis Cole, and I'd like to speak with Mimi Warren.'

Nothing happened.

I pressed the call button again and said, 'Knock, knock, knock! Chicken Delight!'

The female voice said, 'There is no Mimi Warren here.'

'How about I come in and talk with Kira Asano.'

'Do you have an appointment, sir?'

'Yes. Under the name George Bush.'

A male voice came on. 'Sir, if you'd like to make an appointment with Mr. Asano, we should be able to fit you in sometime toward the end of next week. If you do not wish an appointment, please clear the driveway.'

'Nope.'

There was a long pause. 'If you don't clear the drive, sir, we'll phone the police.'

'Okay.'

I turned off the Corvette, got out, crossed my arms, and leaned against the fender. After about fifteen minutes the front door opened and two Asian guys came out and started down along the drive. They wore the same cute little gray jumpsuit some of the kids wore. Gray Army. Only these guys weren't kids and they weren't cute. They were close to my age and had flat faces and eyes that didn't think much was funny. The guy on the left walked with his hands floating out from his legs like he was a gunfighter. The guy on the right bounced a nightstick off his thigh in rhythm with their stride and looked pleased with himself. When they got to the gate I said, 'Hey, Kira didn't have to send a welcome wagon. I'm touched.'

The guy with the priest said, 'You're going to be more than touched if you don't move that shit pile outta here.'

I said, 'Shit pile?'

The gunfighter said, 'You got no business here. You're also trespassing. Beat it.'

I took out my license and held it up. 'Mimi Warren is being sought by the police and the FBI as the victim of a kidnapping. I know Mimi Warren is in there because I saw her. If I have to leave here without speaking with her, I'll call the cops and the FBI and you can play tough with them.'

The guy with the priest said, 'Open the gate, Frank. Lemme kick his ass.' The license impressed the hell out of'm.

Frank ignored him. 'You're mistaken. There's nobody here named Mimi Warren or anything like that.' Frank looked as if he didn't like the thought of the Feds coming around. Probably had a couple of outstanding traffic warrants.

I said, 'There is, and I'm going to stay here until I see her.'

Nightstick gave me you've-done-it-now eyes and slapped his open palm with the priest. 'Open the gate, Frank. How 'bout it?' Neither Frank nor I looked at him.

Frank said, 'You gotta go.'

I said, 'You won't be able to move me without the cops.'

Nightstick said, 'Oh, man.' He was smiling.

Frank said, 'Maybe not.' He was looking at me the way you look at someone when you're remembering things you learned the hard way. He'd probably learned some things the guy with the nightstick would never know. He raised his right arm, and the gate lurched inward.

Nightstick stepped back out of the way, then came around. He was smiling like a loon, gripping the stick tightly with his right hand. 'Last time, asshole. Move it or lose it.'

I hit him on the side of the head with a reverse spin kick just about the time he said *lose it*. The priest spun off against the gatepost and clanged against the gate and he was down on the drive. He didn't try to get up. Frank hadn't moved. He said, 'What style?'

'Tae kwon do. Know a little kung fu. Know a little wing chun, too.'

He nodded. 'Yeah. Saw the kung fu there in the leg move.'

'Where are we?' I said.

Frank shrugged. 'Guess I'll go in and tell'm you're serious about staying. The man says move you anyway, guess I'll come out and give it a try. I'm better than Bobby.'

'Yeah. I guess there's that chance.'

Frank hefted Bobby over a shoulder in a fireman's carry, then went back up the drive. The gate closed. I went back to leaning against the Corvette. I waited.

Twenty minutes later I was still waiting. Frank hadn't come back, and it didn't look like the cops had been called. Maybe they thought I bored easily and would soon grow tired and lax in my vigil. Maybe they were planning to wait me to death. Maybe they were all out back at the pool, grilling hamburgers and drinking cold beer while I stood around out front trying to look tough.

I left the Corvette blocking the gate, walked back along Mulholland and around Asano's ridge to a fire trail, and followed it away from the road. The fire trail angled down into a little erosion gully, then slowly wrapped around the ridge toward Asano's estate. It flattened out across the ridge crest and came out behind a little concrete retaining wall. I scrambled up the slope and the concrete wall and found myself standing by a pool. The pool decking was stained and cracked and needed repair. The pool itself was a fifty-foot oval with a discolored bottom. A slim young man in black racing goggles and a black Speedo suit was swimming laps. He wouldn't notice the Circus Vargus troupe rumbling past.

At the far left edge of the pool was a tennis court. The court looked old and was flaking surface paint. Beyond it, the ground had been terraced in ascending levels up to the house. I walked along the length of the pool and up three stone steps and passed two young women coming around the tennis court. One wore red pants and a white blouse, the other a sleek lapis lazuli one-piece swimsuit. The one in the suit was quite pretty. Neither of them was Mimi Warren. I nodded and smiled and kept walking as if I had just had a nice conversation with the young man swimming laps.

I walked along beside the tennis court until they were out of sight, then turned up a walk past several dwarf orange and lemon and kara tangerine trees. Fruit had dropped to the ground, and no one had bothered to pick it up. At the main house, a boy in the nifty Gray Army uniform was coming out of a set of French doors. I said, 'They told me Mimi would be out by the pool, but I just went there and she wasn't. Any idea where I could find her?'

'Try the community room on the second floor.'

I gave him a big smile and went in. The house was as large and open as it looked from the outside, with high ceilings and blond wood floors and plenty of glass to let in the view. It might have been nice except that the walls needed painting and the floors were due wax and there were cobwebs in the high corners. Maybe when you're founding a revolution, basic maintenance just sort of gets away from you.

Every room and every wall contained large wash paintings of beaches and dunes and flat placid lakes and other lonely places, all in pale, cold colors. There were quite a few tall and spindly steel sculptures. Some of the work was impressive. All of it was signed by Kira Asano.

I was halfway up a wide curving staircase when Mimi Warren and her friend Kerri came around the corner and started down. Mimi's nose was red and her hair looked like she hadn't brushed it. When she saw me she took a half step back up toward the landing, then stopped. 'How did you find me?'

I spread my hands. 'You're supposed to be kidnapped. You go to clubs on Sunset Bouleward, you gotta expect to be found.'

Kerri said, 'Who is this?'

I said, 'Peter Parker.'

Kerri looked confused.

'Most people know me as The Amazing SpiderMan.'

Kerri turned and ran back up the stairs.

'Mimi,' I said, 'you and I have to talk.' Somewhere deep in the house, doors opened and closed and footsteps sounded on hardwood floors.

She said, 'I won't go back.'

'I won't make you go back.'

She said, 'You won't?'

Frank, Bobby, and another man came out of a door on the ground floor and looked up at me.

Bobby's cheek was swollen and beginning to color but he still managed a grin. Probably because he had a Ruger .380 automatic in his left hand instead of a nightstick. He aimed it at me and said, 'Here's where I put the fuck on you, asshole.'

That Bobby. What a way with words.

CHAPTER 25

Frank shook his head like Bobby was backward, and pushed the Ruger down. 'Don't be stupid.' He looked at the third man. 'This is the guy from out front. Elvis Cole.'

The third man was in his early sixties and good-looking in a solid, muscular way. He was deeply tanned and had crew cut hair and the sort of nose you get when you spend a little time in the ring. Kira Asano. He said, 'What's the meaning of this?'

'Gosh,' I said, 'I never heard anyone say that in real life.'

Asano stepped forward and put his fists on his hips.

I looked at Mimi. 'Are you all right?'

She blinked big eyes and scratched herself.

'Answer me.'

She nodded.

I looked back at Asano. 'You're in a world of shit, old man.'

Half a dozen kids had gathered below us in the big room, watching. Asano glanced over them, let his fists drop from his hips, and turned away. 'Bring Mr. Cole along, would you, Frank?'

Frank took the gun away from Bobby and held it down along his leg. Frank looked at me. He wasn't Bobby, all right. 'Come on.'

We followed Asano across a large sunny room with a pool table and into a smaller room that looked out over the tennis court and pool and most of the San Fernando Valley. I didn't see any more of the Gray Army. Maybe there weren't any more. Eddie Ditko had said that once there had been a couple hundred members, but that was a long time ago. Maybe, like the house, the Gray Army's time had passed and its smell had grown musty and it had fallen into disrepair. Old news.

There was a glass desk in the room and some modern chairs and about a million photographs on the walls. On the largest wall there were several mounted samurai swords and a Japanese flag and a portrait of Asano in a Japanese military uniform. He looked young and strong and proud. The portrait had probably been done very close to the end of World War II. Asano went behind the glass desk, crossed his hands behind his back, and stared at me. When Asano walked, he had a tendency to strut, and when he stood, he had a tendency to posture, but there didn't seem to be a lot of confidence to it, more like the strutting and posturing were habits he had developed a long time ago. He said, 'You have no right to be here, Mr. Cole. This place is a private home which you have entered against my wishes. You are not welcome.'

'I rarely am, but that's beside the point,' I said. 'Mimi Warren is a minor whom the police and FBI believe is the victim of a kidnapping. They're looking for her and they'll find her. I'm interested in her well-being.'

Asano smiled reasonably. 'Why would anyone think Mimi has been kidnapped? Does she look kidnapped to you?'

'She staged a phony kidnapping when she ran away from home.'

'Ah.'

'Mimi seems to have a lot of anger toward her parents. I think she saw it as a way to hurt them.'

'Ah.'

'I think you had something to do with it.'

Asano sat down. He put his hands on the desk in front of him and laced his fingers. 'Don't be absurd. I am the leader of a movement, Mr. Cole, a locus for the lifeblood of a system as old as any on earth!' He made a fist and gestured with it.

I said, 'Jesus Christ, Asano, I'm not fourteen years old. Save all the Divine Wind crap for someone else.'

Bobby said, 'Hey.' Bobby had been recruited a long time ago and nothing better had come along. He probably wasn't bright enough to know, one way or another. Frank had been around a while, too, but he was smarter. He put a hand on Bobby's arm. Waiting to see what I had.

Asano made the reasonable smile again. He said, 'If Mimi has done something as foolish as involving the police in a false crime, I certainly know nothing about it. Mimi is free to come and go as she pleases. Everyone here has that freedom. Gray Shield Enterprises and the Gray Army are duly licensed nonprofit political organizations of the state of California.'

'Really aboveboard and oh-so-legal, huh?'

Asano nodded.

338

I said, 'Is Eddie Tang a member?'

Asano's eyes flickered.

I said, 'Here's what I think. Maybe you didn't participate in the runaway or the fake kidnap, but I'll bet you knew about it and that makes you eligible for a contributing charge. And I'll bet you've got the Hagakure. That puts you on deck for grand theft, receiving stolen goods, and accessory before and after the fact.'

When I said it about the Hagakure his hands started to shake and all the hard edges softened and he looked like an old man caught on the toilet. It hadn't been Eddie, all right.

Bobby said, 'Jesus, Frank, shoot the motherfucker.' Frank shifted behind me.

'The Hagakure has to go back,' I said.

Asano said, 'What are you talking about?' His voice sort of croaked and he looked at Frank. It made me wonder who ran the place. It made me wonder a lot of things.

'She's a screwed-up kid with garbage for parents and she came to you looking for something, and you screwed her, too. You had her steal the Hagakure for you.'

'No.'

'The kids you've got out there are here because they've got no place else to go. Not because of any ideal. The Gray Army movement is dead, and having the Hagakure isn't going to bring it back to life.'

Asano stood up. He started to say something, but nothing came out. He looked confused. Frank took a step toward him, then stopped. The Ruger was up now and pointing at me but Frank didn't seem interested in using it. He said, 'If that's the way it is, why aren't you here with the cops?'

'Because the cops are going to want a piece of Mimi for setting all this up and wasting their time. If the cops were here they'd drag her home or maybe to juvie detention.' I looked at Bobby. 'You remember juvie detention, don't you, Bobby?'

Bobby said, 'Fuck you.'

I said, 'Maybe there's a better way to do this than bringing in the cops right now.'

Frank looked at me a little more and the gun lowered. 'What do you want?'

'The kid doesn't want to go home and I won't know what I should do about that until I talk with her. Maybe there's a way to get her back home that will make things right for her.'

Frank said, 'Okay.'

I looked at Asano. 'Either way, the book has to go back. Maybe if the book goes back, nobody has to take a fall. Maybe, if things work out and certain people keep their mouths shut, the cops can be smoothed out.'

Frank said, 'That sounds good.'

Asano went to the wall with all the photographs. There were pictures of Asano speaking to crowds and Asano with his Gray Army recruits and Asano riding in an open convertible in a parade. They weren't recent pictures.

Frank said, 'If no one takes a fall, the Gray Army stays in business.'

'Yeah.'

'Everything stays like it is.'

'Maybe so.'

Asano blinked the way Traci Louise Fishman had blinked, but he wasn't wearing contacts. He said, 'Mimi has indeed been very distraught. Almost certainly due to the state of her home life.'

'Uh-huh.'

'If there were some way to ease those tensions. If there were some way we could bring the child and parents together.'

'My thinking exactly,' I said.

Kira Asano let his eyelids flag closed, and then he raised a finger. 'Get Mimi, would you, Frank? If Mr. Cole can help the child in any way, we should encourage it.'

Frank nodded and left. Asano watched him go, then drew himself up and turned to stare at his photographs, his only army an army of memories.

His shoulders were wide and his arms were muscular and his legs powerful. His neck was taut and corded. Long ago, when his dreams were alive, he had probably been something to see.

CHAPTER 26

When Frank came back with Mimi, I took her out the back and down along the terraced walks and past the rows of little potted fruit trees with their fruit rotting on the ground. Frank and Bobby walked behind us, the Ruger still dangling down alongside Frank's leg.

At the tennis court, I opened the gate and said, 'Let's go out here.'

Mimi and I went to a table and some chairs they had near the outer edge of the court. Bobby started out on the court after us, but Frank pulled him back to wait at the gate.

The court had been cantilevered out over the slope, which fell away sharply and bowled down into a deep ravine. On the fall-away side, the chain link fence hadn't been woven with green fabric so you could enjoy the view while you played. Standing there was like being at the edge of a cliff.

I said, 'You want to sit?'

Mimi went to the table and sat.

I said, 'You don't have to sit if you don't want to.'

Mimi stood.

'You staying here full time?'

'Uh-huh.'

'Anyone forcing you to do something you don't want to do?'

'Uh-uh.'

'Could you leave now?'

'I don't want to.'

'If you wanted to.'

'Uh-huh.' Mimi was staring down at the court. Little scout ants were searching along the white court lines as if they were great white bug highways. Maybe she was watching the ants.

I leaned against the fence and crossed my arms and stared at her. After a while she looked over and said, 'Why are you staring at me?'

'Because I am the Lord High Keeper of the Knowledge of Right and Wrong, and I am trying to figure out what to do.'

She blinked at me.

'Jiminy Cricket,' I said. 'He was also Counselor in Moments of Temptation, and Guide Along the Straight and Narrow Path. You need that.'

Mimi shook her head. 'You can't make me go back.'

So much for Jiminy Cricket.

'Yeah, I could. I could shoot Frank and Bobby and throw you over my shoulder and bring you home.' The skin around her eyes looked soft and nervous. 'But I couldn't make you stay. You don't want to be there and you'd leave again as soon as you could. Besides that, I don't think your going home is necessarily the best thing.'

She looked at me with Traci Louise Fishman out-from-under eyes. Suspicious. She said, 'You don't bring me home, my dad is gonna fire you.'

'He already did.'

'He fired you?'

'Yeah.'

'Why?'

'Because I was supposed to provide security for his family and it didn't stop his daughter from being kidnapped.'

Mimi giggled that sort of nervous, red-nosed giggle, like maybe she was giggling at something else, not what you thought she was giggling at. She took a crumpled pack of Salem Lights out of her pocket and lit one with a blue Bic lighter. She took a quick, nervous puff. I said, 'Was Asano part of that?'

She shook her head.

'You get Eddie to help you?'

She cocked her head. 'How do you know about Eddie?'

'The Blue Fairy told me.'

'You're strange.'

'You know what the yakuza is?'

Shrug. 'I don't care.'

'Eddie's in the yakuza. He's a professional thug. You like him and you think he likes you, but all Eddie wants is the Hagakure.'

She took a nervous drag on the Salem, then pushed it out through the fence and let it drop down the slope. Mid-summer with the brush dry, the whole ridge could burn off.

I said, 'I'm trying to figure out what to do, kid, and you're not helping me. You have supposedly been kidnapped, and the cops and

342

the FBI are involved. They are looking for you and they are looking for the book. They are going to find you, and when they do they are going to take you home. They won't stand around and wonder what's best.'

She crossed her arms and chewed at her upper lip. The lip was chapped and split and had been chewed a lot. 'I won't go back.'

I said, 'Your parents are assholes, and that's rough, but it's not the end of the world. You can survive them, and you don't need guys like Eddie Tang or Kira Asano to do it. You can work past them to be the person you want to be. A lot of kids do.'

For just a moment the nervousness seemed to pass and Mimi grew still. She looked at me as if I were a silly, offensive man and then she rubbed at her face with her hands. She said, 'You don't know anything.'

'Maybe not. If you don't want to go home, there are other places.'

'I like it here.'

'Here sucks. You're going to have to talk to the cops and let them know what's going on and deal with them. They don't like it when people steal valuable things and pretend to be kidnapped and cost the tax-payers a lot of time and money.'

She recrossed her arms so that her right hand was beneath her left arm. The right fingers began to pinch her left side. Hard, nervous pinches. 'You don't understand,' she said slowly. 'I will kill myself first.'

Great. High drama in Teen Town. 'You've been found. Sooner or later you are going to have to talk to your parents.'

'*No.*'

'Now, without the cops involved, is better. There are people that work with kids and their parents who can be there to help. They've been known to help bring a family close together again.'

Mimi Warren made the little smile, then looked directly at me. 'My father is close enough.'

I took slow deep breaths and felt myself grow cold. She pinched at her side and chewed at her lip, then stared down into the valley at things that were too far away to see. Her eyes took on the jumpy vacant look I'd seen on street kids down on Hollywood Boulevard, kids who'd had it so hard back home in Indianapolis or Kankakee or Bogalusa that they weren't right any more and never would be. When she said she would kill herself, she had meant it. 'Mimi, does your father have sex with you?'

The red eyes leaked and she began to rock. She said, 'I hope they

343

changed their minds and didn't give him that fucking award.' She didn't say it to me. She just sort of whispered it.

I said, 'Does your father sexually molest you?'

The right fingers moved faster, digging into the soft flesh of her side and squeezing. She probably didn't even know she was doing it. I wanted to reach out and stop her.

'Does your mother know?'

Shrug. The tears dropped down her cheeks and into her mouth. She dug out another cigarette and lit it. Her fingers were wet from wiping away tears and left gray marks on the paper. She made the giggle and it was confused and crazy. She said, 'Eddie and I are going to get married. He said we're going to live in a penthouse apartment on Wilshire Boulevard in Westwood and I'm going to have babies and we'll go to the beach a lot.' She said it in the to-herself voice.

'You want to stay at my place?'

She shook her head.

'There's a woman I know named Carol Hillegas. She works with kids who have problems like this. What if I take you there?'

She shook her head again. *I'm with people who love me.*

I took a deep breath, let it out. 'Okay. I'm going to let you stay here. I'm not going to call the cops, and I'm not going to tell your parents. You won't have to go home and you won't have to see your father if you don't want to.' I took out one of my cards and I put it in her hand and she looked at it but probably didn't see much. 'That gets me at home or my office, and if I'm not there a machine picks up. I want you to stay here. I don't want you to go nightclubbing and I don't want you to go out with Eddie Tang.'

The giggle.

'Eddie Tang is a bad man, babe.'

The giggle again, and then she made a wet sound. Her slight body shook and heaved and she put her face in her hands and she cried. I put my arms around her and I held her and I glared at Frank. I said, 'I can't tell you things are going to be wonderful. I can't tell you that things will ever be right. All I know is that things have happened to you that shouldn't have and you're going to need help straightening it all out and I will make sure you get that help. Okay?'

She nodded. She was still rocking. She said, 'I'm so messed up. I don't know what to do. I don't know. I don't know.'

I held her until she ran out of tears. I said, 'I'll talk to Carol Hillegas and then I'll give you a call. We can fix this.'

She nodded again.

When I left, Mimi Warren was standing at the edge of the tennis court, staring out at the valley, rocking. Bobby stood in the gate, blocking my way and acting tough. He said, 'Have a good time?'

I went very close to him and said, 'If anything happens to her, I will kill you.'

Bobby stopped smiling. Frank took a step in, then pulled Bobby back. Bobby licked his lips and didn't move. Frank looked at me. 'Forget him,' he said.

I stared at Bobby hard enough to stop his heart, and then I left.

CHAPTER 27

I walked out the long drive toward Mulholland. The gate swung open when I got there, and I went through, and then the gate closed. I got into the Corvette and closed the door and took a deep breath and rubbed very hard at my eyes. I pressed my fingers into my cheeks and under the line of my jaw and behind my neck and over my temples. The muscles in my neck and at the base of my skull and the tops of my shoulders were as tight as spinnaker lines and I couldn't make them loosen.

I drove back along Mulholland to the Stop & Go, and called Carol Hillegas. In the past, when I've had to find runaways who'd taken to the streets, Carol has always proven a help. She knows kids, and counsels them at her halfway house in Hollywood. I gave her the short version and said I needed her help and asked if I could stop by. She told me she'd make some time around eleven. I hung up, then called Jillian Becker. I said, 'I need you to meet me in Hollywood in half an hour.'

She said, 'I'm really very busy.'

'It's about Mimi.'

'Have you found her?' She said it slowly. Scared, maybe.

'Will you meet me?'

She didn't answer.

I said, 'This isn't a time to worry about business. I know where she is and I've spoken with her and now there are some things that have to be discussed. Is Bradley back from Kyoto?'

'Yes.'

'I don't want to involve Bradley or Sheila until after we've talked.'

'Why not?'

I didn't say anything.

After a very long while, she said, 'All right. Where should I go?'

When I got to the halfway house, Jillian Becker was out front, leaning against her BMW. She was wearing a cream-colored pants suit with a white silk blouse and black Sanford Hutton sunglasses with electric-blue mirrorshade lenses. The halfway house was in what used to be a two-story pre-war apartment building on a ratty street called Carlton Way, one block south of Hollywood Boulevard, off Gower. There was a liquor store on the corner where guys with no place to go sat on the curb, and old Taco Bell cups littered the street, and a stack of empty Texaco oil cans on a plot of dead grass, and a tiny bungalow house with a hand-painted sign hanging from the porch that said PALMISTRY. The halfway house had a neat lawn and a fresh coat of paint and was the best-kept property on the street. I think Jillian Becker was hiding behind the sunglasses.

I said, 'One thing about me, I really know how to show a girl a good time.'

She said, 'Is Mimi in there?'

'No.'

'Why do you want me here and not Bradley and Sheila? If this has to do with Mimi, Bradley and Sheila should be here.'

'No,' I said, 'if Bradley were here I would shoot him.'

Jillian Becker stared at me through her mirrorshades, then looked over at the unshaven men sitting on the curb, then looked back at me. She said, 'You really mean that, don't you?'

'Let's go inside.'

We went through the little gate and up the walk and into the house. There was a tiny entry with a hardwood floor and an old-fashioned coat rack and a sign that said LEAVE THE BULLSHIT AT THE DOOR. To our left there was a stair that went up to the second floor, and to our right there was a little reception area with a yellow Formica counter and a telephone and a blackboard for group announcements. A blond boy with long straight hair and a little blue cross tattooed on the back of his left hand was sitting behind the counter. He was reading a worn-out, spine-rolled copy of Robert Heinlein's *Stranger in a Strange Land*. He looked up when we walked in. 'Hi,' I said. 'We're here to see Carol.'

The blond kid closed the Heinlein on a finger, said he'd tell Carol, and came around the counter to take the stairs up two at a time.

Jillian Becker took off the mirrorshades and stood stiffly by the Formica counter. 'What kind of place is this?'

'Halfway house for kids. Most of the kids here are runaways from

347

middle-class homes and middle-class mommas and daddies. Things got a little out of hand back in Ohio. Sometimes things got a lot out of hand. So they end up here in the Land of Dreams hooking or peddling dope or scamming and they get grabbed by the cops. If they are very lucky, the cops give them over to Carol.'

The blond kid came back down the stairs, said Carol was making coffee, and that we could go on up. We did. There was a narrow landing on the second floor and a long hall that went past four dormitory rooms, two for boys and two for girls. A girl who couldn't have been more than twelve was on her hands and knees scrubbing the baseboard. She had a bright pink scar running along the length of her left tricep. Knife. Jillian Becker stared at the scar.

Carol Hillegas's office was at the end of the hall. She appeared in the door, took my hand, gave me a kiss, then introduced herself to Jillian Becker and showed us in. Carol Hillegas was tall and thin and wearing her hair shorter than the last time I'd seen her. There were new streaks of gray in it. She had a long face and thin lips and was wearing a pair of faded Levi's and a green Hawaiian shirt with flowers and birds on it and open-toed Mexican sandals. She wore the shirt tucked into her pants. The office had a new coat of paint, but the secondhand desk was the same and so were the wooden chairs and the textbooks and file cabinets and diplomas on the wall. There was an aluminum-frame sliding window in the north wall. If you looked out, you could see the big red X of the Pussycat Theatre up on Hollywood Boulevard. 'Very nice, Carol,' I said. 'Upgrading.'

'It's all this government subsidy. I'm thinking about putting in a Jacuzzi.'

When we were seated and had coffee, Carol looked at Jillian and smiled. 'What's your position in this case, Ms. Becker?'

'I work for the girl's father. I'm not related to her.'

I said, 'Jillian's here because I'm going to need help with the parents. The more she knows, the more help she'll be.'

'So far,' Jillian said coolly, 'I don't know anything. He hasn't told me what's going on.'

Carol gave Jillian a warm smile. 'He's like that. Secrets give him a sense of power.'

'Bitch,' I said.

Carol laughed, then leaned back in her chair and said, 'Tell me about this little girl.'

I told Carol Hillegas all of it. When I got to the part about the cigarettes, Jillian Becker sat forward and brought one hand to her mouth and stayed like that. I told them about Eddie Tang and following him to the Pago Pago Club and finding Mimi, and then following her to Kira Asano's. When I mentioned Asano, Jillian moved her hand from her mouth and said, 'Bradley opened a hotel in Laguna Beach last summer. Asano had a showing in the hotel gallery.'

I said, 'Would Mimi have gone to the opening?'

'Yes. She probably went down with Sheila.'

I told them about my talk with Mimi, and about her refusal to return home. Then I told them why. 'She said she couldn't go home because her father sexually molests her.'

Jillian Becker drew in a breath as sharp as a rifle's crack. She said, 'My God.' Then she stood up and went to the window.

Carol said, 'You left her at Asano's?'

'Yes.'

Jillian Becker shook her head and said, 'This can't be. I've known these people for years.' She shook her head twice.

Carol Hillegas got up and poured herself another cup of coffee. I'd once seen Carol Hillegas drink fourteen large cups of 7-Eleven coffee in a single Saturday morning. She said, 'Leaving her at Asano's was probably all right. Mimi's there because she feels secure, and that's probably the most important thing right now. In an environment where there is an incestuous relationship, the child loses all sense of security because there is never a safe, nurturing time. The person whom the child should be able to trust most is the source of fear and anxiety.'

Jillian Becker turned away from the window, came back, and sat on the edge of her seat. 'I can't believe Sheila could even suspect this and keep quiet.' She looked at me. 'You've seen how she is.'

Carol drank more coffee and leaned back in her chair. She looked at Jillian and her face took on a more female quality, as if what she were about to say was somehow more female than male. 'The mother might not know. She might only suspect, and there is a high likelihood that she would reject that suspicion out of hand. Somewhere along the line whatever the mother had with the father stopped, and he turned to their daughter. A way to look at it is that the daughter has usurped the mother's power and position in the household. The daughter has proven herself more desirable and more satisfying to the male. More womanly. That's not an easy thing to accept.'

'Sheila has a tough household position,' I said. 'Wow.'

349

Carol looked at me and the female thing in her face was cool. 'Understand that incest is a family problem with a tremendously complex dynamic. It is also one of the most socially shameful things a person can confront. No one wants to admit it, everyone feels guilty about it, and everyone is afraid of it.'

I said, 'Great.'

'Something like this cannot be handled privately. By law, any licensed therapist or counselor has to report a suspected or admitted case of incest to the Department of Public Social Services Child Abuse Unit. The Department dispatches a field investigator who works with the private therapist, if there is one, or the district attorney's office and police, if those two agencies are required. Incest is a violation of the criminal code and charges can be filed, but they usually aren't if the offending parent and family agree to participate in therapy.'

Jillian said, 'What if the parent refuses?'

'As I said, charges could be filed, but if the child won't testify, and most of them won't, there's really nothing that can be done. The child would have to go into single therapy, but unless the parent and child work together, it is very difficult to get past the scars this kind of thing leaves.'

I said, 'What about Mimi?'

'There's no way I can make a diagnosis based on hearsay. You have to work with the client, and it can take many, many hours over many, many weeks. But clearly this girl is demonstrating severe aberrational behavior. She repeatedly inflicts pain upon herself, and she went to bizarre lengths to escape her environment. Most kids want to run, they just run. They don't need to stage a phony kidnapping. The anger this child must be feeling is enormous, and most of it is directed at herself. That's why the masochistic behavior. Another reason is that, subjectively, Mimi is looking for someone who will love her. When a person hurts herself the way Mimi has, they're doing it because they want someone to make them stop.'

Jillian was nodding. 'And the person who makes them stop is the person who loves them.'

Carol Hillegas said, 'Essentially, yes. Sexual abuse isn't love. It's abuse.' She looked at me. 'Mimi is like everyone else. She just wants to feel loved.'

'Should I call the cops?'

Carol shrugged. 'The cops won't kill her. They'll take her in and when this comes out they'll refer it to the DA and to Social Services and they'll get her a counselor. Your instinct was to avoid the trauma of the arrest and the questioning, and in an ideal world that would be the best way to go. Mimi's had enough trauma.'

I said, 'If I can get Mimi and her parents to agree to come in, will you help?'

'Yes.'

'What's the most trauma-free way to do it?'

'The girl should be in a stabilized environment, and should have established some trust with the therapist. If that's me, I'd like to spend some time with her and some time with the parents before we try to bring them together. After we're used to each other, we can begin the group work on neutral ground and see where it leads us.'

Jillian Becker said softly, 'Bradley will never agree.'

I looked at her and leaned forward in my chair. 'Yes, he will.'

She looked at me.

'I'm going to talk to Bradley and Sheila and I'm going to get them to agree to this, but I don't want to do it at Bradley's office. I want you to get them together at home. Can you do that?'

Carol Hillegas said, 'How are you going to convince them?'

I ignored her. 'Can you do that, Jillian?'

'Yes.'

'Will you?'

'Yes.'

I stood up. 'Then let's do it.'

CHAPTER 28

I went to my office and Jillian went to hers, and fifty minutes later she called and told me to be at the Warrens' home at three that afternoon.

When I got there, Jillian's white BMW was parked behind Bradley's chocolate-brown Rolls convertible. The Rolls's top was down and it looked very sporty. Sort of like a tank with the turret blown off. A sky-blue Mercedes 560SL was parked in one of the garages just past the motor court. That would be Sheila.

At three in the afternoon, it was clear and bright and warm in Holmby Hills. Quiet. Mockingbirds chirped and bees floated around the snapdragons and poppies that lined the drive, and high overhead a single light plane buzzed east. Out on the street, somebody's Salvadoran housekeeper walked toward Sunset Boulevard and her bus stop. She didn't look at me and she didn't look up at the plane.

I went to the front door, knocked, and Sheila Warren let me in. She was wearing a white and pink Love tennis outfit and had a short glass containing ice and a dark liquid in her hand. Always after five somewhere in the world. She looked defiant and sullen, a woman who'd had to make too many sacrifices to get where she was. 'I certainly hope I was called off the court for a good reason.'

Sacrifices.

She closed the door and we went into the den. Bradley Warren was half sitting on one of the bar stools, thumbs hooked in his vest's watch pockets, looking sour. The stern affluent businessman as pictured by GQ. Jillian Becker was standing by the other end of the bar, not looking at him and not looking at Sheila. Bradley said, 'Let's get something straight, Cole, and get it straight now. You are not in my employ, nor have you been since you were terminated, so

I don't intend to pay you a dime. If this is just a ploy to maneuver yourself back onto my payroll, you can forget it.'

Sheila said, 'I didn't leave the court to listen to you. If he knows something about Mimi, for God's sake, let's hear him.'

Jillian said, 'I'll wait outside.'

Bradley said, 'You stay here. I want a witness in case this fraud claims I agreed to pay him for additional services.'

Jillian's face was pale. She looked like she had been hoping no one would notice her. 'I can't do that, Bradley.' She started for the door.

Bradley said, 'What do you mean, you can't do that? I want you to stay.'

She kept going. 'Not this time.'

Bradley said, 'What do you mean, not this time? You made me come here. You'd better remember who you work for.'

Jillian stopped at the door. She looked at me, then Bradley. She looked at him for a very long time. 'Bradley,' she said. 'Go fuck yourself.' Then she left.

Sheila Warren laughed. Bradley said, 'Jillian,' but he said it to a closed door. He looked back at me. 'Jesus Christ. I don't have time for this. Tell me about Mimi. Is Mimi all right?'

'No,' I said. 'Mimi is not all right.'

Sheila stopped smiling and put her drink on the bar.

'Mimi has not been in an accident and has not suffered a physical injury and isn't in a hospital somewhere, but she is not all right.'

Bradley said, 'What the hell does that mean?'

Looking at them, I could feel the muscles in my neck and shoulders tighten the way they had tightened when I was with Mimi. I said, 'Mimi wasn't kidnapped. She ran away. I found her and talked with her.'

Sheila said, 'Good Lord, why didn't you bring her home?'

'She didn't want to come home.'

Sheila opened her mouth, then closed it. 'Well, what kind of answer is that? Where is she?'

'I won't tell you that.'

The famous Bradley Warren frown. 'What do you mean? You have to.'

'No. I don't.'

Bradley looked at me the way you look at someone when you're thinking maybe they're up to something. Then he started around the bar for the phone. 'I'm going to call the police.'

I said, 'We're going to talk about some very personal things now. You're not going to want the cops here.'

Bradley stopped, his hand on the phone. Sheila's eyes wobbled from me to Bradley and back to me. She said, 'What's going on here? What's this about?'

I was looking at Bradley. 'Mimi has the Hagakure, Bradley. She stole it to hurt you and she pretended to be kidnapped for the same reason.'

Bradley moved slightly as if a strong wind had pushed him. 'Mimi has the Hagakure.'

'Yes.'

'And you didn't bring it back.'

'No.'

'She stole it to hurt me, and now she is pretending to be kidnapped.'

Sheila said, 'That's silly.' She made a little gesture of dismissal with her left hand, picked up the drink with her right, and had some.

'Your daughter is in trouble. She's got serious problems and she's had them for years and she will probably need professional help for a long time if she's ever going to have a chance to be right. You're going to have to be a part of that.'

Sheila said, 'I don't know what all this is about. Teenage girls get confused. It's hormonal.'

'It has to start now, Bradley. The problems have to come out in the open now and the healing process has to begin.' It was just me and Bradley. Sheila might just as well have been on Mars. 'Mimi will have to go into a halfway house for a while or you will have to leave home.'

Bradley's left eye started to spasm and veins bulged in his forehead and on the sides of his neck. He said, 'I don't know what you're talking about.'

'Tell Sheila, Bradley.'

The spasm got worse. He shook his finger at me. Angry. 'You'd better tell me where the Hagakure is, goddamnit. That book is priceless. It's irreplaceable.'

'Tell Sheila about Mimi.'

Sheila put the glass down again. The defiance and the sullenness were gone. Bad dreams coming true. 'Tell me what?'

'I don't know what he's talking about. What did Mimi say? What's this all about?' You could see his hands tremble.

I said, 'Bradley, your daughter is never going to have a chance to heal until you admit that you've been molesting her.'

Sheila's face faded and went pale and became something ghost-like. She didn't move and Bradley didn't move and then Bradley shook his head and smiled. It was the sort of smile you give to someone you don't know well when you're correcting them. He said, 'That's not true.'

Sheila made a small sound, very much like her daughter's giggle.

Bradley said, 'Mimi made it up. You said she wanted to hurt me.'

Sheila threw what was left of her drink in his face. Her eyes filled and her nose grew red and she said, 'You bastard. You no good shit bastard.' She hit him. She flailed wildly, slapping and punching and calling him a bastard, her face blotchy, spit flying. He didn't move.

The hitting went on until I went over and caught her wrists and pulled her in close to my chest. She said, 'You bastard,' over and over.

Bradley spread his hands the way they do in a comic strip. His you-must-be-mistaken smile didn't waver. 'Why would Mimi say such a thing? It's not true. It's outrageous.' The eye fluttered madly.

I brought Sheila over to one of the couches and sat her down. 'Sheila. There's a woman named Carol Hillegas who is a counselor who's worked with people who've had to go through this. You can talk to Carol, and she will talk to Mimi, and then she will talk to all of you together. Will you do that? Will you talk to Carol?'

Sheila held herself as if there were something hard and painful in her chest. She nodded.

Bradley said, 'I'm going to sue you if you spread rumors about this. There's no proof.'

I left Sheila and went around behind the bar to where Bradley was standing and took out the Dan Wesson.

Bradley backed up until he hit glass shelves lined with liquor bottles and then he couldn't back up anymore. He said, 'Hey.'

I pulled back the hammer until it locked and I pointed the muzzle at the center of his forehead. 'Bradley, your child needs you and you are going to do right by her.' My voice was even and calm. 'Do you understand?'

He did not move. 'Yes.'

'She needs you to be honest about this. She needs you to admit that this should never have happened and that this is not something she precipitated and that she is not at fault. Do you understand that?'

'Yes.'

'The Department of Social Services is going to be notified, and one of their people is going to work with you and a counselor and Sheila and Mimi. It is very, very important for Mimi that you accept the therapeutic process and participate in it. Do you understand that?'

'Yes.'

I stared at Bradley Warren past the Dan Wesson, and then I moved a half step closer. I said, 'I'm told that what has happened here is complex and that you are not what we less sophisticated types call a bad man. That may be. I don't give a rat's ass if you are helped in this process or not. I don't care if you have to fake every moment of therapy for the next ten years. You will see to it that everything that can be done to help your daughter will be done. If you do not, I will kill you, Bradley. Do you understand that?'

He nodded.

'Say it.'

'Yes.'

'Say it all the way.'

'You will kill me.'

'Do you believe that?'

'Yes.'

'Stay here. Don't go back to your office. Carol Hillegas will call you. If you don't come through with this, Bradley, I will be back.'

We stood like that for another few seconds, then I lowered the gun and left.

Jillian Becker was sitting inside her BMW. Even with the mirrorshades you could see that she'd been crying. I went around to her side of the car and squatted down by the window. 'You learned a very hard thing today,' I said. 'Time passes, you'll steady down. You'll see if you can live with it or if you'll have to make some changes.'

She took a deep breath, then sighed it out. 'Do you have to do that much? Make changes?'

'Sometimes. Sometimes you can change what's there, sometimes what's there changes you.'

She nodded and looked toward the house. Big changes coming. She said, 'I was thinking of what Carol said about people who hurt themselves, about how what they're really doing is looking for someone who loves them enough to make the pain stop.'

I didn't say anything.

Jillian Becker started the BMW and put it in gear and looked at me.

After a while she drove away.

CHAPTER 29

When I got home I called Carol Hillegas and told her that I had spoken with Bradley and Sheila and that they were expecting her call. After Carol hung up, I called Kira Asano's place and asked for Mimi. Bobby came on and said, 'Who's this?'

'The Shell Answer Man.'

'Eat shit.'

Frank came on and said, 'Are the cops on the way here?'

'No.'

'She's in the back. Wait.'

In a little while Mimi said, 'Uh-huh?' She sounded like she maybe expected that her parents were really on the other end of the line and about to start yelling at her.

I said, 'It's Elvis.'

'Uh-huh.'

'I spoke with your parents. They're not going to make you go home. You're going to have to leave Asano's, but you can stay at a halfway house Carol Hillegas owns. If that doesn't work out, you can go home and your father will move out, whichever you prefer.'

She didn't say anything.

'Mimi?'

'I don't want to go home.' Dull. I wondered if she was loaded on something.

'I'll come get you tomorrow morning. If you want we can have breakfast and then I'll take you to Carol's place, and I'll stay with you there for as long as you need me to, okay?'

'Okay.'

'Put Frank on.'

There were noises and voices and then Frank came on. 'What's up?'

'I'm going to come get her tomorrow. I'm going to get the book, too.'

'Are you going to be able to keep Mr. Asano out of it?'

'I don't know. I'm not going to bring him into it, but I don't know what Mimi is going to tell the cops when they talk with her. You live up to your end and help me with the kid and I'll see that the parents don't try to press you if the cops come in. I'll tell them that you guys cooperated with me and wanted the best for the girl.'

'That oughta cut a lot of ice.'

'It's what I can do.'

'Yeah.' Frank hung up.

I put down the phone and went into the kitchen and poured myself a glass of apple juice and drank it. I went back into the living room and turned on the evening news. I put my hands in my pockets and shook my head and thought, sonofagun, this thing is coming together. I went back to the phone and called Joe Pike but he wasn't home. I dug through my wallet and found Jillian Becker's home number and gave her a call. Nope. She was out, too. The cat door clacked in the kitchen and hard food crunched. I went back into the kitchen and looked at him eating and said, 'Well, I guess it's just you and me.'

He didn't bother to look up.

I got us a couple of Falstaff out of the refrigerator and put on some music and after a while I went to bed.

At five minutes after eight the next morning my phone rang. I picked it up and said, 'Elvis Cole Detective Agency. Let us get on your case!'

Jillian Becker said, 'What's going on?'

I said, 'What do you mean, what's going on?' This sort of thing is covered in Advanced Interrogation at the Private Eye Academy.

'Mimi called Bradley fifteen minutes ago. She told him she wanted to give the Hagakure back and asked him to meet her. I thought you were supposed to pick up Mimi and bring her to Carol Hillegas.'

'Did Bradley go?'

'Two minutes ago. I told him he shouldn't. I told him he should wait.'

'Are you in your office?'

'Yes.'

I told her I'd call her back, then I hung up and dialed Kira Asano's. I dialed the four numbers I had and each of the four rang but no one answered. I didn't like that. I called Jillian. 'I couldn't get anyone at Asano's. Did Bradley say where he was going to meet Mimi?'

'She wanted to see him at a construction site on Mulholland just east of Coldwater. He said he told her that was silly, that she should come to the office or that he would go to where she was staying but she said she would feel safe there and that's where she wanted to do it. Why would Mimi want to give back the book like this? Why would she want to be alone with him?'

There were a couple of reasons but I didn't like them much. I said, 'I'm on my way now. Call the North Hollywood PD and ask for Poitras or Griggs or Baishe. Tell them you're calling because I told you to and have them send a car. Tell them to hurry.'

Mulholland was five minutes away down Woodrow Wilson, then a single broken-backed sprint west toward Coldwater. Just past Laurel, Mulholland is woodsy and the houses have been there forever, but farther west more and more ridges were being cut and scraped and developed for homesites. A mile short of Coldwater, Mulholland flattened out and signs said HEAVY EQUIPMENT AHEAD. I slowed down. A large ridge grew away to the north, rising off the road toward the San Fernando Valley. The ridge was big and white and had been graded clean. A fresh tarmac road had been cut up to the ridge top and clean white sidewalks paralleling the road had been poured and cement drains set. When all this was finished there would probably be guards and ornate street lamps and no trees and no coyotes and no deer. Just what the locals had in mind when they bought up here ten years ago.

There was a chain link fence running the perimeter of the site. A sign on the wire and pipe gate that should have blocked the road said S&S CONSTRUCTION – KEEP OUT. The gate was open. I turned through the gate, and followed the road up.

The top of the ridge had been sliced off to make a broad flat plateau with a jetliner's view of the valley. On the plateau, the road made a wide circle so that view homes that sold for eight hundred thousand dollars could be built along the rim of the circle. Luxury living. There was a sixty-yard dumpster and two Cat bulldozers and a Ryan backhoe parked on the far side of the circle. Bradley Warren's brown Corniche convertible and a beat-up green Pontiac Firebird were by the dumpster, and Mimi and Bradley were standing by the Firebird. Mimi saw me first. She was wearing a loose red and white cotton shirt over blue jeans and black, high-top shoes. There was a pink leather purse slung over her shoulder and her face looked pale and wild and blotchy from crying. She reached into the purse and took out a small black revolver and pointed it toward her father and I yelled and she shot him. There was one sharp POP. Bradley looked down at himself, then looked back at his daughter, then went forward onto his hands and knees.

Mimi dropped the gun and climbed into the Firebird and screeched away. I jumped the curve and revved the Corvette across the island's rough ground. Bradley stayed on his hands and knees for the time it took me to cross the ridge top and get out of the car, then he keeled sideways onto his side and began to make flapping movements with his arms, trying to get up. 'She shot me,' he said. 'My God, she shot me.'

'Stop trying to get up. Let me see it.'

'It hurts!'

I put him on his back and looked at him. There was pink froth at the corner of his mouth and when he spoke his voice was wet the way it gets when you've a bad cold and the mucus fills your throat and sputters when you try to breathe. There was a red spot about as big around as a medium-sized orange just to the right of the center of his chest. It was growing.

I took out my handkerchief and put it on the spot and pressed hard. 'I have to get you to a hospital,' I said.

Bradley nodded, then blew a large red bubble and threw up blood. His eyes rolled back in his head and he shuddered violently and then his heart stopped.

'God damn you, Bradley!' I was yelling.

I pulled off my shirt and his belt. I bundled my shirt, put it over the red spot, then wrapped the belt around his chest to maintain some pressure. When there is arterial bleeding you are not supposed to use CPR, but when there is no pulse, there's not much choice. I cleared his throat and breathed into his mouth and then pressed hard on his chest twice. I repeated the sequence five times and then I checked for a pulse but there was none.

A single hawk floated high above, looking for mice or other small living things. Out on Mulholland cars passed. None of them saw, and none stopped to help. Somewhere a motorcycle with no muffler made sounds that echoed through the canyons.

I breathed and pressed and breathed and pressed and breathed and pressed, and that's what I did until the cops that Lou Poitras sent found us and pulled me off. All the breathing and pressing hadn't done any good. Bradley Warren was dead.

CHAPTER 30

Six copmobiles came and two wagons from the Crime Scene Unit and a van from the coroner's office and a couple of Staties and a woman from the district attorney's office. The Crime Scene people outlined the body and the gun and measured a lot of tire tracks. The coroner's people took pictures and examined the body and pronounced Bradley Warren officially dead. Bradley was probably glad to hear that. Being unofficially dead must be a drag.

The woman from the DA's office and a tall blond detective I didn't know talked to the Crime Scene guys and then came over and talked to me. The detective had sculptured, air-blown hair that was out of style ten years ago. The woman was short with a big nose and big eyes. I was looking good with blood on my pants and my hands and my shirt and my face. The blond said, 'What happened?'

I told it for the millionth time. I told them where Bradley Warren had stood and where Mimi had stood and where Mimi's car had been parked and how she had taken the gun from her purse and fired one shot point-blank and killed her father.

The blond dick said, 'She drops the gun after she pulls the trigger?'

'Yeah.'

'A sixteen-year-old kid with no gun and you couldn't stop her.'

'I was busy trying to keep her father alive.' Asshole.

A dark cop with a cookie-duster mustache came over with the gun in a plastic bag. He showed it to the woman. 'Gun's a Ruger Blackhawk. Twenty-two caliber revolver. Loaded with twenty-two long rifle ammo. One shot fired.'

The woman looked at the gun, gave it back, and said, 'Okay.' The dark cop left and took the blond cop with him. The woman said, 'What kind of car was she driving?'

'Dark green Pontiac Firebird. Couple of years old. I didn't get the plate.'

'Anyone else in the car?'

'No.'

The woman took out her handkerchief and gave it to me. 'Wipe your face,' she said. 'You look like hell.'

Just before ten, Poitras and Griggs and Terry Ito pulled up in a blue sedan. Griggs was in the back seat. They talked to the woman from the DA's office and then the Crime Scene people and then they got to me. Nobody looked happy. Lou Poitras said, 'Half the cops and Feds in L.A. looking for this kid, Hound Dog, how'd you happen to be up here with her and her old man?'

I told him. As I said it, Ito's face darkened and you could tell he wasn't liking it. Hard to blame him. I wasn't liking it, either. Midway through the telling Jillian Becker's white BMW nosed up to the ridge top and stopped by one of the coroner's vans. Jillian Becker and a short man in a tweed sport coat got out. One of the dicks and the woman from the district attorney's office went over to them. Jillian Becker looked at me. Her face was drawn. Terry Ito said, 'You found the girl, and followed her to Kira Asano's and you decided not to tell anyone.'

'Yeah.'

'Even though you knew the police and the Feds were searching for her.'

I said, 'She looked safe at Asano's so I let her sit until I knew what was going on and then I talked with her. She was a mess, Ito. She had run away and couldn't go home because her father was sexually molesting her.'

Poitras said, 'Jesus Christ.'

Ito took a breath, let it out, and shook his head. He looked out off the ridge toward the valley. The hawk was gone.

I said, 'I wanted to get the kid some help before she'd have to deal with you people.'

Across the ridge top, the woman from the district attorney's office opened the coroner's van and showed Jillian Becker and the short man what was inside. Jillian stood stiff and nodded, then turned and quickly walked back to her BMW. The short man went with her. VP from the company, no doubt.

Poitras said, 'Why'd she kill him?'

'I don't know.'

Griggs was staring at his hands. 'Maybe she just had to,' he said, quietly.

Ito looked at Griggs, then took off his sunglasses and stared at them as if there was a bad smudge on the lense. He put the sunglasses back on. Poitras said, 'As far as you know, she still staying at Asano's?'

'Yes.'

'Let's go get her.'

We got into the blue sedan, Poitras driving, me and Griggs riding in back. I told Poitras to go west on Mulholland toward Beverly Glen. He did. The cop sedan with its heavy-duty suspension rolled easily along Mulholland's curves. Poitras had the windows up and the air conditioning on and no one said anything. All you could hear in the car was the hiss and chatter of the radio. I couldn't understand what the radio voices said, but Poitras and Griggs and Ito could. Cops get special ears for that.

When we got to Kira Asano's, Griggs said, 'Man, this guy must be loaded.'

The gate was open. We went up the drive without announcing ourselves and stopped about halfway to the house. We had to stop because Frank was lying facedown in the drive. His legs were bent and his right arm was under his body and the left half of his head was missing. Poitras and Griggs both leaned to the side to free their guns and Ito called in a request for backup. I said, 'There were about a dozen kids here. Some of them were wearing gray uniforms. There was another guy like the one on the drive named Bobby, and Asano, and Bobby probably has a gun.'

Poitras steered the car out onto the lawn around Frank's body and stopped by the front door. The front door was open.

Poitras and Griggs went around the side past the garage, and Ito and I went in through the front. No one tried to shoot us. There wasn't anyone around to try.

Cabinets had been emptied and furniture upended and Asano's paintings torn from the walls in every room. Poitras and Griggs came in from the back and said they'd found a guy who was probably Bobby with two bullets in his chest out by the little fruit trees. They'd seen no sign of the girl or anyone else.

We found Asano in his office. He was lying on the floor in front of his desk, clutching the grip of a samurai sword. He had been shot once in the chest and once in the side of the neck. The sword was bloodied. There was a short, muscular man sitting on Asano's couch. The man and the couch were sprayed with blood, and the man's eyes were slightly crossed and sightless. There was a slash along the top of his left shoulder and two puncture marks in his abdomen and a black automatic pistol in his right hand as if Asano had attacked him with the sword and he had killed Asano and then staggered to the couch to finish dying. The little finger was missing from his left hand. Somebody said, 'Sonofabitch.' I think it was Griggs.

Ito looked at the left hand and then at me. 'You say Asano had the book.'

'Yeah.'

Ito looked at the left hand again. 'Yakuza.'

We looked through the rest of the house. In an upstairs bedroom we found two girls holding each other under some rags in a closet. They screamed when we opened the door and begged us not to kill them and it was quite a while before they believed that we would not. One of them was Kerri.

We went through every room and every closet. There was no sign of either the Hagakure or Mimi Warren. When we had made the complete circuit and were back at the front of the house again, Ito shook his head. 'So,' he said. 'You left her here because she was safe, huh?'

I didn't bother to look at him.

CHAPTER 31

We brought Kerri and the other girl down to the big open room with the French doors and put them on a couch beneath an enormous watercolor of an old woman sharpening a sword. The old woman was sitting in the snow, and was barefoot, but did not look cold.

The girls were scared and the smaller one had red puffy eyes from crying. We offered them blankets even though it was eighty degrees outside. Kerri kept sneaking glances at me, probably because she had seen me before. She said, 'Are you a policeman?'

'Private eye,' I said. I gave her a little eyebrow wiggle. Elvis Cole, Master of Instant Rapport.

'You're the guy who came here looking for Mimi.'

'Yeah. You know where she is?'

'They took her.'

Poitras said, 'Who's they?'

The other girl pulled her knees up to her chin and locked her arms around her shins. She squeezed her eyes shut. Kerri said, 'These four men came. They just came in and started yelling and shooting and tearing up the house. I saw them shoot Bobby, and then I ran.'

Terry Ito said, 'All Japanese men?'

Kerri nodded.

Poitras asked her when.

Kerri looked at the other girl but the other girl's chin was between her knees and her eyes were still clamped shut. Kerri said, 'I dunno. Maybe seven. I had just got up. I dunno. I ran into the bedroom with Joan and we hid.' Joan was the quiet one.

Poitras looked at me. 'That was before she called Bradley?'

'Yeah.' I said, 'Kerri, was Eddie Tang one of the men?'

'Uh-uh.' She shook her head.

'You sure?'

366

'Uh-huh.'

Ito said, 'You know what they were after?'

'They wanted this book.'

Ito gave me a look, then he and Griggs went out to the car. Pretty soon the same uniforms who had been at Bradley's murder site came, along with a couple of dicks from Beverly Hills and three more guys from Asian Task Force. The uniforms got the girls' names and parents' phone numbers and made some calls to try to get them picked up. The ATF guys brought in big photo albums with known yakuza members and had each of the girls look through them. One of the uniforms and I made instant coffee in the kitchen. I put three cups of coffee on a plate and brought it out and sat by the girls while they turned the pages. I said, 'Kerri, did Mimi say anything to you about leaving here?'

'No.'

'I was supposed to come get her this morning. She and I had talked about it and she said okay.'

Kerri turned each page slowly, lifting the next page and scanning the pictures at the same time. 'I think she changed her mind.'

'Why?'

'Eddie came over last night.' Eddie. Great.

'What happened?'

'They had this big fight. She said he didn't really love her. She said all he wanted was the book and that he didn't care about her and that no one cared about her. Then he left.' Joan finished one album and started another. She hadn't said a word in hours.

'But he didn't come back?'

'Uh-uh.'

In a little bit a couple of the ATF cops came over and Kerri and Joan identified three of the four men who had raided the house. One of the three was the stiff in Asano's office.

A short ATF cop with a puckered scar running along his right jawline said, 'You think this is connected with the torture-murder down in Little Tokyo?' He got a kick out of saying torture-murder.

Ito said, 'Yeah. I think our boy Eddie was making a power grab. He figured Ishida had the book, so he did Ishida to get it. Only Ishida didn't have it. Asano did. So he went after the girl. When she wouldn't come across, he sent in some goons this morning.' He looked at me. 'Sound good to you?'

I gave it a shrug. 'Some of it. Some of it has holes you could put a Cadillac through.'

367

The short cop with the scar smirked.

Ito put his hands in his pockets. 'I'm listening.'

I said, 'Eddie was working the girl a long time before Ishida was done. He'd know Asano had the book.'

'Okay. What about this morning?'

'If the yakuza grabbed her, how'd she get away to kill her old man?'

Ito said, 'I hear a lot of questions. You got the answers?'

'I don't know. I just know something isn't adding up.'

Ito thought about that, and me, then finally shook his head and walked away. 'Well, you had her for a little while.'

Poitras and Griggs and I stood there and watched Ito and the guy with the scar walk away and nobody said anything. After a while, Poitras told me I looked like I'd been through a Cuisinart and asked me if I was okay. I said sure. He wondered if I needed to see a doctor. I said no. He put a hand the size of a manhole cover on my shoulder, gave me a squeeze, and said if I wanted to call him at home later that it would be fine. I said thanks. Charlie Griggs drove me back to my car. Bradley's body was gone. There were just a couple of newsmen poking around, along with a motorcycle cop who was making out like he'd just busted the Hillside Strangler. We sat there a while, in Griggs's car, and he asked if I wanted to have a couple of drinks. I told him maybe later. When I got home I went in through the garage and took off the bloodstained shirt and pants and washed my hands and face in the kitchen sink. I put the shirt and pants in the sink and rubbed the bloodstains with Clorox Pre-wash and let them sit while I went up and took a shower. I used a cloth and lots of soap and hot water and scrubbed myself pink. I used a small brush to get Bradley Warren's blood from around and beneath my fingernails. When I was finished I threw the brush away. *Well, you had her for a little while.*

I put on a loose pair of dojo pants, then went downstairs and put the clothes into the washer. Cold water. I opened a Falstaff, drank most of it, and called Jillian Becker at her office. Her secretary was subdued and distracted and told me Ms. Becker wasn't in. Probably with Sheila. I hung up and drank the rest of the Falstaff. It was so good I opened another. I stood with it in the center of my quiet house and thought about Mimi Warren out there wherever she was and whom she might be with and what she might be doing and I drank more beer. I opened the big glass doors to let in the air, then turned on my stereo and put on an old Rolling Stones album.

Satisfaction. Great bass. I made a sandwich out of some sliced turkey breast and egg bread and tomato and had another beer. *Got family problems? Hire Elvis Cole, The Family Detective. Guaranteed to make things worse or your money back!*

I called Joe Pike.

'Gun shop.'

'It's me. I found the girl.'

He grunted.

'I lost her again.'

He said, 'You been drinking?'

'No.' I sounded fine to me.

He said, 'You at home?'

'Uh-huh.'

He hung up.

Half an hour later Pike was in the living room. I hadn't heard him knock or use a key. Maybe it was teleportation. He was dressed exactly as always: sweat-shirt with no sleeves, faded Levi's, blue Nike running shoes, mirrored sunglasses. I said, 'Are those new socks?'

There was a pretty good-sized pyramid of Falstaff cans on the coffee table. He looked at it, then went into the kitchen and rattled around. After a while he said, 'Come to the table.'

He had put out a ranch omelet with cheese and tomatoes, and whole wheat toast with butter and strawberry jam. There was coffee and a small glass of milk and a little bottle of Tabasco sauce and two glasses of water. The water was all he was having. I sat down and ate without saying anything. The omelet was fluffy and moist and perfectly cooked. The cat door made its noise and the cat walked through the kitchen and hopped up onto the table. The cat watched me eating, his nose working at the odors, then he walked over and sat down in front of Pike and purred. Pike's the only person besides me that the cat will let touch him.

When I finished, I closed my eyes and held my head and Pike said, 'Can you tell it now?'

'Yes.' I drank more coffee and then I told him what had happened to Bradley Warren and I told him why. I told him everything I knew about Mimi Warren, and how she was, and why she was that way. I told him about finding Mimi at Asano's and arranging to bring her to Carol Hillegas's and Eddie Tang and the Hagakure. I told him that there were things that didn't add up and that I didn't have answers for and that maybe I didn't give a damn anymore. Pike listened without moving. Sometimes, Pike might not move for as long as you watch him. There are times I suspect that he does not move for days. When I finished he nodded to himself and said, 'Yes.'

'And you're thinking you had something to do with her killing her father.'

I nodded.

Pike took a bit of egg off my plate and held it up for the cat. 'You were doing your best for her, something that no one in her life has ever done.'

'Sure.' Mr. Convinced.

'Ever since the Nam, you've worked to hang on to the childhood part of yourself. Only here's a kid who never had a childhood and you wanted to get some for her before it was too late.' Joe Pike moved his head and you could see the cat reflected in his glasses. The cat finished the bit of egg.

I said, 'I want to find her, Joe. I want to bring her back.'

He didn't move.

'I want to finish it.'

Pike's mouth twitched. I cleared my place and washed the dishes. I went back upstairs, took another shower, then dressed and put the Dan Wesson under my arm.

When I went downstairs again, Joe Pike was waiting.

CHAPTER 32

It was midafternoon when we got to Mr. Moto's. The lunch crowd was gone and so were most of the employees, except for a couple of busboys mopping the floor and setting up for happy hour. The manager with the hi-tone topknot was sitting at a table with the Butterfly Lady, going through receipts. He stood up when he saw us and started to say something about us not being welcome when I grabbed his throat and walked him halfway across the dining room, bent him back over a table, and put the Dan Wesson in his mouth. 'Yuki Torobuni,' I said.

The Butterfly Lady stood up. Pike pushed her back down. He pointed at the busboys, then pointed at the floor. They went down fast.

I said, 'Yuki Torobuni.'

Mumbles.

'I can't hear you.'

More mumbles.

I took the Dan Wesson out of his mouth. He coughed and licked at his lips and shook his head. 'He's not here.'

I let the gun rest against his jaw. 'Where is he?'

'I don't know.'

I dug my fingers into his throat and squeezed. I said, 'Remember Mimi Warren? I am going to find her and I won't think twice if I have to kill you to do it.'

His eyes opened wider and his face got purple and after a while he gave us Yuki Torobuni's address.

Torobuni lived in a treesy section of Brentwood, just east of Santa Monica, in a large sprawling ranch house more appropriate to a western star than a yakuza chieftain. There were wagon wheels lining the drive and a genuine old west buckboard converted into a flower planter and a gate featuring a rack of longhorn horns. Ben and Little Joe were probably out back. Joe Pike stared at it all and said, 'Shit.'

Ben and Little Joe weren't around, and neither was anyone else. No Torobuni. No guys with tattoos and missing fingers and stupid eyes. After a lot of knocking and looking in windows we turned up a Nicaraguan housekeeper who said that Mr. Torobuni wasn't home. We asked her when he had left. She said he wasn't home. We asked her when he might be back. She said he wasn't home. We asked her where he had gone. She said he wasn't home.

Pike said, 'I guess he's not home.'

'Maybe he's with Eddie Tang,' I said. 'Maybe they're reading the Hagakure and celebrating Eddie's promotion.'

Pike liked that. 'Maybe we should go see.'

When we got to Eddie Tang's there was a black-and-white parked at the fire hydrant out front with the same nondescript cop sedan I'd seen before double-parked beside it. Pike said, 'I'll wait in the Jeep. One of them might know me.'

I nodded and got out. The glass security door was propped open by a large potted plant so the cops could come and go as they wanted. I trotted up the little curved steps and through the open door like I owned the place. There was a landing and a couple of indoor trees and a circular step-down lobby with a brace of nice semicircular couches for waiting and chatting. There was a small elevator to the right and a very attractive suspended staircase to the left that curved up to the second floor. A chandelier that looked like a spaceship hung from the high ceiling and a door under the staircase probably went down to the garage and the laundry facility.

Two kids maybe eleven or twelve were standing by the elevator. One of the kids had a skateboard with a picture of a werewolf on it and the other had thick glasses. The kid with the glasses looked at me. I said, 'What's going on with the cops?'

The kid with the glasses said, 'I dunno. They went upstairs looking for some guy.'

'Yeah? They find him?'

'Nah.' Well, well.

The other kid said, 'We thought they were gonna bust down the door or something but the manager let'm in.'

I said, 'What room is that?'

'212.'

'The cops still up there?'

'Yeah. They're talking with the manager. She wants to screw one of them.'

The kid with the skateboard smacked the kid with the glasses on the arm. The kid with the glasses said, 'Hey, she screws everybody.'

I said, 'Well, you guys take it easy.' I walked across the little lobby and out through the rear door and down one flight of bare cement steps to the garage. There was a little hall with a laundry room across from the stairs. The other end of the hall opened out to the garage. I went out to the garage and walked around. Nope. No dark green Alfa Romeo. Eddie was out, all right.

I went back to the laundry room and lifted myself atop an avocado-colored Kenmore dryer and waited. After about ten minutes I heard the door at the top of the stairs open, so I hopped off the dryer, fed in a couple of quarters, and turned it on. A uniformed cop in his early forties with tight sunburned skin came down the stairs and looked in. I frowned at him and shook my head. 'Damn towels take forever,' I said.

He nodded, continued on out into the garage, then went back up the stairs. I gave it another hour, then I went up to the lobby and looked out front. The cops were gone, and Pike had parked the Jeep across the street. I opened the door for him. We took the stairs to the second floor, went down the hall to 212, and let ourselves in.

Eddie had a narrow entry with mirrors on the walls and ceiling, and some kind of imitation black marble floor. There was a little guest bath on the left. To the right a short hall went to a bedroom that had been refitted as an exercise room, then on to what looked like another larger bedroom. The entry stepped down into a long living room which opened onto a balcony. The living room elled left for a dining area and the kitchen. The living room walls were crowded with trophies for excellence in the martial arts. Hundreds of them. Gleaming first-place cups and championship belts from exhibitions and tournaments all over the United States. Best All-Around. In Recognition of Excellence. Black Belt Master. Over-All Champion. 'Don't worry about this stuff,' I said. 'The guy probably bought'm.'

Pike said, 'Uh-huh.'

Joe went into the kitchen and I went into the bedroom. Eddie had a king-sized walnut platform bed with matching nightstands and a long low dresser and a mirror on the ceiling above his bed. I looked twice at the mirror. It had been years since I had seen a mirror above a bed. On the wall opposite the bed there were about a million framed photographs of Eddie Tang breaking bricks and flying through the air and accepting trophies and competing in martial arts tournaments and raising his hands, sometimes bloodied, in victory. In the earlier pictures he couldn't have been more than eight. Maybe he hadn't bought the trophies after all.

The master bath was as tastefully decorated as the rest of the apartment. Lots of mirrors and imitation black marble and flocked wallpaper. There were dirty underwear and socks in a plastic hamper and stains around the lavatory and in the tub. I looked in the medicine cabinet and the cabinet beneath the sink. There was no toothbrush and no toothpaste and no razor and no deodorant. Either Eddie was lax about personal hygiene, or those things were missing.

I went back into the bedroom. I looked through the chest and the dresser and the nightstand. A stack of well-thumbed *Penthouse* magazines sat on the night-stand along with a couple of old Sharper Image catalogs and one of those globe lamps that makes electrical patterns when you touch it. In the nightstand drawer there were five lavender-scented notes from someone named Jennifer professing her love for him and half a dozen snapshots of Eddie with different women in different places and two postcards from a United Airlines flight attendant named Kiki saying she wanted to see him when she got back to town. There was nothing of Mimi. No snapshots, no notes, no proof of her presence in his life, nothing to indicate a Westwood apartment house or babies or any sort of shared dreams. *I'm with people who love me.* Sure, kid.

There were also no clues to indicate where Eddie Tang might be or if Mimi Warren was with him or, if she wasn't, what had been done with her.

I put everything back the way I had found it and went out into the living room. Pike was waiting by the door. He said, 'There used to be a suitcase in this closet. It's gone.'

I told him what I hadn't found in the bathroom. 'If Eddie went, he'll be back. We can wait.'

Pike stared at the trophies. They were clean and bright and had been dusted regularly. He said, 'Why not.'

Outside, we parked the Jeep down the block in front of a condominium that was being built. We decided to split shifts, six on, six off. I said I'd take the first shift. Pike said that was fine. He walked away without another word.

I sat in the Jeep and waited. Two hours later the same unmarked cop sedan eased down the street and stopped by the fire hydrant. A cop in a brown suit got out, looked into the garage, then got back in his car and drove away. People went in and out of Eddie's building and cars moved up and down the street and a woman walked a little black dog and slowly the sky grew deeper until it was night. There was a nice summer chill in the air and a breeze coming in from the water, and the breeze made the palm fronds move and whisper and remind me of old songs I did not know. If I could just wait long enough, Eddie would come. When Eddie came, I could find Mimi. Waiting doesn't look like much, but it is something very important. Waiting is passive hunting.

At ten minutes after twelve that night, Joe Pike slipped into the Jeep with a brown paper bag. He said, 'I've got it. Take a break.'

I shook my head. 'Think I'll just sit.'

He nodded and took out two sandwiches. He handed one to me and kept one for himself. I didn't open it. I wasn't hungry.

Pike pulled a translation of the Hagakure from the bag. Imagine that. He sat, and read in the dark, and neither of us spoke.

Sometime very late that night I fell into a sort of half-sleep and dreamed I was having dinner with Mimi Warren. We were at a centre table in the big back room at Musso & Frank's Grill, the only diners there. Pristine white tablecloths and shining cutlery and the two of us eating and drinking and talking. I could not hear what we said. I had the same dream every time I dozed over the next three days as Pike and I waited for Eddie Tang. The dream was always the same, and I could never hear what we said. Maybe the saying wasn't important. That we were together, maybe that was what mattered.

On the fourth day, Eddie Tang came home.

CHAPTER 33

It was twenty of ten in the morning. The metal garage gate lifted and Eddie's Alfa cruised past and swung down into his garage. The Alfa was spotted and dust-streaked and there were mud splashes behind the wheel wells. Eddie had driven a long way.

Pike said, 'Now or later?'

'Let's see what unfolds.'

We sat. We waited.

One hour and ten minutes later a long white stretch limo came slowly up from Olympic and stopped in front of Eddie's building. The driver was the midget with the stupid eyes who'd been with Torobuni at Mr. Moto's. 'Better,' I said.

The midget got out of the limo, strutted over to the glass door, and buzzed Eddie's apartment. He got up on his toes for the intercom, then swaggered back to the limo and leaned against the door. He didn't even make it up to the top of the car.

Eddie came out three minutes later in light blue slacks and a navy jacket and a yellow shirt with a white button-down collar and a pink tie. Sweet. Maybe Eddie had been away taking yuppie lessons. The midget climbed in behind the wheel and Eddie got in back, and a few minutes later we followed them down to Olympic, then west to the San Diego Freeway, then south. The limo stayed in the right lane and took it slow. Just before lunchtime, traffic was light, and it was easy to stay back and not worry about being seen. We went south past the Mormon Temple and the Santa Monica Freeway, then took the Century Boulevard exit toward LAX.

I said, 'If he gets on a plane, we've got trouble.'

'No,' Pike said. 'We just shoot it down.'

I looked at him. You never know.

We stayed two cars back and followed the limo onto Century

Boulevard and past the airport hotels and into the LAX complex. Los Angeles International Airport is designed in two levels, the lower level for arriving flights, the upper level for departing flights. Eddie's limo didn't mount the ramp for the departure level. Pike looked disappointed. There went the ground-to-air.

The limo followed the huge U-shaped design of the airport around to the Tom Bradley Terminal, where international flights are based, then pulled to the pickup curb and parked. Eddie got out and went inside. After a while, he reappeared with three Japanese men and a redcap with a load of baggage. Two of the men were in their late fifties and dignified, with dark hair shot through by gray, powerful faces, and stern mouths. The third man was in his early thirties and taller than the other two, almost as tall as Eddie, with a hard bony face and broad shoulders. His hair was short except for a lock growing directly out the back of his head. The lock was long and braided and fell down his back. Well, well, well. 'How much you want to bet,' I said, 'that those gentlemen run the yakuza in Japan?'

'A visit from the home office?'

'Yep.'

'The Hagakure,' Pike said.

I nodded. 'Eddie gives it to Torobuni, Torobuni gives it to them. Everybody moves up.'

Eddie and the three men got into the limo while the redcap and the midget loaded the trunk. When all the bags were stowed, Eddie leaned out of the car, gave the redcap a tip, and then the limo pulled away.

We looped back around to the San Diego Freeway again, headed north to the 1–10, then went east across the center of Los Angeles. We cut just south of the downtown area, then up past Monterey Park, and pretty soon downtown and its skyscrapers fell away to an almost endless plain of small stucco and clapboard houses. Past El Monte and West Covina, the traffic thinned and the houses gave way to undeveloped land and railroad spur lines and industrial parks. The limo settled into the number two lane and stayed there for a very long time, and for a very long time there was nothing to see. We rolled past Pomona and Ontario and by early afternoon we approached San Bernardino. Service roads appeared, lined with Motel 6's and Denny's Coffee Shops and middle-of-nowhere shopping malls featuring BEDROOM SPECIALISTS and INDIAN DINING and UNFINISHED FURNITURE. At the southern edge of San Bernardino, we turned north on the San Bernardino Freeway toward Barstow.

I said, 'How we doing for gas?'

Pike didn't answer.

The San Bernardino forked to the right under a sign that said MOUNTAIN RESORTS, and that's the way we went. A little bit later it forked again, and this time when we followed we began a long slow climb into the San Bernardino Mountains toward Lake Arrowhead. The limo stayed in the slow lane and Pike dropped very far back. Maybe these guys were on their vacation. Maybe they were going to do a little fishing and water-skiing on the lake and grill some wienies down on the dock. That would be fun.

The mountains were vertical giants, rocky and bare except for their shoulders and ridges, which were laced with a stegosaurus-like spine of ponderosa pine trees. Every couple of miles there were signs that said DEER CROSSING or SLOWER TRAFFIC USE TURNOUTS or BEWARE FALLING ROCKS.

It took a half hour to reach a sign that said 5000 FEET ELEVATION, then the highway stopped climbing and leveled out in a heavy forest of ponderosas so improbably tall that we might have been in Oz. Two miles later the road forked again and another sign said BLUE JAY. An arrow pointed toward the left fork. That's where the limo went. That's where we went.

The road was narrow and winding and little clapboard cabins and weekender houses began to pop up amidst the pines. Most had small boats out front or muddy motorcycles leaning against native-stone garage walls. More and more houses sprouted, and pretty soon there was a Pioneer Chicken and a couple of banks and a shopping center and two coffee shops and a Jensen's Market and a U.S. Post Office and crowds of people and we were in Blue Jay. Up so high, Lake Arrowhead was a good twenty degrees cooler than San Bernardino below, and every summer the hordes ascended, desperate to escape the sweltering weather down in the flatland.

The limo didn't stop. It rolled slowly through the three-block stretch that was urban Blue Jay, and then the road forked once more. The town ended and houses reappeared but now the houses were larger and more expensive, big two- and three-story structures with lots of decking and stairs and high slanted roofs to shed the snow. We climbed, then leveled off, and we could see the lake, big and wide and gleaming in the summer sun. There were dozens of boats and skiers on the water, the powerboats and jet skis buzzing like angry mutant wasps.

On the north shore, the limo turned off the main road and eased down a gravel and tarmac lane for a mile and a half past large older homes. Big money was on the north shore. These were old vacation mansions built back in the thirties and forties for Hollywood celebrities and movie moguls who hoped to get away for a little hunting and fishing. Clark Gable and Humphrey Bogart and those guys. Wonder what Bogie would think if he knew a scumbag like Yuki Torobuni was living in his house?

Pike pulled off the road and parked. 'We follow down there,' he said, 'they'll spot us.'

We got out and trotted after them on foot.

A quarter of a mile ahead, the limo stopped at a private gate. The rear window on the driver's side went down and Eddie Tang said something to an Asian man who was leaning against a cranberry-colored Chevrolet Caprice. The guard opened the gate and the limo went in. Pike and I moved off the lane into the woods and made our way past another couple of houses until we got to Torobuni's place. There was a native-stone wall running from the road back into the woods. We followed it until we were hidden from the road, then I went up for a look and Pike continued on toward the lake.

The grounds were ten acres easy, with a looping gravel drive and a huge stone mansion with a mansard roof and a smaller carriage house to the side. Ponderosas and Douglas firs grew naturally about the grounds, and in back there were gardens and flower beds and stone pathways and swings for lazy summer afternoons. The property ran a good four hundred feet in a gentle slope down to the lake. At the lake there was a stone entertaining pier and boat house and four boat slips. The three men Eddie Tang had brought were smiling and shaking hands with Yuki Torobuni at the limo while a lot of guys who were probably just hired muscle watched. Torobuni made a big deal out of pumping each man's hand and bowing and there was a lot of back slapping. Home office, all right.

After they'd had their fill, Torobuni and the Big Shots went inside, and Eddie went over to a thin guy with nothing for a mustache and said something to him. The thin guy went into the main house and Eddie strolled around to the carriage house. After a while the thin guy came out of the big house with Mimi Warren and walked her over to the carriage house. He knocked once, the

379

door opened, Mimi went in, and then the door closed. The thin guy took a walk down to the water.

I stayed at the top of the wall between the branches of a Douglas fir and I did not move until something touched my leg. Joe Pike was on the ground below me.

'Not now,' he said. 'It's too light, and they're too many. Later. Later, we can get her.'

CHAPTER 34

Riding back toward Blue Jay, Joe Pike said, 'We can wait for dusk, then come in from the water. If we come in behind the boat house, the guards won't be able to see us, then we can move up along the wall to the carriage house.'

I nodded.

'Or we could call the cops.'

I looked at him.

Pike's mouth twitched. 'Just kidding.'

At Blue Jay, we turned east along the southern edge of the lake and drove to Arrowhead Village. The village is a two-tiered shopping and hotel complex on the southeast rim of the lake. On the upper tier there's a Hilton hotel and a Stater Brothers market and a video rental place and a narrow road that brings you down to the lake. On the lakeside level there's a McDonald's and an ice cream shop and an arcade and a couple of million gift shops and clothing stores and real estate offices. There is also a place that will rent you a boat.

Joe parked in a spot by the ice cream shop, and took a canvas Marine Corps duffel bag from the Jeep's cargo space and slung it over his shoulder. Probably packed a big lunch. We walked down past the McDonald's to the lake, stopped by a wharf they have there, and looked out. This close, the lake was huge, all dark flat planes and black deep water. There was a little girl with very curly hair on the wharf, throwing white bread to the ducks. She was maybe eight and pretty and gave me a happy smile when she saw me. I smiled back.

Then I looked across the lake again and the smile faded. There was about an hour of light left. Plenty of time to call the cops. I said, 'If we call the cops, they might blow it. The guys across the lake are pros. They're there to protect Torobuni and those other guys, and they won't hesitate to pull the trigger. I want the girl and I want her safe and if it's me over there I won't be worrying about something else when I should be worrying about her.'

He looked at me through the mirrored lenses with no expression. 'You mean us over there.'

'Yeah.'

The little girl tossed her last piece of bread, then ran back up the wharf into the arms of a tall man with glasses. The tall man scooped her up and heaved her toward the sky. Both of them laughed.

Pike said, 'You're riding the edge on this one.'

I nodded.

'Be careful.'

I nodded again. 'No one has ever been there for her, Joe.'

The little girl and the tall man walked back toward the parking lot. Holding hands.

Pike and I went along the shore past boat slips and a tour boat dock and several small shops to a wooden wharf with a flotilla of little aluminum boats around it. There were kids on the wharf, and moms and dads wondering whether or not it would be safe to rent one of the boats so late in the day. At the end of the wharf there was a wooden shed with a rail-thin old man in it. He needed a shave. We went out on the wharf past the moms and dads and kids and up to the shed. I said, 'We'd like to rent a boat, please.'

'I got'm with six- or nine-pony 'Rudes. Which you want?'

'Nine.'

He turned a clipboard with a rental form toward me. 'Fill that out and gimme a deposit and you're all set.'

He came around with a red plastic gas can and got into one of the boats and filled its tank. 'Watch out for those rat bastard ski boats,' he said. 'Damn rich kids come out here and run wild all over the goddamn lake. Swamp you sure as I shit peanuts.' He was a charming old guy.

'Thanks for the tip,' I said.

He looked at Pike's duffel bag. 'You plannin' on doin' some fishin'?'

Pike nodded.

The old guy shook his head and hawked up something phlegmy and spit it in the water. 'Rich little bastards in their ski boats ruined that. You ain't gonna catch shit.'

'You'd be surprised at what I catch,' Pike said.

The old man squinted at Pike. 'Yeah. I guess I would.'

It took twenty minutes to cross the lake. There was mild chop and wakes from the ski boats but the little Evinrude motor gave us a steady dependable push. Halfway across we could make out the houses that dotted the north shore, and a little past that I turned to a westerly heading, looking for Torobuni's.

Pike took the Colt Python out of the duffel and clipped it over his right hip. He snapped a little leather ammo pouch beside it. The pouch held two six-round cylinder reloads. He went back into the duffel and came out with a sawed-off Remington automatic shotgun and a bandolier of Hi-Power shotgun shells. It was a 12-gauge skeet gun with a cut-down barrel and an extended magazine and a pistol grip for a stock. It looked like an over/under, but the bottom tube was the magazine and had been modified to hold eight rounds. Pike had done the modifications himself. He put the bandolier around his waist, then took out eight shells and fed them into the shotgun. Buckshot.

Torobuni's elaborate dock with its boat house and slips and bright yellow sun awning wasn't hard to spot. The stonework was intricate and beautiful and gave a sense of enduring wealth. It was easy to imagine long-ago times when life resembled an Erté painting and men and women wearing white stood on the dock sipping champagne. I said, 'You see it?'

Pike nodded.

From the water you could see up past the dock and the boat house and along the walks that wound through the trees up to Torobuni's mansion. The carriage house was to the right of the main house and about sixty yards up from the lake. On both sides of the property big walls started at the water. There were two guys sitting under the awning and another guy walking up toward the carriage house. One of the guys under the awning went into the boat house, then came back with a third guy. A man and a woman on jet skis buzzed around the point, looped into the cove, then out again. The woman was maybe twenty-five and had a lean body and the world's smallest bikini. One of the guys under the awning pointed at her and the other two laughed. Nothing like America.

Pike said, 'Property to the right is what I was talking about. We put the boat in there and come around the wall, the guys under the awning won't be able to see us.'

The home next to Torobuni's was a sprawling Cape Cod with a sloping back lawn and a new wooden dock. The trees had mostly been cleared from the east side of its property, but Torobuni's side was still wooded and trees kneed out into the water. A sleek fiberglass ski boat was in one of the house's two slips, tied down and tarped, and the house was shuttered tight. Whoever owned the Cape Cod probably wouldn't be up until the weekend.

We stayed well out in the cove until we were past Torobuni's, then turned in and crept back along the shoreline. The sun was painting the western rim of the mountains and the sky was green and murky and cool. End of the day, and you could smell burning charcoal as people fired their barbeques. We tied up by the ski boat, then crept along the shore to the clump of pines at the end of Torobuni's wall. We stepped into the lake and went around the wall and into the trees, Pike keeping the Remington high and out of the water. There were voices from the far side of the boat house and music from the main house and somewhere someone smoked a cigarette, and men laughed. We waited. The sun sank further and the sound of ski boats was replaced by crickets and pretty soon there were fireflies.

We moved up along the wall to the carriage house and waited some more and pretty soon a short guy with thick shoulders and no hair drifted out of the main house carrying a couple of Coors. He came over to the carriage house, kicked at the door, and said something in Japanese. The door opened and the guy with the cheap mustache stepped out. The mustache took one of the Coors, and the two of them headed down to the lake. Pike and I looked in a side window. One large room with a double bed and two lamps and an old wing-back chair and a half bath and no Mimi. I said, 'Main house.'

We slipped through the shadows to the main house, then along its base to an empty room at the front corner of the house. There were two windows and both windows were dark, though the door across the room was open and showed a dimly lit hall. I cut the bottom of the screen, reached through to unlatch the frame, then pulled myself up and went in.

The room had at one time been a child's bedroom. There were two little beds and a very old chest and a high shelf of toys that hadn't been touched in many years. Other people's toys. Torobuni had probably bought the place furnished and hadn't bothered changing the little bedroom. Maybe he had never been in it. Pike handed up the shotgun, then came in and took the shotgun back.

384

Standing in the dark I could hear voices, but the voices were far away.

We went out the door and along the dim hall, first me, then Pike. The dim hall opened onto a wider hall that ran toward the center of the house. There were a lot of old landscapes on the walls and a double door into what was probably a den or trophy room with antelope heads. Halfway down, a guy was sitting in a brown leather wingback chair, smoking a cigarette, and flipping through a *Life* magazine that had to be thirty years old. I took out the Dan Wesson, held it down at my side and a little bit behind, then stepped into the hall and walked toward him. When he looked up I gave him one of my best smiles. 'Mr. Torobuni said there was a bathroom down here but I can't find it.'

He said something in Japanese, then stood up and I hit him on the left temple with the Dan Wesson. It knocked him sideways into the chair and I caught him on the way down and dragged him back into the shadows. No one shouted and no one fired shots. The voices from the back of the house went on. Pike took him from me and said, 'Go on. I'll catch up.' His glasses shone catlike in the dark.

I said, 'Joe.'

He said, 'I'll catch up.' His voice was quiet, soft in the darkness. 'You want the girl?'

We stood like that, both of us holding the man, and then I nodded and let Pike have him. I went back into the larger hall and followed it past the den and into the entry. When Pike caught up with me, there was a fine spray of blood across his sweatshirt.

The main entry was paneled and wide and open the way they made them in elegant old houses. To our right was the front door, and across from the front door there was a stair going up to the second floor. I said, 'If they want her out of the way she'll be upstairs. Maybe the third floor. Old house, the servants' quarters were up under the roof.'

We went up. There was an ornate landing and a long hall running the width of the house and no one sitting in chairs. At the west end of the hall there was another, narrower stair that went down to the kitchen and up to the third floor. Servant's stair. I said, 'Check the rooms on this floor. I'll go up to three.'

On the third floor, the walls were plain and the carpet was worn and it was still very warm from the summer sun. There was a rectangular landing with a tiny bath and two closed doors. I tried the first door. It was locked. I knocked lightly. 'Mimi?'

Inside, Mimi Warren said, 'Huh?'

I put my shoulder against the door and pushed hard and the old jamb gave. Mimi was sitting cross-legged and naked on a queen-sized bed with satin sheets. There were yellow roses in a vase by the bed. Her hair was brushed and her skin was bright and she was wearing a thin gold chain around her ankle. She didn't look scared and she didn't look crazy. She looked better than I had ever seen her. When she saw me, her whole body gave a jerk and her mouth opened. I touched my finger to my lips and said, 'I'm going to get you out of here.'

She screamed.

I ran to her and put my hand over her mouth and pulled her close to me. She made a sound like *uhn* and flailed and hit and tried to bit and the roses crashed to the floor. There was a tall skinny window in the room, open for air, and down on the terrace there were shouts and the sound of running men and then the heavy undeniable *boom!* of Pike's shotgun.

I let Mimi scream and took her around the waist and carried her down the stairs to the second floor. Pike was at the top of the main stair, firing down toward the front entry. I said, 'Back here. Stairs down to the kitchen.'

He fired off three quick rounds, then fell back, reloading as he came.

The servants' stair was long and steep, and a man with one eye appeared at the bottom when we were halfway down. I shot him once in the head and lifted Mimi over him and then we were off the stairs. We went through the laundry and across the kitchen and through a swinging door into the dining room just as Yuki Torobuni and the midget with stupid eyes and the three guys from Japan came in from the outside. Torobuni and the midget had guns. The guy from Japan with the pony tail had the Hagakure. The midget shouted something and Torobuni raised his gun and I shot him twice in the chest. He fell back into the guy with the ponytail, knocking free the Hagakure. The guy with the ponytail threw himself in front of the two older guys and pushed them outside as the midget jumped forward, firing crazily into the floor and walls. Pike's shot gun *boomed* again and the midget slammed backward into the wall, a crimson halo over what used to be his head.

We were halfway across the dining room when Eddie Tang came in through the French doors. He didn't have a gun. I pointed the Dan Wesson at him anyway. 'Get out of our way.'

That's when the door behind us opened and the guy with the nothing mustache put a High Standard .45 automatic against the back of Joe Pike's head. Eddie liked that a lot. 'Man,' he said, 'what a coupla assholes.'

CHAPTER 35

Outside, cars were starting and there was more shooting and men running and then cars accelerating hard on the gravel drive.

The guy with the mustache took Pike's shotgun and .357 and my Dan Wesson. Eddie held out his hand toward Mimi and said, 'Come on, Me. It's okay.' Me.

He didn't snarl and he didn't sneer and he didn't treat her like a dumb kid he had used to get his way. He took off his jacket and put it around her. 'You okay?'

'It's cold.'

He rubbed her arms, cooing to her. He told her that he loved her, and he told her that they were going to be fine as soon as they got to Japan, and he told her everything was going to be just as he had promised. He said those things, and he meant them. Every word. It was not what I had expected, but then, things rarely were.

I said, 'You didn't kill Ishida to get the book. You killed him because he wanted the book so bad he was going to hurt the girl to get it.' The yakuza hadn't taken Mimi from Asano's. She'd gone with them. Just like she'd gone with Eddie from the hotel.

Mimi said, 'Why can't you leave me alone? Why do you have to keep finding me? We're going to Japan. We're going to be happy.'

Eddie gave Mimi a little squeeze and tipped his head toward the Hagakure. 'Get the book.'

She padded over and picked it up and padded back. The jacket fell off and she was naked again, but she didn't seem to notice.

I said, 'These people killed Asano, Mimi. Doesn't that tell you something?'

Mimi gave me the out-from-under look, and there was something angry in her face. 'He thought he was my father. He thought he could boss me just like my father.' Her eyes went red and strained. 'I don't have a father.'

Eddie said, 'Shh,' the way you calm a nervous dog. He snapped at the Mustache Man, pissed and wanting to know where everyone had gone, and the Mustache Man snapped back.

I said, 'You're right, kid. You don't. He bled to death where you dropped him on Mulholland Drive.'

Mimi's left eye ticked.

Eddie said, 'Shut the hell up.'

There was a heavy thud from the front of the house, and loud voices, then another car roared to life.

I said, 'Hey, Eddie, you love her so much, how'd you help? You turn the crank? You say, "What the hell, off the old bastard?"'

Eddie gave me uncertain eyes and I knew then that it had been Mimi. Just Mimi. Eddie probably hadn't even known. She'd gone off, maybe slipped away from him, just done it, then come back and told him, juiced and a little bit crazy. Blood simple. You could see it in his face. Eddie Tang, yakuza murder freak, even Eddie couldn't imagine killing his own father.

Mimi pulled at him. 'Let's go, Eddie. I wanna go now.'

I said, 'She's sick, Eddie. She needs to go back and work with people who know what they're doing. If she doesn't, she'll never be right.'

Mimi said, 'No.'

I said, 'Leave her. I'll see she gets help.'

Mimi said, '*No.*'

The guy with the nothing mustache shouted something, wanting to finish it and go, but Eddie ignored him. Eddie knew there was something wrong, but he was fighting it. 'She goes back, they'll put her in jail for killing her old man.'

I shook my head. 'They'll put her in a hospital. They'll work with her.'

Outside, men crashed around the side of the house. Eddie barked something else in Japanese to the Mustache Man, then turned back through the French doors and yelled. Just as he did, a fat guy with no hair slammed out of the kitchen, waving a gun and screaming. Mustache Man looked, and when he did, Joe Pike took the High Standard out of his hand and shot the fat guy. I hit Mustache Man in the face with a roundhouse kick, and he went down, and then Eddie Tang was back in the house. It had taken maybe a third of a second.

I said, 'That's it, Eddie.' I picked up the Dan Wesson, then edged

389

forward and pulled the girl toward me. She tried to jerk away, but she didn't try very hard. Maybe she was tired.

Eddie's face was dark. 'Don't touch her, dude.'

I pointed the gun at him. 'Get out of the way.'

Eddie put himself in the center of the door and shook his head. 'You want the Hagakure, take it, but Mimi stays with me.'

I looked at Pike. His glasses caught the light and showered it around the room.

'Make your brain work and think about this, Eddie. I'm going to see that she gets help. I'm going to see that she's made right.'

Eddie Tang shook his head. 'No.' He took a step toward us. Me with the Dan Wesson, and Pike with the High Standard, and he took a step toward us.

I aimed the Dan Wesson at his forehead. 'Eddie. Get real.'

Eddie's shirt was wet and sticking to his skin. He yanked off the tie, and most of the shirt came with it. The tattoos writhed and glistened like living things. They crawled up his biceps, over his shoulders, and down across his chest and abdomen. Dragons roared and tigers leaped and samurai warriors locked swords in combat. Red, white, green, yellow, blue. Brilliant primary colors that made him look feral and monstrous and of the earth. He went down low and stared at us.

Pike's mouth twitched.

I said, 'Joe. Not you, too?'

Joe Pike raised the High Standard level with Eddie's heart. 'Your call.'

Some days. I pushed Mimi to the side and put down the Dan Wesson and Pike dropped the High Standard and Eddie Tang launched two spin kicks so quickly that they were impossible to see. Mimi screamed. Pike rolled under the first kick and I pushed myself sideways and hit Eddie's back. Pike came up and snapped a roundhouse kick to the side of Eddie's head and punched him in the back of the neck and the kidneys. Eddie's body tightened like a single flexed muscle and he shook it off. I'd seen Pike crack boards with that kick.

Mimi screamed again and ran forward, scratching and hitting, and Pike pushed her down hard. She stayed there, holding the crumbling Hagakure to her breasts and watching with wide eyes.

We kept Eddie between us, moving on our toes and staying out of reach. Eddie was big and strong and knew the moves from a thousand tournaments, but tournaments weren't real. Real is different. If it wasn't, maybe we'd be dead.

Outside, there were no more shots and no more cars racing away. Voices came through the house and then faded and there was nothing. Maybe everyone was gone and we were all that was left, men alone in a dark wood, fighting.

We moved so that Eddie could never long face either of us. If he turned toward one, the other had his back. Pike would strike, and then me, and both of us worked to stay away from his hands and feet. He was faster than a big man was supposed to be, but having to work against two of us took away his timing. He couldn't get off the way you can get off one-on-one, and after a while he began to slow. We hit the big muscles in his back and his thighs and his shoulders, and he slowed still more. The certainty that had been in his eyes began to fade. It made me think of King Kong, fighting the little men for the woman he loved.

Far away, maybe on the other side of the lake, there were sirens. Something flickered on Eddie's face when he heard them, and he glanced at the girl. When the cops got here, she would go back, and he would go back, but they wouldn't go back together. He made a deep grunt and he tried to end it. He turned his back to Joe Pike and came at me. I backpedaled and Pike came in fast. Eddie ran me back against the doorjamb. He snapped a fist out and the fist hit the jamb and shattered wood and plaster. I rammed the heel of my hand up into the base of his nose and something cracked and blood spurted out and he grabbed me. Pike wrapped his hands around Eddie's face and dug his fingers into his eyes and pulled. Eddie let go and jerked an elbow back and you could hear Pike's ribs snap. I hit Eddie with two quick punches to the ear and followed them with another roundhouse kick that again snapped his head to the side. He staggered, but stayed up, and I said, 'Shit.'

The sirens howled closer and closer until the sound seemed to come from every direction, and then they were at the front of the house. Eddie was in the middle of the room, sucking air, with Pike and me on either side. Back where we started. Only now there was sweat and blood and cops at the door. Eddie looked from me to Pike to the girl, then lowered his hands and stood up out of his crouch as if someone had called time out. The girl said, 'Eddie?'

He shook his head. There were tears coming down his face, working into the blood. He had given it his best, but it hadn't been enough.

I said, 'It's over, Eddie.'

Eddie looked at me. 'Not yet.' When he said it, he looked old.

Eddie Tang stepped over the fat guy and pulled Joe's shotgun from beneath the Mustache Man. He looked at it and then he looked at Joe Pike. There were more voices outside and somebody yelled for somebody else to watch himself. Mimi said, 'Shoot them, Eddie. Shoot them *now*.'

Eddie said, 'I love her, man.' Then he tossed the gun to Joe, bared his teeth like something crazed and primal, and charged straight ahead with a series of power kicks that could knock down a wall. Joe Pike fired four rounds so quickly they might have been one. The 12-gauge blasts in the small room made my ears ring and the buckshot load carried Eddie Tang backward through the French doors and out into the night. The four spent shells bounced off the ceiling and hit the floor and spun like little tops, and outside a cop voice shouted, 'Holy shit!'

When the shell casings stopped spinning there was silence.

For the longest time, Mimi Warren did not move, then she looked at me and said, 'I don't feel anything.'

I said, 'Kid, you've had so much done to you that the part that feels went dead a long time ago.' Maybe Carol Hillegas could fix it.

Mimi cocked her head the way a bird will, as if I'd said something curious, and smiled. 'Is that what you think?'

I didn't move.

She said, 'I'm such a liar. I make up stuff all the time.'

I went to her, then, and put my arms around her, and she started to scream, flailing and thrashing and trying to get to Eddie, or maybe just trying to get away from me. I held on tight, and said, 'It's all right. It's going to be all right.'

I said it softly, and many times, but I don't think she heard me.

CHAPTER 36

The mountain cops were pretty good about it. The sheriff was a guy in his forties who had put in some time with the Staties and knew he was in over his head when he saw the mess. His partner was a jumpy kid maybe twenty-one, twenty-two, and after enough gun-waving the sheriff told him to put it away and go get an extra pair of cuffs out of the cruiser.

They found some clothes for Mimi, then cuffed us and drove us down to the State Police substation in Crestline, about a thousand feet lower on the mountain. The Crestline doc got pulled out of bed to check us over and tape Pike's ribs. Mostly, he looked at Mimi and shook his head.

When the doctor was finished, a state cop named Clemmons took Pike's statement first, and then mine, all the while sucking on Pall Mall cigarettes and saying, 'Then what?' as if he'd heard it a million times.

After I had gone through it, Clemmons sucked a double lungful of Pall Mall and blew it at me. 'You knew the girl was in there, how come you didn't just call us?'

'Phone line was busy,' I said.

He sucked more Pall Mall and blew that at me, too.

The jail was a very small building with two tiny holding cells, one for men and one for women, and from Clemmons's desk I watched Mimi. She sat and she stared and I wondered if she'd do that the rest of her life.

Clemmons called L.A. and got Charlie Griggs pulling a late tour. They stayed on the phone about twenty minutes, Clemmons giving Griggs a lot of detail. One of the Staties brought in the Hagakure and Clemmons waved him to put it on a stack of *Field & Stream* in the corner. Evidence. When Clemmons hung up he came over and took the cuffs off me and then went to the holding cell and did the

393

same for Pike. 'You guys sit tight for a while and have some coffee. We got some people coming up.'

'What about the girl?' I said. Clemmons hadn't taken the cuffs off her.

'Let's just let her sit.' He went back to his desk and got on the phone and called the San Bernardino County coroner.

I went over to the coffee urn and poured two cups and brought them to Mimi's cell. I said, 'How about it?' I held out the cup but she did not look at me nor in any way respond, so I put it on the crossbar and stood there until long after the coffee was cold.

More Staties came and a couple of Feds from the San Bernardino office and they gave back our guns and let us go at a quarter after two that morning. I said, 'What about the girl?'

Clemmons said, 'A couple of our people are going to drive her back to L.A. in the morning. She's going to be arraigned for the murder of her father.'

'Maybe I should stay,' I said.

'Bubba,' Clemmons said, 'that ain't one of the options. Get your ass outta here.'

A young kid with a double-starched uniform and a baleful stare drove us back up to Arrowhead Village and dropped us off by Pike's Jeep. It was cool in the high mountain air, and quiet, and very very dark, the way no city can ever know dark.

The McDonald's was lit from inside, but that was the only light in the village, and the Jeep was the only car in the parking lot. We stood beside it for a while, breathing the good air. Pike took off his glasses and looked up. It was too dark to see his eyes. 'Milky Way,' he said. 'Can't see it from L.A.'

There were crickets from the edge of the forest and sounds from the lake lapping at the boat slips.

Pike said, 'What's wrong?'

'It wasn't the way I thought it was. Eddie loved her.'

'Uh-huh.'

'She wanted to stay with him. She hadn't been kidnapped. She wasn't going to be killed.'

He nodded.

Something splashed near the shore. I took a deep slow breath and felt empty. 'I assumed a lot of things that were wrong. I needed her to be a victim, so that's the way I saw her.' I looked at Joe. 'Maybe she wasn't.' *I'm such a liar.*

Pike slipped on the glasses. 'Bradley.'

394

My throat was tight and raw and the empty place burned. 'She made up so damn much. Maybe she made that part up, too. Maybe he never touched her. I needed a reason for it all, and she gave me that. Maybe I helped her kill him.'

Joe Pike thought about that for a long time. Centuries. Then he said, 'Someone had to bring her back.'

'Sure.'

'Whatever she did, she did because she's sick. That hasn't changed. She needs help.'

I nodded. 'Joe. Once you had the gun you could have wounded him.'

'No.'

'Why not?'

He didn't move for a time, as if the answer required a complete deliberation, then he went to the Jeep. When he came back he had the translation of the Hagakure. He held it respectfully. 'This isn't just a book, Elvis. It's a way of life.'

Tashiro had said that.

Pike said, 'Eddie Tang was yakuza, but he killed Ishida for the girl. He committed himself to getting her to Japan, but we stopped him. He loved her, yet he was going to lose her. He had failed the yakuza and he had failed the girl and he had failed himself. He had nothing left.'

I remembered the way Eddie Tang had looked at Joe Pike, Pike, and not me. 'The way of the warrior is death.'

A cool breeze came in off the lake. Something moved in the water and a light plane appeared in the sky past the McDonald's roofline, its red anti-collision light flashing. Pike put his hand on my shoulder and squeezed. 'You got her,' he said. 'You got her safe. Don't think about anything else.'

We climbed into the Jeep and took the long drive back to Los Angeles.

CHAPTER 37

I spent most of the next day on the phone. I called Lou Poitras and found out that they would be holding Mimi at the L.A. County Correctional Medical Facility for an evaluation. I called Carol Hillegas and asked her to pay Mimi a visit and make sure Mimi had good people assigned to her. The black Fed Reese called me more than once, and so did the woman from the L.A. County district attorney's office. There'd been a lot of conference calling between L.A. and San Bernardino and Sacramento, but nobody was going to bring charges. Nobody was sure what the charges would be. Illegal rescue?

Terry Ito stopped by that evening and said he hoped he wasn't disturbing me. I said no and asked him in. He stood in my living room with a brown paper bag in his left hand and said, 'Is the kid going to be okay?'

I said, 'Maybe.'

He nodded. 'We heard somebody nailed Yuki Torobuni.'

'Yeah. That happened.'

He nodded again and put out his right hand. 'Thanks.'

We shook.

He opened the bag and took out a bottle of Glenlivet scotch and we drank some and then he left. By eight o'clock that night I had finished the bottle and fallen asleep on the couch. A couple of hours later I was awake again and sleep would not return.

The next day I watched TV and read and lay on the couch and stared at my high-vaulted ceiling. Just after noon I showered and shaved and dressed and took a drive over to the County Medical Facility and asked them if I could see Mimi. They said no. I left the front and went around back and tried to sneak in, but a seventy-five-year-old security guard with narrow shoulders and a wide butt caught me and raised hell. It goes like that sometimes.

I bought groceries and a couple of new books and went home to the couch and the staring and the feeling that it was not over. I thought about Traci Louise Fishman and I thought about what Mimi had said. *I make up stuff all the time.* Maybe it couldn't be over until I knew what was real and what wasn't. Some hero. I had brought Mimi back, but I hadn't saved her.

At a little after four that afternoon, the doorbell rang again, and this time it was Jillian Becker. She was wearing a loose Hawaiian top and tight Guess jeans and pink Reebok high-tops. She smelled of mint. It was the first time I had seen her in casual clothes. I stood in the door and stared at her, and she stared back. I said, 'Would you like to come in?'

'If you don't mind.'

I said not at all. I asked if she would like something to drink. She said some wine would be nice. I went into the kitchen and poured her a glass of wine and a glass of water for myself. She said, 'I tried your office but I guess you haven't been in.'

'Nope.'

'Or checking your answering machine.'

'Nope.'

She sipped her wine. 'You look tired.'

'Uh-huh.'

She sipped the wine again. 'The police spoke with me, and so did Carol Hillegas. They told me what you had to do to get Mimi. It must have been awful.'

I said, 'How's Sheila?'

Shrug. 'Her family has come here to be with her. I've been talking to her, and so have the doctors who've seen Mimi. She's going to join Mimi in therapy. She'll probably enter into therapy on her own, too.'

'Have you seen Mimi?'

She shook her head. 'No. I heard you tried.'

I spread my hands.

Jillian put her wineglass down and said, 'Is it always this hard?'

I stared out through the glass to the canyon and shook my head.

Jillian Becker sat quietly for a moment, swirling her wine and watching it move in the glass. Then she said, 'Carol Hillegas agreed with me.'

'What?'

'If the one who makes the pain stop is the one who loves them, then that's you.'

I finished the water and put down the glass and looked out at the canyon some more. The cat door clacked and the cat came in from the kitchen. When he saw Jillian he growled, deep and warlike. I said, 'Beat it.'

The cat sprinted back into the kitchen and through his door. Jillian said, 'What a nice cat.'

I laughed then, and Jillian Becker laughed, too. She had a good, clear laugh. When the laughter faded, she looked at me. 'I wanted to tell you that I'm leaving Los Angeles. There is no more Warren Investments. Even if there were, I would leave. I'm going to find a position back east.'

Part of me felt small, and growing smaller.

'But I'm going to stay here in L.A. for another couple of weeks before I go. I wanted to tell you that, too.'

'Why are you going to hang around?'

She looked at me steadily. 'I thought I might spend some time with you.'

We sat like that, me on the couch and Jillian on the chair, and then she put out her hand. I took it.

Outside, a red hawk floated high over the canyon, and was warm in the sun.

Lullaby Town

AN ELVIS COLE NOVEL

Dedicated with love and respect to
my mother, Evelyn Carrie Crais,
who saved me from the monsters.

There's a quaint little place they call Lullaby Town –
It's just back of those hills where the sunsets go down.
Its streets are of silver, its buildings of gold,
And its palaces dazzling things to behold.

There's a peddler who carries, strapped high on his back,
A bundle. Now, guess what he has in that pack.
No, he's not peddling jams nor delectable creams.
Would you know what he's selling? Just wonderful
dreams!

– from *Lullaby Town**
by John Irving Diller

Welcome back, my friends, to the show that never ends.
We're so glad you could attend.
Come inside! Come inside!

– Emerson, Lake, & Palmer

* published in *The Best Loved Poems of the American
People* selected by Hazel Felleman, Doubleday and Company, 1936, p. 399.

CHAPTER I

Patricia Kyle said, 'Is this Elvis Cole, the world's greatest detective?'

'Yes, it is.' I was lying on the leather couch across from my desk, enjoying the view that I have of the Channel Islands. I used to have chairs, but a couch is much better to relieve one of the rigors of world-class detecting.

She said, 'Were you sleeping?'

I gave her miffed. 'I never sleep. I'm waiting for Cindy to come out onto the balcony next door.' The glass doors leading out to my little balcony were open to catch the breeze that was blowing up Santa Monica Boulevard into West Los Angeles. It was a nice breeze, cool and smelling of salt and sea birds. The open doors were also better to let me hear Cindy.

'Who's Cindy?'

I switched the phone from the left ear to the right. The left ear was still sore from having been hit hard two times by a Cajun with large forearms and no teeth. 'Cindy is a beauty supply distributor who took the office space next door.'

Pat Kyle said, 'Hmm. I'll bet I know what she distributes.'

'Your callousness and insensitivity are unbecoming. She is a very nice woman with a ready laugh.'

'Unh-hunh. I know what's ready.'

'The private-detecting life is a lonely one. After cleaning the guns and oiling the blackjack, what's a guy to do?'

'You could have lunch with me at Lucy's El Adobe Café across from Paramount.'

I said, 'Cindy who?'

Pat Kyle laughed. It was clear and without apology, the way a laugh should be. Pat Kyle is forty-four years old and five feet four, with curly auburn hair and good bones and an athlete's build. When we met six years ago, she looked like the Graf Zeppelin and was having trouble getting out of a bad marriage. I helped. Now she ran four fast miles every day, had her own casting agency, and was engaged to a dentist from Pasadena. Maybe one day I'd learn to like him. She said, 'I'm casting a film for Kapstone Pictures and a director named Peter Alan Nelsen. Do you know who he is?'

'He makes action pictures.'

'That's right. With great success. *Time* magazine called him the King of Adventure.'

'They called him a few other things, too.' Arrogant, demanding, brilliant. I had read the article.

'Yes. There is that.' You could hear something behind her. Voices, maybe. 'Peter has a problem and I mentioned your name. The Kapstone people want to talk with you.'

'Okay.' I swung up into a sitting position and put my feet on the floor. The detective, ready for action.

'When Peter was in film school, he broke up with his wife just after they had their only child. A boy. Peter hasn't seen or heard from his former wife or their son since, and he wants to find them. I told him that finding people is one of your best things. Are you interested?'

'It's what I do.'

'Kapstone has offices at Paramount. I'll leave a pass at the main gate for you to see Donnie Brewster. Donnie's the head of production.' Donnie. A twelve-year-old running a film company. 'Can you be here in about twenty minutes?'

'Let me check my calendar.'

She said, 'Ha. What calendar?'

'Callous. You dames are callous.'

She made the nice laugh again and hung up.

I pushed up off the couch and thought about Kapstone Pictures and Peter Alan Nelsen. The Big Time. I was wearing a white Mickey Mouse sweatshirt with a mustard spot high on the right shoulder. Mickey would be okay, but the mustard spot was definitely unacceptable. Did I have time to race home for the tux? I looked at the Pinocchio clock. Unh-unh. I took off the Mickey and put on a yellow-and-white Hawaiian beachcomber's shirt, a Dan Wesson .38 caliber revolver, and a light blue waiter's jacket. Dress for success. I began to hum. *There's no business like show business.* I turned on the answering machine and listened to the same message I'd been running for two months. *'Elvis Cole*

Detective Agency, we're cheap.' Maybe it was time for a change. You work for a major film company, you need something a bit more show business. *Elvis Cole Detective Agency: There are no small cases, only small detectives – hire the biggest dick in the business!* I decided to leave well enough alone.

I walked the four flights down to the parking garage, got my car, and drove east along Santa Monica Boulevard through the belly of Hollywood. It was October, and the air was cool. I've got a 1966 Corvette convertible, but it wasn't so cool that I had to put up the top. It rarely was. Global warming. With the end of summer, the cars from Utah and Michigan and Delaware were gone, but the cars from Canada were arriving. Snowbirds, come down to beat the cold. At a red light on Santa Monica and La Brea I pulled up next to a maroon Buick sedan from Alberta with a very short man and a very short woman in the front seat and two very short children in the rear. The man was driving and looked confused. I gave them a big smile and a wave and said, 'Welcome to Los Angeles.' The woman rolled up her window and locked the door.

I stayed on Santa Monica to Gower, then turned right and followed Gower down past the Hollywood Cemetery to Paramount.

Paramount Studios is an Olympian structure on the corner of Melrose and Gower with a beige stucco siege wall running around its perimeter. The wall is very high, with a heaviness and permanence that has kept Paramount in business long after most of the other original Hollywood studios have gone. In a neighborhood marked by poverty and litter and street crime, it is free from graffiti. Maybe if you got too near the wall, thugs in chain mail poured boiling oil on you from the parapets.

I rounded the corner at Melrose and tooled up to the guard at Paramount's front gate. 'Elvis Cole to see Donnie Brewster.'

The guard looked in a little file. 'You the singer?'

I shook my head. 'Elvis Presley died in 1978.'

The guard found a yellow slip, stuck it to my window with a piece of tape. 'Not the King. That other guy. With the glasses.'

'Elvis Costello. No. I'm not him, either.'

The guard shook his head sadly. 'Christ, I remember a time, you said "Elvis" there was only one.'

Probably just promoted from parapet duty.

Donnie Brewster was in a two-story earth-colored adobe building with a red tile roof and bird of paradise plants the size of dinosaurs. A receptionist led me to a secretary who showed me into a dark-paneled conference room. In the conference room were Patricia Kyle and a man in his late thirties with a sharply receding hairline and an eight-hundred-dollar sports coat that fit him like a wet tent. What hair he had left was pulled back tight into a short ponytail. Style.

Pat Kyle stood up and smiled and gave me a kiss. She'd been working on her tan since I'd last seen her and it looked good. 'Elvis Cole, this is Donnie Brewster. Donnie, Elvis Cole.'

Donnie Brewster gave me a moist hand and looked nervous. 'Christ, where were you? I thought you'd never get here.'

'The pleasure is all mine.'

Donnie gave me everyone's-out-to-get-me eyes and glanced at Pat Kyle. 'She warned me you thought you were a riot. What you've gotta understand is that this isn't funny.' He held up three fingers. 'There's Spielberg, then Lucas, who doesn't direct anymore, then Peter Alan Nelsen. Peter's grosses total one point two *billion* worldwide over six pictures. He's the third most successful director in the history of film, and he knows it.'

'Hard to keep it a secret from him.'

Donnie rubbed his hand over his scalp and tugged at his ponytail. When he rubbed, he rubbed hard. Maybe that's why his hairline was receding. He said, 'Peter's gifted and brilliant. Gifted and brilliant people are sometimes difficult and have to be handled carefully.' I think he was saying it as much to himself as he was to me. He looked at Pat Kyle. 'Did you tell him what this is about?'

'Yes.' Pat repeated what she had told me.

Donnie nodded and looked back at me. 'That's about it. We need someone who can find the ex and the kid and not waste a lot of time doing it.'

'Okay.'

He sat in one of the swivel chairs, leaned back, and gave me the appraisal look. Getting down to the business of hiring a private eye. 'You charge by the hour or the day?'

'I get a flat fee. In advance.'

'How much?'

'Four thousand, plus expenses. The expenses I bill later.'

'That's absurd. We couldn't pay four thousand in advance.'

'How about six thousand?'

He tapped on the table and gave me his best business-affairs frown. 'You give it back if you don't find what you're looking for?'

'No.'

More tapping. Convincing himself. 'I had our lawyers call around. They spoke to a guy in the D.A.'s office and a policeman named Ito. They say you're pretty good at this sort of thing. How many cases like this have you handled?'

'Maybe three hundred.'

'Unh-hunh. And how many times out of that three hundred did you find the person you were looking for?'

'Maybe two ninety-eight.'

Donnie raised his eyebrows and looked impressed. Maybe he was feeling better about the four grand. 'Okay. We get you going on this, how long is it going to take to find them?'

'I don't know.'

'Well, can't you give me some sort of ballpark?'

I spread my hands. 'If she's living in Encino and telling her friends that she used to be married to Peter Alan Nelsen, maybe I find her tomorrow. If she's changed her name five times and working as a missionary in the Amazon, it takes longer.'

'Jesus Christ.'

I made a little shrug and smiled. Mr. Confident & Assured. 'It's rarely that bad. People usually don't change their names five times and move to the Amazon. People use credit cards, and credit histories list prior residences, and people own cars and driver's licenses and social security numbers, and any of these things are ideal for tracing someone.'

He didn't seem bolstered by my assuredness. He rubbed at his hair again and got up and paced. 'Peter is three weeks away from making a film, and he has to start this crap about finding his family. Christ, he hasn't seen the woman in over ten years. You'd think he could wait until the picture was finished.'

'Insensitive of him.'

Donnie crossed his arms and kept pacing. 'Hey, I know what that sounds like, but you've got to understand. We've got forty million dollars committed to Peter's film. I've already spent eighteen mil. I've got sets and soundstage rent. I've got stars with play-or-pay deals and a crew I'll have to carry. If Peter is distracted, we could run over budget into the tens of millions. We could end up with another *Heaven's Gate*. I could lose my ass.'

Maybe I'd be nervous, too. 'Okay. Then maybe it makes sense to wait until the picture is finished before we get started. The ex-wife will still be wherever she is. I'll still be around. Call me then.'

Donnie rolled his eyes and stopped the pacing and dropped into another chair. 'Did you see *Chainsaw*?'

'Yes.'

'*Chainsaw* was Peter's first picture. He made it for something like four hundred thousand. It grossed four hundred *million* and overnight Peter Alan Nelsen went from parking cars to being Hollywood's new wunderkind. Every picture he's made has grossed a fortune. Every studio in town wants Peter Alan Nelsen's next picture. The biggest actors in the business suck around him for a role and Oscar-winning screenwriters pimp their mothers for a shot at a development deal. You hear what I'm saying?'

'You're saying that Peter gets what Peter wants.'

'Abso-fucking-lutely. Peter being happy is the most important thing there is. Peter wants to find these people, and we want Peter happy, so we're gonna hire somebody.'

I said, 'Make Peter happy.'

'Abso-fucking-lutely.' Donnie slapped his palms down on the table and stood. 'I like you. I like you fine. Peter knows about you, and wants to meet you, so all we have to do now is go over and see him. If Peter's happy, you're hired.'

'Making Peter happy is the most important thing.'

'Right.' Donnie Brewster lowered his voice, like maybe someone else might hear, and leaned toward me. Conspiratorial. 'Tell you the truth, I don't give a rat's ass if you find his ex or not. But if it makes Peter happy to have someone looking, then we'll have someone looking.'

Mr. Sincerity.

He made a little let's-go gesture and started for the door. 'We'll go over to meet him now. Whatever Peter says, just nod and say sure. Whatever he wants, say no problem. He asks how long, say a couple of weeks, max.'

'Make Peter happy.'

'Yeah. Peter being happy is all that matters.'

I looked at Pat Kyle, and then I looked back at Donnie Brewster and shook my head. 'You're asking me to lie to a client. I won't do that. You're also asking me to mislead him. I won't do that, either.'

Donnie stopped with his hand on the knob and looked horrified. 'Hey. Hey, I'm not asking you to do any of that. I love Peter Alan Nelsen like a brother.' He made a nervous glance out the door. Never know who might be listening. 'I'm just saying agree with the guy, that's all, and we'll work out reality later.'

'No.'

'No? What does that mean, no?' He ran back into the room and spread his hands. 'You can't say no to Peter Alan Nelsen!'

'I'm not saying no to Peter Alan Nelsen. I'm saying no to you.'

Confused. 'Hey, you want Peter happy, don't you? Peter's not happy, you won't get hired. You know what a job like this could mean?'

'Ulcers?'

Donnie spread his hands even wider and gave incredulous, like how could I miss it? 'You work for Peter Alan Nelsen, you get on the A list. You get on the A list, you'll be working for the biggest names in the business. You might even get written up in *People* magazine.'

I said, 'Wow.'

Donnie raised his hands to the ceiling and looked at Pat Kyle. Her face was red and she was making a choking sound. He said, 'What kind of guy is this? What kind of guy did you bring me?'

She turned up her palms. 'Someone with principles?'

Donnie began rubbing at his head again and tugging at his ponytail. He rubbed so hard that I thought I saw hair fall, but that might've been my imagination. He said, 'This isn't going to work. Peter isn't going to go for this.'

Pat said, 'Peter and I spoke about Elvis at length. He sounded agreeable to me.'

Donnie gestured at me. 'But this guy's saying he won't play along. You know how Peter is. He can be a monster.' He made the nervous glance again, checking the door and the windows for ears. 'Hey, I love him like a brother.'

Pat said, 'He's expecting us in five minutes.'

Donnie said, 'Holy shit.' I think he was starting to hyperventilate.

I said, 'Donnie. Relax. Breathe into a bag.'

Donnie said, '*You* relax. I got forty million bucks riding on Peter Alan Nelsen and you won't play along. This is Hollywood. Everybody plays along!'

I made a gun out of my hand and shot him.

Donnie slumped into his chair and looked depressed. 'Yeah, yeah, that's just what'll happen, too. In the back.'

Pat said, 'Donnie, Elvis is a professional and he gets results. He has done this before.'

'But not with Peter Alan Nelsen!'

'I told him what Peter is like, and I told Peter what Elvis is like. Peter knows what to expect.'

'Oh, Jesus. Oh, Jesus.'

I said, 'Donnie. Why don't we go see Peter and get it over with? I'm good. I might even find his kid. Think how happy he'll be then.'

Donnie squinted and thought about it. You could see gears moving and lights flashing behind his eyes. 'Yeah, yeah, that's right.'

'Tell him I'm brilliant and gifted. Everybody knows that brilliant and gifted people are difficult.'

Donnie's eyes got big and he slapped his hands on the table again as if he'd just found the Rosetta stone. 'Yeah, yeah. That's it! Brilliant and gifted are difficult.' He jumped up and charged toward the door. 'Let's go see him and get it over with.'

We went to see the monster.

CHAPTER 2

The monster had both floors of a two-story tropical-style plantation house hidden behind a stand of banana and rubber trees at the back of the studio. It had once been a bungalow like any other bungalow, but now it wasn't. Now, there was a veranda across the front and wide-slat Panamanian shutters and a lot of rough-hewn poles lashed together with coarse shipping rope to make you think you were on a tropical island someplace. Sort of like the Swiss Family Robinson's tree house. The roof was thatched with what looked like palm fronds, and running water trickled along a false stream, and a black skull-&-crossbones flag hung from a little pole. I said, 'Do we have to give him an E ticket before he lets us in?'

Donnie Brewster made the nervous frown. 'Stop with the humor, okay? I tell him you're brilliant and gifted, you make with the humor, he's gonna know that you're not.'

Some guys.

Inside, the floors were crude planking and the ceilings were done to match the roof, and Cairo fans hung down and slowly swirled the air. We went down a hall and into a room with two large couches and a little round glass table and posters of the six movies that Peter Alan Nelsen had made. The couches were covered in zebra skin and the posters were framed in what looked like rhino hide and a small, immaculate black man sat at a teak desk. Behind the man was a teak door. Behind the door, someone was yelling. Donnie Brewster rubbed at his scalp again and said, 'Holy Christ, now what?'

The black man nodded brightly when he saw us. Maybe he couldn't hear the yelling. 'Hello, Mr. Brewster. Ms. Kyle. Peter said to go right in when you got here.'

We went right in.

Peter Alan Nelsen's office was as long as a bowling alley and as wide as a check-kiter's smile and done up like the lobby of a Nairobi movie house. Posters from *The Wild Bunch* and *The Asphalt Jungle* and *The Magnificent Seven* hung along one wall and an old Webcor candy machine from the forties sat against the opposite wall between a Wurlitzer Model 800 Bubble-Lite jukebox and a video game called *Kill or Be Killed!* The Webcor featured M&M peanuts and Jujubes and Raisinets and PayDay candy bars. *Nothing beats a PayDay!* A blond woman with a neck like corded rosewood and shoulders like Alex Karras sat side-saddle on a sky-blue Harley-Davidson Electra-glide motorcycle parked at the far end of the office. She was wearing black spandex biking pants with a Day-Glo green stripe down the leg and a matching black halter sports top and pale gray Reebok workout shoes. Her thighs were massive and her calves thick and diamond-shaped and her belly looked like cut stonework. She glanced our way, then slid off the Harley and went to sit by a couple of guys who might've been reserve corners for the Dallas Cowboys. They were slouching on another one of the zebra couches, one of them wearing a Stunts Unlimited T-shirt and the other fatigue pants and eelskin cowboy boots. They glanced our way, too, and then they went back to watching Peter Alan Nelsen.

Peter Alan Nelsen was standing on top of a marble-slab desk, waving his arms and screaming so hard that his face was red. He was maybe six foot two, but skinny, with more butt than shoulders and the kind of soft, gawky frame that probably meant he had been a stiff-legged, awkward child. He had a rectangular Fred MacMurray face to go with the body, and he wore black leather pants with a silver concho belt and a blue denim work shirt with the cuffs rolled over his forearms. The forearms were thin. It was a style and a look that had faded away in the midseventies, but if you were the King of Adventure, I guess you could dress any way you wanted. The King yelled, 'Stop the tape! I don't want to see this crap! Jesus H. Christ, are you people out of your minds?!'

Peter Alan Nelsen was yelling at a neatly dressed woman and a man with a face like a rabbit's who were standing near a 30-inch Mitsubishi television. The man was scrabbling at a videotape machine, trying to eject a cassette, but his fingers weren't doing a good job and the woman had to help him.

Donnie ran forward, rubbing at his hair. 'Peter, Peter, what's going on? Hey, there's a problem here, that's what I'm for!'

The woman at the big Mitsubishi said, 'We showed him a tape of

414

work by the new production designer. He liked it fine until I told him that the designer had worked in television.'

Peter made a loud, moaning sound, then jumped off the desk, raced forward, grabbed the tape from the rabbit-faced man, and threw it out the window. When Peter rushed toward them, the man jerked back but the woman didn't. Peter yelled, 'His quality is all wrong! Don't you people understand texture? Don't you understand image density? Tee-vee is *small*. Movies are *large*. I make *movies*, not *television*!'

Donnie spread his hands, like how could they do this. 'Jesus, Peter, I'm sorry. I can't believe they'd waste your time with a TV guy. What can I do to make it right?' I think he was trying to show me how to make Peter happy.

Peter screamed, 'You can kiss my ass on Hollywood Boulevard, you wanna make it right!' Peter didn't look any happier to me, but Donnie was the expert.

The neatly dressed woman said, 'You're out of your fucking mind.' Then she turned and stalked out, dragging the rabbit-faced man with her. When they passed, I hummed a little bit of 'There's No Business Like Show Business.' Pat Kyle gave me an elbow.

Donnie gave the big smile, telling everybody that he and his old pal Peter were in solid on this one. 'No, hey, Pete-man, I mean it.' Pete-man. 'You want a new production designer, you got one. I mean, we're making *film* here, am I right?'

Peter Alan Nelsen screamed, 'Shit!' as loud as he could, stalked back to the Harley-Davidson, and kicked it over. Hard. There were gouges in the floor where it had fallen before. The blond woman waited until Peter was through, then went over and righted it, her cut muscles straining against the weight. Peter paid no attention. He stood in the center of the floor, breathing hard, hands down at his sides like there was a terrible anger bubbling within him that he didn't know if he could control, but he would give it a game try. Drama. I said, 'I'm Elvis Cole. Is there a problem you want to discuss with me, or should I leave now during the intermission?'

Donnie Brewster said, 'Oh, shit,' and made more of the how-to-keep-Peter-happy hand moves. 'Hey, what a kidder, huh, Pete-man? This guy is the private cop we were talking about. He's –'

Peter said, 'I heard him,' and came toward me. He put out his hand and we shook. He squeezed harder than he had to and stood closer than you stand to someone you don't know. 'I'm sorry you had to see this,' he said. 'These guys give me the weight of making a major motion picture, then do everything they can to screw me up. It gets a little crazy.'

'Sure.'

He jerked his head toward the woman. 'That's Dani.' He gestured toward the two guys. 'That's Nick and that's T.J. They work for me.' Nick was the guy in the Stunts Unlimited T-shirt. T.J. had the eelskin boots. Each of them outweighed him by maybe sixty pounds.

Peter said, 'You see my movies?'

'I saw *Chainsaw* and *Hard Point*.'

'What did you think?'

'Pretty good. *Chainsaw* reminded me of *The Searchers*.'

He smiled a little bit at that and nodded. 'I was a twenty-six-year-old film-school flunk-out when I made *Chainsaw*. I didn't know my ass from a hole in the ground and I ripped off *The Searchers* every way I could.'

Donnie looked up from where he had gone to a phone. 'We were talking about *Chainsaw* before we came over. A dynamite film. Just dynamite. Tremendous gross.'

Peter went to the candy machine, slammed it with the heel of his hand, pulled a lever, and got a bag of M&M peanuts without putting in money. He tore open the bag with his teeth, dropped the paper on the floor, and poured half the bag of candy into his mouth. He didn't offer to share. Dani drifted over and picked up the paper.

Peter went to the big marble desk and sat on it, cross-legged. 'You look about my age. How old are you?'

'Thirty-eight.'

'I'm thirty-nine. We talked to some cop who said you were in the Nam. That true?' He leaned forward and said *the Nam* like they do on television, full of excitement and appeal and unreality. The way Bart Simpson would say it.

'Unh-hunh.'

He slurped up more of the M&Ms. 'The cop said you racked ass over there and got a fistful of medals.'

'What do cops know?'

'I tried to join up, but they wouldn't take me. I got this bone thing in my hips.' He was looking at a poster of John Wayne in *Blood Alley*. It showed the Duke firing a machine gun at some Commies. More shoulders than hips. 'The Nickster was in the Nam, too.' The Nickster.

The Nickster nodded. 'Airmobile.'

Peter said, 'Man, I wanted airmobile bad. Ride the skies. Ace a few Cong. I wasn't so old, I'd'a signed up for Saudi.'

The Nickster said, 'You woulda been a natural, buddy. I'd'a rather had you than half the turds in my unit.'

T.J. said, 'Fuckin' A.'

Peter nodded, regretting the lost opportunity to ride the friendly skies of Vietnam and Saudi Arabia.

Donnie put down the phone and turned back to us, making the big smile and the there's-no-problem-here hand gestures. 'Hey, Pete-man, you wanted that TV putz off the picture, he's yesterday. Gone. A memory. So tell me what you wanna do about a production designer? We've gotta make a decision and start building the rest of the sets.'

Peter said, 'Forget about it, Donnie. I'm into something now.'

Donnie's face pinched and he looked nervous. 'But, hey, Peter. We got a movie to make, man. We gotta get with it. These things won't wait.'

Peter didn't look at him. 'Donnie?'

'Yeah, Pete-man?'

Peter spit a chewed M&M at him. It hit Donnie's right pants leg, hung there a second, then fell. It left a green smear. 'Hit the road.'

Pat Kyle made a hissing sound. Donnie's face went white and his body stiffened as if the M&M had been a turd pie, and for just a moment, his face was clenched and hard and angry. Then, a little bit at a time, the anger was stored away as if little men inside of Donnie were disassembling it block by block. When enough of the blocks were gone, the little men built a smile. It wasn't a very good smile, but the little men were probably tired from all the overtime they put in. Donnie said, 'Sure, Pete-man. Whatever you say. I'll call later. Hey, I'm really sorry you got stuck with those TV clips.' His voice was tight. Trainee in the voice-box crew, no doubt.

Donnie Brewster turned and walked out without looking at me or at Pat Kyle or at Nick or T.J. or Dani. Peter poured the rest of the M&Ms into his mouth, crumpled the wrapper, then laid a hook shot toward a square wastebasket and missed. Dani picked it up.

The Nickster made a whiny voice. 'Sure, Pete-man, whatever you say.'

Peter and T.J. and the Nickster laughed. Dani didn't.

I looked at Pat Kyle. Her eyes were hard and her jaw was tight and she was staring at the floor. *What, and give up show business!* I looked back at Peter Alan Nelsen. Nick and T.J. were rolling around on the zebra couch, laughing and goosing each other and slapping hands. I said, 'Peter. I didn't come here for Pee-Wee's playhouse.'

The laughter stopped.

'I have come because my friend Pat Kyle asked me to come, and I have answered questions about myself because that's the way most people beat around the bush before they get down to business, but now we are at the end of the road. Unless you knock off the bullshit and get to the point, I will walk out of here and you can get someone else to do the job.'

Peter Alan Nelsen blinked at me through surprised, little-boy eyes. T.J. got up from the couch and put his hands on his hips and grinned at me. The Nickster said, 'Oh, man, Peter, this guy wants a piece.'

Dani uncrossed the big arms and came forward until her right hip was pressed against the desk, very close to Peter. Her left quadricep flexed like a beating heart. Peter stared at me for a long time, sort of smiling, but mostly looking like a little boy who'd been caught eating worms and knew it was wrong. He looked ashamed. Peter said, 'Nick, T.J., you guys go grab a beer or something, okay?'

Nick and T.J. glanced at Peter, then walked out, the Nickster making a big deal out of coming very close to me. When they were gone, Peter slid off the desk, dug out his wallet, took out a small color snapshot, and handed it to me. It was creased cleanly once, and yellowed the way old photos are yellowed when they have lain untouched between papers in a box for many years. It was Peter. Much younger and even thinner, with long frizzy hair and a dark maroon T-shirt that said USC FILM. He was sitting on an ugly cloth couch in a plain student's apartment and he was holding a tiny baby. Neither Peter nor the baby looked happy. He said, 'I've got an ex-wife and a son. The last time I saw my son, he was maybe a year old. His name is Toby. We named him Toby after *Toby Tyler, or, Ten Weeks with the Circus*. He's gotta be about twelve now, but I don't know if he's dead or if he's alive or if he's a crip in a ward somewhere. I don't know if he likes pizza. I don't know if he likes Teenage Mutant Ninja Turtles. You see?'

I nodded. 'Your ex-wife never came to you for child support?'

'No.'

'Or alimony?'

He spread his hands. 'For all I know she's on the moon.'

418

I said, 'Peter, you ever think maybe the woman doesn't want to be found?'

He stared at me.

'It's been ten years and you don't exactly lead a low-profile life. If she wanted to find you, she could've. I've done jobs like this before, and what happens is that everyone ends up wishing well enough had been left alone. The kids end up confused and scared and the parents end up fighting the old fights. You see?'

Peter took a deep breath and shook his head and looked around the office. With T.J. and the Nickster and Donnie Brewster gone, the office felt empty and he looked alone. He said, 'I'm worth, what? Maybe two hundred million, something like that? If I've got a kid, part of that's his, right?' Trying to convince me. 'What if he needs a car? What if he can't afford college?'

I said, 'You want to be a father.'

He took back the snapshot of the very much younger Peter Alan Nelsen and his baby son. Toby. Toby Tyler and the circus.

'Unless the kid's dead, I'm a father whether I want to be or not. That oughta mean something, right?'

I said, 'Yes. It should.'

'So Karen's mad. So I schmucked out back then and I blew it. Does that mean that I have to pay for it the rest of my life?'

'No.'

He shook his head and went over behind the marble desk and sat down the way a very old man would sit and he looked at the little picture again. He said, 'You know what's weird? It's like there's a piece of me out there that I don't know and have never seen. It's like I can feel him, like there's this other self, you see?'

I nodded. 'The boy may not feel that way. Your ex-wife almost certainly won't.'

He got up and walked over to the pinball machine and then to the video game and then to the Wurlitzer. He would stand, then move, then stand again, as if he didn't quite know what to do with himself or where he should be or how to say what he wanted to say.

I said, 'Just say it.'

He turned and his face seemed faraway and lost and hurt. 'I just want to say hello to my kid.'

I nodded. 'I don't blame you,' I said. 'I'll help you find him.'

The world's third most successful director took a deep breath, then said, 'Good. Good.' He came across the room and shook my hand. 'Good.'

CHAPTER 3

The black secretary stuck his head in the door and told Peter that someone named Langston needed to see him on the stage right away.

We trooped down out of his office and back into the real world of aliens and oil barons and people who looked suspiciously like studio executives. Patricia Kyle and Peter Alan Nelsen and I walked together, with Dani sort of drifting behind. Somewhere between Peter's office and the soundstage, Nick and T.J. reappeared, Nick giving me tough whenever I looked at him. Had me shaking, that guy. Make you turn in your license, a guy like that. I looked at Peter Alan Nelsen, instead. 'What was your ex-wife's name?'

'Karen Nelsen.'

'Not her married name. What was her maiden name?'

'Karen Shipley. That cop we talked to, Ito, he said you're big with the martial arts. He said you took out some killer from Japan.'

I said, 'What's your son's name?'

'Toby Samuel Nelsen. I got the Sam from Sam Fuller. Great director. You ever been shot?'

'I caught some frag once.'

'What did it feel like?'

'Peter, let's stick to the information about your ex-wife, okay?'

'Yeah, sure. What do you want to know?'

We walked along the little studio back streets and people stopped what they were doing and looked at him. They saw celebrities every day, so they wouldn't look at Mel Gibson or Harrison Ford or Jane Fonda, but they looked at Peter Alan Nelsen, and Peter seemed to enjoy it. He stood tall and when he spoke he made broad, exaggerated gestures as if what was happening had been scripted and he was acting the scene and the lookers were his audience.

Maybe the lookers thought so, too. Maybe, since Peter was the King of Adventure, they figured that a Stearman biplane would suddenly appear and begin a strafing run. Maybe they thought a Lamborghini Contach driven by Daryl Hannah would suddenly screech around the corner, chased by psychopaths in souped-up Fords, and Peter would have to save the day and it would really be something to see. If Daryl Hannah was driving the Contach, Peter would have to move pretty fast. I was planning to get there first.

I said, 'Okay. Do you have any idea where Karen might be living?'

'No.'

'You think she's still here in Los Angeles?'

'I don't know.'

'Did she ever talk about someplace in particular, like, "I'd really like to live in Palmdale one day," or, "Los Angeles is the greatest city in the world. I'll never leave it," something like that?'

'I never thought about living anyplace else.'

'Not you. Her.'

'I don't know.'

'Did she have any friends?'

He pressed his lips together and made a shrug. 'Yeah. I guess so.' Thinking harder. Then, 'I dunno. I was sort of into my own thing.' Embarrassed that he didn't have an answer.

I looked at Pat Kyle.

Pat said, 'Where was she born, Peter?'

'Someplace in Arizona or New Mexico. Phoenix, maybe.' He frowned. 'We never talked about stuff like that.'

'Okay.'

'Why don't you ask me something I know?'

'Okay. What do you know?'

He thought for a while. 'About Karen?'

'Yeah.'

'I don't know.'

I said, 'How did you meet? Did she belong to any clubs or organizations? Did she have brothers or sisters or aunts or uncles or cousins or grandparents?' I figured if I listed enough stuff I would get lucky somewhere.

He said, 'I've got an older sister. She's married to a fat guy lives in Cleveland.' Everything was *I*.

'Great. But that's about you. What about Karen?'

'Oh.' Oh. Then, 'I think she was an only child. I think her people were dead.'

'But you don't know.'

'They were dead.' We walked along a little more, thinking about it. He said, 'Maybe she was from Colorado.'

We went through a pair of twenty-six-foot doors and into a battleship-gray soundstage that was being rebuilt to resemble the interior of a Mayan ziggurat. The doors were open to let in the air and the light. Above and around us dozens of men and women in shorts and T-shirts clung like spiders to scaffolding as they attached vacu-formed plastic panels to a wooden frame. The panels had been cast to look like great stone blocks. There were the sounds of hammers and saws and screwguns and the smell of plastic cement and paint, and somewhere a woman laughed. It was warming as the day wore on, and some of the men had their shirts off.

A heavy man with a Vandyke beard and a roll of architectural plans noticed Peter and started toward us. Peter frowned and said, 'Nick, T.J., gimme some space here, huh?'

Nick gestured toward the beard and T.J. went over and intercepted him. Blocking backs.

We turned left past a couple of guys building something that looked like a sacrificial altar and squeezed between two backdrop flats and over a tangle of electrical cables into a little clearing that had been set up as a sort of office with a desk and a phone and a coffee machine. There was another Webcor candy machine next to the desk. Peter slammed it with his elbow and a PayDay candy bar dropped out. Dani said, 'Peter has a candy machine like this on all of his sets. It's part of his contract.' She said it like a press release.

Peter said, 'Go find Langston, willya, Dani? Tell'm we're hiding back here and ready to rock.'

Dani squeezed back between the flats and disappeared into the darkness. Nick hung back behind the flats, still not liking me.

Peter said, 'Man, I can't take a shit, the pogues aren't after me about something. That's why we gotta hide.' He tore the wrapper off the candy, stuffed most of the bar into his mouth, and dropped the wrapper onto the floor. I wondered how often he brushed.

I said, 'Tell me how you met.'

'I was at USC when I met her. I was casting a film and put up flyers for actors and Karen called for a reading. It was a ripoff of those biker flicks in the sixties. Eighteen minutes, synced sound, black and white. You wanna see it?'

'Is Karen in it?'

'No. I didn't give her the part.'

'Then I don't need to see it.'

'I made an audition tape for her. I couldn't find it, but I got the outtake tape. It was a long time ago, so it's Beta format, but I brought it into the office. We can probably dig out a machine if you wanna see. I did a pretty good job with her.' More of the *I*'s. *I* met. *I* married. *I* lived. Maybe Karen Shipley wasn't real. Maybe, like Pinocchio, she was a wooden puppet he had brought to life.

'What's an audition tape?'

Pat said, 'It's a way for an actor to introduce herself to casting agents. The actor tells you about herself and maybe reads a scene. Peter would've shot a lot more tape than Karen would need, then edited it down to three or four minutes. The outtake tape will be the takes they didn't use in the final product.'

Peter nodded and said something, but his mouth was full of candy again, and I didn't understand what he said.

I said, 'I'll want to look at it. Do you have a still picture?'

He swallowed the wad of chocolate and peanuts and shook his head.

Pat Kyle opened her briefcase and handed me a black-and-white 8 × 10 head shot of a pretty young woman with dark hair and eyes that would be either green or hazel. 'I phoned a friend at SAG and he came up with this.' The woman in the photograph was made up as a waitress with a fluffy apron and cap and a bright the-lemon-pie-is-very-nice-today! smile. She didn't look convincing. KAREN SHIP-LEY was spelled out in block letters along a white border at the bottom of the picture.

I said, 'Pretty. Your friend at SAG say if Karen had an agent?'

Pat opened her briefcase again and took out an envelope large enough for the 8 × 10. 'A guy named Oscar Curtiss, with two esses. He's got an office over here, just off Las Palmas. His address is in the envelope.'

Peter came around next to me and looked at the 8 × 10. 'Jesus, I remember this.' He gestured at Karen's face. 'Nothing unique about the quality. See the nose, it's a little too ordinary. See the mouth, maybe it needs to be fuller.' Peter the director. 'She had these made before we met. I said Christ, what do you want to look like a dopey waitress for? She said she thought it was cute. I said what a fucking waste.' He stared at the picture a little more, then looked at Pat Kyle. 'Can you get me one of these?'

Pat said, 'Sure.'

Peter looked back at the picture, and maybe there was something soft in his face, something less antic and less onstage. 'She got pregnant right away and then there was the kid and I just wasn't into the family scene. I was scrambling from job to job, trying to get a toehold, and she's talking about Huggies. I busted out of film school. It was crazy. So I said, look, this isn't my thing, I don't wanna be married anymore, and she didn't fight it. I don't think I've seen her or the boy since the day we signed the papers. A little while after that *Chainsaw* came along and things happened fast.' He spread the big hands, looking for a way to say it. 'I got larger.'

I said, 'Did Karen work, or was she just a wannabe?'

Pat said, 'Quite a bit of extra work and a couple of walkons. The sort of thing you get when all they need is a pretty face in the background.'

'Where do they send the residuals?'

'She's got four hundred sixty-eight dollars and seventy-two cents waiting for her for some work she did on *Adam* 12. Neither SAG nor the Extras Guild knows where to send it.'

Peter brightened and went back to the candy machine. He slammed it with his elbow and pulled out an Almond Joy. Another wrapper on the floor. 'I remember that gig. I went to the set with her and tried to talk the producer into giving me an episode to direct. The guy gives me the bum's rush. That TV prick. A lousy episodic producer and he's telling me I can't hack an *Adam* 12, he's saying that what they do is "highly stylized." Man, I ain't thought about that prick in years.' It was as if relating something of his to something of hers, he could remember it.

Dani came back between the flats with a fat guy in an argyle sweater. Peter said, 'That's Langston. He's my cameraman. I gotta talk to him about a shot move we're designing through the pyramid set. Is there anything else you wanna know about me?'

'Karen. We were talking about Karen.'

He looked annoyed. 'That's what I meant. Look, I gotta go. If you want anything, it's yours. Use my name. This town, it's like saying open sesame.'

'Ali Baba.'

He smiled. 'Yeah. Just like Ali Baba.'

He walked over to Langston.

Pat said, 'Well?'

I shook my head. 'He knows about him, but he doesn't know about her. How long were they married?'

'Fourteen months.'

I shook my head some more. You do that a lot in this business.

Pat and I went past the electrical cables and between the flats and toward the big doors. We were most of the way there when Peter Alan Nelsen yelled, 'Hey, Cole.'

I turned around. Peter was up on one of the framing catwalks, grinning at me. Dani was with him and the fat guy Langston, and a couple of other people who probably had to do with the construction rather than the design. He said, 'I'm glad you're on this for me. I like your style.' He tossed down a Mars bar. Maybe there was another candy machine up on the ceiling. 'Me and you,' he said, 'I think we're two of a kind. You're my kind of guy.'

I thought about ripping off the candy wrapper and dropping it on the ground, but decided that that would be small. I bit through the paper instead.

Peter smiled wider and said, 'Man, you are wild.'

Pat Kyle shook her head.

We walked out through the big doors and into the light. The paper tasted terrible. If Daryl Hannah was watching, I hope she was impressed.

CHAPTER 4

Pat Kyle and I walked back to the Kapstone offices where someone had set up a Sony Betamax VCR along with several yellow legal pads and sharpened pencils for the taking of notes. There was a check for four thousand dollars in an envelope taped to a Beta cassette on top of the VCR, along with a fresh pot of coffee on a side table with a tray of bagels and cream cheese and lox and sliced tomatoes and red onions. Pat said, 'Would you like company?'

'Sure.'

Pat turned on the machine and inserted the cassette and we watched as nineteen-year-old Karen Shipley Nelsen walked into an empty room and stood next to a stool. She wasn't made up like the waitress now. Now she was wearing faded jeans and an airy white top and red boots and she looked tanned and outdoorsy. The brown hair was cut in a sort of fluffy shag and the eyes were hazel. No makeup.

She looked at someone behind the camera and said, 'What do you want me to do?' The sound coming out of the television was hollow and sort of tinny. Even with that her voice was light and girlish. She giggled.

Peter Nelsen's voice came from where she looked. 'Give us the left and the right and the back. Try not to giggle.'

She showed her left profile, and then her back, and then her right. She said it as she did it, and when she moved she sort of squiggled and swayed and bounced, the way fifteen-year-old girls do when they're acting grown-up and people are watching. 'This is my left side, and this is my back, and this is my right.' And then she giggled. 'Hee hee hee.'

Pat Kyle said, 'Oh, God.'

'She's not impressing you with her talents?'

Pat smiled sympathetically. 'I get tapes like this every week.

Young women and young men come into my office and read for me, and they want you to like them so badly that you can feel them ache, but they aren't any better than this and they never will be any better than this.'

'Then you suspect she has not pursued acting as a vocation?'

She made an I-hope-not shrug.

The shot changed abruptly into a tight close-up. Closer, Karen's eyes showed an absence of line or character. She was talking about herself and trying to look serious. '. . . think my strengths lie in comedy, but I can also do drama. I think I'd make a really good ingenue.'

Peter's voice cut in sharply. 'You sound like an idiot in a malt shop, "really good ingenue." If you're an ingenue, just say it. Say "I'm a perfect ingenue."'

Karen looked unhappy and said, 'Oh, Peter, do I havta?' When she addressed Peter, she looked off camera. When she was acting, she looked directly out of the screen.

Peter's voice said, 'Why am I wasting my fucking time?'

Karen looked unhappy some more, then made a little smile and stared back into the lens and made herself serious and said it. Then she giggled.

It went on like that, cutting from bit to bit. Most of the bits were just fragments, five seconds of this, eight seconds of that, and many of them were repetitious. Peter would ask her a question or tell her to do something and she would answer or do it. There was something hopeful and naïve to her manner, maybe because she was nineteen. She tried hard even when she looked unhappy.

My stomach grumbled and I kept looking at the lox and bagels. I had to keep reminding myself that lunch at Lucy's was only moments away.

At one point, Peter walked into the picture and handed her a couple of script pages. He was wearing an orange Marine Corps T-shirt with a couple of stains on the back. *They wouldn't take me because of this hip thing.* He was young and skinny and built exactly as he was now, all wide butt and coat-hanger shoulders and intense eyes. His hair stuck out in a tremendous natural that, within the small confines of the TV monitor, seemed to be a full three feet across. Karen cleared her throat and read the speech from *Rocky* that Talia Shire says to Sylvester Stallone to give him the courage to go on. She didn't read it well. She giggled when she finished and asked Peter if that was okay. He said no.

The tape lasted twenty-two minutes. Karen Shipley never once mentioned her family or her friends or her hometown. She giggled sixty-three times. I counted. Giggling is not one of my favorite things.

When the tape ended, Pat Kyle turned off the monitor and we went to lunch. Kapstone Pictures paid.

One hour and ten minutes later, full of pork burrito and Dos Equis beer, Pat Kyle resumed work and so did I.

Las Palmas above Santa Monica Boulevard is a community of flat, faceless costume-rental shops and film-editing outfits and little single-story houses with signs that said things like flotation therapy. Women in flowered tops pushed baby carriages and men who looked like they wanted day work stood outside little markets and kids on skateboards practiced jumping curbs.

I stopped in a 7-Eleven on Fountain just past La Brea, bought two dollars' worth of quarters, and ran outside to beat two fat guys to the pay phone on the side of the building. One of the fat guys was in a hurry and the other wasn't. The one who was in the hurry made a face like he had bowel trouble and said *Ah, shit*, when I got to the phone first. The one who wasn't leaned against the grill of a white window-repair truck and sipped at a Miller High Life. Did Mike Hammer use a 7-Eleven as an office?

I fed in a quarter and called a woman I know who works for the phone company and asked her if they had a listed or unlisted number for either Karen Shipley or Karen Nelsen anywhere within the state of California. She said she would have to get back to me, but it probably wouldn't be before tomorrow. I asked if she needed my number. She laughed and told me she's had my number for years. It's something I've been told before.

When I hung up, the fat guy in the hurry started forward. When I fed in another quarter, he raised his hands, rolled his eyes, and went back to the truck. Guess it wasn't a good day. His friend had a little more of the Miller and belched. When he belched, he covered his mouth with two fingers and said excuse me. Polite.

I called another woman I know who works the credit-verification department at Bank of America and asked if she would run a credit check on both Karen Shipley and Karen Nelsen, those names being either primary account names or maiden names listed to another unknown name. She said she would if I took her to a Lakers game. I told her to think of something else because I was going to take her to a Lakers game anyway. She made a little swooning sound, told me she'd get back to me tomorrow, and hung up. Some charmer, huh?

The fat guy was leaning past his truck like Carl Lewis set to come out of the starter's blocks, glaring at me. I showed him another quarter and fed it into the phone. His face went white, he slapped the fender of the truck, and then stormed the long way around the truck and into the 7-Eleven. His friend sipped a little more Miller and shook his head. 'He's asking for a thrombo.'

I said, 'Get him into yoga. That'll help him relax.'

The friend shook his head, looking sort of sleepy and tired, and made a little shrug like they'd been through it a thousand times. 'You can't talk to him.'

I dialed the North Hollywood P.D. and got a gruff male voice that said, 'Detectives.'

'Elvis Cole for Lou Poitras.'

'Wait one.'

The phone got put down on something hard. There were voices in the background and the heavy laughter of men, and then the voice came back. 'I'm putting you on hold. He's gonna take it in his office.'

I got put on hold, then Lou Poitras came on. The laughter and the male sounds were still there, but now they were muted and farther away. Poitras said, 'I got my ass chewed good for trying to fix your last ticket. Don't ask me again.'

'Lou. One might think that our entire relationship is me asking favors of you.'

'So what do you want?'

'A small favor.'

'Shit.'

The fat guy in the hurry came out of the 7-Eleven with a Miller High Life of his own. He leaned against the truck next to his fat friend and looked tired. They drank. If you can't beat'm, join'm.

I said, 'I need to know if you have anything on a woman named Karen Shipley or Karen Nelsen. And I need you to go back ten years on the search.'

Lou Poitras said, 'Anything else?'

I said that should do it.

'You at the office?'

I told him where I was.

You could see him shake his head. 'Some big-time private op, working in a parking lot.'

'Beats sucking off the taxpayers.'

He said he'd get back to me tomorrow and hung up.

Everybody was going to get back to me tomorrow. Maybe there was something going on today that I didn't know about. Maybe that's why the fat guy was in such a hurry. Maybe he knew who to call to find out where the action was, and upon making the call, he and his buddy were going to whatever it was that I didn't know about. Maybe I could go with them.

I hung up the phone, looked at the fat guy in the hurry, and said, 'It's all yours.'

He sipped more Miller and didn't move, giving me who cares? His friend looked at him, then me, and shrugged. Go figure. Some guys are never happy.

CHAPTER 5

The Oscar Curtiss Talent Agency was two blocks below Sunset Boulevard in a small sky-blue clapboard house with a tiny lawn and a porch and a narrow sidewalk leading up to the porch. What looked like a Friedrich air conditioner stuck out of a window on the north side of the house and hummed loudly, water falling in a steady dribble from its underside. A couple of wine bottles were lying on the lawn. *Midnight Rambler*. The bottles were capless and empty.

I parked and went up the walk and through one of those frosty pebbled-glass office doors that no one has used since 1956. There was a large gold star on the door with *Oscar Curtiss Talent Agency* written in an arc above it and what were supposed to be little spotlights lighting up the sky.

Inside, there were three young women sitting on a hard L-shaped couch and a black woman in her sixties sitting at a scarred pecan desk that faced the room. Another frosted-glass door was behind her. This one said *Mr. Curtiss*. The three young women were spread around on the couches in a way that said they didn't know each other. Two of them were reading *Variety*. The other one was chewing gum. There were a couple hundred framed black-and-white head shots on the walls, but I didn't recognize any of them. The carpet was beige and worn and the hard couch was a kind of green and the walls were a sort of mustard and nothing went together, as if the office had been built over the years without regard to style or esthetic. The Friedrich made it very cold.

The black woman looked up and smiled nicely. 'May I help you?'

'My name is Elvis Cole. I'd like to see Mr. Curtiss.' I gave her the card that said *Elvis Cole, Confidential Investigations*. The old cards had a picture of a guy listening at a keyhole. The new cards don't. Without the picture is probably better.

She took the card and nodded pleasantly, still smiling. 'Unh-hunh. And do you have an appointment?'

'No, ma'am. I was hoping Mr. Curtiss could squeeze me in.' I leaned forward and lowered my voice. Confidential. 'It involves a former client of his.'

More smiling and nodding. 'Unh-hunh. Well, why don't you just wait right there while I go see.' She got up, rapped once on the glass door, then let herself through.

I looked around at the three young women and gave them a smile. The two who had been reading were still reading, the one who had been chewing gum was still chewing gum. One of the readers wore a nice pastel pants suit and had a matching briefcase at her feet. She sat so that one foot was touching the case. The other was in blue jeans and knee boots and a purple sweater. The jeans and the sweater were too small, but she had the body for it. I made them early twenties, twenty-five tops. The gum-chewer had her legs crossed and her arms along the back of the couch and was looking at me with pale, steady eyes. She was wearing baggy culottes and pink Reebok tennis shoes and a blousy top that was tied off beneath her breasts so that her belly was bare. It was too cool outside for the top, but that's show biz. Her hair was pale and washed-out, and so was the spray of freckles across her nose. Younger than the other two. Seventeen, maybe. She blew a large pink bubble the size of a goiter, popped it, then used a lot of tongue to lick it off her lips. Maybe sixteen. Run away and come to the big town to be a star. I said, 'Pretty hot outside, huh?'

She blew another bubble, uncrossed her legs, then spread them.

I said, 'Pretty hot inside, too.'

She spread the legs a little wider, then popped the bubble and licked it off. Maybe I was a producer.

The glass door opened and the black woman came out with a short, thin guy pushing sixty. Oscar Curtiss. He had dark circles around his eyes and too many teeth and he was wearing a coarse-weave light sports coat and huaraches and baggy pants like they do in Italian fashion magazines. It looked silly. He gave me the teeth, stuck out his hand, and said, 'Hey, Cole, goodtaseeya.' Then he looked past me at the two readers and the gum-popper, mostly the gum-popper. 'You ladies excuse us for a few minutes, okay? Sydney, I'll see you next.'

The gum-popper nodded and blew another bubble. Sydney. Her knees were bouncing open-closed, open-closed.

Oscar gave her some of the teeth, too, then motioned me into his office. He didn't bother to look at me while he was doing the motioning.

The office was larger than the waiting room, with a lot of plants and one of those heavy, dark wood secretary desks they made back in the forties. It needed to be oiled. There was a leather couch against the wall and another Friedrich in the window behind his desk and more photographs on the walls, but I didn't recognize any of the people in these, either. Maybe Sydney would be there soon and I could recognize her.

He shut the door and followed me in, holding my card. 'Elvis Cole, huh? I like it. It's got catch. It's got pump and pizzazz. You got a nice look, too. You know who you look like?'

'Buddy Ebsen.'

'Nah. Michael Keaton. A little taller, maybe. A little better built. But sensitive and sharp. A guy you don't mess around with.'

'I always thought I looked like Moe Howard.'

'Take my word for it. You got the look and the name. Some of the kids come in here, Christ, they got names flat as piss on a plate. Pat Green. Steve Brown. I say that's no good. I say, you know what you need?'

'Pizzazz.'

'Fuckin' A. Look at Steve Guttenberg. Take away the Guttenberg, whattaya got? Nuthin!' He sat behind the desk and shot a glance at the door. 'Listen, I don't have a lot of time.'

'A long time ago you represented an actress named Karen Shipley. I'm trying to find her.' I took out the 8 × 10 and showed it to him.

He nodded. 'Yeah. Sure. I remember Karen. Great kid. Terrific body.'

'Do you still represent her?'

He handed back the head shot. 'Nah. I haven't heard from Karen in, what is it, ten years, something like that?' He put another glance on the door, anxious to get to other things. 'She musta went to another agency.'

I nodded. 'Did you continue to represent her after her divorce from Peter Alan Nelsen?'

Oscar Curtiss stopped looking at the door and sat forward in the chair and blinked at me. 'That's who she was married to?'

'Yeah.'

'Karen Shipley was married to Peter Alan Nelsen?'

433

'Yeah.'

'*The* Peter Alan Nelsen?'

'Peter Alan Nelsen wasn't Peter Alan Nelsen when they were married.'

Oscar slumped back in his chair and said, 'Jesus H.'

'He was in film school when they married. After he busted out of USC, he divorced her. Now he wants to find her again.'

'Sonofabitch. I remember when she got divorced. She came here with the kid and sat down right over there and said she was divorced and needed to work. I said, sit-ups, Christ, a body like yours you wanna get it back, do sit-ups. Peter Alan Nelsen. Jesus Christ.' He wasn't looking at me anymore. He was staring somewhere in midspace, seeing the old scenes, worrying them through to recall if he'd done anything that could piss off Peter Alan Nelsen. All the worrying made his eyebrows dance around on his face.

I said, 'Do you know how we can contact her?'

'It's been years. Christ, I saw her a couple more times after that, then zippo. *Nada*. I never heard from her again.' The mouth started moving with the eyebrows.

'Okay. Where was she living?'

'It was somewhere over there.' He made a gesture that could mean anywhere in the northern hemisphere.

'That's a little broad, Oscar.'

'Christ, I never visited. She came here.'

'Maybe you've got records.'

He stopped all the moving around and looked at me with the kind of look they give you that tells you that the lights are going off behind their eyes. Getting The Big Idea. He said, 'Maybe I should deal direct with Peter on this. We might be getting a little personal here, you know, and he might appreciate keeping it in the family, as it were.'

I pointed at the phone. 'Sure. He's at the Paramount office now. Give'm a call and tell him that even though he's trying to find his ex-wife and his kid, you're foot-dragging because you want to suck after some kind of deal. He'll like you just fine for that.'

He said, 'Hey, I'm doing a favor here, right? I'm trying to help here, right?'

'Quit being small-time and tell me what you know, Oscar. You're coming across like a chiseler.'

'I look like I'm rolling in it here? I wanna help. I wanna do what I

434

can. But, hey, Peter Alan Nelsen gives you the nod, my friend, you're made in this town.' Peter Alan Nelsen, spitting a green M&M on Donnie Brewster.

'Sure, Oscar.'

He worked it through some more, trying to get a fix on what was real and what wasn't and what he could get if he played it right and how much it could cost if he played it wrong. He said, 'Listen, Elvis, I help you out here, you tell Peter, okay?'

'I'll tell him.'

'You promise?' Like we were in fourth grade.

'I promise, Oscar.'

'Hey, I wanna help. I wanna do anything I can for Peter Alan Nelsen.' Nothing like sincerity.

'Where did Karen live?'

'I'm thinking.'

'Look in your files.'

'Christ, I'm supposed to keep files on people forever?'

'Returned checks. Tax information.'

'Nah.'

'Correspondence. Maybe an old rolodex.'

'Christ, I keep all that stuff I'd be buried in paper. We're talking a lifetime ago.'

'Okay. Maybe there's something else.'

'I'm thinking.'

'You know any of her friends?'

'No.'

'How about family?'

'Unh-unh.'

'Boyfriend?'

He shook his head.

'Did she say if she was thinking about moving away or taking a trip?'

His brow knotted and his face clenched and he hit the side of his head a couple of times with the heel of his hand. Worried that he wouldn't be able to come through and trying to shake something loose.

I said, 'Man, you two were really tight.'

He waved his hands. 'Hey, we never had no big heart-to-hearts. One day she just wasn't around anymore. I thought she dropped me. You know, went to another agency. I didn't hear anything from

435

her and I tried calling the place she lived, but she was never around, so after a while I figured that's it.'

I stood up and walked to the door. 'Okay, Oscar. You tried. Thanks, anyway.'

He jumped up and came around the desk and grabbed my arm. He grabbed hard, like if he didn't something rare would get away. He grabbed the way you grab when the rare thing has visited once before, long ago, and you blew it, and now you're getting a second chance. 'Hey, you know what? I got some old stuff in storage. I'll dig through it. Maybe there'll be something, hunh? Maybe I'll find something that'll help out.' I don't think he meant help me.

'Sure. My phone is on the card.'

'You tell Peter I'm trying, okay? Tell'm I'm bending over backwards. Tell'm I really liked Karen, and I thought the kid was terrific.'

'Sure.'

I opened the door and we went out. The black woman was talking on the phone. The two young women who had been reading were still reading and the Sydney was still blowing bubbles. Oscar gave with the big teeth and made a big deal out of walking me to the outer door. 'Hey, you can tell Peter I'll get on the search tonight.' Putting on the act. 'And tell'm I'd appreciate it if he gives me a call. There's a couple of things I'd like to talk with him about.'

I said I would.

He made the big teeth some more, then left me at the door and sat on the couch next to Sydney with his hand on her thigh. The other two young women were watching him. He said that I worked for Peter Alan Nelsen and that he and Peter were thrashing out a deal together and that things were gonna start hopping around there soon. When he said it, he gave Sydney's thigh a little squeeze.

She watched him with the large pale eyes, blew another pink bubble, then popped it with her tongue. The eyes never once blinked and never once left him.

I walked out. So long, Norma Jean.

CHAPTER 6

The sun was dropping fast, the way it does in the fall, and the air lost its midday warmth and took on an autumn chill as I wound my way up Laurel Canyon to the little A-frame I keep off Woodrow Wilson Drive above Hollywood.

The cat that lives with me was sitting by his food bowl in the kitchen. He's thick and black, with fine shredded ears and broken teeth and the scars that come from a full, adventuresome, male-type-cat life. Sometimes he has fits.

I said, 'Is dinner ready?'

The cat came over and shoulder-bumped against my leg.

I said, 'Okay. How about meat loaf?'

He shoulder-bumped me again, then went back to his bowl. Meat loaf is one of his favorite things. Right up there with Kitnips.

I took a meat loaf out of the freezer, put it in the microwave to thaw, turned on the oven to preheat, then opened a can of Falstaff. It was twenty minutes after five. Business hours were until six. I drank some of the Falstaff, then phoned the Screen Actors Guild and spoke to a woman named Mrs. Lopaka about Karen Shipley. Mrs. Lopaka confirmed everything Pat Kyle had told me and added nothing new. I thanked her, hung up, then dialed the Screen Extras Guild and then AFTRA. Ditto. I called the machine at my office, hoping that there might be a message from the phone company or from B of A. *Nada*. Somebody named Jose wanted someone named Esteban to call him back right away. Jose sounded pissed. I called my partner, Joe Pike.

Pike said, 'Gun shop.' Pike owns a gun shop in Culver City.

'We're on the job again. Backtrack to a woman and child.'

'You need me?'

'Well, I'm here at the house and I'm not yet pinned down by snipers across the canyon, so I guess not yet.'

Pike didn't answer.

'You know the director, Peter Alan Nelsen? He's our client.'

Pike didn't answer some more. Trying to talk with Pike is like carrying on a fill-in-the-blank conversation.

I said, 'Try to make conversation, Joe. It's easy. All you have to do is say something.'

Pike said, 'You need me, you know where I am.' Then he hung up. So much for conversation.

The microwave dinged. I took out the meat loaf, transferred it to a metal pan, opened a can of new potatoes, drained them, put them in the pan around the meat loaf and sprinkled them with garlic and paprika, then put bacon over the meat loaf and put the pan in the oven on high. I like the skin on my meat loaf to be crispy.

The cat said, 'Naow?'

'No. Not now. About forty-five minutes.'

He didn't look happy about it.

I finished the Falstaff, got another, drank most of it on the way up to the shower and the rest of it on the way back down. When the meat loaf was ready, I put out two plates and sliced off the ends for me and a center cut for the cat. He watched me put the end cuts and the potatoes in my plate and the center slice in his. He purred loudly as I did it. I sprinkled Tabasco on mine and A-1 on his, then took the beer and both plates out to my deck. There's a Zalcona glass table out there with a couple of matching chairs and sometimes we eat at the table, but sometimes we take down the center section of the rail and sit at the edge of the deck and look out over the canyon. With the rail, you are separated from the view. Without the rail, you are part of it. We eat there often.

When we were finished, I said, 'Well? How was it?'

The cat stretched and broke wind. He's getting older.

I took the dishes inside, washed them, put them away, then stretched out on the couch with a finger of Knockando to read the latest Dean Koontz when the doorbell rang. It was Peter Alan Nelsen and his best friend Dani. Peter was dressed the same way he'd been dressed earlier, but Dani had shifted to buff-cut blue jeans and a designer sweatshirt with little pearl beads worked into the fabric. The sweatshirt was a pale lavender and looked good on her.

Peter walked in without being asked and said, 'Whadaya say, Private Eye? You ready to rock?' He was squinting a lot and swaying from side to side and he smelled like his clothes had been doused with bourbon.

He staggered into the center of the floor and looked around and said, 'Hey, this is neat. You live here alone?'

'Yeah.' The cat started to growl, a hoarse sound in his chest.

Peter saw my drink. 'What's that, scotch?'

I got a short glass and poured a little of the Knockando. I held the bottle toward Dani, but she shook her head. Designated human.

Peter went to the glass doors and looked out at the canyon. 'Hey, I like this view. This is okay. I got a place up on Mulholland with a view. You gotta come up sometime. We'll have a party or something.'

'Sure.'

Peter saw the cat sitting sphinxlike on the arm of the couch. 'Hey, a cat.'

I said, 'Be careful. He's mean and he bites.'

'Bullshit. I know about cats.' Peter swayed over to the couch and put out his hand. The cat grabbed him, bit hard twice, then ran under the couch, growling. Peter jumped back and shook his hand, then bent over and peered under the couch. I could see the blood from across the room. 'That sonofabitch is mean.'

Dani stood quietly to the side, maybe looking a little sad.

I said, 'Peter, it's late. I'm tired and I was getting ready for bed. What do you want?'

Peter straightened up and looked at me like I had to be kidding. 'Whadaya mean, sleep? It's early. Tell him, Dani, tell him it's early.'

Dani glanced at her watch. 'It's ten after ten, Peter. That's late for some people.'

Peter said, 'Bullshit. Ten after ten ain't nothing to guys like us.' He looked at me. 'I figured we could go out and knock back a few, maybe shoot a little pool, something like that.' He sat down on the couch and threw an arm over the back, forgetting about the cat. The cat growled, and Peter jumped up and moved to the chair across the room.

I said, 'Another time.'

Peter frowned, not liking that. 'Hey, you don't want to party?'

'Not tonight.'

'Why not?'

'Because I'm tired and I want to go to sleep, but most of all because you're so drunk you sound like you're speaking Martian.'

Dani made a soft, faraway sound, but when I looked at her, she wasn't looking at either me or Peter. Peter scowled and leaned forward in the chair. 'You got some smart mouth on you.'

'The rest of me ain't stupid, either.'

He poured himself more of the Knockando and got up and went over to the glass doors. 'I want to know what you've got on Karen.'

'You mean, how close have I come to finding her in the six hours since I started looking?'

'Yeah.'

'She is no longer a member of SAG or SEG or AFTRA, which probably means she no longer acts or works in front of the camera. I spoke with people I know at the Bank of America and the phone company and the police, all of whom are checking their computers for information about her past or present, but I probably won't hear from any of them until tomorrow. I talked with the man who was her theatrical agent, Oscar Curtiss, who is trying to be helpful but probably won't be. It goes like that sometimes. He wanted me to tell you that because he would like to do business with you.'

Peter made a little flipping gesture with his drink. 'Fuck'm.'

I shrugged.

Peter said, 'That's it?'

'Yep.'

'I thought it would go faster.'

'Most people do.'

Peter poured himself another three fingers of the Knockando, took it to the glass doors, and drank it. He stared out at the canyon for a while, then put the glass and the bottle on the floor and turned back to me. It took an effort to get himself turned around, like a tall ship in a wind with a lot of sail. He said, 'I'm calling you out.' Marshal Dillon.

I said, 'Yeah?'

He nodded. 'You're goddamned right. I didn't like the way you spoke to me at the studio today, and I don't like the way you're speaking to me now. I'm Peter Alan Nelsen and I don't take shit.'

I looked at Dani. She said, 'Why don't we just leave, Peter? He doesn't want to party. We can go somewhere and party without him.'

Peter said, 'Hey, Dani, you wanna leave, leave, but I'm calling this sonofabitch out.' Peter sort of swayed forward, squinting the way you do when you're seeing three or four of something that there's only one of.

He said, 'C'mon, goddamnit, I'm serious,' and put up his fists.

440

When his fists went up the cat howled loud and mournful and flashed out from under the couch. He grabbed Peter's ankle and bit and screamed and clawed with his hind legs. Peter yelled, 'Sonofabitch,' jumped sideways, stumbled into the chair, and fell over backward. The cat sprinted back under the couch.

I said, 'Some cat, huh?'

Dani helped Peter up, then righted the chair. Peter said, 'Lemme alone,' and pulled away from her. When he did he fell to his knees. He said, 'I'm all right. I'm all right.' Then he passed out.

I said, 'Is he like this a lot?'

Dani said, 'Pretty much, yeah.'

'I'll help you get him outside.'

'No, thanks. You could get the door, if you want.'

'You sure?'

'I can bench two-thirty. I squat over four.'

Nope. She wouldn't need the help.

Dani lifted him into the chair, then squatted in front of him and pulled him onto her shoulders and stood up. She said, 'You see?'

I got the door.

She moved out past me and stopped on the porch and looked back at me. 'I know it doesn't show, but he really likes you. You're all he talked about this afternoon.'

'Great.'

She frowned, maybe looking a little angry. Defensive for him. I liked that. 'It's not easy being him. Here's a guy with all he has going, and he can't just go hang out, you see?'

'Sure.'

'Everybody in his life is there because they want to screw him. Any time there's a woman, he's thinking it's because she wants to rip him off. Any time a guy says he's Peter's friend, it's because he wants to be in business with Peter Alan Nelsen, the big deal, not with Peter Nelsen, the guy.' She said it as if we were just standing there, as if Peter Alan Nelsen wasn't an outsized yoke across her shoulders.

I said, 'He's got to be getting heavy.'

She smiled softly. 'I can hold him all night.'

I followed her out to a black-on-black Range Rover and opened the right front door. She eased him into the front seat and carefully placed his head on the headrest and buckled the seat belt around him. She tested it to make sure it was snug. I said, 'Everybody's out to screw him but you.'

441

She nodded, then shut the door and looked at me, and there was something soft within the hard muscle. She said, 'Are you going to quit? He pulls stuff like this and most people quit.'

I shook my head. 'I'm liking you too much to quit.'

She made the little soft smile again, then went around to the driver's side, got in, and made a U-turn onto the little road that winds down the blackness toward Laurel Canyon and Mulholland Drive.

I went back into the house and picked up the empty glasses and the Knockando bottle and cleaned up the spilled booze. The cat came out from under the couch and watched me for a while, and then he left. Off to do cat things, no doubt.

When the glasses were put away, I went out onto the deck again and looked down into the dark canyon below. It was open and free and, beneath me there, lights moved along the curving roads.

Maybe they were Dani and Peter, but maybe they weren't.

CHAPTER 7

The next morning I rose early and was out on the deck again while the sun was still low in the east. The canyon below was cold and green with a faint hint of haze, and high overhead a red hawk rode a growing thermal, looking for gophers.

I did slow stretches and then the Twelve Sun Salutes from the hatha yoga and then an easy tae kwon do *kata* and then a hard one, snapping the moves with power and speed and certainty of purpose. It feels clean to do it that way. Sometimes when I practice in the early evening, the two little boys who live in the cantilevered house down the street come over and watch and we talk about things that are important to small boys. I find that they are important to me, too. In the morning, I am always alone. Lately I've noticed that I work out less in the morning and more in the evening. Maybe Peter Alan Nelsen was feeling that way, too.

I showered and shaved and put out two eggs for poaching and made a batter for blueberry cottage cheese pancakes. While I waited for the griddle to heat, I called my answering machine. There were messages from my friends at the Bank of America and the phone company and from Lou Poitras. My friend at the B of A said that their credit check showed that no one named Karen Shipley or Karen Nelsen or listing either of those names as either a maiden or former name possessed a credit card of any kind anywhere within the United States. My friend at the phone company said pretty much the same. Lou Poitras said that Karen Shipley had once gotten a ticket for parking in a red zone but had paid it promptly. Her address at that time was the apartment she had shared with Peter Alan Nelsen. He said that if I found her, I probably wouldn't have to assume she was armed and dangerous, but that I might want to bring along backup just in case. That Lou. He's a riot, isn't he?

I made four pancakes and the poached eggs, then crushed the poached eggs on top of the pancakes, poured a large glass of nonfat milk, and brought the food and the milk to the table. The cat had left during the night. Sometimes he eats breakfast with me, but sometimes he doesn't. When he doesn't, I don't know what he eats. Maybe small dogs.

Karen Nelsen had no phone in either name, but I had sort of expected that. After ten years, the odds were large that she had remarried. The credit cards were another matter. If she had a credit card under Nelsen or Shipley, or with Nelsen or Shipley listed as a former name, she should've turned up. That was odd, but there were explanations. Maybe she had joined a cult and no longer had a name. Maybe she had given over all earthly traits and artifacts to a higher being named Klaatu, and in return Klaatu had blessed her with eternal bliss and escape from snoopy private cops. Or maybe she simply didn't like credit cards. Hmmm.

I had run through all of my leads and I had come up with nothing and it made me feel small. I needed another line. Maybe I should ask Klaatu.

The phone rang and Oscar Curtiss said, 'I think I got a line on Karen Shipley for you.'

I said, 'Thanks, Klaatu.'

'Hunh?'

'I sneezed. What do you have?'

'I dug out that stuff and I found an old address. It's 3484 Beechwood Canyon Place, Apartment 2. It's where she lived after the divorce.'

'Okay. Thanks.'

'I really broke my ass to find this stuff. Christ, I had it in storage in Glendale and I was two hours in traffic. You gonna tell Peter? You gonna tell Peter that I came through?' *Peter making a little flipping gesture with his drink. Fuck'm.*

'Sure, Oscar. I'll tell him.'

Oscar said, 'Oh, man.' Excited at the possibilities.

I said, 'Hey, Oscar? Thanks. I appreciate it.'

Oscar Curtiss laughed. 'Yeah, your thanks and appreciation won't buy dick. Just tell Peter, okay? This town, you're on Peter's team, you're *made*.'

'You bet, Oscar. Made.' *Fuck'm.*

I hung up.

At nine-forty that morning, I looped down Mulholland to the

Cahuenga Pass, then followed the pass down to Franklin Avenue and across the northern part of Hollywood to Beechwood Canyon. Beechwood Canyon starts high, just beneath the Hollywood sign, and winds its way down to Franklin at the bottom of the Hollywood Hills. There is a school at the bottom and a gas station and a lot of large apartment houses that used to be small apartment houses and don't look as nice large as they did small. Urban redevelopment. Between the big places sat small stucco bungalows that were neat and pretty and still managed to look like garages. The higher up the mountain you went, the more you saw of the bungalows and the less you saw of the developers.

3484 was four narrow green stucco apartments stepping up the side of the hill in a line from the street, each one higher than the one in front. Cement steps went up along the left side, the steps cracked and uneven where a couple of ancient yucca trees had lifted them. The front apartment had a little porch with wooden wind chimes and lots of little cactuses in old clay pots that were painted the way maybe Indians would paint them, only the paint was chipped and faded just like the apartments. Four big century plants nested at the street, overgrown with the silver weeds you always see around them. All of it looked clean and all of it looked tended to, but only partway, as if whoever did it couldn't quite get the high spots and couldn't quite get in the corners and couldn't quite get all the grime or the weeds or the litter out. There was no driveway and no garage. Curb parking only.

I drove past, turned around, and parked the Corvette on the steep grade across the street, then went up onto the little porch. The door opened before I could knock and a woman in her seventies looked out past three security chains. She was wearing a paisley housecoat. She said, 'Can I help you?' high and hard, like maybe if she didn't like my answer the sort of help she'd give me was the LAPD's Metro Squad.

I showed her the license. 'About ten years ago a woman named Karen Shipley Nelsen lived here with a baby. I'm trying to find her. Do you have a few minutes to talk?'

She stared at the license, then at me. 'How do I know that's you?'

I took out my driver's license so she could see the picture. Outside on the street a very tall white man and a short, slender Hispanic man walked past. The white guy was bald and wore a tie-dyed dashiki like people used to wear in 1969. The Hispanic guy combed his hair straight back and traced his hand along the lines of the Corvette as they went past. The woman squinted from the picture to the guys on the street, then to me, and said, 'That your car?'

I said it was.

She nodded once, knowing. 'You'd better watch after it. That little sonofabitch will steal it.'

I said I would keep an eye out.

She craned around to watch the two guys on the street until she couldn't see them anymore, then she closed the door and unlatched the chains and opened it wider. 'My name is Miriam Dichester. You can come in, but I think we'll leave this door open.'

'Sure.'

The living room was small and musty, with gray lace drapes and an ancient RCA black-and-white console television and a deep purple wingback couch with crocheted doilies on the arms. A long time ago the doilies had been white. The drapes had probably been white, too. Very old movie magazines sat in neat stacks on either side of the couch, and on the console television were framed photographs of Clark Gable and Walter Brennan and Ward Bond. The picture of Ward Bond was autographed. Ashtrays sprouted from the furniture like mushrooms and an open carton of Kent 100s sat on the coffee table. The air was sour with cigarettes and perspiration and Noxema skin cream.

Miriam Dichester took a single cigarette and a little blue Cricket lighter from her housecoat and fired up. I sat on the couch. She sat on a Morris chair. I hadn't seen a Morris chair in years. She said, 'I watch the street out here and I know. These days, you better watch. That's why I have my place down here by the front. I can keep an eye on anything that comes up that walk.' She waved the cigarette at the little broken walk that went up alongside the building. 'Anything I don't like goes up there, I know about it. I got a little something to take care of it, too.'

I showed her the 8 × 10. 'This is Karen Shipley. Her son's name was Toby.'

'I know who you're talking about.'

I put the picture away. 'Do you know how I can get in touch with her?'

'No, I do not.' She sucked more of the Kent, looking down the flat planes of her face at me. 'I take care of my people. I guess I take care of them even when they don't live with me anymore.'

I said, 'She's not looking at trouble here, Miriam. The ex-husband

446

hasn't seen her or the boy since they were divorced, and he's feeling pretty bad about it. He wants a shot at knowing his son.'

She breathed in the rest of the Kent, then crushed it out. Three puffs, and she had drawn through 100 millimeters down to the filter. She said, 'I don't like this. A woman gets dumped, then the sonofabitch who dumps her wants to come back to stir the pot again. And I'll bet you a high hand to heaven I know what he wants to stir it with, too.'

I gave her a little shrug. 'They're adults, Miriam, they can work that out. The boy isn't. He's about twelve now and he's never met his father.'

She pursed the wrinkled mouth. She was wearing only the upper teeth. The lowers were in a glass by the telephone. She finally took out another Kent and lit up. Succumbing to the inevitable. 'She lived with me for almost a year. She lived in number two, that's the one right behind.'

'Okay.'

'She wanted to be an actress. A lot of them come out here wanting that.' She looked at the picture of Ward Bond and drew heavy on the Kent.

'Only it wasn't happening.'

'She tried, though. She'd ask me to mind the baby so she could go out on readings, and I would, and for a while she worked at one of these carhop places, and I minded the baby then, too. She was good about it. She didn't abuse.' Miriam leaned past me and peered out the open door. The flash of a bird. A passing car.

'How long did that last?'

'Two months. Maybe three.' She leaned back as if whatever had caught her eye was gone. 'I heard her crying one day and I went to see. She said she couldn't keep on like she was going. She said she had the baby. She said there had to be a way to make a life for herself. She was very serious about it. She talked about going to school.'

I thought of the Karen Shipley I had seen on the tape. *Giggle. Do I havta, Peter? Giggle.* 'Did she enroll?'

Miriam Dichester shook her head and finished off another Kent. 'She didn't have the money. And what was she going to do with the baby?'

'Did she have friends? Boyfriends, maybe.' As soon as the one Kent was dead, she fired up another.

'No. She was alone. Just her and the baby. Not even any family to go to. After a while she didn't even leave the apartment. She just sat there, a young girl like that. Then she moved out.'

'She tell you where she was going?'

'She didn't say nothing when she moved out. She just up and left, owing me three months' back rent.'

She leaned forward again to look out the door. This time when she looked, I looked with her. It was catching. I said, 'You seem to like her.'

'I do.'

'Even though she stiffed you on the rent.'

She waved the cigarette at me. 'She paid it back. Couple of years later I got a letter. There was a U.S. postal money order in it for every nickel and the interest, too. How many people you know would do that?'

'A couple.'

'Then all right. There was a little note in there apologizing and saying she hoped I wouldn't think bad of her for what she did but it couldn't be helped.'

'You like her a lot.'

Another nod. More of the Kent.

'You keep the letter?'

She said, 'Oh, Lord, I got so much stuff scattered around.'

'Maybe you could take a look.'

She squinted out past the drapes to the street. 'I go digging around in the back, I can't see the front.'

'I'll watch the front for you.'

'That little sonofabitch is looking to steal something, mark my words. They're coming back.'

'I'll watch. I'm good at watching.' I tapped my cheek under my right eye. Watchful.

She nodded and bustled over to a little secretary that was against the wall near where the living room L'd into the dining room. Three small drawers were fit across the top of the secretary, and she opened them one by one, looking through pens and pencils and note cards and small envelopes and photographs and a crushed flower and newspaper clippings that looked, from across the room, like obituary columns, and things that might've been forty years old. Precious things. She rustled around in it for a while, talking to me but really talking to herself, saying how she'd have to clean the place up, saying that she started to last week but then someone named Edna called and that had been that, no one ever calls until

448

you're about to do something. She went through the drawers and she came up with a small white envelope that had been torn along the top edge. It had been in the little drawer for so long that the ragged tears were crushed flat and smooth and the paper was dingy. She took out a single sheet of folded yellow notepaper and read it and then showed it to me. It was exactly as Miriam Dichester had said it was, Karen apologizing for leaving while still owing money, saying she hoped Miriam hadn't experienced a hardship because of it, saying a check had been enclosed to pay Miriam back in full, including $6\frac{1}{2}\%$ interest, and that she appreciated the kindness and friendship that Miriam had shown her and her son while they had lived with her. There was no return address and no hotel letterhead and no mention of where Karen was or where she was going. The envelope was postmarked *Chelam, CT*.

Miriam said, 'Does it help?'

I nodded. 'It's more than I had before.'

She said, 'You find them, you do right by them, hear?'

'That's my intention.'

'Well, you know what they say about that, don't you?'

'No. What do they say?'

'The road to hell is paved with good intentions.'

When we were in the door the tall white man and the shorter Hispanic man were walking down the street in the other direction. She said, 'You see. I told you they'd be back.'

'Maybe they live down the hill. Maybe they're just out for a walk.'

'My dying ass.' She was a pleasant old gal. 'Mark my words, that little sonofabitch is out to steal something.'

I thanked her and gave her one of my cards in case she remembered anything else, and then I went out to the Corvette. A hundred yards down the street, the white guy and the Hispanic guy were using a two-foot steel shim to pop the door on a white 1991 Toyota Supra.

I yelled and ran after them, but by the time I got there they were gone.

449

CHAPTER 8

Two hours and ten minutes later I was on a United Airlines L-1011 as it punched its way up through the haze layer and climbed out over the Pacific. The air was slick and clear and, below us, the red of the mountains and the desert and the gray of the ocean looked clean and warm. It was your basic outstanding Southern California afternoon. The people around me were relaxed and pleasant, and the flight attendant had a deep tan and when her smile was wide enough she dimpled. She was from Long Beach. Outstanding.

Five and one half hours later we landed at Kennedy airport beneath an overcast layer so thick and so dark that it looked like casket lining. Unseasonal cold snap, the papers had said. Arctic air down through Canada, they'd said. First snow of the season. I had brought a brown leather Navy G-2 jacket and a couple of sweaters and a pair of black leather gloves. It wasn't enough, even for standing around in the terminal.

While I waited for my suitcase at the baggage carousel, three different guys asked if they could borrow cab fare and another wanted to know if I'd found Jesus. An airport security cop arrested a pickpocket. The air smelled like burning rubber. A woman with a baby told me she didn't have enough money to feed her child. I gave her fifty cents and felt like I'd been taken. Maybe I looked like a tourist. I frowned and looked sullen and tried to make like a native. That seemed to work. I got a couple of road maps and a metallic-blue Taurus from Hertz and drove over to the Kennedy Hilton and took a room for the night. Dining-room service was slow and the food was bad and the hostess in the bar had an attitude. A guy on the radio said that the cold air was going to keep pushing down from Canada and that maybe we'd get some more snow. The room cost two hundred a night and nobody had deep tans and dimples.

This was my fourth time visiting New York in eleven years. Nothing much had changed. I ♥ NY.

The next morning I checked out of the Hilton and took the Van Wyck Expressway north to Connecticut. Through most of Queens and the Bronx everything looked dirty and gray and old, but farther along the building density diminished until, as I approached White Plains, stretches of empty land appeared, bordered by stands of trees, and, just north of White Plains, there were lakes. The empty land became fields and the woods grew deeper, and though some of the trees were dark and bare, most were still locked in their explosions of yellow and red and purple, and the sight and the smell of them made me think of squash and wild turkeys and neighborhoods where children yelled 'Trick or Treat!' Maybe the Northeast wasn't so bad after all.

Four miles east of Rockwood Lake, there was a Howard Johnson's Motor Lodge and a green exit sign that said *CHELAM next right*. I got off and followed a state road for a mile and a half through woods and farmland and there it was, a little place of clapboard and brick buildings around a town square, maybe two blocks on a side. There were plenty of trees and lawns, and the streets were narrow and without curbs and looked more like they were made for velocipedes than for automobiles. The overcast and the cold gave a barren quality to the town, but there was still enough green in the lawns and color in the leaves to let you know that, come spring, Chelam would look like one of those quaint little upstate hamlets that are always pictured on the postcards your cousin Flo sends.

I let the Taurus roll down the main street past a Texaco station and a White Castle hamburger stand and the First Chelam National Bank and a barbershop with an honest-to-God barber's pole. A whitewashed gazebo sat on the town square across from a courthouse that was big and old, with a second-floor balcony ideal for mayoral speeches on the Fourth of July. Several big elms dotted the square, their dead leaves a fragile brown carpet over the lawn. Two young women in down jackets stood in the leaves, talking. An old man in a bright orange hunter's parka sat on the gazebo steps, smoking. Next to the courthouse there was a mobile home permanently mounted on cement footings. A big gold star was painted on the side of the mobile home along with the words CHELAM POLICE. Across the square there was a little building just about the size of a pay toilet that said *U.S. Post Office*. Eight years ago Karen Nelsen had gone in there and mailed the letter to Miriam

Dichester. Maybe she had been on her way up to Maine, just passing through when she thought, oh, Christ, I've gotta get this money back to Miriam, and she had stopped and bought the money order and mailed it and continued on her way. But maybe not. Maybe she had stayed the night or had gotten something to eat and had said where she was going and someone would remember.

One block past the post office the town ended. I turned around and drove back to the Texaco station and pulled up to the full-service pumps. An old geez in a stained gray Texaco shirt and a cammie hunting cap was leaning back in a chair beneath a sign that said WE HAVE PROPANE. I turned off the engine and got out and said, 'How about some high-test?'

He tilted the chair forward and came over and put in the nozzle. A dirty blond Labrador retriever was lying between the chair and a Pepsi machine. The Lab had its chin down and its paws out to either side. He didn't move when the old man got up, but his eyes followed the old man to the car. Someone had put down a piece of cardboard for the dog to lie on.

I said, 'Pretty town.'

The old man nodded.

'Picturesque.'

He made a sucking sound through his nose, then hocked up something heavy and spit it toward the road. 'You want me to check the hood?'

'Hood's okay. If I wanted to stay a few days, where would I go?'

'Ho Jo's out on the highway.'

'Here in town.'

He squinted at the gas pump. Nine-forty and rising.

I said, 'There a little hotel? Maybe a boardinghouse? Something established?'

He made the sucking sound again, and this time he swallowed it.

I fed seventy-five cents into the Pepsi machine, pulled out a Barq's root beer, opened it, then sat down in the old man's chair. The dog still hadn't moved, but now it looked at me. So did the old man. Neither of them liked me in the chair. I said, 'Think I'll set for a spell and chew the fat.' Elvis Cole, the Bumpkin Detective.

The old man said, 'Guess you might try May Erdich's place.'

'She the only place in town?'

'Ayuh.' I guess that meant yes.

'Were there any other places, say, about ten years ago?'

'Shit.' I guess that meant no.

'How do I get to the Erdich place?'

The gas pump *dinged*. He put the nozzle back in the pump, then reset the counter. The dog's eyes moved from the old man to me, then back to the old man. Every time its eyes moved, its eyebrows shifted like it was watching a tennis match. It looked like Fred MacMurray.

I said, 'May Erdich.'

He told me, but only after I got out of his chair.

I drove back through the town and found May Erdich's place on a residential street two blocks behind the square. It was a big yellow two-story house with a gravel drive and a covered porch and a little sign out front that said *rooms to let*. Pockets of hard snow hid in the eaves and under the porch, safe from the sun. I parked in her drive and went up to the front door and knocked.

A woman in her late forties opened the door and looked out at me. She had fair skin and a pale green apron over blue jeans and a coarse yarn sweater, and her hair was held up with bobby pins so that wisps of it floated down into her eyes. It was warm in her house, and the warmth rolled out at me and felt good.

I said, 'Are you May Erdich?'

'That's right.'

'My name is Elvis Cole. I'm a private detective from Los Angeles. I'm trying to find someone who may or may not have stayed here about eight years ago.'

She smiled. The smile was where the lines came from. 'A private detective.'

'Pretty hokey, huh?'

The smile got wider and she nodded.

I showed her one of my cards and gave her a little Groucho Marx. 'Sam Grunion, private eye. Secrecy is our motto. We never tell.'

She laughed and slapped the towel against her thigh and said, 'No shit.' I was going to like May Erdich just fine.

She opened the door wider, let me come in, took the G-2, then had me sit on a big overstuffed couch in a room she called the parlor. 'Would you like a cup of hot tea? I just put some up fresh.'

'That'd be great. Thank you.'

She went out through a swinging door. The parlor was neat and clean, with a hardwood floor that showed neither dust nor scuff marks.

She came back with two glass cups of honey-colored tea on a beaten-pewter tray. There was a bowl of sugar with a little gold spoon in it and a few packets of Sweet'n Low and a saucer of sliced lemons and two glass spoons for stirring the tea and another saucer mounded with what looked like homemade blueberry cookies. The apron was gone and the wisps of hair were now neatly under the pins. I took one of the cookies. 'Delicious.'

'Would you like sugar or lemon?'

'I take it plain.'

She made a face. 'Ugh. It's so bitter that way.'

'Private detectives are pretty tough.' I had some of the tea. It was mellow and sweet with mint. Sugar would've ruined it.

She said, 'Is it exciting to be a detective in Los Angeles?'

'Sometimes. Most of the time it's doing things that people never think of when they think of private investigators.'

'Like what?'

'Like looking through phone bills and credit card receipts and being put on hold when you're talking to people at utility companies and the DMV and that kind of thing.'

She nodded, trying to imagine Tom Selleck on hold.

'But sometimes you get to help people and that feels pretty good.'

'Who are you trying to find?'

'A woman named Karen Nelsen. She might've been using the name Karen Shipley. Eight years ago, she would've had a toddler with her. A little boy, maybe three or four years old.'

She sipped more of the tea and thought about it, then shook her head, a little half shake. 'No. No, that doesn't ring a bell.'

I took out the 8 × 10 and showed it to her. The photo had been folded and there were creases that I tried to smooth.

May Erdich leaned forward and smiled the wide smile and said, 'Are you serious?' like maybe I was pulling her leg.

I said, 'What?'

'That's Karen Lloyd. She works at the bank.'

I looked at the picture as if it might've changed. 'She works at the bank?' We exciting L.A. detectives are quick on the uptake.

'She's got a twelve-year-old boy named Toby. I see her in the market. We used to be in PTA together.'

'This woman lives here, this woman and her son, Toby.' Swift, we are.

'That's right.'

I folded the picture and put it back in my pocket. Sonofagun. 'Karen Lloyd.'

May Erdich nodded. 'That's right. She works at the First Chelam. I think she's the manager or something.'

I finished the tea and stood up and May Erdich stood up with me. 'Why are you trying to find her? Did she do something bad?' Her eyes were bright and mischievous, thinking how great it would be if someone in town had done something bad.

I said, 'It involves family business, and you won't be doing her a favor if you tell people that a private cop has been asking about her. Do you understand that?'

May Erdich gave me some Groucho and squeezed my arm. 'Secrecy is our motto.'

'Right.'

She led me to the door. 'You must be a pretty good detective, all the way from Los Angeles to find somebody here in Chelam.'

I put on the G-2 and went out into the cold. 'That's right. I am. In another life I could have been Batman.'

CHAPTER 9

The First Chelam National Bank was a small redbrick building across from the grocery store and next to a place called Zoot's Hardware. There was a single drive-through window for their customers' convenience on the west side of the bank and a small L-shaped parking lot wrapping around the east. Someone had planted a couple of young elms at the edge of the parking lot and their leaves were scattered over the cement. The drive-through window was closed.

I parked in the lot and went in. A teenage boy was filling out a deposit slip at a long table, and a heavy woman in stretch pants was talking to a teller at a blond-wood counter. An old guy in a gray security guard's uniform was reading Tom Clancy. He didn't look up. There were four windows built into the tellers' counter, but only one teller was on duty. Another woman sat at a desk behind the counter, and behind her were a couple of offices, but the offices looked empty. Neither the teller nor the woman at the desk appeared to be Karen Shipley.

I gave the woman at the desk a hopeful smile. She was in her late twenties and wore a bright green top under a tweed suit jacket and a little too much makeup. A name plate on her desk said JOYCE STEUBEN. I said, 'Excuse me. I'm here to see Karen Lloyd.'

Joyce Steuben said, 'Karen isn't in right now. She has a couple of property appraisals, but she should be back around three. Of course, she might come in before then. That's always possible.'

'Of course.'

I left the bank and walked across the street to a pay phone outside the grocery. In L.A., they put phone books three inches thick with the pay phones, but most of the books are stolen and the ones that aren't are defaced. The Chelam book represented something called *The Five-Town Area*. Chelam, Oak Lakes, Armonk,

Brunly, and Tooley's Mill. It was complete and immaculate and was this year's edition, and altogether it was maybe a quarter-inch thick. Karen Lloyd was listed on page 38. Number Fourteen Rural Route Twelve, Chelam. There were six Lloyds. Three in Tooley's Mill and two in Brunly. Karen was the only Lloyd in Chelam. No Mr. Lloyd. I copied her address along with her phone number and put the book back in its case, still complete, still immaculate. Jim Rockford would've ripped out the page, but Jim Rockford was an asshole.

I sat on the bench outside Milt's Barber Stylings and wondered at my good fortune. If Karen Lloyd was in fact Karen Shipley, maybe I could get this thing wrapped up and be on an evening flight back to L.A. In L.A., I wouldn't have to sit outside Milt's Barber Stylings with two sweaters under the G-2 and still be cold. Of course, maybe Karen Lloyd wasn't Karen Shipley. Maybe they just looked alike and May Erdich was wrong. Stranger things have been known to happen. All I had to do was hang around and wait for Karen Lloyd and ferret out the truth.

Portrait of the Big City Detective sitting on a small-town bench, ferreting. In the cold. People passed on the sidewalk, and when they did they nodded and smiled and said hello. I said hello back to them. They didn't look as cold as me, but perhaps that was my imagination. You get used to the weather where you live. When I was in Ranger School in the Army, they sent us to northern Canada to learn to ski and to climb ice and to live in the snow with very few clothes. We got used to it. Then they sent us to Vietnam. That's the Army.

A little bit after two-thirty kids started drifting past with books, and at five minutes before three a dark-haired boy in a plaid Timberland jacket came pumping down the street on a beat-up red Schwinn mountain bike. Toby Nelsen. He was horse-faced and gangly, with a wide butt and narrow shoulders, just like his father. His rear end was up and his head was down and he whipped the bike across the sidewalk and skidded to a stop by the front door of the bank just as a dark green Chrysler LeBaron pulled into the parking lot. He was laughing. A woman who might've been Karen Shipley got out of the Chrysler. A dozen years older than the Karen Shipley in the videotape, wearing a tailored rust-colored top coat and heels and tortoiseshell sunglasses. Together. Her hair was short and set off her heart-shaped face nicely and she stood straight and confident. She didn't bounce or wiggle. Toby raised his hands over his head and yelled, 'I beatcha by a mile!' and she said something and the boy laughed again and they went into the bank. I crossed the street after them. Elvis Cole, Master Detective. We Always Get Our Mom.

When I got into the bank, Karen Shipley was seated in one of the back offices, talking on the phone, and the boy was at a little coffee table, writing in a spiral notebook. I went to the end of the tellers' counter again and waved at Joyce Steuben. 'I'm back.'

Joyce Steuben looked around at Karen Shipley, still on the phone. 'She's on a call now. Can I tell her who wants to see her?'

'Elvis Cole.'

'Would you like to have a seat?'

'Sure.'

I walked back to the little round table and sat down across from the boy. He was writing in the workbook with a yellow pencil and didn't look up. Fractions. He was big for twelve, but his face was smooth and unlined and young. He looked exactly like his father, and I wondered if he knew that. I said, 'You Toby Lloyd?'

He looked up and smiled. 'Yeah. Hi.' He looked healthy and happy and normal.

'You're Karen's son?'

'Yeah. You know my mom?'

'I'm here to see her. I saw you guys racing down the street. You were really flying.'

His smile flashed a yard wide. 'I really creamed her today. Usually she wins.'

Karen Shipley said, 'Mr. Cole? May I help you?' She was standing in the little passage at the end of the tellers' counter.

I got up and went over and shook her hand. The handshake was firm and dry and poised, and she looked at me with a clear confidence that she could meet my every banking need. No wedding ring. Up close, and with the sunglasses off, you saw that she was the woman in the video, yet not. It was the face, yet not the same face. As if she had stepped into the transmogrifier with Calvin and Hobbes and had been changed. Her voice was lower and there was a light network of lines around her eyes and she looked better now than she had then, the way most women do as they move into their thirties. I said, 'I hope so. I'm going to be moving to the area, and I'd like to discuss financing for the purchase of a home.'

She opened the gate and gave me a warm, professional smile. 'Why don't we go back to my office and talk about it.'

'Sure.'

Her office was neat and modern, with a polished executive's desk and well-tended green plants and comfortable chairs in which people with legitimate business could sit and look at her. A Toshiba *My Café* coffee machine sat on a lowboy filing cabinet between a couple of smoked-glass windows that looked out on the parking lot, and on the wall behind her desk there were framed photographs and certificates and diplomas. Official-looking men and women were standing with Karen in the photos, and in some of them the official-looking people were presenting Karen with what looked like plaques and citations. Some of the citations were on the wall. *Greater New England Banking and Trust Award. PTA Meritorious Service Award. Appreciation Award from the Five-Town Area Rotary.* A framed real estate license hung beneath a diploma from the State University of New York for a bachelor's degree in finance. *Gee, Peter, do I havta?* It had been awarded two years ago. I blinked at her and maybe smiled a little. It had been a long time since she'd made herself up like a waitress. She said, 'Would you like coffee?'

'No, thank you.'

She went around and sat behind the desk and folded her hands and smiled at me. 'All right. How can I help you?'

I got up and closed the door.

She said, 'You don't have to do that.'

I left the door closed and went back to my seat. 'It's better if it's closed,' I said. 'I'm afraid I've come to you under false pretenses.'

She made a small frown, wondering what I was talking about.

I said, 'I'm not moving to the area, and I don't want to finance a house. I'm a private investigator. From Los Angeles.'

Her left eye flickered and she didn't move for several seconds. Then she made an effort at the professional smile and sort of cocked her head to one side. Confused. 'I'm afraid I don't understand.'

I took out the 8 × 10 of nineteen-year-old Karen Shipley made up like a waitress, unfolded it, and put it on her desk. I said, 'Karen Shipley.'

She leaned forward and looked at the 8 × 10 without touching it. 'I'm sorry. My name is Karen Lloyd. I don't know what you're talking about.'

'Your ex-husband, Peter Alan Nelsen, hired me to find you.'

She shook her head, smiled patiently, then used a pencil to push the picture back toward me and stood up. 'I don't know anyone named Peter Alan Nelsen and I've never been to Los Angeles.'

I said, 'Karen. Come on.'

'I'm sorry. But if you're not here to discuss business with the bank, I think you should leave.' She came around the desk and opened the door and stood there, right hand on the knob. Outside, Joyce Steuben glanced at us from her desk and a woman with blue hair took money from the teller.

I picked up the 8 × 10 and looked at it and looked at the woman with her hand on the knob. They were one and the same. I had not lost my mind. 'Ten years ago you and Peter Alan Nelsen were divorced. Your theatrical agent was a guy named Oscar Curtiss. You lived in an apartment house on Beechwood Drive owned by a woman named Miriam Dichester for almost a year, and then you skipped out on three months' back rent. Twenty-two months after that, you mailed a U.S. postal money order for four hundred fifty-two dollars and eighteen cents to Ms. Dichester. It was postmarked Chelam. This is you in the picture. Your maiden name was Shipley. Then you were Karen Nelsen. And now you're Karen Lloyd.'

She was gripping the door knob so hard that the tendons in the back of her right hand were standing out like bow strings, as if the force of the grip was not so much to hold on to the knob as it was to hold together something that had been carefully constructed over many years and was now in danger of being pulled apart. Her eye gave the flicker again. 'I'm sorry. I don't know what you're talking about.'

'Don't know.'

She made the professional smile, but it didn't quite work this time. 'I'm sorry.'

I held up the picture. 'This isn't you?'

The little smile again. 'No. We do look alike, though, so I can understand your confusion.'

I nodded. Outside, the woman with the blue hair put money in a plain white envelope and put the envelope in her blouse and walked away. Joyce Steuben talked on the phone. The guard read Tom Clancy. Nobody seemed ready to jump up and give me a hand, but then they rarely do. I said, 'Peter doesn't want anything from you. He doesn't want to impose on you or to interfere with either your life or the boy's. He just wants to meet his son. He seems sincere in this. You're not going to gain anything by acting this way.'

She didn't move.

I spread my hands. 'Karen, you're found.'

She made a little shrug and shook her head. 'I hope you find whoever you're looking for. I really do. Now if you don't mind, I have work to do.'

She didn't move and I didn't move. Outside, a black man in a New York Yankees baseball cap approached the teller and Joyce Steuben hung up the phone and began to write on a yellow legal pad. Somewhere in the back of the little building the heating system clicked on and warm air came through the vents. I said, 'If there's nothing to anything I've said, call the guard and have him throw me out.'

She squinted to make the left eye stop moving. The knuckles on the hand holding the knob turned white. Neither of us said anything for quite a while. Then the tip of her tongue appeared and wet her lips. She said, 'I'm sorry that you've wasted your time, but I know nothing about any of this.'

I took a deep breath and let it out and then I nodded. 'Karen Lloyd.'

'Yes. That's my name.'

'Never been to Los Angeles.'

'Never.'

'Don't know Peter Nelsen.'

'I can understand your confusion. I do look very much like the girl in the picture.'

I nodded again. The black man finished his transaction and left and the teller walked over to Joyce Steuben's desk and sat down. Toby Nelsen appeared in the teller's window, reached through, took a pencil, then disappeared again. Karen Shipley stood very still, legs together, elbows tight at her sides, right hand on the knob and left hanging down at her side. The left was red as if blood had pooled there. I folded the 8 × 10 and put it in my pocket and stood up. 'Sorry,' I said. 'You do look very much alike.'

'Yes.'

'I'll be seeing you.'

'Have a nice day.'

I walked past her and past Joyce Steuben and around the end of the tellers' counter and out past the guard to the front door. I stopped and looked back at her. She had not moved. Her face was tight and contained and her right hand was still gripping the knob of her door. She stared at me a little longer and then she stepped back into the office and shut the door. Toby was concentrating on the math workbook and did not look up.

I went out to the parking lot and stood by my car beneath a sky that had grown heavy and dense and the color of shale. There was a cold wind coming from the northwest and a formation of large black crows beating their wings a hundred feet overhead. Because of the wind, the crows were pointing in one direction but traveling in another. I wondered if they knew it, and, knowing it, understood it, or if they were simply oblivious, carried along by a force that was felt but not seen. The same thing happens to people, but most of the time they don't know it, or when they know it, they think it an action of their own devising. They are usually wrong.

CHAPTER 10

Just after four o'clock I drove back to the Howard Johnson's and took a room for the night. I brought in my things, pulled off my clothes, then went into the shower, letting the hot water cut at my scalp and my neck and my shoulders. I let it cut for a long time. When I got out, I drank a glass of water, got dressed, and went down to the bar.

The bartender was a red-haired woman in her early forties with white lip gloss and heavy silver earrings that looked like little Rorschach patterns. She was cutting limes with a very large knife with a wide, flat blade. She said, 'You're the guy from Los Angeles.' These small towns.

I nodded. 'Really packing'm in tonight.' I was the only one in the place.

'Wait'll you have one of my drinks. You'll see why.'

'Unh-hunh.' You come to these small towns, the people think they're a riot. 'The beer cold?'

'Yeah, but it's flat.' You see?

I asked her for a Falstaff, but all they had was Rolling Rock. She put down the knife and went to a refrigerator with a see-through door and took out a long-necked bottle. She said, 'I always wanted to go out to Los Angeles. What they say about the smog true?'

'Yep.'

'Bet it's nice, though.' She opened the bottle and put it and an icy glass on a little napkin in front of me. I had some.

'It is.' I took a little more. Second pull and the bottle was almost empty. Maybe Rolling Rock just sort of naturally went down easy after a hard day of dealing with women who hung on to their lies as if the lies were living things. I had most of the rest of it.

The bartender said, 'I was a kid, I wanted to go out there. I used to think about it all the time, palm trees and people roller-skating at the beach and cruising down the freeways in a convertible.' The knife went through another lime. *Thunk*. 'Sometimes things just sort of get away from you.' *Thunk*. She stopped cutting and looked at me. 'You want a piece of lime in your beer?'

'No, thanks.'

'I heard people in California put lime in their beer.'

'No.'

She looked disappointed.

I left a two dollar tip and went next door into the restaurant. Two guys in plaid flannel L.L. Bean shirts and bright orange hunter's caps sat at a formica counter, holding heavy white coffee mugs in coarse hands. A chalk board that said *Today's Special: Homemade meat loaf* sat on a little easel on the counter across from a row of booths. Farther back, there were tables and chairs for people with a greater sense of formality. I sat in a booth by the windows with a delightful view of the parking lot.

A short woman in a black waitress outfit brought a menu and a glass of ice water, and asked whether or not I'd care for a drink before dinner. The first Rolling Rock had been so good I told her that I'd have a second. Without lime. She wrote on a little pad and said, 'We have a special tonight. It's the meat loaf. It's very nice.' She was in her sixties.

I handed back the menu without looking at it. 'Then that's what I'll have.'

She gave me an approving smile and went away. I felt the warmth of her smile and was glad that someone approved of me. Karen Shipley probably didn't. *You have me confused with someone else*. Not much you could do with that. A stranger walks in off the street and tells you that everything you've worked for was about to change. Who you gonna call? Gumshoebusters?

The waitress came back with the beer. An older couple strolled in and took a table in the dining room. Formal. A single guy in a gray business suit came in carrying the *New York Times* and sat at the counter, well away from the two guys in the orange hunting caps. He opened his *Times* to the real estate section. I drank the Rolling Rock and marveled at how good Karen and the boy and the Rotary awards had looked together, and wondered if that would continue with Peter on the scene. With Peter around, maybe their lives would disintegrate and Karen would fall into prostitution and Toby would end up running with a dope-fiend vampire motorcycle gang and the Rotary would take back their awards. It happens all the time with Hollywood families.

The waitress brought the meat loaf on a heavy white plate like the kind they used in cafeterias in the forties. The slice of meat loaf was wide and thick and weighed almost a pound. There was a large portion of creamed potatoes and about a million green peas, and a thick brown gravy had been ladled over the meat loaf and the potatoes. Nurture food. It smelled wonderful. She said, 'Can I get you anything else?'

'Tabasco sauce and another Rolling Rock.'

She brought the Rock and the Tabasco. I applied both liberally. Tabasco is great for clearing the sinus and putting the ruination of lives into perspective. So is the Rolling Rock. The meat loaf was excellent.

What's wrong with this picture? Peter Alan Nelsen was a celebrity, and the profits from his pictures were subject to stories in *Newsweek* and *Time*. Karen would read those stories and know that her ex-husband, the father of her child, was worth millions. Many people, perhaps most, would go after a piece of that, yet she hadn't. Either for herself or for the boy. Interesting. Maybe Peter wasn't the boy's father. Maybe Peter had done such hateful things to Karen that this was her way of punishing him and he deserved it. Maybe Karen was a nut case.

At five minutes before seven a tall guy with a nose like a chayote squash came in and looked around. He was wearing a bright turquoise shirt with a squash-blossom string tie and black slacks and a black duster. The black slacks were a half inch too short and the pointy black shoes were cut a half inch too low, so you ended up seeing a lot of black socks with little red triangles. He looked at me and the guy with the *Times* and the couple in the back and then he left. Probably looking for the disco.

I worked on the meat loaf and the potatoes and the peas and a growing depression. There were questions, and the questions bothered me, but I hadn't been hired to answer questions or even to get Karen Shipley to admit that she was Karen Shipley. I had been hired to find her whereabouts and I had done that. The rest was up to Peter Alan Nelsen. So what if Karen Shipley didn't like it, and so what if I didn't like it. They don't pay me to like it.

I ordered two more of the Rolling Rock to bring back to my room. A couple more Rock and I'd probably like it just fine.

Out in the parking lot the guy in the string tie met a white

Thunderbird and said something to the driver. They talked for a minute, then the guy in the string tie got in on the passenger's side and the Thunderbird crept away around the side of the motel.

The waitress brought the beer in a little brown paper bag and the check and a single peppermint. I signed for the check and went out through the lobby. My room was on the ground floor, off the parking lot on the west side of the motel, halfway down a two-story row of rooms and just past a little alcove with an ice machine and a Pepsi machine and a stair leading up to the second floor. The Taurus was parked outside my room and a green Polara station wagon was parked closer up on the street side of the lot. A Peterbilt eighteen-wheeler took up most of the far end of the parking lot, looking like a supertanker in dry dock. No white Thunderbird.

When I got to the stairwell, the guy in the string tie and another guy stepped out. Guess they put the Thunderbird on the other side.

The guy with the string tie said, 'Hey, Joey, you think this is the guy?'

Joey was shorter and wider than me with a round cannon-ball head and caviar zits and a thick fleshy body that made him look sort of like an overgrown Pillsbury dough boy. He was wearing a blue Navy pea coat open over two layers of flannel shirts. The shirttails hung out. He said, 'Yeah, this is him. Looks like a fuck from out of town who don't belong around here. Like he needs a little help to find his way home.' He was maybe twenty-six, but he looked younger. He also looked mean.

The guy with the string tie nodded and made a sort of snickering sound. The snickering sound was a nose whistle. 'Fuckin' A. Let's get him on his way.'

I said, 'Are you guys for real, or is this going to be on *America's Funniest Home Videos*?' They sounded like Leo Gorcey and Huntz Hall. Brooklyn or the Bronx or Queens, but I couldn't tell which. New Yorkers all sound alike.

The guy with the string tie took out a piece of pipe maybe ten inches long and Joey took a half-step forward. Joey said, 'We got a message for you, Mickey Mouse. Pack your fuckin' mouse ears and go back to Disneyland.'

I blinked at them. 'Did Karen Lloyd put you guys on me?'

The string tie waved the pipe so I could see it better. 'You don't ask questions, fuck face. You just do what we say.' He was breathing hard and the nose whistle was loud. Even Joey looked.

I said, 'That's some nose whistle. Is it natural or did you have to stick something up in there?'

Joey said, 'This fuck thinks we're kidding.'

Johnny Style swung the pipe from somewhere out around the North Atlantic.

I stepped to the inside and hit him in the forehead with the two bottles of Rolling Rock. The broken glass cut through the bag and beer sprayed back along my arm and across the wall and the sidewalk. Johnny Style said, 'Unh,' and dropped the pipe and fell backward over a curb stone. Joey sort of waddled forward, throwing a lot of overhand rights and lefts without much in the way of control, trying to do it the way he'd done it in schoolyards and on playgrounds for most of his life.

I sideslipped and hit him twice in the face and once in the neck and drove a straight kick from the tae kwon do into his solar plexus. He stopped swinging and made a sort of coughing sound and stepped back. Surprised.

I said, 'What's this got to do with Karen Lloyd?'

Joey made the coughing sound again, then something hard hit me behind my right ear and I went down. Third guy in the Thunderbird. I kicked up and punched, but I don't think I hit him. My eyes weren't working too well and it was hard to see through the starbursts. Joey leaned over and punched me some more in the ribs and again in the back of the head, saying, 'You fuck! You fuck!' He was slow, and he was stupid, but he was strong. He lifted my head by the hair and sort of shook my head and said, 'Get out of town and keep your mouth shut or we'll turn you into a fuckin' piece of hamburg. You got that? You got that, you fuck?' I tried a claw move at his eyes, but I missed. The guy with the string tie said, 'Jesus Christ, I gotta get to a hospital.'

Joey kicked me again, then there were footsteps and, a long time later, an engine fired to life and faded away into the buzz of the highway.

I lay with my face pressed down into the parking lot, and no one came and no one saw. It was cold. Cars moved past on the service road, but none pulled in. Out front there would be people coming and going for the bar, but not back here. After a while I pushed myself up and tested my balance and went to my room.

I took four aspirin and peeled off my clothes and looked at myself. You get kicked in the lower back and you worry about the kidneys, and you get kicked in the ribs and you worry they're broken. I leaned forward and back and from side to side and raised my arms over my head. The places where I was kicked throbbed with a sort of a dull ache and when I raised my arms the right side of my back below the shoulder blade hurt but not the way it would hurt if anything was broken. I urinated. There was no blood. Kidneys were okay, but I'd have to check again later in the night.

I closed the toilet lid and sat on the seat and felt myself living. I felt the blood move and the lungs work and the muscles pull against bone. I hurt, but it was better than being in the hospital, and it was better than being dead. I had been hurt bad before, and I knew what that felt like. This wasn't bad.

I took a very cold shower, and then I dressed and went out to the ice machine and brought back a tub of ice. I undressed again and took another four aspirin and put some of the ice in one of the snowy-white Howard Johnson towels. I stacked the pillows at the head of the bed and sat against the pillows with the ice on my head. An hour later I dressed and put on my jacket and walked back to the bar. It was nine-forty-five. The bartender was gone and the bar was closed and so was the restaurant. That's life in Chelam.

I went back to my room and put more ice in the towel and lay there for a very long time thinking about Karen Shipley.

CHAPTER 11

The next morning my back felt stiff and hard, and the place behind my ear ached with a doughy, immediate presence. I took more of the aspirin, soaked in a hot bath to loosen the back, and then did yoga, starting with the simplest stretches and working my way through the spine rock and the cobra and the spine twist. The back hurt quite a bit at first but warmed and felt better as I worked.

By twenty minutes after nine I was back in Chelam. I drove down Main Street past the bank to the town square, turned one block south, then turned again and parked in front of a place that had at one time been a showroom for John Deere tractors. Now, it was empty.

The threat of snow had passed without incident, and the day was bright and clear except for a scattering of cottonball cumulus clouds that moved through the sky to the south. It was warmer. I walked back to the grocery store one block north and stood by the pay phone and looked at the bank. Karen Shipley's green LeBaron was in the lot. I could go into the bank and confront her, but chances were good that she would continue to deny that she was Karen Shipley. Chances were equally good that she would deny knowing the three leg-busters who had come to the Ho Jo. I could go in with the sheriff, but that would bring in the press and Peter Alan Nelsen. The press would like it, but Peter Alan Nelsen probably wouldn't. Also, I didn't like the way it felt for Karen Shipley. There was something acutely desperate and unprotected about Karen Shipley denying that she was Karen Shipley even as she stared at her photograph, and I didn't want the sheriff and the town and the press to know what it was before I knew what it was. Also, going to the sheriff seemed like a wimpy thing to do. There were alternatives. I could lie in wait for Karen Shipley and, when she stepped out of the bank, pistol-whip her into admitting her true identity. If that didn't work, I could shadow her every move until, in an unguarded moment, she revealed her true self. Or maybe I could just ask around. Hmm. Asking around seemed easiest and a lot less trouble. After all, Karen Shipley had lived here for eight years. The people here knew her and knew of her, and if I talked to them, I might learn what they knew and see what they saw. If I knew enough and saw enough, maybe I'd know what in hell was going on and what to do about it. Elvis Cole, detective in search of intelligence.

Rittenhauser's Diner was down the block, two doors past the barbershop. I went in and sat at the counter. A pinch-faced short-order cook in a blue apron was standing with his arms crossed near the cash register. He was watching a tiny Magnavox color TV that was sitting on a gallon can of pork and beans next to the register. Oprah Winfrey. Something about fat men being better lovers. He picked a clean coffee mug from a wire rack and filled it and put the mug in front of me without my having to ask. He said, 'What'll it be?'

'Three eggs, scrambled. Rye toast. Maybe put some mushrooms and some cheese in the eggs.'

'Sharp cheddar?'

'How about Swiss?'

'You got it.'

He made the eggs and a little patty of hash browns and two large pieces of rye toast. When it was done, he put it all onto a heavy white plate, then he put the plate in front of me. I said, 'Nice looking plate of eggs.'

He said, 'Unh,' and went back to the Oprah.

I ate some of the eggs. 'Just moved out from California. Transfer. Met Karen Lloyd at the bank yesterday.'

'Unh.'

'Nice looking lady.'

He said it again.

'You know if she's married or seeing someone?'

'Nope.' An obese man in his sixties told Oprah that he could ejaculate twenty-six times a day. He attributed it to his bulk. The cook looked interested.

'Nope, you don't know, or nope, she's not seeing someone?'

'Ain't none of my business.' The obese man said that when he was thin, he was sexually dysfunctional.

'She been working at the bank long?'

The cook leaned closer to the television. Something about high-fat content leading to increased fluids production.

I said, 'Great day for a nuclear holocaust, huh?'

The cook nodded and cut himself a piece of cherry pie, still staring at the Oprah.

Maybe looking for intelligence in Chelam was going to be harder than I thought. I decided to shadow her every move.

Being a stranger in a small town is sort of like being a Martian in Mayberry. You tend to stand out. Aunt Bea sees you hanging around a parking lot, pretty soon Barney Fife is looking at your driver's license. Opie rides by on his bike, pretty soon you got Andy in your shorts. Everybody in town knows you're there, and then you get your thugs in string ties asking why you're still around. You see how this works?

I drove back to the Howard Johnson's, changed rooms, then drove down to the Hertz office in upper Westchester and traded the blue Taurus for a white one. I couldn't do much about Aunt Bea and Opie, but I could make it tougher for Joey and his pal with the tie.

By nine-fifty I was back in Chelam. By nine-fifty-two the new white Taurus was parked in a little alley outside the John Deere showroom and I had picked the lock on a side door and let myself inside. From the showroom I could see the bank and the grocery store and a fair part of Main Street. Aunt Bea and Opie might wonder about the Taurus, but it was better than having them wonder about me.

Between ten-thirty and noon eight people pulled up to the First Chelam, went in, did business, and came out. None of them were fat guys with caviar skin or people who wore string ties, but I held hope.

At five minutes after twelve Karen Shipley came out and got into her LeBaron. She was wearing a tweed pants suit and brown flat-heeled shoes under a slim leather topcoat, and she carried a briefcase. She pulled out of the lot and turned south, and I hustled out to the Taurus and went after her. Twenty minutes later we turned into a shopping mall in upper Westchester where Karen went into a little café. A man in a gray suit took her hand and kissed her on the left cheek and they sat at a window table. I sat in my Taurus. Midway through the meal she opened the briefcase and took out some papers and gave them to the man. He put on tortoiseshell half-glasses, read the papers, then signed them. She put the papers back in her briefcase and they resumed their lunch. Business.

At ten minutes before two Karen was back in the First Chelam and I was back in the John Deere showroom. Opie and Aunt Bea were nowhere to be seen.

At three o'clock Karen Shipley came out again, climbed back into the LeBaron, and drove half a mile out of town to the Woodrow Wilson Smith Elementary School. Toby got into the car and they drove back across Chelam to a single-story medical building with a little sign that read *B. L. Franks, D.D.S. & Susan Witlow, D.D.S., a dental corporation*. They stayed for just under an hour.

After the dentist, we went back through Chelam along a two-lane county road between fields and woods and a scattershot of ponds and small lakes until we turned down a broad new black-topped road past a stone sign that said *Clearlake Shores*. Someone had come in with a bulldozer and carved out a housing development around a couple of lakes that were too round and too sculptured to be natural. Most of the lots were still unimproved, but some of them had houses under construction, and some of them held completed houses warm with life.

Karen Shipley pulled into a one-story brick colonial with a wide cement drive and white pilasters and virgin landscaping. Maybe a year old. Maybe less. Four white birch trees and a live oak had been planted in the front yard. The trunks on the birch were only a couple of inches thick, the oak was maybe a little thicker. They weren't much now, but if you gave them a little time they would grow tall and strong and you would be glad you stayed with them. There was a basketball backboard suspended over the drive at the lip of the garage. Toby and Karen went inside through the front door and lights came on. They didn't come out again. Home.

I cruised through the development and parked in some high weeds near the county road and watched the house until the sky was dark. Joey and the guy with the string tie didn't show up. Shadows didn't skulk across the landscape. The new house and its hopeful landscaping didn't look like a place where people hid in fear or sicced leg-breakers on unsuspecting private eyes, but then they never do. When my stomach made more noise than the radio, I drove back to the Howard Johnson's.

Each day was pretty much the same. Toby would head for school on his red Schwinn mountain bike, then Karen would leave for the bank. She would get to the bank before anyone else and unlock the

472

door. Joyce Steuben would get there two or three minutes later, and the teller would roll up by nine, just before the bank opened. Bank customers would come and go, and sometimes during midmorning or in the early afternoon Karen would drive to a house or a building or a piece of unimproved land where she would meet two or three people and they would look and smile and point, and then Karen Shipley would go back to her office.

Every day between four and four-thirty Toby would pedal up to the bank and go in and stay until Karen left, sometimes as soon as Toby arrived, sometimes not until five. They would go home, Karen sometimes stopping to do a quick errand on the way, but most times not. Once, they drove fourteen miles to a McDonald's, and once they drove to the next town to see the new Steven Segal film. One day Toby didn't come to the bank. Karen left early and drove to the school where the Woodrow Wilson Smith Barking Bears took on the Round Hill Lions in a basketball game. I went in through the rear of the auditorium and watched from the stage. Toby played right forward and he was pretty good. Karen sat on the lowest bleacher and cheered hard, once screaming at an official and calling him a jerk. The Barking Bears lost 38 to 32. Karen took Toby out to a place called Monteback's for a malt. Portrait of the successful single-parent family in action.

At six-oh-five on the morning of the fourth day it fell apart.

I was driving down the county road toward Karen Shipley's when Karen Shipley passed me going in the opposite direction, an hour before she usually left.

I turned around in a gravel drive and waited for a pickup with a beagle in the back to pass, then pulled out and followed her. She went past Chelam, then picked up the state highway and drove most of the way to Westchester. Traffic heading down toward the city was dense and made keeping her in sight easy. She stayed in the right lane and took an exit marked *Dutchy*. Less than a mile off the interstate she pulled into the parking lot of an abandoned Eagle service station and parked. There was no one else around. I stayed behind an old guy in a 1948 Chevy for another half mile, then pulled over, parked off the road, and walked back through a jumble of birch and elm trees until I was behind the Eagle station. She was still in the car.

The cold air and the winter woods smell made me think of when I was a boy, hunting in the autumn for squirrel and whitetail deer, and I felt the peace that comes from being alone and in a wild place.

473

I wondered if Karen Shipley felt that peace, and if that was why she came.

At twenty-two minutes before seven a black Lincoln Town Car with smoked glass and a car phone antenna turned off the road and parked behind her. The door opened and a dark man with a thick neck and a wide back got out. He was in his early forties and taller than me, and he wore an expensive black Chesterfield topcoat and gray slacks and black Gucci loafers shined so cleanly that he probably kept them in his refrigerator. He took a green nylon bag out of the trunk of his Lincoln and walked over to Karen's LeBaron and gave Karen an off-white smile, but I don't think he was trying to be friendly. Karen got out without smiling back. She took the bag and tossed it into the passenger side of the LeBaron. They talked. Karen's mouth was tight and her eyes were edged on a frown and she stood with her bottom pressed against the LeBaron. The dark man reached out and touched her arm and I could see her stiffen from eighty yards away. He said something else and touched her again and this time she pushed his arm away and as fast as she touched him he slapped her. It was a single hard pop that turned her head. She didn't scramble away from him and she didn't scream for help. She stood there and glared and he raised his hand again, but then he lowered it and went back to the Lincoln and drove away with a lot of spinning tires and spraying gravel and roaring engine. I copied down his license number.

Karen Shipley watched him drive away and then she got back into her LeBaron and started the engine and put her face into her hands and cried. She slapped the LeBaron's steering wheel and screamed so loudly that I could hear her even with the windows up and the engine running.

She cried for another five minutes and then she dried her eyes and checked her makeup in the rearview mirror, and when it was perfect she drove away.

I ran back through the woods and pushed the Taurus over a hundred on the roads back to Chelam and picked up Karen Shipley again just as she turned into the bank's parking lot. I pulled up beside the grocery and watched. It was six-fifty-two. Still plenty of time before Joyce Steuben or the teller would arrive.

Karen got out of the LeBaron and carried the duffel bag into the bank. Ten minutes later she came out with the duffel now deflated and folded into a tight roll. She walked across the street to a public waste can in front of the hardware store and threw the duffel away.

Someone in a green and white Chevy Blazer drove by, beeped his horn, and waved. Neighborly. Karen Shipley did not wave back. She walked with her eyes forward and her face set all the way back into the bank. She looked tired and old. Older than the lemon-pie girl in the 8 × 10.

I sat in the Taurus in the empty grocery store lot and watched the town come to life. A rural town with small-town ways. The air was cool and smelled of maple and the coming of Halloween. I turned on the radio. A man and a woman were discussing all the fine recipes you could make with pumpkins and the other autumn squash. A little bit of butter. A little cinnamon. A little sugar. After a while I turned off the radio.

Fall used to be my favorite time of the year.

CHAPTER 12

I called the New York State Department of Motor Vehicles from a pay phone at a Shell station just off the interstate and said, 'This is foot patrol Officer Willis Sweetwell, badge number five-oh-seven-two-four. I need wants and warrants on New York plate sierra-romeo-golf-six-six-one. And gimme the registration on that, too.' They either go for it or they don't.

There was a little pause, then a guy with a deep voice said, 'Wait one.' Score for the Jack Webb.

The deep voice came back on and told me there were neither wants nor warrants on six-six-one, and that it was registered to the Lucerno Meat Company at 7511 Grand Avenue in lower Manhattan.

I said, 'You don't have an individual on that?'

'Nope. Looks like a company car.'

I said, 'Thanks for the help, buddy. Have a good day.' Cops like to say 'buddy.'

I took the Merritt Parkway down through White Plains, then went across the peninsula to the Henry Hudson Parkway and down along the western rim of Manhattan with the Hudson River off to my right. A green treesy park followed along the river with joggers and old people and kids who should've been in school hanging out and laughing and having a good time. I passed Grant's Tomb and the Soldiers and Sailors Monument and then the Hudson parkway became the West Side Highway and the green strip of park was gone and the road ran along the waterfront. Lee J. and Marlon, slugging it out. You hear that the Hudson is ugly and barren, but I didn't see any dead fish or floating bodies, just a couple of nice sailboats and about a million Japanese container ships and a Cessna floatplane tied to a short pier.

At the Holland Tunnel I went east along Canal, crossing lower

Manhattan between Little Italy and Chinatown. The buildings were old and made of red brick or yellow brick or stone, some painted and some not, each webbed with a tarnished latticework of fire escapes. People jammed the sidewalks, and yellow cabs roared over the streets without regard to traffic lanes or bicyclists or human life, and no one seemed to see anyone else, as if each person was inalienably alone and liked it that way, or at least was used to it.

Lucerno's Meat Packing Plant was in a two-story redbrick industrial building between a tire wholesaler and a textile outlet, four blocks from the Manhattan Bridge. There was a drive and a large crushed-gravel parking lot on the side where Econoline vans and six-by trucks turned around and backed up to a loading dock. Five cars were parked at the far end of the lot, out of the trucks' way. The second car from the end was the black Lincoln.

I pulled into the lot past the six-bys, whipped a snappy turn like I was trying to get out of the place, put it into reverse, backed up, and crunched the Lincoln nicely. I turned off the Taurus, got out, and made a big deal out of looking at what I had done. The Lincoln's left front headlight was popped and the chrome around it crumpled and the bumper compressed. A couple of black guys in dirty white aprons up on the loading dock were watching me. One of the black guys went into the warehouse and yelled something, and then a little guy in a white jumpsuit and a clipboard came out. I walked over and said, 'I was trying to turn around and I backed into that Lincoln. Do you know who owns it?'

The little guy came over to the edge of the dock and stood with his boot tips hanging over and looked at the cars. *Lucerno's Fine Meats* was embroidered on the back of his coveralls with red thread and FRANK was sewn over his left breast pocket. His face was sour and lined, like maybe he'd just checked his lunch pail and discovered that his wife had given him a roach sandwich. He said, 'Jesus Christ, where'd you learnta drive? Wait here a minute.' He went back into the warehouse. The two black guys finished loading a dolly of white boxes into a six-by. They took the boxes off the dolly two at a time and slid them into the six-by so hard that the boxes slammed into the truck with a heavy thud. Tenderizing the meat.

In a little while Frank came back and said, 'Forget it. You're off the hook.'

I looked at him. 'What do you mean, forget it?' Best-laid plans.

477

'Just what I said. You had a bad break, but we're not gonna bust your chops about it. Take off.' The old smash-their-car-and-offer-to-pay-for-it routine wasn't getting me very far.

I said, 'The headlight's smashed and the bumper's pretty dinged up and the frame around the light is busted. Maybe the owner should come take a look.'

'It's a company car. Forget it.'

'I don't want to forget it. I'm responsible. I oughta pay something to somebody.'

He gave me Desi looking at Lucy, the look saying, Jesus Christ, what did I marry? 'I'm giving you a pass, *capisce*? What, are you stupid?'

I said, 'You know, that's the trouble with America today. Everybody's looking for a pass. Nobody wants to own up. Well, not me. I own up. I take what's coming to me. I pay my way.' Maybe I could appeal to his national pride.

One of the black guys adjusted his crotch and laughed. He had two gold inlays on the right side of his mouth. Frank took a deep breath, let it out, and said, 'Look, I got work to do. You came in here, you busted the car, and you came looking for someone to do right by it. Great. But I'm standing here telling you that it's okay. I work here. We seen what happened and it's okay. I'm telling you that you ain't gotta pay a dime, you ain't gotta say you're sorry, you ain't gotta do dick. Okay?'

'But you don't own the car?'

He spread his hands and blinked. 'What?'

'And you don't own the company.'

'What?' His voice was getting higher.

'If you don't own the car and you don't own the company, then how do I know you've got the right to tell me it's okay?'

He shook his head and looked at the sky. 'I can't fuckin' believe this.'

'Tell me who drives the car,' I said. 'Maybe the guy who drives the car should tell me it's okay.'

'Jumpin' Jesus fuckin' Christ with a hard-on.'

'It seems only fair.'

One of the black guys said, 'Oo-ee.'

Frank threw down the clipboard and stalked back into the building. The two black guys flashed a lot of inlay work and gave each other the Spike Lee treatment. After a little while Frank came back with a large, bald man in his fifties with pop eyes and a melon head and a voice so soft that it might have come from a sick child. He told me that he was the manager and he gave me his card. It said *Michael Vinicotta. Lucerno Meats. Manager.* He said that if my insurance company wanted to speak with anyone, they could speak with him. He told me that he very much appreciated my concern and my consideration in trying to make sure I had done right by the owner of the car, but that restitution by me was neither sought nor needed.

I said, 'Maybe we should leave the cars where they are and call the police and get an accident report.'

He said, 'Get the fuck outta here or there's gonna be more broken than a goddamned headlight.'

I went back to the Taurus and drove around the block and parked in a garage on Broome Street. I walked back to a pastry shop across from Lucerno's and bought a double decaf espresso and sat in the window. Maybe I should go back and pretend to be Ed McMahon and tell them that the guy who drove the Lincoln had just won the Publisher's Clearing House Sweepstakes for a million bucks. That sounded better than the old busted-headlamp routine, but now they knew I wasn't Ed McMahon. Probably should've tried that one first.

Most of the way through my third espresso the fat guy with the caviar skin came out of Lucerno's. Joey. He was wearing the white coveralls and insulated work boots and the same blue Navy pea coat that he had worn at the Howard Johnson's. Well, well. He wasn't the guy in the Lincoln, but he was close enough.

I paid for the espressos and followed Joey two blocks east to a place with a big sign that said SPINA'S CLAM BAR. I watched through the front glass as he took a stool at the end of the bar and said something to the bartender. The bartender put a glass of draft beer in front of him, then set up an iced tray and started opening clams. Four other guys sat at the bar, but no one seemed to know anyone else and no one seemed particularly talkative. Another half-dozen people sat in little booths. It was the kind of place you could go in your work clothes.

When the tray was filled with clams, the bartender put it in front of Joey and then walked away to see about the other guys. Joey was slurping a clam off its shell when I walked up behind him and said, 'Say, Joey.'

Joey turned and looked at me and I thumbed him in the throat. His face went red and his eyes got big and he grabbed at his throat and started to cough. Most of a clam popped out and fell on the floor.

I said, 'You oughtta not eat so fast, you're going to choke.'

The bartender came down. 'Is he okay?'

I said sure. I said I knew how to do the Heimlich. A couple of the people at the other end of the bar looked over, but when they saw the bits of clam all over the place they turned away. The bartender went back to his other customers.

Joey sort of half fell and half slid off his stool and pushed a slow right hand at me. I pushed it past with an open hand then thumbed him in the right eye. He went white this time and stumbled backward and fell over his stool into the bar and down to the floor.

The bartender and the other four guys at the bar looked at me. I said, 'Think I did the Heimlich a little too hard.'

The nearest guy said, 'You want I should call an ambulance?'

'Maybe in a bit.'

Joey was scrambling around on the floor, holding his face with one hand and trying to get up. He screamed, 'You poked out my fuckin' eye! I'm gonna be blind!'

I pulled him up and led him farther back into the bar. The bartender and the other guys were making a big deal out of not seeing it. I said, 'Nah. I took it easy. Let me see.'

He let me see. I thumbed him in the other eye.

Joey made a sort of gasping sound and grabbed at the other eye and tried to turn away but he was against the wall and there was no place to go. The eyes were red and tearing but he would be fine.

He said, 'You sonofabitch, you're supposed to be gone. We got rid of you.'

'You did a lousy job.'

He lurched forward and threw another right hand and I pushed it past just like the first and drove a spin kick to the right side of his head. It slammed him sideways into the bar and he fell down again. The guys at the other end of the bar and a couple of people in the booths stood up. The bartender said, 'Hey, I'm gonna call the cops.'

I said, 'Call'm. This won't take long.'

I reached down and pulled Joey up again and sat him on the stool and dug out his wallet and looked at his driver's license. *Joseph L. Putata. Jackson Heights.* I put the wallet back in his pocket. 'Okay, Joey. What's a used rubber like you got to do with Karen Lloyd?'

One of his eyes was looking up and the other was sort of rolling around and he was blinking a lot. He shook his head, like he didn't know what I was talking about. 'I dunno. Who's Karen Lloyd?' His hands were down at his sides.

'The lady at the bank.' Maybe she hadn't sent them.

Joey's eyes started coming together and he looked scared. 'Oh, shit, I told him we run you off. I said you were outta here.'

'Who? The guy in the Lincoln?'

The bartender said, 'I just called the cops.'

Joey looked from me to the bartender, then back to me. Confused along with the scared.

I said, 'Why'd the guy in the Lincoln want me to forget about Karen Lloyd?'

'I dunno. He said you were bothering her. He said she was a friend.' He looked even more scared, like talking about the guy in the Lincoln brought it out in him. 'I told him you were gone.'

'Who is he?'

'Who?'

'The guy in the Lincoln.'

Joey looked at me like I'd just beamed down from the *Enterprise*. 'Jesus Christ, you don't know?'

'No.'

He looked at the other people at the bar and then he lowered his voice. He said, 'We're talking about Charlie DeLuca. Sal DeLuca's kid.'

'So?'

Joey shook his head and put on a face like he was about to wet his pants. 'Sal DeLuca is the godfather, you dumb fuck. The *capo de tutti capo*. He's the head of the whole damned mafia.'

CHAPTER 13

It was twenty minutes before five that afternoon when I turned down the neat, clean blacktop off the county road above Chelam and pulled into Karen Shipley's drive. The sun was most of the way down in the southwest, and would set in another hour. The LeBaron was parked in the garage.

Toby Lloyd was pounding a basketball on the drive, hopping sideways and swiveling his head as if he were being covered by David Robinson and Magic Johnson. I parked about thirty feet back to give him room to work the ball and got out. 'Hi. Remember me from the bank?'

'Sure.' He bounced the ball a couple of times, then turned and launched one toward the basket. It banged off the backboard and went through the net.

I said, 'Gotta be tough shooting in the cold. Gets your fingers stiff.'

He nodded and scooped up the rebound. 'You want to see my mom?'

'Yeah. She inside?'

'Sure. C'mon.' Elvis Cole, friend of the family, comes to call.

He led me through the garage and a laundry room and into their kitchen. The walls and the ceilings and the floors and the appliances were still new-house bright, without the ground-in dirt that comes as the years put their wear of life on a place. A thick spaghetti sauce was simmering on top of a Jenn-Air range, a fine spray of the sauce a red shadow on the enamel. Toby yelled, 'Hey, Mom, there's somebody here to see you!'

We went out of the kitchen and through the dining room and into the living room. Karen Shipley came out of a hallway from the back of the house in a pink sweatshirt and faded blue jeans and white socks with little pompoms at the heels. She said, 'What did you say, hon?' Then she saw me.

I said, 'Hi, Karen.'

There was a small part of a moment as she saw me when her eyes flickered and her breath might have caught, but then she forced a pretty good smile for the boy like everything was fine. 'You're still here.'

'Unh-hunh.'

More of the smile for the boy. 'Tobe. Mr. Cole and I have something to discuss. Would you leave us alone for a while?'

'Okay.' Like he was used to having to be out of the way when she talked business and that was just fine with him. He charged back through the kitchen and the laundry.

The living room was large and comfortable, with a vaulted beamed ceiling and peg-and-groove floors and Early American furniture across from a used brick fireplace with a mantel. Colonial. A white and orange cat was asleep on the couch.

Karen Shipley said, 'You're wasting your time, Mr. Cole. My name is not Karen Shipley.'

I said, 'You're owned by the mob.'

She went very still, and then her left foot moved as if her balance had abruptly and without warning shifted and she had to catch herself. Her mouth opened, then closed, and she wet her lips. She did not look away from me. Outside, Toby bounced the basketball. There was a faraway electric hum from something in the kitchen and something else behind me in the living room. Clocks. She said, 'That's,' and then she said, 'Silly.'

'Two hours after I saw you in the bank four days ago, three men came to the Howard Johnson's and told me to forget about you and get out of town. I didn't. This morning you met a man driving a black Lincoln Town Car at a secluded place off the road near Brunly. The man in the black Lincoln gave you a nylon duffel bag, then made advances on you which you refused. He struck you. The man left first and then you brought the duffel to the bank. The Lincoln Town Car is registered to the Lucerno Meat Company in lower Manhattan and was driven by a man I've identified as one Charlie DeLuca, son of Sal DeLuca, head of the DeLuca crime family. I went to the meat plant and observed one of the three men who had come to the Howard Johnson's. His name is Joseph Putata. That links Putata to Charlie DeLuca. I didn't see what was in the bag, but I'd bet it was money, and I'd bet you wash it for the

DeLucas by running it through an account without reporting it to the IRS. I'd also bet that if I went to the cops with this, they'd be pleased as peaches to see me.'

Karen Shipley's eyes got red and wet, and she sat down next to the cat with her hands in her lap. She said, 'Oh, damn,' over and over.

I went into the kitchen, turned off the Jenn-Air so that the sauce wouldn't burn, then drew a glass of water and brought it out to her. She sipped it.

I said, 'The three guys gave you away. Where would you get three guys like that?'

'I'm sorry. I didn't think they would send anyone to do that. I didn't mean for them to threaten you.'

'It's okay. I've been threatened before.'

'I'm not a bad person. I don't like this.'

'I know. I saw the way it was with DeLuca.'

Karen Shipley wiped at her eyes, then got up and went to the big triple-glazed window and looked out at her son. Bounce. 'What happens now?'

'I don't know. I'm trying to figure that out.'

She looked back at me, surprised. 'What do you mean? Haven't you told Peter?'

'No.'

'And you haven't told the police?'

'No.'

'But those men beat you up.'

I said, 'I knew something was wrong and I wanted to find out what it was. Cops deal with the law. The law isn't usually concerned with right and wrong. Ofttimes, there are very large differences.'

She shook her head as if I'd spoken Esperanto.

I said, 'All you do is launder their money?'

'Yes.'

'Ever done any other crimes for them? Drugs, murder, stolen goods?'

Surprised again. 'Of course not. What do you think I am?'

'An employee of the mafia.'

She looked away and crossed her arms. Embarrassed. Back at the boy. Bounce, bounce. 'When I met Charlie DeLuca all I knew about the mafia was Al Pacino. I was working as a waitress on Seventh Avenue in the Village and Charlie introduced me to his father and

484

the old man said he could help me get a better job and I said sure. Nobody said anything about the mafia.'

'They never do.'

'I came out to Chelam and met with the woman who used to be the manager here and she hired me as a teller. I rented a little house. I started taking night classes at the college in Brunly. I didn't see Charlie again for months.'

'Then he needed a favor.'

She gave me the eyes.

I said, 'It would've been Charlie's father, Sal. He would've said that he was in a bind with a couple of business partners and he needed a place to put some money and could you open an account for him that no one would know about and maybe transfer the money out of the country without reporting it to the IRS.'

She shook her head and made the kind of smile you make when you feel stupid and used. 'Is it so obvious?'

I made a little shrug. 'You weren't thinking in terms of crime. You were helping a friend. It's the way they do it.'

'He had gotten me the job. He had been so nice.' She uncrossed the arms and walked back across the room to the hearth. Embarrassed again and angry because of it. The orange and white cat stretched, then sat up and stared at her. 'Toby was in nursery, I was in school, I was studying for the real estate exam, I had a life. It was months before I heard from Sal again, and when he called I was surprised. I didn't think there would be a second time. The third time it was Charlie, and then the calls were every few weeks, and then every week, and then there it was. The *New York Times* runs an article on organized crime and they feature the DeLuca family. That's how I found out. I'm laundering money for the mafia. I'm taking the cash profits they're making from prostitution and gambling and whatever else they do and I'm cleaning it for them. I called Charlie. I said I can't do this anymore and Charlie comes to the bank and he says that I will keep doing it for as long as they want because I'm a stick of furniture and then he locks the door to my office and takes out his penis, and I thought, oh God, he's going to rape me, he's going to use me to show me what I am, but he doesn't. He urinates on the carpet and he says, you see, this is what I can do, and then he left.'

She was trembling as she said it. The cat hopped down from the couch, walked over to her, and rubbed against her ankles. I don't think she felt it.

I said, 'If you want out, go to the cops. You're in with Charlie and Sal. That's worth something. You could cut a deal.'

She shook her head again and walked back to the window and looked at the boy. The cat followed her. He wasn't as big as the cat who lives with me, or as scarred, but he was okay. 'No. Going to the police means witness protection. We'd have to give up everything we have.'

'Looks like you're giving up a lot right now.'

Her eyes hardened and an edge came to her voice. 'All I had when I left Los Angeles was my son and a lot of bad memories. I wanted a job with a future. I wanted an education. I wanted to work and see the work pay dividends and be a worthwhile person. I am. I have a good home. I do a good job with my boy. He's not on drugs and he does all right in school. Witness protection means we change our name and our life and start over. I won't do that. I've already started over and I've built the thing I wanted to build and I don't want to lose it. I've come a long way from stupidville.'

'Far enough to make it worth being owned by the mob?'

The eyes went back to the boy and turned red again. 'I don't know what I can do, but I'll find a way out. It's been eight years, but I will find a way out. I promise you.' She wasn't saying it to me. She was saying it to the boy.

I looked around the house. I looked at the cat. I looked at the boy bouncing the ball. It was a good house, well put together and warm and filled with the things that a family home should be filled with. It couldn't have been easy. *Peter, do I havta?* I said, 'I know what you can do.'

She made a tired little laugh and looked back at me. 'What shit. You're here, and Peter's here, and any chance I might've had to get away from these people is gone. There isn't anything else I can do.'

'Sure there is. You can hire me to get you out of this mess.'

CHAPTER 14

We were sitting on the Early American furniture across from the fireplace, me on the couch, Karen on one of the wingback chairs, drinking white wine from glasses that were simple and without adornment. The cat had left the room. She said, 'They give me money, and I transfer it out of the country without reporting it to the Treasury Department. Any deposit over $10,000 we're supposed to file a form with the Treasury Department, but I don't. That's what it's all about, taking in the money and not reporting it. I put the money into an account, then transfer it to a bank in Barbados. In, then out. It doesn't seem like much, does it?'

I said, 'Who gives you the money?' I was looking for a way out for her. I didn't know what that would be, but maybe if I heard enough, something would present itself. It's the scattershot approach to the detective business.

'Either Charlie or a man named Harry. It's usually Harry, but sometimes it's Charlie.'

'Who's Harry?'

'Just this guy. He works for Charlie and he's usually the one who brings the money.'

Outside, the sun was dropping down and the sky was taking on a deep blue cast, but there was maybe a half hour of good light left. Toby was still working the ball. 'I'm surprised you see Charlie. The top guys like Charlie and Sal always stay away from stuff like this. They use guys like Harry. Something goes wrong, Harry takes the fall. That's what he's paid for.'

She sipped some of the wine, then set down the glass as if the wine had lost its taste. 'This is common to you, isn't it? You deal with things like this all the time.'

'Not exactly like this, but close enough. People look for ways to trap themselves and they usually find what they look for. I see people at their extremes.'

'Are you good at what you do?'

'Not bad.'

'I'm surprised you found me. I took great care to hide myself. I erased my maiden name from all my credit records. I took the name Lloyd from a billboard.'

'You left a trail a mile wide.'

She picked up the wine again and had some, as if she needed the wine to help her talk about these things. 'I want you to know that what I've built, I've built without their help and without their money. I didn't use Peter's help and I didn't use theirs.'

'All right.'

'Three days after I made the first transfer, a man came to the bank and gave me an envelope containing one thousand dollars. I called Sal and told him to take the money back, but he wouldn't. He told me that friends have to take care of one another, that kind of thing. He was sweet and charming, and it was a thousand dollars, so I let myself get talked into keeping it. That first time, after I got used to the idea, it was even sort of exciting. Do you see?'

I nodded.

'But after more calls, and more money, it wasn't. I knew it was wrong and I was scared, and finally they said, okay, if you don't want to get paid, we won't pay you. But they had already paid me a total of sixty-five hundred dollars, and I had spent it.' She got up and went back down the hall again and came back with a 5 × 7 manila envelope. She opened it and shook out a small stack of papers and handed them to me. 'Over the past three years I've put forty-two hundred dollars into various charities. I didn't want to keep any of the sixty-five hundred. That's all I can do.'

I looked. The receipts totaled forty-two hundred dollars. Twenty-three hundred dollars until a clean conscience. Extremes.

She said, 'Does this help at all?'

'If you got caught and went to trial, or if you went to the cops, maybe. Other than that, no.'

She nodded. 'Oh.'

'Has Charlie ever mentioned any other way he launders money?'

'No.'

'How about the woman who hired you, was she in their pocket?'

'I don't think so.'

'Do they own anyone else at the bank now?'

'No.'

'Does anyone else at the bank know what's going on?'

'No.'

'Is there a paper record that passes between you and the DeLucas?'

'No.'

Maybe the scattershot approach wasn't going to work so well. Sort of like trying to find intelligence. 'How about a record of the bank transfers?'

'Not for the first few times. The first few times, I was scared and I didn't want there to be a record so I erased it from the computers. Then I got scared to not have a record and I started keeping a file.'

'Okay. That's something. I'll need to see it.'

She nodded. 'All right. I can print out a transaction record at the bank.'

I said, 'Is there anything you can think of that maybe I'm missing?'

'I don't think so.'

The cat came down the hall and walked across the dining room and into the kitchen. Karen Shipley Nelsen leaned toward me and clenched her hands together. 'What about Peter?'

I spread my hands. 'I have what we in the trade call an ethical dilemma. I've taken Peter's money to find you, and now I have. I owe him that information.'

She stared at me, still clenching the hands.

'I've found people before and kept their secrets, but that won't work here. Peter wants to find his son and he has unlimited resources with which to do it. If I tell him that I couldn't find you, he will simply hire someone else and they will find you. You weren't that hard to find.'

Her jaw tightened. She wasn't liking it much, but she knew that she didn't have to like it.

I said, 'What does Toby know?'

'He doesn't know anything about the DeLuca family or how I'm involved with them. I don't want him to know.'

'What does he know about Peter?'

'He knows that his father's name is Peter Nelsen, and he knows that his father left us because he didn't want a family and he didn't want to be married. We don't talk about it. He doesn't know that his father is the guy who makes movies and has articles written about him.'

489

'You should think about telling him.'

She stood up and went to the window and looked out at her son. The ball was sitting motionless on the drive and Toby was sitting against one of the birches. She said, 'Tell me the truth. Do you see any way out of this?'

'Guys like the DeLucas, they won't do something out of the goodness of their hearts. If we want something, we'll have to give something.'

'Like what?'

'They might let you go if we could put one of their people in your place. That way they don't lose anything. Would you walk away from the bank?'

'Yes. Yes, I'd walk away.' Her face was pale when she said it.

I nodded. 'Okay. That's a place to start. I'll ask around, find out about the DeLucas, see what's there that we can give them or what we can use as leverage. What you can do is get together all the information you have about the accounts and about what you know about Charlie and Sal. Don't leave anything out. Even if it seems small or silly or beside the point.'

'Okay.'

'I'll go to Charlie and give him a little push and see what happens. Charlie won't like it, but there isn't any other way. Is that all right with you?'

She nodded.

'Maybe I can get you away from the DeLucas before we bring Peter in. If they're away and you're not a part of them anymore, it might work.'

She nodded again.

'If it works, Peter doesn't have to know about the DeLucas and they don't have to know about Peter.'

She was looking hopeful. 'That's what I want.'

'But it may not work out that way. It may get messy and you have to be ready for that, too. Focus on DeLuca. DeLuca is who is important. Not Peter. Do you understand?'

'Of course.'

'We'll take it a step at a time.'

She nodded some more, then we stood up and went to the door. When we got there, she said, 'How much?'

I looked at her.

'How much do you want for this?'

'Fifty billion dollars.'

She stared at me and then she nodded and made a little smile.
'Thank you, Mr. Cole.'

'Don't mention it. We're a full-service agency.'

CHAPTER 15

I called Joe Pike at seven-thirty that night, L.A. time. 'It's me. I'm in New York on this thing, and it's heating up. Looks like the mafia is involved.'

'Rollie George.'

'You got his number?'

Pike gave me a phone number. 'Where are you staying?'

I told him.

'Wait ten, then call Rollie. Try to survive until I get there.'

He hung up. That Pike. Some partner, huh?

Fifteen minutes later I called the number and a deep male voice said, 'I've got an apartment on Barrow Street in the Village, just east of Seventh. You need a place to stay, it's yours.' Roland George.

'How ya doin, Rollie?'

'Can't complain. My friend Joe Pike says you want to know some things about your classic, all-American-style mafia.' He dragged out *mafia* into three long syllables. Street black.

'The DeLuca family.'

'Figured it might be the Gambinos, you being the guy who burned Rudy when he was out on the coast.' Nobody in the rest of the world refers to Los Angeles as 'the coast.' Only New Yorkers.

'A woman named Ellen Lang did him. I was just along for the ride.'

'They after you?'

'No. This is something else.'

'Whatever you want, it's yours, you know that.'

'Sure.'

'Whatever I've got, whatever I can get for you or for Joe, it's yours.'

'I'm coming in tomorrow morning. From Chelam, Connecticut.'

'Come in after the traffic, say about ten. Take you an hour. I'll meet you downstairs in front of the building at eleven-thirty.'

'All right.'

He gave me the address and we hung up.

The next morning I retraced the route I had driven before, this time turning off the West Side Highway on Twelfth and picking up Bleecker at Abingdon Square and following it down through the Village to Barrow.

Two black men and a very old Boston terrier were standing in front of a redbrick building at the east end of Barrow by Fourth Street. One of the men was younger and tall and muscular in a plain navy suit with a white button-collared shirt. The other was in his early sixties in a dark brown leather trench coat and had maybe looked like the younger guy a couple of lifetimes ago, before twenty-two years with the NYPD's Organized Crime Control Bureau and two 9mm high-velocity parabellums in the liver had taken it away from him. Roland George. The little black and white Boston terrier sat at his feet, rear legs stuck out at odd angles, its pushed-in, once-black face white with gray, staring at nothing through eyes heavy with cataracts. Its tongue was purple and didn't fit in its mouth. It drooled. Roland's dog, Maxie.

Eleven years ago, Roland George and his wife, Liana, had been driving up the Rahway Turnpike from a weekend at the Jersey shore when a dark brown Mercury had pulled up alongside them and two Puerto Rican hitters had cut loose with a couple of Sig automatics, payback from a Colombian dope dealer whom Roland had busted. Roland survived the bullets and the subsequent crash, but Liana did not. Maxie had been left in the care of a neighbor. They had had no children. Roland George took a forced medical retirement, drank heavily for a year, then sobered up to write thick, violent novels about New York cops tracking down psychopathic killers. The first two didn't sell, but the last three had ridden the *New York Times* bestseller list to a couple of penthouse apartments, a twenty-eight-room home on a lake in Vermont, and substantial contributions to political candidates favoring the death penalty. Fourteen weeks after Liana George died, the two Puerto Rican hitters held up a Taco Bell in Culver City, California, and were shot to death by a uniformed police officer named Joe Pike. That's how Joe and I knew Roland George. Roland still wore the wedding ring.

I pulled to the curb, got out, and Roland shook my hand. His grip was hard and firm, but bony. 'You hungry?'

'I could eat.'

'Let Thomas here put your car in the parking garage across the street. There's an Italian place we can walk to not far from here.'

'Sure.' I gave the younger man my keys, then leaned down and patted Maxie on his little square head. It was like petting a fire hydrant. 'How ya doing, old boy?'

Maxie broke wind.

Roland shook his head and looked concerned. 'He's not doing so well.'

'No?'

'He's gone deaf. He's got the arthritis, he's blind as a bat, and now he can't hear. I think he sees things.'

'Growing old is hell.'

'I bear witness to that.'

Thomas said, 'Shall I pick you up at the restaurant, Mr. George?'

'That's all right, Thomas, I think we'll walk back. Be good for old Max.'

'Very good, sir.'

Thomas climbed into the Taurus and pulled away. I said, 'I never heard anyone say "very good, sir" in real life before.'

'I keep trying to break him of it, but, you know, he's working his way through Columbia Law.'

Roland and I turned off Barrow onto Fourth. To get Maxie going, Roland had to lift him to his feet, then give little tugs on the leash to point him in the right direction. Maxie's tongue stuck out and a ribbon of drool trailed along the sidewalk and his back legs lurched along with a mind of their own. The arthritis.

As we walked, Roland's eyes flicked over faces and storefronts on both sides of the street, sometimes lingering, mostly not. Still a cop. He said, 'Sal DeLuca is your old-line dago. Came up as a hitter through the Luchesi mob back in the forties, and by the time that broke up, he had a big enough crew and enough power to form his own family. Sal the Rock, they call him. These dagos are big on the names.'

'What are they into?'

'Gambling and loan-sharking and the labor rackets here in lower Manhattan. We're in DeLuca family territory right now.'

I looked around for shadows lurking in doorways or people with tommy guns, but I didn't see any. 'How can you tell?'

'Over in OCCB they got a territory map hung on the wall with New York carved up so it looks like its own little United States, here to here the DeLucas, here to here the Gambozas, here to here the Carlinos, like that. A bunch of guys called *capos* each have their own crew of soldiers and run their own businesses, but the *capos* all answer to the *capo de tutti capo*, the boss of the bosses.'

'The godfather.'

'That's it. In the DeLuca family, that's Sal. Charlie's got his own crew, and his own business, but he's still got to answer to Sal. Most of the time, the *capo de tutti capo* retires, he passes it on to his kid. He's lined things up so that the kid has the biggest crew, the most money, like that. Sal bought Charlie a meat-packing plant.'

'I've been there.'

Rollie made his hand like a gun and touched his temple. 'He's a nut case. Absolutely out of control. They call him Charlie the Tuna. You see, with the names? They call him the tuna because he's put so many guys in the ocean.'

Great. Just what you want to hear.

We turned off Fourth onto Sixth and started south toward Little Italy. When we were waiting for a light to change, Maxie suddenly growled and ran sideways, back legs moving faster than his front legs, drool trailing from the corners of his wide shovel mouth like wet streamers, trying to bite something that wasn't there. A couple of guys in watch caps waiting next to us traded looks and moved out of range.

Roland looked sad and said, 'It's hardest when their minds go.'

Maxie snapped at the air until he wore himself out and then he broke wind again and sat down. One of the guys who had moved away frowned and shook his head. I said, 'Sounds like digestion problems, too.'

Roland made more of the sad nod. 'Yes.'

When the light changed, Roland helped Maxie up and got him pointed in the right direction and we crossed.

We turned off Sixth onto Spring and went into a little place called Umberto's. A bald guy in a vest hustled up to Rollie with a lot of smiling and a lot of *buon giorno* and brought us to a booth across from the bar. A couple of dozen people were already eating and more than half of them were speaking Italian. Dark eyes moved with Rollie and voices lowered. The maître d' snapped his fingers and a kid with spots on his face brought water. Maxie sat on the floor next to Rollie and panted. When the maître d' and the kid were gone, I said, 'They don't mind the dog?'

'Max and I been eating here for years. When I was with the cops, I kept book on half the guys in this place. We nod, we smile, it's like a game we play. This place is owned by the Gamboza family.'

'Here in DeLuca territory?'

Rollie sipped his water and nodded. 'Used to be there were only five core families, with everybody killing everybody else over territory and business, but now there's eight, nine families and these guys all like to make like they're Lee Iacocca, everybody polite, everybody doing business with everybody else as long as the other guy pays *rispetto*. You know *rispetto*?'

'You want to do business in another guy's territory, you don't just move in. You pay respect. You ask permission and you give him a piece of the action.'

'Yeah. Vito Ratoulli, the guy owns this place, he's a soldier for Carlino. He pays the DeLucas six percent of his gross to do business here. Vito makes the best calamari diablo around, he treats DeLuca with respect, old Sal even comes here to eat sometimes. Works both ways. Some of DeLuca's people have businesses in Carlino territory.'

The maître d' came back and put a large white plate between us. There was a little white bowl of olive oil and basil in the center of the plate and a dozen paper-thin slices of prosciutto fanned out around it and a row of small hot rolls around the edge of the plate. The rolls were warm and slick with olive oil and little pieces of garlic. Rollie folded up a slice of the prosciutto, swirled it in the olive oil, ate half of it along with one of the little rolls, then gave the rest to his dog. He said, 'You like spicy food?'

'Yes.'

Rollie told the maître d' that we wanted the calamari. The maître d' went away. I said, 'What part of Italy are your people from?'

Rollie made a booming laugh. 'You eat enough macaroni, you lose your taste for red beans and fatback.'

I said, 'Why'd the families make peace?'

Rollie spread his hands. 'Organized crime isn't just the dagos and the kikes anymore. The brothers up in Harlem used to be under the mafia's thumb, but now you got civil rights. The black man figures he can do his own crime and not have to pay the dago. You got your Crips and Bloods and they ain't just street punks anymore. You got your Jamaicans and your East Indians, and those cats come up here believing in voodoo and shit. They don't give a damn about no Sicily. You got your Cubanos and your Chinese Triads and all these little bastards from Southeast Asia. Shit.' Rollie frowned and thought about it. 'The families knew that if they didn't hang together, they'd be run out of business, but it ain't an easy peace. There's still plenty of bad blood. No one likes showing polite, and no one likes showing respect, and a lot of bodies were buried before the families decided how they were going to divide up the crime and the territory. Your DeLucas and your Gambozas hate each other all the way back to Sicily, but they hate the niggers and the chinks worse. You see?'

'Anybody do business with the other guys?'

'Shit.'

'I want Charlie DeLuca to turn loose somebody he owns.'

Rollie ate another piece of prosciutto. 'Charlie the Tuna isn't a guy you can talk with.'

'They never are.'

Rollie smiled. 'You got anything to give him?'

I shook my head.

Rollie made a little shrug. 'I'll ask around. Maybe I can help you out.'

'I figured I'd go talk to him, see how he feels about it. You know where I can find him?'

'Try the meat plant.'

'I did. He's sorta tough to see.'

'Probably ain't there most of the time, anyway. The wise-guys own these businesses, but they don't like to work. Try a place called the Figaro Social Club up on Mott Street, about eight, nine blocks from here.'

'Okay.'

Rollie frowned at the last piece of prosciutto, picked it up, then swirled it in the oil. 'This guy, he gets hot, he ain't so good at controlling himself. That's why he's always in trouble. That's why his daddy has to clean up after him.'

'I know.'

'He's a nut case, Elvis. Certifiable.' He spoke slowly. 'This ain't L.A.'

I said, 'Rollie, in L.A. we got Richard Ramirez and the Hillside Strangler.'

Roland stared at me for a minute, then nodded again and ate the prosciutto. 'Yeah. I guess you do.'

Maxie suddenly charged sideways, snapping and barking at something that only he could see. Roland George got the sad look again and gently reeled him in and mumbled soft things that the dog could not hear and petted him until he was calm. I thought I heard him say Liana.

After a while the little dog took a deep breath and sighed and sat at Roland's feet. He broke wind loudly. Everyone in the restaurant must have heard, but no one looked. Showing polite, I guess. Paying respect, I guess.

When the calamari came, it was excellent.

CHAPTER 16

The Figaro Social Club was on Mott Street, squeezed between a shoe repair shop and a place that sold fresh ground coffee, looking sharp with one of those padded doors upholstered in red naugahyde. The naugahyde was cracked and had maybe been wiped down in 1962 but not since, and the doorstep and the gutter were littered and oily and wet. A small CLOSED TO THE PUBLIC sign was hanging on the door. I thought it all looked sort of crummy, but maybe I was just suffering from West Coast Bias. On the West Coast, big-time mobsters spent a lot of money and lived in palaces and acted like they were related to the Doheny family. Maybe on the East Coast such behavior was considered gauche. On the East Coast, the well-established mobster probably went in for the rat-hole look.

I pushed through the red door and stood in the entry for a moment, letting my eyes adjust. Charlie DeLuca and a couple of guys built like bread trucks were sitting at a bare wooden table, shoveling in pasta with some sort of red sauce. Behind them, Joey Putata and a short, muscular guy were wrestling a full beer keg onto the bar. An old guy in a white barman's bib yelled at them to go easy with the goddamned thing. In the back of the place a tall bony man with a long face and a hatchet nose was shooting pool by himself. His shoulders were unnaturally wide, as if he should have been twins but wasn't, and he was X-ray thin, with pale skin pulled tight and lean over all the bones. His hair was black and shaggy and stuck out in spikes on top, and he wore black Ray Ban Wayfarer sunglasses and black roach-killer boots with little silver tips and tight black pants and a black silk shirt buttoned at the neck. All the black made the pale skin look as white as milk.

The bartender saw me first and flagged his hand. 'Hey, can't you read? We're closed to the public.'

'I know. I'm here because I want to see Mr. DeLuca.' You give them the mister when you're hoping for cooperation.

DeLuca and the two guys at his table looked over, and so did Joey Putata. When Joey Putata saw me, he stopped wrestling with the beer keg and said, 'Oh, shit.' He hadn't said anything about the clam bar.

'My name is Elvis Cole, Mr. DeLuca. I want to talk with you about Karen Lloyd.' I was laying it on thick with the mister.

DeLuca blinked at me, then looked at Joey Putata. 'I thought you got rid of this fuck.' Probably wasn't laying it on thick enough.

Joey said, 'Hey, Charlie, we gave him the word. I took Lenny and Phil with me. We gave him the word real good.'

Charlie turned back to me and went back to work on the pasta. I think he was eating tongue. 'You're the creep from Disneyland, right?'

'Nope. I'm the creep from Los Angeles.'

'What's the fucking difference? It's all talking rabbits out there anyway, ain't it?'

The two guys sitting with Charlie and the little bartender thought that was a good one. One of the guys sitting with Charlie had big arms and a lot of gut and a gray sharkskin jacket over a blue shirt. His collar tips were long and stuck out over the jacket. Twenty years out of style. He said, 'Hey, Charlie, you think this mook knows Minnie Mouse? You think he plays hide the salami with old Minnie?' Everybody laughed except the guy back at the pool table. He was staring at the pool table and holding the cue stick as if it were a guitar, gently bobbing his head in time with the music.

Charlie said, 'You got some nut coming here. Didn't Joey tell you to knock it off and go home?'

'Joey didn't do a good job.'

Joey said, 'Hey, fuck you.'

Charlie turned back to me with the same hard eyes he was giving Joey. 'Joey's a piece of shit. I got guys who can do better, Mickey Mouse.' He turned enough to look back toward the pool table. 'You think you can do better than this piece of shit, Ric?'

The guy with the pool cue nodded, still staring at the pool table. Ric. He looked almost seven feet tall.

Charlie said, 'You're bothering my friend Karen, Mickey Mouse. That's not good.'

'Not anymore, Charlie. Now I'm working for her because she's working for you and she wants to stop. You see?'

Charlie stopped with the knife and fork and said, 'Karen.'

'She'd like to retire.'

'Karen been talking to you?' He wasn't liking it.

'I found out some things and I asked her about them. She's hoping we can work something out.'

Charlie put down the knife and fork and made a little hand move to the guy with the twenty-year-old clothes. 'Tudi, see if he's wired.'

Tudi came around the table and patted me down. I stood with my hands raised and sort of out to the side while he did it. He took out the Dan Wesson, opened it, pushed out the bullets, closed it, put the bullets in my left pants pocket and the Dan Wesson back in my shoulder rig. He took out my wallet and tossed it to Charlie DeLuca. Tudi started at the tops of my shoulders and went down each arm and my back and my front and my crotch and each leg. He took off the G-2 and went over the seams and the fabric, and then he took off my belt and checked that, too. While he did it, Ric knocked pool balls around and Charlie DeLuca looked through my wallet. Tudi said, 'He's clean.'

DeLuca closed my wallet and tossed it back to me. 'I never met a private dick before. Private dicks around here know they fuck with Charlie DeLuca, they end up with the fish. You know what they call me?'

'Charlie the Tuna.'

'You know why they call me that?'

'They can't think of anything better.'

Joey said, 'You see? The guy's a wiseass. I couldn't help the wiseass wouldn't listen.' Whining.

Charlie said, 'Shut up, you piece of shit.'

Joey shut up.

I said, 'Karen wants to move on. Maybe we can work something out so that you get what you want and she gets what she wants.'

Charlie nodded, two guys sitting around a bar, shooting the breeze. 'What's your cut? You fuckin' her?'

'No cut. I'm just trying to help a friend.'

'Yeah. You know the old saying, if it ain't broke, don't fix it?'

I said, 'There are ways we can work this. You can find another bank to launder your money.'

501

He smiled and spread his hands and looked at Tudi. 'Tudi, you know what this guy is talking about, launder our money?'

Tudi said, 'Shit.'

I said, 'Okay. How about you move someone else into Karen's place. She'll stay on until they're in place, and then she'll leave. That way you don't lose a thing and everything stays just as it is.'

Charlie made the smile again and did more with the hands. 'I don't get this guy. I say one thing, he says another. Maybe he don't speak English out there in Disneyland. Whatta they talk there, mousetalk?'

Tudi went, 'Eep, eep.' Everybody thought that was a riot.

I said, 'Karen wants out, Charlie. She's leaving.'

Charlie pushed his plate of pasta carefully to the side and leaned forward. 'Try to get this through your head, mook. What she wants does not matter. Do you know what matters?'

'What you want.'

'Right. And you know what I want right now?'

'To fit into size-34 pants.'

Joey said, 'You see, Charlie? You see? A wiseass.'

Charlie DeLuca's eyes went dark and he looked at me the way you look at a parking ticket you've found under your wiper blade. He said, 'I want you to watch this.' He turned and made the little hand move to Joey Putata. 'Come here, piece of shit.'

Joey glanced at the short, muscular guy and then at the bartender, and then he walked out to stand in front of Charlie DeLuca's table. The principal's office. 'What?'

'You told me you got rid of him. I sent you on the job to get rid of him, and here he is. I don't like fuckups, piece of shit.'

Charlie wasn't looking at Joey; he was looking at me. Joey was staring at Charlie, sweating now, scared and wondering what was going to happen, and everyone else was staring at Joey. Except for Ric. Ric made a nice, smooth shot and the *clack* of the balls was the only sound in the bar.

Charlie said, 'Smack yourself, piece of shit.'

Joey said, 'C'mon, Charlie, please. I took Lenny and Phil. We gave him the word.'

Charlie still didn't look at him; he stared at me. 'Do it, piece of shit. Hit yourself in the face.'

Joey sort of slowly raised his right hand and looked at it, then slapped himself in the face. It wasn't very hard.

'Close your hand.'

Joey started to cry. 'Hey, c'mon, Charlie.'

'Piece of shit.'

Joey closed his hand and sort of punched at his jaw.

'Harder.'

Joey hit himself harder, but it still wasn't very hard.

Charlie said, 'Ric, this piece of shit needs some help.'

Ric put down the pool cue and moved up by the bar, head still bobbing to music only he could hear. When he moved, he sort of glided, as if the tight pale skin were laid over steel cables and servo motors instead of muscle. He took off the Wayfarers and put them away in the black shirt and then he took out a stainless-steel Smith & Wesson 10mm automatic. You don't see many 10-mils. Style.

Joey said, 'Hey, Charlie, hey, I'll do it, look at this.' This time his lip split.

Charlie nodded. 'That's better, piece of shit. Now a couple more.'

Joey hit himself twice more. The second time opened the split and blood ran down Joey's chin and dripped onto his shirt. Ric put away the 10mm. Charlie DeLuca got up from the little table and came around and looked at me. 'You see the way it is.'

I said, 'Sure.'

'I want you gone. Ric, you and Tudi walk this fuck outta here and show him that I get what I want.'

I said, 'Does this mean I can't stay for lunch?'

Ric peeled himself away from the bar and the guy with the big arms took out a short-barreled Ruger .38 revolver. He showed it to me, then put it in his coat pocket just like they do in the movies. Ric didn't bother with the 10mm. I guess he just brought it out on special occasions.

Charlie DeLuca was turning away as if he were going around the table to finish his tongue when he hit Joey Putata a wide, looping right hand that caught Joey blind and knocked him over a couple of chairs and down to the floor. Joey covered up and DeLuca kicked him in the kidneys and the back and the legs, yelling, 'Piece of shit, rotten piece of shit.' He grabbed a fork from somebody's plate and stabbed Joey in the fleshy part of the shoulder. Joey Putata screamed and Charlie went back to kicking him. Tudi and the bartender and the other guys watched, but took a step back as if they didn't like what they were seeing and they were frightened that they might be pulled into it. Except for Ric. Ric glided up behind Charlie and put his hands on Charlie's shoulders and mumbled until Charlie stopped kicking and cursing and was finally standing there, breathing hard and finished with it. Ric the cooler, talking down the nut case. Charlie went back to the table, sat, but stared at the plate as if he didn't recognize what was in front of him.

The little bartender said, 'Jesus.'

Ric straightened his jacket, then came back over to me and pushed me through the red naugahyde door out into the light. It took Tudi a couple of steps to catch up. I said, 'He gets sort of carried away, doesn't he?'

Ric said, 'Shut up and let's go.'

We went up along the street, then turned into a little alley. The alley was black and wet and gritty, with dumpsters and steel garbage drums sprouting like mushrooms along the base of the buildings. A couple of six-wheeler vegetable trucks were parked to the side, enveloped by restaurant steam venting from greasy pipes. Surly white kids and Puerto Rican kids in dirty aprons hung around outside of the kitchen doors, smoking and scratching at tattoos that someone had cut into them with Bic pens and sewing needles. Rotten cabbage was the big smell. I said, 'Gee, fellas, I think I can find my way from here.'

Tudi said, 'We get finished with you, mook, you ain't even gonna be able to find the hospital.'

Ric didn't say anything.

Tudi took the little .38 out of his coat pocket and pointed it at me and that's when Joe Pike stepped out from behind one of the vegetable trucks, twisted the gun out of Tudi's hand, cocked it, and pressed it against Tudi's right temple. It had taken him maybe a tenth of a second.

Pike said, 'Do you want to die?'

CHAPTER 17

It happened quickly and without apparent effort, as if Pike had somehow assembled himself from the air and the trucks and the earth.

Tudi blinked and looked confused, response lagging behind event, and then his eyes bulged and he sucked in a single sharp breath. 'Jesus Christ.' His right hand stayed up and out, as if he were still holding the gun.

I said, 'You're five minutes too soon. I was just about to let these guys have it.'

Pike's mouth twitched. He never smiles, but sometimes he'll give the twitch.

Pike is maybe six-one and lean, all taut cords and veins. He was in straight-legged blue jeans and Nike running shoes and an olive-green Marine Corps parka over a gray sweatshirt and G.I. pilot's glasses so dark that they were without depth or dimension. He cocked his head to look at Ric. He had to look up.

Ric lifted his hands to the sides, letting Pike see that they were empty. He moved with great care, but he didn't look scared. Outside in the light, his skin was so pale I wondered if he used makeup, his eyes black dots set far back in dark hollows, angry weasels staring out of ice caves.

Pike said, 'Your call.'

Ric smiled. His teeth were small and yellow and angled backward like a snake's. If he bit you, you'd have a helluva time getting away from him. He reached out and pushed Tudi's gun hand down. 'He's got your gun, stupid. All you're holding is air.'

Tudi looked at his hand, maybe wondering where his gun had gone. 'The guy japped me.'

Pike stepped back and lowered the gun.

I gave Tudi the tsk-tsk. 'First Joey the Potato, now you. Charlie's gonna love it.'

Tudi's face was red and angry. He looked at his empty hand again like maybe he had made a mistake the first time, like maybe if he looked again, it wouldn't be empty and he could shoot Pike and me and he wouldn't have to tell Charlie that he'd been japped by a guy who came out of nowhere. Only when he looked, the hand was still empty. He looked back at Pike, then grunted and charged, head down. Pike's right knee snapped up hard, and Tudi popped over as if he'd been jerked backward by a leash. He hit the ground flat on his back with a loud slapping sound and that was the end of it.

'Dumb,' I said. 'This man has the market cornered on dumb.'

Ric smiled some more. 'He thinks he's good. All these guys, they think they're good.'

Pike was back to looking at Ric. 'How about you?'

Ric reached down with the emaciated white scarecrow arm and picked up Tudi and lifted him over his shoulder like a bag of dirty laundry. Tudi had to go two-thirty-five, at least. It was a long way to lift two-thirty-five. 'We'll talk again,' he said.

Pike nodded, then opened Tudi's gun, shook out the bullets, and dropped the gun into a steel garbage drum. We walked away, me leading and Pike walking backward, keeping an eye on Ric until we got to the street, then we moved against the traffic down toward Broome, trying to blend in with the natives.

I said, 'How'd you find me?'

'Went by Rollie's when I got in and dropped off my stuff. He said you'd be here. He said you were going to go one-on-one with the mafia.' He shook his head, unimpressed. 'The mafia.'

'What they lack in skill, they make up for in numbers. Except for Ric. Ric is maybe pretty good.'

Pike shrugged, still giving it unimpressed. You want to impress Pike, you've got to use the neutron bomb.

We picked up a cab at the corner of Mott and Broome. The cabbie was an older guy with a bald, misshapen head and a lot of ear hair. He said, 'Where to?'

I told him an intersection near Rollie's. 'You know where that is?'

He flipped down the flag on the meter. 'Hey, I'm driving the Big Apple thirty-five years.'

We went west on Broome.

The cabbie said, 'You guys here on business?'

'Yeah.'

'You from California?'

I said, 'We're from Queens.'

The cabbie laughed. 'Yeah, right. I got you made for somewhere out west, L.A. or maybe San Diego.' So much for blending with the natives.

We picked up Pike's things and the Taurus from the parking garage across from Roland George's building, and worked our way out of the city and then north through the countryside to Connecticut and Chelam. While we drove I told Pike about Peter Alan Nelsen and Karen Lloyd and their son, and Karen's involvement with the DeLuca family. Pike sat in the passenger seat and never once moved or spoke or acknowledged what I was saying. As if he weren't even in the car. Maybe he wasn't. You hang around Pike enough, you begin to believe in out-of-body experience.

Twenty minutes after four we pulled off the highway into the Ho Jo, and I used the phone in my room to call Karen Lloyd at the bank. She said, 'Charlie called.' Her voice was low, as if Joyce Steuben might be outside the door, listening.

'I thought he might.'

'He was livid. He told me I shouldn't have brought you in.'

I said, 'It's not anything we didn't expect, but we had to try. Did you print out a record of the transactions for me?'

'Yes. I have them here.'

'Okay. I need to see them.'

'Don't come to the bank.' There was a pause, as if she had to think through the variables and find the best one. 'Come to the house, say at seven-thirty. We'll be finished with dinner then and Toby will be doing his homework. Is that all right?'

'Fine.'

There was another pause and then she said, 'Thank you for trying.'

'Don't mention it.'

I put down the phone and looked at Pike. 'We'll go out to her place at seven-thirty.'

Pike nodded, then went out to the lobby and checked in, taking one of the rooms adjoining mine. I stood in the door and watched him bring in an olive-green Marine Corps duffel bag and a long metal gun case that looked like something for a Vox guitar. Anyone saw it, they'd think Pike played bass for Lou Reed. After he was settled he came back into my room and we looked at each other. It

507

was four-forty-five. He said, 'Anything around here to do until seven?'

'Nope.'

'Any good places to eat?'

I shook my head.

Pike looked out of my window down onto the parking lot and crossed his arms. 'Well,' he said. 'We didn't have it this good in Southeast Asia.'

Nothing like support from your friends.

At five o'clock we went down to the bar and drank beer, then enjoyed an early dinner in the restaurant. I had a very nice chicken-fried steak. Pike had lentil soup and a large mixed vegetable salad and four slices of whole-wheat toast and a thick wedge of Jarlsberg cheese. Vegetarian.

The female bartender who was thinking about moving to California came in from the bar and kidded around with us until two older couples in heavy coats and loud shirts walked in and then she had to go back to the bar. The two older couples didn't eat. They just drank.

After a while we bought four beers to go and took them back to my room and watched the local New York news. The weather forecast said that the skies would continue to clear for the next few days, but that then another front would move down from Canada bringing cold and snow. The sports report was fine, but the hard news stories were mostly about subways and city strikes and local personalities and things indigenous to New York. They seemed alien and sort of empty.

Midway through the newscast, a male anchor with a lantern jaw and a rough-hewn face and squinty eyes reported a federal study that concluded that the L.A. basin had the dirtiest air in the country. He grinned when he said it. The black female co-anchor grinned, too, and reported a corollary story that Angelenos drive more than urbanites in any other major American city. The jut-jawed anchor grinned even harder and said that maybe Los Angeles wouldn't have such a bad smog problem if they put in a subway to the beach. That got a big laugh from everybody. Especially the weatherman.

Joe Pike said, 'Assholes.'

I turned off the television.

It was ten minutes before six.

We sat and stared, neither of us saying much, and then Joe Pike

508

went into his room. After a while I heard his water running. I took off my clothes and did a little yoga, stretching to warm myself, then working through the cobra, and the locust, and the wheel pose, but I couldn't concentrate. I tried doing push-ups and sit-ups instead, but with no better luck. I kept losing count. After a while I got off the floor and called the local news station in New York and told a young woman that I wanted to speak to the jut-jawed anchor. When the young woman asked me why, I said that I wanted to call him a prick. She wouldn't put me through.

Pike stayed in his room and I stayed in mine, and at twenty minutes after seven we went down to the Taurus and drove to Karen Lloyd's.

Tough guys like me never miss home.

CHAPTER 18

The air was crisp and cold and the sky was a velvety black as we parked in Karen Lloyd's drive and walked up to the door. I rang the bell and Karen Lloyd answered. When she saw Joe Pike, she said, 'Oh.'

I said, 'Karen Lloyd, this is Joe Pike. Joe, this is Karen Lloyd. Joe is my partner. He owns the agency with me.' Dark, and he still wore the glasses.

Pike said that he was pleased to meet her. Karen looked uneasy but she said hello. Another person invading her life.

The three of us went into the dining room. There was a 9 × 12 manila envelope on the table and a glass of white wine next to it. Most of the wine was gone. I said, 'Where's Toby?'

'In his room, doing homework. I told him that people were coming and that I had work to do. He has his radio on. He won't be able to hear us.'

'All right.'

Karen picked up the 9 × 12, handed it to me, then picked up the wineglass. 'This is what I had in the computer.'

'Okay.'

Pike and I took off our jackets. When Pike took off his jacket, Karen leaned forward and made a little sound like *ssss*.

Pike had two bright red arrows tattooed on the outside of each deltoid when he was in Vietnam. They pointed forward, and looked like the kind of red arrows you see on jet intakes or rocket nozzles or other dangerous things. With the jacket off and Pike in a sweatshirt with no sleeves, you could see the tattoos as clearly as if neon tubes had been laid beneath his skin. Karen looked away, not wanting him to catch her staring. People do that.

The orange and white cat came in from the hall, walked over to Pike, and rubbed against his ankles. Pike bent down and held his fingers out. The cat began to buzz. Karen said, 'Do you like cats, Mr. Pike?'

Pike nodded.

She said, 'His name is Tigger.'

Pike nodded once, then stood and walked into the kitchen. Karen said, 'Excuse me, the bathroom isn't that way.'

Pike went through the door without looking back.

I said, 'He isn't looking for the bath. He's looking for how someone might get into your home, or get out, and for where they might hide while they are within it.'

She blinked at me.

'It's one of his more colorful habits.'

The back door opened and Pike went outside. Karen went to the window and tried to look out at him, but she couldn't see out of the light and into the darkness. No one ever can. 'What a strange man.'

'Perhaps, but he is someone that you want on your side. He will never lie to you, and he will give you every piece of himself.'

She looked doubtful. 'Has he been your partner for a long time?'

'Yes. Since I bought the agency. We bought it together.'

She looked out of the window again. Worried. 'What if he scares Toby? What if one of the neighbors sees him and calls the police? Then we'll have to explain.'

'No one will see him and no one will hear him. You ever see a ninja movie? That's Pike.'

She squinted out the window some more, then came back to the table and picked up her glass. 'How can he see at night while he's wearing those sunglasses?'

I gave her a little shrug. There are some things even the great and wonderful Oz does not know.

In a little while Pike came back and we went through the records. Karen got more wine.

There were two hundred fourteen entries made into eight different First Chelam account numbers, all of which were immediately transferred into two accounts in Barbados. The records were spread over six pages of computer printout, showing single-spaced rows of numbers without meaning, dates to the far left, account numbers to their right, amounts to the right of that, destination accounts on the far right, with dates going back four years and eleven months. I would read the sheets, then pass them to Pike, and he would read them. Karen watched us and drank the wine. It was sort of like reading a phone book with phone numbers but without names.

I said, 'Let's start with the most recent deposit and you can walk us through every transaction.'

'God, they're all the same.'

'You told me that most of the deposits come through Harry, but some of them come through Charlie.'

'That's right.'

'Then they're not all the same. There are Harry deposits and there are Charlie deposits.'

She nodded and said, 'All right. What are you looking for?'

'I don't know. All we can do is dig into what we have and see if something presents itself.'

'Oh.'

'Most of the time, in what we do, there are no clear or ready avenues. Detectives look for clues, and clues tell you what's going on and what to do about it. Do you see?'

'Of course.' She didn't look convinced. I think she was trying to relate it to banking.

'I'll need a pad and a pencil.'

She got up and went down the little hall and came back with a yellow legal pad and a Paper Mate Sharpwriter pencil. She also got more wine. She seemed tired, but I didn't think it was just the booze. Her hip brushed the jamb when she came back through the door. I said, 'Let's start with the transaction I saw in Brunly. Tell us how it was arranged and who arranged it, and how you were told to do what you did and as much as you know about where the money came from and where the money went. Don't leave anything out. Things that you take for granted we don't know anything about. We'll do that one, and then we'll walk through every transaction for as far back as you can remember.'

She nodded gamely, and we began.

We went through as much of each transaction as she could remember, starting with the latest and working backward. She remembered more than she thought she would because a lot of what had happened was repetitious. Most of the answers were the same. Charlie's secretary at the meat plant would set the meetings just as she would for Charlie and any other business associate. At the meetings, Charlie would tell Karen which of the eight First Chelam accounts the money should go into and into which of the two Barbados accounts it should be transferred. There were no

512

receipts given and no statements mailed and nothing to prove that someone named Charlie DeLuca was either putting cash into the First Chelam Bank or moving money from one account to another. Karen assumed that someone in Barbados checked to make sure that the right amount of money was being fed into the accounts, but she wasn't sure.

Somewhere in the middle of it, Toby came into the hall and looked at us with big eyes. 'Mom?'

I said, 'Hi, Tobe.' Mr. Bright and Cheery.

Karen put down her wine and gave him the Barbara Billingsley smile and went over to him. 'Hey, pal, you get the homework done?' She'd had three or four glasses of wine by then, but she was doing okay.

'Unh-hunh.'

'You know Mr. Cole? And this is Mr. Pike, his associate.'

Toby smiled uneasily, knowing that something wasn't right, that his mom didn't get sauced and have late-night meetings with guys sporting tattoos and sunglasses to talk over wrap-around financing and short-term mortgage envelopes. He looked nervous. 'You okay?'

She ran a hand through his hair and looked sad. 'Sport, it's been a helluva day. Why don't you get ready for bed?'

He glanced at Pike and me, then he gave his mom a kiss and went back down the hall. Karen watched him go and then she turned and trudged back to the table and Barbara Billingsley was gone. Karen Lloyd's face was older.

I said, 'You want to knock off until tomorrow?'

She shook her head. 'No. Let's get this done.'

Two hours and eleven minutes later we had filled the legal pad with two columns. HARRY had been written above one column and CHARLIE had been written above the other, with deposit dates on the left of the columns and amounts in the middle and destinations accounts on the right. There were seven different account numbers under the HARRY column, but only one account number under the CHARLIE column. All of the HARRY accounts were transferred to the same Barbados destination. The CHARLIE account went to the other Barbados location. There were one hundred eighty-one entries under the HARRY account and thirty-three entries under the CHARLIE, with all of the HARRY deposits coming every Thursday, as regular as the sunset. The HARRY deposits were from $107,000 to $628,000, and they were spread more or less equally among the seven accounts. The CHARLIE deposits were different. They started about twenty-eight months ago, and sometimes they would be made twice in one week and other times there would be eight or nine weeks between them. Irregular. The first couple of years the deposits were relatively small, with nothing over $9,800. A little less than five months ago the deposits went from four figures to five, with a high of $68,000. All of the deposits since then had been large, but still much smaller than any of the HARRY deposits.

We stared at our numbers and our chart, and Pike said, 'You see it?'

Karen said, 'What?'

I turned the yellow pad around so it would be easier for her. 'Harry brings money, and Charlie brings money, but only Charlie tells you where to put the money.'

She nodded. 'Yes.'

'Look at it. Every time Harry brings money, it goes into one of seven accounts, but it never goes in the eighth. Every time Charlie brings money, it goes in the eighth and never into any of the other seven.'

She frowned and brought the pad closer. The frown made her look more strained, but now there was maybe a little hope. 'I've never thought about it, but I guess that's right. Do you think this means something?'

I made a little shrug. 'I don't know. I'm looking at things in a certain way and they're adding up, but maybe they add up in other ways, too. Maybe the Harry accounts are DeLuca family accounts, and the Charlie account is a personal account. Maybe the money Charlie gives you is the piece that Sal cuts for him, and maybe it's bigger than the piece Sal cuts for the other *capos*, so Charlie and Sal don't want anyone else to know to keep peace in the family.'

Pike grunted. 'Or maybe not. Maybe it means something that we can use.'

Karen looked from me to Pike and then back to me. The hope you could see in her faded. She said, 'It seems iffy.'

'It is iffy. If you want certainty, go to the cops. There's witness protection.'

Her face set, then she got up and went to the hearth. The cat followed her with his eyes. 'We've been through that.'

'It's still an option.'

'No. It is not. It is not an option for me.' Her frown deepened and she stared at the mantel. The pictures of her and Toby were there.

She chewed her upper lip, then looked back at me. 'Charlie's secretary called back this evening. She said I'm supposed to meet Charlie tomorrow. I told her no. I said that I'm not going to do it.' That's why the drinking.

Pike said, 'Bad move.'

Her nostrils tightened and she looked at him. 'What do you know?'

I said, 'He's right. Charlie's already pissed, and we shouldn't make it worse. Pike and I will be there, and we won't let him hurt you.'

She pulled herself erect and stepped away from the hearth and gave me the sort of eyes she must've given herself ten years ago when she'd decided to change her life. Hard, focused, don't-get-in-my-way eyes. 'No. It's not about being scared. It's about not wanting it in my life anymore. I've got Peter coming back. I've got you in my home. I'm not going to pick up his money. I'm not going to take any more deposits from Harry. I've made up my mind. Do you understand?'

I said, 'Yes, ma'am.'

Pike nodded once, and his mouth twitched.

Karen Lloyd said, 'Will you need me for anything else tonight?'

'Nope,' I said. 'I think that about covers it.'

She went to the front door and opened it. The cat slipped out and was gone. She said, 'I appreciate what you've done, and I don't mean to be abrupt, but it's late and I'm tired. If you need to speak with me tomorrow, you can call me at the bank.'

'Sure.'

'Good night.'

She closed the door before we were off the porch.

Pike said, 'Tough lady.'

'Unh-hunh.'

'Maybe too tough. Like she's got something to prove.'

I nodded.

Outside, the night air was crisp and chill and sparkling in its clarity, smelling strongly of oak and elm. Orion hung sideways in the southern sky, and a three-quarter moon hung in the east. We walked out onto the lawn and stood by the Taurus and watched Karen Lloyd's house. One by one, the lights went out and the house grew dark. With every light that died, the night grew closer.

I said, 'A long time ago, she made the choice to be the way she is. She earned the job and the house and the position within the community. She rose above the bad thing in her life and has tried to get it out of her life and is trying again. I think she made gutsy choices. Be a shame if she had to regret them.'

Pike moved in the dark, and the orange and white cat came from beneath the car and rubbed against him. Pike bent and picked up the cat and held him close. 'You're right when you say that Charlie's already pissed. She doesn't show when he expects her, he might drive around to find out why. He might try to make sure it doesn't happen again.'

'Think you could stay close to her, keep him from doing that?'

Pike's mouth twitched in the moonlight. 'Unh-hunh.'

I nodded, and Pike put down Karen Lloyd's cat and we got into the Taurus. The final light went out in Karen Lloyd's house, and all was darkness.

CHAPTER 19

Roland George called at 7:32 the next morning and said, 'NYPD owns a guy named Walter Lee Balcom. Busted him seven weeks ago on two counts of murder and one count kidnapping and about two dozen ancillary counts. Most of them smut and sex crimes.'

'Do the DeLucas run porno?'

'No. That's the DeTillio family. But Walter's not mob. He's just been around for a long time and knows people who know people who know people. He's been singing up a storm to try to cut a deal, and Charlie DeLuca's name has come up a few times.'

'Can I talk with him?'

'Ten o'clock at the Hall of Justice, downstairs, room B28. I'll meet you there.'

'Right.'

Rollie hung up.

At a quarter before ten I pulled into the parking garage next door to the Criminal Courts Building on Centre, just north of Foley Square in Chinatown, then walked across and down to subbasement B. A fat cop sitting behind a narrow table asked my business. I told him I was looking for Roland George in room B28. The fat cop looked through a little box, took out a pass with my name on it, and jerked a thumb to the right. 'That way.'

Subbasement B of the Criminal Courts Building looked like a breeding ground for cops with green cement walls and tile floors that were maybe a thousand years old and the faraway smells of disinfectant and urine. Cops of both sexes moved through the halls, uncomfortable in spotless, starched uniforms, called in by prosecutors to rehearse before appearing in court. Defense attorneys on their way into or out of interview rooms glared at the cops with angry eyes that were looking to cut a deal for clients everyone knew were guilty. The lawyers looked like chronic gamblers. The cops looked like drunks.

When I got to B28, Rollie George and a fireplug-shaped guy with a blond crew cut were standing outside the door. Rollie said, 'Elvis, this is Sid Volpe. Sid's with the Justice Department, and he's the guy who's letting us see Balcom.'

We shook. Volpe's hand was dry and hard. He said, 'I got you sandwiched in between the IRS and the feds. You can have him for twenty minutes starting now, so let's not waste time.'

We went in.

Walter Lee Balcom was a pale man in his late forties with fine, straw-colored hair that was thinning on top. He was sitting at a narrow wooden table, chain-smoking Lark cigarettes and wearing gray prison fatigues. A boxy Nagra reel-to-reel tape recorder sat to his side on the table, along with a couple of gray legal pads. There were four metal chairs scattered around the table, but there weren't any pencils or pens or other sharp things.

Walter Lee Balcom gave me a nice smile as we walked in. 'Hello, Mr. Volpe, hello, Mr. George, is this the gentleman you told me about?' His voice was soft and papery.

Volpe said, 'This is him, Walter.' Volpe sat in one of the chairs and turned on the Nagra. 'Don't let Walter's manner fool you, Cole. Walter recruited a sixteen-year-old male prostitute named Juan Roca to help him kidnap a nineteen-year-old nurse's aide named Shirley Goldstein. They took her over to a tank farm outside Newark where Roca raped her and tortured her to death with a butane torch while Walter here got it all on videotape. Then Walter walks out in front of the camera in a Groucho Marx nose and shoots Roca four times in the chest and back with a .45 automatic butt-packed with hollowpoints.'

Walter Lee Balcom sat impassively while Volpe said it, using the stub of one Lark to light another. The air smelled of pipe tobacco from the Larks.

Volpe said, 'There's no business like show business, right, Walter?'

Walter said, 'That wasn't me in the videotape, Mr. Volpe. That was someone made up to look like me.' A voice like whispers.

Volpe said, 'Shit,' then grinned at Rollie. 'This asshole is so fucking perverted even the goddamned DeTillio family wouldn't touch half the smut he handled.'

Walter shrugged, as if this were all part of a meaningless conversation he was having with strangers at a bus stop.

I said, 'Do you know many organized-crime figures, Walter?'

Another shrug. A deep puff. 'A few. I've been in the industry for quite a long while. It has always been profitable.'

'Do you know Charlie DeLuca?'

'Not personally. I know who he is, of course.'

Rollie said, 'We're told that DeLuca's name has come up a few times in the songs you been singing.'

Shrug. A whisper. 'You hear things.'

Rollie crossed his arms and sat back in the chair. 'Your kind of business, they've got to be dirty things.'

Walter made the nice smile again. 'One man's garbage, Roland.'

Sid Volpe leaned across the table and hit Walter Lee Balcom in the face with the back of his left hand. Walter went backward out of the chair and landed on the floor. The broken Lark landed on the table next to the pack, its coal still red and smoking. Walter Lee slowly got up, righted his chair, and sat again. There was a trickle of blood from his right nostril.

Volpe said, 'It's *Mister* George, Walter.'

Walter made an embarrassed smile. 'Yes, of course. My apologies.' Walter took a fresh Lark out of the pack and lit it with what was left of the coal. Volpe took a white handkerchief out of his pants and tossed it onto the table next to Walter. 'Get your nose.'

Walter dabbed at his nose.

Roland watched without moving, then said, 'Thanks, Sid. I think we can take it from here.'

Volpe said, 'Whatever you want,' then got up and left.

When he was gone, Rollie turned off the Nagra. 'You want some ice for that, Walter?'

'No. Thank you.'

Rollie said, 'When I was starting out, we used to call these rooms the garden rooms. Can you guess why?'

Walter shook his head the slightest bit, made the gentle smile.

'We called'm the garden rooms because this is where we took out the hoses. You see?'

'Ah.' The smile.

'I didn't like it then, and I don't like it now, but I don't like you, either. I just can't abide beating on a man when he can't fight back. Even a piece of trash like you.'

'Ah.'

'Just so we understand each other.'

Walter nodded and took more of the Lark. Rollie crossed his arms and settled back.

I said, 'I'm looking for a handle on Charlie DeLuca, Walter. Do you have any ideas?'

'As I said, I don't know him.'

'But you hear things.'

'Yes. But none of it has been of particular interest to my friends with the Justice Department.'

'I don't have to worry about building a case or following the rules of evidence. This is private. I have reason to believe that Charlie might be involved in something that he doesn't want the rest of the family to know about.' Rollie's eyes shifted over to me when I said it. 'You got any idea what that might be?'

Walter shook his head. 'No. I'm sorry. I know quite a bit about what the DeTillios are into, and the Gambozas, but really very little about the DeLucas.'

'Could be anything, Walter. Maybe he's cheating one of the other capos. Maybe he's ripping off Sal.'

Walter shook his head. 'I'm sorry.'

I sat back in the hard chair and crossed my arms and looked at him. 'Okay, forget that angle. I'll take any dirt you can give me.'

Walter closed his eyes and drew in deep on the Lark. 'There are maybe other people who might help you.'

'Like who.'

The smile. 'Mr. DeLuca often used an intermediary to acquire films featuring young women of color. I'm told that he had a taste for black hookers, especially those who had appeared in films and videotapes.'

Rollie said, 'Who told you this stuff?'

'A fellow named Richie. A sometime customer of mine. He spoke of Mr. DeLuca with great familiarity. He said they were associates.'

I said, 'Does Richie have a last name?'

Walter gave me sad and shook his head. 'I'm sorry.'

Rollie said, 'So the man likes kink with black chicks. Mob dagos been going for the dark meat since the speakeasy days in the twenties. Sal ain't gonna give a shit about that.'

'It's more than just a taste for the dark, Mr. George.' The smile, the cigarette glowing hotly. 'I'm told that his passion is short-lived, but that he pays very well. I would think that if anyone would know something, a person in that position might.'

'You got a name?'

'There was a woman named Angelette Silver, though she's no longer in the trade. I believe she works in a florist shop on 122nd Street, in Harlem.' The smile. 'But she may not be likely to help.'

'Why not?'

'Charlie uses them up rather quickly, you see. He can be quite a violent man.' Walter's eyes twinkled when he said it, as if somehow the knowledge of it was delicious. Then he shook his head sadly. 'Their parting wasn't on the best of terms.'

'But he pays very well.'

The smile. 'Yes. For every buyer there is a seller, for every seller, a buyer.'

Rollie said, 'Shit.'

I said, 'Walter, you in here ratting on the mob, aren't you scared they'll nail you?'

The smile, the Lark. 'I've always been willing to sell what no one else would sell, Mr. Cole. I find it quite' – the smile grew broader and the Lark glowed hotly – 'gratifying. Do be careful with Mr. DeLuca. He's quite mad, you know.'

'That's what they tell me, Walter. Thanks.'

'I hope this has helped you.'

'Sure, Walter. Maybe it has.'

Volpe opened the door and tapped his watch. 'The guys from the Bureau are here.'

Roland nodded, and then we went out into the hall, leaving Walter Lee Balcom sitting quietly at the table, smoking and smiling a gentle smile to himself.

CHAPTER 20

Out in the hall Rollie said, 'What's this business about Charlie being up to something?'

I told him what I had.

When I finished, he said, 'You figure Charlie's got his own private little nest egg growing down in Barbados.'

'That's what I need to find out. If he does, then I can use it to make him turn loose my client.'

Rollie nodded. 'What kind of money we talking here?'

'Forty, sixty grand at a crack during the last five months. Smaller money before.'

Roland whistled. 'That's serious crime. Sal wouldn't mind the nickel-and-dime stuff, postal scams, unregulated hijacking, that kind of thing, all the *capos* got something going, but fifty grand.' He shook his head.

'Could Charlie's crew be turning that kind of cash with nobody knowing about it?'

'No way. When these guys talk about family, they really mean it. Guys in Charlie's crew got brothers, cousins, uncles in all the other DeLuca crews. These guys get drunk together, they have barbecues. It'd be easier to keep a secret in a newsroom.'

'So if Charlie's got something going, he's keeping it from his own crew.'

'That's a pretty good bet.' Rollie looked thoughtful, then watched as a trim Chinese woman came out of the elevator and walked down the hall to a door with frosted glass. She had nice calves. When the door was closed, he looked back at me. 'Course, Sal might be the only other guy in the family who knows. Sal might be skimming a little off the top for Charlie 'cause it's his kid.'

'I thought about that.'

'And if Sal's in on it, you're screwed.'

I spread my hands. 'It's a position I'm accustomed to. Do me another favor?'

'Name it.'

'Can you check the JD files for anyone named "Richie" in the DeLuca family?'

'Sure.' Then he said, 'Elvis?'

'Unh-hunh.'

'What he said in there about Charlie being nuts, you remember that.'

I gave him a smile. *Dawn Patrol.* Errol Flynn courageous in the face of certain doom.

I left Rollie downstairs and took the elevator up to the lobby where I used a pay phone to get the number for the New York City Florists Association. The Florists Association told me that there were four flower shops on 122nd Street, two in Morningside Heights, one in Harlem, and one in East Harlem. They had no listing for an Angelette Silver as a licensed florist, and they couldn't tell me in which shop she might work. I copied down the names, addresses, and phone numbers of the four shops, thanked them, and hung up.

I got change at the little cigar stand they have there in the lobby, then went back to the phones and called Victor's Floral Gifts and asked to speak to Angelette Silver. A businesslike woman who sounded to be in her forties said that she was sorry, but no one by that name worked there. I thanked her, hung up, and called the Gilded Lily. A man with a heavy, masculine voice told me that he didn't know anyone named Angelette, but that he was certain he could meet my every need without her help. I thanked him and hung up and called Rudy's Florist. Rudy didn't know anyone named Angelette, either, though he did know a guy named Angel. Would that do? I said that I thought not. The fourth shop was a place called Your Secret Garden. An older woman with a soft southern accent answered.

I said, 'May I speak with Angelette Silver, please?'

There was an uncertain pause. 'You mean Sarah?'

There were voices in the background, then something covered the mouthpiece, then a heavy male voice came on. 'You got the wrong number. Nobody by that name works here.' He hung up. Hard.

Hmm.

I picked up the Taurus from the parking garage, then took Canal

523

over to the West Side Highway, then went north past the Village and the Lincoln Tunnel on my way up to 122nd. Maybe I was on to something. Walter Lee Balcom had put me on to Angelette Silver, who very likely was living under the name Sarah, and maybe Angelette Silver could connect me either to someone named Richie or someone who knew what Charlie DeLuca was up to. If I could just keep Charlie DeLuca from killing either Karen Lloyd or me until I knew who or what that was, all of this might work out. Stranger things have been known to happen.

On the Henry Hudson Parkway at 86th Street, halfway up the island and along the Hudson River, I spotted a metallic-brown Chevrolet following me four cars back and one lane over.

I swung south on Broadway, then east on 86th, then south again on Columbus, but he stayed with me, always four cars back, once gunning it through a red light to keep his position. Pretty good. I wondered if it was Ric.

An eight-wheel flower truck was parked on Columbus in the right-turn lane at the corner of 76th Street. Traffic was backed up and horns were blowing and people who wanted to turn right had to work their way slowly around the truck. I turned right with them and slowed it down even more, staying hidden behind the flower truck until the traffic had cleared ahead of me. I goosed the Taurus half a block down, then threw it into park in the middle of 76th Street and was out of the car and walking back up the sidewalk when the metallic-brown Chevrolet came around the corner. It wasn't Ric.

The guy behind the wheel played it well. Traffic was backing up again and more horns were blowing and the other cars were putting on their blinkers and trying to get around the Taurus, so he put on his blinker and got into line to get around the Taurus, too.

I walked out into the street behind him and went up around his car and put the Dan Wesson in through the driver's side window. 'Surprise.'

He was a medium-sized guy in his early forties with a precise manner and a nice tan and thick hair. He kept both hands on the steering wheel, left in the ten o'clock position and right in the two o'clock position, just like they teach in driving school. He was staring at the gun. 'Jesus Christ, put that away. Where the hell do you think we are, Beirut?'

Around us, drivers were blowing their horns and a fat guy with a three-day stubble called us assholes and told us to get out of the street and nobody seemed to mind too much that I was holding the Dan Wesson. Just another story in the naked city.

'Take out the wallet very slow. If you jerk, I'll shoot you.'

He did it, still with his eyes on the gun. He said, 'I don't know what in hell you've got going on here, but it's not worth pulling the trigger.'

'We'll see.' I really know how to throw a scare into them.

I took the wallet and opened it. Nothing said MAFIA. Nothing said HIRED KILLER. What I saw was a California driver's license in the name of one James L. Grady, address c/o James L. Grady Confidential Investigations, Los Angeles, California. I blinked at it a few times and then I blinked at James L. Grady.

James L. said, 'Will you stop pointing that goddamned gun at me now?'

I didn't stop pointing the gun at him. A pretty woman driving past in a white Mercedes gave us the finger. I said, 'Who hired you?'

'Peter Alan Nelsen.'

'Peter Alan Nelsen, the film director?'

James L. Grady gave me snide. 'Yeah. He said he hired you to find his ex-wife, but he figured you were stiffing him and he wanted to find out. I picked you up in Chelam with the ex and the kid, and I've been following you around ever since.'

'Ever since.'

'Peter came in last night. He's staying over at the Ritz-Carlton. He wants to see you.'

I stopped pointing the gun at him and he snatched back his wallet. A guy passing by in a red Nissan truck called me a shithead. So did James L. Grady.

CHAPTER 21

Peter Alan Nelsen had the Presidential Suite on the top floor of the Ritz-Carlton, overlooking Central Park. I followed Grady's Chevy to the curb, where we let a couple of guys who looked like they'd just mustered out of the French army have our cars, then we went inside.

James L. used a house phone and said, 'This is Grady. I'm in the lobby with Cole.'

He listened for a minute, then hung up and gestured with his chin. 'Elevator's over there.'

He stayed a half step in front as we crossed the lobby, looking very spiffy in his coat and tie, like a successful exercise-equipment importer or a high-end insurance executive. He didn't look like a guy who could follow me for a week without my noticing. If he did, I probably would've noticed him.

In the elevator, he leaned against one wall with his arms crossed and I leaned against another, and neither of us looked at the other. Invisible lines. The elevator was quiet and still and somehow made closer by the faraway hum of the electric motors. It was a long way up to the top floor. I said, 'How come I didn't make you?'

He shrugged, still not looking at me. 'I'm good at it. Also, I didn't have to maintain continual contact. Once I knew where you were staying and where the woman lived and worked, it was easy.'

'You didn't have to worry about losing me because you could always pick me up again.'

'Unh-hunh.'

I nodded. 'I put the plane ticket and the Ho Jo on plastic. There were the phone calls charged to my office number in L.A.'

'You weren't trying to hide. You didn't expect anyone to look.'

I stared at him for about twelve floors. 'Fed.'

Grady smiled. 'Secret Service. Fourteen years.' He finally turned and looked at me. 'I'm impressed you picked me up. I was back and I was loose. I don't get picked up even when I'm living in the other guy's shorts. You're good.'

I spread my hands. Maybe Grady wasn't so bad after all.

We got off at the top floor and followed the noise to the Presidential Suite. Nick met us at the door and gave me the big smirk, then jerked his thumb through the door. 'Inside, hotshot.' The Nickster.

Inside, a quadraphonic stereo system was blasting out Fine Young Cannibals, and the air smelled like Jiffy Pop popcorn and cigarettes. Peter Alan Nelsen was talking to a couple of guys in baggy suits out by the terrace, and a guy with a loud green tie was speaking into a phone by the bar. One of the guys with Peter was wearing a paisley ascot and was smoking a purple cigarette. Dani and T.J. were slouching on the palatial furniture, and a thin woman going for the Tama Janowitz look sat next to T.J. with her hand on his thigh. Dani gave me a little wave. There were open bottles of Absolut vodka and Jack Daniel's bourbon on the bar, and Nestlé's wrappers on the floor. Most of the Absolut was gone. It probably wasn't like this when the president was in residence. Grady frowned at the mess and gave disapproving. Nope, it wasn't like this with the president.

Peter saw us and turned away from the two guys by the terrace without excusing himself and said, 'Well, it's about goddamned time. Dani, turn off that shit and get these Broadway fruits out of here.' Broadway fruits. Always sensitive.

The guy with the ascot looked peeved. He said, 'Peter, we have the backers in place. If you'll agree to direct the play, we can be on the boards by next fall.'

Peter said, 'Nick, give Dani a hand with the fruits.'

Nick pulled the phone away from the guy at the bar, then pointed at the two guys by the terrace and showed them his famous thumb-jerked-at-the-door move. High verbal. The guy with the ascot said, 'I'm sure we can reach some sort of agreement,' but Peter wasn't listening; he was already over with me and Grady. Nick and Dani hustled the three Broadway people out. The Tama Janowitz went with them.

Peter said, 'Jesus Christ, you were supposed to find my kid and let me know. Instead, I gotta hire somebody to find you. I thought we were pals.' He looked hurt.

'There were things I wanted to find out and do before I called you in.'

'Like what?'

'I can't tell you.'

'Bullshit. I didn't hire you to do things. I hired you to find my kid. What're you trying to do, jack up the price?' Now he was giving me suspicious.

I said, 'If you had waited, I would've called. Karen needs to prepare the boy, and there are things going on in her life that she needs to straighten out. That's what's been taking the time.'

Peter grunted when I said it and looked interested, forgetting about the hurt and the pissed. 'You talked to her about me?'

'Yeah.'

'What'd she say? She excited?' He was leaning forward now, wanting to hear about himself.

'She's got a life here, Peter. She's scared that your coming in is going to change that. You need to be sensitive to that.'

'Sure, sure. I'm sensitive. I'm caring.' He made a little hand move to show me how sensitive and caring he was. 'How about my kid? Is Toby okay?'

'Yes. He plays basketball. He seems happy.'

'Good, good.' Peter was moving around now, looking pleased with the way things were working out. Karen wouldn't be pleased, but there you go. 'So maybe you weren't trying to fuck me over. You were trying to smooth things out and that takes time. I can understand that.'

'Thanks.'

He gave me beaming. He was wearing a blousy white tuxedo shirt, black jeans, and black leather jump boots. The boots hadn't been polished in about three hundred years. 'I knew you were on my team. You're my kind of guy. We're two of a kind.'

I spread my hands. Two of a kind.

James L. Grady cleared his throat. 'You need me for anything else, Mr. Nelsen?'

Peter said, 'You got the address on my kid?'

Grady took a small spiral notepad from his jacket, tore out a sheet, and handed it to him. 'Yes, sir. Home and work addresses for the ex-wife.'

Peter gave the slip of paper to Nick without looking at it. 'Terrific, Grady. You're on the A list, just like Cole. A couple of A-team players.' He made another little hand gesture to Nick. 'Pay'm off, Nickster. Give'm something extra for the good work.'

Grady said, 'Just what we agreed to, Mr. Nelsen. I don't need extra.'

'Whatever.'

James L. started out with Nick, then turned back and looked at me. 'Good work finding the woman, Cole. I'll see you around.'

'Sure.'

He went out.

Peter strutted around the room, giving everyone more of the beam job. 'I'm excited. I'm jazzed. I'm ready for action.' He strode to the bar and picked up the phone. 'This is Peter Alan Nelsen. Have my cars ready in five minutes.' He hung up before whomever he had spoken to could answer, then he addressed the room. 'Everybody get ready. We're going to see my kid.'

I said, 'Peter, I know you want to see your son, but going out there like this isn't the way to do it. The boy doesn't know you're here.'

'I'll tell him.'

'He doesn't even know that you're his father. He needs to be prepared.'

Peter stopped grinning and frowned at me. 'What are you talking about? What does he need to prepare for? I'm not some kinda test.'

'Peter, think about it. The smart way is to take it slow. You don't want to screw it up with Toby before you begin.'

The frown got deeper. 'What are you saying? Are you telling me not to go?'

Dani said, 'Maybe we should let them know. It's not polite to just barge in.'

Peter said, 'Goddamnit, what's the big deal? He's my son, isn't he? She's my ex-wife, isn't she? How come everybody's turning against me?'

Dani said, 'Nobody's turning against you, Peter.'

I said, 'It's better if you wait. Let me set up a meeting with Karen.'

Peter suddenly made the big smile again and came over and pounded me on the back. 'You wanna set up a meeting, that's okay by me. Tell her Peter Alan Nelsen is back. Tell her I came three thousand miles to see my kid and I'm on my way. She's gonna be thrilled. The kid's going to be thrilled. Why wouldn't they?' He slapped me on the back again and then he told everybody he was going to take a leak and after that they would leave.

I said, 'But, Peter.'

He waved his hands. 'Trust me on this. I know people. I know the human heart. It's why I'm me.' Then he strode out of the room. Whistling.

I took a deep breath, let it out, then went over to where Dani was standing with the Nickster and T.J. The Nickster said, 'Hey, the guy's happy. Why you wanna piss on his parade?' Dani just looked at me the way you look at someone when you want him to help you.

I said, 'I'll call his ex-wife and let her know. There's a Howard Johnson's just off the freeway outside of Chelam. Neutral territory. Have him come there, to the restaurant. That's where she'll be.'

Dani nodded. 'I'll try.'

I strode out of the room, too, but I wasn't whistling.

CHAPTER 22

I went down to the lobby and used a pay phone by the men's room to call Karen Lloyd at the bank. It was not a call that I wanted to make. 'Yes?'

'It's me. Peter's in New York. He hired another detective who followed me to you. He knows where you live and he's coming out there now.'

She took a deep breath, then let it out with a soft hiss. 'My God. He's coming to Chelam now? Right now?'

'Yes.'

'We can't just spring it on Toby like this. Toby doesn't know anything. He'll be terrified. I don't want Peter coming to the house.'

'I've arranged for him to meet you at the Howard Johnson's. I'm leaving ahead of him so I'll be with you when he gets there.'

'That sonofabitch. Can't you stop him?'

'I thought about shooting him, but that seemed a bit drastic.'

'Not to me.' She didn't say anything for a while. 'Did you tell him about the DeLucas?'

'No. That's up to you, but he's going to know sooner or later.'

'That bastard.'

'Stay focused on DeLuca. We can talk to Peter. We can find a way to work it out.'

She said, 'Oh, that's shit,' and then she hung up. She didn't sound as thrilled as Peter had said she'd be, but maybe that was just me.

When I got to the Ho Jo it was four minutes after three that afternoon, bright and clear and smelling of autumn. Karen Lloyd and Joe Pike were sitting at a table in the front of the bar. Karen was wearing a maple pants suit and pale red lip gloss and she seemed calm and contained, but it was the kind of calm you feel in a hospital waiting room. This early, they were the only two people in the bar.

Karen said, 'Where is he?'

'A few minutes behind me. Did you meet Charlie?'

She gave me annoyed. 'No. I said that I wouldn't, didn't I?' She was holding a tall glass with something clear in it. 'I don't want to talk about that. All I can think about is Toby. I'll have to sit down with him tonight. I'll have to tell him about his father. It's all happening so fast.' She made a little head shake and had some of the drink.

'You may not want to talk about Charlie, but we need to. He's your more serious problem.'

'It doesn't feel that way.'

'It will.' I told her about Walter Lee Balcom and Angelette Silver. 'Did Charlie call to find out why you didn't show up?'

'No.'

'Did anyone who looked suspicious come into the bank, or watch you from a car, or follow you?'

'Of course not.'

I looked at Pike. He shook his head.

Karen said, 'You were watching?'

Pike nodded.

Even more annoyed. 'I didn't see you. I didn't know you were spying.'

Pike made a little head shrug.

Karen tapped at the table, then took more of the drink. Not a happy lady. Feeling the control slip away, but trying to make the best of it. 'All right. But I would think that your going to see Charlie and my standing up to him finally convinced him that I'm serious.'

Pike said, 'It's not over.'

Karen frowned at him. 'He can't want to make a stink about this any more than I. If I get in trouble, he gets in trouble. Isn't that right?'

I said, 'Guys like Charlie don't let it go.'

She made the little head shake again and closed her eyes. 'I'm sorry, but I just can't deal with this. I've got Peter to think about. I've got Toby. My God, how am I going to tell him that yesterday he didn't have a father but today he does?'

Pike leaned forward. 'Tell him you've got some good news.'

Karen closed her eyes again and said, 'Please.'

Four minutes later, Peter arrived. At first I thought that maybe Rommel and his Panzers were pouring through the pass, but then I realized it was Peter. Two black presidential stretch limos followed T.J. riding point on a candy-apple-red Harley-Davidson cop house special, T.J. in a heavy buckskin coat and World War I aviator's goggles, circling the parking lot and revving his engine as the two presidentials skidded in. Peter Alan Nelsen climbed out from behind the wheel of the first limo and the Nickster climbed out of the second. The waitress and the bartender went to the windows to look. Karen looked at them looking and chewed at her lip.

Dani and a couple of scared-looking guys in formal black chauffeur suits got out of the back of the first limo. Everybody could have easily fit into one, but why have one when you can have two?

I watched Karen Lloyd–once–Karen–Nelsen watch them and I touched her arm. 'It's going to be fine.'

'Of course it's going to be fine.' She took a sip of her drink.

Peter came in first, with Dani beside him and Nick and T.J. sort of behind. Karen folded her hands neatly on the table in front of her and watched Peter the way you watch someone in the next yard, sort of detached. For a moment they looked at each other across the room, then Peter walked over and stopped at the edge of the table. 'Hi, Karen.'

'Hello, Peter.' Her face was without expression and she did not stand up.

I said, 'This is Dani. That's Nick and T.J.'

Everybody nodded and said howareyas. When Karen looked at Dani, Dani's big thighs jumped.

Peter sat down and Dani pulled up a chair from the next table. Nick and T.J. went to the bar. Peter looked at Joe Pike and said, 'Who's this?'

'Joe Pike. He has the agency with me. Remember?'

Peter looked back at Karen. 'It's been a long time, Karen. You look great.'

Karen nodded politely. 'Thank you.'

The waitress came out from behind the bar. 'What's everybody having?'

Peter said, 'I want a Budweiser. The guys at the bar, they're with me so give'm whatever they want.' He gestured at Karen's drink. 'What's that?'

'Vodka tonic.'

'Give her another.'

Karen said, 'No. Thank you.'

533

Peter said, 'You don't want another?'

'No. But thank you.' She pronounced the words slowly and carefully, as if she and the chair were in balance but the words might upset that balance. 'I'd rather do what we have to do, so that I can get back to the bank.'

Peter looked confused. 'It's over ten years.'

Dani said, 'I'll have a Perrier, please.'

The waitress eyed Peter past her order pad. She hadn't written anything down. 'You look like someone.'

I said, 'Bring the Bud and the Perrier, okay?'

The waitress put her hand on the side of her neck and rolled her eyes in recognition. 'You're the guy who makes movies. I saw you on *Arsenio*.'

Karen's jaw knotted.

The waitress said, 'You're Peter Alan Nelsen!'

Karen's jaw knotted harder and the corners of her mouth pulled down.

Peter nodded, turning on the smile. 'That's right. In the living 3-D.'

'Wow.'

Karen said, 'Oh, for Christ's sake,' and glared at the waitress. 'We're trying to have a discussion here, and you're not part of it.'

'You don't have to get snippy.'

'And you don't have to act like some sort of idiotic teeny-bopper. Just bring the drinks.'

The waitress gave Karen the ice treatment and went over to Nick and T.J.

Peter said, 'Jesus Christ, she probably just wanted an autograph or something.'

'She can get it later. I'm the vice-president and manager of the bank here, and I am a mother. I have responsibilities. I can't waste my time.'

Peter looked like a little kid who'd just been told to go to bed and didn't like it.

Karen said, 'I know you want to see Toby, but I'd rather you wait. He doesn't know that you're here and he doesn't know who you are or anything about you. Give me this evening to talk to him and then you can see him tomorrow.'

Peter liked that even less.

Karen said, 'If you come out now, you'll just scare him.'

Peter shook his head. 'Hell, what's he got to be scared of?'

I said, 'Any child would be scared, Peter. One day he's comfortable with his life, the next a strange man walks up to him and says, hi, I'm your old man. Everything he knows changes, and everything becomes an unknown. Do you see?'

Peter frowned and sort of pooched out his lips. 'Whose side are you on?'

'The kid's. I'm also on yours and Karen's.'

Dani said, 'You've seen this kind of thing a lot, haven't you?'

I nodded. 'A couple of hundred times.'

Peter made a big deal out of sighing. Disappointed that he wasn't going to see his kid. 'Shit.'

Karen said, 'I'll tell him this evening, Peter, and that way he has the night to get used to the idea and maybe even excited about meeting you. Then you can meet him tomorrow. You can come to the house. If it goes well, the two of you might go to dinner. You could take him to Dasher's in Brunly. It's his favorite.'

'All right. Sure.' Peter was starting to nod, thinking that it sounded pretty good.

Karen said, 'One thing.'

'What?'

She looked at Dani, then at Nick and T.J. 'It would be less threatening if it were just the two of you.'

'Me and Dani?'

'You and Toby.'

Dani shifted uncomfortably in her chair. Peter leaned back and looked uncertain. 'I never go anywhere without the guys. What if I get mobbed?'

Karen flattened her hands on the table. 'You're not going to get mobbed in my home, believe me.'

Peter looked at me, even more uncertain. I nodded. He made a little shrug and then he looked back at Karen. 'Okay. That sounds fine. That sounds like you've got it all figured out.'

She gave him the flat, cool, vee-pee eyes. 'I do. I've been figuring it out for the past ten years, so I'm good at it.'

Peter nodded again. 'Okay. If that's the way you want to play it. We can check in here. It'll be fine.' This wasn't Peter Alan Nelsen. The real Peter Alan Nelsen had stayed in the city and this was Mr. Reasonable, Peter Alan Nelsen's alter ego. Sure. That was it.

The waitress went through a little swinging door they have behind the bar and came back with a fat guy and a skinny black guy with a marcel. She pointed at Peter. Karen watched them for a moment, then said something under her breath and stood. She looked tired again, the way she had the night before when we were going through the bank records and Toby had come out. She said, 'Thank you for meeting me here instead of coming to the bank, Peter. And thanks for waiting to see Toby. If we continue to cooperate, I know this all will work out to the good.'

Peter looked surprised when she stood, and he took her forearm. 'Hey, where you going?'

Karen stiffened as if someone had thrown a switch and she didn't look tired anymore. She looked hard and bright and she stared at his hand without moving.

Peter said, 'What?'

Karen's eyes flicked up from the hand to Peter's left eye and held there. Locked on.

Peter gave embarrassed and let go her forearm. 'Sorry.'

Karen nodded once, giving him okay, then gathered her purse. 'I have work.'

'That's it? We don't see each other for ten years, and you have work? I've got a lot to tell you. I'll bet you've got questions.'

Karen shook her head and smiled at me. 'Do you see?'

Peter said, 'What's the smile?'

Karen held her purse with both hands and let out a deep breath and looked at him. She said, 'Peter, I'm not the same person you knew. I'm not a little bubblehead who wants to be an actress and is impressed when you talk about image density and emotional composition. I'm also not impressed by your success. I don't want your money.'

'Hey, who said you did?' Defensive.

'Because I'm not the same, I won't respond to you the way I used to. If I had never seen you again, it would've been fine. But you're Toby's father, and Toby has a right to meet you and know you and judge for himself. I'll work to that end, but don't expect anything more.'

Peter made a big deal out of spreading his hands. 'I don't understand this hostility.'

'Think about it.'

He said, 'Hey, I'm not looking to get you into the sack. We were married, for Christ's sake. That should mean something. We have a son.'

She stared down at him, her face without thought or consideration. 'No, we don't,' she said. 'I do.'

She brushed past me and walked across the bar and out the door.

Peter stared after her, his face sort of pinched and confused, and then he shook his head. 'I can't believe it. She didn't look happy to see me.'

'She wasn't.'

He looked at me. 'Maybe you were right. Maybe I should play this a little easier.' He was nodding to himself. 'You've seen this a lot. You know about this.'

'Sure.'

'Okay, you were right. Peter Alan Nelsen can admit when he was wrong and you were right.'

I spread my hands.

He suddenly leaned forward and looked hopeful again. 'This didn't go too badly between me and Karen, did it? Not for a first meeting?'

I shook my head. 'No,' I said. 'It went great. She could've shot you.'

CHAPTER 23

Pike and I had an early dinner, then went back to our rooms for a fun-filled evening of TV news and East Coast sports. Peter and Dani and Nick and T.J. took three adjoining rooms on the opposite side of the Ho Jo, but didn't join us for the dinner or for the sports. They left in both of the limousines. Taking advantage of the night life, no doubt.

Word of Peter's presence spread, and a news crew from a local television station came out and poked around. A tall thin woman was the on-camera talent. You could tell because she walked fast and every place she went, a short pudgy guy with a minicam followed. Seeking the truth. A few minutes after they got there, a carload of high-school kids cruised by, too. Running down rumors. The tall thin woman interviewed the high-school kids. Truth is where you find it. After that, everybody left. Not much news to be had sitting around a Ho Jo.

The next morning Karen Lloyd phoned me at seven-fifteen. Joe Pike was already gone. She said, 'I've spoken with Toby. Tell Peter to be at my home at four o'clock this afternoon.' Her voice sounded tired and strained, as if she hadn't gotten much sleep.

'How'd it go?'

'How do you think?' She hung up.

I called Peter Nelsen's room. On the fourth ring Dani answered. I told her about being at Karen Lloyd's at four. She said that she would tell Peter and then she asked if I would like to have breakfast with them. I said that I had things to do, but that I appreciated the offer. There was a little pause and then she said that it might go better this afternoon if I was at Karen's with them. I told her that I would be. She thanked me. She thanked people a lot. I hung up, showered, dressed, ate a short stack of Howard Johnson pancakes

538

and two poached eggs, then drove back to the city to seek out Angelette Silver.

Your Secret Garden was a small shop on 122nd Street between a shoe-repair place and a Rexall Drug Store, along the eastern edge of Morningside Heights, just above the West Side.

As you go north through the West Side, climbing through the nineties and passing into the hundreds, white faces give way to Hispanic and black, and by the time I got to 110th, I was the only white guy around. I kept thinking of Natalie Wood and Richard Beymer, but no one was dancing down the streets singing *When you're a Jet*. I guess they didn't think much of George Chakiris.

A little bell rang when I went into the flower shop. Your Secret Garden was cool and humid and alive with the sights and smells of flowers and greenery and planting soil and soft classical music from tiny Bose speakers hanging from the ceiling. In the front of the shop there were cans of fresh flowers sitting on risers and a refrigerated cooler with glass doors showing ready-made floral arrangements. There was a little counter about halfway back with a workspace behind it where a black man and a black woman maybe in her sixties were building a flower arrangement. The black man was maybe five-eight, with the long arms and ropey neck of a guy who could've fought welterweight. An FTD sign sat on the counter.

In the front of the shop a slender black woman in her late twenties was arranging baby's breath in a can filled with daisies. She was wearing green pants and a light blue smock like orderlies wear. When the little bell rang, the man and the older woman in the back and the slender woman with the daisies glanced up at me and stared. The man gave me hard eyes for a time, then went back to working on his arrangement. Wouldn't see many white guys in here.

The slender woman came over and smiled. 'May I help you?' She was pretty except for a two-inch scar splitting the left side of her upper lip and two smaller scars cutting the brow above her left eye. They weren't old scars. A little name tag on her smock read *Sarah*.

I said, 'Hello, Angelette. My name is Elvis Cole. I need to talk to you about Charlie DeLuca.'

Her smile fell away faster than a sinking heart. She glanced at the man behind the counter, then back at me. The man was staring at us. He couldn't hear, but he knew something wasn't right. She said, 'You the police?'

I said, 'Charlie DeLuca's holding a woman I know. She wants out, and I'm trying to find a way to make him let go.'

She glanced again at the man behind the counter and made her voice low. The man stepped away from the flowers he was working with and wiped his hands on a gray cloth. She said, 'We don't talk about that. If you not the police, you better get out of here.'

'You were with Charlie, weren't you?'

Looking at the floor now. 'I was with a lot of men. William was in Dannemora and I had three kids to feed.'

'Sure. It must've been tough.'

She looked up, angry. 'William been out nine months and he's stayin' out. We both out. We got a man let us run this place.'

I nodded. The shop was a nice shop. Clean and fresh. Not like Dannemora. Not like walking the streets. I said, 'Charlie hurt your eye?'

'That's no never mind.'

'You know a guy named Richie?'

'I don't know nobody.'

William put his hands down on the cash register and gave me the jailhouse stare. The older woman came up behind him and put a hand on his right forearm that he didn't seem to feel. They couldn't hear us, but they knew what we were talking about. Funny, how that works. I said, 'My friend has a child, too, Angelette. She's got a life that she doesn't want to lose, just like you don't want to lose this life.'

William pushed past the older woman and came out from behind the counter carrying a two-foot length of galvanized pipe. Even with the smock you could see the strong forearms and the hard shoulders. Dannemora weight room. 'You better get on out of here, man. She ain't on the street no more and she ain't goin' back. She don't want nothin' to do with you.'

'I just want to talk to her.'

'You ain't gonna be talkin' to nobody with this pipe upside your head.'

I took out the Dan Wesson and cocked it and pointed it at him. I didn't like coming into their lives and I didn't like pulling the gun. But I didn't like what was happening to Karen Lloyd, either. I said, 'That's her choice, William. Not yours.'

The older woman made a low moaning sound and began to wring the gray cloth, rocking herself back and forth.

540

I said, 'Five minutes and I'm gone, Angelette. I won't bother you again.'

William stepped closer. Guess you been to Dannemora, you're not so impressed by the gun. 'I ain't saying it twice, Mister Man. There ain't no Angelette here. There ain't no bad things here.'

Angelette looked up at me for a time, then nodded once to herself, like maybe she'd seen something she could live with or couldn't live without. 'You got deliveries to make, William. Why don't you get to'm.'

William's eyes got wider and he pointed the pipe at me. 'He ain't nothin' here. He ain't the police. You ain't got to talk to him.'

She was looking at him steadily, and when she spoke, her voice was soft. 'He's trying to help his lady, William. What you gonna do, hit him with that pipe? You get violated, then what? You be back in Dannemora, where I'm gonna be then, makin' more dirty movies?'

'Don't you say that.'

'Workin' those streets again?'

'Don't you say that.' He blinked hard twice, then looked down at her as if it had taken a physical effort to move his eyes from me to her.

She said, 'Make your deliveries, William. When you get back, he'll be gone and everything gonna be just like it was before. Please, William.'

The older woman said, 'You better listen to her, William. You do like she say, now.' The older woman was still back behind the counter, looking scared and wringing the gray cloth and rocking.

William stared down at Angelette for a little longer, then the jailyard eyes softened and he turned and walked back behind the counter and through the little work area and out the back door.

Angelette watched him until he was gone, then took a deep breath and let it out, as if with his leaving some inner tension within her had been removed. 'It hurts him that I had to do what I did while he was away. It shames him.'

'He loves you very much.'

'Maybe.' She took another deep breath, then looked at me. 'My name is not Angelette. Angelette a street name.'

'Okay.'

'My name is Sarah Lewis.'

'Sarah. That's nice. Nicer than Angelette.'

She crossed her arms and made a sharp little laugh that was

somehow hard and pained. 'Stop talkin' trash and tell me what you want.'

'I think Charlie DeLuca's up to something that he doesn't want the rest of the family to know about. If I can find out what it is, I can make him let go of my friend.'

'I ain't seen Charlie DeLuca since before William got out. That must be five, almost six months ago.'

'How'd you meet him?'

'On the street. That's the way he likes to do it, with the street girls. He see somethin' he likes in a dirty movie, then him and his bodyguards come up here and he gets some of it.'

'He always up here with the bodyguards?'

She laughed. 'Man, he don't take a pee without them bodyguards. Got this one creepy guy, all tall and white and skinny, look like a goddamn vampire.' Good old Ric.

'You hear the bodyguards say anything?'

She shook her head. 'No. They stay down in the car while we up in the room. You know.'

I said, 'A guy named Richie might know something. I think he supplies Charlie with the movies.'

She thought for a second, then shook her head. 'I don't know no Richie.'

'Did Charlie ever talk business with you?'

'Not the kind of business you talkin' about.' The older woman was working with the flowers, carefully turned away.

'He ever complain about anything to you, like what a crummy day it was, like how a big deal went bad?'

'Look, I know what you want, but it wasn't like that. Charlie takes a liking to a girl, he comes around a lot and he spends big, but he don't stay around too long. He never stayed with a girl longer than three weeks. He likes to hurt and you complain one time too much and then he beats the hell out of you and moves on.'

'He never said anything about what he does?'

'No.'

I said, 'You know any of his other ladies?'

'Just to see. You know, out on the street, walkin' around. We'd be on the corner, we'd talk about him.' She brushed at her mouth, past the big scar. 'It's pretty easy to tell who he been with.'

'You know who he's with, now?'

Her eyes flashed hot. 'How I know that? You think we stay in touch? You think Mr. Charlie send me love letters?'

542

'It's important, Sarah. Could you find out?'

She crossed her arms again and stared at me, maybe thinking she'd had enough of this, but then maybe thinking she'd come this far. She uncrossed the arms and went behind the little counter and used the phone. While she spoke, the older woman sneaked glances at me between a spray of lilacs.

Sarah Lewis put down the phone, then came back and said, 'He seeing some gal named Gloria Uribe. She lives over on 136th, up above a bar called Clyde's.'

'Thanks, Sarah. I appreciate the help.'

'Won't do no good, you talkin' with her, though. She'll be too scared to say anything, even if she knows more than me. Any girl with Charlie is that way.' Sarah brushed at the lip again, as if it itched. It was a bad scar, the kind that comes from a deep cut. When Charlie hit her, he had hit her hard, and probably more than once.

I went to the door.

'You really think you gonna find a way to put the hurt on Charlie DeLuca?'

'Yeah,' I said. 'I do.'

She squinted at me from the hurt eye, then made one of the nods to herself again and opened the door. 'All right. You find a way to hurt him, you hurt him a little bit extra. You hurt him for Angelette Silver, you hear?'

The older woman had stopped pretending to work and was staring at me. I nodded at her, then looked back at Sarah Lewis.

'I was planning to.'

The older woman smiled and turned away, and I left.

CHAPTER 24

Clyde's was a knothole of a bar in the bottom of a four-story building that was mostly fire escapes and clotheslines. Three or four women in tiny red dresses and rabbit coats sat listlessly at the bar while a couple of guys in long coats leaned against a Pontiac out front laughing about something. One of the guys had a gap in his teeth like Mike Tyson.

I put the Taurus across the street in a bus stop, then walked back. The two guys kept laughing but watched me come. There were no more white guys up here than there were down on 122nd Street. If I were them, I'd probably watch me, too.

I went into a little open stairwell next to Clyde's and found the apartment-house mailboxes. *G. Uribe* was on box 304.

The guy with Mike Tyson's teeth looked in at me and said, 'Say, man, who you lookin' for?'

'Gloria Uribe. She around?'

'Naw, she workin'. She better be, she know what's good for her.'

'You her business manager?'

'Naw, man, she Haitian or Cuban or somedamnthing like that. They got their own people to take care of'm. I got somethin' on the fourth floor just as good, though. No waitin'.'

'No, thanks,' I said. 'My heart belongs to Gloria.'

He said, 'Shee-it, you the poe-lice, all right.' His buddy laughed and they knocked fists.

I gave him the okay-we-both-know-I'm-a-cop face. 'What's your name, homeboy?'

'Luther.'

'Luther, make a friend on the force. Gloria do a good business?'

'Fair to middlin'.'

'White guys?'

Luther nodded and winked at his friend. 'You sniffin' 'round 'bout that gangster with the big car. You from Organized Crime?'

'Maybe.' Maybe. Did Eliot Ness say maybe? 'Tell me about the big car. He here often?'

'Two, three times a week.'

'There any pattern to when he comes around?'

Luther gave me pained. 'Man, all these questions grinding my brain, you know?'

'Unh-hunh.'

I dug out a twenty and passed it to him. He didn't look impressed. 'Tha's pretty thin pickin's.'

'It's the budget crunch, Luther.'

'I hear that.' He made the twenty disappear. 'He came around twice last week. On Tuesday, then again Friday. Usually a Friday.' He looked at his friend and the friend nodded.

I said, 'What do the bodyguards do while he's with Gloria?'

'Shee-it, he ain't had his posse around in three months.'

I looked at him. 'He's been seeing Gloria Uribe for three months?'

'Hell, he been coming around longer than that.' Luther squinted at his friend again. 'What, four, five months now?'

The friend nodded, unh-hunh.

Luther looked back at me.

I said, 'He's been seeing Gloria Uribe for maybe five months, and when he comes, he comes alone?'

Luther frowned and gave me the heavy-eyelid treatment. 'How many times I gotta say it, a lousy twenty bucks.'

Luther's friend yawned and stared at something down the street.

I thought about it. In my business, you look for things that are out of the ordinary because out of the ordinary things usually mean clues. Sarah Lewis had said that Charlie DeLuca never stayed with a woman for longer than three weeks and that he never went anywhere without bodyguards. Of course, that was a long time ago and maybe Charlie had changed his ways. Maybe Charlie and Gloria were in love and all the getting together without bodyguards was to discuss wedding plans. Then again, maybe not.

I said, 'Luther, Gloria just a streetwalker, or does she do outcall?'

'She walkin' when times are hard. Things looking better, she be strictly outcall. You can tell when she outcall, 'cause her nose in the air.'

Luther's friend laughed like hell.

A white Caddie DeVille pulled to the curb and a slender, mocha-colored young woman in a tight dress and black-and-white cowboy boots got out. The Caddie's driver was an Asian guy in his fifties. She said something to him, then glanced at Luther and went into Clyde's. Luther frowned after her. 'I got business to tend to.'

'Thanks for the help, Luther. I appreciate it.'

'Just don't say nuthin' 'round that wop gangster. I don't wanna wind up on no pizza.'

'Sure, Luther. Count on it.'

Luther and his buddy disappeared into Clyde's.

I walked up the two flights to the third floor and down a short hall to 304 and knocked. No answer. Somewhere at the other end of the hall a baby was crying, and somewhere else a rapper was banging out a gangster line. Ice-T. *Drama*. No sounds came from within Gloria Uribe's apartment. I knocked again, then took out the wires I keep in my wallet and let myself in.

Gloria Uribe had a one-bedroom with a bath and a tiny kitchenette. The walls were discolored and paint was peeling from the ceiling, but it wasn't an unclean place. A tattersall sofa with a beaded slipcover sat opposite a Victorian china cabinet that had been polished a deep, purple mahogany. The kitchenette and the bath were neat and clean, and the bedroom was a spotless vision in pink: pink satin comforter, pink Princess telephone, pink lace pillows, pink walls and ceiling. She had even found a pink clock-radio, which sat next to the bed on a nightstand. The nightstand was brown.

I wanted to find her trick book. Streetwalkers don't keep them because they don't have regular customers, but call girls do. They use the book to keep track of their appointments and such details of their trade as client preference and past fees. If I found Gloria's trick book, I would know when Charlie DeLuca was with her and when he wasn't and what they did when they were together. I might even learn what was going on.

I started with the nightstand, then looked behind and beneath the bed and between the mattress and the box springs. I found two boxes of Softique tissues, one open, the other not, and a box of Trojan prophylactics, ribbed. I went through her vanity and a small chest of drawers with a forest of little knickknacks on top. Bottom drawer of the chest, there were a black snakeskin whip, a black vinyl body harness, two pairs of police-issue handcuffs, and a black

546

rubber mask with a couple of little holes that I guess you were supposed to breathe through. Nice.

I looked through the rest of her bedroom and her closet and then I went into her bathroom. The trick book was wrapped in a freezer-strength Baggie and taped to the underside of her lavatory, along with a little vial of crack cocaine. It had taken me exactly eight minutes and forty seconds to find it. Cops probably do it in less.

I took the book out into the living room, sat on the couch, and looked through it. There were entries dating back ten months to the beginning of the year, and sure enough, exactly five months and one week ago, there was the first mention of Charlie DeLuca. He had seen Gloria on three consecutive days the first week they had met, then five times the following week. The notes were mostly abbreviations, but the abbreviations were obvious. I read them and tried to feel detached and professional, but all I managed was smarmy and embarrassed. None of the notes related to Charlie's business or to anything Charlie might've said about his business.

I looked through every day of every week up until the present and noticed that starting in the fifth week, whenever Charlie's name appeared, another name appeared, too. Santiago.

Hmm.

I flipped back to the beginning of the book again and this time went through looking for *Santiago*. His first mention was during that fifth week, with Charlie. Maybe Charlie had brought him along. I kept looking. Sometimes Gloria wrote the full name, sometimes she just wrote *S*. For the next few weeks, every time there was an *S*, there was also Charlie's name, but after that sometimes there was just the *S*. Luther had said that Charlie had been around last Tuesday and Friday, but there was no mention of him on those days in the book, just Santiago. Maybe Charlie didn't come around to see Gloria anymore and maybe that's why she didn't list him. Maybe he came to see Santiago.

Hmm, again.

Santiago was penciled in for tomorrow at four-thirty in the afternoon. A Friday. Hmm. Charlie wasn't scheduled, but that was okay. Neither was I.

I closed the trick book, put it back in its plastic bag, then retaped it beneath the lavatory in Gloria Uribe's bathroom and let myself out. When I got down to the street, Luther and his friend were back leaning against the Pontiac. Luther grinned when he saw me, flashing more of the Mike Tyson teeth. I said, 'Luther, you know a guy named Santiago, comes around here sometime?'

Luther stopped grinning and shook his head. 'I don't want no part of that.' He pushed off the Pontiac and walked past me into Clyde's.

I looked after him, and then I looked at Luther's friend. Luther's friend shrugged.

I said, 'What was that all about?'

Luther's friend said, 'Santiago's her pimp. Few years ago, when she come here, Luther try to get her in his stable and Luther and Santiago have a thing. Santiago 'bout kill Luther. Stick him with an ice pick.'

'Oh.' Great. 'He run any other girls around here?'

'Nah. He been moving up. He some kind of Jamaican gangster now, and he doin' real well. Drives a nice car, wears a fine cut of clothes. I think Luther feelin' jealous.'

'Hunh.'

Luther's friend pushed off the Pontiac. 'I better see about Luther. You don't see about him when he get like this, he sulks.'

'Right. Thanks for the help.'

Luther's friend went into Clyde's.

It was two-forty-five. Still plenty of time to get back to Karen's by four.

I took my time walking back to the Taurus, remembering what Roland George had told me about the Italian mafia hating the Jamaicans and the Cubans and the Asians. Maybe I was on to something. Maybe this was a clue. Maybe if I could ferret out its true and hidden meaning, Karen Lloyd and Toby Lloyd and Peter Alan Nelsen could all live happily ever after. Just like in a movie.

For all of the drive back to Chelam, I wondered what Charlie DeLuca might be doing with a Jamaican gangster named Santiago. All I had to do was find out what.

CHAPTER 25

I got back to Karen Lloyd's home at twenty minutes before four that afternoon. Karen's LeBaron sat in the drive, but Toby's red Schwinn mountain bike wasn't leaning in its spot against the garage. I parked on the street to leave room for Peter. Karen answered the door in a long beige skirt and a sea-green top with a large ornate necklace that looked like something a Zulu chieftain might wear. Her makeup was freshly applied. She said, 'Thank God you're not Peter.'

'Yes. I've often thought that myself.'

'I'm trying to get the place straight.'

The carpet had been vacuumed and the magazines on the hearth tidied and the pictures on the mantel dusted and arranged symmetrically according to size, the largest frames centered around the Early American electric clock, the smallest at the ends. Pike was sitting at the table, sipping tea and staring at the world through his dark, expressionless glasses. I said, 'Where's Toby?'

Karen said, 'School. He wanted to stay home, but I said no.'

'Okay.'

'I told him that our lives weren't going to stop because of this. I said that we're still going to be the same people and live here and that he would go to the same school and still have basketball practice.'

I looked at Pike and Pike raised his eyebrows. I guess it had been like this all afternoon. I said, 'Consistency is important.'

'That's right. It is.'

She stood in the center of the room, left hand on her left hip and right hand under her chin, inspecting plant location and knick-knack placement.

'Are you nervous?'

'Certainly not. I'm tense. That's different.' She glanced at the

Early American electric, then at her watch. Whatever she saw there didn't agree, so she went to the mantel and added two minutes to the Early American. She straightened a copy of *Good Housekeeping* that was on an end table next to the couch, picked up a piece of thread from the rug, then went down the hall and into her bedroom. There was a quality of tension to the way she moved that I hadn't seen before.

Pike said, 'News crew came to the bank, sniffing around about what she was doing at the Ho Jo with Peter Alan Nelsen. She had the guard throw them out.'

'Ah.'

'She left early and came home. She's been cleaning all day.'

'She's scared. Someone who threatens her sense of identity is about to invade her home.'

'Awful lot of cleaning for someone about to invade your home.'

'The zen of housecleaning allows one to reach inner peace.'

Pike nodded again and sipped more tea. 'I've always found that to be true.'

I went into the kitchen, made a cup of coffee, then went back into the dining room and sat down with Pike. Karen came out of the hall, stared at the living room for thirty seconds, then went back down the hall. Zen.

I said, 'Charlie make contact today?'

Pike shook his head.

'I don't like it. Guys like Charlie don't let it go. They freak out and try to teach you a lesson. He must be working something.'

Pike nodded. 'You get anything?'

I told him about Gloria Uribe and the Jamaican. Pike said, 'The mob doesn't mix with those guys.'

I shook my head. 'Nope.'

Pike said, 'Hmm.'

At eight minutes before four a black stretch limo came roaring up the street and pulled into the drive. I said, 'They're here.'

Karen came back down the hall and went to the window. The sea-green top had been replaced by an elegant black sweater and a small but tasteful string of pearls.

Car doors slammed and Karen stepped away from the window. She drew herself up and placed her hands at her sides. 'Damnit, I was hoping Toby would get here early.' She seemed pale, but maybe it was the light.

I said, 'Let's hide and pretend no one's home.'

'Very funny.'

I'm a riot, you get me going.

She stood in the center of the room and did not move until the doorbell rang. Then she looked at me and said, 'I will bet you twenty-five million dollars that the first thing he says will mark him as an asshole.'

'Why be defeatist?'

The doorbell rang again, and she walked to the door and opened it. Peter stalked in with Dani behind him. Nick and T.J. had been left at home. Peter said, 'Jesus Christ, you really live out in the goddamn sticks, don't you?'

Karen gave me the flat eyes. 'You see?'

The room felt smaller with them in it and the ceiling no longer felt high and peaked. Peter looked around like he was thinking of buying the place, and Dani stood to the side, sort of out of the way, one hand holding the other.

Karen said, 'Would either of you care for something? I have soft drinks and beer and I made iced tea.' The corners of her mouth were tight.

Dani said, 'No, thank you.'

Peter said, 'I'll take a brewski. You got a Bud?'

Karen went into the kitchen without saying anything.

Peter winked at me and smiled. 'She's doing okay, isn't she? If you'd known her back in L.A., you'd never believe it.'

I said, 'Peter. Go easy on that.'

He looked confused. 'What?'

Karen came back with a bottle of St. Pauli Girl and a glass and a napkin on a Dansk tray. Peter took the bottle but not the glass. 'You know I never use a glass.'

Karen said, 'I forgot.'

'Sure.'

Karen offered Dani a seat on the couch, then took one of the wingback chairs. I sat at the dining-room table with Joe Pike. Peter had some of the beer and went over to the mantel and looked at the pictures. It was five minutes to four and we were having just a fine ole time.

Peter said, 'Guess it was too much to hope you'd have a couple shots of me up here.'

Karen made her lips into a small hard rosebud.

'You know, for the boy.'

She looked out the window, then checked her watch.

Peter crossed the living room and sat on the other wing chair. He spread his legs under the coffee table and held the beer without drinking it. He said, 'I'm not trying to create a problem for you.'

Karen said, 'Of course.'

'I just want to know my son.'

'He should be here anytime.'

Peter nodded and drank some of the beer and didn't say anything. Karen stared out of the window. Dani stared at the floor. Pike sat immobile, safely hidden behind the dark glasses. Maybe if I asked he would loan the glasses to me and I could pretend I wasn't here, either. I made a little face at him to see if he was looking, but he didn't react, so maybe he wasn't. Of course, he might be pretending that he wasn't. You never know with Pike.

At ten minutes after four Peter said, 'I thought the kid was supposed to be here at four.'

Karen leaned forward a fraction of an inch. 'Don't call him "the kid." His name is Toby.'

Peter spread his hands and nodded and stared off into space some more.

At fourteen minutes after four Karen's orange and white cat came out of the hall, walked across the living room, and sniffed at Peter. Peter reached down to pet it, then thought better of it and drew back his hand. Guess the scratches hadn't healed from before.

At twenty-two minutes after four Karen looked at her watch, then at the Early American clock, then frowned. Toby should've been home.

At twenty-eight minutes after four Peter put his hands on his knees and stood up and said, 'What the hell is this? Is the boy coming or not?'

Karen stood up with him and her nostrils were tight. 'He's having a hard time, Peter. He was nervous about meeting you. He didn't sleep well and he's scared.'

'What'd you tell him about me, that I eat rat turds?'

Karen made a hissing sound and went into the kitchen and picked up the phone. 'I'll call the school.'

Peter walked around in a little circle, then sat down again. Dani put a hand on his shoulder.

Six minutes later Karen came out, worried. 'They said he left forty-five minutes ago.'

I said, 'How long is the ride from school?'

'No more than ten minutes.'

Peter said, 'Jesus Christ, you think he ran away?'

Karen got her purse and her keys from the hutch in the dining room and went to the front door without saying anything. I got up with her, looking at Pike. 'I'll go with her. You hang here.'

Pike nodded, the black lenses moving just enough to catch the light.

Peter said, 'Hey, I'll come, too.'

Karen said, 'No,' and when Peter started to get up, Pike gently pushed him back down. 'Not this time.'

Peter said, 'Hey,' and tried to get up again, but Pike kept him in the chair, standing so close that Peter couldn't get the leverage to rise. Peter said, 'What in hell you doing?'

Dani stood and took a step forward, but I shook my head once and she stopped. Pike leaned down close to Peter, Pike's face maybe six inches from his, letting Peter stare into the glasses, and said, 'It's better if she goes without you.' Pike's voice was soft and even.

Peter squinted into the dark and stopped trying to get up. 'Sure.'

Karen was already climbing into the LeBaron when I got out the front door. Her back was stiff and her jaw was tight and she overcranked the engine, grinding the starter gears.

We drove to the school and circled the campus twice and then went into town and back out to the school. We took a shortcut that Karen thought Toby might've taken, but he wasn't there, either. We drove for over an hour and we saw no sign of him until we were heading back toward her house on a part of the road that was between two wide, flat fields overgrown with a heavy wild rye that was dying from the cold.

I said, 'Stop the car.'

She said, 'What?'

When the car was stopped, I got out and walked off the road to Toby Lloyd's red Schwinn mountain bike. Its rear wheel was broken and its frame was crushed and the handlebars were bent backward and together so that the handgrips were touching and it looked the way a bike looks when it's been run over by a car.

I researched for Toby Lloyd in the high grass around the bike, but I couldn't find him.

Charlie DeLuca had finally made contact.

CHAPTER 26

Karen Lloyd got out of her car and ran to the edge of the field. When she saw the bike, her eyes got wide and she put her hands on the sides of her head and she yelled, 'Toby?' first scared and then angry, like maybe this was a bad joke and he would jump out and yell boo. She pushed past me into the rye and the timothy and the pumpkin vines, screaming her son's name and running one way and then another. 'Toby?'

I caught her and held her and she said let go and tried to pull away. I said, 'He's not there. They wouldn't hurt him. They want you on their side and they know that if they hurt him they'll lose you.'

'I want to find him.'

'We'll find him. We'll go back to the house and wait for Charlie to call.'

'Oh my God. What am I going to do?' She was breathing hard, as if her subjective reality had suddenly been hypered on to a higher plane. 'How could they do this? How could they know?'

'There's only one school here. They probably hung around until Toby started for home and then they picked him up.'

'But his bike.'

'I don't know.'

'Did they just run over him?'

'No.'

'My God. What did they do to him?' She turned and ran back to the car and I followed.

Five minutes later we knew.

Charlie DeLuca's black Lincoln Town Car was sitting in Karen's drive behind the limo. Ric was in the passenger's side with the window down and country-and-western music on the stereo. Reba McEntire. He still had the black Ray Bans and the black spiked hair and the deathly white skin. A brand-new red Schwinn mountain bike was leaning against the garage, the price tag still on the handlebars. Karen said, 'Oh, thank God.'

Ric peeled himself out of the Town Car as we parked. He was wearing a triple-layered black leather English jacket with an acne of metal studs. When the jacket pulled open you could see something stainless-steel and shining under his left arm. The ten. 'Let's go inside.'

Karen said, 'Is my boy all right?'

'Let's go inside. Charlie's waiting.'

Karen ran toward the door, and Ric and I followed.

Peter and Dani and Toby Lloyd and Charlie DeLuca were sitting in the living room, Peter and Charlie in the two wingback chairs and Dani and Toby on the couch. Charlie DeLuca was laughing at something that Peter was saying, and they were each holding a bottle of St. Pauli Girl. Toby was sitting on the edge of the couch, hands between his knees, staring at Peter with a kind of nervous curiosity. Joe Pike was standing against the wall by the fireplace, arms crossed and weight on one foot. When Ric came in, Pike put his weight on both feet but didn't uncross his arms. Charlie DeLuca smiled at us like he was everybody's favorite uncle and said, 'Here they are, now.'

Karen went directly to Toby and gripped his upper arms and looked him in the eyes hard enough to read something written on the inside of his skull. 'Are you all right?'

'Sure, Mom.'

'Did anyone hurt you? Or threaten you?'

The boy was looking confused and embarrassed. 'What do you mean?'

Ric nodded at Pike, took off his Ray Bans, and rubbed at his eyes. Guess one pair of dark glasses in the room was enough.

Charlie smiled at me. 'You're still here, hunh? I figured for sure you'd be back ridin' Dumbo, knew what's good for you.'

I gave him a little hand shrug. 'Maybe we didn't understand each other.'

Peter was smiling, like he had a joke. 'You're not going to believe why Toby's late, Karen. Go ahead, Charlie, tell her. Listen to this.'

Go ahead, Charlie. Old friends.

Charlie settled back in the wing chair. 'I backed over his bike at school. Can you imagine that? I felt so terrible that I waited around until he came out so I could buy him a new one. Hey, a bike is like

555

a horse, right? You're a kid, your bike is your best friend. I felt like such a dufus.' Dufus. Putting on the show for Peter, and Peter eating it up.

Karen stared at Charlie as he said it and then she looked back at her son. 'You went with this man to buy the new bike?'

'Well, yeah. Sure.' Talking fast and knowing that he was in trouble. 'We went to Quisenberry's. He said he wanted to pay for a new bike and he asked where they sold them in town and I showed him.'

Karen looked from Toby to Charlie and then back to Toby, then she slapped him so hard that it sounded like a .22 pistol fired indoors. 'Don't you ever go away with a stranger again!'

Toby's head snapped to the side and Dani gasped and Peter said, 'Hey! What'd you do that for?'

Karen said, 'Shut the fuck up.' Her face was white now, almost as white as Ric's, and she was trembling.

Toby looked scared. 'He knew you, Mom. I thought it'd be okay.'

Charlie said, 'Tobe, I'm afraid your mom's upset and she's got a right to be. It's my fault.' Good old Uncle Charlie. He looked back at Karen, and he didn't look so much like Uncle Charlie anymore. 'All of this never would've happened if I hadn't come all the way here from the city for a meeting, and you know what? I'm stood up. I'm left hanging. I need this, right? To be insulted like this?'

Peter nodded, in perfect agreement with his new friend Charlie. 'Hey, I get a clown working on a picture does that, I set him straight.'

Charlie smiled. 'That's right, Pete. Sometimes you just gotta set people straight.'

Peter nodded again and shot a wink at his son.

Karen said, 'Toby. Go to your room and close the door.'

Toby's face darkened, but he went out. When he was gone, Karen turned to Charlie and said, 'You bastard.'

Peter gave surprised. 'Jesus Christ, Karen, the guy's apologized fifteen times. Toby's okay.'

She didn't look at Peter. Her eyes stayed with Charlie and her chest rose and fell and the skin at the corners of her mouth turned a sort of purple color under the makeup.

Charlie said, 'Believe me, I know how she feels. You warn kids about strangers, but kids are still kids, right? They make mistakes. I know how I would feel if anything happened. You wouldn't want anything to happen, would you, Karen?' Giving it to her slow.

Karen shook her head. 'No. I wouldn't want anything to happen.'

I said, 'We get the drift.'

Ric said, 'No one asked you.'

I said, 'Did anyone ever tell you you look like Herman Munster?'

Charlie's eyes made a slow-motion move from Karen to me, then he got up from the chair and walked over. A vein pulsed in his right temple. He said, 'Some guys never get it, Ric. Some guys, you tell'm and tell'm, they never get it, and they end up in trouble.'

I nodded. 'Some guys, trouble is a way of life.'

Peter was giving confused. 'What are you guys talking about?'

Charlie took another step closer. He was maybe six inches from me, red-faced and snorting, staring with eyes that were now dead and fishlike, and you could see how he got the name, Charlie the Tuna. 'You got brain damage from too much sun? You wanna go over the top right now?' His voice was a sort of a hiss.

Peter said, 'Hey, this doesn't need to get out of hand.'

Ric said, 'It's cool,' and came up behind Charlie, putting a hand on either shoulder, working him just like he had worked him with Joey Putata, whispering, talking until the snorting and the pulsing had stopped. Keeping Sal DeLuca's kid in control of himself. I wondered if they paid him extra for this.

Peter said, 'Hey, Charlie, you all right? You want a glass of water?'

The deep-sea eyes submerged and Charlie made a little move that stopped Ric. Charlie stepped back and picked up his coat and Ric held it open so that Charlie could work into it. Charlie said, 'I'm fine, Peter. Just a little misunderstanding, that's all. Misunderstandings happen.'

Peter said, 'Hey, sure.' Everything okay now.

Charlie looked at Karen again, then buttoned his coat and went to the door. 'It was a pleasure to meet you, Peter. Christ, you know *Chainsaw* is one of my favorite pictures. I bought a videocassette. Seventy-nine ninety-five. I musta seen it – what? – over a dozen times, Ric?'

Ric said, 'A dozen.'

Peter said, 'You'll never have to buy another. Give Karen a call and let her know your address. I'll send you tapes of all my movies.' He hoisted the St. Pauli Girl and made a little salute.

Charlie smiled. 'I'll give Karen a call.' Then he looked back at Karen and shook his head. 'C'mon, Ric.' Ric opened the door and they left.

Joe Pike peeled himself away from the wall and went across to the window and looked out.

Peter said, 'Jesus, I don't know why you had to make such a big deal about it, Karen. Toby's fine.'

Outside, a car door opened, then closed. Toby yelled 'Bye' from his room. Watching out his window. An engine started. A car pulled away. Pike drifted back to the wall.

Karen went through the dining room and into the kitchen, closing the door quietly after her.

Peter said, 'What's her problem?'

I left them in the living room and went to the kitchen after Karen Lloyd. She was standing at the sink, staring through the garden window at her backyard. There were little clay pots on the shelf in the window for growing herbs. Some of the pots were planted, but some of them weren't.

She said, 'The man came to my home. He actually came to my home. He was threatening my child.'

'Mobsters will do that.'

She stared at the backyard some more, and I thought she was going to cry, but she didn't. Every tendon in her body was standing out. I *will* change my life. I *will* maintain control. You had to admire it. She said, 'Oh my God, what am I doing to us? What if they had hurt my son?'

I reached out and touched her back. She didn't pull away. I said, 'They didn't and they won't. Charlie wants you on his side. He hurts the boy, he knows he's lost you.'

She nodded, thinking about that but not believing it. 'I want you to watch out for him. Will you do that? Will you and Mr. Pike stay with us until this is over?'

'Yes.'

She turned away from the window and looked at the door to the living room. 'I'm going to have to tell all of this.'

'I don't see any way around it.'

She closed her eyes and looked tired. 'Christ,' she said, 'that's going to be worse than dealing with Charlie.'

CHAPTER 27

I left Karen Lloyd in the kitchen and went back out into the living room. Toby had come back and was sitting on the couch with Peter. Pike was gone. Outside, probably. Peter said, 'You want to come visit me in California?'

'Sure.'

'Hey, you come out,' Peter said, 'I'll make the studio send their jet. They got this jet, it does nothing but fly jerks to places they don't need to go. The studios are scared shitless of me. I got a house in Malibu on the beach. Johnny Carson lives a couple doors down. So does Steven Spielberg and Sly Stallone and Tom Hanks. We can hang out. Won't that be great?'

'Unh-hunh.' Maybe meaning Spielberg and Stallone, maybe meaning the jet. Dani was smiling and nodding at how wonderful it would all be. Every boy's adventure come true.

Outside, I could see Pike on the driveway, palms together over his head, standing on one leg. Tree pose. Seeking focus and balance and escape from chaos. Peter said, 'What's your favorite car?'

'What do you mean?'

'I mean, what's your favorite car? You see TV, you see cars driving around, you look at magazines. You gotta have a favorite car.'

'I kinda like red cars.' He had never thought about it.

Peter spread his hands and beamed. 'Hey, you come out, we'll get a red car to drive around. How about that?'

Toby made a face like his father was speaking Venusian. 'You'll buy a car because I'm there?'

'Sure. You're my son. We'll buy a fuckin' helicopter, you want.'

Toby sort of giggled, maybe for the helicopter, but more likely because Peter had used the F word.

Peter said, 'Dani, go get the thing.'

Dani grinned and went out to the limo and came back with a couple of good-sized boxes. Peter said, 'Open'm up, champ.' Champ. Just like Ward Cleaver talking to the Beave.

Toby opened them. The boxes contained a top-of-the-line JVC professional videotape camera, a turbo-charged videotape player and electronic editor, some blank tapes, and copies of all of Peter Alan Nelsen's movies. I figured the setup would retail out at about thirteen grand, excluding the movies. Toby said, 'Wow.'

Peter patted him on the leg. 'Now you can make your own movies. Just like your old man.'

'Will you show me how?'

'Bet your ass.' Peter leaned forward and ruffled his hair. 'You're Peter Alan Nelsen's kid, and things are going to be different from now on. Your life is going to undergo *enormous* improvement.'

What a thing to say to a twelve-year-old.

Peter said, 'Whatever you want, it's yours. Anything you wanna do, we'll do it. I'm thinking about buying a couple of motorcycles so we can go riding together. Would you like that?'

'Yeah!'

When Karen came out of the kitchen, Toby said, 'Look at what Peter gave me.'

Karen didn't like it much. 'It looks expensive.'

Toby said, 'We're gonna get motorcycles. We're gonna go riding together.'

Karen didn't like that at all. 'Motorcycles are dangerous, Peter. Toby is too young.'

Peter said, 'I'll get'm a trail bike. We won't ride on the street. We'll ride in the woods.'

Karen's jaw clenched and her eyes went hard. 'That's not the point. Toby lives here. Toby lives a certain way and too many expensive gifts will distort his values.'

I said, 'Tobe. Peter and your mom have to talk. Why don't you go outside for a little bit.'

Peter said, 'The boy and I were just getting to know one another.'

Karen said, 'I know, but this is important. You can get to know each other after.'

Toby went out the front door and pretty soon there was the *thump thump thump* of the ball on the drive. Karen looked at Dani. 'Could we have some privacy?'

Dani flushed and said that she'd keep Toby company and went out.

Peter said, 'What?'

Karen sat on the couch and tucked her skirt under and stared at the man she had married when she was seventeen years old and lived with for fourteen months. Then she took a sharp, quick breath and told him about her involvement with the mafia. No preamble.

Outside, the deepening twilight was purple and chill and punctuated by the bounce of the ball and an occasional laugh or word. I could see Dani and Toby and most of the drive, but not the hoop. Someone would shoot the ball and the ball would arc up, but then it would be gone, passing from my line of sight. It didn't matter. You could tell if they made it or not by their faces and the sounds they made and by how the ball rebounded. If someone ran to one side or the other, the ball had caromed off the side of the hoop. If someone ran fast straight ahead, they had lofted an air ball and it was rolling into the garage. If the ball gently came back to them or they trotted forward to the hoop, they had made a basket. You didn't see the event, you saw the results of the event. I had read a book on modern astronomy which had said that both Neptune and Pluto were predicted long before they had ever been seen because of peculiarities in the orbits of the other outer planets. It made me think that planets weren't so very different from people. Seeing what happened around them was enough to tell you where they were and what they were.

When Karen Lloyd was finished, Peter looked at me and said, 'Is this for real?'

'Yep.'

He stood up and gave impatient. 'No. I mean, is this really real? This guy who was here, Charlie, he's a criminal, he's in the *mafia*?'

I said, 'It's really real, Peter.' Something only someone in show business would have to hear. 'The DeLucas are one of the largest mafia families in New York. I've talked to Charlie about letting Karen out of the setup, but he's said no.'

Peter made a big deal out of looking around the room before he looked back at Karen. He was grinning, like this wasn't really real after all, like maybe we were clowning around. 'You're in the mafia.'

'No. I'm not in the mafia. I'm involved with the mafia.' Her voice was edged. The edge hadn't been there a few minutes ago.

'Does the boy know?'

The jaw knotted again. 'Stop calling him "the boy." He has a name.'

'Jesus Christ, all right. Toby. Does Toby know?' Now Peter was giving us irritated.

'No. This is illegal, Peter. What I'm doing is against the law. You don't tell a child something like that.'

I said, 'This is why I didn't call. We were trying to get this straightened out before I brought you in.'

Peter said, 'Jesus Christ.'

'If Karen goes to the police, she'll have to cut a deal with the states and the feds. She can do that, and her testimony will put Charlie and probably Sal away, but then she'd have to go into witness protection.'

Karen said, 'We'd have to change our names. We'd have to move and go into hiding. I won't do that to Toby or to me.'

Peter said, 'But the guy's here threatening our kid.'

I said, 'Charlie did what he did today to get a message across. He won't do anything else if Karen makes the pickups that he tells her to make and continues to launder the money.'

Karen said, 'I've asked Elvis and Mr. Pike to move in here until this is over.'

Peter blinked at me. Surprised. 'I didn't know you were staying here.'

'I wasn't staying here. I'm going to stay here *now*.'

Peter frowned, thinking about it and not liking it. 'How long is this going to take?'

I told them about Gloria Uribe and the Jamaican named Santiago, and that maybe Charlie was going to meet with Santiago sometime tomorrow.

Peter was shaking his head. 'You're gonna follow him around and hope you see a connection? Christ, that could take years.'

'It's what we can do.'

Peter went to the window. Outside, Toby passed the ball to Dani, who shot and missed. She laughed when she missed and said something that I couldn't understand. Peter said, 'All right. If that's the way things are, that's the way things are. I'll take care of it.' He was looking sort of pleased with himself.

Karen said, 'What do you mean, you'll take care of it?'

Peter made a little no-big-deal gesture with his right hand. 'I'll talk to the guy. I'll pass a little cash and smooth him out. I'll take care of you, Karen.'

The skin beneath Karen's right eye began to jump. 'You'll take care of me.' Her voice was soft.

'Sure. We don't need all this running around and following.'

I said, 'Peter, this isn't some mid-level union fixer looking for a payoff.'

'I know what this guy is.' Annoyed.

I said, 'No, you don't. This guy is a professional nut case who made his bones when he was sixteen years old by killing a man. This guy is not going to do what you want because you're from Hollywood. He's *capo* of the largest crew in the DeLuca family, and one day he's going to be boss of all the other *capos*. If he wants to pal around with people from Hollywood, he'll buy a studio.'

Peter leaned toward me, giving me the Donnie Brewster treatment. 'And I'm telling you I can smooth this guy out. I come three thousand miles and find out the mafia got my family, I know what to do. I'm Peter Alan Nelsen.'

Karen leaned toward him. 'We're not your family.'

Peter's face went red and he blinked behind the thick glasses. 'Hey, I'm just trying to help. I'm just trying to take care of the boy. All this following around and waiting, something could happen. Someone could get hurt.'

Karen said, 'Elvis knows how to do this. If you come barging in, you'll mess it up.'

Peter rolled his eyes and made a big deal out of waving his hands. 'That's right, that's right. I don't know anything.' He looked at me, and then he looked at Karen, and then he shook his head. Mr. Incredulous. 'You got no idea how lucky you are. There must be four hundred million women out there wish they had been married to me. You oughta wake up and take advantage.'

Karen's face went very white and a small dimple appeared below the corners of her mouth, and she said, 'You arrogant sonofabitch. Get out of my home.' You could hear her breathe.

Peter slammed out of the door. Outside, the ball stopped bouncing and the voices grew hushed.

Neither of us said anything for a time, and then Karen went to the window and looked out. She lifted her hands and looked at them and said, 'My God, I'm shaking.'

I nodded.

She put one hand in the other and held them down, looking again at whatever was on the other side of the glass. 'I guess I'll have to let him own me a little while longer, won't I?' I didn't know if she was talking about Peter or Charlie, but maybe it didn't matter.

'Yes,' I said. 'I guess you will.'

She nodded. 'Okay. If that's what it takes, I can do that.'

'You're doing fine.'

'I'm surviving.'

'Sometimes that's enough.'

'No,' she said. 'It used to be. But it isn't anymore.'

CHAPTER 28

Karen Lloyd put out blankets and pillows and towels for Pike and me in a little spare room that she used as a home office. There was a couch and a desk in the little room, and just enough floor space for one of us on the couch and one of us on the floor. Pike said he'd take the floor.

We drove back to the Ho Jo, got our things, and checked out. The waitress who had always wanted to visit California was in the lobby when we paid. She said that she hoped she would see us again soon. I said anything was possible. By the time we got back to Karen Lloyd's, Peter and Dani were gone, Toby was in his room, and Karen had gone to bed. Twenty minutes after seven. Guess it had been a rough day all the way around.

At nine-forty-two the next morning Pike and I cruised past Clyde's Bar on 136th Street, Pike's head moving slightly to check out the fire escape, the alley, the street, the people. Luther and his buddy weren't around, and neither was their Pontiac, but maybe sixty or seventy thousand black people were on their way to work or school or doctor's appointments or the market. Pike said, 'Be tough to maintain a low profile around here.'

'Maybe we could do the stakeout in blackface.'

Pike's mouth twitched.

I felt as obvious now as I had before, but neither was the first time I had felt that way. The first time had been in 1976, not long after I had left the Army, walking with a man named Cleon Tyner in Watts. It was a feeling that everyone was staring at me, even though I could see that they were not. When I told Cleon, he said, now you know what it's like to be black. Cleon Tyner had died in Beverly Hills ten years later, shot to death by an Eskimo.

I said, 'Gloria Uribe is on the third floor, 304, up two flights of stairs, on the east side of the building.'

'What time is Santiago coming?'

'Four.'

'Let me out.'

I pulled to the curb, let him out, and drove around the block. My third time around, Pike came out from the alley and slipped into the car. He said, 'Maintenance entrance in the back next to an old coal chute, but no way up to the third unless you come through the lobby. You can get up the fire escape in the alley, but a guy coming here for business wouldn't use it. Thirty-foot drop to the roof from the next building.'

'So anyone who comes or goes is going to come or go through the lobby.'

Pike nodded. 'We try to hang around here all day, everyone on this street is going to know it. So will the woman.'

I turned south on Fifth and dropped down Central Park toward the Village. 'We can pick up Charlie. If Charlie doesn't come, it doesn't matter if Santiago shows up or not.'

Pike grunted and settled back in the seat. 'Let's do it.'

I pulled to the curb by a pay phone, called information, and got the numbers for the Figaro Social Club and the Lucerno Meat Company. I called the social club first and asked if Charlie DeLuca was there. A guy with a voice like a rusty gate said no. I called the meat plant and said, 'Charlie's office, please.' A woman came on and I told her that my name was Mike Waldrone and that Charlie's dad Sal had said that I should call and could I speak to him. She told me that he was on the other line and asked if I wanted to hold. I said no thanks, hung up, and went back to the car. 'Meat plant,' I said. 'Piece of cake.'

Twenty-eight minutes later we parked the Taurus just off Grand around the corner from the meat plant, walked back to a fruit shop with a little juice bar in the window, ordered a couple of papaya smoothies, and sat down to watch for Charlie DeLuca. Elvis and Joe go hunting in the city.

Econoline vans and eight-wheel delivery trucks came and went and guys in stained smocks loaded and unloaded packages of meat. At nineteen minutes after ten Ric the Vampire came down the sidewalk carrying a little white bag and took it into the meat plant. Danish, no doubt. At eleven-fifty-one Charlie and Ric came out and got into the black Town Car. Charlie was wearing a three-thousand-dollar Johnson & Ivers topcoat and climbed into the front seat. Pike and I hustled back to the Taurus and followed them northwest up across the Village to a little café two doors down from Foul Play Bookstore on Abingdon Square. Charlie went into the restaurant and Ric stayed in the car. In the café, Charlie met three other men, also in Johnson & Ivers topcoats, and sat in the window where they laughed and talked and read racing forms. Power lunch, no doubt. Who will we rob today? Who will we kill?

An hour and ten minutes later Charlie came out and got into the Town Car, and he and Ric drove to the Figaro Social Club, *members only*. Ric went in with him this time, instead of staying in the car. Shoot a little pool, drink a little espresso, hang out with the other wiseguys. They still hadn't cleaned the front door.

Neither Charlie nor Ric came or went for the next two hours and twenty-five minutes. A couple of old men hobbled in and another old man hobbled away, and strong younger men with broad backs and sturdy necks drifted in and out, but Charlie never moved. Probably weren't a lot of command decisions to be made at a meat plant, anyway.

At ten of four Pike said, 'Maybe it's a pass.'

At four Pike said, 'We can forget the Jamaican connection.'

At six minutes after four Pike said, 'You wanna check on this Santiago guy, anyway?'

At eleven minutes after four Charlie DeLuca came out and got into the black Town Car, and Pike said, 'He's alone.'

I looked at Pike and gave him Groucho Marx eyebrows.

Charlie pulled away from the curb and went up Bowery to Fourteenth, then across to Eighth and uptown past the theater district and the porno parlors and the street hustlers and a guy carrying a placard that said TRAVIS BICKLE WAS RIGHTEOUS. Heading north. Maybe north to Morningside Heights and Gloria Uribe and a guy named Santiago, but maybe not. He could always turn off to New Jersey.

This time of day the streets were crowded with cars and yellow cabs, and the cars and the cabs accelerated and swerved and stopped without regard to lanes or reason. Yellow cabs roared past the pedestrians who lined the street corners, some speeding up the closer they came to the warm bodies, others veering sharply across traffic, passing within inches of other cabs and cars, and nobody bothered to slow down. Everyone drove as if they were in Beirut, but that made it easy to follow him. In the chaos that was the approaching rush hour, we were just another random particle.

Pike loosened his .357 in its holster.

We stayed north on Eighth for a long time and then Charlie turned off Broadway onto Eighty-eighth and then over to Amsterdam, and suddenly we weren't going toward Morningside Heights and Gloria Uribe anymore. Pike said, 'Change of plans.'

'Unh-hunh.'

Charlie DeLuca pulled to the curb in a No Parking zone on Amsterdam Avenue. A young guy maybe thirty with a rat face and pimples and two sweatshirts came out of a doorway carrying a white, legal-sized envelope and got into the Lincoln. The Lincoln pulled away and we followed. Less than two blocks up Amsterdam the Lincoln again pulled to the curb and the pizza-faced guy got out. He closed the door as soon as he was out and walked away without looking back. He didn't have the envelope. The Lincoln started up Amsterdam again.

Pike said, 'Let me have the kid.'

I jerked the Taurus to the curb and Pike was out of the door before the Taurus stopped moving. I gunned it back into traffic and stayed with Charlie up Amsterdam into Morningside Heights and finally to Clyde's Bar. Well, well.

Luther and his friend had shown up and were leaning against their Pontiac. Luther didn't look happy. I drove around the block four times before I found a place to park and then I went back to see Luther. Luther smiled nastily when he saw me and said, 'Figure I be seeing you again. The Godfather roll up around five minutes ago. He upstairs now.'

'I know. How about Santiago?'

Luther nodded, slow, maybe remembering the ice pick. 'Yeah. He up there, too. So's the woman.'

'What's Santiago wearing?'

'Camel hair coat. Hat with a little pink feather in the band. Boots with these real skinny heels.'

'Great, Luther. Thanks.'

Luther gave me the slow nod, considering. 'You really a cop?'

'Luther,' I said, 'I am the right hand of God.'

Luther nodded again, and the nasty smile came back. 'If you plannin' on smitin' the sinners, I be glad to help.' He pushed back his long coat and showed me a little Rossi .32 snub-nose stuck in his pants. He remembered the ice pick, all right.

'Strictly surveillance this time around. Any smiting will have to come later.'

Luther shrugged and closed his coat. 'I be here.'

I went back across to the Taurus. Six minutes after I got settled Charlie and a tall black man in a hat with a pink feather and a camel overcoat came down and got into the Lincoln. When they passed Luther and his buddy, the tall black man said something to Luther and laughed. Ice-pick joke. Luther slid his right hand under his coat and watched the tall black man with sleepy eyes until he was in the Lincoln. It was going to take more than an ice pick the next time.

I followed the Lincoln down to 135th Street, then east across the island to Second, then straight down Second to the Queensboro Bridge and across the bridge into Queens.

We worked our way down off the bridge into an area of row houses and basketball courts and four- and five-story residential buildings. The sidewalks were crowded and most of the faces were black or brown, but not all of them, and many of the signs were in Spanish. The Lincoln pulled to the curb outside of a little coffee shop named Raldo's Soul Kitchen, and Charlie and the tall black guy went inside.

I looped around the block and parked in front of a barbershop, then walked back to Raldo's and looked in through the window. Charlie and the tall black guy were sitting at a booth with a shorter black guy and another white guy. The white guy looked sort of working class and the black guy looked like a fashion-row closeout with small eyes. Charlie handed the white envelope he had gotten from the guy on Amsterdam to Santiago, and Santiago handed it to the other black guy. Chain of command. I went back to the Taurus and waited.

Sixteen minutes later Charlie DeLuca and the two black guys and the other white guy came out of Raldo's and walked to a green Jaguar Sovereign parked up the block. The black guy with the small eyes opened the trunk and took out two brown-paper grocery bags and gave one of the bags to Charlie and the other to the working-class white guy. Charlie's bag was bigger and looked like it weighed more. As soon as they had the bags, the white guy went to a brown Toyota Celica and Charlie came back to his Lincoln and the two black guys got into the Jaguar. Nobody shook hands and nobody said so long, but everybody looked happy. Also, everybody went in different directions.

Portrait of the detective in crisis. Stay with Charlie or go after the black guys or the guy in the Toyota? Staying with the black guys would be hardest, and if they made me so soon after their meeting with Charlie, they'd tell him, and he might get scared and stop whatever he was doing. I went with the white guy in the Toyota.

We drove north to the Long Island Expressway, then east to 678 and then south through the heart of Queens to an exit that said Jamaica Avenue. Two blocks east of the Jamaica Avenue exit, the brown Toyota turned into a little parking lot next to a bright, modern cast-cement building with a sign that said BOROUGH OF QUEENS POLICE.

He parked in an empty spot next to a Volkswagen bug and got out with the brown-paper bag. He opened the Toyota's trunk, tossed in the bag, then took out a cop's blue-on-blue NYPD uniform and a gray gym bag. He closed the trunk, then carried the uniform and the gym bag into the station house.

I sat in the Taurus in the Borough of Queens Police parking lot for a very long while until a couple of cops with thirty years on the job gave me the bad eye, and only then did I drive away.

Amazing what you learn if you just wait and watch.

CHAPTER 29

I called Rollie George from a pay phone outside a Korean market and gave him the license numbers off the cop's Toyota and the Jaguar Sovereign. I told him that one of the black guys might be known as Santiago, and I asked him to get me anything on them that he could.

Rollie grunted. 'I don't like we got a cop in this. Maybe he's undercover.'

'Maybe.'

'Yeah.' He didn't say anything for a minute, but there was a lot of breathing. 'You know, Elvis, I haven't asked who you're working for.'

'I know.'

After a while Rollie said, 'Okay. I'll run these and get back to you.'

'Thanks, Rollie.'

He hung up without saying good-bye.

By the time I got back to Karen Lloyd's, the sun was settling comfortably in the trees to the west and the arctic air had made its predicted move down from Canada, dropping the temperature and clouding the skies.

Joe Pike was sitting in one of the wing chairs with the cat in his lap and Karen Lloyd was making noise in her kitchen. I had the car, but Pike beat me back. One of life's imponderables. I said, 'You made good time.'

'I followed the kid with the pimples to an apartment building on Broadway and 96th Street. Name on the post drop was Richard Sealy.'

'Aha. Richie.'

'Un-hunh. I called Rollie a little bit after you. He'll run a make.'

There was more noise from the kitchen. Heavy glass tumblers set hard on a counter. 'You been here long?'

'Long enough.'

More noise. Drawers slamming shut. I looked toward the noise, but Pike didn't. 'Everything okay?'

'Nope.' Pike's mouth twitched.

Karen Lloyd came out of the kitchen with a bucket of Kentucky Fried Chicken. Her mouth was narrow and tight, and she took short, quick steps. She said, 'We're having the Colonel. I want you to come here and look at this.' She put the Colonel on the table and went back through the kitchen toward the garage. I looked back at Pike. 'You get it like this, too?'

Pike's mouth twitched again.

I went back through the kitchen. Karen was standing in the laundry room at the door to the garage with her arms crossed. The door to the garage was open. 'Look at what that bastard did.'

I thought she meant Charlie DeLuca, but she didn't. A gleaming new blue and white Yamaha snowmobile was parked next to her LeBaron. 'It's going back. I told Peter about the gifts. I thought we had it straight, but this is what I find waiting for me when I got home with Toby.' No questions about the mafia. No *Did you discover what's going on?* No *Did you find out where he gets the money?* No *Are we going to get out of this alive?*

I said, 'That louse.'

She turned red. 'It's not an appropriate gift. Toby's too young.'

'Sure.'

'It's dangerous. Can't you see that?'

'It's not as dangerous as motorcycles, and I don't think it'll skew your son's values if he gets a nice gift from his father.'

She shut the door on the garage. 'I wouldn't think that you'd understand.'

Karen went back into the kitchen and put out the rest of the things she had brought from the Colonel and then she called Toby to the table. He came out sulky and silent. She asked him what he would like to drink and he said nothing. She asked him if he wanted rolls and the cole slaw and he said no. She asked him if he wanted a breast or a thigh and he said he didn't care. Sore about the snowmobile, I guess. Pike made himself a cheese sandwich and ate as if he were alone.

We were most of the way through the chicken when the white van that said WKEL-TV turned into the drive and the tall, thin woman got out. The weenie with the minicam got out with her. When Karen saw them coming through the big front window, she said, 'Oh, Jesus Christ.'

I said, 'Would you like me to get it?'

Karen shook her head and went to the door. 'No, thank you. This is my house, and my problem.'

The doorbell rang just as Karen opened the door. The tall, thin woman tried to step in past Karen, but Karen wouldn't get out of the way. The tall woman gave a nice local-news on-camera smile and put out her hand. Karen didn't take it. 'Hello, Ms. Lloyd. Janice Watkins, WKEL-TV. I do local color and human interest, and I was fascinated when I heard that Peter Alan Nelsen, the filmmaker, is your husband.' Janice Watkins seemed neither to mind nor notice that Karen hadn't taken her hand. Probably used to it.

Karen said, 'You've made some sort of mistake. I'm not married.'

The smile didn't falter. 'Ex-husband, then. I know how that is, I've got two.' She chuckled. Establishing rapport.

'I'm sorry, Ms. Watkins. I don't know what you're talking about.'

A corner of the smile gave way. 'Peter Alan Nelsen and his entourage are staying at the Howard Johnson's.'

Toby craned around the bucket of chicken, trying to see. Pike pushed the bucket out of his way.

The thin woman said, 'You've been seen with him. So has your son. Everyone is saying that Toby Lloyd is Mr. Nelsen's child and that Mr. Nelsen has journeyed across the country to find him.' *Journeyed*. She was working up the human-interest angle, all right.

'I've never been married to Peter Alan Nelsen and I don't know what you're talking about.'

The smile faltered. 'You weren't?'

'No.'

'Is Peter Alan Nelsen the boy's father?'

'No.'

Janice Watkins blinked. She tried to peek past Karen to see if Peter Alan Nelsen was lurking inside. I waved at her.

Karen Lloyd said, 'You've interrupted our meal. Do you mind?'

Janice Watkins narrowed her eyes. 'Ms. Lloyd, I have this information on very good authority.'

Karen Lloyd leaned toward Janice Watkins. 'Ms. Watkins, chew a used rubber.' Then she slammed the door.

Toby was staring at his plate when Karen came back to the table. His face was red and her face was tight and pale. When she picked up a piece of original recipe, her hand trembled and she put it back down.

Toby said, 'Why did you tell'm he wasn't my dad?'

Karen lifted the piece of chicken again and this time took a small bite. She didn't answer. After a while Toby got up, took his plate into the kitchen, then went down the hall to his room.

Karen Lloyd put down her chicken and said, 'Shit.'

At seven-fifty that evening the doorbell rang again and this time when Karen answered, Peter Alan Nelsen came in without Nick or T.J. or Dani. He said, 'I've been thinking about this and I've got a way to make everybody happy.' Toby must've seen the limo, because he came out of his room.

Karen stiffened as if someone had injected her with Super Glue and said, 'He can't keep that thing.' First words out of her mouth.

Peter started to say something, but then he didn't. Showing restraint. 'I'm not a dope. I know I'm here at a bad time. You're trying to straighten out this thing with the DeLuca people, and you've got me here, and you've gotta be worried about Toby. Lemme lighten the load for you. How about I take Tobe back to L.A. with me until you guys get this worked out?'

Toby said, 'Yeah!'

Peter looked from Karen to me and then back to Karen. He spread his hands. 'Toby'll be safe, and I'll be out of your hair, and you can take care of what you need to take care of. When it's done, you can give me a call and Toby and I will come back and we can work out our family situation.'

Toby was giving it the ear-to-ear. 'Great! Can I meet Sylvester Stallone?'

Peter said, 'Sure.'

Karen said, 'No.'

Peter frowned. 'No, he can't meet Sylvester Stallone, or no, he can't go to L.A.?'

Karen went back to one of the wing chairs and sat down. Her knees were together and so were her hands. 'He has school. He has basketball.'

I said, 'It might make things easier.'

Peter said, 'Jesus Christ, Karen, it won't kill him to miss a few days of school.'

Toby said, 'I can get Miss Garrett to give me the work. I won't fall behind.'

'No.'

Peter said, 'What do you mean, no?'

'It would be too disruptive. Who knows how long this is going to take?'

I said, 'I think it's a good idea.'

Karen flashed the hard eyes at me. 'Nobody asked you.'

Peter rolled his eyes and looked at the ceiling. 'Hey, am I being an asshole here or what?' Getting loud.

Karen said, 'Watch your language in front of my son.' They were starting to shout.

Peter gestured wide with the arms the way he had when I'd first seen him, reading the riot act because a couple of executives had been trying to fob off a TV guy on him. 'Hey, Karen, a *mobster* was here with *our son*. Do you remember that?'

Karen pushed up out of the chair and made a shooing gesture to Toby. 'Toby, I want you to go to your room.'

Peter said, 'Lemme take the kid back to L.A. He'll be safer there than here. You think I won't bring'm back?'

Pike stuck his fingers in his ears.

I said, 'Peter, maybe now isn't the time to talk about it.'

Peter whirled around and glared at me. 'I'm Peter Alan Nelsen and I'm tired of fooling around.' He wheeled back toward Karen. 'If you played it smart, I could set you up. You wouldn't have to worry about a thing and you could do whatever you want. You could even be an actress again. I'm Peter Alan Nelsen, and I could make you a star.' Like she was still nineteen and always would be.

Karen Lloyd put her hands on her hips and laughed at him. 'You arrogant asshole.'

Toby started crying and yelled, 'Why won't you let me go with him? Why are you being like this? You're gonna make him go away and I hate you!' He ran down the hall and slammed his door.

Pike still had his fingers in his ears.

Peter was giving us confused and frustrated, as if he were trying to explain that two plus one equals three and Karen just couldn't get it, and the frustration was giving way to suspicion, like maybe she got it but was pretending she didn't because something was going on. He squinted at me, then back at her, and then he nodded and made an oh-I-get-it smile and said, 'You're fucking this guy.'

Karen Lloyd slapped him. It was a hard, quick shot that took him off guard and backed him up. I stepped in between them, taking his wrists and keeping his hands at his sides and pushing him

575

backward. Karen yelled, 'You piece of shit. You rotten piece of shit. Why'd you have to come back? Why couldn't you leave us alone?'

Peter jerked away from me and threw a punch that seemed to float down from heaven. I stepped outside of it, then stepped back in very close and pushed him up against the door and told him to relax. He tried to bite me and then he tried to butt me with his head, and when he did, I punched him once in the stomach. He made an urp-ing sound and went down onto his hands and knees and threw up on Karen Lloyd's beautiful bleached-oak floor. I hadn't wanted to hit him, and I was glad the boy wasn't there to see it.

Peter stayed on all fours, head hanging down, and made little burping noises. 'I'm sick.'

Pike said, 'Take deep breaths.'

Karen stood by the mantel, holding herself. Pike went into the kitchen and came back with a roll of Scot towels.

Peter took the deep breaths, then staggered to his feet and shook his finger at me. 'Goddamnit, you're fired. You're off the fucking payroll. I'm gonna make sure you never work again.'

I said, 'Clichéd, Peter. I expected more originality from the King of Adventure.'

Peter burped some more and then he lurched out the front door. In a minute the limo pulled away and Pike held out his hand. 'I'd better make sure he gets home.'

I tossed Pike the keys and he left.

Karen Lloyd and I stood without moving in the now quiet house, and I said, 'Peter's idea was good.'

She shook her head.

'It's smart to get the boy out of the picture. It's smart if Peter's gone, too. It would give you more room.'

She shook her head again. 'If he wanted to help, he could just leave. He doesn't need Toby. This is just more of the same old Peter Alan Nelsen bullshit. Peter wanting everything his way.'

'Karen,' I said, 'think about it. They've threatened your life. They made a move on your son. Falling behind in history doesn't rate with getting him out of here. Do you see?'

She made a little blowing move with her mouth and then she crossed her arms and sat on the edge of the hearth, leaning forward so that her elbows touched her knees. She gave me a short glance, and then she looked at the floor, and then she uncrossed her arms and put a hand on either side of her head and squeezed, like maybe she was trying to keep her head from bursting. She said, 'I'm not crazy. I am not crazy. *I'm not crazy.*'

'Nope,' I said. 'You're scared, but it isn't Charlie DeLuca who scares you, though it should be.'

She shook her head and closed her eyes. 'I'm too tired to argue.'

I said, 'This is your house. You bought the couch and the table and the wood in the fireplace. You secured the loan for your car. You buy Toby's clothes, and you've made a good life.'

She shook her head some more.

'But now comes Peter, and you're scared that it won't be yours anymore. You'll be the woman who was married to Peter Alan Nelsen, and Toby will be Peter's son.'

She stopped shaking her head.

'You're scared of losing yourself.'

Two tears squeezed out of the inside corners of her eyes and ran down her cheeks. 'You sonofabitch.' She might've been talking to me, but maybe not.

I said, 'Don't think about Peter. Think about Charlie. Charlie is who you have to focus on. Charlie can hurt you and Toby a lot worse than Peter.'

She brought one hand up and rubbed at the tears but still did not open her eyes. 'Do you think I'm stupid?'

'No.'

'It sounds so stupid, worried about losing myself. It sounds weak and silly, like something one of those idiot *Cosmo* feminists would whine about. I don't want to be weak. I don't want to be stupid.'

I made a shrug. 'Pride isn't male or female. It's human.'

'I'm a vice-president at the bank. I have a real estate license and I am a certified financial planner and I've been president of the PTA twice and vice-president of the local Rotary.' The tears were coming harder.

'Unh-hunh.'

'I have a B.A. in finance. I am Toby Lloyd's mother. I will not lose those things.'

'No. You won't.'

'I will not lose who I am.'

'I won't let you.'

She opened her eyes and looked at me.

'Saving selves is one of my best things.'

She rubbed at the tears again and then she put her face in her hands and sat very still. I guess she wasn't convinced.

I used the Scot towels on the floor, then put them in a white plastic trash bag and took the bag out and put it into a blue garbage can in the garage. It seemed twenty degrees colder than it had been at dusk, and the north wind rattled tree limbs and dead leaves and pushed dark shapes across the lawn. Thunder rumbled many miles to the east, a winter storm moving with the front. When I went back inside, Karen Lloyd had gone to bed.

I turned off most of the lights and went down the hall to the room where Joe Pike and I were bedding. Karen Lloyd's room was at the end of the hall in the back of the house, and Toby's room was across from Karen's, in the front. Both of their doors were closed, but I could hear them crying, she in her room and he in his. I felt a very great urge to knock and say the word or make the touch that would make them feel better. I went into my own room and I closed the door.

You do what you can, but you can't do everything.

CHAPTER 30

When I woke the next morning, the sky was dark with clouds and the air was as cold as the edge of a hunting knife. The snow above us waiting to fall was a physical thing, heavy and damp and alive with turbulence.

Toby was sullen and Karen was unhappy and nobody said very much as we went through the house and prepared for the day. Karen drove into the office early and I took Toby to school. Pike stayed at the house, waiting for Roland George to call. Neither Toby nor I spoke on the way to school, but when I dropped him off I told him to have a good day. He didn't answer. It was as if the bad feelings and restless, logy sleep had carried over into wakefulness.

At nine-forty-two that morning Roland George called. I took it in the living room. Pike picked up in the kitchen. Roland George said, 'The Jag you saw is registered to a Jamaican named Urethro Mubata. Came up here in 1981. Fourteen arrests, two convictions, assault, armed robbery, like that. He's mostly in the dope business.'

'Not exactly a good-will ambassador.'

'Unh-unh. He did eight months at Rikers for possession with intent and another fourteen at Sing Sing for attempted murder. When he was at Ossining, he did cell time with a man named Jesus Santiago, another Jamaican. Santiago served out, but Mubata's on parole.'

'Santiago in for pimping?'

'That's it. Sorta curious how this guy Mubata got the forty grand for a new Jaguar when his employment of record is being a busboy at Arturo's Tapas Stand in Jackson Heights.'

Pike said, 'What about Sealy and the cop?'

'Sealy is a hype, registered in the methadone program at St. Vincent's. He's a nobody with a string of minor busts, mostly hijack and street boosting, run a little policy, steal a few stereos, that kind of thing.'

'Is he part of DeLuca's crew?'

'It's not in the files, but it's possible. The guy's a drop of pus, but he's a known associate. Hard to figure, though. Hype like this, Charlie DeLuca shouldn't be having anything to do with him.'

Pike said, 'He shouldn't be having anything to do with a police officer, either.'

'Yeah.' Something hard came into Roland's voice. 'The officer in question is employed by Kennedy Airport Security. He is not undercover.'

'Okay.'

I hung up. Joe Pike came into the living room from the kitchen and said, 'I make it for a hijacking setup. Something coming into Kennedy.'

'It sounds right, but why's Charlie sneaking around? He gets a tip that something worth stealing is coming in, he uses the Jamaicans to pull the heist, then they split the take with him. Big deal. Why does he want to keep it from Sal?'

'Because he doesn't want to split the money.'

I thought about it some more and shook my head. 'It's not a world breaker. Charlie shows a little initiative, he makes a few extra bucks. What's Daddy going to do?'

Pike said, 'There's the hype.'

I nodded. The hype didn't figure. You want to keep secrets, you don't do business with a hype. 'Maybe Charlie doesn't have a choice. Maybe, whatever he's doing, he can't do it without the hype.'

Pike grunted. 'Makes you wonder what he's got going, that he can't do it without a hype.'

I said, 'Yes, it does. Maybe we should ask the hype and find out.'

'What if the hype won't cooperate?'

'He'll cooperate. Everyone knows that a hype can't keep secrets. They have low self-esteem.'

We put on our coats and our guns and made the drive into Manhattan in less than fifty minutes.

We parked by a subway entrance near 92nd Street and Central Park West, then walked two blocks to an eight-story gray-stone building with painted windows and a lot of crummy shops on the ground floor and a fire escape.

Pike said, 'Third floor in the back. Three-F.'

We entered the lobby of the apartment building between a place that sold discount clothing and a place that sold donuts. The lobby had a white and black linoleum floor, circa 1952, probably the last year it had been waxed, and someone had scotch-taped a little handwritten sign that said *out of service* to the elevator. Someone else had urinated on the floor. You watch *Miami Vice* or *Wiseguy*, the criminals always live in palatial apartments and drive Ferraris. So much for verisimilitude.

We walked up the two flights, then down a dingy hall past a stack of newspapers four feet tall, Pike leading. An empty plastic Cup•A•Soup was lying on its side atop the newspapers. Three-F was the third apartment on the left side of the hall. When Pike got to the door, he stood there a moment, head cocked to the side, and then he shook his head. 'Not home.'

'How do you know?'

Shrug. 'Knock and see.'

I knocked, then knocked again. Nothing.

Pike spread his hands.

I said, 'Why don't we be sure?'

Pike shook his head, giving me bored.

There was only one lock and it was cheap. I let us into a studio apartment that was just as attractive as the rest of the building. Bags of fast-food wrappers and potato-chip empties in the kitchenette, stacks of the *New York Post* and the *National Enquirer* along the walls, paper cups packed with dead cigarettes by a throw-pillow couch, and the sour smell of body odor and wet matches. Nice. No Richard Francis Sealy, though. Maybe Pike could see through walls.

We went back down to the mail drop in the lobby. Most of the little mailbox doors had been jimmied – junkies looking for checks – and most of the boxes were empty. The top box had a little plastic sticker on it that said: *Sal Cohen, 2A, mgr.*

We went back up to the second floor and found 2-A. I knocked hard on the door three times. Somebody threw a series of bolts and then Sal Cohen scowled out at us from behind what looked like eight security chains. He was little and dark, and he had a Sunbeam steam iron in his right hand. He said, 'The fuck you're knocking so loud?'

New York, New York. The attitude capital of the universe.

I said, 'Richard Sealy in three-F, he's a pal of ours. He was supposed to meet us here and he's not around.'

'So what?' Mr. Helpful.

'We're movie producers. We're going to produce a movie and we want him to be the star. We thought you might know when he'd be around so we could get him in on this.'

Sal Cohen blinked at me and then he blinked at Joe Pike. 'Yeah?'

'Yeah.'

Sal smirked. 'What bull. I know cops when I see'm.'

Pike walked away down the hall.

I stepped closer to the door, lowered my voice, and tried to look furtive. I have never in my life met a cop who looked furtive, but there you go. 'Okay,' I said, 'we're on the cops. We need your help in locating Richard Sealy so that we might topple the organized crime structure in our city.'

He said, 'You find him, you get me the eight months' back rent the little bag of shit owes.'

'You got any idea when he'll be around?'

'No.'

'You know where he works?'

'That lazy sonofabitch, work? If he worked, he wouldn't be eight months back on the rent. None of these lazy bastards work.'

'You know where he spends his time?'

'Look down at Dillard's. He's always down there, shooting pool and trying to buy dope, else he's running around with those crazy Gamboza bastards.'

'Gamboza bastards?' Pike came back and stood next to me.

Sal nodded and squinted out at us. 'Yeah.'

'As in the Gamboza family?'

'Yeah.' More squinting.

I said, 'Richard Sealy hangs out with the DeLuca family.' Sal laughed, and it came out like a series of sharp hacks. 'Hey, you just fall off the lamebrain truck, or what? I run this building thirty-five years. Those fucking Gamboza bastards grew up right over there on Wilmont Street and so did Richie Sealy. They useta throw rocks at the niggers and steal their money, the little bastards, Richie Sealy and Nick and Tommy Gamboza and that nut case Vincent Ricci. Jesus Christ, the DeLucas.' More of the hacking laugh. 'Richie's about as close to being a Gamboza as you can be without the blood. Why else you think I gotta put up with a junkie eight months back on his rent? I heave him out, those bastards would cut out my heart and fry it in a pan.'

I said, 'But how does he fit in with the DeLucas?'

Sal squinted at me past the security chains like I was a new release from Bellevue. 'He don't. Nobody around here got anything to do with the fucking DeLucas. The Upper West Side is owned lock, stock, and short hairs by the Gamboza family. DeLucas got lower Manhattan. This look like lower Manhattan to you?'

I was seeing it. 'Sonofabitch.'

Sal Cohen said, 'No wonder this city's down the toilet, fucking cops like you.' Then he slammed the door.

Joe Pike and I walked down the flight of stairs and out onto the street and looked around at deepest, darkest Gamboza country. Nary a DeLuca in sight.

'Well, well, well,' I said. 'Now I'm beginning to see why Charlie's keeping this secret.'

Pike nodded.

'The Delucas and the Gambozas hate each other, but they have an agreement. They're supposed to be standing together against the foreign gangs.'

Pike's mouth twitched. 'Doesn't look that way, does it?'

'Nope.'

Pike's mouth twitched a second time. Hysterics, for Pike. 'You think whatever these guys are stealing at Kennedy, it's something that would make a lot of people mad?'

'I've got some guesses.'

Pike nodded again. 'Let's go down to Dillard's and see if your guesses are right.'

CHAPTER 31

You had to walk up a long wooden flight of stairs to get to Dillard's. The stairs were dark and the finish was worn off the center of each tread. A sign at the bottom of the stairs said DILLARD'S POOL & BILLIARDS, LADIES WELCOME. Another sign said NO MINORS, UNDER 21 NOT ALLOWED.

We went up the stairs and into a big room with a high ceiling and maybe twenty tables and a splintered floor that went pretty well with the stairs. A dozen kids in black leather jackets over white T-shirts shot pool and smoked and sucked on red cans of Coca-Cola as if this were still 1957, only most of them had long shaggy hair or buzz cuts. Pool cues like prison bars stood upright on racks against the walls, and fluorescent lights on the ceiling made everyone look dead. One of the lights flickered. A sixty-year-old bald guy with knotty arms sat behind a short bar where you could get beer or soft drinks. He was reading a copy of *Sporting Times*. I didn't see any ladies and no one except the guy behind the bar looked over sixteen. I didn't see Richie Sealy, either. Pike said, 'I'll check the back.'

Pike went across the big room and into a little alcove where a couple of signs said *restrooms* and *exit*. I walked over to the guy behind the bar.

He watched me come over the top of his paper and squirmed around on his stool. Nervous. I said, 'We're looking for Richard Sealy. Is he around?'

The old guy glanced toward the rear of his place, where Pike had gone, then back to me. He didn't fold the paper or put it down. 'You guys with the cops?' First Sal Cohen, now him. Maybe if we let our hair grow.

I said, 'Richard Sealy.'

More of the nervous. 'Look, I'm straight now, okay? I did the

584

nickel and I'm good at my parole and I live straight, so whatever Richie's got going, I don't know.' He shot little glances at the kids and kept his voice down, hoping no one would hear. They probably thought he was tough, and he didn't want them to know he wasn't.

I gave him a hard cop look like I'd seen Robert Stack give in old *Untouchables* reruns. 'We just want Sealy.'

In the back, a fat kid with glasses laughed too loud and then a gray metal door that said GENTLEMEN opened next to a pay phone and Richard Sealy came out. He was wearing the same two sweatshirts and the same fingerless gloves and he was smiling. Thirty-five years old and he was hanging out with kids.

The old guy said, 'No shooting.'

I looked at him. Life at the Longbranch.

Pike came out of the back as Richie went over to a green table where a couple of kids were shooting eight-ball. Richie grabbed a pack of Marlboros off the edge of the table, lipped out a cigarette, fired up, then bent over to line up a shot. Someone had taped a poster of Heather Thomas in a bikini onto the wall. Heather looked okay.

Pike moved along the far wall past the pool cues and came up behind Richie. When he was ten feet from Heather Thomas, I walked over and came up from the near side. 'Hey, Richie.'

Richie let out a cloud of the Marlboro and looked at me. 'I know you?'

'Sure.'

Richie squinted through the smoke and rubbed at the inside of his left arm. He looked sleepy. 'Where I know you from, Gino's?'

I said, 'Let's take a little walk. We got something to talk about.'

Joe Pike came up from the other side and stood very close to Richie without expression. The kids shooting eight-ball stopped and looked over.

Richie glanced at Pike, then me. 'What the fuck? I don't know you.'

'Come on.' I put my hand on his arm. 'We've got mutual friends.'

'Hey, I'm in the middle of a game here.' Eyes flicking faster now, Pike to me, Pike to me.

I went in closer until we had him sandwiched and made my voice quiet. 'Tommy Gamboza sent us, Richie.'

Surprised. 'Tommy wants to see me?' Almost a little excited, like maybe Tommy had sent us around to tap him for the secret order,

585

like we'd drive somewhere and he'd get to take the blood oath to become part of La Cosa Nostra.

'Yeah.' I took him under the arm and pulled him toward the stairs. Pike looked back at the kids and told them that the game was over.

Richie said, 'Hey, if Tommy wants to see me, how come he didn't come himself? How come he didn't send Tony or Frankie to get me? I don't know you guys.'

'We're imported, Richie. Vegas.' You say Vegas, they know it's bad.

He jammed on the brakes, pulling up short. You see how it is with Vegas? 'Hey.'

I leaned close and whispered in his ear. 'The Gambozas know you're selling them out to Charlie DeLuca.'

Richie Sealy's knees went weak and he sort of slumped. If I hadn't been holding his right arm he would've gone down the stairs like a runny egg. 'Oh, Jesus,' he said. 'Oh, Jesus.'

We took him down the stairs and around the corner into a little alley that smelled of grease and ammonia and put him into the wall against a metal dumpster. I held his collar and Pike patted him down and came up with a sharpened screw-driver and two ten-dollar packs of white powder. Pike opened the bags and poured out the powder. I said, 'Don't you know this stuff is bad for you, Richie?'

'I don't know what you're talking about. I don't know anything about Charlie DeLuca. I swear to Christ on my mother's life.' These junkies.

I said, 'Richie. The Gambozas know. Vincent Ricci saw with his own eyes. Are you calling Ricci a liar?'

'Hey, no way, but, you know, like maybe he made a mistake –'

I jerked his collar once. 'Knock off the shit.' Elvis Cole, Professional Thug.

Richard Sealy started to cry.

I said, 'The Gambozas know that something is going on, but they don't know what. You know how they hate that bastard Charlie DeLuca. You know what Tommy thinks.' I didn't know what Tommy thought, but if the blood between the DeLucas and the Gambozas was as bad as Roland George had said, whatever Tommy thought couldn't be good.

'Yeah. Yeah, I know.'

'Okay. They told us, give him one chance. They said, if he comes

586

clean with you, let him live, but only if he comes clean and gives the whole thing.' I looked at Pike. 'Isn't that what they said?'

Pike nodded.

I looked back at Richie. 'You hear that?'

Richie was sobbing. A ribbon of mucus ran down across his mouth and along his chin. He said, 'I can't say anything. I can't.'

I slapped him. 'You made fools out of those guys, you moron. Ricci, Tommy, the Gamboza brothers. They grew up with you. They loved you like family and you have made them look like turnips, and you have done this with the help of Charlie DeLuca. Can you imagine how this makes Tommy and Nickie feel?' Elvis Brando. One step away from the Great White Way.

Richie Sealy was nodding and shaking his head at the same time and his eyes looked like dried apricots. He said, 'Jesus Christ, we're talking Crazy Charlie DeLuca. Charlie the Tuna. Charlie will kill me. He'll cut out my eyes, for Christ's sake, can't I make it up to Tommy another way?'

I shook him and said, 'Moron. You're worried about Crazy Charlie. Why do you think the Gambozas brought us in for this?' I looked at Pike again. Pike reached behind his back and brought out a twelve-inch Buck hunting knife. It was so bright you could shave in the reflection.

Richard Sealy tried to backpedal away, but the dumpster was there. 'Okay,' he said. 'Okay. Whatever you want.'

'What do you and Charlie have going?'

'I tell him when some of the dope shipments are coming in through Kennedy.'

'Gamboza dope.' There it was.

'Yeah. Sure.'

'What about the Jamaicans? What about the cop out in Queens?'

'Jesus Christ, Tommy knows everything.'

I pulled Richie close. 'Tommy knows all and sees all.'

Pike sighed and looked away.

Richie said, 'Charlie sells the information to the Jamaicans. The Jamaicans hijack our stuff and sell it and then they give Charlie a piece.'

'Is this DeLuca family, Richie, or is this just Charlie? If it's family, we're talking war.' War. Mario Puzo, eat your heart out.

'I don't know, but I think it's just Charlie. Charlie's the guy turned me. He came to me and said he'd cut me in and I could have all the smack I wanted. It was Charlie's idea. You gotta tell Tommy that.'

'Sure.'

'I don't never see anyone else.'

'So Charlie is violating the agreement the DeLuca family made with the Gamboza family. He's in business with the Jamaicans to steal from another family and Sal doesn't know.'

'No. Sal doesn't know. Jesus Christ, Sal would have a fit. Tommy should know that. Sal, that old gumbah.'

I looked at Pike and Pike looked at me. Pike said, 'What do we do with him?'

Richie said, 'Hey, I come clean. You said I come clean, Tommy said you should let me off.'

Pike said, 'He tells Charlie we know, it's over.'

Richie said, 'Hey, I won't tell Charlie nothing. I swear to Christ.' He was crying again.

I looked into Pike's flat dimensionless glasses and saw little reflections of myself. Pike waited. I turned back to Richie and pulled him close again. 'Here's what you're going to do. You're going to walk out of this alley and go to the Port Authority bus terminal and you are going to take a bus to Miami. You will not speak with Charlie DeLuca or the Jamaicans or anyone else about this, do you understand?'

'Yes.'

'If you do, Tommy Gamboza swears that he will find out. If you do, the entire Gamboza family will seek you out no matter where you might hide, and we will kill you. Do you understand?'

'Yes.'

'Get out of here.'

He ran out of the alley, knocking into a garbage can, then bouncing off a wall, then disappearing around the corner and into the street.

Pike said, '"Seek you out"?'

'Too dramatic?'

Pike frowned.

Everybody's a critic.

CHAPTER 32

Karen Lloyd gave me confused. 'He's stealing from other criminals?'

'Yes.'

'How can you go to the police with that?' She was leaning against the front edge of her desk at the bank with her arms crossed. Pike and I were sitting in the two chairs opposite. It seemed colder in Chelam than it had in New York, but maybe that was because it was later and the damp clouds and the cold air pushing down from Canada had gained greater purchase over the woods and the fields and the small clean buildings.

I said, 'We won't go to the police. We'll go to Charlie. He isn't just stealing money and hiding it from his father and the other *capos* in his own family, he's stealing from another family in direct violation of a treaty that the DeLucas made with the other families.' I gave her what Rollie George had given me, how the families had divided up territory and crime, and how nobody much liked it but everybody had been living with it. 'Until now.'

She nodded, seeing it as a banker would see it, IBM and Xerox negotiating a market arrangement. 'All right. He's violating a trade agreement.'

'Yeah. Only he's got more to worry about than the Securities and Exchange Commission. If the Gambozas found out that Charlie DeLuca was stealing from them in collaboration with the Jamaicans, they'd kill him and they'd probably try to kill Sal, too.'

Karen blinked at Pike, then at me. 'Does Sal know?'

'Probably not, but it doesn't matter. If he doesn't know, it makes things cleaner because we only have to deal with Charlie. If Sal's in on it, then we have to deal with him, too. A little more complicated, but the outcome is the same.'

She wet her lips, getting anxious with it, thinking it through and seeing the potential, but unwilling to commit until all the *i*'s were dotted and the *t*'s crossed. She shook her head. 'Even if he goes along, we'll still know. Charlie's going to think that. He's going to think that the only way to keep himself safe is to kill us.'

I said, 'He'll think about it, but we'll set things up so that he can't. We'll bring in Rollie George. We'll make sure that other people know what we know, and we'll prove it to Charlie so that he knows it, too. If he kills us, he gets screwed. Do you see?'

She wet her lips again and made a very small nod, still thinking it through. 'We go to Charlie, we say that he has to let go of me or we tell the Gambozas.'

'Yes.'

'We tell him that people we trust know, too, so that if anything happens to us, the Gambozas will still be told.'

'Yes. If we die, he dies. We make this deal, it's a deal we honor forever. We can't change our minds. Do you see?'

She nodded again, stronger. 'Of course. When are you going to do this?'

'I'll call Rollie this evening and maybe drive down to the city to talk with him. He knows people in publishing and on the cops we can trust. We'll have to get together with them and set up what we know and how to prove it to Charlie. It'll take a couple of days.'

'And then we do it.'

'Yep. We do it.'

She wet the lips again and looked at Pike, then me. 'What if it doesn't work?'

'If it doesn't work, we go to the Gambozas and you go in to the cops for witness protection. It isn't what you want, but it's the best hand we've got.'

She made a hissing sound and her eyes sort of fluttered for a moment, but then she nodded. 'Yes. I believe it's the best we can hope for, too.' She went around behind her desk and sat with her fingers laced in front of her, very much like she did the first time I came into her office. Businesslike. 'I've thought about what you said last night. I've decided that you're right. It would be best for everyone if Toby went back to California with Peter until this is resolved.'

'Okay.'

'Peter can take Toby as soon as possible. I'd like him to be in California before we meet with Charlie.'

'All right. I'll stop by the motel and set it up.'

She nodded tightly. 'Thank you. I'll tell Toby when I see him after school.'

Pike and I drove to the Howard Johnson's looking for Peter, but the limo was gone. We went in to the front desk and asked if they knew when Mr. Nelsen would be back. They said they didn't, but that his friends were in the bar and that they might know. We went into the bar.

Nick and T.J. were sitting at a little round table, drinking Heinekens and eating hamburgers. Nick said, 'Hey, look, it's Mike Hammer and his sidekick, Tonto.'

T.J. laughed with his mouth full.

I said, 'Where's Peter?'

Nick said, 'Peter said you're canceled, pal, so he's taking care of business himself. We don't need you anymore.'

I said, 'What do you mean, Peter's taking care of business?'

'He got tired of waiting around. He and Dani went to straighten out the wop.'

'He and Dani went to see DeLuca?'

'Yeah.'

'When?'

'A little while ago.'

Pike moved next to me.

'Where?'

Nick gave me the smirk. 'Hey, fuck you. It's not your business.'

Pike stepped in close, took out his .357, and touched it to Nick's upper lip. 'Tonto wants to know.'

Nick stopped smirking and T.J. stopped laughing. Nick said, 'Some meat place. He got the address from the operator.'

Pike and I ran out of the Ho Jo and pushed the Taurus hard back along the state road to the expressway and then down to Manhattan.

We were half a block from the meat plant when a brown Nissan Sentra nosed out of the parking lot and into the street. Two guys I hadn't seen before were in the front seat and Ric was in the back with Dani and Peter. Peter's head was sort of lolling to the side.

Pike said, 'We get the chance, we take them in traffic.' He took out his Python and held it in his lap.

I let the Sentra make its first corner, then I jerked the Taurus around and caught up to them going east on Canal to climb the Manhattan Bridge across the East River to Brooklyn.

The bridge was electric with late-afternoon congestion as thousands of cars raced for home before the bridge gridlocked. If the bridge was locked now, what we were trying to do would be easy, but the bridge wasn't locked. Traffic coursed and bumper-to-bumper cars weaved from lane to lane, cutting each other off, hitting their brakes and making it hard to keep the Sentra in sight. Pike rolled down the passenger window and climbed out to sit on the door, but it didn't help. Eight cars ahead of us and two lanes over, the Sentra took the second exit ramp over the Brooklyn shore and that's where we lost it.

Pike said, 'Off-ramp.'

I blew the horn and cut in and out between three cars and knocked the bumper off a green Dodge station wagon, but I kept going.

We jumped across the two right lanes and hit the off-ramp in a skid and followed it down in a great looping arc over factories and waterfront and chain-link fences and bridge supports, Pike standing as tall as he could in the window, trying to spot the Sentra, finally yelling, 'Got it.'

The Sentra was below us in a U-Stor-It yard under one of the on-ramps leading back to Manhattan. The two guys were out of the Sentra's front seat and Ric and Peter and Dani were getting out of the back. One of the guys from the front was wearing a red leather jacket with very wide shoulders. The other had a gun out. Revolver.

We came off the ramp at the rear of the storage yard on the wrong side of a ten-foot chain-link fence. I said, 'Faster to go over it.'

We went up and over and came out between two corrugated-metal storage sheds eighty yards away as Ric took out the stainless-steel ten, pointed it at Peter, and said something to the guy with the revolver. Peter was standing with his hands up the way he'd had actors stand in his movies. Eighty yards away, you could see that his face was white and his eyes looked scooped out behind the thick glasses. Dani was maybe a half step in front of him. Peter said something to Ric and put out his hands, maybe saying please don't shoot, and Ric raised his gun to eye level and Dani went for him. I yelled, but it didn't do any good. Ric's gun popped once and the right back quarter of Dani's head blew off. Then I had the Dan Wesson out and Pike had his .357 and we were firing at them, eighty yards away, me screaming at Peter to get down, but Peter standing there, still with his hands up.

The guy with the revolver went down.

Ric ran toward the Sentra, firing as he went, and the guy in the red jacket pulled out a black automatic. Bullets slapped into the little corrugated sheds around us with the sound of hammers hitting garbage cans and left silver streaks on the tarmac where they hit and bounced into a concrete bridge support. The guy in the red jacket fired fast, *bapbapbap*, and then he went for the Sentra, too. I shot him in the back. He fell in through the Sentra's front passenger window as Ric roared away, fishtailing into storage sheds and a boat trailer, and then through the far gate.

When the Sentra was gone, the storage yard was still.

We got to Dani as fast as we could, but there wasn't anything to do.

Peter said, 'He told that guy Ric to kill me.' He was talking fast and there was a knot below his left eye, like maybe someone had hit him there. His hands were still in the air. 'Just like that, he said kill'm. I said I'm Peter Alan Nelsen. I said you can't kill me. He said, you wanna bet? And then these guys were bringing us out here and they were gonna kill me.' Me. Me and I.

I stood up. 'Dani.'

He was hopping from foot to foot, confused and squinting at me. 'What?'

'They killed Dani.' I said it carefully, each word distinct.

He gave me more of the confused and said, 'What?' Pike was squatting next to her body and I was standing over her, and Peter and I were talking about her, but he hadn't looked at her and he hadn't said anything about her. He said, 'I told'm you can't do this to me. I'm Peter Alan Nelsen.'

I went over to him and said, 'Put down your hands.'

He put down his hands.

I punched him in the chest with my right hand. He fell backward and landed hard on his butt and said, 'Hey, what did you hit me for?' Surprised.

I grabbed him by the hair and lifted him as high as I could and I hit him in the face. His nose popped with a little spray of blood and I hit him again. He started to cry. I said, 'Who's lying right there? What's her name?'

'Dani.' He still wouldn't look at her.

'Look at her.'

'No.' Blubbering now.

I knotted his hair between my fingers and turned his face toward the body and pointed at her. 'Look at her.'

He clenched his eyes tight. 'No!'

I slapped him hard on the left side of his face two times and then I dug my fingers at his eyes, prying them open. I said, 'Look at her, you sonofabitch. Dani's lying there and not you. They killed Dani. Do you see her? They didn't kill you.' Peter covered his face, peering out from between his fingers at what was left of the woman who picked up his candy wrappers. I said, 'Do you see her, Peter?'

He coughed out a great whooping sob. 'Dani.'

I let go of him.

He rocked forward and crawled toward her body. 'It's my fault,' he said. 'Oh God, it's my fault.'

I didn't say anything. I was breathing hard and something sharp throbbed behind my right eye.

Peter sat on his knees next to her, and touched her muscular arm, and cried all the harder. It made me feel ashamed.

Pike came up behind me. 'Ric will go to DeLuca. Things will happen fast now.'

'Yes.' I took a deep breath and let it out. 'Peter?'

'What?' He didn't look at me.

'Did you tell Charlie that we were on to the Jamaicans?'

He nodded, still not looking at me.

'Did you tell him we knew about the secret accounts?'

Another nod.

It felt cold and damp and ready to snow. Above us, the roadway vibrated with cars and trucks and thousands of people. Around us was a city of millions. We'd fired maybe fifteen high-velocity pistol rounds, yet no one came.

Pike said, 'Charlie will panic. He'll do the first thing he thinks of and that means he'll come for us and for Karen and the boy. He won't want anyone around who knows about the accounts or the Jamaicans.'

I looked down at Dani. 'We'll have to leave her.'

Pike said, 'Yes.'

I lifted Peter Alan Nelsen to his feet. He didn't look at me or at Pike and he didn't resist; he stared at Dani's body.

I said, 'Did you hear? Did you understand?'

Peter nodded.

'All right.'

Pike took Peter by the arm and led him back to the car.

I took off my G-2 jacket, ripped my name out of the inside collar, and put it over Dani's head. Then I followed after them.

CHAPTER 33

I stopped at the Texaco station in Chelam and used the pay phone to call Karen Lloyd at the bank. I had to pull off the shoulder rig and the Dan Wesson and leave them in the car. No jacket. The old guy in the hunting cap was still sitting in the hard chair and the old retriever was still lying on his piece of cardboard. The retriever wagged his tail when he saw me.

I told Karen that something had gone wrong and that she should pick up Toby from school and go home. She wanted to know what. I told her that I was at the Texaco station and would tell her when she got home. I said, 'Are the printouts of the DeLuca transactions at your house or at the bank?'

'The bank.'

'Bring them.'

At ten minutes of four we parked in Karen Lloyd's drive and went into the house. Karen was in the living room, looking nervous, and Toby was with her. Peter was sort of slack-jawed and distant and walked as if his knees were stiff. They stared at him. Karen said, 'What's wrong?'

'Plans have changed.'

Peter said, 'They killed Dani.'

'What?'

Peter went to the couch and Joe Pike went past them down the hall to Karen's study.

I said, 'You guys are going to have to go away for tonight. Maybe a couple of nights. Throw whatever you need into a bag.'

Karen started to ask another question, then looked at Toby. 'Tobe. Do what he says. Go pack an overnighter.'

Toby took a couple of steps back along the hall, then stopped.

Joe Pike came back with his duffel bag and took out a 12-gauge Winchester autoloader and a box of Remington Long Range Express shotgun shells. Number 4 buck. The autoloader had an illegal 14-inch barrel and a pistol grip in place of a stock. When Karen saw the shotgun, she said, 'Oh my God. What is happening here?'

Pike took a Browning .32 automatic in an ankle holster out of the bag and showed it to me. 'You want the backup?'

'Yes.'

He handed it to me and I put it on. I made sure the safety was off. *'Tell me what happened*!'

I told her. I told her that at about the time Pike and I had been in her office, explaining what we had found out and what we were going to do with it, Peter and Dani had gone to see DeLuca and that now Dani was lying beneath an on-ramp to the Manhattan Bridge in Brooklyn. When I said the part about Dani, Karen's face went gray and she said, 'You stupid sonofabitch.'

Peter looked at the floor.

I pulled my pants leg down to cover the Browning and Karen said, 'What are we going to do?'

'It's not just Charlie anymore, but there's still maybe a way to do this without the cops. Before, we had it contained and we could have worked it so that we were dealing only with Charlie, but now that's different. We shot two DeLuca soldiers. One of them is dead and the other might be. Charlie's going to have to explain where the dead guys are and how they got dead.'

'So what will he do?'

'He'll hit us. He'd rather lose the laundering setup than risk the other *capos* or the Gambozas finding out what he's been doing.'

Karen said, 'Maybe we can talk to him. Maybe we should call him.'

'It's past that.'

'What can we do?'

Pike said, 'Sal.'

Karen looked at Pike, then me.

I nodded. 'Sal's our only way out. Charlie's thinking he's got to end it. He's got to get all of us before we send up the flare. So we go to Sal and we lay it out for him just like we were going to lay it out for Charlie. Sal won't want the Gambozas or the other families to find out what Charlie has been doing any more than Charlie.'

Karen nodded, maybe looking hopeful. Toby had worked his way back to the living room and she had her arm around him. He was staring at Peter.

'Did you bring the account records?'

She got them out of her purse in the dining room and gave them to me.

I said, 'Joe will stay with you. Does Charlie know about May Erdich's place?'

Karen shook her head. 'I don't think so.'

'Go there. If they come here looking for you tonight and don't find you, they might get the idea to look around. They'll check the Ho Jo, so don't go there. Get a room with May Erdich. If it goes okay, I'll come to May's when it's done.'

'All right.'

Maybe Peter could feel the weight of Toby's eyes. He looked up and he said, 'I got her killed. I'd make it better if I could, but this is what I've done.'

Toby turned and ran down the hall.

Peter Alan Nelsen, the King of Adventure, put his face in his hands and sobbed like a baby.

I borrowed Pike's coat and pulled it on. It was a little big, but it fit well enough. I folded the account records and put them in the right outside pocket.

Karen said, 'Peter.'

Peter's shoulders shook and what you could see of his face looked red and splotched.

Karen said, 'Goddamnit, Peter, we don't need to listen to this.'

Peter cried harder.

Karen crossed her arms and looked out the window, and then she walked over to Peter Alan Nelsen and put her hand on his back. Peter gulped air and made a deep, racking sob and hugged her around the hips and cried into her skirt. Karen Lloyd stared at the ceiling and patted his back.

I walked out of the house and climbed into the Taurus and drove hard through the falling darkness all the way down to Manhattan and Sal DeLuca's.

CHAPTER 34

Sal 'The Rock' DeLuca had three adjoining brownstones just east of Central Park on 62nd Street. One block in from the park a homeless woman with two children was building a little hut out of cardboard against somebody's front gate while a wino staggered by and offered her a drink. The wino didn't look where he was going, tripped over something, stumbled around in a wide orbit with a lot of hand waving, then fell onto the cardboard and threw up. The homeless woman kicked him in the balls. Anywhere else in America, East 62nd Street was a place you'd avoid after the sun went down, but not in New York. In New York, people paid millions to live on East 62nd Street. There were trees on East 62nd. The French Embassy was around the corner.

Charlie DeLuca's black Lincoln Town Car wasn't around, but a couple of guys in a maroon Mercedes were. If Sal knew what Charlie was up to with the Jamaicans, I figured that Charlie would come to Sal first for damage control. If Sal didn't know, then Charlie would charge straight out to Chelam and try to end it before Sal found out. The black Town Car not being around was a good sign, but maybe Charlie had come with somebody else. He even might've taken a cab.

I made the block twice, then parked on Fifth and walked back, trying to figure a way to see Sal without getting killed. The two guys in the Mercedes watched me as I walked past.

The homeless woman and her children were huddled in their little cardboard house and the wino was sitting with his back against the building, holding his crotch with one hand and his bottle with the other. I made a big deal out of weaving as I walked and stopped a couple of times as if I had to steady myself and then I sat down next to the wino and studied the block. There were no fire escapes to creep up and no alleys to slip within and no second-story landings to leap to in a single bound. There were only the two guys in the Mercedes and another guy hanging around on Sal the Rock's top step. Phoning for an appointment probably wouldn't work.

The wino burped softly and gingerly fingered his crotch.

I said, 'Pretty nasty shot she gave you.'

He nodded ruefully. 'Women have been my ruination.'

'Is there any wine left in your bottle?'

The wino lifted the bottle and looked at it forlornly. 'Alas. *Non.*' Our breaths were fogging in the cold night air.

'May I have it?'

He placed the bottle carefully on the sidewalk. 'My world is yours to share.'

I picked up the bottle and wobbled across the street.

The two guys in the Mercedes and the guy standing on the top step watched me, but it was the guys in the Mercedes I was worried about.

I leaned against one of the trees for a while and pretended to drink, then continued along the sidewalk until I came to Sal DeLuca's. When I got to Sal's, I sat on the bottom step.

The guy on the top step said, 'Beat it, rummy.' He was a little guy with a squinty face.

I mumbled something and hugged the bottle.

'Hey, asshole, I said beat it.' He pounded down the steps and grabbed me by the back of the jacket and tried to lift me. When he lifted, he pulled me to him and I pushed the Dan Wesson into the soft flesh beneath his ribs. I said, 'If you give it away, you die first.'

He stopped moving and stared directly into my eyes.

I said, 'Take me up the steps. Walk like you're helping me. We're going inside. Do you understand?'

'Yes.'

'Is Sal DeLuca in there?'

'Yes.'

'Is Charlie DeLuca in there?'

'No.'

'Who else is in there?'

'The old man. Vito and Angie. The staff.' I didn't know who Vito and Angie were, but it didn't seem to matter.

'Let's go.'

We went up the steps, walking close so that the gun was hidden between us.

Halfway up, the passenger side of the Mercedes opened and one of the guys got out. 'Hey, Freddie.'

I dug the gun into Freddie's side a little harder. 'Tell'm you're getting me something to eat.'

Freddie told him.

The guy at the Mercedes laughed and called Freddie an asshole.

We went up the rest of the way and Freddie let us into a long marble entry with a high ceiling and ornate stairs. The house was quiet. I said, 'Take me to Sal.'

'You gotta be crazy.'

'If I was crazy, I'd have said take me to your leader.' I gave him another prod.

We went down the long entry, then through a living room that looked like it was maybe a hundred years old and then into a wood-paneled den with a fireplace. Sal DeLuca was sitting with a couple of well-dressed guys close to his age, the two guys on one couch and Sal on another, facing each other across a little table. Vito and Angie. They had hard, lined faces, and one of them had a gray mustache, and both of them looked at me with the sort of mild curiosity you reserve for a strange dog with a skin rash. *Capos.* Mafia executive material.

Sal looked surprised. 'What do you want?'

Then Sal saw the gun.

Sal DeLuca was in his early sixties and maybe five ten but he was very wide, with the sort of muscular density that allows great strength. He would've been very strong when he was younger, and he was probably very strong now. They don't call you Sal the Rock because you're wuzzy. He had a round face and protruding eyes and a wide mouth and fleshy lips, sort of like a frog's. He was wearing a deep blue smoking jacket. The last guy I'd seen in a smoking jacket was Elmer Fudd, but I didn't tell him that. Instead I said, 'Two of your soldiers were killed today in Brooklyn. I'm the guy who killed them. Charlie DeLuca is partnered with a Jamaican gangster named Jesus Santiago. No one knows it yet, but they're stealing dope from the Gamboza brothers.'

The guy with the gray mustache said, 'Hey.'

The other guy said, 'You gotta be outta your fuckin' mind.'

Sal DeLuca didn't say anything, but when I mentioned Charlie, something cold flickered in his eyes and I felt scared.

I said, 'I wanted you to find out first, Sal. I didn't want it to get around before you knew.' I lowered the Dan Wesson.

Sal said, 'Vito.'

The guy with the mustache hopped up and took the gun. Vito. I said, 'There's a .32 on my right ankle.' He took that, too, and put both guns on the little table between the two couches. Sal picked up the Dan Wesson with his left hand, felt its weight, and then he looked at me and nodded. 'You got balls, I'll give you that. What's your name?'

'Elvis Cole.'

'That's a stupid fucking name.'

'Better than Elvis Jones.'

Sal made up his mind about something and leaned back in the chair, still holding the Dan Wesson. 'Okay. You got fifteen seconds to tell me something that will save your life.'

CHAPTER 35

Sal said, 'Freddie, you wait in the hall.'

Freddie looked nervous. 'He had the gun, Sal. I couldn't help it.'

'Wait in the hall.' The cold thing still alive in his eyes.

Freddie went out into the hall.

Angie said, 'Sal, you don't believe this shit, do you? Guy comes in like this, a stranger?'

Sal made a little hand move. 'So now he has to prove it.'

I said, 'Take something out of my right front pocket?'

Sal nodded.

I took out the computer sheets and gave them to him.

'What the fuck is this?'

'Transaction records of your money-laundering operation through the First Chelam Bank. You remember Karen Lloyd?'

Sal nodded again.

I glanced at Vito and Angie. 'You want to do this alone?'

Sal said, 'You're not from New York. Where you from?'

'California.'

He made a little head move, like that explained it. 'This is my brother Vito. This is my cousin Angie. We're family here. You understand family?'

'Yes.'

'Say what you came to say.'

I walked them through the eight accounts. I showed them how the deposits in Charlie's private account went from nickel and dime to the mid-five figures starting about five months ago, when Charlie had met Gloria Uribe and through her fell in with Jesus Santiago. I told them that Charlie had turned a Gamboza hype named Richie Sealy and that the hype fed information to Charlie about incoming Gamboza dope shipments and that Charlie then sold the information to the Jamaicans so that they could hijack the dope. I told them about following Charlie to Queens and the meeting that I had witnessed between Charlie and the Jamaicans and the cop from Kennedy airport. I told him about Peter and Dani and what had happened in Brooklyn under the Manhattan Bridge. I spoke slowly and carefully and I gave them names and addresses and times of day.

When I was finished, nobody said anything. Angie was chewing at his upper lip and Vito was staring at the fireplace. It was a long time before Sal moved or spoke, and when he did it wasn't to me. 'Vito, we hear anything about the Gambozas getting ripped off?'

Vito shrugged, not wanting to commit himself. 'Something about maybe some niggers took down a load of Gamboza dope. Who listens? We got no financial interest in dope anymore. We gave that up to the Gambozas.'

Sal shook his head. 'We traded with them, Vito. We gave them our piece of the dope for their piece of the labor.'

Angie said, 'Hey, Sal, this mook's talking about your kid, for chrissake. I think he's fulla shit.'

Sal went over to the fireplace and stared at the dead coals, already knowing it was true. He said, 'We got somebody in the coroner's over in Queens?'

'Yeah.'

'Check it out.'

'Jesus Christ, Sal. It's Charlie.'

'Check it out. Who's running the nigger whores for the Gambinos?'

'Marty Rotolo.'

'Call'm. Find out about this Gloria Uribe.'

Vito picked up the phone and punched in a number and spoke in a voice that was difficult to hear. He spoke for a few seconds, then hung up, but he stood with his hand on the receiver, not moving for maybe five minutes. Sal moved less than Vito. The Rock. When the phone rang, Vito picked it up and listened without saying anything. When he finished with that call, he made two more and then put down the phone and turned back to Sal. 'They found a woman's body when they found Carmine. Under the Manhattan Bridge.'

'Dani,' I said. 'Her name was Dani.'

'Stevie says Charlie's catting around with the Uribe woman. He said the Gambinos don't know anything about her because she's Jamaican. She's mixed up with some other Jamaican named Jesus Santiago.'

Sal made a soft hissing sound, steady and high-pitched, as if some core of deep pressure within him had been tapped. Angie said, 'Jesus Christ, Sal.'

Sal went to the door and told Freddie to come in. 'Find Charlie and tell him I want to see him.'

Freddie glanced at me. 'Sure, Sal.'

'Don't tell him anything else, Freddie.'

'Sure, Sal.' Freddie left.

Sal went back to the dead fireplace and looked at me. Calm. Like I hadn't just told him these things about his son. The Dan Wesson was almost hidden by his thick left hand. 'Okay. So maybe you're not full of shit. What do you want?'

'Karen Lloyd.'

'And if I don't want to give her up?'

'I give Charlie to the Gambozas.'

Angie gave with, 'So what? So we give a shit about the fuckin' Gambozas.'

I shrugged. 'Play it out that way. The Gambozas will kill Charlie for showing them up and then they'll move on you, and probably the rest of the families will, too. Everybody had an agreement and the DeLuca family broke it.'

Angie said, 'Bullshit,' and threw up his hands.

Vito didn't throw up his hands. Vito stood slow and easy, and went over to Sal. 'Not bullshit, Angie. He's right.' Vito stared at Sal when he said it and Sal stared back at him. 'Charlie's selling out another family to do business with an outsider. The fuckin' Jamaicans, for Christ's sake. Our word won't be shit. The families will turn their backs on us.'

Sal nodded.

'The family comes first.'

Sal looked at his brother, and the cold thing was suddenly very bright and alive. 'You don't have to tell me what's what, Vito.'

Vito spread his hands.

No one said anything more to me. Angie went out and came back with coffee and hard cakes, and the three of them sat on the two couches by the fireplace, drinking the coffee and eating the cakes in silence. I wasn't offered anything and I wasn't spoken to. After a while I went to an overstuffed chair across the room and sat down. Vito made more calls, and a couple of times big men knocked and looked in and would start to say something in English, but when they saw me they would switch to Italian. Angie went out twice and Vito went out once, but Sal didn't go out at all. He sat and stared, and I was glad he wasn't staring at me.

We sat like that in Sal DeLuca's den for almost six hours.

At ten minutes before five the next morning, Freddie came in with Charlie and Ric. Charlie's hair was mussed and his collar was open and he looked anxious, like maybe he had been looking for someone and he hadn't been able to find them. Ric still looked like a vampire, all hard bones and white, leathery flesh. Charlie was saying something about why the hell this couldn't wait until morning when he saw me and you could see the fear jolt through him like a galvanic shock. He scrabbled under his coat for his gun, but Vito slapped the gun out of his hand.

Sal said, 'Freddie, close the door.'

Charlie said, 'That's the sonofabitch killed Carmine and Dante.' Trying to cover, doing a lot of arm waving and loud talking, as if the loud talk might convince Sal and Vito and Angie that whatever I'd said was lies. 'He's trying to force us outta the bank. Jesus Christ, what's he doing here?'

Sal's left hand snapped out and caught Charlie beneath the right eye. It was a hard shot and it caught Charlie by surprise. He yelled, 'Hey!'

'Shut up and listen to this.'

Charlie shut up. Ric settled back against the bookcases and watched, choreographing the dance in his head, seeing himself move fast and perfect.

Sal looked at me again for the first time since he had sent Freddie away to find Charlie and said, 'Tell him.'

I went through it for Charlie just like I had for Sal. The more I said, the more Charlie fidgeted, moving from foot to foot and picking at his hands and visibly sweating. The more Charlie moved, the more Sal didn't move. When I finished, Charlie said, 'This is bullshit. This is *merda*. Whattaya listening to this guy for?' He looked at Angie. He looked at Vito. 'Uncle Vito. Hey, Angie. Who's family here?' He looked back at his father. 'Whattaya listening to this guy for?'

Sal put the blank, frog eyes on his son and said, 'I listened because I got no doubt in my heart that you would do this, and watching you now, I know you did.'

'Whattaya talking about? That's horseshit.'

Sal hit Charlie with the back of his right hand so hard that

Charlie staggered backward. Vito looked at Ric, and Ric made a little head move, saying he wasn't in it, and Vito nodded.

Charlie was taller than Sal, and younger, but where there was something flabby and mean about Charlie, in Sal it was hard and vibrant, even at sixty-five. The Rock. 'You're a piece of shit, Charlie.' What Charlie had said to Joey Putata. Charlie tried to cover up, but Sal slapped him again and again, steady, rhythmic shots. Sal held my Dan Wesson in his left hand and slapped with his right. 'You double-crossed the fuckin' Gambozas. You made the family into liars, and you ain't even got the balls to admit it. Be a man, Charlie. Face me and tell me that you've done this horrible thing.'

I looked at Ric again, but Ric didn't seem to be watching or hearing. His eyes were flagging closed and his head was gently bobbing in time with some dark music.

Charlie stumbled into a chair, trying to get away. His face was purple and ribbons of snot leaked down across his mouth. 'It's not true. I dint do nothing. I swear I dint.' Like a little kid.

Sal said, 'I gave them my word, Charlie. This family made peace with the other families and you've broken it. You understand that? You know what that costs?'

Charlie scrambled away from the chair and covered up against the wall. He said, 'Please, Daddy.'

Sal grabbed Charlie by the throat and shook him. 'I keep hoping you'll come around, but that day is never going to come, is it? I put you in business, I make it easy for you, but you're always gonna be a fuckup.'

Charlie slipped out of Sal's grip and fell to the floor, then tried to crawl away. Sal hit him harder, grunting with every blow.

Vito looked embarrassed and Angie looked confused and I wished I wasn't there seeing it. Sal followed his crawling son around the room, hitting him until Charlie ended up on his side, curled into a ball behind a heavy leather chair. Sal stood over him, breathing hard and hitting and saying, 'Be a man, be a man,' until finally Vito said, 'Jesus Christ, Sal,' and went over and pulled him away, lifting Sal DeLuca off his feet and talking to him and calming him down. Moving the Rock.

Then it was over. Sal stood in the center of the room, the Dan Wesson at his side, breathing hard and watching his blubbering adult child for what seemed like forever. Maybe violent insanity ran in the family.

He shook his head and seemed to see me again, as if for a time I was gone but had now returned. 'Okay,' he said. 'Karen Lloyd walks. Is that what you want?'

'Part of it. There's something else.'

'What?'

'The woman who died in Brooklyn.' I looked at Ric. 'He pulled the trigger. I want you to give him up to the cops.'

Ric moved the steel-girder shoulders and peeled himself away from the bookshelves, the leather jacket falling open.

Sal looked at Ric and then looked back at me. 'I ain't never gave one of my people up to the cops and I never would. My guys know that.'

Ric made a little smile.

'That's the deal, Sal. Take it or leave it.'

Sal the Rock DeLuca shook his head. 'No cops.' He raised the Dan Wesson, aimed it between my eyes, then turned and shot Ric once in the chest.

Ric saw it coming and yelled, 'No!' and tried to move, but the slug caught him. It pushed him back into the bookshelves and then his heels slid out from beneath him and he fell to the floor.

Charlie made a gargling sound and whimpered.

Ric tried to get up, but his feet kept slipping.

Sal shot him again.

Ric clawed under his jacket and came out with his gun.

Sal shot him twice more, smoke from the caps rolling across the room like smog spilling through the Glendale Pass into the San Fernando Valley.

There were shouts in another part of the house and the sound of men running and then someone was banging on the door. Freddie came in first.

Sal was as calm as if he had taken out the trash. 'Freddie, get a couple of those big plastic bags and take care of this.'

Freddie swallowed and stumbled backward out of the room.

Sal looked down at his son and then looked at me, his eyes empty and bottomless. 'Good enough?'

I nodded.

'Okay, you got what you want. Now I get what I want. The Gambozas must never know. What we speak of here stays here, buried forever. Will you bury this? Will you keep my kid safe?' Sal and Karen Lloyd, each worried about their children.

I nodded again. 'We bury it. We keep everyone safe.'

Vito said, 'We got loose ends, Sal. Other people know.'

Sal said, 'We'll take care of the loose ends, Vito.' He looked back at me. 'You want anything else?'

'No.'

'Then it's a done deal. Get the fuck out of my sight.'

CHAPTER 36

I walked out of Sal DeLuca's brownstone to a fine powder of snow on the streets and the sidewalks and the cars parked at the curb. The air was cold and the Manhattan skyline to the east was clear and pink in anticipation of the rising sun. To the west and the north, though, the clouds were still heavy and dense and promising more snow. The drunk was gone, but the little cardboard house remained, quiet and white in the early morning light. Cars belched fog-breath out on Fifth and 62nd, and men and women in heavy coats walked fast along the sidewalks, leaving gray trails. Somewhere there was music playing, but I didn't hear the notes clearly and couldn't make out the song. I slipped a twenty-dollar bill into the little cardboard house and went back to the Taurus.

I drove across Central Park, then up through the city and the Bronx and Yonkers and White Plains. I drove slowly and listened to a pretty good classic rock station that played a lot of John Fogerty and CCR. *Run Through the Jungle*. Nothing like a little Creedence Clearwater Revival at six in the morning after spending the night with the Godfather. Four miles above White Plains, I pulled into a rest stop overlooking a lake and started to shake. I shook for what seemed like hours but was probably only a couple of minutes. I let the motor run and the Taurus's heater pump on high, but I wasn't shaking from the cold.

A tan and white RV was parked broadside to the view, and had probably been there all night. A man and a woman in their sixties came out with coffee cups and went to the rail, looking out at the lake. They watched the lake for a while and sipped the coffee and held hands. When they turned and came back to the RV, the woman gave me a friendly smile. The license plate on their little mobile house said *Utah*.

At a quarter to ten I parked on the street in front of May Erdich's house. Toby and Joe Pike were standing in brown leaves and snow, tossing a beat-up Wilson football, and Peter was sitting on May's front step, watching them. Peter looked cold.

Karen Lloyd came out of the front door as I went up the walk. I said, 'It's over.'

She shook her head, like maybe I was lying. 'You got Charlie to go along?' Pike and Toby stopped throwing the ball. Toby ran over to stand by his mother.

'Sal. Charlie doesn't have anything to do with it anymore. It's Sal, and Sal says you're out of it. Charlie will do whatever Sal says.'

She gripped one hand with the other. 'I can stay at the bank?'

'Yes.'

'No more Charlie? No more deposits?'

'It's over, Karen.'

Peter smiled and crossed his arms but stayed on the front step.

Karen came down the steps and hugged me and then she hugged Pike. She started crying, holding us tight and digging her fingers into our shoulders as if only by holding us here could it be real. When she did it, Peter looked at his feet.

Karen let go and stepped back, smiling and crying and thanking us. She said, 'Can we go back to the house?'

'Sure. Any time you want.'

Peter looked up and said, 'Karen, I'm glad. I couldn't be happier.'

Karen smiled at him, then looked at her son. 'Tobe. Let's get our things. Let's say bye to May.'

They went into the house together. Inside, there was movement and warmth and the pounding footsteps of Toby running down a long hall.

Peter uncrossed his arms and pushed away from the top step. He said, 'I've gotta get Dani. I want to bring her home and take care of her.'

I nodded. 'The police will have questions. We'll have to figure out what to tell them.'

He made a little shrug. 'I'll tell them the truth. She died saving my life because I'm a jerk.'

Pike said, 'You can't.'

Peter looked at him.

I said, 'I gave my word to Sal that we wouldn't let what Charlie was doing get out to the Gambozas. You tell the cops or *People* magazine or anyone else you know how Dani died, the Gambozas or someone who works for them will put it together. When they do, the deal with Sal will be over. He'll come for you.'

'I don't care about me.'

'He'll come for Karen and Toby.'

Peter pursed his lips and looked at the ground. He didn't like it, but he was learning to live with things that he didn't like. He said, 'It makes me feel like I'm cheating her.'

'You are, but it's all we can do. Do you understand?'

He pursed his lips some more, but he nodded. The front door opened and Toby brought out his overnighter, put it on the porch, then went back inside and closed the door. Peter watched him. 'They think I'm full of shit.'

I didn't say anything.

'I'm thinking I've gotta get back to L.A. I've got the picture going into production soon. There's no point in me staying around.'

I stared at the house for a while. My back hurt and my neck was stiff and I wanted to go to bed. 'You shouldn't have come back here expecting them to think of you as husband and father. You could've earned that, perhaps, but you didn't think in terms of earning. You thought it was your right. You demand what you want and you get it, usually, and that makes you think that you can get whatever you demand.'

'I didn't come out here wanting to fuck it up.'

'I know.'

'I wanted this to work out. I wanted them to be a part of my life. There are empty places.'

'Maybe the way to look at it is that you should've worked to be a part of their lives and hoped to fill the empty places they have.'

Peter pressed his lips together and looked at the ground, like maybe there was something interesting there. Elm leaves, dried and brittle in the cold. 'Shit. I've gotta go.'

He walked across the leaf-strewn yard and got into the limo and drove away. There was still a little snow on the windshield when he left.

Pike and I waited at the Taurus until Karen and Toby came out. Karen was smiling and said, 'I feel like a celebration. Would you like to have a late breakfast? On me, of course.'

'Whatever you want.'

We went to the Chelam diner and sat in a booth and had eggs and sausage and pumpkin pancakes and home-fried potatoes, but it wasn't much of a celebration. There was a curious letdown feeling between us, as if there were unresolved business still at hand. When Toby was finished, he got up and played a video game. *Space Command*. A guy with a ray gun trying to kill thousands of little bugs. Karen watched him uneasily.

I said, 'At loose ends?'

She nodded. 'Does it show?'

I said, 'There's a lot to think about. There's still Peter in your life.'

She nodded again. 'It's that, but it's more than that, too. It's as if a very large object has moved across the sky, but only we've seen it. These other people here in the diner, Joyce Steuben at the bank, no one else in town has seen it.'

I nodded. It's always like that.

She said, 'I don't know what I'm going to do. I thought I did, but now I don't.' She turned away from her son and looked at me. 'I fought so hard to keep what I have here in Chelam and at the bank. Now that I've got it, you know what keeps coming to mind? Maybe I can get a better job closer to the city or up in Boston. Maybe I can find a better high school for Toby. Isn't that crazy?'

I made the same little shrug for Karen Lloyd that I had made for Peter Alan Nelsen. 'Not crazy. It wasn't a choice you could make before. Now you're free to make any choice you want.'

She sort of smiled at that and looked back at her son. 'Yes, I guess I am.' Then the smile became a little laugh that was light and open. It was the first time that I had heard her laugh.

After a while Joe and I went to the Taurus and Karen and Toby went to her LeBaron and the four of us drove back to her house beneath gray skies expectant with snow. We went inside and packed our things while Karen made phone calls and Toby dug around in the kitchen for something to eat. Twelve years old, and you're always hungry. When my bags were packed, I called United and booked two returns on a flight they had leaving from Kennedy at six-forty that night. When I told Pike the time, he said, 'Didn't they have anything sooner?'

At twenty-four minutes after noon the black limo turned into the drive and Peter Alan Nelsen came to the door. Karen let him in. She said, 'I thought you had gone back to Los Angeles.'

Peter said, 'I want to start over. I know that me coming here is going to create problems for you, and changes, and I want to do what I can to help you through them. I don't want you and the boy to think I'm an asshole. I want Toby to get to know me, and I want to get to know him, and I want to work out things like visitation and holidays and getting together. I want to pay child support, but only if that's okay with you. Can we talk about this stuff?'

Karen Lloyd said, 'Oh, shit.'

Peter said, 'Please.'

Karen Lloyd made a little whistle and tapped her right hand on her thigh and looked at the television. The television was not turned on.

I said, 'Sounds pretty good to me.'

Karen shook her head and frowned.

Peter said, 'C'mon, Karen. *Please.*'

I said, 'For Christ's sake, meet him halfway.'

Karen crossed her arms and the frown grew deeper. 'We'll see.' Give'm an inch.

The phone rang and Karen Lloyd went into the kitchen and answered it. When she was gone, Peter said, 'What do you think?'

I spread my hands. 'We'll see.'

Karen came back and said, 'It's a man named Roland George.'

I left them to stare at each other and went into the kitchen. Rollie came on with a tight, clipped voice. 'You heard?'

'What?'

'On the news ten minutes ago. Sal DeLuca was shot to death in his health club, four in the head, close range, sometime around ten this morning. You know anything about it?'

'I think it was Charlie. If it was, I think he'll want us next.'

I hung up and went back into the living room and told Karen and Peter and Joe Pike. When I told them, Peter said, 'You mean the sonofabitch is coming back here?'

'Yes.'

Karen said, 'I knew it couldn't be this easy. I knew it wasn't over. What are we going to do?'

'Get into town where there's people. When you and Toby are safe, Joe and I will see what we can do with Charlie.'

Karen called Toby and we went quickly out the front door and into her LeBaron. I told Peter to get in the back and I told Karen that I would drive. Neither of them objected.

Toby said, 'Is it those men again, Mom?'

We pulled away from her house and went down the clean new tarmac street and turned onto the main road toward Chelam. It was twenty-eight minutes after noon.

We had gone about two miles when they found us.

CHAPTER 37

They came up behind us in two cars, a green Dodge station wagon and the black Town Car, just as the snow began to fall.

Pike saw them first. 'Behind us. Turned out from a side road, maybe a half mile back.'

I pushed Toby's head down. 'Get on the floor. Make yourself as small as you can and wrap your arms around your head.'

I pushed Karen down on top of him.

The Town Car pulled into the left lane and the wagon stayed in the right and they came on hard. Pike reached under his jacket and took out his .357.

I pressed the LeBaron's pedal to the floor, but the Town Car inched closer and then there were gold specks flashing around it and something hit the rear of the LeBaron two times, *bam bam*, like rocks thrown by a kid hiding behind a tree. The right rear tire blew and Karen Lloyd made a sharp gasping sound and Toby said, 'What was that?'

The LeBaron nosed up and I swung us to the right, and then we were off the road and bouncing across an untended pumpkin field, ripping through weeds and a barbed-wire fence and a couple of white birch saplings. I gunned the engine and forced the LeBaron across the field, sideways half the time and near out of control, until the flat right rear dug into the loam maybe three hundred yards from the road and the LeBaron wouldn't go any farther. I said, 'Everybody out.'

The station wagon and the Town Car skidded to a stop on the road and doors banged open and eight men pushed out, five of them with shotguns. Charlie DeLuca had been driving the Town Car and Joey Putata was one of the guys in the wagon, but I didn't recognize anyone else. Ric was conspicuous by his absence. No one now to keep Charlie calm, no one to rub his back and say the quiet things and keep Charlie DeLuca among the land of the sane. Sal the Rock had learned that. Charlie was certifiably, stark-raving, bad-to-the-bone out of control.

I shoved the driver's side door open and fell out, then pushed my seat forward and pulled Karen and Toby out after me. Pike went out the passenger's side and the .357 boomed twice. Peter followed Pike, and then the five of us were crouched down among the pumpkins behind the LeBaron.

Two of the guys up on the road started blasting away with their shotguns, but then someone did a lot of arm waving and they stopped. Three hundred yards with shotguns was silly.

The little pumpkin field was maybe five hundred yards on a side, bordered to the east and the west and the south by thick stands of birch and elm and maple trees. Behind us to the south there was a little ramshackle feed shed that looked to be maybe a hundred years old. I squatted down next to Karen and said, 'Does anyone live around here?'

'Maybe a couple of miles that way.' She pointed southwest.

'Is there a road behind us?'

She scrunched her face, trying to think but not having an easy time of it. 'There must be. Some kind of farming road.'

Toby said, 'Yeah, there is. It's a utility road. Dirt.'

'How far?'

'Maybe a mile and a half. It's on the other side of all these fields. It comes out by this little airport where the crop dusters fly, but there won't be anyone there. They close it down in the winter.'

Pike said, 'If we can get there, maybe we can make a farmhouse.'

The snow fell harder, swirling and piling up in little white pockets on the LeBaron and on the pumpkins, thick enough in the air to make the men on the road indistinct and shadowy. Two of the shadows went off to the left and two of them went right and four of them started off the road directly for us. Classic pincer move. Probably taught that at the mafia academy.

I said, 'They're going to try to envelop us, faster guys moving out on the flank, the other guys coming slow up the middle to drive us toward them.'

Pike said, 'Unh-hunh,' and opened the duffel. He took out the shotgun and a cartridge box and began filling his pockets with the shells. Twenty-five rounds in the box, but he found places for all of them.

Peter was squatting next to Karen and behind Toby. He had put an arm around Karen's shoulders without thinking about it. Or maybe he had. He said, 'Maybe we could dig in here and hold them off.'

Pike shook his head. 'Not with twenty-five rounds.'

I duck-walked to Karen and Peter and knelt close to them. Their faces were white and their eyes were squinty and drawn. 'We're going to have to split up. Pike and I will go out to the flanks. You guys move straight back across the field and try to get to the farm road. Do you understand that?'

They both said, 'Yes.'

'Stay low and run as fast as you can just like you've seen people do on television. Try to keep the car between you and the four guys coming across the field. They're coming slow because they know we have guns, so you'll have time. Work your way to the feed shed and get behind it, and then work your way to the woods using the shed as cover.'

Peter nodded and Karen said, 'Yes.'

'Don't stop until you get to people. Then call the police.'

Karen wasn't looking into my eyes. She was watching my mouth, getting every word. Hanging on by her fingernails.

Peter said, 'I don't want to run off. I want to do something.'

'You are doing something. You're helping this woman and your son get to a safe place. That's your job.'

Peter glanced down at the woman that he used to be married to and their son, and he nodded. 'Sure. Okay.'

I turned to Toby. 'Tobe, you think you can find the road through the woods?'

'Sure. You just keep going south.'

'Okay. You get to the road, which way to the airfield?'

'East.'

I looked back at Karen and then at Peter. 'Do it.'

Karen said, 'They're going to kill us, aren't they?'

'They're going to try. But Joe and I won't let them.'

Her eyes were big and darting. She held tight to Toby's arm. 'How can you stop them? There're eight of them and we're trapped here in the middle of nowhere with them.'

Pike chambered a round into his shotgun. 'No,' he said. 'They're trapped with us.'

I gave Karen a little nod and then she crabbed away, holding on to Toby's shirt with her right hand, crouched low and stumbling through the frozen weeds and the pumpkins. Peter followed close after them.

Pike said, 'How many rounds you got?'

'Just what's in the gun.'

He gave me disapproval.

'I know,' I said. 'You can't take me anywhere.'

He handed me the .357, butt first, then gave me a little leather pouch with three speed-loaders. Be prepared.

'You ready?'

'I'm ready.'

'Let's do it.'

We fired six quick rounds at the four men coming across the field, then Joe broke left and I broke right, moving low and fast, and then he was behind me and gone.

The snow was a glistening powder across the field, piling up in little mounds that scattered without sound as I moved. Charlie DeLuca saw us break, and the three guys with him opened up, firing with the shotguns and their pistols, still better than two hundred yards out. Panic shots. I guess they hadn't expected us to try to outflank the flankers. Charlie yelled something at the guys who had gone into the woods, but with the snow and the wind and the distance you couldn't make out what he was saying. Pellets rained on the field around me and a great orange pumpkin exploded, but I didn't stop and I didn't look back. I stayed low and moved hard and wondered if the guys in the woods were making better time coming my way than I was making going theirs. Then I didn't think about it anymore and pretty soon I was in the trees.

I moved twenty yards into the tree line and stopped between two white birch to listen. If the flankers had moved fast, maybe they were already behind me. They weren't. Thirty yards upwind toward the road, limbs snapped and dead leaves crunched and it sounded like the Fifth Marines were on the march. City kids come out to play. This deep in the trees, you couldn't see the field. They didn't know Karen and Peter and Toby were falling back and they didn't know Pike and I had moved into the tree line. Out in the field, the pistols and the shotguns had stopped firing and Charlie was yelling, but I couldn't hear what he was saying. If I couldn't hear, the flankers couldn't hear. They were making so much noise that even if Charlie had been understandable, they wouldn't have heard.

I moved deeper into the trees and found a place beside a fallen elm and waited. In the woods the snow fell only slightly, caught higher in the tree canopy by dead leaves and vines and branches. Some of the earlier snow had melted and the water had leached down the trees, making their bark feel velvety and damp and enhancing their good smell. Except for the coming of the flankers, it was quiet. Calm. The natural state of the woods.

Joey Putata and a guy in a blaze-orange hunting jacket pushed their way through a tangle of vines hanging from a dogwood tree. The guy in the orange jacket had heavy sideburns and the kind of coarse virulent beard that had to be shaved three times a day and a little hat with a feather in the band. Joey Putata was carrying a 12-gauge Mossberg slug gun and the guy in the orange had a Ruger Redhawk .44 Magnum revolver. Joey's eyes were still black and green from the beating Charlie had given him, but here he was, tramping through the woods. Some guys are stupid all the way through. The guy in orange ducked down under a branch but didn't duck far enough. The branch knocked his hat off and a slug of fresh snow fell down his back. He said, 'Sonofabitch,' and then they stopped.

Joey Putata said, 'You think we're far enough?'

The guy with the hat said, 'How the fuck I know? Let's go that way and see if we can find Tony and Mike.' Tony and Mike must be the other flankers.

From a very long way off there were two quick *booms*. Joey got excited and said, 'Maybe we got'm.' When he said it, he shoved the guy with the hat, and the guy with the hat turned sideways and saw me. I shot him once in the chest. The .357 slug hit him square in the sternum like an express-speed brick and punched him back into the vines. I said, 'Hey, Joey. Don't you ever learn?'

Joey brought up the Mossberg, but he didn't bring it up fast enough. I shot him once in the neck and then I was moving back toward the field.

When I came out of the tree line, Pike was running toward the LeBaron. Charlie and the other three guys were gone and so was the black Town Car.

Pike said, 'He took off a couple of minutes ago, heading away from town.'

I came up next to Pike and reloaded the .357. 'He's betting that the others are making for a road behind us and he's gone to look for it.'

Pike cocked his head. 'I don't figure he's looking. I figure it's the side road he came at us from and he knows just where it leads.'

'Great.'

We set off south across the field, running side by side past the little feed shack and falling into an easy rhythm. When we made the woods, it was easy to see where Karen and Toby and Peter had passed. The damp mat of dead winter leaves was kicked up and branches and small winter-dead saplings were broken.

The narrow dirt utility road was less than a mile in from the main road, closer than Toby had thought. We came out of the trees and went east, pounding along as the road cut through the woods, striding in tandem and feeling the cold air cut into our throats. There were foot tracks and fresh tire tracks in the snow, but the tire tracks didn't necessarily belong to Charlie's Town Car. They could have been anything. Pike said, 'I see it.'

The road broke out of the little section of woods and cut across flat white fields of pumpkins and squash and winter truck. Half a mile farther down the road, there was an orange wind sock flapping in the wind and a utility shed and a corrugated-metal hangar. If the wind sock wasn't orange, we would never have seen it against the snow. A couple of Piper Pawnee crop-dusting planes were next to the hangar, tarped and tied down, as winter-dead as the leaves.

The black Lincoln Town Car was parked by the utility shed and people moved between the planes.

We hadn't come out of the woods in time. Charlie DeLuca had them.

CHAPTER 38

Pike and I picked up our pace, running on either side of the road, our breath great white plumes in the snowy air. We ran hard until we drew close, then we throttled back, trading speed for quiet as we moved up to the hangar. The shadow shapes we had seen when we came out of the woods were gone.

Charlie's Town Car was parked at a skew outside the corrugated-metal hangar, already collecting little pockets of snow on the windward side. The two Pawnees were on the field side of the hangar, and, before them, a couple of rusted water mules used for aviation gasoline and pesticides. Somewhere upwind, Karen Lloyd yelled and there was a single sharp *pop*, pistol, but the wind and the snow carried away the sound.

Pike said, 'They'll be in the hangar or in the fields behind the planes.'

We went to the hangar, looped around the corner, and saw them through a dust-streaked window built into a door. Karen Lloyd was on her knees, crying, and Charlie DeLuca was holding Toby by the hair, pointing a Browning .380 automatic at his right temple. Toby was crying, too. He was probably crying because he was scared, but he might've been crying because a fat guy was hitting Peter Alan Nelsen in the face and knocking him down. He would hit Peter and knock him down, and Peter would get up and go after him again. The fat guy was thick through the middle and the hips and the shoulders and the back, sort of like an overstuffed sausage, but it was hard fat. There wouldn't be a lot of stamina, but there was plenty of mean. Peter kept trying to get to Charlie, but the fat guy kept beating him up. Karen was yelling something about doing whatever Charlie wanted if only he'd stop. It was hard to hear them through the glass.

I touched Pike's shoulder and pointed past them to the big sliding doors at the back of the hangar. The doors were open.

Pike nodded, and we slipped under the window and took one step toward the field when the two other guys who'd been with Charlie DeLuca came around the corner. One of them was tall and the other wasn't. The shorter one had a dead cigar in his mouth and what looked like a .32 revolver in his right hand. The taller one was grousing about the cold, and neither of them knew we were there until they saw us. Joe Pike hit the shorter guy with an outside spin kick that sounded like it broke his neck. The taller guy said, 'Hey,' and fired what was maybe a Rossi .38 into the ground, and I shot him high in the chest. Blood squirted out in a little geyser, and he looked down at it and then started pressing on the blood, trying to make it stay where it was. Then he fell over.

Inside, there were the sounds of fast movement and Karen screamed something and there was the peculiar high shriek that only young children can make. Someone started shooting and bullets slammed through the side of the hangar, well wide of us, and then the shooting stopped.

We looked in through either side of the window in time to see Charlie drag Toby through the hangar doors. Karen followed them. Peter was lying on his side and the fat guy kicked him twice, then took a blue revolver from under his jacket. He pulled Peter's head back and put the revolver into Peter's mouth. Pike shot him in the top of the left shoulder with a load of number four. The fat guy fell backward and Pike shot him again.

We ran back between the two Pawnee crop dusters just as Charlie came around the hangar with one arm locked around Toby Lloyd's neck, looking for us. The Browning .380 was pressed under Toby's ear. Charlie's face was bright red and there were veins standing out on his forehead. He was checking the roofline. Batman and Robin always come down from the roof. He screamed, 'You're mine, you sonofabitch. I'm gonna cut out your fuckin' guts and fry'm in a pan!'

Karen came around the corner behind them, tears washing her face, her hands tight and clawed. She wanted to run to Toby, but she was scared if she did the nut with the gun would kill him. She yelled, 'Toby!'

Charlie DeLuca dug his pistol so deep under Toby's jaw that Toby shrieked again and wet his pants. Charlie yelled, 'I'm gonna kill him, you chickenshit motherfuckers, you don't come out here. I'm gonna blow his fuckin' eyes out.'

I glanced at Pike. Pike's flat black lenses were locked on Charlie DeLuca, the shotgun resting easy along the Pawnee's metal wing strut. Pike's a better shot than me. Maybe the best I've ever seen. I said, 'He's going to do it. He's going to kill the boy.'

'Yes.'

I gave him the .357 and took the shotgun. 'Can you make the shot?'

Karen screamed, 'Help him, please. Somebody help!'

Pike said, 'I can make the shot, but not with his gun on the boy that way. He could jerk when he dies.'

Karen screamed, 'Toby!'

Peter stumbled out of the hangar and said, 'Let go my kid, you fat fuck!' There were cuts over both eyes and his nose was broken and his lips were split. There was so much blood on his face that he looked like he was wearing makeup. 'I'm Peter Alan Nelsen, and I will kick your fat fucking ass!'

Karen screamed, 'Peter! No!'

Charlie DeLuca smiled and swung the Browning toward Peter and said, 'Kick this.' Then he fired once.

Peter fell down, and Karen and Toby screamed, and I stepped out from behind the Pawnee and yelled, 'Charlie!'

Charlie DeLuca swung the .380 back toward me, pulled the trigger, and something tugged at the top of my shoulder. Then I felt something solid wash past me from behind and there was a loud noise and the back of Charlie DeLuca's head blew out like a big rig tire filled with red paint. Pike's Python. Charlie was dead before he started to fall.

Toby kicked away from what was left of Charlie DeLuca and ran to Peter, yelling, 'Daddy! Daddy!'

Blood was spilling from the top of Peter's left thigh, but he made it to his knees and dragged himself over to Charlie DeLuca and started punching the body. If Peter could get up, I figured I should get up, too. I did okay at it, but my ears were ringing and my shirt felt wet. I looked down and opened my jacket and saw that my shirt was turning black from the top down. Then Pike was there, peeling back the shirt. 'Doesn't look bad. Caught it across the top of the trapezius.'

'Sure.'

Pike went over to Peter, took off his belt, and wrapped it tight

622

around Peter's leg. Then he came back to me and used his sweatshirt as a compress on my shoulder. I burned where the bullet had torn through the muscle and there was a tingling feeling, but it could've been worse. Peter blinked at his leg and at Charlie DeLuca and then he grinned at me. 'We got the bastard. We got him.'

'Yes,' I said. 'We did.'

He began to laugh. 'It's over.'

Karen was laughing then, too. Nervous and scared and letting off the tension by laughing. 'Yes,' she said. 'God, yes.'

Karen came over and hugged me. Toby helped Peter to his feet and they came over and hugged me, too.

Some days, I guess you're more huggable than others.

CHAPTER 39

We left the bodies at the airport and went into town to see Chelam's only doctor, a young guy with a beard and glasses name of Hocksley. Karen Lloyd drove.

The doc was good about it. He practiced out of his home just four houses down from May Erdich's place, the kind of guy who wanted to know his patients and bring babies into the world and watch them grow. Idealistic. You know the type. When he cut off my shirt and Peter's pants, he whistled and said, 'Man, I haven't seen anything like this since I left the Bronx General ER.'

'Hunting accident.'

'Sure.'

He swabbed us down and cleaned us out, then put in a couple of stitches and gave us each two injections, something clear to fight infection and something white to fight tetanus. He also gave us some orange pills for the pain. He said, 'Don't suppose I should call the police about this.'

I said, 'Mind if I use your phone?'

I called Rollie George and told him where I was and what had happened. While I told him, the doc crossed his arms and listened and absently stroked his beard. When I hung up, he said, 'Think I should maybe go take a look?'

I shook my head. 'It won't do any good.'

He looked at Peter. 'You look familiar.'

'I've got one of those faces.'

We left the doctor, dropped Toby with May Erdich, and drove back to the little airfield. The snow had stopped falling but not before a gentle skin of white had been pulled over the road and the airplanes and the bodies in the field. Joe Pike and I unshipped the tarps from the two Pawnees' engine cowlings and covered Charlie

624

DeLuca and the three guys who'd died with him and then we sat in the LeBaron to wait.

A couple of Connecticut state cars got there first, followed by a plain blue sedan with somebody from the Connecticut AG's office. They came in the right way, without the sirens or the lights, and I liked them for it. The guy from the AG's office walked over to us and asked who we were. I told him my name and Joe's, but I didn't mention Karen or Peter, and he didn't ask. He said that he had been told something about bodies at another location. I told him how to get to the pumpkin field and that there were two bodies on either side of the field in the woods. He nodded and went back to the uniform cops, and then he and a car full of the uniforms drove away to take a look. Twenty minutes later a tan car with an FBI emblem on the side door and a white Ford from the New York State Attorney General's office pulled in just ahead of a gray Cadillac limousine. Two guys got out of the FBI car, and a bald guy and two women got out of the N.Y. car. Rollie George and his dog got out of the limo. The law student was driving. Everybody except the bald man smiled when they saw Rollie and shook his hand and told him it was good to see him. Nothing like palling around with a big-time novelist at a murder scene.

Karen said, 'Shouldn't we be out there with them?'

'No. We sit and wait and see what they say.'

They went as a group to the spot between the two airplanes and lifted the tarpaulin and looked at what was under it. Maxie sniffed at Charlie's body and lifted his leg and Rollie had to pull the dog away. One of the women laughed. They stood over the bodies for a long time, sometimes glancing back to the car, but mostly not. Everybody seemed in agreement with what they were talking about except the bald guy. You could see it in his face. He made sharp gestures and once he pointed at our car. They talked some more, and then Rollie George walked over to us and bent down by the driver's side window. He gave Karen the sort of reassuring smile your grandfather might give, and if he recognized Peter, he didn't say anything. He leaned close to me and said, 'Can we have the bad cop?'

I said, 'Yes. If my people don't get named and don't have to testify.'

He nodded. 'It looks like there's more than one officer involved. It looks like there might be several with Kennedy security who took part.'

I nodded back at him. 'I sort of figured that.'

Rollie smiled at Karen again and then he and Max walked back to the little group around Charlie DeLuca's body. There was more talk and the bald guy liked it even less and made more of the sharp gestures until one of the women he had ridden out with said, 'Oh, shut the fuck up, Morton.'

The feds and the people from the two AG offices came to the car for Pike and me and walked us around the site asking us questions. Most of the questions were about Charlie DeLuca and the Jamaicans and the cop I had followed to the Queens precinct house. I didn't mention Charlie DeLuca's secret account, or that he was doing something that Sal didn't know about, or the Gambozas. The Jamaicans probably didn't know whose dope they were stealing and neither, probably, did the cop. If they did, and if they told, that was between the DeLucas and them. You do what you can.

When the AG people were finished with their questions, they brought us back to the car. None of them looked at Karen Lloyd or Peter Alan Nelsen, or spoke to them. It was as if they weren't there. One of the women and one of the feds went with a couple of Staties to the pumpkin field. They weren't gone long. After they got back, there was more talk and then Roland George came back to us. He said, 'I think we've done about all we can do here. You can go now.'

Karen Lloyd said, 'Is that all?'

'Yes, ma'am.'

'You don't need to question us? You aren't going to take us in?'

Peter said, 'Karen.'

Rollie George smiled and walked away.

Karen looked at me. 'They're keeping us out of this? Even with people dead?'

'Yes. Start the car and let's get out of here.'

We drove to Karen Lloyd's house in silence and parked in the drive beneath the basketball hoop until Peter had his story straight. The people from the AG's office were going to release Dani's body to him with no questions asked, but he would need to know what to tell Nick and T.J. and the press. Peter Alan Nelsen's bodyguard had been murdered and there would be questions. He was going to have to lie, and he was going to have to maintain the lie for the rest of his life. He said, 'I can do it.'

Karen said, 'You'd better.'

He frowned at her and then he got out of the LeBaron and got into

626

his limo and drove away. Karen watched him go. 'Do you think he can?'

I nodded. 'Yes. He's learned a lot.'

'I hope.' She let out a sigh. 'I hate this. I hate it that once you let someone into your life, they're part of your life forever.'

I said, 'Part, maybe, but not all. You're still you. You're vice-president of the bank. You're twice president of the PTA. You're a Rotarian and a member of the Library Committee. Maybe, without having gone through what you went through with Peter, you wouldn't be any of those things. Maybe you would be less.'

She turned and looked at me, and then she leaned across and kissed me, and then she turned in the seat and kissed Joe Pike. She said, 'I'll do what's best for Toby. I've always been able to do that. What happens now with the DeLucas?'

I looked out the window at the house and the basketball hoop and Toby's bike leaning against the garage wall. Then I looked back at her. 'I don't know. Sal and Charlie aren't running the family anymore. They'll have a new boss.'

She made her lips into a little rosebud and then she nodded slowly. 'Do you think he'll try to make me keep doing this?'

Pike leaned close to her and patted her arm. 'Go live your life. You let us worry about that.'

Karen Lloyd took a deep breath, let it out, and got out of the car.

CHAPTER 40

Pike and I collected our things, said our good-byes, and drove down to the city where we took a fourteenth-floor room at the Park Lane Hotel on East 59th Street. It was a nice room with a view of Central Park.

We took turns in the shower, then dressed and walked to the Museum of Modern Art on 53rd. They call it MoMA for short, which is dumb, but they had Vincent van Gogh's *The Starry Night*, which is anything but. Score one for New York. I had always wanted to see it, and now sat for the better part of an hour staring into its depths and textures. Pike said, 'I know how he felt.'

'They say he was mad.'

Pike shrugged.

We walked up to West 71st Street and had an early dinner at Victor's Café 52. Cuban food, which rivaled and in some ways surpassed the excellent fare found at the Versailles on Venice Boulevard in Los Angeles. I had the chicken steak and black beans. Pike had the white bean soup and fried plantains. We both had beer. Score two.

It was still light when we finished, so we walked across the three long blocks of Central Park, past the lake and Bethesda Fountain and something that called itself the Boathouse Café. The café was closed. People were jogging and riding bikes and a couple of kids were flying a model airplane. No one seemed about to do crime, but the mounted police were in high profile. After the sun went down, it might be different. I asked Pike, 'Are you afraid?'

He shook his head.

'Would you be afraid at midnight if we were alone?'

He walked a moment. 'I have the capacity for great violence.'

I nodded. So did I. But I thought that I might still be afraid.

Pike slipped his hands into the pockets of his parka and we

walked past a smaller pond where an older man and a couple of young girls were sailing a model sailboat. A man and a woman decked out in serious biking apparel were standing with a tandem bike, watching them. We stopped and watched them, too, and I wondered how deeply into winter the pond could venture before it would freeze. The brisk fall wind carried the boat well across the pond. Pike said, 'Elvis?'

'Yeah?'

'I remember being afraid. I was very young.'

We watched the old man and the girls and the boat, and then we left the park and walked down to the brownstones that used to belong to Sal DeLuca. There were no limos at the curb or thugs hanging around the stoop. There was a black bow on the door.

Joe stayed on the corner at Fifth Avenue and I went up to the door and rang the bell once. In a little bit Freddie opened the door and looked out at me. His face was flat and without expression. 'Yeah?'

'You hear about Charlie?'

'We heard.'

'I'm at the Park Lane.'

'Swell. Have a party.'

'Tell Vito. Tell Angie. I'll be there until this is squared away.'

Freddie gave me the patented tough-guy sneer. 'We got no business with you.'

'That's where you're wrong. Tell Vito and Angie. The Park Lane.'

The next morning there was a three-inch article on page six of *The New York Times*. It reported that a prostitute named Gloria Uribe and a man believed to be her pimp, one Jesus Santiago, were found shot to death in a warehouse in lower Manhattan. Authorities had no leads as to the circumstances of their deaths. In a separate article on page eighteen a Jamaican national and known drug dealer named Urethro Mubata was found murdered in the front seat of his late-model Jaguar Sovereign in Queens. His throat was cut so deeply that the head was almost separated from the body. Police speculated his death to be the result of a drug deal gone sour. The *New York Post* reported that Richard Sealy, a drug addict, had been found dead in a Port Authority men's room with multiple fractures of the head, neck, both arms, and left leg. Guess junkies don't rate the *Times*.

Loose ends were being tied.

Two days later, in the afternoon, I was walking down Central

Park West across from the Hayden Planetarium when a blue Cadillac Eldorado pulled up beside me. Pike was maybe forty yards back and across the street. Vito DeLuca opened the door and looked out at me. 'Get in.'

I got in. Freddie was in the front seat, driving. Vito was in back, alone. Vito said, 'I'm *capo de tutti capo*. You know what that means?'

'You're Marlon Brando.'

Vito smiled, but there was something hard and tired in it. The weight of responsibility. 'Yeah. You killed a lot of our guys.'

'Charlie's people.'

'Some of the *capos*, they don't like it. They think something should be done.'

'What do you think?' Out the window, past Vito, I could see Joe Pike moving closer, talking to a guy who was selling Middle Eastern food from a little cart.

Vito looked out the window but saw only people on the street. 'I think Charlie came very close to bringing dishonor to the family. He was my nephew, my blood, but Sal was my brother. Sal knew how a man acts. You behaved like a man behaves. These guys, they talk about California and granola and Disneyland, I say, Christ, he put ten of our guys in the ground. If he was Sicilian, I'd kiss him on the mouth. He could be a made guy.'

'What about Karen Lloyd?'

Vito turned back and looked at me. He said, 'Sal DeLuca was *capo de tutti capos*, and when he spoke, he spoke for the family. The DeLucas honor their word. *Capisce?*'

'Charlie wouldn't.'

'Charlie's dead.'

I nodded.

'She's out. She will never be seen by DeLuca family eyes again. The DeLuca family will always honor that.'

He put out his hand and we shook. When we shook, he squeezed my hand hard, so hard that it cut off the blood. More than one rock in the family. He said, 'The agreement works both ways. Does the woman know that?'

'Yes.'

'Does her husband? The movie guy?' Peter Alan Nelsen, the movie guy.

'Yes. I'll be responsible for them.'

He nodded. 'That's right. You will. For the rest of your life.'

630

He let go of my hand and I got out of the limousine and walked across the street. Joe Pike and I went back to the hotel, called Karen Lloyd at her bank, and told her what Vito DeLuca had said. We checked out that afternoon.

CHAPTER 41

October moved into November, and three weeks later, on a pleasant Sunday afternoon, I was on my deck grilling salmon steaks and Japanese eggplant for Cindy, the beauty supply distributor, and Joe Pike and another woman named Ellen Lang. Ellen Lang had been a client once, several years ago, and since then she and Joe Pike have seen each other, time to time. She had a deep tan, and when she laughed there were dimples high on her cheeks. Laughter came easier to her now than in that earlier time.

Joe Pike and Cindy and Ellen Lang were inside, making salad and garlic bread and mint tea, when the phone rang. Someone inside answered it, and Ellen Lang came out and said, 'There's a call for you. It's Peter Alan Nelsen. The director.'

I said, 'Wow. Maybe this is my big break.'

She said, 'Oh, you.'

Ellen stayed with the salmon and I went inside and took it in the kitchen. On the counter next to the sink, Pike sliced the long French bread and put it on a tray while Cindy watched him. Cindy had soft auburn hair and expressive brown eyes. I liked watching her watch Pike's precise moves.

Peter said, 'They're coming out to visit.'

'Karen and Toby?'

'Yeah. He's got a week off for Thanksgiving and I asked'm to come out.'

'Great.' I already knew, because Karen had called and told me.

'She doesn't want him traveling alone, so she's coming, too.'

'Even better.'

'She's not coming by herself. She's bringing some guy.' She had also told me that.

'She's got a life, Peter. That's a good thing. Why don't you get a date and the four of you can go out one night. Leave Toby with me.'

632

'I know. I know.' He didn't say anything for a little bit. 'Listen, when they're out, I'm gonna bring Toby to the set, take'm to Disneyland, that kind of thing. You think you could sorta be around some of the time? At first.'

Pike finished cutting the garlic bread and Cindy took it outside. She wriggled her eyebrows as she passed and gave me a yum-yum smile. She smelled of daisies. Yum, all right. 'Sure, Peter. Not the whole time. But if you need me around at first, sure.'

'Hey, thanks. I really appreciate that. I really do.' He sounded relieved. 'I'm out at the Malibu house. You wanna come out?'

'I've got company.'

'Another time, okay? You ever wanna come out, you don't even have to call. Just come.'

'Sure.' Elvis Cole, detective to the stars.

I hung up and Pike said, 'What's up?'

'Karen and Toby are coming out and he's scared. Growing up is a scary time.'

'He asks you a lot. Maybe he should try growing up without you.'

'He calls me less now than he once did. He'll call me less still. He's getting there.'

Pike nodded. 'Yeah. I guess he is. Karen getting any chaff from the DeLucas?'

'Vito's been good at his word. All of the DeLuca accounts through the First Chelam Bank have been collapsed and the funds in the Barbados accounts have mysteriously vanished.'

'So she's free.'

'Yes. She's as free as you can be when you've got the memories she has, but, like Peter, she's getting there, too.'

Outside, Ellen Lang moved the fish to the side so it wouldn't overcook and Cindy put the garlic bread in the center of the grill. Pike washed off a yellow pepper, cored it in the sink, then sliced it into thin rings. Each ring was uniform, no thicker or thinner than any other ring. When the pepper was cut, he added the rings to the large salad that had already been built and we took it out to the deck.

Ellen Lang says that if you stand on my deck and close your eyes, with a breeze coming up the canyon to blow across your face, it's easy to imagine that you're flying free through the sky, over the city with Tinkerbell and Mark and Wendy, off to Never Land to find the lost boys.

I haven't told her, but I've always thought that, too.